To: Ron

A LoT of gREAT,
CONTEL meMoRiES!
GOD BLESS!
Bob B
Jeremiah 29:11

Acquisition

Robert W. Zinnecker

Outskirts Press, Inc.
Denver, Colorado

Outskirts Press, Inc.
http://www.outskirtspress.com

ISBN: 978-1-4327-7248-2

Outskirts Press and the "OP" logo are trademarks belonging to Outskirts Press, Inc.

PRINTED IN THE UNITED STATES OF AMERICA

ACKNOWLEDGEMENTS

I am indebted to my wife Elaine, my brother Roger, and my children, Tim, Karen, Diana and Brad. I am also grateful to my friends and associates, Mary Currant, Sarah Matthews, Deborah Newkirk, Susan Roberts and Paul Zielinski. Without the support and wise counsel of my family and friends, this book could not have been published.

BIBLICAL QUOTATIONS

PROLOGUE

In the 1940s, a French opportunist and gambler named Philippe Legrane came to the west Texas oil country. Legrane quickly made his fortune and acquired several small telephone companies and a small power company that provided services in or near the oil fields. Legrane recognized the opportunities in both industries for growth through acquisition. He formed an acquisition company and named it LEGENT for Legrane Enterprises. Later, he sold off the power company and concentrated on telephony. With the backing of New York City investment bankers, he began an acquisition program focused on family-owned telephone companies.

In the early 1950s LEGENT became a publicly traded company based in Dallas, Texas. At the same time, two telephone directory advertising salesmen, working for a Kansas City company, watched LEGENT's acquisitions take away many of their clients. They studied the locations of LEGENT's operations and noted that there were few in the Midwest and plains states. They enlisted the backing of a Chicago-based financier named Charles Corbin who had many contacts in the investment banking community and in state and national government. They organized an acquisition company named Dynacom and began to acquire small telephone companies.

In the early 1960s Dynacom became a publicly traded company based in Chicago and the acquisition pace peaked. It slowed down in the 1970s with the breakup of the Bell system and the rise of telephone competition. Digital technology and optics began to be applied to telephone networks in the 1970s and 1980s. Cellular technology burst on the scene in the 1980s and LEGENT was an early adaptor of the new wireless technology. They invested heavily in cellular systems and made minimal upgrade to their wire line networks, especially in the more rural portions of their operation. Dynacom, meanwhile, continued to modernize its networks with digital switching and fiber optic cabling. It mounted a small fledgling cellular operation.

Fewer independent companies were placing themselves up for acquisition. LEGENT and Dynacom competed intensely for those companies that fit well with their existing operations by paying extraordinary prices. These acquisitions were made by paying multiple thousands of dollars on a per line served basis. Many acquisitions were done on a "pooling of interest" basis where stock in the acquiring company was exchanged for the equity in the acquired company, thus saving the former owners tax problems.

With fewer companies being acquired, the basis for acquisitions in the latter part of the 20th century were done by teams of lawyers, accountants and merger and acquisition ("M&A") specialists that performed "due diligence" reviews and computed acquisition values on the basis of multiples of earnings before interest, taxes, depreciation and amortization (EBITDA) which represented free cash flow in the company to be acquired.

The acquiring systems began to divest themselves of portions of their holdings which they could not run efficiently. Most of these holdings were in rural areas adjacent to well-run smaller companies. These instances reversed the acquisition process as smaller companies acquired properties from the larger companies. At the same time, "aggregators" emerged, acquiring both smaller individual companies and portions of the larger companies' systems. The surviving Regional Bell Operating Companies (RBOCs) from the breakup of AT&T in the 1970's, began to consolidate into fewer companies. Against this backdrop, both LEGENT and Dynacom continued their feverish growth efforts while at the same time attempting to stave off being acquired themselves.

Technology turned traditional telephony into today's telecommunications industry. The process of dividing long distance revenue amongst the companies was also changing. Historically, long distance revenue was divided based on who initiated the call, who switched the call, whose network carried the call and where the call terminated. This system used the average revenue per message, settlement amount per message and "line haul" schedules to properly compensate companies for what they did in providing service. A new cost allocation process based on both capital investments in providing service as well as operating costs for various services came into use. This system focused on originating and terminating minutes of use over the networks. In some cases, more urbanized companies with lower costs of service paid into state "pools," which were then re-distributed to companies with higher costs of service. In several jurisdictions, LEGENT was a payer and Dynacom was a payee. This further irritated the competitive relationship between the two companies.

The impacts of all these changes caused companies to find new ways to achieve adequate returns on investment. The local exchange portion of the network was still regulated by individual states and the national regulatory structure was governed by the Federal Communications Commission. The states focused on assuring that competition flourished, telephone rates remained reasonable and service evolved to "state-of-the-art" status. State and federal governments had long used the telephone carriers as a means to collect needed funding for social programs and this continued with the addition of special fees and surcharges placed on telephone service to fund such things as educational and library access to the Internet. The resulting charges amounted to a significant premium on telephone services compared to similar services provided by cable television and cellular competitors. The landmark Communications Act of 1996 set in motion further changes in industry regulation. In a few cases, state regulators de-regulated rate structures while maintaining control over service quality. Cellular service began to eat into the wire line customer base and growth rates in many companies dropped off significantly.

As the 20th century drew to a close, cable television companies intensified their efforts to take customers away from telephone companies. They did this by packaging telephone services with traditional Community Antenna Television (CATV) services and Internet access. Those telephone companies who had modernized their networks with optic cables and who had gotten into CATV and Internet-based services responded with packages of their own. The trend, however, was a slow but steady decline in the number of wire line telephone customers in the more urban portions of the country and a flattening of the wire line growth in the rural areas.

Faced with this changing environment, an aging Charles Corbin, ever on the lookout for a new acquisition, knew that Dynacom needed to make a significant investment in cellular technology to augment its wire line predominantly fiber optic network. Philippe Legrane had taken his profits and retired to his winery in France when LEGENT stock reached an all time high in the 1980s. The LEGENT management team, moved to acquire its most competitive rival.

In the small Michigan village of Farnsworth, the Warner family operated the local telephone and CATV companies over a broadband network facing minimal competition. They could not have anticipated how the fallout from the LEGENT's acquisition of Dynacom was about to impact them.

(1)

The bus driver signaled for a left turn, waited for two cars and a pickup truck to pass, and turned into the side street just before the stoplight. The stoplight was one of three in Caro. With a hiss of the brakes, the bus came to a stop in front of an ivy covered grey stone building. A wide porch took up half the front and the side. A red neon arrow pointed down a staircase at the left of the building's face to a café in the basement. A faded Indian Trails Bus Station sign hung from one of the stone pillars that supported the porch overhang.

The bus driver hoisted himself out of his seat and without turning said, "This is it mister, this is Caro." He then proceeded to open the baggage area underneath the bus seating area. The lone remaining passenger, McCann, stepped down to retrieve his bag. The canvas tote he carried clashed with the hand tooled leather two-suiter that the driver pulled from the baggage area. The driver eyed him again just as he had when McCann had boarded the bus in Chicago. It was clear that the pinstriped suit, Florsheim shoes and $50 tie that McCann wore weren't the clothes his passengers usually wore. It was also clear that he hadn't dropped anyone dressed like that in Caro in quite a while. At six feet one, McCann was well built and carried his 200 pounds well. His black hair, brushed with a bit of gray at the temples, dark blue eyes, tanned face and rugged features gave him a Marlboro Man appearance, less the dangling cigarette. He had a way of gazing intently at people in a manner that made it seem as though those blue eyes were boring right through them. The driver looked away as McCann regarded him intently.

McCann took his bag, palmed a $5 bill into the driver's hand while bidding him goodbye and turned toward the steps. At that moment an urgent shout arrested him.

"Mr. McCann! Hello – welcome to Caro! I have a car right over here!"

McCann turned and recognized an older version of the man he had known 25 years ago. Leonard Olzewski was heavier now and his hair was thinner. His choice of clothes, McCann observed, hadn't changed much. The checkered sports jacket clashed with his brown slacks and the green floral tie did nothing to help matters.

McCann turned toward him and extended his hand. His smile was thin.

"Hello Leo, how are you? Are the papers ready?"

He mentally kicked himself. He hadn't waited for the real estate broker to respond before getting down to business. Oh well, it was hard to shed habits learned in 20 years of corporate America. He would have plenty of time now to change his ways.

Leonard Olzewski pulled a rumpled handkerchief from his hip pocket and hastily wiped his ruddy face. It was as if by this gesture that he expected to prepare himself in his client's eyes for the business to be done this day.

"They're all ready. Mr. Penay at the Farnsworth State Bank has us scheduled for 3:00 p.m.," he responded quickly.

McCann guessed that Fred Penay probably didn't have much on his calendar that would interfere with the transfer of ownership of a 100-acre farm, the payoff of a mortgage that the bank had held for over 30 years and the deposit of $250,000 into a new checking account.

"Excellent, Leo. Let's not keep him waiting. I know you are both busy."

Olzewski led the way to a station wagon parked nearby. McCann threw his bag and tote in the back and slid into the passenger's seat.

"How are the kids Leo?"

Olzewski pulled away from the curb and headed up Caro's main street. McCann observed that the view hadn't changed much in the last two decades. A pizza place had gone in where the dress shop had been, and a video store had replaced the old hardware store. There were a few vacant, yet clean, storefronts and the bank continued to be the most prominent structure in the business district. The county courthouse looked older but much the same as he remembered it.

"You wouldn't know them Mr. McCann. They're all grown up. Anna is going to get married and Rosa is in Detroit working for Ford. Martha is teaching in Farnsworth so we get to see her quite often."

"Any grandchildren yet?" McCann asked, making conversation.

"None are married. We keep hoping." Olzewski said quietly, looking straight ahead.

"I'm sorry Leo, I should have known that" McCann felt guilty and promised himself to pay more attention before asking personal or sensitive questions. He made sure that he didn't ask about Lottie. Leo's wife was the cross he had carried for thirty years of marriage and quite well known throughout the county seat for her flamboyant lifestyle. He was sure that Leo's real estate business was hard pressed to keep her in clothes and liquor.

The twelve-mile trip to Farnsworth took fifteen minutes. McCann noted that most of the farms along the way looked well maintained. The crops of corn and beans looked promising and the landscape was as featureless as he remembered. The interior of Michigan's "thumb" was clearly not a place that attracted tourists.

His attention perked up as they approached Farnsworth. The farm buildings at the edge of town had been replaced by a Laundromat and a row of rather drab looking townhouses.

"Progress in Farnsworth Leo?" McCann asked pointing to the townhouses.

"That's not what I would call it," Olzewski responded. McCann concluded that Leo's realty firm hadn't earned commissions on the sale of townhouses in Farnsworth.

The downtown business district, if you could call it that, was five blocks, with a stop light at the intersection of Main and Cedar. The Farnsworth State Bank occupied the southeast corner of the intersection. Other than some new windows, the bank remained the same two story brown edifice that had anchored this corner of town for over half a century. McCann noted that the Federated department store in the middle of the block before the light had a wooden sign overhanging the old façade. A bright red barn set against a blue sky and the words "Barnes' Loft" in Algerian script didn't quite cover the old "Federated" sign.

"Something else is new," McCann remarked.

"Donna Barnes leased the old Federated and opened up a clothing store about five years ago. She's doing reasonably well…caters to the farmers and their wives."

McCann's pulse quickened at the mention of the name. Feelings from 20 years ago surfaced and he fought them back.

"I think I may have known her when I worked on the farm in the summer" he said.

"She found religion too," Olzewski remarked in a condemning tone.

"I didn't know she lost it," McCann replied, remembering nights long ago.

"Her old man didn't know she did," Olzewski said with meaning in his voice. "He knows she has it now. She quotes scripture to him and he doesn't like it much."

McCann remembered Ed Barnes and his religion quite well. Part of McCann's attitude towards organized religion sprang from those memories. He wondered if Donna Barnes' newfound religion was any different from her father's.

The two men walked in the front door of the bank. A tall thin man wearing a dark gray suit and white shirt stood as they entered and motioned them to come through the low wooden gate that separated the office area from the teller's cages to the right of the entrance. McCann felt as though he had stepped back in time. Fred Penay hadn't changed much in over two decades. He had aged well, and a casual observer would not guess that Penay was senior to McCann by fifteen years.

"How good to see you, Wilson," Penay said, extending his hand. "How are you, Leo?"

"We came straight here as soon as Mr. McCann arrived," Olzewski replied.

"Good, good. Please sit down. I believe everything is ready," Penay replied, motioning McCann and Leo to chairs opposite the desk. He sat and produced a folder bulging with several documents.

"The wire transfer that you sent, Wilson, has been applied to the accounts owing to various businesses in Farnsworth and Caro. I have received receipts from all of the creditors releasing any claims they had against the estate. That has freed the bank to sell the farm to you to satisfy its mortgage. As you already know, there is nothing else in the estate of Fred and Ella Harms other than the farm and the various furnishings and equipment associated with it. Do you have any questions?"

"None," replied McCann.

"Good, good. Upon receipt of your check for the amount owed to the bank, I will sign the release of the mortgage. As the administrator of Fred and Ella's estate, I can tell you that several people here in Farnsworth were relieved to receive payment of their claims."

"I'm pleased," McCann said, not meaning it.

"Now, Leo, do you have the closing statements and transfers?" Penay asked, putting on a pair of half glasses that suddenly made him look his age.

"Right here, Mr. Penay. I'm real pleased to see this property in Mr. McCann's possession," Olzewski said, producing a small folded sheaf of papers from his inside jacket pocket. "You will find everything in order."

"I'm sure I will, Leo. You always do good work," the banker said sincerely. McCann had to bite the inside of his lip to keep from smiling. Penay was ever the gentleman. Leo had done very little to sell the farm except hold the real estate listing. It was Penay's call to McCann that had produced the eventual sale.

"Wilson, do you have a check for the balance of the mortgage?" Penay asked, peering over the rim of his glasses at McCann.

McCann reached into his suit coat pocket and produced a cashier's check. The amount was in six figures. He passed it to Penay and watched Olzewski's eyes widen expectantly.

"Good, good," replied Penay. "I will deposit this check to the estate's account as well. Here is the deed and the keys to the house. I believe the outbuildings are locked, and the keys to the locks and the vehicles are in the kitchen. Is that correct, Leo?"

"Absolutely. I checked them all myself just last Monday" Olzewski replied. "When will you be drawing a check for me, Mr. Penay?"

"I have it right here, Leo," Penay said as he handed Olzewski his commission on the transaction. "I believe that concludes our business here today and I thank you again for an excellent job."

Olzewski knew that he was being dismissed. He stood uncertainly and held out his hand to McCann. McCann took it without rising and smiled up at the realtor.

"Thank you, Leo, for all your help," He said.

"Will you need a ride out to the house?" Olzewski asked tentatively

"No, I think I can get out there on my own. Thanks anyway."

Olzewski hesitated, obviously wanting to say more. He swallowed and plunged ahead. "I'm real glad you came back Mr. McCann. I'm only sorry it had to be because of what happened at Dynacom."

There it was, out in the open. They obviously read the *Wall Street Journal* even here in Farnsworth. Penay raised his head slightly and looked McCann full in the face. He said nothing.

"That's in the past, Leo. This is a new day," McCann replied quietly, repeating a phrase he had used many times in the past 20 years. On previous occasions he had been in quite a different position. He didn't like this one all that much.

"Yes, well, I'd best be going. Lottie will be expecting me." Olzewski replied.

McCann thought to himself, "Lottie will want to count the commission and figure out how to spend it before the week is over." Olzewski turned and left the bank.

"Wilson, I'm sure Leo meant no harm," Penay said quietly.

"It's all right Fred. It only hurts when I think about it. That happens almost every day now. I expect it will get better. I have one more piece of business for you. I'd like to open a checking account."

Penay was obviously surprised. He was more than surprised when McCann reached in his coat pocket and produced a second cashier's check in the amount of $250,000 and handed it to the banker.

Fred Penay didn't usually open checking accounts for new customers at the bank. He made an exception for Wilson McCann. He kept up a polite banter while he completed the paperwork. When his offer of a ride to the farm was quickly accepted, he chatted about the current prices for beans and corn and the general economic climate of the area during the mile and one half ride to the Harms place. McCann said little and Penay dropped him off with repeated offers to be of help in any way possible. McCann's responses were quiet, short and appreciative and, Penay thought, slightly cold.

On his way back to the bank, Fred Penay wondered aloud, "Why did he come here and what does he want?" He didn't have any answers to his questions. Penay was a patient man. Perseverance had seen him and his bank through good times and bad. At the bank, he removed a folder titled "McCann-Dynacom" from his desk drawer. He took out a folded piece of newspaper containing an article headlined "McCANN – BAILEY COUNTER OFFER REJECTED – DYNACOM ACQUISITION APPROVED". As he read the article yet again, he was confident that the answers would come in due time.

Five men sat at a table in the back of a weathered frame house just off Highway 31 in the crossroad community of Brutus in Michigan's Emmett County. Two were dressed appropriately for the area in work pants and shirts. Two were dressed in suits, shirts and ties. One was dressed in a golf shirt and slacks. It was this latter man who held a folder bulging with real estate papers. He looked at the two suits and pulled a property deed from the folder.

"I think everything is in order here gentlemen. Do you have a check?" he said. Out of the corner of his eye, he noted the expectant looks on the faces of the two in work shirts.

"May I see the property transfer papers and the deed?" the smaller of the two suits asked. His partner, a tall sandy haired man, looked on passively.

"Certainly."

Scanning the papers quickly, the shorter man turned slightly to his partner and nodded. "It's all in order, Ross," he said, waiting.

The taller man reached inside his suit coat and removed a plain white envelope. He extracted a bank draft and handed it to the golf shirt, who looked at it briefly, showed it to the two work shirts and placed it on top of the folder.

"I think we are finished, gentlemen," He said.

"Not quite," the tall man responded, looking at each of the others for a moment. "I want to reemphasize that this transaction is not to be discussed with anyone. If any of you are approached by anyone seeking information as to the buyer's intentions for this property, you are to say that you do not know anything about that. Just give them my number. In return for your agreement to keep this transaction as confidential as is possible, we have paid you an extra five per cent over the agreed upon purchase price. He paused for effect. "Is that clear?"

The two work shirts and the golf shirt nodded. Five per cent of the agreed upon purchase price was ten thousand dollars. Split three ways, it was good money in this part of the state.

All five rose. The two work shirts shook hands with the two suits and the suits left. The golf shirt and the two work shirts looked at the check, congratulating themselves on their good fortune. Each wondered why the sale of one hundred acres of Emmett County land was such a hush-hush matter.

The two suits got into a Chevrolet Trail Blazer and headed east from the main intersection in Brutus. About three miles down the road, they passed a small brick building. A wooden sign reading "LEGENT" had been fastened over a somewhat larger brass sign that read "Dynacom Communications". Two miles further brought them to Burt Lake. They turned right and accelerated south along the road around the lake until they came to a large home secluded among the trees. Once inside, the taller man dialed a number and spoke briefly.

"The purchase is completed. They have been reminded to keep quiet. But I must warn you this is going to leak out at some time. Someone will read about the land sale and begin to ask questions about Wolverine Property Management. People are going to wonder what's going on."

Two hundred miles south of Burt Lake in Lansing, the Governor of the State of Michigan smiled. "We will deal with that when it comes, Ross," he said.

(2)

Wilson McCann stood in the driveway and looked around. The farm was much as he remembered it. The barn set against the side of the hill. The large hip-roofed tool shed directly behind the house dwarfed the smaller cribs and sheds. The house itself was non-descript. Fred Harms had not spent much on the buildings, preferring to put his money into more land and equipment instead. His mother's sister had had to make do with what she was given or could earn from selling produce from the garden and eggs from her chickens. As he looked out over the fields behind the barn, the memories flooded in. He had been a senior in high school when his father died. His mother needed all the financial help she could get to make ends meet for the two of them on her meager salary as a clerk in a large law firm. When Fred Harms offered summer employment for Wilson, he and his mother realized it was an opportunity not to be missed. The money would get them through the winter in Chicago when heating bills in their apartment would eat into their funds. Both felt that the physical labor under the direction of his uncle, together with the chance to get away from the city for the summer would do Wilson good.

The work had been hard. Fred Harms was a stern, hard working farmer. He was also fair to his only nephew. "Fair" was a word that Wilson James McCann had come to use often. Fred Harms believed in a fair day's work for a fair day's pay, in that order. Wilson had worked on this farm every summer until he graduated from the University of Illinois. He reflected often that he was the better for it.

And now the farm was his. All 100 acres of it. Fred Harms had finally run out of energy, time and money. He had died slumped over a piece of farm equipment in the middle of a 10-acre field. His wife died two years later of congestive heart failure. The long years of hard work, the unrelenting pressure of unpaid bills and the constant pressure to put another year of promises into the ground had broken their two hearts. At least that was what McCann surmised.

Fred Penay had called two weeks before the Dynacom acquisition counter offer had been rejected. The day after McCann had sat in Charles Corbin's office at Dynacom headquarters and been relieved of his duties, he returned Penay's call. His only goal had been to get out of Chicago as fast as he could and to go somewhere to heal. He had avoided the press today by taking a cab to the bus station. No one would expect the former CEO of a nationwide telecommunications company to ride a bus to Michigan's "Thumb"!

The two checks plus the wire transfer had totaled $600,000. It was a minor part of McCann's severance package from Dynacom. The wire transfer of $100,000 had paid off the creditors in Farnsworth and Caro and freed the bank, as administrator of the Harms estate, to sell the farm to pay off the bank's mortgage. The first check for $250,000 had taken care of that. The second check established his operating funds for as long as he stayed in Farnsworth. His mother, now living quietly in Ft. Myers, would not benefit frm her sister and brother-in-law's estate consisting of this farm and its furnishings and equipment which now belonged to McCann. McCann took some comfort from the knowledge that the $1,000,000 annuity that he had purchased for her five years ago would take care of her very nicely.

He turned, picked up his bag and tote and walked to the back door of the house, inserted the key and turned the handle and entered the kitchen. The kitchen was just as his aunt had left it a year ago when she died except that it had been cleaned by the ladies of her church and the perishables removed. He opened a cupboard door and idly scanned the dishes, glasses and other china that were inside. "K-Mart specials" he muttered to himself. If it came to a choice between decent table china and a new plow to work the land, the plow always got the nod.

He reflected on the similarities between the approach of Fred Harms to his farm and that of Charles Corbin, the Chairman of Dynacom. Both had been quick to invest in plant and equipment and slow to take care of their people. In doing so, both had incurred excessive debt, and that in the end had brought them down.

ACQUISITION

"That's in the past; this is a new day," McCann said aloud. The question was what to do with the days ahead. He didn't have an answer.

He walked through the living room and into one of the two bedrooms. It was the one where he slept as a teenager and college student. He placed the suitcase on the bed and opened it. Two suits. Two pairs of slacks. Assorted underwear; three pairs of socks. A pair of white shirts in original packaging filled the space not used by his shaving kit. A pair of boat shoes was jammed into a corner.

"I'll need a different wardrobe for my new line of work," he muttered to himself as he hung the clothes in the musty closet.

He pulled off his tie and suit coat and walked back to the kitchen. The keys to the outbuilding locks were where Leo had said they would be. "Better find out what I bought," he thought to himself as he went outside.

Unlocking the padlock and opening the hasp, the big tool shed door rolled back at his push. He flicked the light switch and looked around. A 12-year old Ford Ranger pickup with its hood up faced the doorway. Behind it, an even older Buick LeSabre sedan with two flat tires sat heading away from him. A John Deere gleaner occupied the far corner and a John Deere tractor sat beside it. Both looked to be in good shape. Various pieces of farm equipment filled the other far corner. A fluorescent shop light added to the light coming in through a window over a work bench that held an assortment of tools.

He opened the driver's side door to the pickup and saw that the keys were in the ignition. He climbed in and turned the key. The engine growled once and died. He switched it off and climbed out, pocketing the keys.

A battery charger with 15-foot cables sat on one end of the bench. He plugged it in, carried the cables to the pickup and connected them. He turned the charger on and watched the needle move to the 12V symbol on the gauge. The charger began to hum.

"Maybe I'll have wheels by tonight," he said to himself, remembering the BMW that he had left in Chicago to be picked up by Dynacom's fleet manager.

Walking to the barn, he unlocked the door to the stable area. The door rolled back with only minor effort, and the familiar smells engulfed him.

The stalls were empty and the feed alley had cobwebs stretching across it. A battered Philco radio sat on a shelf at the end of the alley. The stairs to the loft area were at his left and he climbed up into the second story of the barn. The mows to the right and left of the stairs were empty and the one directly ahead of him held about three feet of hay and cornstalks. What few cattle were left on the farm had been sold to pay off an account at the feed store.

He was about to go back down the stairs when a faint whimper from the mow in front of him caught his attention. He looked into the mow and could see an outline of something or someone lying back in the hay. Climbing the first three pegs of the ladder to get a better look, he saw an emaciated black and white Border Collie lying in the hay. The dog was so near dead that he couldn't lift his head. McCann knew that it must have been in the barn when Olzewski checked the farm last Monday. When Leo locked the door, he had locked the dog in without food or water.

McCann quickly found an old coffee can and filled it with water from the tap at the end of the feed alley. He returned to the mow and lifted the dog's head to drink from the can. The animal lapped the water greedily and lay back. McCann repeated the process one more time before lifting the dog to the edge of the mow and considering how to get it down to the main floor. It was then that he heard the sound of a vehicle in the driveway and the slam of its door.

"In the barn! I need some help!" he called as loudly as he could. The dog's eyes flickered fearfully but it didn't move.

He heard someone enter the barn and start to climb the stairs. A man in his early 30's stepped into the loft and looked at McCann. He had a Caterpillar Cap pushed back on his head.

"Hello, I'm Jim Marks. What have you got there?" he asked.

"I just found this dog and he's near dead. Can you help me get him down?" McCann replied.

Marks came to the edge of the hay to see the dog. "Oh Teddy, what have you done now?" he said.

"You know this dog?" McCann asked.

"Yes sir. He belonged to the Harms. Since they're gone, he hangs around here until he gets hungry. Then he comes to our place or waits in front of the Barnes' Loft for Donna to feed him."

The mention of Donna Barnes caused McCann to quickly look up. "Why would he do that?"

"Donna sort of took care of Mrs. Harms after Fred died. Took her to church, brought her groceries, drove her to the doctor and the like. She made over Ted and feeds him when he comes around. He mostly hangs around here."

Together, the two men lowered the dog to the floor of the loft.

"I've got some bread in the truck; I'll get a few slices and see if he will eat." Marks said as he started down the stairs. "By the way, I'm guessing you are Wilson McCann?"

"That's right," McCann replied. "I just got here."

"I know. I stopped in at the bank and Mr. Penay said you were out here." Marks said over his shoulder as he disappeared. "News travels fast here!" thought McCann to himself as he stroked the dog's head.

Marks returned shortly and broke several slices of bread into pieces and slowly fed them to the dog along with more water. Soon, the animal raised his head and tried to stand.

"Let's carry him down. I'll get some hay and make a bed for him," McCann said. Marks looked at McCann's pin striped suit pants and white shirt and said that he would get the hay and carry the dog down. McCann led the way carrying the coffee can.

"I'm meaning to get some work clothes as soon as I can get that old pickup in the tool shed running," he said.

"Are you planning to work the place then?" Marks asked, looking up.

"I'm not sure yet what I'll do. I worked here for uncle Fred during several summers about 20 years or so ago."

"You like farming? There's not a lot of money to be made on a 100 acre farm." Marks muttered his observation quietly, as if in testimony to a sad fact.

"I can't say that I liked it much when I was younger but Fred taught me a lot about planting and harvesting and caring for livestock and such," McCann said reflectively, thinking of his uncle's stern directions as to the right and wrong of everyday farm chores.

"The battery in the pickup is probably dead. It hasn't been moved since Ella died. I'll give you a jump if you want," Marks offered.

"Thanks. I have it on the charger but that will take a while."

"Good thing I came along when I did. By the way, I live one mile straight east of you. My wife and I bought the old Heeley place"

McCann extended his hand. "I'm glad to meet you. I take it you like farming?"

Marks lifted his cap and scratched his head, looking at the ground. "It's not easy on a small acreage. My wife does some bookwork for businesses in town to help out. But we feel that the farm is a good place to raise our children. I wanted to ask you if you would be interested in leasing me the back 40 acres for the coming year. Mrs. Harms let me work it on shares the last year before she died."

McCann had made a living out of judging people and putting people in the right jobs to get the right results. His immediate reaction to Jim Marks was that he was the right man to trust to get a job done.

"I don't know just yet what I am going to do with the farm. But when I do, I'll certainly consider that. What did you have in mind?"

"Well, Mrs. Harms took a third and I took two thirds and we split the cost of seed and fertilizer. I'd really like to just pay rent and take the crop this time" Marks replied. He looked McCann straight in the eye as he talked. "I'd be willing to pay the going rate per acre and trust the Lord to provide a good crop and a good price."

McCann thought the reference to the Lord a bit unusual. "Give me your phone number. I'll call you when I decide something. It won't be long." McCann said as Marks prepared to drive his pickup closer to the tool shed.

The two men connected the two pickups using a set of jumper cables that Marks pulled from behind his seat. McCann turned the Ranger's ignition switch. It growled, caught and came to life. The gas gauge showed half a tank and he let the engine run as Marks disconnected the cables and stowed them in his truck.

"I don't think you'll be calling me until you get your phone hooked up," he said casually.

"Where do I do that, at the co-op?" McCann asked.

"The co-op was bought out ten years ago by the Warner family," Marks replied. "Doug Warner runs it now. He goes to our church." Marks hesitated and then continued. "By the way, do you go to church Mr. McCann?"

McCann would have been offended by this question under normal circumstances. He hadn't darkened a church door in five years. But he liked this young farmer and his straightforward manner.

"I haven't found one I like yet," he said evenly.

"You'll like ours. It's the United Methodist, located one block off Main behind the bakery. Charles Hastings is a great pastor," Marks said enthusiastically as he climbed into his truck.

"I'll consider that a testimony," McCann replied, digging deep into his vocabulary to use a word that hadn't crossed his lips in a long time. "I'll get my phone hooked up and I'll call you when I decide what I intend to do with the farm."

"Thanks. See you in church. Oh — and welcome to Farnsworth" Marks said in his easygoing manner as he started the pickup. He leaned out the window smiling. "If you need any dog food, the Agway is a good place to get it. I'll be seeing you, Mr. McCann"

"I usually go by Wils," McCann replied, smiling.

Marks returned the smile. "Right, good luck in whatever you decide to do with the farm. I hope you'll consider my proposition" Marks smiled back

"Which one, the 40 acre rent or the church on Sunday?"

"Both" Marks yelled as he backed down the driveway and drove away.

"He didn't even ask me what I was doing here," McCann thought to himself as he returned to the barn to check on the dog. "I like that young man."

The dog was standing and drinking the last of the water in the can when McCann walked into the barn. He turned to McCann and licked his hand.

"Looks like you're feeling better Ted" McCann said as he scratched the dog's ears and watched its tail wag east and west.

He turned toward the barn door. The dog slowly followed him outside and up to the pickup. Without warning, he summoned his remaining strength and jumped into the passenger's seat through the open door. He lay down and began to lick his paws.

"Looks like I've found myself a co-pilot," McCann grinned as he slid into the driver's seat and reached across the dog to close the door.

He drove the pickup out of the tool shed and stopped to close the door. The dog remained where it was. McCann slid behind the wheel, scratched Ted behind his left ear, drove out the driveway and headed toward Farnsworth.

For the first time in six months, Wilson McCann was whistling.

Donna Barnes was straightening a pile of sweaters and looking over her shoulder at the clock on the back wall when the door opened. Wednesday afternoon was always slow and she turned with her smile at the ready." Good afternoon, can I help…" her voice trailed off as she recognized McCann. He was older, thicker, and darker than he had been as a teenager going into manhood but there was no mistaking the jut of his jaw and the black wavy hair. In his pinstriped suit pants, white shirt open at the collar and wing tipped dress shoes, he looked strangely out of place. She thought she saw traces of hay in his pants cuffs and he had what looked like dog hair on one trouser leg. She caught her breath and started again.

"Hello Wils. I heard you bought the farm."

His smile was thin and questioning. "Hello, Donna. It's been a long time. Leo told me that you bought the old Federated store."

"I'm actually leasing it but I have an option to buy. I'm hoping that business will support a decision to do that."

The way she said it sounded entirely too businesslike. But she was talking to a business man wasn't she?

"I stand corrected. I have an old friend of yours in the pickup. Found him in my hay mow," he said, pulling a straw of hay from his cuff.

"I don't know if I can take two old 'friends' showing up in one day" she said putting a twist on the word.

"I understand he takes to you and spends time lying in front of the store" McCann replied, catching the emphasis she had placed on the word "friends."

"Ted!" she exclaimed and he saw a light in her eyes that hadn't been there before. "You found him in your hay mow? What was he doing there?"

"Mostly dying from lack of water and food." McCann replied tersely. He put up his hand as she began to exclaim again. "It's okay! A young man named Marks came along just when I was trying to get him down from the mow and get some water into him. He told me that Ted hangs out here when he is not at the farm or over at his place. I thought you might be able to tell me what to feed him seeing as how you have experience. We fed him some bread and he drank a lot of water and he seems to be better. He even jumped into the pickup for our trip to town!"

She relaxed and smiled. "Purina 1 for dogs is what Ella fed him. I feed him the same – when he's here. I keep a bag in the back for him. I'll get it if you are going to take over." The last was said as a question, and she looked at him steadily when she asked it.

"If you're asking am I staying for a while, I guess the answer is yes. I'll take care of Ted if he wants to stay with me," he said, smiling.

"He'll stay there forever if you feed him." She said it like a schoolteacher and he didn't miss the message. She was challenging him to be responsible, just like she had many years ago when they were young. He glanced down at his shoes and then at the counters holding jeans, shirts and work shoes. "I don't think I am properly dressed for my latest venture. These probably won't hold up long at the rate I'm going. I'll need a couple of pairs of jeans, two work shirts, some socks and a pair of those Wolverines."

She was glad for the distraction of doing business. She quickly pulled two pairs of jeans from the middle of a stack on one counter, a flannel shirt from another and waited expectantly as he took them.

"You're pretty good at guessing a man's size," he smiled. "Can you guess my shoe size too?"

"I've been doing it for a while. You know...just like you in your field." She was sorry the minute the words left her lips for she saw the smile vanish and the firm set to the jaw return. "I'd guess 10 ½ - am I right?"

The smile didn't return but the face softened a little. "Right on," he said.

"Do you want work or hiking?" she asked

"What's the difference?" McCann was glad that Donna had turned away to reach for the boots. She was not as dashingly beautiful as she had been as a girl going into young womanhood but she was somehow even more attractive in the grey skirt and white blouse with her hair neatly pinned up. The glasses she had so hated were gone and he wondered if she wore contacts.

"About $30" she replied, turning and holding up two contrasting pairs of boots.

"I'll take the work boots then. I'm sort of on a fixed income now." He was smiling again as he said it.

"Right you are! You knew that hikers were more expensive." She smiled back.

"Just in Farnsworth. I could get them less expensively in Chicago," he said, opening the door for what he knew she would ask before he left.

"And will you be going back there soon?" she asked, as she added two pairs of work socks and started to write up the sales slip.

"That depends on a lot of things," he replied evenly. "You know what happened to Dynacom I presume? Fred Penay and Leo Olzewski obviously do and maybe Jim Marks too although he was too nice to bring it up."

She put her pen down, leaned on the counter and looked him straight in the eye. "Yes, Wils, I do know what happened. At least what I read in the papers. I know how hard it must have been for you after all you put into the company"

He was strangely glad that the last remark didn't sound bitter or cynical. "Someday perhaps I can tell you my side, but not now." He said this with some finality as he handed her his credit card.

"Sorry Wils, I don't take credit cards. Can't afford to pay the banks their cut off the top. Strictly cash or, in your case, I can write you up a bill and you can send me a check." Her tone indicated that he was still someone special to her. She hoped that it showed and that it made up for her earlier gaffe.

"You might have to check with Fred Penay at the bank to be sure I'm good for it. He has my account now." McCann smiled as he pulled bills from his wallet. "This should cover it." She made change and got the bag of dog food from the back of the store. Together, they walked to the pickup where he placed the dog food and the sack of clothing in the bed. The dog leaned out the window and she scratched his ears.

"So Teddy, you have a new master. Take good care of him." Donna started for the store.

"Jim Marks said you took Ella to church." He said it matter-of-factly but there was a question there as well. She turned and his heart jumped a little just like it had when he had walked into the store and caught his first sight of her.

"Yes, I did. Near the end both Fred and Ella became believers" she said, waiting.

"In what, hard work?" he said, with a bit of a sneer.

"Fred and Ella changed a great deal in the years after you were here, Wilson. I'm sorry that you didn't get to know them during those years. Perhaps some time I can share a bit of what their lives were like if you can find the time," she replied, seemingly oblivious to his sarcasm.

McCann took a deep breath and started to turn away. He looked back at her. She was waiting for a response.

"Marks asked me to come to church," McCann said. "Do you also attend the United Methodist Church?"

"Yes I do, and I'd be pleased to see you there." There was a deeper meaning there although he couldn't grasp it. "Well, I'd best be going. Now that Ted's supper is assured, I need to lay in some supplies for myself. I wouldn't want you or any of the good citizens to find me in the hay mow dead from lack of food." The attempt at humor sounded like more sarcasm and she frowned.

"Good luck Wils — and thank you for your business. Take good care of Ted." With that she turned and went back in the store.

Wilson McCann gunned the motor of the Ranger and backed out into the street to head toward the Erlig supermarket on the edge of town.

"Well, Ted, I guess I need to watch my mouth a little better," he said as he patted the dog. Ted curled up on the seat and looked up at him with what seemed to be reproachful eyes.

(3)

McCann's mood when he woke the next morning was somber and he definitely didn't want any people contact. He fed Ted and examined the house and its furnishings more closely. He noticed that the living room was furnished more comfortably than when he had spent his summers here. A worn Bible lay on an end table under a crystal lamp. He opened the drapes to the window facing the road. Light flooded the room and it felt almost cozy standing in the bright sunshine. He wandered outside with the dog at his heels and went to the tool shed. It was obvious that the Buick had not been driven in some time and would require some work to get it operational. He checked the tractor and noted that the battery was disconnected. He re-clamped the leads and pressed the starter button while holding out the choke. The tractor roared to life, music echoed from the tape player mounted inside the rear fender. It was a choral version of "Amazing Grace." He quickly shut the player off. He could not in his wildest dreams, imagine Fred Harms playing "church music" while he tilled the soil!

He opened the door wide and drove the tractor out. A chain was hanging from a hook near the workbench and he attached it to the rear frame member of the Buick and to the draw bar on the tractor. Making sure the Buick was in neutral, he carefully pulled it through the door and into the yard. It sat there, lop-sided on its two flat tires, covered with dust, bird droppings and a few rust spots. He made sure it was far enough out of the shed to permit him to get the tractor and pickup in and out. He unhooked the chain while Ted watched expectantly from the doorway.

McCann checked the tractor's gas gauge and saw that the tank was half full. He drove it into the lane behind the barn and out to the fields beyond. Half way out, he turned the tape player back on and listened to the music as he drove along. The fields were overgrown with a combination of sweet clover, alfalfa and wild carrot. He wondered again why he had chosen to buy the place and come here.

Wilson McCann had risen quickly at Dynacom. He had joined the company right out of college as an economic forecaster in the Engineering/Planning department. His forecasts of the rural economy in the company's operating area had proven quite accurate and, as the company grew and acquired more properties, he grew with it. Eventually he moved into the Finance department and his knowledge of the operating territory and the economy soon resulted in his promotion to Chief Financial Officer. It was there that he came under the eye of Charles Corbin, the company's aggressive Chairman. Corbin had led the company through an era of unprecedented growth and expansion. His contacts in the financial community and in Washington enabled Dynacom to pretty much get what it wanted when it wanted it. A combination of cable manufacturing and service industry capability contributed to Dynacom's success. Unfortunately, Corbin was not a man to delegate authority. He filled Dynacom's board with a combination of Wall Street financiers and Washington "wannabes" who knew who their patron was and who did not cross him. That was the beginning of Dynacom's problems. A succession of CEOs quickly came and went and a succession of acquisitions quickly soured, leaving Dynacom with disorganization in its management team and debt on its Balance Sheet. McCann had cured the Balance Sheet problems with a progressive divestiture and consolidation program. As CFO, his plans were quickly adopted by Corbin as his own and pushed through over the objections of an expansion minded CEO with no financial background. When the CEO left, McCann stood ready to move up and Corbin quickly promoted him. McCann was ready to solidify Dynacom's position with more consolidation of operations and cost cutting as he modernized both the manufacturing facilities and the company's communication networks. As profits rose and financial strength returned, Corbin looked around for the next big "deal". He found it in SATCOM, a large wireless provider. The match was ideal from an operating standpoint. However, the acquisition turned on Dynacom's ability to finance a staggering amount of debt. The interest coverage alone, had sponged away most of McCann's hard won cost cutting gains. When the economy began to decline,

McCann knew they were in trouble. Profits dropped and soon Dynacom's stock price did as well. A planned public offering of stock to refinance a large portion of the SATCOM debt was shelved.

It was at this juncture that LEGENT showed up with an offer to buy Dynacom and take care of its problems. The per-share offer was ridiculously low but the prestige associated with the LEGENT deal was such that Corbin couldn't ignore it. It was to be the crowning achievement of his life. In addition to the glory, Corbin would be Vice Chairman of LEGENT and a member of its Strategic Planning Committee. When McCann and a group of management recommended a plan to further streamline Dynacom and go it alone, Corbin and his handpicked board quickly vetoed it.

McCann and his group had turned to Stu Bailey for help. Stu was a venture capitalist in New York City. He quickly put together a "White Knight" package and mounted a battle for control of Dynacom. Corbin and his board rejected the bid. Dynacom's stock soared on the news of the counter offer and fell equally as fast when Dynacom's board rejected it. LEGENT lowered its offer, Corbin recommended that Dynacom proceed and the deal was done.

The press had gone crazy. Articles in the *Tribune, Wall Street Journal* and *Business Week* made McCann and his group the bad guys in a deal which had gone bad for the small shareholders. Corbin was quoted saying that McCann had let his position as CEO go to his head and that his "Visions of Grandeur" had resulted in a lower bid from LEGENT. The day of the shareholder vote, two LEGENT men arrived in McCann's Chicago office and told him to clear out. McCann had exited through a rear door to evade the press gathered outside his office. Arriving at his condo in the Chicago suburbs, he encountered more TV crews staked outside. It was then that he remembered the call from Fred Penay. His anger, humiliation and hurt were enormous. His mother called from Florida to console him but she really didn't understand any of it. He had holed up in the condo for a week while he alternately fielded phone calls from the media asking for reactions that he would not give and making calls to Farnsworth to buy the farm. Then, two days ago, he had risen in the middle of the night, exited the condo through the rear entrance and walked five blocks to a newsstand where he called a cab and headed for the bus station.

ACQUISITION

All this ran through McCann's mind as he stopped the tractor and looked out over the fields. His anger returned. He knew that he had been right about Dynacom and he knew that he could have grown the company. Even the SATCOM acquisition would have paid for itself over time. If only he had been given a chance! He silently cursed Charles Corbin and his group of sycophants.

What should have been a very satisfying part of his life had gone sour. He had worked hard all his life. Even the summers on this farm had been hard under Fred Harms' unrelenting drive to try to make a living. He had worked hard in college. He wasn't a party animal like many of his friends. He had studied hard, spent his summer savings sparingly, and had little social life. On the few occasions where he had "loosened up", the relationships had been shallow, short and selfish. He had basically used people to satisfy his immediate needs for friendship and moved on.

That was really how he had treated Donna Barnes during his summers here. Donna was the daughter of one of Farnsworth's leading businessmen. Her father was also a pillar in the Presbyterian Church. His strict Christian principles had grated on his daughter and Wils McCann was just the young man to exploit her rebellion. Their summer relationship had been fast to take shape and fast to end when he went back to college each fall. Donna needed him as a part of her rebellion against her father and he needed Donna to survive his summers on Fred Harms' farm. He grudgingly admitted to himself that, despite the hard work and his Uncle's stern manner, Fred had taught him to love the farm, how to operate the equipment, care for the livestock and to resolve problems on his own, without requiring a lot of help. Those summers had been the birthplace of his strong self-reliance and independent nature. As he looked around the fields, he was surprised how much he felt at home in coming here.

Then, the summer before his senior year of college, Donna was gone. She had left Farnsworth abruptly in May and hadn't returned. As the summer passed, he heard that she had taken a summer internship with a missionary arm of the church and was working with children in some remote village in Eastern Europe. McCann couldn't imagine Donna reading Bible stories to kids and while he missed their relationship, he had become so self-reliant to the point that he didn't need her to get through the summer. In fact, the summer of his junior year had not been as much fun anyway. Donna had seemed more serious than during previous summers. She had, on several occasions, tried to talk to McCann about his future and what he wanted to do. She had even asked once if he felt anything for her as a part of that future. He had quickly changed the subject and she did not bring it up again. He noticed that something had come between them and that their relationship had become more distant but he did not care.

He substituted trips with local girls who were only interested in a good time to the VFW hall for Saturday night dances. That had satisfied his needs for female companionship and he left Farnsworth that fall vowing never to come back. And, he hadn't until now. He had sent flowers for Fred and Ella's funerals and donated $5,000 each to the local hospital foundation in their memory and that was that, until now. Yet in all those years, he often had remembered his days here in these fields and in the barn with a sense of satisfaction.

He looked back at the house and barn. He had $13,000,000 in cash, stocks and bonds, no friends and this run down farm to show for his life. Even the condo and his car had been owned by Dynacom and provided to him as part of his employment. Dynacom had been his home and his family and now they were gone. He turned the tractor and slowly drove back to the house. Ted trotted along behind, darting off into a field at intervals to flush a pheasant or partridge from the clover. He put the tractor in the tool shed and started for the house. He looked at the Buick.

"A picture of my life," he said aloud. "Proud, dirty and with two flat tires."

He spent the rest of the day wandering over the fields on foot with Ted. His mood did not lighten and he was no closer to knowing what he wanted to do than when he had arrived. He felt as though something inside of him had died. His bitterness at the way things turned out at Dynacom gripped him just as it had in Chicago. Standing in the corner of the back field, he leaned against the fence post and stared out over the landscape. He realized he must do something or this bitterness would consume him, but what?

The next day was Saturday. A UPS truck pulled into the yard and disgorged three large boxes. They contained the personal effects from his office including his laptop computer and printer. At noon, the mail man drove in, welcomed McCann to the area, and told him he would need a mail box out at the end of his drive. He handed over a letter from the superintendent at the condo asking when McCann's furnishings would be picked up. McCann decided it was time to turn on the phone. A small sticker on the kitchen wall phone advising that "To re-establish service – simply pick up the handset" caught his eye. When he picked the handset up and listened, a friendly voice advised him that while service hours were normally Monday through Friday, he could ask for weekend reconnection by dialing the repair center and giving his address. A number was provided. McCann was well aware that there would be a premium for weekend reconnection and hung up the phone.

"A quarter mil in the bank and I'm too tight to spring for an $85 connection fee!" He said to Ted who wagged his tail in obvious understanding of his master's mood.

He walked into the living room and sat down. Picking up the Bible from the lamp stand, he idly began leafing through it. He noted that the "Presented to" page was filled out showing that the Bible had been given to "Fred and Ella Harms on the occasion of their wedding" and the date. The "Family Religious History" page was also filled out, showing that both Fred and Ella had "Accepted Jesus Christ as their personal Savior" at the Farnsworth United Methodist Church about five years ago.

McCann stared at the page. He had last seen Fred and Ella Harms twenty-one years ago when he boarded the bus back to Chicago at the end of his final summer on the farm. They had looked old and care worn even then. Fred had died at age 76 and Ella two years later at age 78.

He began to flip the pages again and an envelope dropped to the floor. He picked it up and removed the card from inside. It was a birthday card. The front said "To my darling wife on her birthday".

During his four summers on the farm, McCann had never heard Fred Harms call his wife by any other name than her own. His manner was direct with her at all times and McCann did not remember any tender moments between them. Fred worked the fields and tended to the livestock and Ella kept the home, mowed the grass in the yard and took care of her chickens.

When an extra pair of hands was needed to bring in the hay or the grain or to help with the livestock, she donned a pair of jeans and helped out.

He opened the card. Below the pre-printed "With all my love" was a scrawl that he recognized as that of his Uncle. It said, "We have been brought together in our love for the Lord and our love for each other and I love you very much. Thank you for being my wife."

McCann laid the card aside, returned the Bible to the lamp stand and stared out the window. What had happened here five years ago? The thoughts expressed in the card were not from the man he knew to the woman he knew. Something had changed Fred and Ella Harms' lives. He remembered Leo Olzewski saying that Donna Barnes had "got religion" and Jim Marks had said that Donna had taken care of Ella after Fred's death and had taken her to church. McCann decided he would take Jim Marks up on his invitation to attend church the next day. Perhaps he would find the answers there to what had changed the Harms and what he was looking for in his own life.

Sunday morning was gloomy with rain misting the windshield of the Ranger as he headed into town. He wasn't sure what time the UMC church service started but he remembered that the Presbyterians had started at 11:00am when he and Donna had attended many years ago. Donna's father hadn't been fooled by their Sunday morning attendance at services. He continued to voice strong disapproval both of Donna's life style and her choice of a boy friend. Perhaps, he thought, the Methodists were on the same schedule.

The church sign showed 10:45am as the starting time for the morning worship. People were already going in as McCann parked the Ranger down the street from the church. He started up the walk only to be arrested by a shout from behind him.

"Mr. McCann — good to see you!" it was Jim Marks, accompanied by a short pleasant looking blonde with a page boy haircut and two small children.

McCann waited as the family came up. He extended his hand.

"I decided to take you up on your invitation," he said.

"It's great to see you here! This is my wife Lona and our children Trent and Susan," Marks said, shaking hands vigorously.

They walked into the church together and Lona Marks turned to McCann, "Won't you sit with us?"

"I'd be delighted," McCann responded as he followed them down the aisle. He was immediately sorry as they went all the way to the third row from the front before sitting down. Trent Marks squirmed in next to McCann and leaned his four-year old body against him. McCann tousled the boy's hair and looked away. In so doing, he locked eyes with Donna Barnes who was sitting on the right hand side of the aisle one row behind him. Her gaze was expectant and he smiled and nodded. She returned the smile and looked down at her bulletin.

He scanned the church. He was surprised to see a drum set and two guitars on the platform behind the altar. The heavy lectern and pulpit he remembered from his visit many summers ago, as part of an ecumenical youth party had been replaced by a smaller lectern which stood at the side. The large overstuffed chairs that had stood behind the pulpit had also been removed. It was clear that things had definitely changed at the UMC.

McCann had never been much of a churchman. He had gone with Donna during the summers to the Presbyterian Church and to youth events in the community. His mother usually went to the Methodist church near their Chicago apartment when she went, mostly on holidays such as Thanksgiving, Easter and Christmas. McCann went to church sporadically during his career at Dynacom. He had stopped going altogether five years ago. He hadn't missed it.

The pastor, a tall, thin man in his late thirties seated himself in the front row and three musicians and a pianist ascended the platform and began to play softly. On cue, the congregation rose and sang the "Gloria Patri". It was followed by a short Pastoral prayer. Then, from somewhere in the rear, a projector clicked on and words to various choruses were displayed on the back wall of the platform. The congregation began to sing and McCann noticed several raised hands as the music reached a lively beat.

On one chorus, the congregation clapped in accompaniment to the music and he noted that Jim Marks and his family clapped along. Trent Marks looked up at McCann quizzically as he stood stiffly. He began to wish he had not come.

The music ended with another prayer and the congregation sat as they sang two verses of "How Great Thou Art". The drummer and the two guitar players exited the platform as the last words were sung and the pianist did likewise as the pastor stepped behind the lectern.

"Turn in your Bibles to Matthew 6:25 please," he said, opening his own.

"Today I would like to talk to you about worry and seeking God's kingdom," he paused and then began to read the passage. McCann noted that Jim and Lona Marks had Bibles open on their laps and were following along with heads bowed. The two children were quiet. His attention snapped back to the reading as the pastor concluded

"......But seek first His kingdom and His righteousness; and all these things shall be added to you. Therefore do not be anxious for tomorrow; for tomorrow will care for itself. Each day has enough trouble of its own."

The pastor looked up and stepped out from behind the lectern. "Two questions – what are you worried about and what are you seeking?" He said as his eyes moved over the congregation.

"Two answers," McCann thought to himself, "Nothing" and "I wish I knew."

For the next twenty minutes, Charles E. "Chuck" Hastings spoke quietly and effectively on his text. McCann was impressed. "He would make a good marketing plan presenter," he thought to himself.

It was obvious that Hastings knew the Bible and was comfortable in expressing his understanding of its truths. McCann glanced around as the Pastor reached the end of his message. All of the adults and most of the children were listening closely to what was being said.

"So, I challenge you today. If you do not know Jesus Christ as your personal Savior, commit your life to him and accept His plan for your life. Follow His direction to seek God's kingdom and His righteousness and let Him carry the burdens of your life. If you have not done this, please talk with Him now as we pray. If you would like to talk with me, I will be at the front of the church following the service."

The congregation rose as one and bowed their heads. The pastor prayed and closed the service. People began to collect themselves and start for the rear of the church. McCann noticed a young couple walking slowly to the front to talk with the Pastor.

He turned to see if Donna Barnes was still in her seat and saw that she was sitting with head bowed in prayer. Jim and Lona Marks also sat and bowed their heads.

McCann walked up the aisle and out of the church. He noted that many of the congregation were dropping envelopes and money in offering plates on either side of the church door. He had wondered what had become of the Methodists' customary taking of the offering during the service.

He drove home slowly. What was he seeking here? Why was there a feeling of unease that accompanied his anger whenever he thought of Dynacom and his past? He changed into his jeans and ate his lunch. He took Ella Harms' Bible and sat on the back steps of the house with Ted. The air held the smell of the coming of fall. He flipped the pages of the Bible restlessly and then turned to the verses that the Pastor had read that morning. He noticed a cross-reference at Matthew 19: 30 and turned to it. He read

"But many who are first will be last, and many who are last will be first."

He thought of his rise to power at Dynacom and his rapid fall from it. He thought of Jim Marks and his family sitting with their heads bowed in prayer and he thought of Donna Barnes' expectant glance at him this morning.

Wilson McCann, former CEO of Dynacom, buried his head in his hands and cried for the first time since his mother had told him thirty years ago that his father was dead. As his body shook with sobs, Ted rested his head against McCann's knee and waited.

(4)

Stu Bailey put down the phone and leaned back in his chair. It was Monday morning in New York City. His back was to the door to his office. He looked out the window and could just make out the top of the Empire State Building over the tops of the buildings opposite his office on 3rd Avenue. He quickly reviewed in his mind what he had just heard. He turned and pressed a button on the phone. His secretary answered, "Yes Mr. Bailey?"

"Jeanine, I need to talk to Wils McCann."

"Yes sir, I'll try to reach him."

Bailey looked out the window again. He couldn't believe it. LEGENT was already shedding pieces of Dynacom! Was there an opportunity for a quick killing there? His instinct told him there was but only if the right combination of leverage and management could be brought to bear. Was it worth a look? There would certainly be plenty of bidders.

His phone buzzed. "Mr. McCann's phone at his condominium has been disconnected Mr. Bailey."

"Call Lois Kemp at LEGENT, she is in charge of the Dynacom personnel integration. See if she knows where he is." He said, leaning forward. Where had McCann gone? No one had heard from him in a week. The Tribune articles reported that he hadn't been available for comment after the LEGENT representatives had showed up at his downtown office and told him to clear out.

His secretary, Jeanine, leaned in the doorway. "She says that the Superintendent at the condo complex says he is in a small town in Michigan called Farnsworth. Says they sent him a letter asking him where he wanted his furnishings sent. LEGENT sent his office things there by UPS. He hasn't called the complex."

"Thanks, I'll find him," Bailey replied turning to a laptop on his credenza. He opened his e-mail and looked up McCann's personal e-mail address.

Only a few people knew it. Stu Bailey was one. He typed rapidly. "Come on Wilson, read your mail!" he muttered to himself as he typed. He finished the message and hit "send".

He turned in his chair and pressed his intercom button again. "Jeanine, LEGENT has a bid package out on some of the Dynacom property. Call Lois Kemp back and tell her I want to be placed on the bidders list to receive a package and I want that address in Michigan for McCann. Then call Sadler Consulting and tell them I need a team to do some due diligence at LEGENT starting in two weeks. Then, get on the net and see if you can get a phone number for that Michigan address."

"Yes sir," Jeanine replied resignedly. "So, this is how <u>you</u> find him?" she thought to herself as she began punching Lois Kemp's phone number up. "I suppose this means more nights and weekends of chasing Stu Bailey and Wilson McCann's rainbow?" she thought. Oh well, she was single and would use the extra money to pay off her townhouse at Hilton Head. "I just hope I get to spend at least a week there this year," she thought.

In his office, Stu Bailey was already loading a CD-R/W into his laptop and getting ready to review the Dynacom numbers in the database it contained. Maybe this time it would produce a winner! While the system loaded, he began jotting the names of potential investors on a yellow pad with a purple felt tip pen.

McCann rose with the sun and fixed his breakfast. He filled a pan with dog food and set it on the back steps. Ted would be back from his morning rounds soon and would eat. McCann picked up the phone and gave his name and address to the Service Center representative that answered the ring.

"We'll have service connected this afternoon, Mr. McCann," she said in a businesslike manner. "We're offering free installation of a Digital Subscriber Line or DSL. Are you at all interested?" She said it matter-of-factly and didn't seem to anticipate a taker.

"I'm surprised," He said. "Do you have it available in this area already?"

Her voice took on a more expectant tone. "Oh yes, there is a Digital Subscriber Line Access Module within a quarter mile of your place. Are you interested?" He could almost see her fingers hovering over the keyboard waiting to punch in the Universal Service Code or USOC for DSL service.

"Yes I am, how much?"

"Full 1.54 service for $49.95 a month with a six month minimum" she replied almost glowing.

"Sign me up. You can get my credit information from Qwest in Chicago."

"Thank you Mr. McCann. Our service technician will be there this afternoon to install the necessary equipment."

McCann hung up the phone and turned to one of the boxes sitting in the kitchen. He opened it and began to remove its contents. A laptop computer in a Targus case and an ink jet printer were the last two items to be unpacked. A plastic bag held a printer cable.

He looked around the kitchen. No place to put a computer and printer here. He walked through the house checking for phone outlets. He found one in the master bedroom behind a dresser and one in the living room behind a small writing desk. He decided on the living room and moved the laptop and printer to the writing desk. There was not a lot of space left. He cabled the two devices together and plugged the laptop into an electric outlet. He thought of his office in Chicago and the eight-foot curved mahogany desk that had been its centerpiece. The anger and unease rose in him again. "The first shall be last all right!" he said aloud.

He finished unpacking the boxes and storing their contents. Then he went outside and walked to the brow of the hill behind the barn. He gazed out over the fields and watched the wind moving the clover this way and that like waves on the ocean. An idea began to grow in McCann's mind. He walked down the hill and into the fields. He looked more closely as he went along, until he was almost in the center of the six-acre field. He turned a full turn slowly and as he did so, he surveyed the entire field. He crossed the lane and did the same in the next field. Then, he walked to the end of the lane and repeated his survey in the back field. Together, the three fields represented almost twenty acres.

He turned and started back to the house. He heard a car door slam and Ted barked and ran towards the building. Rev. Charles Hastings stood at the top of the rise and watched McCann approach.

"Good morning Mr. McCann." The preacher smiled and extended his hand. "I see you are out in the fields early today."

McCann shook hands and noted the strength of the preacher's grip. "Just looking things over a bit," he remarked.

"Fred and Ella often walked in the fields in the evening holding hands," Hastings said.

"In the summers I spent here, I never saw them as much as touch one another." McCann said it as a challenge and the minister was quick to rise to it.

"I am sure that is quite true. But during the time I knew them, they became a loving couple," Hastings replied easily. "I understand that they were your Aunt and Uncle. Would you like to know more about their last years together?"

McCann hesitated, and then responded "I have a pot of coffee on the stove that I can heat up. Why don't you come in and have a cup and tell me."

The two men went into the house and Hastings seated himself at the kitchen table as McCann turned on the burner under the coffee pot and got out two mugs. "Cream and sugar?" he asked.

"No, I drink mine black. In fact I drink too much of it black!" Hastings said, leaning back in his chair.

"A minister with a bad habit? Perhaps you need prayer," McCann said, wanting it to sound smug. It came out lighthearted and Hastings laughed easily. "We all need prayer Mr. McCann".

"You can drop the 'Mr.', Reverend" McCann said as he watched the coffeepot start to percolate.

"I will if you drop the 'Reverend'. My name is Charles but most of my congregation calls me Chuck".

"Most of the people I thought were my friends call me Wils," McCann replied quietly.

The minister sat forward in his chair. He looked at McCann thoughtfully. "I do not understand big business of the type you have been involved in, Wils, but I read enough to know that corporate matters do not always run smoothly or in the best interests of those who work for large corporations or own their stock. I understand that your departure from Dynacom resulted from an attempt to stave off an acquisition through a leveraged buyout that failed."

"You understand the basics pretty well." McCann smiled thinly as he turned to face the minister. "What most people don't know about or understand is the behind the scenes maneuvering and the sell-out of loyalties that accompanies these types of deals."

"Sort of like Jesus and Judas?" Hastings smiled quietly, looking down at his empty mug.

"Yes except there was more than one Judas in the Dynacom deal." McCann said with a touch of bitterness.

"And you have come here to recover from that situation? I should have thought that there were many more exotic places that a man of your position and financial resources could have gone." Hastings had said it casually but there was depth to his question and McCann immediately resented it.

"I don't know why I came here Chuck. I had to get away and I took the first bus out of Chicago. I bought this farm and now I wonder why I did that as well.

"Perhaps you'll find the answers in time. I'll pray for guidance for you as you seek them."

McCann's resentment faded quickly as the minister looked at him directly. He turned to the coffee pot and turned off the burner. He poured the mugs full to the brim and sat down at the table opposite Hastings.

"Did Fred Harms find the answers to what he was looking for?"

"Yes Wils, I believe he did. Fred was like many of us. He was seeking answers in the wrong places. He was working himself to death and losing ground every day. He changed when he began to look for answers in other places than on this farm and the latest prices of beef, milk, wheat and eggs."

"I can guess where he found them. I think you call it getting 'Saved'." McCann said it sarcastically.

Hastings ignored the sarcasm and continued pleasantly. "Ella began coming to church with Donna Barnes and found a loving and supporting family in the church. Later Fred began to come as well.

They simply came on Sunday morning at first and then began to participate in other activities of the church. Finally they dedicated their lives to Jesus Christ and rededicated themselves to each other."

Hastings lifted the mug to his lips and his eyes locked on McCann's. McCann raised his own mug and drank slowly. He sat it down quietly and leaned back.

"And you have come out here to see if I am a candidate to repeat the process. Well, Chuck, I don't think I am."

"I came out here to welcome you to the community and to thank you for coming to our church. I came out here to invite you to come again any time you're of a mind to. I came out here to offer my hand in friendship and to say that I would be honored to help you in any way I can. If your life needs changes, that's something between you and God."

Hastings had set his mug down and circled it with his hands as though warming them as he said it. He sat leaning slightly forward looking intently into McCann's eyes. He had not said it harshly or in argument. It was clear to McCann that this man was as solid as a man could be. His dislike of preachers had been strong over the years and this man did not merit it.

"I'm sorry I spoke as I did. I appreciate your coming out. I am not much of a churchgoer but if I decide to go to church, I'll come to yours." As he said it, he impulsively reached across the table and took the minister's hand.

"I'd best be going. May I offer a prayer?"

"Fine" McCann responded, noting that Hasting continued to grip his hand and feeling somewhat self-conscious about it.

Hastings said a short prayer, downed the rest of his coffee, stood and moved outside. McCann followed feeling strangely better for the minister's visit.

"Good luck with whatever you decide to do Wils," Hastings said as he opened his car door. McCann noted that the car was an older model Chevrolet. The pay for preachers obviously hadn't improved. He felt guilty as he thought about the pay that men and women, with less ability than this man's, had drawn at companies like Dynacom.

"Come again Chuck" he replied, meaning it.

He walked down to the barn and pulled the door wide. He climbed the stairs to the mows and spent 10 minutes looking up into them and running capacity calculations through his mind. Then, he went below to the stables and walked around thinking.

As he emerged from the barn, a panel truck with "Farnsworth Tele. Coop" on the side pulled into the yard. Two hours later, Wilson McCann was at his laptop surfing the Internet for the current beef prices!

Midway through his surfing session, McCann's laptop gave him the "you've got mail" message. He sat back for a minute and stared at the screen. His chest felt tight and his mood, which had been the best since he had arrived, turned sour for just a moment. The only people who would know his e-mail address were people from Chicago and New York City. People he didn't want to talk to; people that would bring back the pain and the anxiety. He clicked on the "cancel" button and went back to surfing.

Twenty minutes later, he turned the laptop off and started to rise from his chair. The phone rang. He had connected a small digital answering machine to it. He waited until the message came in and then played it back.

"Wils! I need you to call me back right away! Something has come up that I think you will be interested in! What are you doing out there anyway?" He stood there listening to Stu Bailey's voice like it was from another world. Stu Bailey was his friend. More correctly, Stu Bailey was his friend as long as it put money in Stu's pocket. Stu was his "business" friend. Right now, he didn't need a business friend!

He pushed the "erase" button on the answering machine and the robotic voice responded "message erased – that was your last message". He hoped so.

He picked up the phone and dialed the Telephone Company service center number. When the representative answered, he identified himself and made his request. "I need a new telephone number and I need it to be unlisted"

"Is there a problem, Mr. McCann?" she asked.

"No, no problem. I neglected to ask for an unlisted number this morning and this number has already been given out."

"I'm sorry about that. I will make the change right away. That will add $1.45 to your monthly bill for the non-listing. Can I do anything else?"

"No, I think that should take care of it, hopefully" he said, making a note of the new number she gave him and putting down the phone. "But I wonder if it will?" he said to himself.

McCann walked outside and got into the Ranger. Ted looked up at him expectantly. "Get in if you want to go" he said. The dog leaped into his lap and then into the passenger's seat. He sat with his nose to the window and his tongue lolled out.

He backed the Ranger up and turned down the driveway and into the road. He drove to the first corner and turned left up a paved road, which angled off sharply to the left. A mile up the road, he spotted "Marks" on a mailbox and turned left into the driveway. The house stood on one side of the road and the Barn and outbuildings were on the opposite side. A small garage behind the house, with its doors open, housed Jim Marks' pickup and a small Dodge Neon. The yard was neat and the grass had recently been cut. A swing set and slide sat at the rear of the yard. Lona Marks opened the back door to the house. "Hi Mr. McCann! How are you?" She called from the doorway.

"Fine, Mrs. Marks. Is Jim around?"

"He's over in the barn working on his tractor," she replied.

"Thanks," McCann turned and walked toward the barn. A car and a milk tanker whizzed by on the road as McCann waited to cross. Jim Marks was under a large tractor working on a hydraulic line.

"Good morning neighbor!" McCann said cheerfully.

Jim Marks rolled out from beneath the tractor and looked up at him. A big smile spread across his face.

"Mr. McCann – er - ah – Wils – it's good to see you!" He said, rising to his feet and extending his hand. McCann shook it strongly.

"I'm sorry we didn't get to talk with you after the service. When someone comes forward, we always stay to pray for them." Marks said.

"I understand completely." McCann said, wishing that he did. "I've come to talk with you about your proposal. You want to rent the 40 acres opposite the farm on your side of the road?"

"Yes, but I'd access it from the road. I wouldn't cut the fences or anything." Marks offered expectantly. McCann was impressed by the sincerity in his voice.

"Well I have a somewhat different proposal in mind." He said, eyeing

Marks carefully. He noted a little hesitation in Mark's expression. "Don't worry, I think you may like it." He said reassuringly.

"What I propose is that you help me get the hay off those three fields behind the barn and help me get the other two fields south of the barn into wheat before the freeze sets in. In return, I'll let you work the back 40 for free."

He could see the surprise register in Marks' eyes. It was replaced by a look of wariness. "What do you mean about helping you get the hay in and the wheat in?" he asked.

"I think Fred has a mowing machine and a rotary rake in the tool shed. I'm not sure what shape they're in but I think I can get the three fields cut and raked. I'll need someone to bale them and help me get the bales into the barn. I can plow and disk the other two fields but Fred's planter looks like it has seen better years and I don't know how to mix the wheat, fertilizer and alfalfa seed properly to plant."

Jim Marks leaned against the tractor wheel and considered. "I don't have a baler, been wanting to get one but we just don't have the money. I've been keeping my eye on a used one at George Whyte's but I can't afford it this year. We could get a custom baler to do it. He'd charge you by the bale."

Wilson McCann thought of the business deals he had pulled off over the last 20 years. He had always done the unexpected. He had always reached for more than was there on the table and he had usually won. Dynacom had prospered because of it. The thoughts made him edgy. He mentally shook the feeling off.

"Tell you what Jim, I'll buy that baler and when you can afford it, you can buy it or a half interest in it. Now, have we got a deal?"

Marks hesitated, "And you're saying I can work the back 40 and keep the entire crop?"

"That's what I'm offering – deal or not?" The phrase was one that McCann had used many times. It usually came out hard. This time it came out softly. Jim Marks wasn't the type of man who inspired hard dealing.

Marks extended his hand, "Deal!" He stepped back and continued, "Do you want me to draw up some papers or will you?"

"We just did all the paperwork necessary when we shook hands. I guess I'll go down to George Whyte's and buy that baler. Then, I had better get home and get to work. I'll expect you over next week sometime to start work. Oh, and by the way, I think it would be easier for you if you cut a gate in the line fence between us to get onto the 40. It will save you some time."

"I'll be there and ---thank you Wils," Marks responded.

As McCann drove away, Lona Marks walked into the barn. "What did he want Jim?" she asked.

Marks told her. She slipped her arm about his waist and softly whispered, "Thank you Jesus." They stood there together each wondering what on earth the former CEO of one of the country's largest Telecommunications firms wanted with 20 acres of baled hay and 20 acres of winter wheat. For his part, Wilson McCann rested his left arm on the window of the Ranger and whistled a tune as he drove into Farnsworth. Ted lay quietly in the seat beside him, beginning to like this stranger who had entered his world.

George Whyte's implement dealership was located at the east end of Farnsworth's main street. It consisted of a relatively small showroom with a large garage behind it. Numerous pieces of farm equipment and tractors both old and new occupied the lot to the left of the dealership as it fronted on the street. McCann pulled into the lot and turned off the Ranger. "Stay here Ted," he said as he stepped down. Ted turned his head from the window and sagged back down on the seat.

McCann looked around him. There were three hay balers lined up against the fence at the back of the lot. One had a flat tire and one was in pretty bad shape. The third appeared in reasonably good shape. Next to it sat an old McCormick-Deering Farmall "A" covered with years of dirt and grime, its two back tires flat. McCann had learned to drive a similar tractor during his first summer on Fred Harms' farm.

He walked into the dealership and, ignoring the salesman who leaned on the parts counter, walked back to a small office at the rear. A small, older man, with thinning brown hair, dressed in a John Deere shirt and brown pants was working at a computer.

"George, how are you?" McCann said it quietly but the man turned as though someone had poked him in the back. His face was long and narrow and his nose was hooked. Wire rimmed glasses gave him the look of an unhappy nearsighted rat. He jumped to his feet and extended his hand.

"Wilson McCann! I heard you were in town! I want to thank you for cleaning up all those bills that Fred ran up!" He said it in a rush. McCann thought back over the years and decided that his dislike for George Whyte hadn't changed since he had first met him years ago when Fred Harms had purchased equipment from him.

"It was the least I could do considering all you did for Fred and Ella," McCann replied, the oil he spread into his voice made the words seem almost sincere. Whyte bobbed his head and chuckled to himself.

"Yes, we did a lot of business with Fred. I'm just sorry that he never seemed to get on top of things. I always hoped that he would have a good year and be able to pay back what he owed but it never seemed to happen."

McCann had seen the figures. Harms' steadily growing debt to the George Whyte's Implement Company had been further increased by interest rates that were about 2 points higher than the going rate at Fred Penay's bank. But, Fred and Ella couldn't qualify for a loan at the bank. George Whyte had fed annually off of the Harms' need for equipment and for credit. McCann only wished that people like George Whyte and Charles Corbin could be made to give account of how they handled their wealth. The thought of Corbin made McCann's jaw set.

"How much are you asking for the hay baler next to the "A" out there George?" McCann asked.

"Oh, that one is in great shape Wilson, a neighbor of Fred's named Jim Marks has wanted to buy it for a year or more. I keep telling him to take it on credit but he insists on waiting until he has the cash."

"How much?" McCann said again.

"What do you want with a hay baler anyway Wilson?" Whyte countered.

McCann smiled his most pleasant smile. The words were clipped. "How much?" he said.

Whyte swallowed. "$3,000 and its worth every penny, don't you want to look it over?"

"I'll give you $2,500 for it" McCann replied.

"Oh Wilson, I couldn't sell it for that, I've got that much in it, but for you, I'll take $2,750."

"I appreciate that George" McCann said thinly. "Do you still deliver?"

Whyte laughed, "Of course, we always deliver the goods Wilson!"

McCann thought to himself, "You certainly delivered the goods to Fred Harms." He turned and looked out the window. Whyte waited expectantly, rubbing his hands together.

"Does Phil Willard still own the Agway?" He asked without turning.

"Yes he does, but Phil's getting up in years. I don't know how much longer he'll keep it." Whyte replied.

McCann turned abruptly, "Tell you what George, you throw in that old Model A Farmall sitting next to the New Holland and I'll give you your $2,750."

"Done and done!" Whyte exclaimed, "But what do you want that old piece of junk for?"

"I'll write you out a check. You can deliver the New Holland to Jim Marks' farm and the "A" to the Agway." McCann reached into his shirt pocket and produced his checkbook.

"Your credit is good with me Wilson, no need to pay cash," Whyte said quickly.

"I thank you for that George but I prefer to pay now" McCann replied as he wrote out the check.

"You working with Jim are you Wilson?" Whyte inquired.

"You might say that", McCann replied. "Why?"

"Well… you know… he and Lona are a little different," The implement dealer said smugly as he sat and began writing out a receipt.

"How so?" McCann looked steadily at Whyte.

"Well, he and Fred Penay and Phil Willard all started going to the UMC when that new preacher came to town and now they are all Bible thumpers!" Whyte said, as he handed over the receipt.

"Interesting, I understand Donna Barnes goes there as well." McCann said evenly.

"Yep, she sowed her wild oats and then switched churches just to make her daddy mad. She's a regular now!"

McCann could feel the heat rising under his collar. "Thanks George, be sure to send the "A" down to Phil. I'll tell him to expect it." He turned and walked out the door and climbed into the Ranger and drove away.

George Whyte leaned back in his chair. "What in the world is he doing here and what is going on?" He said out loud. He picked up the check and smiled. "Oh, well. No concern of mine!" Having so said, he went back to punching away on his computer terminal.

The Agway was at the west end of town. As McCann drove down the main street heading west, he let his temper cool. George Whyte was the same little weasel he had always been, that was for sure. He and Mac Woods at the drug store had always been a pair to watch. He glanced to the side as the thought passed through his mind. The drug store was to his left next to the "Barnes Loft". Donna Barnes was standing at the counter in her store talking with a customer. Without thinking, McCann hit the horn one long note. Ted jumped up and looked out the window. Donna turned to look and McCann waved. She raised a hand in reply and he continued down the street.

The Farnsworth Agway was a hub of activity. It supplied the needs of gardeners, bird feeders and pet owners in the area. It also offered light engine repair service and sold a full line of seed grain, fertilizers and auto and tractor parts. Phil Willard was in his late 60's. He looked, McCann decided, as he entered the store and spotted the proprietor behind the counter, like Andy Devine, the actor who played "Jingles" in old TV westerns.

"Hello Mr. Willard," McCann said, smiling.

"You've got the better of me son, I'm sure we've met but I can't think where," Willard picked up a pair of half glasses from the counter and put them on as he spoke.

"Wilson McCann, I used to come to Fred Harms' farm in the summers many years ago," McCann replied, smiling.

"Wils McCann! Well I'll be! What are you doing here son?"

"I bought the Harms place and I'm living out there for now." McCann replied.

"Well, it's good to see you! I heard that you were a big business tycoon in Chicago. What are you doing here?" The question was asked so innocently that McCann had to smile.

"I imagine quite a few people are asking that. I'm not sure I know myself." He replied.

"Well it's good to see you son! What can I do for you?"

"Actually you can do quite a bit. I just bought an old Farmall "A" from George Whyte and I told him to deliver it here. Do you think you can put four new tires on it and get it to run? It may need an engine overhaul and a new battery."

"That old A has been sitting in George's lot for over five years. But I know the fellow who traded it in and he took good care of it. With new tires, a battery and a good steam cleaning, I'll bet you we can have it purring like a kitten." Willard responded. It was obvious that he would enjoy doing just that. "What else?"

"I'm going to plant 20 acres of winter wheat and I'll need seed, fertilizer and alfalfa seed to plant with it to turn it to hay in a year. I'm not sure how much. Jim Marks is going to plant for me. He'll know what to order. I'll have him call you and order. Is that alright?"

Phil Willard crossed his arms over his ample stomach. His eyes were alive and his smile broadened. "Jim and Lona Marks and those two kids of theirs are the salt of the earth. You are lucky to have them for neighbors. I'll be glad to fill the order. What are you going to do with winter wheat?"

"Well that leads me to my third request, Phil. I'm planning to use that wheat next year together with some oats that I intend to plant next spring and some of your good beef cattle chow mix to feed some beef cattle." I'll need a winter's supply of feed this winter however."

Willard unfolded his arms and began to scribble on a pad. "How many head? Where will you get hay to feed them?"

"Jim Marks and I are going to bale the hay off those three fields behind the barn and put it up. I bought a used New Holland Baler off George Whyte's lot along with the 'A'."

Willard paused and looked over his glasses. "Did you check it out before you bought?" he asked carefully.

"No but Jim Marks did. I trust his judgment."

Willard went back to scribbling. "You're a good judge of character son, both good and bad – if you know what I mean?"

"I think I do Mr. Willard," McCann smiled back.

"Phil" Willard said, extending his hand. "By the way, now that I think of it, did I see you in church on Sunday?"

McCann tensed slightly, "Yes, I was there. I didn't see you."

"I don't see so good without these blamed glasses! I thought I saw some-one new walking out when I was coming out of our prayer room. I lead a prayer group during the morning service. We lift up Pastor Chuck and the service and pray for God's direction. It must have been you." He looked at McCann and McCann dropped his eyes.

"It was me. Jim Marks and Donna Barnes both asked me to church. I understand you and Fred Penay go there as well."

"That we do. Fred was away on Sunday but he'll be back teaching his Sunday school class this coming Sunday. You should try it out."

McCann tried to imagine the banker teaching a Sunday school class. He had a hard time doing so.

It was not as hard to picture Phil Willard leading a prayer group. Somehow, he felt that this church thing was beginning to meet him at every turn. It bothered him. People like George Whyte were the type he was used to dealing with. He hadn't met many people like Jim, Fred and Phil in the last 20 years. He absently thought of Stu Bailey's message on his phone earlier. Men like Jim Marks were the type of people who gave their friendship without a reason to do so. Phil Willard had obviously changed from the rather boozy, scatterbrained but likable man that McCann remembered from his past. Fred Penay was much the same and yet his quiet demeanor seemed more peaceful now as McCann thought about it. What had happened here?

He thanked Willard for his help, made a deposit on the repairs and purchases and left to Willard's cheerful "Come again son, when you have more time to visit." He headed back to the farm quite satisfied with the way his day was going. He hadn't had a day like this in over two years. Ted licked his paw and watched him out of the corner of his eyes. McCann reached over and scratched the dog's ears. "Can you handle 20 beef cattle, boy?" he asked him. The dog's tail moved slightly in reply.

(5)

The next morning, McCann was up early. He moved the mowing machine out of the tool shed and installed a new bar from several standing beside the workbench. He backed the tractor in and pulled the hay rake out into the yard and hosed about a year's worth of dirt and grime off it. Next he did the same with the mower. Then, he backed the tractor up to the mower and hooked it on. Using a grease gun from the shed, he lubricated the tractor, mower, and rake. He checked his watch and noted that the time in eastern Nebraska would be about right, so he went inside. He turned his laptop on and found an address and phone number for a large cattle-feeding operation northwest of Omaha and called. Ray Priestly's rough voice answered and he could hear the lowing of cattle in the background. Ray was obviously on his cell phone.

"Ray, its Wils McCann"

"Wils! How in the world are you? What are you up to? I heard that some other outfit bought that company of yours. Are they going to take good care of us out here in the hinterlands?"

"I'm sure they will, Ray. How's the cattle feeding business these days?"

"You know how it is, Wils. Feed prices are up, beef prices are down and I got more than I can say grace over. If I didn't love it so much, I'd quit and move to town!"

Ray Priestly ran one of the largest cattle feeding operations in eastern Nebraska. He had been one of Dynacom's largest customers in that state. McCann had toured his operation as part of a field visit six years ago. He smiled to himself as he remembered walking down the long troughs in his wing tipped shoes while Priestly explained the nuances of cattle feeding to him.

"Ray, I want to buy 20 head of cattle to feed this winter on a farm in the thumb of Michigan. I know that pales in comparison with the 3,000 head or so you care for but I need to start somewhere and I know you know how to pick 'em."

There was a long silence at the other end of the connection. McCann could hear the restless moving of the cattle and the clank of the feed canisters. Finally Priestly spoke.

"Wils, are you putting me on? You are going to feed beef cattle through the winter? Is this some sort of tax deal you got going?"

McCann laughed. "Ray, I bought a hundred acre farm that I used to work on when I was going to college, I'm living here on it and I want to feed some beef through the winter. I know it doesn't make any sense to you, and it doesn't to me either. But somehow, I want to do it. Can you help me?"

There was another long silence before Priestly spoke again. "There's a fella west of Saginaw that I met at a convention two years ago that I'll call. He can give you whatever you need. Is this a cash deal?"

"Yes it is and I'd be happy to pay you for your trouble, Ray," McCann said, meaning it.

"Wils, when you cleaned up our telephone system, you helped me and my business. I sure as the world don't know what you are up to but I'm happy to help out. Tell you what, I'll call this fella and tell him to bring you over 20 yearlings, cash on delivery. I'll vouch for you. When do you want 'em?"

"In about two weeks, Ray. I appreciate it," McCann said sincerely.

"Wils, you get them critters through the winter and I'll come out there and see 'em in the spring!"

"You've got a deal!" McCann said, enthusiastically.

Later, he began to mow the field directly behind the barn. He turned the tape deck up and sang along with it. Round and round the field he went. "At least I'm not in Chicago going round in circles" Wilson McCann thought to himself. As he neared the center of the field on his final pass, two pheasants and a rabbit darted across the freshly mown hay and into the adjoining field.

In New York, Stu Bailey put down the phone and yelled. "Jeanine! They are saying that number in Farnsworth is not in service! Are you sure you gave me the right one?" Jeanine sighed and began to re-enter the number from her pad. The robotic voice on the other end repeated the phrase, "The number you have called is not in service, please check your number and call again."

"I'll check information," she called back to Bailey. A few minutes later, she appeared in the doorway to his office. "They say that Wils has an unlisted number and they won't give it out."

"What about the e-mail I sent? Any answer?" Bailey said impatiently.

"Boss, I don't check your personal e-mail. Did you get an answer?" Jeanine leaned against the doorframe and waited.

Bailey swiveled his chair and punched the keyboard to his desktop computer. Incoming e-mail messages began to scroll down the screen.

"Nothing! What is going on? Why doesn't he answer? If we got through once on the phone, why can't we get him now?"

Jeanine signed. "I think it is safe to say that Mr. McCann got your first message, doesn't want to talk to you and changed his number and de-listed it."

"It makes no sense. I'm his friend! We do business together!" Stu Bailey sounded like a spoiled child who had just had his favorite toy taken away.

"Jeanine, call Global and get me a charter. What is the nearest airport for business jets near Farnsworth?"

She sighed, "I don't know but I'll find out. Is that what you are going to do? Go see him?"

"You bet your life I am. This is a deal that is made to order for Wilson McCann!" Bailey said, turning back to his computer.

She turned and went back to her desk. "Maybe Wilson McCann is tired of doing deals," she thought to herself as she punched in the Global number.

Two hours later, she turned off the lights, locked the door and went home. Stu was on his way to Michigan. She wondered if there was a motel or hotel in the "Thumb." If not, Stu might find himself sleeping in the compact rental car she had rented at the little airport near Caro. It was the only one they had according to the rental agent. Oh well, tomorrow would be peaceful at least.

It was dark by the time Stu Bailey turned the two year old Dodge Neon into the parking lot of the rather shabby motel on the south end of Caro's main street. He figured that Farnsworth was smaller than the county seat and its only motel would probably be worse than this one. He had grabbed a chicken sandwich at the McDonald's and wolfed it down on his way to the motel. He checked in, took a quick shower in the rather dirty shower stall and went to bed. He intended to be knocking on Wilson McCann's door by eight in the morning. He already knew where McCann was. He had remembered him talking about his summers on his uncle's farm and had put two and two together. A call to the county clerk's office in Caro had given him the address. Tomorrow, he would find out what Wilson McCann was doing here, why he wasn't returning phone calls or e-mails and when they could start putting together their next deal. He smiled at the thought of it. Wilson McCann was one of the best technology managers he had ever met. He knew the former Dynacom operations like the back of his hand. Now, there was a chance to put that knowledge to work in a way that would make McCann, and of course Stu Bailey, a lot of money. He intended to take advantage of that opportunity.

Wednesday morning dawned warm and sunny. McCann was up at 6:00a.m. His body ached in places he hadn't imagined possible. He had always been a man who worked his body regularly to keep in shape. His condo had access to a workout center and his office building had one as well. He had used them early and late to maintain his lean, athletic look. But one day of riding a tractor and mowing hay had reminded him that there was more to physical strength than stationary bikes, rowing machines and treadmills. He eased himself into a chair and waited for the coffee to perk. Ted, having been fed, curled up just outside the kitchen door and went back to sleep. The smell of freshly mown hay wafted through the doorway and McCann closed his eyes and inhaled it. He let his mind drift back to his summers here as a teen. He had learned much about hard work here on this farm. Yesterday it had felt good to use his back and muscles instead of his brain.

Dynacom had "died." He had come to think of it that way. The company hadn't been acquired. It had been killed and Charles Corbin and his gang of sycophants had been the killers. The press, of course, had seen it differently. To them, Corbin was simply delivering another deal in a career of deals and Wilson McCann was guilty of trying to deny the shareholders a reasonable return on their investments in order to satisfy his own personal ego and those of his venture capitalist friends. The fact that Wall Street had ignored McCann's track record and generally given bland support to Dynacom's demise only served to create more pressure on McCann and his group as they attempted to save the company. He rose and paced the kitchen as the coffeepot began to perk. Yesterday's good feelings were gone as he reviewed again in his mind the events that had led him here. Finally, he took a mug from the sink, rinsed it out and poured it full of the coffee and walked outside. Ted rose, wagged his tail and lifted his head to be stroked. McCann bent to scratch his ears and his mood quieted. He walked to the brow of the rise behind the barn and looked out on the fields. By mid morning, the hay would be ready to be raked. Already, his mind was filling with plans for the activity of the day. He turned toward the house and began to whistle. Ted cocked his ears and trotted along behind him.

After eating his breakfast, he went to the tool shed and began to move several small pieces of equipment to one side to gain access to a steel framed hay wagon that stood against one side of the big shed. Three of the four tires on the wagon were flat and he had to use the tractor to pull the wagon to the front where he could reach it with an air compressor hose. Luckily, all three tires held air. Grabbing the tongue with both hands, he pulled the wagon out into the yard and hosed it down.

He switched the tractor from the wagon to the rake and was just turning when the sound of wheels in the drive caused him to turn. A Subaru Forester pulled up the drive and stopped. Donna Barnes stepped out and closed the door. She held a paper cup of coffee in one hand and a paper bag in the other. Both said Dunkin Donuts on them.

"Well, farmer McCann, where will you plow today?" she smiled.

He paused to let his gaze travel over her. She was dressed in a pair of light tan slacks and a dark blue blouse and wore black, low-heeled shoes. Her hair was down and framed her face. He was struck by the fact that, at age 40, Donna Barnes was even prettier than she had been at age 17.

"We make hay today M'Lady! We do not plow the earth." He said laughingly as he bowed.

"Such gallantry! Here, have a donut!" She responded.

"Did you come out with a care package for the poor bachelor farmer?" he asked teasingly as he reached into the bag and selected a cake donut. "Where's my coffee?"

"Sorry, I only have two hands. Yours is in the Forester." She said, indicating the door.

He opened it and took out the cup from the console. The inside of the Forester was immaculate. A magnet in the shape of a scroll that read "I can do all things though Him who strengthens me" was attached to the glove box.

"What brings you out here so early?" He asked, turning toward her.

She sat down on the step. Ted came and nuzzled her hand and she fed him the half of a donut before reaching into the bag to take out another.

"I heard you were expanding your operation and wanted to see it." She smiled, taking a sip from her cup.

He moved to sit on the step beside her and she pushed Ted away to make room for him. It felt good to sit beside her. She inhaled the smell of the hay and leaned back against the door.

"I see. Is this the UMC prayer chain in action?" He looked straight ahead as he said it.

"Yes, I stopped at the Agway for gas and Phil Willard told me he was working on a tractor for you. Isn't one tractor enough or is your operation even bigger than I thought?" She smiled.

"What else do you know about my recent activities?" he parried.

"I know that you did something yesterday that may help Jim and Lona Marks in more ways than you can imagine." She said as she looked at him intently. He looked away. He found her green eyes vaguely disconcerting.

"How so? All I did was to tell him he could work the back forty."

"At no cost to him except helping you get in some hay and plant some winter wheat. Those forty acres gives them a chance to bring in a crop next summer that will pay off a short term bank loan that comes due."

"You seem to know a lot about everyone's business." He said it stiffly.

"Jim and Lona are in our prayer group at church. They have shared their situation and asked us all to pray that God would make it possible for them to work that land. I don't think I am breaking any confidences when I tell you that they see you as an answer to that prayer." Her voice was soft and she was looking down into her coffee cup as she said it.

He looked at the wagon sitting in the yard. He felt uneasy and didn't know why. "And what do *you* pray for in your group, Donna?" he asked. He knew instantly that he shouldn't have said it. He saw her stiffen and then she seemed to relax and stared out at the barn. Her voice was soft as she replied. "I pray that God will use me in ways that he sees fit and that he will grant my desire to serve him in a foreign mission field."

McCann was shocked. He stared at her in total disbelief. It wasn't the first part of her answer that had surprised him but the second.

"But, you own a business. You've lived here all your life. How in the world can you even think of something like that?" As he said it, he stood and turned to face her. She looked up and met his gaze. She took another sip from her coffee and lifted her eyes again.

"The business I own is one I can liquidate in three months. I am hoping it will be profitable enough to provide for my preliminary training and enable me to raise the funds I need to be fully trained and accept an appointment."

"I can't believe it!" He said it questioningly.

"Wils, during the fourth summer you were here, something happened. I realized that my rebellion and wild behavior was wrong. I paid a price for it. I also realized that I was resisting God. I realized that it wasn't my father's religion but what God expected of me that was important. I tried to make you see that I needed something deeper. I found it. I found a deeper walk with God through faith in Jesus Christ. I have been on four church sponsored trips to South America and three to Eastern Europe in the past 20 years and I feel led to become a missionary to Eastern Europe. I have another trip already scheduled for this fall."

It all came out in a rush. It explained so many things that his mind reeled with the impact of it all. She had not been the same that third summer so many years ago. She had been more serious. They had continued their physical relationship but something was changing. He could sense it. When he had left for college at the end of that summer, there was something different about Donna. Something had come between them. The next summer she was gone and he had spent it in the company of other girls in other places, mostly at the VFW on weekends. He had looked older than he was and "carding" wasn't practiced in those days. Getting beer or even mixed drinks had been easy for him. Finding girls who were interested in a good time had been just as easy. Their paths had diverted. Yet, at the end of the summer he had felt emptier than in the past as he packed for his return to college. He had sought her out and was told that she was in Eastern Europe on a mission trip for her church and would not be back until mid September. Now, he thought, I am learning what Paul Harvey calls "The rest of the story." He turned away for a moment to gather his thoughts and when he turned to face her, she was standing there looking at him. There was the hint of a smile on her face. He tossed the remaining coffee into the grass and wadded the cup in his hand.

"I hope it all happens just the way you want it to." He said it quietly, looking into those green eyes.

She stepped forward, tossed the dregs of her coffee in the grass and wadded her own cup and put it in the paper bag. She reached for his left hand and held it.

"And you, Wilson, what are you looking for?" She looked into his eyes and he felt that she could see to the depths of his soul.

"I don't know." He responded, unwilling to have her stop holding his hand.

"I will pray for you." She said quietly, bowing her head. But, before she could begin to speak a dusty Dodge Neon pulled into the drive. She instinctively dropped his hand and stepped back. A heavy set man in gray slacks, rumpled white shirt and tie derricked himself from the car.

"You are one hard man to get hold of when you want to be!" he said loudly, as he moved toward them.

Donna looked at McCann's face. It had changed dramatically. His jaw was set and the coffee cup in his right hand was being squeezed into an even smaller lump. She sensed that his whole body had stiffened. He did not extend his hand to meet the one offered by the stranger.

"Hello Stu," McCann said thinly.

"Stu Bailey is my name, ma'am," the venture capitalist said turning towards her. He extended his hand again and she took it briefly.

"Donna Barnes, I'm a friend of Wilson's." She said it looking not at Bailey but at McCann.

"What do you want, Stu?" McCann asked

Bailey hesitated, looking again at Donna. She moved toward the Forester. "I have to be going. I open the store at 10:00am. When will you be baling hay this week Wils?"

McCann was surprised by the question. "I … I… ah, probably tomorrow if Jim brings the baler," he stammered awkwardly.

"I close at noon. I'll come out and drive the tractor for you to help load," she said getting into the Forester. "Nice to have met you Mr. Bailey." She closed the door before McCann could reply and backed around the Neon and down the drive. McCann watched her drive away, feeling angry with Bailey for being there.

"A very attractive lady! The two of you looked very romantic as I drove in! Is that what you came here for?" Bailey said it jokingly but McCann colored and he clenched and unclenched his hands before replying. When he did so, he put as much venom into his voice as he was capable of.

"I came here to get away from people like you Stu!"

Bailey wasn't fazed by the sting of the response. In fact he had expected it. "Better to get it out and out of the way quickly," he thought to himself.

"Wils, whether you want to accept it or not, I truly want to be your friend. I consider you one of the most intelligent men in the business and I respect your integrity. I know the Dynacom deal didn't turn out the way either of us wanted it to but I still feel that what we tried to do was the right thing to do under the circumstances."

McCann turned away and looked out over the fields. Bailey waited. The whole purpose of this trip hinged on what Wilson McCann would say next.

"I'm sorry Stu. I had no right to say that. You have never been anything but straight with me. It's just that the last six months have been almost more than I can bear and I seem to have lost everything I worked for and believed in."

Bailey sighed. "What happened was business, Wils. Not every deal has a happy ending. But the only real losers are those who are good at it and who quit playing. I don't intend to quit playing and neither should you."

"What do you want, Stu?" McCann's voice was a little softer as he turned and looked at the rumpled venture capitalist.

"Can we go inside where I can put my laptop on a table or something?"

"Come in. Have you had coffee? I've got this morning's batch still on the stove," McCann said, stepping toward the door

Bailey turned and walked to the Neon. He reached inside and pulled a small case containing a laptop computer from the back seat and walked toward the door. "I had an egg sandwich and coffee at McDonalds," he said as he sat the case on the kitchen table. "I could go for another cup."

McCann turned on the burner under the coffee pot, placed a cup in front of Bailey and watched as he booted up the laptop. His sense of apprehension had returned. He felt that he was being drawn back into some black hole that he had just escaped from.

"Look at this," Bailey said.

McCann stood behind him and read the e-mail on the screen. It had a LEGENT logo in the upper left corner and was from a LEGENT executive that McCann knew quite well. It was three sentences long and said that LEGENT planned to divest itself of all its Telecommunications investments in Minnesota, Iowa, Michigan and Wisconsin within the next year.

"I've run the numbers, Wils," Bailey said, as he closed out the e-mail and brought up an EXCEL spread sheet. The spreadsheet was a summary of investment, equity, revenue and costs for the four states mentioned in the e-mail.

"You are talking about $300 million at minimum," McCann said quietly. Two emotions gripped him at almost the same time. He knew these properties and he felt an immediate rush of excitement at the opportunity to acquire and operate them. At the same time, he felt that he was sliding back into an environment that he had come to dislike intensely during the past year.

"You always could do the math," Bailey said, looking up at McCann and leaning back in his chair.

McCann turned to the stove and brought the coffee pot to the table. He poured a cup for Bailey and none for himself. He turned and placed the pot on the stove and spoke without turning back to Bailey.

"And…my role is?"

"Investor initially and CEO if and when we acquire the properties." Bailey sipped his coffee and waited.

"Are we buying to operate or are we buying to slash and burn and re-sell?" McCann said, staring down at the coffee pot.

Stu Bailey leaned forward in his chair. This was the moment of truth as to whether McCann could be enticed into getting involved. He wanted to lie but knew he couldn't.

"Cut the cost structure, consolidate, integrate the systems and sell out within five years. We can't raise the money without that in the plan." He said it quickly and took another sip from his cup. McCann's back was still toward him.

"Thanks for being honest, Stu. I'm not interested," McCann said, as he took the lid off the coffee pot and poured the dregs into the sink beside the stove.

"Wils, I can't do this deal without you as the CEO if we get it. The inves-tors want someone with a proven track record to head it up or they won't commit."

McCann smiled as he turned to face Bailey. "There are plenty of people with proven track records and they don't have the baggage I carry as far as LEGENT is concerned."

Bailey stood and faced him across the table. "Charlie Corbin is not going to impact this deal, Wils. LEGENT knows that what we did was in the best interests of the shareholders, the Dynacom people and the customers. They respect you and your ability. Having you on board actually makes the offer more acceptable. They are concerned with their customer service image and they will want to make assurances that any potential buyer will operate in the customer's interests. You bring that to the table."

"For five years," McCann said tersely.

"I've already said that my investors won't want to operate this thing beyond five years."

"Even if the operation is returning a good profit to them from improved earnings?"

"Wils, you know that even if you get the return on investment up to the highest level, you can't return enough in five years to offset what the gains can be from a buy/restructure/sell scenario. Investors aren't willing to commit for longer terms than that."

"What about using it as an acquisition vehicle and building it?" McCann asked. He felt he was being drawn further into this than he wanted to be. But his desire to analyze the possibilities overcame his reluctance.

"It would take an entirely different set of investors. I don't think I could put it together," Bailey admitted honestly. Stu Bailey recognized his capabilities and his limitations. He had good contacts and good resources but he also knew that there were major investment banking firms that would look at him as a penny ante player.

He powered down the lap top and closed it. "So, you prefer sitting here on this farm and playing gentleman farmer and holding hands with your lady friend?"

McCann refused to be baited. Bailey had been honest with him. He could have been otherwise. He pulled a chair out from the table and sat down. He looked up at Bailey.

"I don't know why I came here, Stu. I had to get away. I ran and I hid. For the first time in almost a year, I am doing something productive even if it is just bringing in a hay crop. I've met some nice people here. They are as confused about why I'm here as I am. I just need time to think things through."

Bailey looked down at him. Here sat one of the industry's best operating managers in jeans and flannel shirt admitting that he didn't know what he was doing here. Bailey thought for a moment, trying to figure out what to say next. He reached into the side pocket of his laptop case and produced a thick brown envelope. He laid it on the table, put the laptop into the case and zipped it shut.

"My jet is waiting at the Caro airport. I've summarized the whole deal and printed it off. All I ask is that you take the time to read it and then call me. I won't even ask for your unlisted phone number. If I don't hear from you by Monday, I'll not bother you again."

"I don't think you will hear from me." McCann said it quietly.

Bailey extended his hand. "Friends?" he asked.

McCann took his hand and shook it. "Friends," he said.

Stu Bailey went out into the sunshine, took a deep breath and walked to his car. He put the laptop in the rear seat and got in. McCann watched him from the steps. The Neon backed out the drive and headed down the road. McCann inhaled deeply and walked toward the tractor. It was time to rake 20 acres of hay. As he circled the fields in ever smaller rounds and the rows of raked hay became a design under the sunny skies, his mind turned often to the opportunity that Stu Bailey had brought, uninvited, into his life. He found himself running the numbers through his mind, creating scenarios for operation and formulating plans for transition, consolidation and integration. They came naturally to him from his years of experience. There was no doubt in his mind that the operation of such properties could and, if he were to take charge, would be successful.

At the end of the day, the hay was raked, the tractor and the rake were in the tool shed and McCann sat on the back step. Ted was stretched out at his feet. The envelope lay beside him on the step, unopened. He had brought it out intending to open it and read the material inside. He had hesitated and then laid it down. Ted rose to sniff it and then resumed his position. As the sun dropped low in the western sky, McCann rose and went inside. He took the envelope with him and laid it on the kitchen table.

He picked up the Bible from the small desk in the living room and opened it. His eyes fell upon a verse which had been circled in heavy black ink. It was in the 29th chapter of Jeremiah:

"For I know the plans that I have for you, declares the Lord, plans for welfare and not for calamity to give you a future and a hope."

A note, in the same heavy black ink, was in the margin. It read "Jeremiah 31:17a."

McCann turned the pages and saw the same heavy black ink encircling half of the referenced verse: *"And there is hope for your future, declares the Lord."*

He closed the Bible and laid it on the desk. He had felt an absence of hope for several weeks. Coming here had given him an opportunity to fill his days with simple tasks and simple decision making. He did not fully understand why he had impulsively done what he had done the past two days but doing it had given him a measure of peace. The moments this morning with Donna had given him a glimpse into another person's dreams in a way he had not experienced for a long time. Stu Bailey's arrival had pulled him in another direction. If this all-wise, all-knowing God had a plan for his life and if that plan had any hope, he couldn't see what it was.

He returned to the kitchen and took the envelope from the table. He opened it and withdrew the papers inside. There was a narrative, several worksheets and some graphs. He tossed the envelope into the wastebasket beside the stove and returned to the living room. He picked up the Bible and sat in the overstuffed chair. He was about to read the documents when he heard Ted whine and scratch at the back door. He set the papers and the Bible aside and returned to the kitchen. Ted had his nose pressed against the screen. His tail wagged expectantly.

"What do you want?" he said, as he opened the door. Ted came into the kitchen and trotted into the living room where he lay down beside the chair. McCann's eyes widened in amazement. During the few days he had been at the farm, Ted had not stayed in the house overnight.

"So, you have decided to move in?" McCann asked. Ted's tail moved back and forth twice and then he curled it around him, lowered his head to his front paws and closed his eyes. McCann resumed his seat in the chair and absently reached down to scratch the dog's ears before reaching for the papers that Bailey had left. He read through them rapidly. His understanding of what was contained in the papers, the numbers and graphic presentations, was clear. It was a well written, concise plan for the acquisition of LEGENT'S operations in four states including the financial presentations and a three-year operational plan. McCann noted that the plan called for the "appointment of a Chief Executive Officer with significant industry leadership experience and capability."

He dropped the papers to the floor beside Ted who didn't raise his head. He picked up the Bible and began to idly flip through it. He remembered being asked to memorize the 23rd Psalm as a boy and turned to it. He read it through and leaned back in the chair and closed his eyes. He began to recite the Psalm aloud from memory. Ted raised his head and looked up at him. Then, the dog lowered his head, stretched his legs, rolled on his side and went back to sleep. Behind the barn, a rooster pheasant crowed.

(6)

The next two days were the most physically painful that McCann had ever experienced. Jim Marks arrived at 9:00 a.m. with the baler pulling a hay wagon and Phil Willard arrived shortly thereafter with the "A" on new rubber and sporting a wax job! Willard was soon picked up by one of the men from the Agway and Jim and Wils went to work.

By the time Donna arrived shortly after noon with lunch in a large picnic basket, they had baled three wagonloads of hay and were unloading the third into the barn. McCann was in good physical shape but lifting and throwing the big rectangular bales was taking its toll. His shirt was soaked with sweat and he had to stop at regular intervals just to catch his breath. Marks on the other hand didn't seem to be even breathing hard. He ate quickly and returned to the field while McCann and Donna finished their lunch.

"Are you sure that you want to be a farmer?" she asked, smiling, as McCann stood and groaned.

"I didn't know it was possible to hurt in every area of your body at one time from three hours of work," he responded.

"You have been pushing a pencil and riding a desk chair too long," she teased.

"Okay, miss Country Gal, let's go see what you have to offer," he teased back as he helped her to her feet. She was clad in jeans and a short sleeved denim shirt. Her hair was pulled back in a ponytail. Without a trace of makeup, he thought she was as beautiful as most of the "trophy wives" of some of his high-toned business acquaintances in Chicago.

She climbed onto the "A" and started it in one smooth motion. He stood on the draw bar behind her and inhaled the scent from her hair. They drove back into the field just as Marks filled the hay wagon and stopped to unhitch it from the baler. The field was two thirds empty. With two more fields to bale, McCann was beginning to wonder if he could make it to nightfall.

At 3:00 p.m., Marks finished baling the first field and started on the second. With Donna driving, McCann had an opportunity to rest between trips to the barn with each wagonload. The two of them were able to get three more loads into the mow before Marks had to begin baling and dropping the bales in the field instead of into the wagons. They simply stood and watched as the field became a checkerboard of bales.

At 5:00 p.m., Lona and the children drove into the yard with dinner in a big cardboard box. Jim stopped the tractor and joined them as they laid it out on the bed of one of the wagons. The six of them ate slowly. McCann wondered if he would be able to get out of bed the following day and realized that he had one field to load by hand and that come tomorrow, another field would be baled. The west mow in the barn was already two thirds full. He wondered aloud how he was going to get the hay into the upper portions of the east mow and all of the south mow.

"Tomorrow, I'll bring an elevator with me when I come. No problem at all," Jim Marks said cheerfully. When I'm finished, we'll load the rest by hand and haul it up here and use the elevator in all three mows to get them in. What are you going to do with all this hay anyway?"

McCann lifted his head slightly and saw that the three adults had paused in their eating to await his reply.

"I have 20 head of yearling beef scheduled to be delivered in two weeks." He said it quietly and saw the surprise register on Donna's face. She picked up a chicken leg from her plate and held it thoughtfully as she looked at him.

"Then, you'll be feeding them through the winter? You'll be staying through the winter?"

"Jim is going to plant some winter wheat for me. I figured I should stay to see if it grows." He said it lightly but he could see that she did not see the humor.

"I…I must get home," she said, standing and putting the uneaten chicken leg back on her paper plate.

"What's the hurry? We still have a couple of hours of daylight left!" Marks said as she turned to go.

"Jim, can't you see that Donna and Mr. McCann are about through for the day? They aren't used to your sun up to sun down days!" Lona Marks admonished her husband. McCann felt the flush come to his face as she said it. He felt ashamed that she could see how spent he was. He turned away and followed Donna to her car.

"I appreciate you coming out and helping me today," he said, as she opened the car door.

"Wilson, what are you trying to prove here?" she flared

He felt the sting in her words. He felt he needed to give her some explanation and wasn't sure he knew what it was.

"I don't know, Donna. That is the honest truth. I need something to work at until I know what I want to do. I thought I would spend the winter here. Feed some cattle, try to figure out where I go from here."

"And that man who was here yesterday? What about him? He isn't buying hay and beef cattle!"

"He is a friend of mine from New York. He wants me to become involved in a deal to buy some Telecom properties in the Midwest and manage them for him."

He saw her lips tighten into a hard line. "And...?"

"I told him I wasn't interested." He said it simply but at the same time he was slightly irritated that she had elicited so much from him.

She looked up at him and placed her hand on his arm. She lowered her head and spoke again more softly, "I'm sorry, Wils. It isn't any of my business what you do or what you don't do. I had no right to pry."

He placed his left hand on hers. "It helps to have someone to talk to."

She looked up at him again. She took a deep breath and let it out slowly. "I'll bring dinner out tomorrow night after I close the store."

He looked into her eyes and the soreness in his body dissolved. "Thank you," he said simply.

Jim Marks put down a freshly cleaned chicken bone and looked at his wife. The two of them had been watching Donna and Wils as they stood together. He reached for Lona's hand. "Let's thank the Lord for the good day today."

Together, they bowed their heads and prayed silently as Donna Barnes drove slowly out of the yard and Wilson McCann turned and retraced his steps toward the barn.

With the exception of the use of the elevator, the next day was a repeat of the day before. Marks arrived early and the two men worked steadily loading the wagons, hauling the bales to the barn and storing them away. Lona and the children came again at noon with lunch and they ate quickly and returned to the field. Clouds were gathering in the western sky and Marks grimly forecast a thunderstorm for the evening. McCann forced his unwilling body to work faster as they raced against the gathering storm clouds.

McCann told Jim that Donna was coming with dinner but Marks declined to stay when they finished at 5:00 p.m. He hooked the baler and elevator together behind his tractor and with a wave of his hand was gone. McCann closed the double doors to the barn and put the tractor and wagon in the tool shed. He was washing up when he heard a car drive into the yard. The first raindrops spattered against the kitchen windows as Donna stepped inside with a picnic basket in her hands.

"Whew! It is going to get nasty out there!" she exclaimed as she ran her fingers through her hair.

"Good thing we didn't wait on you to get that last load in the barn." McCann smiled as he buttoned the last button on a hastily donned shirt and tucked it into his jeans.

"My timing is always perfect," she grinned. "You and Jim must have put in a day."

"We did. He never seems to stop. I loaded three loads and he loaded five. If he hadn't brought that elevator, I would be lying out there in the field getting wet!"

"Well, let's get some food into you to restore that energy."

She began to open the basket and bring out food and a thermos. McCann spotted thick steak slices between equally thick slices of sourdough bread. A container of potato salad and another of coleslaw appeared. Slices of cherry pie wrapped in plastic wrap finished off the basket. He saw that there was food for three. He was glad there were only the two of them to eat it.

Sensing his gaze, she smiled, "I brought food for both of you but I guess you'll have leftovers tomorrow instead."

McCann dropped into a chair and reached for a sandwich. As he did so, a thought struck him.

"Do you want to talk to your plate before we eat?" he said, the sandwich gripped in his right hand.

She shot him a quick look and, catching his meaning, bowed her head.

"Lord, thank you for this day, for your blessings and for this food. Make us better servants for you. Amen." She said it quietly and then sat in the chair opposite him.

"What's in the thermos?" he asked amiably as he began to chew on his sandwich.

"The elixir of life for farmers, cold tea!" she replied, opening the thermos and getting a pair of glasses from the cupboard. McCann thought she looked quite at home in this kitchen and seemed to know where everything was. She turned toward him as she poured the tea into one of the glasses and set it before him.

"You look at home here," he said.

Her glance was questioning at first and seeing no hidden meaning, she smiled. "I spent many an hour in this kitchen with Ella and Fred. It became a second home for me."

A flash of lightning lit up the western sky and a clap of thunder rocked the window panes. Rain began to pour down and soon they could hear the water running in the downspouts outside. A second flash and another clap brought Ted from somewhere in the house to lie at McCann's feet.

"You have a friend."

"He decided he liked me enough to move in the other night."

"He is a good judge of character," she replied without looking up.

"Even in my case?" he said, looking at her intently.

She raised her eyes to his and put her sandwich down. She took a drink from her glass without taking her eyes from his. "Wilson, tell me about Dynacom."

He felt his emotions running like a river towards a waterfall. Suddenly, he didn't want them to stop. The dam he had built up over the past several months burst and he wanted to pour it all out to her. He took a deep breath and spoke in a voice that he hardly recognized as his own.

"I put my whole life into Dynacom. I worked hard, I played the game as well as I knew how and I finally reached a place where what I did counted for something. We were making money. I was making money. Wall Street loved us. The morale of our people was high. Investor confidence was good. Our investments to improve and expand our services were paying off and we had added strategic balance to our product lines. Then, Charlie Corbin had to do one more deal. He bought SATCOM largely with venture capital."

"You mean debt?" she interjected.

"Big time debt. Our earnings went south in a hurry. The capital plan had to be cut in half and our service didn't keep pace with other companies. Morale started to decline. I worked night and day to come up with a way that we could digest the SATCOM acquisition and get things back on track within five years. It depended in large part on the success of a stock offering to refinance a good portion of the debt. The market started to decline just about the time we were ready to go in. That was when LEGENT showed up and Charlie decided it was time to sell out and close out his career with his greatest deal ever."

She took another sip from her glass. "And you decided the time was ripe to step in and try to buy Dynacom for yourself? You and that man who was here this week?"

He looked at her closely and decided that there was no sarcasm in the question. She was really leading him on to get it all out there on the table.

"The LEGENT deal meant the end of everything that I and hundreds of others had worked for years to build. No one in management wanted the deal. The employees didn't want the deal. Wall Street didn't move our stock price more than fifty cents when they heard about it. I knew that LEGENT would close offices, cut staff, cut programs and that their bureaucracy would stifle all the innovation we had built into our thinking. I couldn't sit back and watch that happen. Stu Bailey and I had been friends for a long time. He had helped us with a couple of acquisitions in the past and he felt he could recruit the necessary investors to put together a leveraged buyout of the company by management. I felt that was in the best interests of the company, its people and its customers."

He impulsively reached across the table for her hand. "As God is my judge, Donna, I didn't do it to put money in my pocket. I did it to preserve a dream and the people who gave that dream life."

She withdrew her hand and continued to look into his eyes. "So, you gambled for that which you had given your heart and soul to and you lost."

McCann's temper flared and he slapped his hand on the table. The glasses bounced and Ted raised his head. Lightning flashed and thunder rolled and the rain came down harder. He sagged in his chair and looked at her. He had the desire to lash out at her and say something cutting. But, he saw in her eyes not condemnation but something else. Was it pity? No, he decided, it was sorrow. He lowered his eyes and said what he knew to be true.

"Yes, I lost my dream."

"And you have come here because you have lost your dream? Why?"

"The media made it look like I was only trying to enrich myself at others' expense. They followed me everywhere asking their questions. They couldn't believe that a CEO would care about the company's people or customers more than personal gain. I couldn't take it anymore. Fred Penay had called me just about the time the deal fell through and told me that this farm was on the block because of debts that Fred and Ella had run up. He said that Fred had told him once that I was the only family member who had ever even cared enough to come here. He wanted to know if I had an interest in helping to sell it off and taking care of the debts. I needed a place to run to and this seemed as good as any."

"And now?" she prodded.

He took another deep breath and sat back in his chair. "I don't know. When I came here for those four summers many years ago, I thought I hated it. Fred worked me hard and wasn't the most pleasant person to be around. But, he was fair and he didn't ask me to do anything that he wouldn't do himself. When each day was done, I could see what I had accomplished. I wanted that feeling again."

She leaned back as well before she spoke again. "Fred had a dream too, Wils. It was almost too late, but he found something better. His priorities changed and he was a different man from that time on."

He stood and walked to the window to look out. Rain was cascading off the barn roof and puddles were already forming in the driveway. The day was growing darker. He automatically reached for the light switch and flicked it up. Nothing happened.

"The electricity must have gone out," he said, turning towards her.

"There are candles in the cupboard over the stove — and matches in a jar."

He brought out two candles in glass holders and lit them. The light bathed the table top with its clutter of food and cast shadows into the corners of the room. The interruption had released some of the tension that he felt. He leaned against the cupboard and turned to look at her. She hadn't moved. Her body was relaxed against the chair and she seemed to be waiting for him to speak.

"Donna, there is something else I need to get off my chest."

She continued to look at him but he could sense that the tension he had felt had now taken hold of her. She waited, saying nothing.

"Those summers we spent together — I wish they had been different. I feel like I used you and I am sorry — so very sorry."

Tears formed in Donna's eyes and slowly rolled down her cheek. "I wish they had been different, too, Wilson. I used you to get at my father. I was wrong and I have regretted it for many years. I wish things could have been different, too. I paid a heavy price for what we did."

He sensed something hidden there. He also sensed that to ask about it would be something that would lose her forever.

"That third summer...the summer before the one you were gone... I wasn't interested in hearing anything but doing what we had been doing for the past two summers. I felt you had changed and I wanted no part of getting serious. I had decided on a course for my life and I wasn't going to let anyone interfere with that. I am so very sorry. Could we start over?"

She looked away and stared out the window into the darkness. The yard light cast its dim light into the heavily falling rain. He sensed that she was re-living some awful moment and was struggling to master it before she answered.

"What we had cannot be restarted, Wils. You and I have followed far different roads since then."

"But both roads led back here. Maybe that is part of God's plan too," he said, hopefully. It was important not to lose her or this moment. He felt a wall between them starting to rise. "Let's take these candles into the living room and sit. These chairs are getting hard and my body is one big bruise!"

She laughed and the moment held. They finished their sandwiches and the rest of the meal, took their pie, tea and the candles into the living room. They sat them on the coffee table and sat together on the couch. Ted came and lay at their feet, rolled onto his side and went to sleep. The rain continued to fall and the wind howled around the eaves. Wils leaned back into the softness of the couch and hoped that the evening would never end. His body throbbed but he hadn't felt such peace in a long time. Donna kicked off her flats and curled up at the opposite end of the couch holding her glass of tea in one hand. Her green eyes reflected the candlelight.

McCann finished his pie and sat the dish on the coffee table. He leaned back again. "Tell me about your life since then," he said.

She hesitated and he sensed that she was struggling with where to begin. "The fourth summer you were here at the farm, something happened that changed my life forever…"

He sensed that whatever it was, it had left a deep scar in her. "What happened?" he asked quietly.

"I can't tell you that. Not now…maybe not ever…" Her eyes held a plea as she said it.

He waited as she gathered herself. She looked away and continued, "I went on a missionary trip to the Czech Republic…that's where I'm going this fall. There were people there with practically nothing that were happier than I was. I worked among them and they showed me what it meant to be a follower of Jesus Christ. It wasn't the religion of my father. It was a personal relationship with Jesus and turning my life over to him that brought me a happiness that I had never known before. I came home and made peace with my father even though he considered my new faith another radical reaction. I went to business school, learned marketing, and took a job in Bay City and learned retail marketing from the ground up. I became involved in a church there and was active in their missions work, including going back to Czech twice and to Peru once on mission trips during the next 10 years. I moved to Saginaw and was store manager for a retail chain there for four more years. I went on additional mission trips during that time. During my last trip, Dad was ill and needed someone to care for him. The Federated store had closed and there was a need for a retail clothing store in Farnsworth and the Barnes Loft opened six years ago. I am saving to go to school and get training that will enable me to go as a full time missionary."

She reached for her glass and found it was empty. Rotating it between her hands, she looked away. McCann rose and got the thermos from the kitchen and poured the rest of the tea into her glass. She looked up at him and smiled faintly.

"I am impressed," he said. "How is your father now? I mean, how do you and he…?"

"Get along?" she finished for him, "I love and respect him and he loves me although he never says so. Our faith is different. His is more traditional and mine is more contemporary. He still stresses the 'do's and don'ts' of religion. We debate the meaning of portions of the Bible quite often."

McCann sipped his tea. There was something between her and her father that she wasn't telling him. He was unsure of what to say. He wanted her to keep talking but she seemed willing to sit and gaze into the candlelight. He sat his glass down and leaned back against the cushions. "Tell me about Fred and Ella," he said.

Donna leaned forward and smiled. "When Pastor Chuck came to Farnsworth six years ago, he began to call on people in the community. He called on Fred and Ella and helped Fred with some sort of work on the farm on his first visit. Fred was impressed and appreciative. Pastor Chuck asked them to attend church. Fred didn't come but he brought Ella for a while and he would go down to the café and have coffee and read the Sunday paper during church. Ella didn't have many friends as I am sure you know."

"I can't think of any during the time I was here," McCann replied.

"Anyway, she made some friends at the church and began to come to a small group."

"And you brought her, didn't you?" McCann smiled as Donna looked at him in surprise.

"Yes I did. She was so sweet. I came to love her as a substitute mother."

Donna's mother had died the year before McCann had spent his first summer in Farnsworth. He had often wondered if Donna's rebellion against her father and his God was because of that loss.

"And Fred?" he asked.

"Fred would have nothing to do with church or Ella's new found friends. Then, he cut his foot open with an axe and was laid up for a month. People from the church came out and took care of the chores and Pastor Chuck came every day to call on him. The term "Christian" took on a whole new meaning for Fred. When his foot healed up, he started coming to church with Ella and within two weeks he was bringing her to the small group. They gave their hearts to Christ and were baptized. Fred even began to tithe. Did you know that?"

"He didn't have much to tithe from if the records I saw were any indication," McCann replied

"They had found something far more valuable than equipment and cattle and land. They found Jesus and they found each other. I never saw two people more in love than Fred and Ella for the next two years. But, Fred was too far in debt and George Whyte was squeezing him to pay up. He owed at the Agway and at my store...."

"I thought you didn't give credit" McCann smiled

"I made an exception for Fred and Ella. Anyway, he owed here in Farnsworth and in Caro..."

"I know, I bought the farm remember?" McCann interjected.

"I'm sorry, of course, you know all about the debts. Anyway, Fred died in the field and I helped Ella out and Jim Marks worked the land. We sold off the cattle and what equipment they owned outright. And then Ella died. They had two years of happiness and she had two more years of happiness in the church. I think both of them thought of you often and wished that they had been closer to you and your mother."

"A missed opportunity," McCann sighed.

"Are you and your mother close?" she asked.

"We talk about once a month on the phone and I went to see her twice a year until the LEGENT thing hit. I haven't seen her in a year. She is happy and has a circle of friends at the resort where she lives. She benefited from my success at Dynacom."

Donna leaned toward him. "Wils, do you have any close friends?"

"Define 'close,'" he replied uncomfortably. She was probing into areas that he felt uneasy about.

"Come on, Wils! Don't play word games with me!"

He leaned forward and dropped his gaze. "No, I don't suppose I do. Dynacom was my family and my focus. I didn't have time to develop any deep friendships."

She leaned back and took another sip from her glass. "I'm sorry for you, Wils."

"Don't be. I have a lot of money, a farm and people who respect my business ability. I just need to figure out what to do with the rest of my life." He said it defensively and regretted it. She looked away and placed her glass on the table. The drumming of the rain outside occupied the space between them.

"There are people here who will be your friends if you let them. They won't care how much money you have or don't have and they won't base their friendship on how many acres you own or how smart you are. People like Jim and Lona and their kids, Phil Willard, Fred Penay...."

"And you?" he interrupted her.

"Yes, Wils, I would like to be your friend. Not in the way we were years ago but a friend in the right way."

He smiled, "Would I have to go to church, read my Bible and pray every day?"

"Those are things I will be praying for but they are not a condition of my friendship nor will they be conditions of the friendship of the others."

"Then, I accept your offer of friendship, Miss Barnes." He smiled and extended his hand. She smiled back and took it. They sat there for a moment and their eyes locked. She withdrew her hand and stood.

"I've got to be going."

"You'll get wet if you do," he said, unwilling to see the evening end.

"I have to get home and check on Dad. He doesn't get around well anymore."

He accepted the answer and followed her to the kitchen where she gathered the remains of the meal and put them in the refrigerator. The rain had eased and he found himself wishing the opposite were true. Where was a good clap of thunder and flash of lightning when you needed it?

"Thanks for dinner, I owe you one. And, thanks for the help yesterday and …for tonight," he said.

"You can take a day off tomorrow. It doesn't look like you'll get much farming done with this rain."

"I need to get the barn ready for the steers and get the plow on the tractor."

"You sound like a farmer already. I'll be seeing you." She smiled at him as she went out the door into the night.

McCann stood in the doorway and watched her drive away. He watched until her taillights turned onto the highway a quarter mile away and disappeared. Ted stood beside him with his ears perked forward.

"She is quite a lady," he said to the dog. Ted wagged his tail in total agreement.

(7)

Doug Warner parked his GMC Yukon in front of the Farnsworth State Bank and went inside. He was 10 pounds over his playing weight of 240 while at Michigan State University as a reserve line backer. His hair was completely gray despite his 45 years. He wore jeans, cowboy boots and a white shirt inside a denim jacket with *Farnsworth Tele. Coop* stitched in maroon over a gray candlestick telephone logo. He nodded at the tellers and walked directly to Fred Penay's desk.

"Morning Fred," he said, as he sat in the chair opposite Fred's desk.

"Good morning to you, my friend. What brings you in so early this morning?"

"I need money – a lot of money," Warner responded with a smile.

Penay leaned back in his chair and returned the smile. "Who doesn't?"

"Not as much as I do."

Penay knew that the Farnsworth Telephone Cooperative was in sound financial condition. Its name belied the fact that 10 years ago, the Warner family had bought out the rest of the Coop's members, paid off the Rural Electrification Administration debt and began to modernize the network with much of their own money. He leaned forward and looked at Warner expectantly.

"LEGENT is going to put 12 exchanges serving 15,000 customers and all of their Michigan cellular business on the market within the next 30 days. I want to make a bid. I figure it will take $45 -50 million to get 'em."

Warner sat back in his chair and waited as the banker digested this bit of news. Penay swiveled his chair sidewise to the desk and absently doodled with a pencil on a note pad. He looked up at the clock on the wall and then back at Warner.

"Unless you and your mother have a rich relative I don't know about, you're going to need about $30 million or so."

Warner smiled to himself inwardly. Fred Penay was one of FTC's board members and he took his responsibilities seriously. Doug was glad to know that Penay remembered the amount of free cash FTC had available on its balance sheet.

"You've got it! I can raise $10 million from within the family interests. That leaves $40 million. Can I put down the bank for the rest?" he said, knowing the answer.

Penay didn't rise to the bait. He looked back at the clock. "Not today you can't."

"I know that Fred. But you must know where I can go to raise that kind of capital outside of traditional Telecomm sources." Warner's tone was all business.

"Doug, you know that I don't have that kind of contact. But, someone who has come to town lately may."

"Who?" Warner leaned forward.

"Wilson McCann."

Warner leaned forward. This was news! He knew McCann from telecommunications media and had heard him speak once at a national Telecomm showcase.

"What is Wilson McCann doing in Farnsworth?"

"His uncle was Fred Harms. He worked on Fred's farm for four summers between his junior year in high school and his senior year in college. When Ella died, the bank and several of the merchants here and in Caro made claims against the estate. I'm the administrator. There were no wills. I called Wils and asked if he was interested in buying the farm and equipment, paying off the bills and then liquidating it. Surprisingly, he agreed. The only change in plan is that he showed up here about 10 days ago and moved in. He bought a baler from Whyte and he and Jim Marks just put up 20 acres of hay. I understand from Jim that he plans to feed 20 head of beef cattle through the winter."

Warner scratched his head in perplexity. "Why? Why would he come here and try to be a farmer? He could command a six figure salary and lots of perks from at least three holding companies that I know of."

"I don't know. I suspect that he is pretty beat up over the Dynacom deal and has come here to lick his wounds and decide what to do next. I think he could use a few friends. Why not pay him a visit?" Penay swiveled his chair back to face Warner and leaned forward.

Warner sat back. He thought for a minute and rubbed his chin. "I don't know, Fred. Wils McCann has a reputation as a tough, hard-nosed operator and his try at buying out Dynacom looked pretty selfish to me."

"Things aren't always what they seem, Doug."

"The properties in the northern lower peninsula are old Dynacom properties that LEGENT got in the acquisition. I guess I could go out and ask him his opinion on their worth and see what his reaction is. It might give me some insight as to whether to ask him about sources for financing."

"It couldn't hurt. I hear that he knew the Dynacom network like the back of his hand."

Warner smiled. "For a small town banker, you seem to hear a lot."

Penay smiled back as Warner rose and made his way to the front door. "This is all very interesting," he said to himself as he leaned back in his chair.

Wilson McCann wakened to a sodden, gloomy day. Puddles of water stood in the drive way and in a low spot in the front pasture field. He started the coffee pot and put dog food into a pan for Ted who had tracked mud into the kitchen. With an old dish towel, McCann wiped the dog's paws and underbelly dry.

"Days like this, I wish you had stayed in the barn," he said to the dog. Ted wagged his tail and began to eat.

After breakfast, they walked outside to the tool shed. The aluminum roof had shed the water and the inside of the big building was perfectly dry. McCann checked the fuel tank outside the shed and noted that it was about one quarter full. He made a mental note to call Phil Willard and order a re-fill. He backed the big tractor around to the front of a four-bottom plow and made the three point connection to the tractor and hooked up the hydraulic lines. Then he raised the plow and lubricated it. Plowing today was out of the question but he wanted to be sure the equipment was ready when the fields were. He checked the big double disk toward the rear of the shed and went to the barn. The feed storage bins and auger system needed to be checked to make sure they were ready when Phil delivered the mix that Jim Marks would order up for him. Halfway through that chore, he looked at himself in the reflected steel of the bins. His shirt was becoming grimy and ragged from his week's work and his jeans were already worn above the knees from bouncing hay bales off them into the wagon or up into the mow. His hands were red and cracked and he had blisters on both hands. Yet he felt that the soreness in his muscles and the rough appearance of his clothing were badges of progress in an attempt at a different life. He did need some additional work clothes though, he thought. That gave rise to anticipation of seeing Donna again. He had wanted her to stay last night. He hadn't wanted the night to end. But, she had made it clear that her friendship now was different than the relationship that they had shared during his summers on the farm. He knew better than to try to make it more than it was and he was glad for what it was. He sensed that Donna cared about him. He wasn't sure what direction that feeling would take if he pushed for more than friendship. He decided he didn't want to lose it by trying to find out.

He cleaned and lubricated the augers, snapped them on and off to make sure they worked as they should and rolled the big door back that led into the feeding pens at the south end of the barn. A light rain was beginning to fall. Ted sat down and stared out into the pasture as if waiting for something to chase.

"Are you any good at herding beef cattle, boy?" McCann asked as he scratched the dog's ears.

Ted looked up and his tail cleared an arc of dust on the floor.

Donna Barnes ran the comb through her hair one last time and looked in the mirror. At age 40, she was, she thought, still attractive. She wore very little make up. Over the last twenty years, there had been a few local men and at least two from her the mission trips that had indicated an interest in developing a relationship. She had politely let them know she wasn't interested. From the time she was a senior in high school, only one man had held any interest for her and now he was back. Downstairs, tucked away in a closet where no one would see it, was an album filled with press clippings about Wilson McCann and his rise to and fall from power at Dynacom. Just when she thought she could focus on running the Loft, taking care of her aging father, and trying to save enough money to achieve her dream of overseas mission work, he had come back into her life.

Their relationship during the first three summers he had spent in Farnsworth had been fun and physical in that order. She was ashamed to think of how she had behaved. She had been in full rebellion against her father and against a God who had taken her mother from her just when she had needed her most. And she had paid a heavy price. She had gone away in late spring before he had returned to the farm for the fourth time. As spring turned into summer, she applied for and was granted a place on a mission team to Eastern Europe. By the time she returned to Farnsworth, her life had risen from the dark hole into which she had fallen. He had gone back to college but she was forced to hear of his exploits from certain young women in the community. In public, she had called him a "Casanova" and laughed lightheartedly. In private, she had sobbed out her hurt. Gradually, she had replaced her love for him with a love for Jesus Christ that had grown and deepened until the hurt was gone. At least she had thought it was gone until he had returned.

She had wanted to stay with him last night. Her mind was torn between what she knew to be right and what she knew to be wrong. She felt like she was seventeen again. Her confusion was just as great as it had been then. She sensed that McCann had been changed by what had happened to him. She also sensed that he was looking for something to replace the great loss in his life just as she had found the answer to the sorrow she had experienced long ago. She knew she could be part of that replacement. "Another acquisition" she had murmured to herself as she drove home last night. But she had been down that road once and had reaped the harvest of her own sowing. She had set herself to a future in God's service and was determined to place His plan for her life first. Her offer of a different kind of friendship had been based upon that.

She picked up her overnight bag from the bed and went out into the hall. She looked in on her father, sitting propped up in bed with the morning newspaper spread out before him. He was thin and pale. His white hair was still full and it framed his face as he turned to look at her.

"I'll see you Sunday evening, Dad," she said from the doorway. "Mrs. Willard will bring in a meal tonight and tomorrow night."

"So how is your friend the gentleman farmer doing?" he asked pointedly.

The way he said it took her back again to the time when he had raged against her behavior and her promiscuity and her general "sinfulness." She had hoped that over time, their relationship would have healed to where he could forget the great chasm that had been forced between them. She knew that he had forgiven her and that their relationship had healed. The forgetting was what continued to be hard.

"Wils and Jim got the hay in. I'm afraid he is finding out that farming is harder than sitting at a desk. See you on Sunday." She turned quickly and went down the stairs before he could reply.

A few minutes later, she pulled the Forester out onto M-81 and headed west for the interstate to Detroit. Her mind was troubled and she began to pray aloud for guidance. Why had Wilson McCann come back into her life?

McCann washed up, shaved and put on a pair of slacks and a golf shirt. As he came into the kitchen, Ted wagged his tail in anticipation. Together, they went to the Ranger and got in. He drove into Farnsworth and found a parking place on Main Street. It was close to noon and he hoped that Donna would be available to have lunch with him. When he entered the store, a dark haired girl in a faded sweater and blue slacks was at the counter. She looked to be about seventeen years old but her eyes looked thirty. They gave her a melancholy demeanor.

"May I help you?" she asked politely, trying to affect a smile.

"Is Donna – ah - Ms. Barnes around?"

"No, she went to a style show in Detroit. She won't be back until

Monday. Is there anything I can do? I run the store for her when she has to be away."

McCann's disappointment must have showed and her sad eyes took it in. Just then, a baby began to cry in the back room. She moved quickly to the rear of the store and soon emerged with the child against her shoulder.

"I'm sorry, it's time for his feeding. Was there something I could help you with?"

He reflected that this was the third time she had offered to help. The child continued to wail and she walked back and forth by the counter trying to quiet him. McCann quickly picked up two work shirts and a new pair of jeans and brought them to the counter. He paid in cash and told her to keep the change. The baby continued to cry as he left the store with the clothes under his arm.

Why hadn't Donna told him she was going away for the weekend? He was temporarily irritated and pushed Ted roughly out of the driver's seat as he got in. He realized he had no right to know her schedule and that his reaction was typical of his attitude towards being inconvenienced. He had driven into town expecting to spend more time with Donna. He was disappointed and confused. Ted looked at him quizzically and then turned to look out the window at a passerby. McCann reached across and ruffled his coat.

"Sorry, boy."

He drove to the Agway and checked to see if Jim had given Phil Willard the instructions for the feed order. Phil said that he had and that the Agway would deliver it the next week. On an impulse he asked Willard if he wanted to go to lunch and Phil readily accepted. Ted was sound asleep in the Ranger and the two of them walked down the street to the Diner. On the way, Willard chatted away about the blessing of the rain and how fortunate McCann had been to get the hay in before it started. McCann's mind was elsewhere.

They entered the Diner and sat in a booth to the right of the door. Three booths on each side flanked three chrome-legged tables and chairs up the middle. From behind the counter, a dark haired woman about forty called out a greeting to Willard and came forward with her pad to take their order.

Her blue jeans were tight and her scoop neck peasant blouse left little to the imagination. Her hair was full and framed her face. That it was coal black suggested it was exceptional or colored. McCann felt a strange stirring of remembrance but couldn't place her face.

"Coffee, tea or me?" she smiled suggestively at Willard. He smiled right back and seemed not offended by her brazen manner. She leaned against the side of the booth and looked McCann over appraisingly. He found it some-what stimulating and at the same time discomforting.

"Sally, you are too old for me!" Willard joked. McCann could tell that this must be a daily routine that the two of them played out at lunch time.

"You could leave your wife at church and go off to the lake with me on Sunday," she responded.

"I'd rather you bring those kids of yours to church and sit in my Sunday school class," Willard replied. "By the way, this is Wils McCann. He just moved into his Uncle Fred Harm's place north of town. Wils, this is Sally McHugh. She owns and runs this place."

She straightened immediately and the playful smile left her face. Instant recognition hit McCann with the mention of her name.

"Well, I'll be _____!" She covered her mouth with her hand to smother the rest of the sentence. McCann smiled broadly.

"Sally! It's been a long time."

Willard looked from one to the other, his face puzzled. McCann lowered his gaze and Sally McHugh took a deep breath. McCann looked at Willard and struggled to find the right words to say.

"Sally and I got to know each other when I was working on Fred's farm during the summer."

"Got to know each other pretty well as I remember it!" She said, her voice resuming its more brazen tone. "Wils here taught me to 'Chug-a-lug' beer at the VFW on Saturday night!" She leaned in toward Willard and low-ered her voice. "I taught him a couple of things, too." She leaned back and let her gaze travel over McCann's face. "You look good." She said softly.

McCann saw something cross Phil Willard's face. He wasn't sure what it was. He looked up at Sally. Her eyes met his and didn't flinch.

"So, you have children? How many?"

She put her hands on her hips. "Three…one from my first marriage and two from my third. The oldest is 22. The youngest is 13. How about you?"

"Still single," he replied. "What does your husband do?"

"Last I knew, the last one was working construction in Washington State. The first one lives in Detroit and the second one lives in Caro."

Phil Willard continued to look uncomfortable. He put down the menu he had just taken from behind a napkin holder. He glanced at McCann and looked up at Sally. "A Tuna Melt with a side of Slaw and Decaf coffee for me. How about you Wils?"

McCann hesitated. He started to reach for the menu.

"The special today is Shepherd's pie." Sally interjected.

"Sounds good, decaf for me also."

She scribbled on her pad and turned toward the counter. As she walked away, McCann watched the sway of her hips. Sally was still a very attractive woman.

He looked at Willard. Phil lowered his eyes as if studying the grain in the wood of the booth's tabletop.

"Sally is a piece of work isn't she? But God still loves her."

"Her name was Ormsby, right?" McCann asked.

"Yes. Ormsby. Then Fields. Then Bishop. Then McHugh. She didn't bother dropping her married name when Chuck left. She bought this place three years ago from the money she gets from the first two and she's done a good job with it. I keep hoping I can get her to bring those kids to church and settle her lifestyle down. I truly believe Sally has a lot of good in her. Her kids are model citizens."

McCann looked down. "I'm afraid that she and I were a bit on the wild side when I … when I spent the summers here. Donna had gone off on that church trip and I wanted to have a little fun when the work was done. Sally seemed more than willing to have a good time."

Willard took a deep breath. "Kind of like Donna had been the previous summers? I'm sorry I don't mean to pry but…"

"No, it's true. Donna and I had a lot of fun the first summers I spent here. Then, she started to get too serious for me. I didn't want anything serious. I just wanted to sow my wild oats, I guess."

"Well, Sally is still sowing hers. I just hope she doesn't reap a whirlwind."

McCann decided to change the subject. "I stopped in at the Loft this morning. Donna wasn't here. I met a young woman with a baby. She said Donna went to a style show in Detroit."

"That is Darcy. She was another Sally in the making until Donna took her on and gave her a job. The baby's father is a young man from one of the leading families in town. He is also trying to find his way. So far, he hasn't seen fit to make an honest woman out of Darcy."

McCann smiled. "Another prayer project of yours?"

Willard smiled back. "I have many on my prayer list, including you."

Somehow, McCann was not offended. He was beginning to like Phil Willard more and more as he got to know him.

The door opened and Willard looked up. A tall muscular gray haired man entered and smiled as Phil raised his hand. He strode to the booth and slid in next to Willard as he moved over.

"Good morning, Doug," Willard said motioning toward McCann. "Meet Wils McCann. He's new in town, owns the Harms place."

Doug Warner leaned back and smiled as he extended his hand. "I was just talking about you over at the bank."

McCann's face showed surprise and then suspicion. "Is my account overdrawn or something?" he said, trying to make it sound light.

"No not at all. I was just talking to Fred Penay about a little deal I would like to make and he suggested I talk to you. My family owns and operates the Farnsworth Telephone Cooperative." He looked sideways at Phil Willard. "Phil is on our Board."

McCann's mind flashed back to the industry he had spent his career in. He tried to remember what he knew about the Farnsworth Company. He continued to search his memory as he spoke.

"I didn't know that a Coop could be a family-owned company."

"Our family bought out the Coop owners ten years ago. We paid off the REA five years ago and we just didn't bother to drop the word Coop from the name."

McCann's memory locked onto a piece of information and his face showed it.

"Warner! Your name is Warner, right? I remember meeting you and your mother at a convention where I spoke."

Doug Warner smiled broadly. "You talked about fiber in the network and the need for companies to start getting involved in the Internet."

"I remember it! Did I make any sense at all?"

"You did to us. We went home and began to modernize our network and we were an ISP long before anyone else in the Independent part of the industry here in Michigan."

"And your mother?"

"My mother is Chairman of our Board and I am the President and CEO."

Sally McHugh appeared with McCann's and Willard's orders. She gave Doug Warner a dazzling smile. "Well, you big hunk of manhood. What will you have today?"

Doug Warner smiled up at her. "Sally, you are absolutely beautiful today. And your appearance isn't half bad either! You know what? God loves you! I'll have a cheeseburger and a Diet Coke."

"God loves me and you'll have a Cheeseburger. Ha!" She turned toward the counter and McCann got to watch those hips a second time.

"So what's this big deal you are working on? As a Board member, I have a right to ask!" Phil Willard said.

Warner leaned forward and lowered his voice. He looked intently at Wilson McCann and then at Willard. When he spoke, his eyes bored into McCann's.

"LEGENT is going to sell some of its properties, including all of its property in Michigan. I want to put together a proposal to buy the Michigan properties. Fred told me that you know those properties and that you know some people who might be able to help me pull that off."

Stu Bailey dipped a shrimp into the cocktail sauce and popped it into his mouth, neatly disposing of the tail on his plate. The man opposite him in the small restaurant in downtown Manhattan waited expectantly.

"So, is he in or out?"

Bailey took a sip from his Sprite and leaned back in his chair. "I know Wils McCann as well as anybody and when he reads the material I put together and left with him, his juices will start to flow and he will definitely want to be part of this deal."

"And. . . .if he doesn't?"

"There are others in the business that we can get to run the operation until we get ready to unload it."

"Not with his knowledge of the service areas and the network. Not with the respect he has within the industry. Remember, Stu, we want to unload this baby in five years and we want it to have a new coat of wax on it when we do. Getting money today is a lot different than it was a year ago. Global Crossing and WorldCom have changed things. A lot of people don't think there is money to be made in Telecom any more. Wilson McCann can put that coat of wax on for us."

Bailey took another shrimp. He didn't want to admit that his trip to Michigan had left him less than sure of Wilson McCann's interest in being part of any deal. McCann had been bitterly hurt by the failure of their attempt to save Dynacom. His move to Michigan and his actions in buying a farm, not to mention baling hay and talking about feeding cattle, were uncharacteristic of the hard-charging executive that Bailey knew.

"Don't worry, Ed. I'll deliver Wilson McCann. There is money to be made here. The prices are lower because of Global Crossing and WorldCom. These properties are rural and they are stable and, for the most part, they reflect a modern network that Dynacom put in place before Charlie Corbin's ego resulted in the sale to LEGENT. Now, how much can we count on your firm to put into the kitty?"

"One hundred and fifty big ones, if you get the rest raised, McCann is the CEO and we get two board seats." Ed Feldman responded. He leaned back and watched Bailey closely. "Where will you get the rest?"

"Triad will raise one hundred million and the rest will come from smaller venture capitalists." Bailey replied, finishing his shrimp. "Are you having dessert?"

"Dessert will be when you call me next week and tell me that Wils McCann is in on the deal. Are you picking up the tab?"

Bailey picked up the bill from its leatherette pad and scanned it. Six shrimp cost $24.99! A Sprite was $4.25? What was this world coming to?

"Got it, Ed!" He said, dropping his Platinum VISA card on top of the bill and motioning to the waiter.

Five minutes later, the two men parted. Feldman hailed a cab and headed back to his office on 3rd Avenue, south of 42nd St. He was not at all convinced of the viability of this deal. There were a lot of opportunities to invest money these days and Telecommunications companies, however small and stable, were not a place one went looking for dramatic returns. If Wilson McCann was part of the deal, he would feel better. McCann was a strong, ethical operator who knew the business. If he was in, Feldman would pull the trigger on the financing. If not, well, there were other places to put one hundred and fifty million dollars. He looked out the cab's window at the New York City skyline. Ever since September 11, 2001, he had felt uneasy living and working here. He didn't need any more uncertainty in his life.

Bailey decided to walk the ten blocks back to his office. Four bucks a shrimp and three hundred million for telecommunications networks! He began to whistle as he walked along.

McCann looked at Doug Warner and then at Phil Willard. Willard's expression was one of surprise. Warner waited expectantly. McCann let out a breath and leaned back.

"You are the second person in three days to want me to help him buy LEGENT property," he said for effect. He got it. Warner's face showed his surprise. Willard looked at McCann with interest and waited.

"How do you know they are for sale?" McCann went on.

"I have a friend who is a Trade Association staffer in Wisconsin. A friend of his at LEGENT told him on the Q.T. that LEGENT was getting ready to pull out of the state. He started following the rumors and found out that it's four mid-western states, not just one," Warner replied, the surprise of McCann's statement still evident in his tone of voice. "Who else is going to bid on the Michigan properties?"

McCann took a sip of his coffee and followed it with a bite of the Shepherd's Pie. He considered how much he wanted to tell Warner. His impression of the big, gray headed man was positive, much the same as his initial impression of Jim Marks had been in the barn on his first day here.

"I would be breaking a confidence to a very dear friend if I told you what

I know. I can tell you this. The other party will bid on all four states, not just Michigan."

Warner's face sagged. "That would take a lot of money." He said quietly.

"I figure about three hundred to four hundred million — minimum." McCann replied. Phil Willard was in the process of taking his first bite from the Tuna Melt. He quickly washed it down and whistled through his teeth.

At that moment, Sally McHugh plopped a cheeseburger and Diet Coke in front of Warner and turned her smile on McCann. "Anything else for you boys?" she asked. McCann shook his head and Willard did likewise. Sally looked from one to the other and realized that she had intruded. "Wave if you want me," she said rather suggestively and for the third time in an hour, McCann watched the hips move back behind the counter.

Doug Warner carefully cut his cheeseburger in half and took half in one big hand and considered it before taking a bite and chewing slowly. For a moment, all three men devoted themselves to their food. Finally, Warner lowered the remains of his half Cheeseburger to his plate and looked directly into McCann's eyes.

"Do you think a little outfit like ours would have a chance if we could put the money together? For just the Michigan properties I mean?"

McCann considered for a moment and decided that Doug Warner was the kind of a man you could talk straight with.

"You would need to sweeten the pot if you wanted them to break it up into pieces instead of selling the whole."

"How much sweetening?" Warner was holding his half Cheeseburger again.

"Twenty per cent above the normal selling price." McCann watched his face as he said it. Warner put his burger down and leaned back against the cushion of the booth.

"That makes it about $60 million for just the Michigan piece," he said quietly.

"And that could be a minimum if they get a lot of interest in the entire package," McCann said. Warner might as well know what kind of a game this was. McCann had the scars to show. He didn't want to see Doug Warner scarred.

Warner sat forward, took the other half of the cheeseburger in his hand and bit off about a third of it. He chewed methodically and said nothing. Phil Willard finished his slaw and waited. McCann pushed a few peas to the side of his plate and took another sip from his coffee. Warner drank deeply from his Diet Coke and set the glass down firmly on the table.

"Mr. McCann …"

"Wils."

"…Wils, how much would you charge for three hours of your time?"

"Am I hauling hay, plowing a field or talking to you?" McCann smiled.

"You would be talking to my Board about what kind of a deal it would take to try to do this and how we would have to go about it. You would also be sharing your knowledge of the part of the LEGENT property here in Michigan that Dynacom used to own."

McCann took another bite of the Shepherd's Pie. The mashed potatoes, ground beef and peas were layered and were the best he had eaten in a long time. He would have to make it a point to stop in here more often. Visiting with Sally McHugh would be an added benefit.

"Mr. Warner…"

"Doug."

"…Doug, as you no doubt know, my last endeavor ended quite badly. You have no doubt read the accounts in the financial press …"

Warner raised his hand to stop him. "They don't understand our industry and they didn't understand what you were trying to do." Warner broke in.

"And you do?"

"I think you were trying to save a good company with a good record of service and shareholder value from being snapped up at a ridiculous price by a company whose record on both scales is mediocre."

McCann looked at Warner. The big man's face was very serious. For the first time in six months, Wilson McCann felt a part of the industry he had given a good measure of his life to.

"Doug, I have to make a phone call to a party in New York. After I make that call, I'd be glad to sit down with your Board and talk about anything you want . . . at no charge."

Phil Willard took a drink from his coffee and whispered "Thank you Jesus." Both McCann and Warner heard him.

(8)

The Director of the Communications Division of the Michigan Public Service Commission sat in the Governor's outer office. He wasn't happy to be here. He didn't like the idea of being asked to come to the Governor's office. The Governor was a Republican. The Chairman of the Commission, the Director's boss, was a Republican. One of the other two Commissioners was a Republican. The Director was a Democrat and he was three years away from his State Civil Service pension. He had been in his post for 15 years. He had been in the Division for 40 years. He was looking forward to retirement. He was not happy with the way things were decided in the regulatory environment these days. With all the competitive local exchange carriers wanting a piece of the incumbent's business, with the long distance carriers wanting into local service and the regional Bell operating company wanting into long distance and with all the mergers and acquisitions, life was no longer simple for a regulatory staff person. "The time was," he thought to himself as he watched a Michigan State Trooper tap away on a notebook computer on a desk to the right of the door to the Governor's office, "when nobody gave a turnip about who owned what or provided what as long as what they owned was operated well and what they provided was good service." Well, those days were gone. The regional Bell operating company was not even headquartered in Michigan anymore and the second largest carrier wasn't either. Frankly, he felt the dozen or so family owned companies that operated within the state provided a much better grade of service to their customers and a lot less headache to him and his staff. But, unless things changed, most of them would soon be gone, devoured by other non-Michigan based companies.

"The Governor will see you now." The secretary to his left said as she looked over her half glasses at him. She was in her late forties and wore a gray pinstriped pant suit. Her hair was pulled back in a bun and she wore a minimum of makeup. The Governor was known to be straight laced and his inner circle was composed of men and women who shared his views.

He rose and walked through the door into the Governor's office. The Governor didn't rise to greet him as he entered. His desk was clean with the exception of a single file folder in the middle of his desk pad. He motioned the Director to a chair opposite the desk. The Director noticed the well worn Bible on the desk. The Governor had a reputation as a man with an axe in one hand to cut into state bureaucracy and a Bible in his other to guide his way.

"Well, Fred, what do we know?" he asked, leaning back in his chair.

"Nothing for certain sir. Just rumors at this point but LEGENT'S VP-Regulatory for the Midwest would like to meet with the Chairman next week."

"Do you think it's about the sale?"

"It could be sir."

The Governor leaned forward and folded his hands together on top of the folder. "I've been looking at the quarterly service results you sent over. The Independents continue to provide service levels above the standard, the Regional Bell Operating Company is at standard and LEGENT is below standard. Is that right?"

"Yes sir, that is correct."

"Fred, who would you think would be interested in buying the Michigan properties?"

"Probably one of the acquisition consortiums. I think that there might be one or two of the independents who would like pieces of the Michigan property but they would have a hard time getting financing and LEGENT will want to sell all the states together if they can."

"Is there anyone who can operate the LEGENT properties and provide top notch service over a fully modern network, especially in the northern Lower Peninsula?"

The Director considered the question carefully before answering. He had heard rumors that the Governor and his staff had taken a significant interest in the economy of Michigan's northern Lower Peninsula. The Chairman of the Commission had recently asked for an evaluation of the

Telecommunications network north of a line from Alpena on Lake Huron to Ludington on Lake Michigan. Half of the LEGENT property in the state was north of that line.

"The RBOC could but they won't invest in the network there. They are having a hard time keeping their heads above water in the metro areas. No. 2 won't expand into that area either."

"How about one of the Independents?"

"There are two in the area and only one is interested in expanding. We expect the other to be acquired within the next two years."

"By who?"

"One of the acquisition consortiums."

The Governor leaned back again. He clasped his hands behind his head and rocked slightly in his chair. The Director noted that the Governor's chair didn't squeak as his own did when he leaned back in it.

"Tell me about these acquisition consortiums."

"They are basically led by a combination of former industry executives and a group of venture capitalists. Over the past two years, there has been a lot of money available to fund the acquisition of smaller companies. Most intend to build a multi-state operation and either take it public to make a killing or to sell it off to another company. They are even selling to each other."

He said the last with some degree of heat and the Governor took note.

"You don't think much of them, do you, Fred?"

"Their record on service and rates is not the best, in my opinion, Governor."

The Governor leaned forward again and looked the Director straight in the eye. His voice was measured and his tone was very direct.

"Fred, I realize that this is uncomfortable for you, coming here without the Chairman's knowledge. I do not like putting you in that position. But, I need to be kept informed about this situation as it moves along. I want you to come and see me after LEGENT meets with the Chairman and when you have a better idea of who may bid on these properties. I want you to be brutally frank in expressing your opinions about what is happening. You have a long and distinguished record in the agency and you know far better than many how important it is to have a first rate network in this state. We are in the information age and it is critical to the state's economic competitiveness that we assure that those who seek to operate within the state meet the standards for service that we have set. Will you do that for me?"

The Director looked at the Governor thoughtfully. "May I inquire why this particular matter is important enough to receive this level of interest?"

"Not at this time, Fred. When I can, I will share more with you. Until then, I need your help. Will you do that for me?"

"Yes sir."

"Thank you, Fred. On your way out, please make an appointment to see me in ten days."

He made the appointment with the gray haired Secretary and left. On his way back to his office, he pondered why the Governor was so interested in the sale of a bunch of rural telephone exchanges. But, he had survived four changes in party leadership at the Commission and he didn't intend to do anything right now that would keep him from surviving until he was pension eligible.

As the door closed, the Governor turned toward another door at the side of the office. It had been slightly ajar and now opened. A tall man with a full head of sandy hair entered. He collapsed into the chair which had just been vacated by the Director.

"Well, Ross?" The Governor asked.

"It's obvious he doesn't know about the project. It's also obvious that he shares your desire to provide good service. It also is obvious that the Director doesn't like LEGENT or the acquisition consortiums. In my opinion, we have to stay close to this thing and make sure that LEGENT sells to the right people. If we get some fly-by-night group that is only interested in making a quick killing, it could scuttle the project but good!"

The Governor leaned back and clasped his hands behind his head again. "And the Chairman? What do you think? Should we tell him?"

"No. He's there because of what he did to help get you elected. He has close ties to the industry. He'll talk to one of them and the project will leak before you are ready. The price of the LEGENT sale will escalate, or LEGENT will decide to stay, along with their lousy service and the opposition will jump all over the project and you. I would trust Fred more than the Chairman right now. I've checked him out and he is a man with a high degree of integrity. He is also three years from retirement and he isn't going to do anything to mess that up. We can bring the Chairman in when we need to but now is not the time."

"You're right, of course." The Governor responded. "But, stay close to it, Ross."

Wilson McCann shook hands with Doug Warner, and he and Phil Willard turned right and headed down Main Street towards the Agway and McCann's Ranger. Warner turned left, rounded the corner and headed up Cedar Street towards his office.

"Tell me a little more about Doug and the company," McCann said, as they approached the Ranger.

Willard leaned against the front fender. "Solid as a rock…both Doug and the company. He is a local boy who puts a lot of himself into anything he does. He's married to a beautiful gal and they have two great daughters. He is on the Board of our church, Vice President of the County Chamber of Commerce and sits on the Economic Development Board. The company is first class in everything it does. He is way ahead of LEGENT in the types of service he provides and the costs are reasonable. He treats his people fairly and …."

"You make him sound like a Saint!" McCann laughed.

"Doug was always a good man but he wasn't always the kind of husband and father he needed to be." Willard responded, looking serious. "He and his wife were about to split when Pastor Chuck came to town. They started talking football at the diner and Doug went to church and kept coming. Pretty soon his wife and the girls came and they found a new life in Christ and…"

"…and now he's 'born again!'" McCann finished for him. "That story seems to repeat itself quite often here! By the way, what were you thanking Jesus for back in the diner?"

Phil Willard straightened and clapped McCann on the shoulder. "For sending you here!" he said firmly, and turning, headed on down the street.

McCann watched him go. His mind was churning. He had come to Farnsworth uncertain of his future. He had no plan. He was just running away from his former life. The farm, Stu Bailey's proposition, his feelings for Donna Barnes and now this new wrinkle and behind it all, this business about Jesus having a plan for your life! If that were true, how did all this fit together? How does one know what that plan is? One thing was certain; he was not finding his new life in Farnsworth boring!

He watched Phil turn into the Agway and then he climbed into the Ranger. Ted licked his right hand and thumped his tail rapidly against the passenger door. "I wonder what tomorrow will bring." McCann said out loud. Ted cocked his head quizzically and perked his ears forward as if expecting McCann to answer his own question.

Jim Wolfe turned his Explorer into the drive of the rented house in Mackinaw City. It was 2:00 p.m. and he had decided to knock off early and go fishing. LEGENT wouldn't care. They didn't care about anything, it seemed to Jim. He parked the SUV and turned off the engine and sat there thinking. It was not good to think too much but he couldn't help it. A year ago, he had been State Manager for Dynacom in Lansing. Now, he was Area Superintendent for LEGENT'S Northern Michigan Area. He had made the choice and LEGENT was only too happy to freeze his salary and let him move north. They had paid the cartage for his family's household, nothing more. His new job was one he could do in his sleep. It was the once a week conference calls and the unplanned, unscheduled meetings that drove him up the wall. It seemed that all LEGENT wanted to do was talk about empowerment and communication and "bottom up" management. That was the difference, Jim thought to himself. They talk about it, we did it!

His mind turned back to similar conference calls and meetings with Dynacom's management team. You were expected to know the objectives and to deliver a plan to meet them. You were expected to know the issues and have a plan to address them. You didn't just talk, you acted. Wilson McCann would have had no part of all this empowerment talk! He would have demanded action and he would have gotten it.

"What are you doing home this early?" June Wolfe leaned against the driver's side door of the Explorer. She was short, dressed in a University of Michigan sweatshirt and shorts. She was "five foot two with eyes of blue" and Jim had loved her from the first time he saw her on the U of M campus fifteen years ago.

"I thought I would knock off early and go fishing. At least there are some results from that." Jim smiled as he leaned out the window and put his left hand on her arm.

"Another conference call about 'The power of one'"?

"Yep. The Southern Area's Out of Service over 24 hours is up twenty per cent over last month and all they do is talk about it. I give them our results and they say 'thank you' and 'keep up the good work'."

June Wolfe sighed. She had never seen her husband this way in the fourteen years they had been married. He had always been a hard worker and he enjoyed his work. He only put two things ahead of it, his faith in God and his family. She had always felt protected and secure in the knowledge that her husband would take care of her and their two boys and that he would do it in a way that was pleasing to God. The last six months had been like some sort of bad dream. First, the LEGENT takeover of Dynacom, and then, the "integration" of the two companies that left very few Dynacom managers in any significant position within the new company. Then, Jim chose to take a two level demotion to the Superintendent's job instead of taking a staff job in Fort Wayne, Indiana. She was immediately glad as it would move the family away from the city of Lansing and closer to her family in Alpena. But, in her heart, June Wolfe knew that her husband was made for greater things and she knew that down deep he was not a happy man.

"Come inside, I'll fix you up a snack and you can stay out as long as you want. Just come home smiling. Okay?"

Jim climbed down from the Explorer and put his arm around his wife's shoulders as they walked into the house. Maybe if he prayed hard enough, God would give him peace about the situation.

As he began to change into his fishing clothes, his pager went off. He looked down at the display and noted that it contained the number of the Director of the Emmett County Economic Development Corp. Jim knew her well. He decided to return the call in case there was some service issue at stake. Jim was determined not to let his service indices falter despite LEGENT'S lack of investment in the network of the Northern Area. He dialed the number on his cellular as he began to lay out his fishing gear. The voice on the other end was cheery.

"Hello, Joyce, how goes it?"

"Just great, Jimmy! How about with you?"

"Well, if I could get away from my customers, I'd go fishing and it would be great." He said lightly.

"Sorry about that! Some of us have to work until five! I guess you are an executive!"

Wolfe snorted into the phone. "Hah! I sure am. I'm in charge of White Tailed Deer and Pulp Forests!"

"Hey! Don't knock it. I need those deer and trees to expand my county's industrial base."

"So, what's up? Need a fiber line into some back woods property to serve a new industrial plant you've persuaded the Outer Mongolian government to invest in?"

The tone on the other end of the line turned serious. "Something like that, Jim. Or it could be. I was wondering if you had ever heard of a company called Wolverine Property Management. You being an old U of M alum, I thought it might be something you would know about."

Wolfe thought for a moment. "No, never heard of it. Why?"

"About two weeks ago, they bought 100 acres of land near Brutus. The two guys that sold the property said it was all very hush-hush and won't talk to me about it, and the real estate guy that handled the deal practically choked when I asked about it at the Rotary meeting today."

"It's probably some outfit thinking they can build a golf course or a resort hotel and attract people up to the Burt Lake area. Tell you what, I'll check with some of my contacts in Lansing and let you know if I turn up anything interesting."

"Thanks Jimmy! Catch one for me!" With that she hung up.

Wolfe decided to wait until Monday to make a few calls to his contacts in Lansing. The fish were waiting. He kissed June full on the lips and grabbed a well worn Bible from the kitchen table and headed out into the sunshine.

(9)

Nick Hardesty walked across the service bays of the Rambaugh Daimler Chrysler dealership and entered the glassed-in office with a sign over the door that read "Service Manager." His dark blue uniform pants and shirt were greasy and his shoulder length hair looked like it had been in the same grease trap. His hands were fairly clean because of the red oil rag he kept twisting as he walked. He was 18 years old and stood six foot one in his work shoes. He was a disappointment to just about everyone, from his father who owned and operated the Hardesty Insurance Agency to Darcy Evans, the mother of his child. He had finished high school in May ranked 75th in a class of 86. He had few friends and spent most of his time hanging around the dealership where he had worked since graduation. His rusted Ford Mustang still had three payments to go on it.

Fred Erlack, the Service Manager, looked up as Nick entered. He did not indicate that Nick should sit so he stood there waiting. Erlack extended a paycheck and spoke quickly. "I can't use you any more, Nick. Sales are off and we have to cut back. We just don't need an extra set of hands just to sweep up and do lube oil and filter jobs. You should take your old man up on his offer to send you to trade school and learn a trade."

So there it was, three months and out. Nick took the check and turned to leave. It wasn't in his nature to beg, but he spoke quietly from the doorway. "Thanks, Mr. Erlack. If something comes up where you need someone, let me know."

Erlack was already scanning some parts invoices. Without looking up he said, "Sure, Nick, I'll do that. You can keep the uniform shirt and pants if you want 'em."

Nick left and Erlack heard the Mustang come to life out on the side street. "What a loser! His old man is going to kill him when he finds out," he thought to himself as he stacked the invoices in his out basket.

Upon returning to the farm, McCann walked the fence lines of the two pasture fields and found only two breaks in the fence. These he fixed quickly using a fence repair kit in a leather bag that he found in the tool shed. He judged that the upper of the two fields to be planted to winter wheat would be ready for plowing the next day. The lower would have to wait another day or two to be sufficiently dry.

He hosed down the Buick and hooked up the air compressor from the tool shed to inflate the tires. Three would hold air but the fourth had been irreparably cut when he had dragged the car from the shed. He looked at the spare and decided to forego putting it on. By that time it was dinnertime and he fixed his dinner and ate it in the kitchen. Ted lay at his feet, hoping for a handout while he washed the dinner dishes. Going into the living room, he picked up the Bible and flipped the pages. His eyes fell upon a passage that was underlined in red ink. It was in 2nd Corinthians 9, verses 6 through 9:

Now this I say, he who sows sparingly shall also reap sparingly and he who sows bountifully shall also reap bountifully. Let each one do just as he purposed in his heart; not grudgingly or under compulsion; for God loves a cheerful giver. For God is able to make all grace abound to you, that always having all sufficiency in everything, you may have abundance for every good deed: As It is written, He scattered abroad, he gave to the poor, His righteousness abides forever.

He thought about his life. Certainly he had been blessed with success and material wealth beyond his dreams. He could now say that, despite the LEGENT/Dynacom acquisition. He read the underlined verses again. What had he sown over his career? He had worked hard and diligently. He had tried to treat others fairly and had been honest in his dealings. He had not been one to give money to causes but he had, on occasion, supported various community projects within the Dynacom service area from his own pocket. He had given many young men and women an opportunity to excel and had watched in satisfaction as they had done so. He had reaped bountifully until the LEGENT acquisition. Had he sowed as bountifully? He knew that he had not always been as considerate of others as he could have been. His excuse was that the good of the business did not, at times, allow for consideration of others' feelings.

As he pondered it all, it became clear to him that his aloofness and drive to put the needs of Dynacom first in his life had resulted in few friends beyond his close business associates. He reflected that the way he had been treated upon the conclusion of the LEGENT acquisition had in fact been the "reaping" of what he had sowed. The needs of the business had been met by his dismissal.

He began to think of his future. How could he put more balance in his life in the future? Was there a way to "sow bountifully"? Could he make his knowledge and ability available to those who obviously could use it, like Doug Warner? Should he involve himself in Stu Bailey's plans to put together another acquisition? Could he find a way to utilize his personal wealth and experience in some manner that would provide him the satisfaction he had gotten from his career, as well as some balance to what he could now see had been a rather narrowly focused life?

He sat there as the darkness slowly invaded the house. He ran the events of the past year through his mind again and the old anger and anxiety came back. He thought of the past week and all that had happened since he came to this farm. He thought of Donna Barnes, Stu Bailey, Jim Marks, Phil Willard and Doug Warner, and then he noticed that the anger and anxiety had faded away and that he was beginning to have some anticipation for the days ahead. He noted that someone had written a reference to Proverbs 11:24 in the margin of the Bible next to the verses he had read:

There is one who scatters, yet increases all the more, and there is one who withholds what is justly due, but it results only in want.

He knew now which kind of sower he had been up to now. He went to bed, wondering whether, as he sowed his fields with winter wheat, he could sow some kind of good here in Farnsworth. Ted, his head on his paws, watched him go.

Saturday dawned bright and sunny. McCann took his time over his breakfast and used his computer to check on his brokerage account and 401k, noting that most of his telecommunications stocks were down. The continuing decline in technology stocks and the poor earnings results from some of the nation's larger carriers were depressing that segment of the market. He reviewed the business news on the Internet and made a mental note to re-start his *Wall Street Journal* delivery at his new address. The activity stimulated him and his mind moved quickly over the statistics and information displayed on the screen, prompting him to make two minor adjustments in the allocation of his 401k and making notes of three actions he wished to take within his brokerage account. He shut down his Internet access and opened up his spreadsheet software to load various pieces of information from the file that Stu Bailey had left with him and added other bits of information from his memory of the operations. Then, he built a model based on the information together with his perspectives as to the financial characteristics of LEGENT'S Michigan property.

He called Stu Bailey's New York City office and left a message for Stu to call. He knew that Bailey would be checking his messages from time to time during the weekend as he always did. Next, he opened his Outlook file and placed a call to Jim Wolfe's number in Lansing. Wolfe knew the LEGENT property in this state as well as anyone. A recording told him that the number had been disconnected and he hung up the phone in frustration. LEGENT had no doubt closed the Lansing office. He wondered where Wolfe had been transferred or if he had left the company, and decided to call one of his contacts at LEGENT'S headquarters on Monday and find out.

Finally, he closed and saved the worksheets and opened a word processing system where he created an outline of a proposed acquisition strategy for Farnsworth Telephone Coop's bid on LEGENT'S Michigan property. Having completed that, he saved the file, closed the computer and headed for the tool shed.

The big tractor roared to life with the turn of the key and he headed out into the field. Four hours later, what had been a hay field was turned into a pattern of straight dark rows. McCann sat at the end of the last set of furrows and surveyed what he had done. He had enjoyed the work.

The power of the tractor, the smell of the soil as it turned over and the steadily growing number of black rows had given him a sense of satisfaction he had not felt for some time. He stepped down from the tractor and scooped up a handful of the rich dark soil and let it run through his fingers. He thought again of the scripture that he had read the previous night. Would he reap sparingly or bountifully from his new life? He sensed that there was a piece of the puzzle as yet not found. With more time to think now, he was sure he would find it. He climbed back up into the tractor's seat and, on impulse, turned on the tape deck. The strains of "Amazing Grace" filled the air and McCann headed the tractor back to the tool shed.

He awakened on Sunday morning with the thought to go out and check the other field. But, at the same time, he felt an urge to go to church. He debated with himself while he scrambled two eggs and fried some bacon. Finally, he decided to go to church. He showered and shaved and put on his suit, white shirt and tie. He paused to check his appearance in the mirror. His face was a little darker from his work outside. Otherwise, he reflected, he looked like the same man who only a few months ago had led one of the country's telecommunications companies. The thought brought an instant surge of emotion as he remembered the meetings, the high level discussions on policy and the satisfaction of being "the man in charge." For a moment, he felt tempted to call a friend at a placement agency and submit his resume for another go at leading a company. He poured himself another cup of coffee and sat at the kitchen table thinking. He let his mind go and thought of the various possibilities that might be available to him if he were to get back into the business world. As he drained his cup, he realized that a return to that life did not hold the appeal for him that it once had. He thought again of the last two weeks and the dramatic change it had brought to him and how much enjoyment he had taken from working outside in the fields. He decided that, for now, he would play the cards as they were dealt to him and see which way he was led.

"I guess I'll just stay here a while and see what happens," he said to Ted.

The dog rose from his place near the door and, wagging his tail, walked to McCann's side, laying his muzzle on McCann's knee.

"Besides, what would I do you with you? I can't let you go back to wandering and begging!" he said as he scratched the dog's ears.

The church was almost full when McCann entered. He saw Jim and Lorna Marks and their children seated in the third row from the front. Their pew was full. He turned to look for a seat in the back. Phil Willard motioned him to a seat toward the back on the right side of the sanctuary.

"I'm so glad to see you here!" Willard whispered as McCann sat down and the organist began to play the prelude. McCann looked around and noted that the girl from The Barnes Loft was seated three rows in front of him with her baby. A scruffy looking young man sat next to her. McCann wondered if this was Phil's "Prayer Project". He noted that Doug Warner sat in the middle of the sanctuary beside a striking blonde and two teenage girls. Fred Penay and his wife were seated in the row in front of Warner.

The service was similar to the previous week except for a congregational recitation of the Apostle's Creed. McCann found himself moving his lips to mask his lack of knowledge. He hoped Willard wouldn't notice.

After the Creed, Chuck Hastings walked to the center of the platform and, opening his Bible, read the morning scripture from Galatians 6:7-10:

Do not be deceived, God is not mocked; for whatever a man sows, this he will also reap. For the one who sows to his own flesh shall from the flesh reap corruption, but the one who sows to the Spirit shall from the Spirit reap eternal life. And let us not lose heart in doing good, for in due time we shall reap if we do not grow weary. So then, while we have opportunity, let us do good to all men, and especially to those who are of the household of the faith.

McCann's mind jumped back to his Friday night musing over the scripture in Corinthians. He pulled a pen from his inside coat pocket and jotted the scripture reference Hastings had read on his bulletin. Phil Willard's eyes followed the movement of the pen and he suppressed a smile before looking back to the minister.

"What have you sown in your life?" Hastings asked as he closed his Bible and placed it on the podium. "Some of you are playing games with God. You think you can get away with it but you won't. Paul says that if we sow from our own selfish wills, we will reap corruption. What does he mean by corruption? He means death! You will go in the grave and the grave will swallow you up and your remains will deteriorate and that will be it. But, we have an alternative. Through faith in Jesus Christ, our selfish nature is replaced by a new nature that is led by the Holy Spirit. Under His control, we stop playing games with God and our spirit-led actions give evidence of a newfound faith."

"Some of you have begun to walk with Christ and you are trying to lead that spirit controlled life. But, it is tough at times. We grow weary of trying to do what Christ would have us to do. Paul says that we should press on. He says we should run the race to the finish. He says that we should seize upon every opportunity to do good and we shall reap our rewards if we do not grow weary."

He paused and McCann looked around the sanctuary. Most faces were waiting expectantly. Some heads were bowed. He noted that the young man next to Darcy was staring at the minister in rapt attention.

Hastings moved toward that side of the platform and began again. "Many of us have been blessed by God with great abilities and talents. Are we using them for God? Are we willing to seek God's plan for our lives? It is only when we seek God's plan and submit to his will for our lives that we can truly accomplish great things. Perhaps your life is confused right now. Perhaps you don't know what God's plan is for your life."

McCann felt a strange stirring in his heart and mind. It seemed that Hastings was talking just to him. It felt uncomfortable and he glanced out of the corner of his eye to see if Willard had noticed it too. But Willard's attention seemed to be riveted on the minister. McCann found himself flashing back to his conversations with Donna and the minister. He knew that he had been given unusual abilities and he had been given more than an average amount of the world's goods. He knew that he had not always used his ability and wealth to advance the interests of anyone other than himself. As Hastings continued to speak, McCann wrestled within himself over what was becoming an increasingly difficult question. What was God's plan for Wilson James McCann? He had never given that question a moment's thought until he had come to Farnsworth. Now it seemed he was confronted with it almost every day.

As the congregation stood to sing the final hymn, Hastings invited those who wished to come forward to the altar to pray. McCann watched as the young man seated next to Darcy went forward and knelt at the altar. Phil Willard stepped in front of McCann and went forward to join him. Willard put his arm around the boy's shoulders and McCann could see them heave as the boy sobbed quietly.

At the conclusion of the service, McCann left quickly through a side door. His mind was troubled. He started the Ranger, head down.

"Wils! Wait up!" It was Doug Warner coming out of the same side door.

McCann waited on the sidewalk as Warner approached. "Some of us get together for a sandwich out at the Four Corners every Sunday after church. I'd like you to join us if you don't have other plans."

McCann did not want to be around anyone at this particular moment but he was sensitive to the sincerity in Warner's voice. He considered for a moment and knew that he needed some human company rather than an empty farmhouse with a dog for company.

"I'd like that very much," he lied, smiling.

"Great! Go back to Main and turn right. It is four miles east at the junction with M-53. I'll gather up the wife and kids and meet you there."

McCann walked to his pick-up and drove slowly out to Main Street and turned right. The land east of Farnsworth was low-lying scrub country and there were few houses. Those that occasionally appeared were old and weather beaten with derelict cars in the front yards. A few had cattle standing in barnyards outside of dilapidated barns. The road rose in the last mile and the scrub died away as he neared the junction. The "Log Cabin" restaurant, a gas station and an auto repair shop occupied three of the four corners. A run-down house occupied the fourth. He pulled into the restaurant parking lot and waited.

In about five minutes, Doug Warner's Yukon pulled in beside him followed immediately by a familiar Dodge Neon. He was pleased to see Jim and Lona Marks and their children in the car.

Warner introduced McCann to his wife, Lori, and their two girls,

Chris and Cheryl. McCann walked along with the two men as the women led the way into the restaurant. Trent Marks lagged behind and walked beside McCann. The boy looked up expectantly and McCann tussled his hair.

"How are you today, Trent?" He asked, looking down at the upturned face.

"Fine!" the boy responded, pleased to have his name remembered.

Susan Marks walked with the two Warner girls, impressed with the two teenagers. McCann noted that the two girls made sure to talk and joke with the much younger one and include her in their conversation. He was surprised to see such grown up behavior from two teenagers. His experiences with teens had been few, and the ones he had met during his career were mostly the spoiled children of other executives. Those teens usually wore "grunge" clothing and had a set of CD player headphones attached to them or they were so engrossed in their latest Game-Boy as to render any attempt at conversation useless.

Lori Warner was every bit as charming as she chatted with Lona Marks. McCann contrasted the two women. Lori was tall, blonde and dressed in the latest fashion. She was the epitome of the "trophy wife" that he had seen so often at business meetings, conventions and social events. Lona, also blonde, was wearing a pair of gray slacks and a blouse that didn't match. Yet the two women obviously respected each other and seemed, to McCann's observation, to be almost like sisters in their behavior toward one another.

Warner ordered a table set for 11 and McCann wondered who else would be joining them. He got his answer five minutes after they sat down when Phil Willard and his wife came in. If Phil Willard looked like Andy Devine, McCann was certain that his wife could have doubled for Aunt Bea from "Mayberry RFD." The younger women and the two teenagers each gave her a hug before she sat down. Phil Willard was obviously in a good mood, and as he seated himself, raised his hand to quiet the group.

"Praise the Lord! I have great news! Our prayers have been answered! Nick Hardesty accepted Christ as his savior this morning and he asked Pastor Chuck to marry him and Darcy next Saturday."

This news was greeted by a chorus of "Amen's", "Praise the Lord" and

"Thank You Jesus." McCann noted that the two teenagers joined right in with comments of "Wow!" and "Neat."

Willard raised his hand again and the group grew silent. "Now for the bad news! Nick lost his job yesterday. We have to begin to pray for employment for him and a place for his new family to live."

All heads were bowed immediately and McCann bowed his as first Lona Marks and then Doug Warner prayed, thanking God for his answers to prayer for Nick and asking for him to work out his plan for Nick and Darcy's new life together. As they prayed, McCann surveyed the room through partially closed eyes. The restaurant was slowing filling with Sunday noontime patrons. Most of them appeared to be locals coming from church or the golf course. A few appeared to be travelers passing through. Most of the people seemed to ignore the excitement and praying. A few looked at the group and then looked away. McCann's feelings of uneasiness with all of this were somewhat allayed by the fact the group was the largest in the restaurant.

Phil Willard closed this ad-hoc prayer time by praising the Lord for his goodness and asking the blessing on the food. It was obvious that this was a part of a typical Sunday meal together by this group and no one seemed to question Willard's role as the leader of the group.

Conversation resumed and meal orders were taken. McCann, seated next to Trent Marks, helped the youngster order a hot dog with fries and Lona Marks commented that this was Trent's "usual Sunday fare."

"Where is Donna?" Chris Warner asked during a lull in the conversation.

"She went to a style show in Detroit," answered Martha Willard.

"Boy will she be excited when she hears about Nick and Darcy!" chimed in Cheryl Warner.

"I can't wait for the wedding!" responded Chris.

"Do you think Donna will be Maid of Honor ----again?" asked Cheryl.

"Darcy couldn't get a better one, could she, Lona?" Lori Warner said, smiling.

"Well, other than the guys we got…we didn't turn out too bad!" Lona responded.

Doug Warner turned to McCann and answered the question that was obvious in McCann's face.

"Donna was Maid of Honor for our wedding and for Jim and Lona's" he said.

"We've got to find her a man!" Chris said with some feeling.

McCann noticed Jim Marks look at him out of the corner of his eye. He felt his face begin to redden. It was obvious that the Warners did not know that Donna had been at McCann's place helping with the haying. Martha Willard smiled and set her menu in the center of the table.

"Donna is going to be a missionary," she said quietly.

"But when?" responded Chris, turning toward the older woman.

"When the Lord provides a sponsor or sponsors," Martha said.

"It is very hard to run a business, care for an aging parent, and try to line up potential support and make time for training." Phil Willard commented as the food arrived. "Donna has done well to get away occasionally for two weeks of service abroad. That experience will help when the Lord provides an opportunity."

The food arrived and the conversations died down as each person began to eat. Doug Warner looked at McCann from his place at the foot of the table and asked, "Did you make your phone call yet?"

"No, I plan to do it tomorrow."

"Our Board meets on Thursday at 10:00 a.m. in our conference room. Would that work for you?"

"I can make that if Jim here doesn't need me to plant wheat!" McCann said, smiling at Jim Marks, who was in the middle of taking a big bite from his roast beef sandwich.

"Have you got those fields plowed and worked?" Jim inquired, when he had finished chewing and taking a big swallow from his iced tea.

"One is plowed and the other will be tomorrow. I'll have them both worked by Wednesday night."

"When do the cattle arrive?" Marks asked, ignoring an elbow gently pushed in his ribs by his wife.

"I'm thinking end of the week or early next. They will call before delivery."

"I'll have the feed out on Wednesday," Phil Willard put in.

"Mr. McCann, you sound like a very busy man!" Lori Warner said, smiling.

"I'm learning that the life of a gentleman farmer is a busy one... you can drop the 'Mr.' and call me Wils." McCann said, smiling back.

"Who will take care of your cattle when you aren't around?" asked Lona Marks.

"I plan to be here through the winter and into spring. I'll sell them then," McCann replied.

"Keeping up that farm and taking care of cattle and meeting with our Board ...you may need to get yourself a hired hand," Lori Warner said, smiling at him.

Cheryl Warner turned in her chair and gave her full attention to her mother. A huge smile spread across her fifteen-year-old face. "I know! He could hire Nick! Nick's good at fixing things and he needs a job!"

Lori Warner's smile faded slightly as she looked across the table at her two daughters. "How do you know so much about Nick and what he can do?" she asked.

"Mom! Darcy loves Nick and she has been praying for him... we all have been praying for him and..."

Her mother's smile brightened again and she raised her hand, palm out to stem the tide coming from across the table. McCann was glad for the change in the direction of the conversation. As the conversation went on around him, his thoughts turned to the Pastor's sermon of the morning. What was he sowing? As he thought back over his life, he realized that most of his actions had been to benefit either his own career and self-interest or that of Dynacom. As he looked around the table, he saw that from the youngest to the oldest, these people had a much more balanced life than his had been. He said little and listened as the teens speculated on where Nick and Darcy would live and what Nick would do and how neat it was that God had heard their prayers. The parents added a comment here and there and seemed to take great satisfaction in the whole of it. Phil and Martha Willard ordered apple pie and basked in the general goodwill of the entire group. McCann ordered a cup of decaffeinated coffee, to hold the cup and hide behind more than to savor the coffee. He noticed that

Martha Willard was watching him quietly from her end of the table with a little smile on her face.

The bill arrived amidst much discussion over who would pay for whom and Doug Warner put his hand on McCann's right arm as he reached for his wallet with his left.

"This one is on me. We are very glad you could join us."

"Thank you. I've enjoyed it as well." McCann said as he rose with the others. "I would like to e-mail you an outline of what I might cover with your Board on Thursday."

"Great! My e-mail address is on my card," Warner replied, handing McCann a business card.

As they walked to their cars, Phil and Martha Willard fell in step beside McCann. Martha Willard looked up at him with that same little smile.

"Where did you go to church before coming here, Wils?"

McCann lowered his head and looked away across the highway. He hesitated as a large tractor trailer truck thundered by on its way north.

"I haven't made much time for church," he said looking at her, "…until coming here, that is."

"Well, there is a first time for everything in life and sometimes the best is followed by a better life. I will pray that yours will be everything God wants it to be. It is a pleasure to finally meet you. Phil has mentioned you on several occasions. Fred and Ella Harms were my very good friends."

Giving him her hand, she looked up at him and smiled again. She withdrew her hand and turned to her car. Feeling awkward, McCann placed his hand on her shoulder and said "Thank you, Martha, I'm glad to know you."

On the way back to the farm, he pondered what was happening to him. When he reached the farm, he went inside and, for the first time in several months, he called his mother in Florida and told her about the farm, the cattle that would be coming, the people that he had met and that he had gone to church two Sundays. She chatted about her friends in the development and the many activities she was involved in. Before he hung up, Wilson McCann told his mother that he missed her and she quietly replied "Love you, son."

ACQUISITION

As he placed the phone back in its cradle, he realized that it was the first time that they had told each other that they loved each other in many, many years. Then, Wilson McCann did something else that he had not done in many years. He leaned back in the recliner and took an afternoon nap. Ted curled up at his feet and took one too.

(10)

The sun was up and shining brightly as he let Ted out the next morning. He felt refreshed and ready for the day's activity. He ate his breakfast and sent an e-mail containing the outline he had prepared to Doug Warner.

He took a deep breath as he picked up the phone and dialed Stu Bailey's number in New York. Jeanine answered on the second ring.

"Hello, Jeanine. It's Wils McCann. How is that condo in Hilton Head?"

"It's a townhouse, Wils, and if I could ever find time to go there, I could enjoy it!"

McCann laughed. "A beautiful, intelligent, sophisticated lady like you should know how to get Stu to give you some time off to check out your investment."

"You know how Mr. Bailey is, Wils. He is always working on the next big deal! But, the pay is good. When I'm 65, I'll probably enjoy it!"

"You'll be too old then, Jeanine! That's what - another 40 years?"

Jeanine was 42. She had often wished she was 25 again. She wouldn't even mind being 42 if someone with Wilson McCann's good looks, money and charm would take an interest in sharing his life with her. An ill-conceived affair with a married lawyer from one of the firms Stu used in his acquisition work had turned out all wrong and she hadn't pursued anyone else. She thought about making some sort of suggestive response to McCann but decided against it.

"Hold on, Wils. I'll put you through to his Eminence! It is good to hear from you. I understand you are a farmer now?"

"Tractors, barns, cattle, the whole thing!" McCann responded. "I've even found someone to share my life with!"

Bailey had told Jeanine a little about his visit to Farnsworth. She immediately had visions of the "mousy little shop owner" that he had described.

"Really? What's she like?" she asked.

"It's a he and his name is Ted," McCann replied. There was dead silence on the New York end of the line. It dawned on him what must be going through Jeanine's mind. "He's a Border Collie!" he blurted.

"Oh!" was all Jeanine could muster. "I'll put you through to Stu."

The excitement in Bailey's voice was obvious as he answered the phone. "I was waiting for your call, Wils. I had lunch the other day with Ed Feldman and when he heard you were coming in on the deal, he made a commitment for funding."

McCann took a deep breath. "Stu, I've been thinking about this and I've come up with another idea."

"Great! When can you fly out here and meet and we'll listen and then get rolling."

"Stu, there is a local company here that wants the Michigan properties. I'd like to try to help it get them."

Bailey leaned back in his chair. "You mean some sort of joint bid? Or are you saying they would buy them from us after our deal is done?"

"Neither. I'd like to help them bid on the Michigan properties alone."

A slow realization of what McCann was saying began to take hold of Bailey. He looked out the window, frowned and thought. This was not going the way he had expected.

"Exactly what are you getting at, Wils? Are you coming in on the deal I outlined or not?"

"No, Stu, I haven't changed my position. I don't want to go back to trying to run a company for a group of money men to sell in five years."

It came out in a rush. He had tried to make it less harsh than it sounded. He could hear Bailey's breathing on the other end of the line. "I'm sorry, Stu. I didn't mean that the way it sounded. It's just that I am not ready to go back to running a company right now. I need to get a grip on where I want to go with the rest of my life."

Bailey's tone was hard and even as he sat forward in his chair. "Wils, you are one of the best operating men in the business. You can make yourself a lot of money and have a lot of fun taking these properties and putting them in shape to be sold to the highest bidder when this telecom slump is over. What are you talking about – getting a grip on your life? You are one of the best! People will follow you! It's what you are cut out to do!"

"God's plan for my life, eh?" McCann said quietly

"What?" Bailey said.

"Nothing. Stu, are you willing to help me help this smaller company put together a bid for the Michigan properties?"

"Wils, what are you talking about? This is small potatoes! There's only what? 15,000 to 20,000 access lines in Michigan? Who are these people you are talking about? They can't be very big! What's in it for you? Are you trying to take over this company?" Bailey sounded almost beside himself. In the outer office, Jeanine put down her pencil and decided to quit pretending not to listen.

"It's the Farnsworth Telephone Coop. It's owned by the Warner family. They....."

"A coop! You mean it's an REA company and it wants to buy access lines? What kind of nonsense are you talking about?" Bailey was really beginning to lose it. He took a deep breath and leaned back in his chair. "Okay, let's start over. Tell me again what you are talking about."

Ten minutes later, McCann had finished outlining what he knew. Bailey had been busy alternatively jotting notes on a yellow pad and punching keys on his lap-top. He looked at the screen and down at his notes.

"Wils, this is a small deal. With the lack of interest in Telecom these days, no one is going to touch it, least ways no one in the Big Apple. Why don't you come in with us on the whole package and we'll get Feldman and the banks to agree to sell the Michigan portion to the Coop when we sell it off in five years."

Now it was McCann's turn to take a deep breath. "Okay, I'll work with you but only as an advisor. I won't be CEO and I want Farnsworth in on the deal from the start as a partner with first rights on the Michigan portion of the property."

"Feldman won't commit unless you are CEO, Wils!"

"Turn on the charm and persuade him, Stu."

Bailey swore. Five minutes later, he hung up the phone and slammed his fist down on his desk. Jeanine busied herself typing a letter from the dictation machine on her desk. She could hear Bailey pacing back and forth in his office. A few moments later he emerged with his jacket on.

"I'm going out. I'll be back after lunch," he said shortly as he left.

"So much for the overtime money!" Jeanine said to herself as she continued to type.

McCann sat looking at the phone for a few moments. He picked it up and entered a familiar number in Lansing, Michigan. In response to his inquiry, he learned that Jim Wolfe was now District Manager for LEGENT in its Northern District of Michigan, based in Mackinaw City. He made note of the number and dialed. Jim Wolfe's voice mail advised that he was "either out of the office or away from my desk but your call is important to me so leave a message and I'll get right back to you."

McCann left his message, rose and walked out into the sunshine. His head hurt and the muscles in his shoulders were tight with the kind of stress that had often been part of his days at Dynacom. Ted wagged his tail expectantly at the edge of the drive and cocked his head to one side as McCann strode purposefully to the tool shed and rolled the big double doors back. He started the big tractor and moved it to the gas pumps at the side of the shed to fill it with gas. He checked both it and the plow carefully before going to the remaining field. He plowed the field during the morning and changed the plow for a double disk and worked both fields by evening. As he drove the tractor into the shed and rolled the door shut for the night he realized that the stress that he had felt after his phone call to Stu Bailey was long gone. In his mind he began to question whether his decision to agree to participate as an advisor in the acquisition had been the right one. Doug Warner and his family-owned company would need all the help they could get to acquire the additional access lines and survive in an increasingly competitive industry. He felt comfortable in his ability to provide that help but he was beginning to think that satisfaction in life lay elsewhere.

As he put the tractor in the tool shed, he looked at the barn. The paint had long since faded. Even the double doors leading to the hay mows and the large stable entry doors were beginning to lose their color. An idea began to take shape in his mind as he prepared and ate his evening meal. He cleared away the dishes and picked up the phone book. He looked up Phil Willard's home number and called. After a brief apology for disturbing Phil at home, he told him what he had in mind. Willard's enthusiasm crackled over the line and McCann replaced the phone with a smile on his face. Perhaps if he couldn't help Farnsworth Telephone and Doug Warner, he might sow something good in another field of endeavor after all!

Earlier that morning, the Director of the Telecommunications Division of the Michigan Public Service Commission leaned back in his chair and looked at the two men opposite him. Both wore expensive suits and were groomed to perfection. The older man smiled and the Director found himself wondering how much it had cost to cap all those teeth. He would be glad when LEGENT was gone from Michigan. He detested working with paid professional lobbyists like this one and the LEGENT functionary who sat beside him. He had listened attentively as the two men had outlined LEGENT'S intentions to sell its property in the state and to "assure that the good citizens of the state continue to receive the very best in telecommunications service from the buyer through a very careful selection process." They had also assured him that the Commission would be "kept informed every step of the way" as the sale was concluded in a manner "that protects our citizens as well as LEGENT'S shareholders." He knew who would receive priority between the two! But, it was the Commission's job to protect the ratepayer's interests.

He knew it was time to state the Commission's position clearly and forcefully. He ignored the consultant's million dollar smile and concentrated his gaze on the LEGENT man.

"I appreciate you coming in to advise us as to LEGENT'S decision. I also appreciate your willingness to work with the Department's staff to assure an orderly process as we consider any potential sale application. The staff's primary function, as you are aware, is to protect the ratepayers of this state. We will want to assure that the current LEGENT customers will not be disadvantaged by any potential sale and that any costs attributable to the sale are borne by LEGENT and not by the customers. We will also want to assure that any benefits arising from the sale which should properly be assigned to the ratepayers accrue to them. I will assign a person from the staff to serve as your contact point and to lead the staff's presentation during the Commission's hearing relative to the sale. I must say at this juncture that the Commission takes a dim view of the practice of buying and selling properties in such short time frames, as there are usually disruptions in customer service that arise from changes in ownership. It has been less than a year since LEGENT purchased, with the Commission's approval, the former Dynacom properties."

The LEGENT man looked at his companion and seeing that the response to this would have to come from him, cleared his throat and leaned forward in his chair.

"We recognize the Commission's jurisdiction in these matters and that is why we wanted you to be informed prior to the commencement of any sale activity. We also recognize and appreciate the Commission's concern over activities of this nature. When we purchased the Dynacom property, the telecommunications marketplace was expanding and we felt confident that we would remain in the Midwest for some time. Unfortunately, as you are well aware, things have changed. It is in the interests of the company and its shareholders to consolidate operations where it is economically feasible to do so and to divest operations which cannot be operated efficiently."

Before he could continue, the Director spoke quietly. "If LEGENT found that its approved rates were not covering its operating costs in Michigan, it could have requested relief from our order in the Dynacom case which froze rates at their pre-sale levels."

The LEGENT man started to retort but his companion laid a well manicured hand on his knee and smiled broadly. "We are well aware of the Commission's position on rate relief for LEGENT after the Dynacom purchase. I think we have completed our business here today and if there is nothing further, we will run up and say hello to the Chairman and be on our way."

The Director bit back his irritation at the man. Proper regulatory relations etiquette would dictate that the Division Director would have been invited to any meeting with the Commission Chair. It was obvious that LEGENT planned to meet separately with the Chairman in an attempt to further lobby the conditions governing the sale. "Oh well," he thought to himself, "staff will have its day in court." He stood and extended his hand.

"Do you have any ideas on who might be potential bidders?" he asked, smiling.

The two men had been waiting on the question and were surprised that it had not come earlier in the meeting. The LEGENT man looked out the window before answering.

"I presume the usual players will be interested, along with the RBOC and maybe one or more of the larger Independents."

"By 'usual players', I presume you mean the aggregators?" The Director said as he came around the desk.

"Well, yes, I suppose so."

The Director had one more message to deliver and now was the time to deliver it. "Gentlemen, I can assure you that the Commission is most interested in seeing the property sold to people who have a genuine interest in improving and expanding service to customers within the state as against those who are merely trying to accumulate assets, build stock prices and sell out in five years. I hope you will keep that in mind and I hope you will make LEGENT'S senior management aware of that fact. Thanks for coming in."

The LEGENT man's face turned a bit grayer and the lobbyist's wide smile disappeared as they waited for the elevator to take them to the Chairman's office. They were well aware that the Telecommunications Staff of the Michigan Commission had a great deal of power and would have a lot to do with the success or lack of it in disposing of these properties.

Back in his office, the Director picked up his phone and dialed a number in the Governor's office. He related the highlights of the meeting and was gratified when the voice at the other end of the line closed the call by saying, "That's exactly the message the Governor would have given them if he had been present. Keep us posted."

(11)

On Wednesday McCann rose early and watched as Jim Marks pulled into the yard with a load of seed and fertilizer. Marks surveyed the two fields and smiled. "You do good work for a desk-jockey!" he said.

"I had a good teacher. He didn't have equipment that was as modern as this but Fred made sure I knew how to plow and work a field. It was just one of the many things I learned during those summers here."

"Did you enjoy your summers here?" Marks asked, eyeing him.

"I was a typical kid. Liked the out of doors and running anything with a motor in or on it. I can't say I liked taking care of cattle and cleaning out barn stalls and gutters. But, the harvesting, haying, planting and working with the equipment were fun. I don't think I fully appreciated how much I learned from Fred. I was too busy resenting how hard he worked me," McCann replied honestly.

I didn't know Fred then, of course," Marks commented. "But from what I've heard about him, I would guess that the term 'firm but fair' applied?"

McCann smiled back. "Firm for sure and fair mostly. As long as I did my work and didn't wreck his old pick up running around at night, he treated me alright. He paid me the going rate for a field hand and Ella saw to it that I ate well."

"They were already part of the church family when Lona and I moved here. I'd have to say that next to Phil and Martha, Fred and Ella were the kindest to us. We couldn't have asked for better friends and neighbors."

"I'll just leave my truck here and walk home through the fields. I'll be here bright and early in the morning. I trust you will be able to get up early?" Marks was grinning again.

McCann started to reply but was stopped by the arrival of an old Ford Mustang in the driveway. A thin wisp of smoke came from the dual exhausts as the driver shut down the motor and opened the door.

He was dressed in faded jeans and a cotton work shirt. His hair was over his ears and just above the collar but it was clean and looked like it had recently been cut. The transformation in Nick Hardesty was really quite spectacular, McCann thought, as he approached.

"Are you Mr. McCann?" he asked looking down at the ground.

Marks was still feeling his oats. "Well I'm sure not. And that only leaves one other, Nick!"

McCann offered his hand. "I'm Wils McCann. I'm glad to meet you Nick. I imagine Phil Willard talked to you about what I have in mind?"

The big grin on Jim Marks' face was replaced by one of questioning incredulance. He adjusted his cap, scratched his ear and waited expectantly.

"Phil …I mean Mr. Willard said you might have some painting you needed done." Hardesty said looking McCann full in the face for the first time. Wils noticed how blue his eyes were. The look on Nick's face reminded McCann of the way Ted had looked up at him in the hay mow when he found the dog half dead.

"My barn and those three outbuildings all need to be painted. I'm guessing you will have to put a good oil-based primer on first and probably at least two coats of paint. I'll pay you by the hour and that includes the time you need to find the paint and ladders to get the job done. I'd expect you to start on the outbuildings. After the first one's done, I'll decide if I like your work and if I do, I'll expect you to finish the whole job."

McCann's tone was forceful. He had automatically reverted to the demanding CEO that he had once been. He had laid out the task in no uncertain terms and had made it clear what his expectations were. Now, as he waited, he wished that he had been a little less direct. Nick Hardesty scuffed one boot in the dirt and looked sidewise at the two story barn. When he looked back at McCann and spoke, his voice was equally direct.

"And what's the hourly rate?"

"$15.00 an hour, fair enough?"

Nick Hardesty tried hard not to swallow but failed. $15 an hour was half again as much as he had been making at the garage. Jim Marks looked at McCann dumbfounded and then looked away at the barn. He knew that the job McCann had outlined would keep Nick Hardesty busy six days a week until it was too cold to paint. Something must have gotten in his eye because he rubbed it away and swallowed hard.

"I've got a set of extension ladders that you can use Nick," he said quietly.

Hardesty extended his hand. "Thank you Mr. McCann."

McCann took the hand and held it momentarily. "One more thing, I'll expect you on the job at first light. If you want to move in here and use the spare bedroom, I'll make it available to you and take $25 a week out of your pay for food."

Jim Marks adjusted his cap for the second time and scratched his other ear. A smile tugged at the corner of his mouth. He cleared his throat loudly and spat into the grass beside the drive.

"Thanks. I'd take you up on that, but I'm getting married next Saturday and I need to find a place for my family."

McCann smiled again. "So I heard. Tell you what, if you don't find a place for your family, you can all move in here and Darcy can take over the cooking and cleaning while you finish the job. I'm getting a little tired of doing my own cooking anyway. How's that?"

Jim Marks stuck his hand in his hip pocket and lowered his head to where he had to peak out under the brim of his cap to look at McCann. The "Thank you Jesus" that came up in his throat was somehow stuck there.

Hardesty's young face betrayed his surprise. "You don't understand, Mr. McCann. I have a small baby and...."

"I've met your wife to be and I've met your son. I haven't been around babies much in my life. Maybe the change will make a better man out of me. Now, do we have a deal or not?"

"Yes sir! When do I ... I mean ..."

"Get started? Now! Get busy figuring out how much paint, primer and equipment you'll need. There is an air compressor in the tool shed. You might be able to fit a paint sprayer on it and use that. You can move in tonight and bring Darcy and the baby out after the wedding on Saturday. By the way, as your employer, I'd expect an invitation to the wedding!"

Hardesty extended his hand again. "Thank you. I appreciate what you are doing."

"I'm getting my barn and outbuildings a good coat of paint. Phil Willard tells me you have a lot of ability in that regard and I'm expecting a good job." McCann tried to sound gruff but couldn't quite carry it off. Jim Marks smiled and reached into the Mustang to pull out a clip board with a pad and pencil on it.

"Come on, Nick. I'll help you figure out what you'll need. You can run me home when we are done."

As the two men turned toward the barn, the phone rang in the house. McCann walked rapidly into the house and picked it up.

"Wils! It's Jim Wolfe. I just got your call. This is a pleasant surprise! By the area code and NNX, I'd judge you are in the Thumb of our fair state! What are you doing there?"

"I could always depend on you to know what is going on in Michigan, Jim. I'm disappointed that you didn't know I was here!" McCann replied as he eased himself into a chair. "What are you doing in Mackinaw City? That's a long ways from the hallowed halls of government in Lansing!"

Jim Wolfe had been one of McCann's favorite managers at Dynacom. His contacts with Wolfe had been few but positive over the years. The young man knew his operation and ran it as though it was his own. He knew the state and he knew how to get things done and keep his customers happy. McCann had always admired Wolfe's integrity and while he didn't understand Jim's rather straight-laced lifestyle, he respected him for the results he consistently delivered from the Wolverine state. The sound of his voice immediately brought back many fond memories.

"LEGENT decided they could take care of Lansing from Chicago and that I needed to re-locate as far away from Lansing as they could send me. So, I chose to come here and here I am. I am in charge of their Northern District which covers everything north of a line from Bay City to Manistee."

"LEGENT doesn't know a good manager when they see one," McCann said quietly. "I'm sorry, Jim. How is your family?"

"June is happy. We're closer to her folks. The boys love to hunt and fish and there's a lot of that here."

"And how are you?"

There was a pause on the other end of the line. "I'll get by. This job isn't much of a challenge and won't be until the plant deteriorates to a point where the customers start to get testy."

McCann could hear the sarcasm in Wolfe's voice. He knew down deep that Jim Wolfe was suffering from his association with Dynacom and Wilson McCann. He also knew that LEGENT would not be spending a lot of capital dollars in the north country of Michigan. He drew in his breath and decided to level with Wolfe.

"Jim, I need to tell you something and I need for you to keep it between us. Then, I need your help. If you decide that what I'm about to ask is not ethical, I'll understand."

Once again there was a pause at the other end of the line. "First, tell me what you are doing in Michigan and how you are. I've read all the newspaper reports and I've watched the TV reports and I know that the last six months couldn't have been easy for you – or fair to you."

McCann smiled to himself. Most people would have immediately wanted to know what the reason for the call was. It was a tribute to Wolfe that he was just as interested in the welfare of others as he was in that.

"I'm living on my Uncle's old farm. I bought it and I'm planning to plant some winter wheat and to raise some beef cattle. I'm trying hard to figure out what I want to do with the rest of my life."

Wolfe's chuckle came clearly over the connection. "Well, I'll be darned!"

McCann hastened on. "Jim, I know I can trust you. LEGENT is planning to sell some of their mid-western properties including Michigan. Some people are starting to line up to bid for it and I've been asked to help them. I think you know one of them. His name is Doug Warner and he and his family own the Farnsworth Telephone Cooperative."

"Doug Warner! I know him. He's a good man. His family is the best! But he can't handle the kind of money it would take to buy several states!"

"He may not even be able to handle the Michigan properties, and that is all he is interested in. I'm thinking of advising him as part of a joint bid with some Wall Street money men and bankers."

There was a pause again at the other end of the line. Wolfe's voice had less excitement in it when he spoke again.

"Is it the same crowd that tried to help us when LEGENT bought us out?"

McCann sensed the hesitancy in Wolfe's voice. Jim Wolfe was not the kind to associate with Stu Bailey and his type. He was an operating man first and foremost. He had not been exposed to finance people beyond those in Dynacom's regional and corporate offices who oversaw his capital and income and expense budgets. It was natural for him to be wary, especially in view of how the takeover battle had turned out.

"Some of them," McCann said evenly, waiting.

"And what do you need from me?" Wolfe asked.

"I need the names of people in Lansing who we can work with to ensure that the state looks favorably on our application. No one knows that scene better than you do, Jim."

"Wils, I'm on the LEGENT payroll. I am not happy to be there but I have a family to support and there aren't many jobs that pay what this one does. LEGENT froze my salary at the level I was making at Dynacom and I owe them for that. I'm going to copy three pages out of the Directory of State Government into an E-file and send them to you. I'm going to underline six names that you should talk to. I can't do more than that. I'm sorry but I have to be honest with my employers even though I don't respect them."

"I appreciate that, Jim. I have no desire to jeopardize your employment."

"Thanks. I wish you all the luck in the world."

When he replaced the phone, Wilson McCann sighed. He didn't like using Jim Wolfe and he realized that he had just done that. Wolfe now knew something that could impact his career and his family. McCann could only hope that somehow Wolfe would come out of whatever happened with a better situation than what he had now with LEGENT.

When he walked outside, Marks and Hardesty were gone. Ted ran up, wagging his tail. McCann stooped to scratch his ears and pat his head.

"Well, Ted, I hope I know what I'm doing."

Ted continued to wag his tail and McCann took that as a good sign.

Jim Wolfe leaned back in his chair. He wasn't at all sure that what he had agreed to do was right. He owed Wilson McCann a lot. He didn't like the way LEGENT was running things in Michigan but did that give him the right to provide assistance to a possible purchaser of the properties? And what would a new buyer mean in terms of his own future? He knew Doug Warner and respected him for his knowledge and leadership within the Michigan telecommunications industry and for his personal faith in Christ. He and Doug and their wives had spent several hours together during a state convention talking about their faith. He quietly prayed for an extra measure of wisdom and then brought up the State Government Directory on his computer. He highlighted the pages he had told McCann about and copied them into a separate file. Then, he underlined six names and telephone numbers and saved the file. He brought up his e-mail message screen and typed a quick note to McCann and attached the saved file. He clicked on "Send" and the deed was done.

He remembered the call from Joyce at the Emmett County Economic Development Corp. and went back to the Government Directory. He selected a number and dialed.

"Ryan" said a voice on the other end of the line.

"Hello Dan. It's Jim Wolfe."

"Jimmy! How are things in the north country?"

"The deer and the fish are flourishing! When are you coming up?"

"Ha! When the Governor loosens the purse strings and we can visit our field offices again!"

Dan Ryan was one of the liaisons between Michigan's Office of Economic Development and the various County agencies throughout the state.

"I'll keep watch on the deer and the fish for you and you can call me when you are ready to spend a day in the woods," Wolfe said, smiling into the phone.

"I'm in the woods most of the time down here anyway!" Ryan replied. "Why do I have the idea that you didn't call me up to talk about deer and fish?"

"You're as perceptive as ever, Dan! What do you know about Wolverine Property Management?"

The silence on Ryan's end of the line was deafening. Wolfe waited. Finally Ryan spoke. "Nothing...why?"

Wolfe knew that there was more there than Dan Ryan was willing to share. He decided to be straight with the government man.

"I got a call from Joyce at the Emmett County EDC asking what I knew about a big land purchase down near Brutus. She said the buyer was Wolverine Property Management."

Wolfe waited again. Finally Ryan spoke. "Jim, I have more to do than worry about a sale of a bunch of scrub brush in Emmett County. If you want, I'll ask around and see if I can find out anything meaningful, but I suggest you forget about it."

Jim Wolfe had been around Lansing long enough to recognize when he was being deterred from trying to find an answer.

"That sounds like good sense, Dan. Let me know when you want to come up and see those fish."

"I will. Good to talk to you, Jim."

Wolfe hung up his phone. His call had touched a nerve. He wondered where the nerve endings were. Just then, his phone rang and one of his field crews reported that a contractor had cut a feeder cable in Levering, Michigan. He spent the rest of the morning taking care of that crisis. But the Wolverine Property Management name kept popping up in his mind and wouldn't go away.

McCann spent the afternoon working on his presentation for the Farnsworth Telephone Board. He incorporated the facts and figures from Stu Bailey's material into it and put together a list of considerations and a time line of milestone events for the process. He found it easy to work at this. Strategic planning had always been one of his strengths. He did not look up when Nick's Mustang returned. He heard the tool shed doors roll back and the rattle of paint cans being stored there. At five o'clock, he heard the doors roll closed and the Mustang pull out of the drive. He closed the laptop and walked to the kitchen window. The smaller outbuilding was covered with a coat of primer. "Progress is being made!" he said to Ted, who looked up from where he had been sprawled in the sunlight from the window and wagged his tail. To him, progress would be when his dinner was in his dish. He waited expectantly as McCann poured it into the bowl and sprayed a little warm water on it from the faucet at the kitchen sink. As soon as the bowl was on the floor again, Ted rose and began to eat.

Nick Hardesty and Jim Marks arrived the next morning within minutes of each other. Marks had tied a set of aluminum extension ladders to the top of the seeder and the two were untying the ropes and lowering the ladders to the ground as McCann emerged from the house in his wing tips, suit pants and white shirt.

"Going to a funeral?" Marks asked, smiling. "You don't look like a planter this morning!"

"I'm going to be planting seed of another type," McCann replied, returning the smile. "You made a good start on that outbuilding Nick; I think I'll keep you on."

Nick lowered his gaze at the compliment. It was obvious that compliments for work well done had been few and far between in his experience.

"Jim, I am sorry but I made a commitment to talk with Doug's Board today. Can you get along without me?"

"Well, I should charge you extra but I guess Nick can help if I need it," Marks replied.

Nick headed for the tool shed and Jim began to fill the seeder. McCann looked at his watch and went back inside to finish dressing. When he emerged, he had knotted a dark maroon silk tie at his throat and had his suit coat over his right arm. His briefcase, containing the laptop, was in his hand. Marks was already in the field, and Nick had driven the pickup full of seed and fertilizer down to the end of the lane where Jim could get to it easily when the seeder needed refilling. Nick was making an adjustment to the spray nozzle he had fitted on the compressor. He looked up as McCann put his coat and briefcase in the Ranger.

"I charged the nozzle to your account at Mr. Willard's. Is that okay?"

McCann smiled. "It's fine Nick. Did you find a place for your family?"

"No sir, not yet. But Donna and Darcy are working on it."

At the mention of Donna's name, McCann remembered that he hadn't seen or heard from her since the night of the rain storm. He thought of going inside and calling to see if she would have lunch with him and thought better of it. The Board meeting might run late.

"Donna's back then?"

"Yeah, she got back on Sunday night. She and Darcy are getting the orders ready for the Christmas season."

McCann started to respond when the phone rang. He turned and went into the house and picked up the phone, reminding himself mentally that he should get a cellular phone or at least a portable.

"Hello."

"Wils, its Donna."

He leaned his back against the cupboard, enjoying the sound of her voice. "Long time… no see."

"I went to Detroit to a style show. I got back on Sunday night."

"I know, I've been kept informed," he laughed.

"So I hear! Wils, It is so good of you to give Nick work and to offer to provide a place for he and Darcy and Damon."

McCann kept his voice light. "They can all move in anytime. I only eat well when you bring something from town. I was hoping for Dunkin' Donuts some morning this week but no such luck."

Her laugh made him smile into the mouthpiece. "We are looking for a place for them here in town but what Farnsworth has to offer isn't much. They may take you up on it. Are you ready to do a middle-of –the- night feeding?"

McCann grinned, "I'm not equipped!"

"With a bottle, silly!" she laughed. He wanted the moment to last forever but the clock on the kitchen wall was moving towards the hour when he needed to be with Doug Warner and his Board.

"Listen, I have a meeting this morning with Doug Warner and his Board. Can I stop by when I'm through?"

There was a pause at the other end of the line and he could sense that she was trying to understand the meaning behind what she had just heard. Her reply was reserved. "Sure, stop by."

McCann wanted to explain but thought better of it. This would be better done face to face. He said goodbye and hung up the phone. He stepped out into the sunlight and watched for a moment as Nick sprayed a coat of red paint on the side of the outbuilding. He got into the Ranger and headed into Farnsworth.

The Farnsworth Telephone Cooperative building was a blend of the results of REA financing and, more recently, Warner family ownership. The outside of the building remained the same red brick and gray concrete as when it was built in the 1950's. Four oak trees framed the walk to the glass and steel front entry, two on each side. The company name was the anodized aluminum lettering unveiled at the building's dedication. Inside, however, the difference was dramatic. The lobby was done much like the finest offices in any of the country's major cities. The use of rich carpeting and mahogany wall treatments and office furniture was everywhere. The receptionist was seated directly opposite the front door and two service representatives sat at desks to the right of the door. The desks had wide front overhangs to accommodate customers who could sit in rich high-backed chairs to conduct their business. As McCann entered, the receptionist looked up from her recessed computer screen and smiled.

"Good morning, Mr. McCann, Mr. Warner is expecting you. He asked me to take you to his office. You can wait there until the Board is ready to meet with you."

McCann returned the smile. "I'm impressed! How did you know my name?"

"Mr. Warner described you to me this morning when we were going over his schedule for the day. Please come with me. Would you like some coffee?"

"Thanks, I had a cup earlier this morning. That will do for now," he replied.

McCann followed her through a mahogany door to the left of the lobby and down a hallway carpeted in sculpted Berber. As he walked, his glance took in the offices on either side of the hall. In one, a technician was sitting at a computer terminal with a large flat screen monitor. The screen displayed a network which McCann assumed to be Farnsworth's feeder cable system. Two indicators were blinking on the screen. He knew that these would indicate either construction of maintenance locations and that the technician was probably part of Farnsworth's Network Operations Center. In another office, a man and a woman were seated at winged desks with computer terminals and printers. The woman was watching as billing notices were printed. The man was reviewing a large computer printout. "Accounting," McCann thought to himself. In the last office on the right, an attractive middle aged woman was talking with a young man dressed in Levis and a flannel shirt. "Human Resources," guessed McCann.

"Right in here, Mr. McCann. Make yourself comfortable. I will tell Doug that you are here." She opened the door and ushered him into Doug Warner's office. The room was at least 14 feet wide and 25 feet long. A conference table and six chairs were directly opposite the doorway. A couch, end tables and lamps were along one side and two overstuffed chairs fronted the massive, walnut desk. A bookcase/credenza was against the wall behind the desk and McCann noted another recessed computer screen in the left pedestal of the credenza. The far wall of the office was entirely glass looking out over a landscaped area about 20 feet wide that ended at a wrought iron fence.

He settled into the couch and sat his briefcase down. A moment or two passed and there was a quick rap on the door frame. A young man in a white golf shirt with a University of Michigan logo stepped in.

"Good morning, Mr. McCann. I'm Ted Lark. I understand from Mr. Warner that you may be using a computer assisted presentation to the Board and I would be happy to set that up for you."

McCann rose and extended his hand. "I'm glad to meet you. I will be using my laptop. It's here in my bag."

McCann took the laptop from its case and Lark took it in both hands and quickly scanned the ports at the back of the computer. "Very nice. We will hook our projection up to this and you will be all set. May I take this with me now and get it set up for you?"

"Thank you, I appreciate that," McCann said, smiling at the obvious interest in his equipment. It was state of the art and loaded with every option available. He was also aware that at this time next year, his laptop would be outmoded.

"No problem. I'll leave it in 'sleep mode' for you. I'm glad to have met you."

Lark left and McCann walked behind the desk to look at the various pictures and mementos that Doug Warner had placed on the credenza and some of the shelves in the bookcase. There was a picture of Doug with his family, one of the two girls in soccer uniforms and one of an elderly couple. The man was standing and the woman seated in the classic pose. The woman's gray hair framed a strong face with eyes that seemed to look right through the camera into his. McCann saw the resemblance to Doug Warner in the man's face. They were obviously Warner's father and mother. He did not have a similar picture and the thought pained him. He had never given things like that a thought. His office in Chicago had many pictures on the walls and bookcase shelves. Most were of him with various industry leaders, politicians and community leaders. All of them were in a box somewhere in a moving and storage company's warehouse. He had one picture of his mother in his billfold. He made a mental note to buy a frame for it. He thought to himself that there was still time for him to get a picture of the two of them to go with it. Perhaps this winter he could find a way to get to Florida…

His thoughts were interrupted as Doug Warner strode into the office. He smiled broadly as he noted McCann looking at the picture.

"Good morning, Wils! That's my mom and dad. He died five years ago. You'll meet mom in about fifteen minutes. She's the chair of our Board."

"I know. As I remember, she was also President of the State Association's Board at one time."

"Right, now I'm on the Board. Dynacom had a man named Wolfe on it until LEGENT took over."

"I spoke to Jim just this week. He's in Mackinaw City now. LEGENT closed the Lansing office and made him their Northern District Manager."

Warner sat down in one of the chairs in front of the desk. McCann remained standing behind the desk. "If we get these LEGENT properties, what do you think our chances would be of getting Jim to work for us?" Warner asked, looking intently at McCann.

McCann was impressed with Warner's thinking. Jim Wolfe would be the perfect fit in such a position. Not only would he bring outstanding knowledge of the properties with him, his knowledge of the operation of State

Government and his personal business philosophy would be right in line with that of Doug Warner.

McCann had to admit to himself that his initial reaction to Warner's plan to attempt to buy the LEGENT properties in Michigan had been skeptical. But, the more he was exposed to Warner and his thinking as well as the efficiently handled reception he had received at the office this morning, his skepticism was beginning to diminish. This was no starry eyed dreamer. The man sitting opposite him with his cowboy boots stretched comfortably out in front of him was a solid thinker. Warner was the kind of man Wilson McCann would have liked to have had working for him at Dynacom. The thoughts of what might have been returned quickly and he moved around the desk to sit in the other chair as he responded, forcing his mind to focus on today and now.

"That's an excellent idea! Jim Wolfe would fit in very well in an expanded operation."

Warner smiled. "I have a couple of folks here who can handle more responsibilities as well. Janice Fox, the lady in the last office on the other side of the hall is our operations manager and Ron Layne, our Treasurer, is also ready to take on more. But, we have to succeed first. I'm interested to hear what you have to tell us about how to do that."

McCann reflected that his "Human Resources" stereotype had been wrong. He was seldom wrong in his reactions to people and their roles. It was clear that here in the smaller, independent segment of the industry, he would have to refine his judgment.

"You had a chance to look over my outline?" he asked.

"Yes I did. It looks great. I encourage you to give it to us straight from the shoulder. I want the Board to be fully aware of what we are talking about and the risks and opportunities that attach to it. I need to share one thing more with you before you talk with the Board. We are taking a fifteen-minute break while Ted sets up your lap-top and then you can make your presentation."

"And the one thing is?"

"We have two people on the Board who are dead set against any expansion of Farnsworth's operating territory or any other step that will require giving up any element of control or placing our dividend in jeopardy."

"George Whyte and Joe Rambaugh?"

Warner's face showed his surprise. "You've obviously been talking to someone or you have been reading some PSC reports!"

"The latter. What I don't understand is how those two men each have a ten percent ownership in Farnsworth Tele."

"Very simple. Both George and Joe held a lot of farmer notes for equipment, trucks, cars, etc. When we bought the Telephone Company, it was owned by its members. The farmers who owned stock in the Coop couldn't sell their stock without George and Joe giving their okay because, in many cases, the stock was pledged as part of the security for those notes. George and Joe simply bought up the shares themselves and held it. Rather than fight to get it, our family accepted the minority ownership and, in most cases, we have operated quite well despite occasional disagreements on how capital should be expended."

"A dissenting minority could make things a little more troublesome for you."

"If push comes to shove, my mother still has enough influence in Farnsworth to bring George and Joe into line. There are other implement and car dealers in the Thumb!"

"Small town politics?"

"Exactly, if that is what it takes!"

"How about your other Board members?"

"As you know, we have a seven member board. Phil Willard and Fred Penay will support the company action if they believe it is prudent. Our attorney, Arthur Boyington is from Detroit and will also support the company if the action is prudent and proper. My mother and I are the other two votes."

"People sometimes disagree on what is 'prudent' and what is 'proper'," McCann replied. "To attract those with the money to support your attempt to acquire these properties, you may have to give up additional control of your company. Are you prepared to do that?"

Warner sat up in his chair and thought for a minute before answering. "When our family acquired Farnsworth Tele., we dedicated ourselves to improving and expanding service to our customers, to making a positive contribution to the economic development of the communities we serve, to taking care of our people, and to improving the shareholder value of our company. We also dedicated ourselves to doing everything in a way that testified to our family's faith in Jesus Christ. My mother and I will not vote to do anything that does not honor those goals."

McCann was impressed by the sincerity of Warner's convictions. He fully understood the first four aims as ones which he had held as CEO of Dynacom. He had never met anyone who had given such a strong commitment to their faith. He was about to respond when Ted Lark stuck his head in the doorway.

"We are ready to continue, Mr. Warner", he said.

"Thanks, Ted. Let's go, Wils" Warner said as he stood.

McCann followed him out and back down the hall to a door which had been closed before. Warner opened it and stepped aside as McCann entered. The conference room was even larger than Warner's office. The boat-shaped conference table was actually six different walnut topped tables fitted together. The ten captain's chairs surrounding it were richly padded leather. At one end a white board was exposed from a walnut wall cabinet whose doors had been swung back and out of the way. McCann's lap-top rested in a combination wall cabinet, wet bar and media center at the other end of the room. On the shelf below it a video projector was turned on. A twenty foot mouse cord ran to one of the chairs where he assumed he was to sit. The white board displayed a computer graphic "ready."

The gray haired woman from the picture stood has he entered. She was dressed in a dark blue pants suit and white blouse with a high collar. A cameo brooch was at her throat.

"Mr. McCann. I'm very pleased to meet you and I want to express our appreciation to you for taking the time to visit with us," she said, as she extended her hand. Her grip was firm and reassuring. Isabel "Belle" Warner was every bit the industry leader that his experience told him she was. At 82 years of age, he could sense that her intensity level had not diminished.

"Thank you, Mrs. Warner. I've heard many good things about you and am pleased to finally meet you," he said, releasing her hand.

"Please call me Belle. Let me introduce our Board. I think you already know Phil and Fred. This is Arthur Boyington, our counsel," She said as a sandy haired man in a stylish suit and white shirt stood and extended his hand. His eyes behind the wire rimmed glasses were appraising McCann as they shook.

"Mr. McCann, it's good to meet you."

Belle Warner guided him to the next man who was dressed in a tweed sport jacket, brown slacks, and a white Oxford dress shirt with no tie.

"Joe Rambaugh, Wilson McCann."

McCann reached out his hand to a man who could have doubled as Broderick Crawford. His thinning hair was swept back and his body was heavy and muscular. His dark eyes bored into McCann's as they shook hands.

"My pleasure! Welcome to Farnsworth! I understand you are Nick Hardesty's new employer!"

McCann was not surprised to hear that Rambaugh knew of his offer to Nick. Phil Willard had already told him that Nick had been employed at the auto dealership until last week. He held Rambaugh's hand for just a second longer and squeezed hard. "Yes, he is working on one of my sheds as we speak!"

"Good for him!" Rambaugh said as he sat down.

"I understand you know George," Belle said as Whyte stood to shake hands with McCann. A wide smile crossed the implement dealer's face.

"Of course! We have already done a piece of business. How are you, Wils? How is that Baler working out for you?" Whyte's tone seemed almost mocking and McCann noticed that his eyes were on Belle Warner as he spoke.

"Jim and I have already put it to good use, George." McCann responded smiling as he held out his hand. He could feel Belle's gaze on him as he spoke.

"Good! Good! Let me know if you need any help with anything," Whyte said, as he released McCann's hand and sat down. McCann had the urge to wipe his hand on his suit pants but resisted it.

McCann walked around the table and shook hands quickly with Phil Willard who smiled encouragingly and with Fred Penay who said, "It's good to see you again Wils", without smiling. McCann wondered at the banker's serious demeanor.

With the introductions over, Belle motioned for McCann to take a seat and resumed her own at the far end of the table. Doug sat directly opposite her. She looked across the table at Doug and motioned with her hand that he should take the floor. He swiveled his chair to look directly at the others arranged down both sides of the table and began to speak.

"We learned about ten days ago that LEGENT has decided to put their properties in the Mid-West states up for sale. That includes the properties in Michigan. Those properties are highlighted in red on this map."

He pushed a button on a small remote device in front of him and the "ready" symbol on the board was replaced by a map of Michigan showing all of the operating territories of the various telecommunications companies. The LEGENT properties were displayed in a prominent red.

"You are all readily acquainted with our operating area, but I'll show it in contrast in this one."

He pushed the button again and the map re-appeared with the Farnsworth Tele areas displayed in a deep green.

"The LEGENT operating areas serve approximately 15,000 customers, which is roughly equal to our customer base. If we were to acquire these properties, it would double our size in both revenue and customers served. The LEGENT properties have a network investment that is about 80% of ours. As I was thinking about the possibilities of pursuing this, I became aware that Wils was living here in Farnsworth. Wils, as you know, is the former CEO of Dynacom, which owned the properties in question prior to their acquisition by LEGENT. I've asked Wils to talk with us about these properties and about what might be involved in acquiring them. He has considerable experience in acquiring and merging properties from his time with Dynacom."

"You didn't make the sale on the last one though!" smiled Joe Rambaugh, as he looked across the table at McCann. The challenge in his eyes as he said it was evident. George Whyte looked down at the papers in front of him and smirked. McCann felt his blood pressure start to rise and stretched his hands out on the table in front of him. He resisted the thought of a sarcastic remark and said, "No, Joe, we didn't, but we tried." He could feel Belle Warner's eyes on him again.

Doug Warner clicked off the map and sat back in his chair. "Wils has prepared an outline of the comments he will make and I have reproduced it for you in your Board packet. I'm going to ask him to go through it with us and then, with the chair's permission, we will do a Q & A session. You need to know that I am very serious about this possibility, but I want to fully air any thoughts that each of you may have. Wils, will you begin, please?"

McCann moved the mouse a little closer to him and clicked it. The "ready" disappeared and a black and white slide with bullet points appeared. The heading said "ISSUES."

"This acquisition, if you are successful, will double your size as Doug has indicated. A successful acquisition has some issues connected with it. The first is a potential decrease in ownership. Unless you have about $50 million lying around somewhere, you will need to raise capital. In the current industry situation, capital is difficult but not impossible to obtain. Most investment firms will want to have an ownership position and they will want Board representation. As this is primarily a family owned company, you will have to consider a decrease in the percentage of the total enterprise that you will own. Second, if you utilize debt capital, there is the cost of money to consider. Third, there is the issue of securing approval from the regulating agency, in this case, the Public Service Commission. Their primary interest will be in protecting your customers and those of the acquired property from any rate impacts due to the acquisition. They might even require a rate freeze for a period of time. There is also the issue of whether you can mount a successful acquisition against the type of competitor that will emerge for these properties. Most investment firms will be reluctant to assist you because of your relative size compared to acquisition companies or "aggregators" that have greater scope and with whom they have done business in the past. Lastly, there is the issue of the costs of making the acquisition attempt. You can expect significant legal and accounting costs and you will experience some impact on the day-to-day productivity of your operation, as your management's attention is diverted to this process."

He clicked the mouse again and the "ready" indicator replaced the Power Point slide. He looked around the table. Willard, Belle, Doug and Arthur

Boyington were looking at him expectantly. Fred Penay was looking down at some notes he had been scribbling on his pad. Whyte and Rambaugh were looking at each other. He clicked the mouse again and a new Power Point slide titled "Approach."

"I've taken the liberty to outline an approach here that you could follow. It is patterned on one that I have used in the past." He glanced at Penay and saw that he had the banker's attention now. "It involves associating your company with a consortium that is planning to make a bid for the entire LEGENT property that is for sale not only in Michigan but throughout the Midwest. The condition would be that you would acquire the Michigan property for yourself, but would join in a single bid for all the properties. You would form an acquisition company that I have called 'Farnsworth Acquisition Co' or 'FAC' for purposes of this presentation. You would use this separate entity to purchase the LEGENT property in Michigan and, upon completion of the acquisition, you would close down FAC and continue to operate the acquired property as a separate entity."

Fred Penay looked up from his notes and asked, "but why would we do that? Why wouldn't we just have Farnsworth Tele acquire the property and operate it as part of Farnsworth?"

Before McCann could respond, Boyington spoke, "It is highly unlikely that the Michigan Commission would allow Farnsworth to simply combine the two operations. They would want records kept entirely separate for some time and would only consider merger of the two properties when they were satisfied that rate payers in each company were not unjustly impacted. I'm sure Mr. McCann is well aware of the Commission's track record in these types of transactions."

McCann felt immediate relief at the attorney's grasp of the situation. It was clear that Arthur Boyington was well versed in doing business before the state's regulatory agency. He noted that a slight smile had crossed Doug Warner's face at the exchange. The smile quickly faded as Joe Rambaugh spoke.

"Who is this consortium you spoke of? Is it the same group you used to try to buy Dynacom?"

McCann could sense the skepticism in the auto dealer's voice as he said it. He took a breath and looked Rambaugh squarely in the face.

"I am not at liberty to divulge the names of the companies and people involved beyond saying that one of the principals is a man I worked with on the Dynacom proposal."

To his credit, Rambaugh did not avert his gaze. "And what is in this for you?" he said, casting a sidewise glance at Belle Warner.

McCann felt his temper begin to rise. Before he could respond, Doug Warner broke in.

"Let's be clear of one thing here. I invited Wils to share his knowledge of these types of efforts with us. We have not made any decisions on this matter yet and we certainly have not decided on a course of action. I am confident that Wils has outlined a possible approach to accomplishing this. There may be others."

Rambaugh refused to be deterred. He swung his gaze to Warner. "He just said he knows this consortium is planning to make a bid. How do we know that he doesn't have some plan up his sleeve that could result in Farnsworth getting into something beyond our capability and losing our company to a bunch of Wall Street Bankers? With all due respect to Mr. McCann, I think it is very strange that he shows up here in Farnsworth and makes a show of buying farm equipment from George and saying he's going to feed cattle through the winter and going to church with you and young Marks and now he's telling us how to lose control of our company!"

Belle Warner tapped her pen loudly on the table in front of her. All eyes swung to her as she leaned back slightly in her chair and spoke very quietly.

"We are not here to get into Mr. McCann's reasons for coming to Farnsworth or raising beef cattle. We are here to listen to his expertise in the field of acquisitions and to consider whether we should give any further consideration to possibly making a bid for the LEGENT properties here in Michigan. I am going to ask that we hold any further questions or comments until Mr. McCann is finished. Will you please proceed, Mr. McCann?"

Rambaugh dropped his pen on the pad in front of him and leaned back in his chair, folded his arms across his substantial stomach and interlaced his fingers. Whyte's thin features were swathed in an oily grin. Boyington and Penay were both looking down at their notes. Only Phil Willard continued to look directly at McCann expectantly. Had it not been for that and Belle

Warner's calm smile at him, Wilson McCann would have walked out. He fought to control his rising temper and looked down at his notes. Clearing his throat, he continued his presentation, moving through a series of slides that contained a timeline with milestone goals for each stage of the process and a final set of slides that contained financial analyses of both Farnsworth and the LEGENT Michigan properties on a separate and combined basis. A final slide set showed the estimated costs of the acquisition and current costs of investment capital followed by the combined operation with those costs included and a projected Income statement for a three year period following the completion of the acquisition. The entire presentation had taken an hour.

"Thank you, Mr. McCann," Belle Warner said. She had clearly re-taken control of the meeting when Rambaugh had made his statement. Doug Warner sat quietly opposite her.

"Are there any questions?" she looked around the room.

Penay asked several questions relative to the financial projections and the cost of capital. Boyington asked several more about the various steps in the acquisition process and, at one point, said he felt that some of the milestone goals were a bit aggressive. McCann responded that this could quite possibly be the case. Whyte and Rambaugh were quiet. Phil Willard leaned forward and looked directly at McCann. The sincerity in his gaze was apparent. "Wils, if this was your company, would you attempt this?"

McCann was somewhat taken back by the question which was the only one Willard had asked. His thoughts raced as he sought to put a proper answer together. He leaned back in his chair and pushed the mouse away from him.

"I honestly don't know, Phil. On the one hand, the competitor in me would want to try it. But, these things can take something out of a person and a company. I'm not sure whether I would try or not."

For the first time, he saw a smile cross Fred Penay's face. It seemed that the banker had relaxed a bit and his face showed a friendliness that had been absent previously. Boyington made a brief note on his pad. Rambaugh started to say something and thought better of it and sat back in his chair, waiting.

ACQUISITION

Belle Warner closed a leather portfolio in front of her with a snap. She leaned forward, resting her arms on the table in front of her. "It is now 11:45 a.m. and we will break for lunch. I understand that Doug has ordered lunch to be brought in at noon which will give you a chance to check for any messages you may have in your offices. I need to run home for a minute and will eat there. Mr. McCann, if you are free, I would like you to join me."

(12)

McCann was taken aback by the invitation and his frame of mind was to immediately decline and leave. Yet there was something in the way she had invited him and the look on her face that made him think twice before answering. "I really hadn't planned……"

"Please?" she said with a smile and laid a hand gently on his left arm.

"Thank you, I'd be happy to," he said quietly, acquiescing to the smile.

"We'll re-convene promptly at 1:15 p.m.", She said as she looked at Doug. It was clear that she expected him to deal with the outburst by Rambaugh during lunch. Doug smiled and placed his hand on McCann's shoulder as he retrieved his lap-top and stored it in his bag.

"Thanks, Wils. That was just what we needed to hear. I'd like to talk with you some more tomorrow if it is convenient. Enjoy your lunch. Mother wants to get to know you."

McCann wondered what was meant by the latter comment. He would know soon enough. Belle Warner led him out of the room and down the hall to another door that opened into a parking lot at the rear of the building. She clicked a fob in her hand and the lights flashed on a Cadillac Deville DHS parked facing the doorway.

"Get in, Wils, I'll drive," she said. He noted that she had dropped the "Mr. McCann."

McCann settled into the leather seat and waited as she expertly backed the car out of its space and headed it out onto a side street. She turned left at the first intersection and crossed the main highway heading north out of town. She turned right at the first corner and the car began to climb a slight rise. The neighborhood quickly changed from newer homes to older larger ones hidden behind good sized trees. At the end of the street, a circular drive led to what would have been referred to as a "Stately Mansion" in years past. The two story brick and frame house sat at the top of the first rise and looked down on those they had driven by. Above the home on the next rise, another newer sub-division was accessible from another street.

She had not said a word during the three-minute drive. They got out and she led him up to the front door, framed between two pillars that ran to the second story. Before entering, he turned and looked down the rise through the trees. A good portion of Farnsworth was visible. She stopped and stood behind him in the doorway.

"At one time, this was the 'big house" in town," She said. "Now it's just another 'older home'."

"It has a lot of character," he replied, turning to go inside.

"My husband and I built it when the children were in grade school. The school was across the highway then. It was only a block to school and they could come home for lunch every day."

"You have other children besides Doug?" he asked.

"A daughter, Nancy. She died in an automobile accident fifteen years ago."

"I'm very sorry," he said.

She led him into a dining room that overlooked the back yard. The sun was streaming in through the windows and the yard was awash in color. A table was set for two. She had obviously been planning this part of his day well in advance. She rang a small bell and a young woman appeared.

"Maria, this is Mr. McCann. We will take our salads now. Wils, I hope you like chicken Caesar salad."

"It's one of my favorites. Thank you," he replied, as they both sat. She looked out the window for a moment as if gathering her thoughts. Maria brought the salads and a pitcher of iced tea. Belle bowed her head and said a brief prayer thanking the Lord for the food and asking his continued blessing on her family and on "this new friend who has offered his assistance to us." He had automatically bowed his head as she prayed and as he looked up she handed him a small covered basket that he found contained four fresh rolls. He took one and sat it on his bread plate and waited.

"No doubt, you are wondering why I invited you up here for lunch," she said, as she took a roll and began to butter half of it.

"Yes," he said quietly.

She took a bite and chewed for a moment before speaking.

"Joe Rambaugh made you angry, didn't he?"

He hesitated a moment and then answered quietly, "Yes."

"He made me angry also but not for the same reason. You see I have the same questions he has but I am not as impertinent as to ask them in a meeting you had been invited by the Warner family to speak at."

He noted the use of the words "Warner Family" and smiled thinly. She continued.

"Wils, why are you here? Why is one of our industry's better leaders living on a small farm and planting winter wheat and talking about feeding beef cattle when our industry is in such chaos?"

He took a bite of the salad and looked out the window before answering. He could feel her gaze upon him just as it had been during the meeting.

"Belle, several people have asked me that since I came here. I'll tell you what I told them. I don't know. I guess I am trying to figure out what to do with the rest of my life."

She considered his answer and ate some of her salad and took a sip from her tea. "I took the liberty of doing some background checking when Doug talked with me about having you talk to our Board. I hope you don't mind. I know that you have no family other than your mother whom you seldom see. You have never been married and you have never had a close relationship with anyone outside of Dynacom. Those relationships were strictly business and you have few close friends. My friends in the industry tell me that you are a man of great vision and great talent. From this knowledge, I have formed some conclusions. Would you like to hear them?"

He dabbed at his lips with his napkin and sat back in his chair. He looked at her and his mind ran back over the years to his high school English teacher. Judith Bingham had taken him under her wing. She had chided him when he didn't do as well as he could have. She had believed he could do better. She had led him to push himself into areas such as Shakespeare that didn't particularly appeal to him. She had recommended him for honors at the school. She had been his sponsor. In his mind he could hear her in that dusty classroom in Chicago, as she sat behind her old oaken desk looking up at him on his last day of school as a graduating senior. "You have it in you to become something special, Wilson. Don't fail." He had never forgotten the moment. He had never thanked her. She had died fifteen years ago and he had sent flowers to her funeral. Belle Warner was a slightly taller, slightly thinner version of Judith Bingham. He swallowed and said "yes," very quietly.

"You gave your life to a company. You worked hard and you sacrificed to achieve great success for it and for yourself. Then, someone took it away from you. You tried to get it back and you failed. Now, you have nothing left to fall back on. You have no family, you have no friends and you have no faith. Yet, through all of this you are still a man of great vision and great talent. There are those who feel that you are selfish and out to further your own self-interests. The fact that you are willing to listen to an old woman dissect you this way says a lot about you. May I ask you a very personal question?"

She had said it all in a very straight-forward manner. There had been a time in his life when he would have resented her and what she said. That time was long past. Instead he found himself liking her more and more. "We've come this far. Why not?" he said.

She did not return his smile. Instead, she took another sip from her tea and sat the glass down as she spoke. "What exactly is your relationship with Donna Barnes?"

He was shocked at the question. It was not what he had been expecting. "I don't know what you mean," he said, as he looked away and out over the yard.

"Many years ago, you came here as a young man and took advantage of a young woman who was at a very difficult stage in her life. You used her and you never looked back. Even if I put that action down in the category of 'sowing one's wild oats' it is an action that is contrary to what I have come to know about you."

Her words stung him, and he felt condemned. While he knew she had hit the mark, he found himself trying to justify himself to her.

"We were young, we had a lot of fun together but it was only a summer romance ....."

"For two summers as I recall," she interjected. "What happened the third summer?"

"She started to get serious and I wasn't ready and we sort of each went our way and that was the end of it."

"And now you have come back and Donna has been out to your farm helping you and...?"

"We are just friends. Ask Donna! That is what she wants. She wants to be friends."

"You are not a Christian are you, Mr. McCann?" she asked as she took another bite of her salad.

The change in questioning began to bother McCann. He shifted in his chair and crossed his legs under the table and took another bite of his salad. What was she driving at?

"I believe in God and in doing good and trying to live a good life," he replied.

"But you haven't accepted Jesus Christ as your personal Savior and turned your life over to him?"

"No, I have never been part of that movement. Frankly, I have never had time to become involved in a lot of church related activity. I had a company to run. I have never killed anyone or cheated anyone or ran around with someone else's wife. I have supported charitable causes and worked for the good of my fellow man whenever I could. I think that should count for something!" He said it defensively and was immediately ashamed of the way he sounded.

She smiled at him and continued to eat her salad. "It does count for something, Wils. It just doesn't count enough. You need Jesus. You need to put Him first in your life. You need to turn your life over to His leading. He will show you what His purpose is for you and he will show you what to do with the rest of your life. Would you care for some dessert?"

He laughed out loud. "Belle, you are amazing. You just psycho-analyzed me, asked me about my relationship with a woman I hadn't seen for over 20 years and now you are trying to convert me! Yes, I would like some dessert, if only to prolong this conversation so you can really get inside my head!"

She laughed with him but quickly regained her serious look. She rang her little bell again and Maria appeared to clear away the salad plates. She re-appeared with two large pieces of deep-dish apple pie. Belle took a big bite of pie and looked at him. She placed her fork beside her plate and leaned toward him over the table with her elbows on either side of the plate as though to give her support.

"Wils, I have known Donna since she was in grade school. She often came here to lunch with my children when she was little. She found the Savior before I did but now I think of her as my daughter in Christ, the daughter that I lost before I knew the Lord. I think very highly of her. I do not want to see her hurt."

"And you think I will hurt her in some way?"

"You have the potential to. She loves you."

He dropped his fork on the dish with a small clatter. The look on his face was one of incredulity. Before he could speak, she continued in a very matter-of-fact tone.

"She has since those summers long ago. I have always wondered why she didn't find someone and get married. One day, several years ago, I asked her why. She told me she had fallen in love with someone years ago, suffered a great hurt and would never do so again. I think that someone is you. I think you should carefully consider your feelings for her. She has found someone she loves more now. Jesus. She wants to serve him as a missionary. I could finance that desire for her but the Lord has not directed me to do so. I have one other question for you before we are through. What are your intentions regarding this LEGENT acquisition business?"

McCann felt relieved to move back to the question of the LEGENT properties and away from the subject of his relationship with Donna. He felt the need to share openly with her about his contacts with Stu Bailey, his initial refusal to be part of the acquisition and what he had committed to. He told her that he thought he could convince Bailey to agree to make Farnsworth a part of the acquisition group if he acted as an advisor to the group. He assured her that he had no personal agenda in the LEGENT property acquisition. When he had finished, she folded her napkin and sat back to take one last drink of tea.

"Wils, I love the Lord. I am going to pray that you come to know him in a personal way. I love my family and I will do whatever is appropriate to protect them and their stake in Farnsworth Tele. I have no desire to see

Farnsworth Tele become a pawn in a Wall Street chess game. I love Donna Barnes as a daughter and I don't want to see her hurt. I like you. I feel you are a man who can be trusted. If we decide to pursue this LEGENT acquisition, we will need the advice of a man like you. I ask that you forgive an old woman for prying into your life and making observations about it. I trust that we can become and remain friends."

He reached across the table and took her hand. "I would like that very much," he said.

She led him through the house, pointing out various pictures of her family and mementos from their lives. There were pictures of Doug in his football uniform and his girls in their soccer uniforms, pictures of Doug and Lori on their wedding day and pictures of Belle's husband beside a D-9 Caterpillar Tractor at a construction site. McCann thought again of how barren his own life experience had been outside of Dynacom.

They walked out onto the deck and looked out over the yard and down on the town before returning to the car. She dropped him next to the Ranger with a smile and a firm handshake.

"Thank you for sharing with us today," she said as he leaned in the window.

"Thank you for sharing with me today," he smiled.

He sat in the Ranger thinking about his luncheon with Belle Warner. He was getting a little tired of everyone playing psychiatrist with his life. At the same time, he was beginning to feel that Chuck Hastings, Donna and Belle were probably right. He had built his whole life around Dynacom and when he lost that, his life was an empty shell. He was also bothered by the resurfacing of his feelings for Donna. He had never felt strong affection for anyone. His relationship with his mother had become distant, once he began to rise within the company. There was no one else that he had ever felt close to. Donna's expressed desire to keep their relationship on a "friends only" basis contradicted what Belle had told him. Was it possible that Donna had feelings for him that matched his for her? He wondered if he should try to find out.

He remembered that he had told Donna that he would stop by when he was done at Farnsworth Tele. He wasn't ready to do that right at the moment. He decided instead to stop at the diner and sort out his thoughts before seeing her. The diner was empty except for an older couple in one booth and a truck driver drinking coffee and reading a paper at a table near the door. Sally McHugh, in a red denim shirt and blue jeans was behind the counter. He slid into an empty booth close to the front window and she walked over. She smiled good-naturedly. "Coffee, Tea or Me?"

"Decaf coffee, thanks," he smiled back.

"What brings you to town all gussied up?" she asked, leaning against the back of the booth and eyeing him appraisingly. "Somebody die?"

"No, just doing a little business down the street."

"Ah! None of my business obviously! I'll get your coffee." She said it in a friendly way and walked away. The denim on the jeans was doing its best to hold everything in and straining mightily. He watched her, thinking about her failed marriages and her three kids. Despite her background, he felt that she might have built more into her life than he had. She returned with a steaming mug of coffee and a small cream pitcher. She sat it before him and slid into the booth opposite him.

"So, how is the farming going?" She said it in a teasing tone of voice.

"Well, ma'am, we got the hay baled and in the barn, the wheat going in the ground and paint going on the buildings. The beef should be here next week and winter's on its way!" He drawled it out in an imitation of a laid back farmer.

She leaned back and smiled. Sally had a friendly face. He smiled back and, without giving much thought to what came out of his mouth, said "Sally, have you ever been in love?"

She laughed loudly. The old couple turned their heads and stared. The trucker raised his head a bit over his paper but quickly resumed reading. McCann lowered his head and took a sip from his coffee. He could feel the redness creeping up from his collar.

"I mean…you've been married three times… did you love each one of them?" he said lamely, still looking down at his mug of coffee.

She leaned forward and smiled. "I married three different times and I guess at the time I must have loved each of 'em. The problem was that I kept finding someone else that I thought I could do better with. In the end, I ended up with no one and three kids that I do love very much. I guess by the standards some in this town set I'm a tramp. But, I have three good kids, I have a decent business here and I go out on Saturday night, have a few beers and enjoy myself. I have a good life."

McCann smiled at her candor and took another sip of his coffee.

"How about you Wils? You ever been in love?"

"No… never." He said it quietly.

"All that money they say you have and all that jetting around the country in company planes and you never met someone?" She sat back as she asked it, eyeing him closely.

"I was too busy building a company and making 'all that money'," he said.

"Maybe you and I should pick up where we left off!" She was back to the teasing tone of voice.

He smiled at the memory. "Yeah, we could go over to the VFW, have a few beers and go down by the river and park in my Ranger pick-up!"

"No! We would have to take my Mustang! I've seen Fred Harms' old pick-up! You should trade that thing in and get a new one. I hear you can afford it!"

It was his turn to laugh. "I've got to wait until spring to see what my beef cattle bring!"

She leaned forward again and put her hand on his arm. "Wils, if you ever need someone to talk to, I'm available."

He put his other hand on top of hers. "Thanks Sally. I appreciate that."

Donna's hand was on the door handle when she saw them, their heads together, smiles on their faces, her hand on his arm and his hand on hers. Donna turned and went back down the street the way she had come. Neither of them saw her.

McCann stopped by the Barnes Loft twenty minutes later. Darcy told him Donna had gone home early as she wasn't feeling well.

McCann thought about the meeting at Farnsworth Tele as he drove home.

ACQUISITION

His irritation at Joe Rambaugh returned whenever he thought of the auto dealer and his remarks. McCann knew that Rambaugh and Whyte would be a problem for the Warners if they decided to make a bid for the LEGENT properties. His mind began to explore ways to mitigate or eliminate their opposition. He parked the Ranger, gave Nick an encouraging "Looks Good" salute and went inside. He made two phone calls: one to his financial planner in Chicago, and the other to a private investigator in Detroit. His instructions to each were brief and he asked for results within 48 hours. He changed his clothes and thought about how much more comfortable he was beginning to feel in jeans and a flannel shirt than in a suit and tie. Ted waited by the bedroom doorway, wagging his tail. McCann had the urge to go out and help Nick with the painting but knew that would appear to be cutting into Nick's potential earnings. He decided instead to go for a walk. He paused briefly beside the lamp table and picked the Bible up. He looked at it for a moment and decided to take it with him. Ted trotted along at his left as they walked out past the barn and down the lane. Nick, stripped to the waist and standing on the third rung of a nine foot step ladder, watched them go.

The sun was bright and warm on his face as he walked down the hill behind the barn and out into the lane. He walked past the newly sown field on his left and the pasture field where the beef would graze next week on his right. He could hear Jim Marks' tractor to the south as he finished planting the wheat in the other field. He considered walking back to watch him but he wanted to be alone. He continued walking until he reached the back fence line and sat down under a tree. Ted watched him for a moment and then curled up at his feet. McCann began thumbing the Bible idly. His eye fell on a penciled note next to a verse in the book of Romans. It said "Rom-Rd 6". He noted that it was beside Romans 10:13: "For whoever will call upon the name of the Lord, will be saved."

He turned back to the beginning of the book of Romans and began to turn the pages. Another penciled note read "Rom-Rd 1" appeared opposite Romans 3:1: "There is none righteous, not even one."

He turned the page and "Rom-Rd 2" appeared opposite Romans 3:23 which read "For all have sinned and fall short of the glory of God."

On the opposite page, two verses in the 5th chapter were notated. "Rom

Rd-3" was beside the 12th verse that read "Therefore, just as through one man sin entered into the world, and death through sin, and so death spread to all men, because all sinned ---. "Rom-Rd 5 was beside the 8th verse that read "But God demonstrates His own love toward us, in that while we were yet sinners, Christ died for us."

He turned the page, looking for "Rom Rd – 4". He found it beneath the last verse in the 6th chapter. "For the wages of sin is death but the free gift of God is eternal life in Christ Jesus our Lord."

It was obvious that these verses were marked so as to be read in order by number. He returned to the one marked "Rom Rd 1" and read them in order:

1. *There is none righteous, not even one.*
2. *For all have sinned and fall short of the glory of God.*
3. *Therefore just as through one man sin entered into the world, and death through sin, and so death spread to all men because all sinned....*
4. *For the wages of sin is death but the free gift of God is eternal life in Christ Jesus our Lord.*
5. *But God demonstrates His own love toward us, in that while we were yet sinners, Christ died for us.*
6. *For whoever will call upon the name of the Lord will be saved.*

He closed the Bible and leaned back against the tree. Why had Fred or Ella marked these verses in this manner? He was beginning to think he understood the meaning when Ted rose to his feet and barked. A figure was standing on the hill beside the barn. At first he thought it might be Marks but as the man began to walk down the hill and start down the lane, he could see that it was Chuck Hastings. His first impression was to go and meet the preacher. Ted bounded forward to do just that. McCann, however, remained seated beneath the tree. He placed the Bible beside him on the ground and waited. With Ted trotting along beside him, Hastings walked up.

"This gives new meaning to the term 'Gentleman Farmer'," he said, looking down with a smile. He was dressed in sneakers, jeans, a blue oxford shirt and sleeveless sweater. Without being asked, he sat down beside McCann, glancing down at the Bible and then looking out across the fields.

"I guess you could say that I am enjoying the fruit of my labors, except I don't have any fruit yet," McCann replied.

"I don't blame you a bit! What a glorious day! The Bible says 'This is the Day that the Lord has made; I will rejoice and be glad in it!' I see you are reading the Word today too!"

McCann picked up the Bible between them and held it. He flipped it open and thumbed until he came to Romans. "Someone did a lot of marking in it. I thought you were supposed to treat the Bible more respectfully!" He said, pointing to one of the notations.

"Fred and Ella were always making notes in their Bible. Ah! The 'Roman Road'!" the minister said, leaning over to see where McCann's finger was pointing.

"What is that?" he asked.

"The Roman Road to Salvation" Hastings responded. "Six verses in Romans that present the good news of the gospel of Jesus Christ, God's plan for our lives!"

McCann shifted uneasily and looked away from the minister. "As I said before, I don't think I'm a candidate for the process."

Hastings looked away as well and smiled warmly. "Ah, but I think you are Wils! We all are. It depends on whether we decide to make the election to become a serious candidate. When we do, God answers. You have done some rather good things since coming to Farnsworth. That tells me that you may be a better candidate than you think."

"I presume you saw your latest convert painting my buildings?" McCann asked.

"I did indeed. In fact that is why I came out today. I needed to talk to Nick about the wedding on Saturday. As long as I was here, I thought I'd see how you were doing. As I remember, I found you in the fields on my last visit."

"They call it 'becoming one with the land'."

Hastings rose and McCann did as well. The minister turned to face him. "What you did for Jim and Lona Marks and what you are doing for Nick Hardesty were acts of great kindness. I also understand that you have been helpful to the Warners on a decision that they are praying and seeking God's will on."

McCann lowered his gaze. "It seems as if I am under the magnifying glass whatever I do. Thus far, at least three people, yourself included, have tried to analyze me. I'm not sure if I like my every move and motive being questioned."

Hastings studied McCann carefully before he responded.

"I'm sorry if that offends you, Wils, but you have made a positive impression on many people in the community in a very short time. By your own admission, you are seeking to find a sense of purpose for your life. There are several people in Farnsworth who would like to help you find that purpose."

"No hard feelings, Chuck. It's just that everyone I talk to lately seems to feel that I need to 'find Jesus 'as the cure to my needs."

"That is something I pray for you and for all who come to our community not knowing Him. God will work that out in His own time if you are open to it. In the meantime, I'll continue to pray and offer my friendship and a listening ear when you need one."

"Sally McHugh said much the same thing about two hours ago," McCann said, as they started to walk back toward the house.

Hastings smiled broadly "Ah yes! Sally McHugh. She is another whom I pray for."

"Sally says that she enjoys life," McCann responded.

"I am sure she does. She is a good mother and a good businesswoman and has a very lively personality. Unfortunately, her lifestyle does have a bit of a wild side to it!"

"You seem to be blessed with two ' sinners' to occupy your prayer life — Sally and me!" McCann replied.

"Yes. Two people that have some very good and admirable qualities who I pray will find a personal relationship with the Savior." The minister replied as they climbed the rise to the barn. Nick Hardesty had completed the east and south walls of the granary and was half way down the west side. "See you Saturday, Pastor," he called from his step ladder.

"I'm looking forward to it, Nick!" Hastings called back.

The two men walked to Hastings' car and the minister opened the door. "May I offer a brief prayer before I go?"

"Please do," McCann replied.

"Father, I thank you for Wils and for his life. I pray that you will guide him to the answers he is seeking and that you will lead him to a path of full and complete relationship with you. Amen."

"Come again, Chuck", McCann said, extending his hand.

"I shall," Hastings replied, as he got in his car and started the engine. McCann watched as he backed down the drive and drove away.

Ted rubbed his muzzle against McCann's leg. McCann scratched his ears and together they headed for the house, the Harms' Bible held in his left hand.

(13)

As he stepped inside, the phone began to ring. He recognized the voice of the senior partner of the Chicago firm that handled his personal finances and investments.

"Wilson, I have just been informed that you plan to move $11 million into your cash account. I must seriously advise against this. You are selling some investments that, while their return is not what we would have hoped for are none the less above what you might achieve anywhere else. You also do not need the tax losses that these sales will create!"

"Max, I appreciate your concern for my interests, but I want that money liquid and I want it done as quickly as possible," he said firmly.

"Am I entitled to know what you are planning to do with it?" Max's voice had lost none of its concern.

"Ever heard of Farnsworth Telephone Coop?" McCann asked, smiling to himself as he imagined Max punching the name into his desk-top computer.

"It's not listed! Is it a private company?"

"Family owned."

"Family owned? Wilson what are you doing?" Max's voice had risen two octaves.

"I plan to make some investments and I need to get liquid to do that. Max, I have trusted you and you have always taken care of my interests. Let's just say that those interests have changed."

The resignation was heavy in Max's voice. "As you say, but I still strongly advise against this course of action."

"Thank you Max, and don't worry so much." McCann said lightly. He hung up the phone and thought of calling Donna but thought better of it. If she wasn't feeling well, her father might answer and McCann was sure he would not be pleasant to talk to.

He sat down in the recliner and put his feet up. He thought over the day's events and his talk with Belle Warner. He thought of Sally McHugh and her "wild" lifestyle. Lastly, he thought of Chuck Hastings and his prayer. "Quite an assortment of acquaintances I have here, Ted," he said to the dog who was curled up beside the chair. Ted didn't bother to raise his head.

Jim Marks poked his head in the back door at 5:00 p.m. to tell him that both fields were seeded. McCann thanked him and asked him in but Marks said he was in a hurry to get home. Nick Hardesty poked his head in the back door a few moments later to tell him that the shed and the granary were done and that he would start on the barn in the morning if McCann was satisfied with his work. The two went out and looked both buildings over. McCann was pleased with the work and said so. The young man grinned with pleasure.

"Have you found a place to stay?" McCann asked.

"I'm on my way to see Donna. She and Darcy have been looking this evening," Nick replied.

"She must be feeling better," McCann said.

"I didn't know she was sick," Nick replied, as he got into the Mustang. He drove off in a small cloud of blue smoke, leaving McCann standing in the driveway scratching his head.

Early the next morning, the phone rang and McCann received the report of the private investigator in Detroit. He took several notes and told the man where to send his bill. He needed a lawyer and thought for a moment of calling Arthur Boyington's firm in Detroit. He decided against it. "Possible conflict of interest there," he thought. Instead, he called an attorney in Chicago who had handled several of his personal affairs as well as some minor work for Dynacom. He outlined what he wanted done and asked that he be informed as to the status by Tuesday morning.

As soon as he hung up the phone, it rang. It was Doug Warner.

"Good morning, Wils. I wanted to get back to you and to thank you for talking with the Board yesterday."

"Glad to do it Doug. What was the reaction?"

"Probably what you might expect. Joe and George are all out against the idea. Arthur feels we should proceed to draw up a plan. Phil and Fred wanted to give it some additional thought. We are to re-convene next Wednesday."

"Anything more I can do?" McCann asked.

"Is there anything you can share about the consortium?" Warner asked, hopefully.

"Let me talk to Stu and see where they are at and I'll get back to you."

"Thanks…and Wils?"

"Yes?"

"I wanted to apologize for Joe Rambaugh's comments yesterday. They were uncalled for and I wanted you to know I told him so after you and mother left."

"No problem. I enjoyed having lunch with your mother. She is quite a lady!" McCann replied.

"She said you had a pretty good discussion. I think she has taken a liking to you."

"I have for her as well." McCann said, smiling to himself.

He hung up the phone and, thinking of Donna, called the store. Darcy answered and said that Donna was busy at the moment so he said he would call back. Forty minutes later, the cattle feeder from Hemlock, Michigan, called to advise that the cattle would be delivered on Monday morning and that, "on Mr. Priestly's recommendation," he would accept a personal check in payment. McCann thanked him and assured him that everything was ready for their arrival.

He hung up the phone and called Donna again. She answered on the first ring.

"Are you feeling better?" he asked cheerfully.

"I'm fine," she replied tersely.

He could feel the iciness in her voice. He tried again.

"I came by yesterday but Darcy said you weren't feeling well and had left early."

"I'm fine," she said again.

"Donna, is something wrong?"

"No. Should there be?" The icy tone remained.

"You sound sort of … upset. Did I do something wrong?"

"What you do does not concern me, Wils. By the way, we found a place for Nick and Darcy and Damon. So you won't be inconvenienced. You can entertain at will. Now I am very busy and must go."

McCann felt his frustration rising. What was going on here? He tried again.

"I was wondering if we could have dinner tonight somewhere."

"I'm sorry, we have rehearsal practice for the wedding tomorrow. Perhaps one of your other friends could entertain you. Good bye, Wilson." With that, she hung up.

McCann slammed the phone back in its cradle and, for the first time in two weeks, he swore.

The phone rang again and he snatched it up, hoping it was Donna. A very professional woman's voice advised him that his Chicago attorney would need a Power of Attorney to execute the documents he wanted and that she would e-mail a form to him immediately. She asked if he could sign it and fax it back. He told her that he had an electronic signature in his lap-top and would affix it and e-mail it back to her. She was pleased and thanked him. He hung up the phone again and stood waiting for it to ring again. It didn't. He turned the lap-top on and went outside. He walked aimlessly around the yard. Nick Hardesty watched him from the top of a twenty foot aluminum extension ladder. McCann ceased his pacing and looked up.

"I understand you found a place to stay," he said.

Hardesty descended the ladder and stood dusting the paint scrapings out of his hair. "Yeah, Donna and Darcy found a little house on the south side of town. I just hope I can keep the rent up."

"That's good. Nick, did Donna say anything about me?" McCann watched as Nick shuffled his feet and looked away.

"Well, no ... not exactly."

"What do you mean, 'not exactly'?" McCann asked, boring in. Nick looked down at his feet and scratched his ear.

"She came back to the store yesterday in a huff. Later, she told Darcy that you hadn't changed a bit and she never wanted to see you again. Wils, what did you do? Donna's never like that!"

McCann stood there, soaking it in. Suddenly an idea came to him. "Nick, you said she came back to the store and was upset. Did Darcy say where she had been?"

"Yeah, she had seen your truck parked down by the Diner and decided to go down and meet you there. Darcy said she hadn't been gone five minutes when she came back and said she was going home. Darcy called her later to see if she felt good enough to go look at the house and she said she was 'over it' - whatever had made her feel bad."

For the second time in the last hour, McCann swore. Nick turned away and looked up at the barn.

McCann put his hand on Nick's shoulder. "Sorry, Nick. I apologize for that. I need to go into town. Keep up the good work. It looks like the barn is going to take a full coat of primer and a couple of coats of paint. That old wood is just like a sponge. Don't work too late. You need to get ready for your rehearsal."

Nick watched him go, the Ranger's back tires spitting gravel. "One day he's walking in the fields with a Bible and talking to the Pastor. The next, he's getting Donna all upset and cussing up a storm. I guess it's none of my business, Ted," he said. Ted wagged his tail and watched as Nick climbed back up the ladder and resumed his scraping.

Joe Rambaugh sat back in his leather desk chair and looked out the window at the main street of Farnsworth. The most recent monthly dealership report lay on his desk. The results were even worse than the previous month. Joe's theory was that the service shop should cover the operating expenses of the dealership and any used vehicle losses. That way, the profits on new vehicle sales would flow directly to the bottom line and into his pocket. For five years, the plan had worked. For the last fourteen months, the results were mixed and most months were like this one, declining new car sales and declining service work. This was the fifth straight month with a loss. Car sales across the country were down and the trade media was openly questioning Chrysler's plan to reverse its fortunes. In a small town like Farnsworth, the importance of regular returning customers was critical. Lately, some of the regulars hadn't been returning and were driving their vehicles an extra two or three years due to their own financial situation. All in all, the next few months didn't look much more promising than the last five.

The finance company that handled his floor planning had called that morning. His floor-planning note was due in two weeks. His building and the Farnsworth Telephone Coop stock were pledged as collateral for the money needed to pay for new car inventory and to cover operating losses beyond the normal floor-planning period allowed under his relationship with the auto maker. Now, Doug Warner wanted to embark on some wild goose chase that would probably mean a decline in the book value of the Coop stock. The stock was worth $4.5 million based on the latest Farnsworth audited financials. He could borrow $2.7 million based on that value. He needed to either renew or make a payment on the $3 million floor-planning note. At the rate things were going, what with the economy in the toilet and no one coming into the show room or to the service desk, he would need another half million by the end of the year just to keep operating.

He had thought of calling Warner and offering to sell the Farnsworth shares. But Warner wouldn't pay beyond book value at best and probably not that. The Coop would need all its cash if their Board decided to pursue this acquisition. He silently cursed Wilson McCann for showing up now to offer encouragement to Warner.

He and George Whyte had both raised opposition to the Board's consideration of the proposal. But, the bottom line was that the Warners controlled 80% of the stock and Phil Willard sure wasn't going to oppose his church-going friends! He wasn't sure where Penay stood on the idea but probably the banker would go along. After all, the Warners and McCann both did business with the bank. Rambaugh kept his payables account with the Farnsworth State Bank but all of his investments and savings were with a big bank in Detroit. There wouldn't be a lot of concern at Farnsworth State Bank for his problem. He thought of calling Boyington to see where he stood but the lawyer would probably not be very forthcoming outside of the boardroom.

He watched as Wilson McCann sped by in Fred Harms' old Ranger. He had heard that McCann left Dynacom with millions in his pocket and here he was in this one-light town driving a twelve year old truck. There just wasn't any justice!

One block further west and on the other side of the street, George Whyte was having similar yet different thoughts as he surveyed the financial statement he had just pulled off his computer. Sales were flat, service revenues were actually up on a month-to-month basis and he had no debts to worry about. The three town houses that he owned west of town were all rented and had been for two years. It was the Farnsworth Telephone Coop stock that worried Whyte, but not for the same reasons as Rambaugh. He had picked up the stock for just under $1 million. It now had a book value in excess of $4 million. Whyte picked up the copies of the overheads that Wilson McCann had used in his presentation to the Farnsworth Tele Board. Whyte reasoned that if he owned 10% of the stock, he owned 10% of the access lines that the Coop served. McCann had used a number of $5,000 per access line as a potential acquisition price for the LEGENT properties. If Whyte could sell his 10%, it was worth $7.5 million at that rate. The problem was how to get it! He knew Doug Warner wouldn't pay that much and there was no one that he knew with that kind of money. He believed that the value of the Farnsworth Telephone Coop would be diluted by Warner's plan to go after the LEGENT properties. If that happened, his investment might only be worth $2 million at best.

Whyte scratched his head as he muddled the problem over in his mind. Who would pay a reasonable price for the stock? It was clearly time to divest himself of it and put the money somewhere else. In George Whyte's shrewd mind, there was only one rule that worked: "Get yours while the getting is good."

He rose and walked into the showroom that fronted on Main Street. Wilson McCann sped by in his old pickup. Suddenly an idea formed in Whyte's mind. McCann supposedly had money. If he thought $5,000 per access line was the right price for the LEGENT properties that Warner wanted, perhaps he might think that a 10% ownership in Farnsworth Tele was a good investment.

Whyte smiled to himself as he walked back to his office. He would call Doug Warner this afternoon and offer his 10% interest for $6 million. He knew Warner wouldn't be able to meet it and that would allow him to turn to McCann. If things went the way he felt they would, he could be rid of a big concern and pocket a tidy sum at the same time. Let McCann put his money where his mouth was. He would find out soon enough that the "players" weren't just in Chicago or New York!

He had never told her that he loved her. It wasn't that he didn't love her. He did. It was just that it was so hard for him to express himself in that way. He was proud of her. Her indiscretions of the past were long forgiven. He wished that they could sit down and talk about faith in God and religion and how to worship the Lord without always seeming to disagree.

Ed Barnes leaned back against the pillows. He could hear the housekeeper, Florence, moving about in the living room below him. He probably should get up and brush his teeth and go down and sit in his favorite chair and look out the window. He had read the morning paper and The Upper Room devotional for the day. He liked to remain here in his bedroom until Donna had gone off to the store in the morning. She always brought him his breakfast and gave him a peck on the forehead before leaving. Why was it so hard to tell someone that you loved them?

He hadn't gone to church on a regular basis for almost a year. He had gone at Easter and it had just about done him in. He missed the old hymns and the Apostles Creed and reading the scripture responsively. The minister at the Presbyterian Church wasn't a great speaker. In fact, he was sort of dull in Ed's opinion. But, preaching wasn't what it was all about anyway. It was the reverence he felt when he entered the old church and heard the organ play "Amazing Grace" or "All Hail the Power of Jesus Name" or some other hymn. No drums and guitars for him! He knew that Donna enjoyed the United Methodist Church with its new music and the minister who often sat on a stool to speak. Where was the reverence in that?

Yet, deep down in his heart, he was happy that she had come back to the church even if it wasn't his church. He looked fondly at the old Dickson Bible that lay on his lamp table beside the bed. He had just read this morning in 1st Corinthians how Paul had rebuked the church in Corinth for division. Paul had said that it was God who gave the increase. Surely that was true in his daughter's case. He knew that she would not have come to a strong faith in God through Christ based upon his own faith. He had made many mistakes in trying to raise a teenage girl alone. But that was past and he was glad for the happiness that radiated from her when she returned from church each Sunday and from her small group Bible study each Wednesday night.

He thought of the pain he had seen in her eyes last night. It had something to do with this man McCann, he was sure. McCann had been the source of her hurt many years ago and now he had returned. Ed had heard bits and pieces about the man over the years. He had risen to power in a large corporation and then made a grab for even more power and had failed. Now, he had come to Farnsworth to lick his wounds. And now Donna was sad again. He knew that she loved this man. He had seen it in her face when she was young and he had seen it again just last week when she came home from helping McCann on his farm. He had prayed for McCann's salvation each night before he went to sleep. Last night, Donna had come home almost in tears. Ed was sure it had to do with McCann. Last night he had prayed even more fervently that God would work out His plan for Donna and for this stranger that had come back into her life. He felt frustrated that he couldn't do something. But all he could do was sit here and look out the window and pray.

"There is something I can do," he thought, "something I have never done." With that, he reached for the pad of paper that lay beside the Bible. He used it to make notes to himself of things to try to remember. At least he hadn't gotten to the place where he didn't remember what the notes meant!

He took his pen and began to write slowly. The emotion of his writing brought tears to his eyes and his heart began to beat a little faster. He continued on, the pen scratching over the paper. Word after word, long held back, began to flow under his hand. His emotions were driving him now in a way that they hadn't for many years. He found himself breathing more heavily as he wrote.

When the first pain hit, he ignored it and kept writing. When the second surge hit, he leaned back against the pillows and took a deep breath. He had finished what he wanted to say. With one final effort, he signed the paper, "Dad."

When the third pain hit, his fingers released the pen which fell to the covers. His head fell back against the pillows and his eyes closed as if in sleep. He had told his daughter that he loved her, for the first and last time.

The pad lay on his covers. The single page read:

My Darling Daughter:

I love you! I have wanted to tell you that so many times and just couldn't seem to say the words. I am so very proud of you and I know that your mother would be too. I am thankful that, while our methods of worship may differ, we serve and love the same Savior.

I want you to know that I am praying for you and for your happiness. I am praying that God will work out his plan for your life in a wonderfully abundant way. I want you to know that whatever happens along the way, God loves you and I love you. I am sorry that it has taken me so long to tell you how much I care.

Dad

Donna was straightening some sweaters on a rack near the doorway to the storage room at the back of the store when McCann came in. He strode toward her and she turned to face him. The jut of his jaw and the look in his eyes told her that he was upset. She raised a hand in reflex, "Wilson, I don't want to talk…"

He grabbed her elbow and spun her around and through the doorway into the storage room. He kicked the door shut behind them and spun her around to face him.

"How dare you…!" she said sharply, putting both hands on his chest to push him away. She could hear the phone ringing in the store and Darcy moving to answer it.

"I dare because I care!" he said it quietly but firmly as she struggled to free herself. "I care more for you than you will ever know. I will do anything I have to if it means not losing you! If friendship is all that we can have, than I won't lose that!"

He pulled her to him and kissed her. At first, she continued to try to push him away. Then, as he held her, she put her arms around his neck and returned his kiss.

As Darcy opened the door she saw them together. With any other phone call, she would never have intruded. But she knew this was different.

"Donna … it's Florence at the house. She just found your Dad…she called 911…you better go home now!"

(14)

The EMT told Donna that it was a massive heart attack. He tried his best to assure her that her father hadn't lingered, that the attack had been sudden and final. They had tried to revive her father but it was to no avail. McCann called Belle Warner and she arrived within ten minutes. McCann called the funeral home and arranged to have the body taken away. He sat in the living room opposite Donna and Belle who sat together on the sofa. This was the first time he had ever been inside this house. They had always met somewhere away from the house where her father wouldn't make a scene. The few occasions that he had met Ed Barnes had not gone well. He sat with his hands clasped between his knees. Belle had one arm around Donna's shoulders and her other hand held Donna's. She sat quietly, her head bowed.

The funeral director and his assistant arrived quickly and McCann took them upstairs. As the body was moved from the bed, he stood against the window looking out on the street. As he turned, he saw a pen and pad lying on the floor. In the rush of the EMTs' work, they had been brushed aside. He bent to retrieve them and saw the note. He started to read and realized his mistake. He laid the pen next to the old Bible and followed the other men down the stairs. The director returned to ask Donna to come to the funeral home to discuss final arrangements as soon as she felt up to it. McCann waited on the front porch until the hearse drove away. He took the pad inside and walked to where the two women sat. He squatted down in front of Donna and gave her the pad.

"This was on the floor beside the bed," he said quietly, handing it to her.

She took the pad and read what was written on it. Her head sagged forward and sobs racked her body "Oh Daddy! Oh Daddy! Oooooh!" she wailed as Belle Warner wrapped both arms around her and pulled Donna to her. She continued to sob into Belle's shoulder. McCann rose and looked into Belle's eyes.

"Is there anything I can do?" he asked.

"Please stay a while," Belle said. "She will need all the support we can give her."

And so he stayed through the rest of the morning and into the afternoon. Phil and Martha Willard came for a while and sat and talked quietly with them. Lori Warner came in the middle of the afternoon with food and Lona Marks came shortly thereafter. The two younger women took Belle's place on the sofa and flanked Donna.

Later, Reverend Halford, the Presbyterian minister came and went, soon joined by several elderly men and women, apparently friends of Ed's from the Presbyterian Church. Towards evening, Darcy, Nick and the baby came. Belle said she would stay the night and went home to get her things. One by one, the others expressed their condolences and left. Only Phil and Martha Willard remained when Donna rose and went into the kitchen. Lori had started a pot of coffee earlier and Donna poured herself a fresh cup as McCann stood in the doorway.

"Donna...I'm so sorry...about today...I mean...I had no right..." He stammered, bracing himself against the doorway as she looked at him.

"What you said... in the store.....did you mean it?" She regarded him quietly, her eyes red rimmed and puffy.

"I had no right to treat you that way. I am so sorry ...."

"Did you mean it?" She looked down at her mug of coffee.

"Every word," he said quietly.

She put the cup down on the counter and crossed the room to where he stood. Wrapping her arms around him, she put her head on his chest. He held her close.

"Just hold me," was all she said.

Belle Warner had entered through the front door quietly. She saw them standing there in the doorway to the kitchen. She quickly stepped into the living room and waited, her head bowed in prayer.

Nick and Darcy were married the next morning. Chris Warner stepped in to be Maid of Honor in Donna's place and Cheryl and her mother hosted a quiet reception in the church fellowship hall. Donna came just long enough to hug the bride and kiss the groom. McCann shook hands with Nick and told Darcy how pretty she was and then he drove Donna back to the funeral home. Visiting hours were set for 5:00 p.m. A Steady procession of Ed's friends from the Presbyterian Church, community businessmen and women, and Donna's friends from the UMC came and went. McCann felt badly out of place and found himself spending much of the afternoon and evening in a small alcove off the main viewing area. During a lull, Donna came and sat down on a chair next to him. She took a folded piece of paper from her pocket and handed it to him. He recognized the page from the pad he had found in Ed's bedroom. He read it and looked at her, waiting for her to speak.

Tears welled up in her eyes. "He told me he loved me. He never had said that to me before."

"His generation kept things pretty much inside." McCann offered quietly.

"Did your father…I mean?"

"No. I don't remember him ever saying that he loved me," McCann said, looking down at the floor. "You are very fortunate to have that letter. It was his 'going home' gift to you."

"I wish… I wish we could have talked more…you know?" She said, looking out the small window at the back of the room.

"I know."

The funeral was at 10:00 a.m. on Monday at the Presbyterian Church. The Reverend Halford presided and Chuck Hastings gave the Invocation and Benediction. McCann had arranged to have the delivery of his beef cattle delayed one day. The Presbyterian Church Ladies Group served a dinner in the church basement following the graveside services and McCann excused himself and went up the stairs to the entrance door. Doug Warner fell in beside him and they walked out to the street together.

"Got a minute?" Warner asked.

"Sure. What's up?" McCann responded.

"George Whyte called me Friday afternoon and offered to sell his 10%

interest back to the company for $6 million." Warner watched for McCann's reaction.

"Not asking much, is he?" McCann smiled.

"More than we could pay. He thinks the LEGENT acquisition is a mistake and wants out before he loses out."

"Sounds like George," McCann responded, waiting.

"I'm worried, Wils. If George sells to some outsider, it could make everything a lot more difficult. At least George was here in Farnsworth."

"The Board meets tomorrow?" McCann asked.

"Yes. We, mother and I that is, have prayed and we feel we should go forward. I have talked with Phil and he feels the same. I think Fred and Art will go along. I'm sure Joe and George will vote against it. I plan to push ahead anyway. I'll call you after the Board meeting to make arrangements to meet with you and representatives of the consortium."

"Sounds good," McCann smiled. He turned to face Warner. "What is it you 'born again' believers say? 'The Lord will provide!' isn't that it?"

Warner smiled, "Yes, I guess we do!"

McCann started to turn away and said, "You gotta believe."

Doug Warner scratched his head as McCann walked away down the street towards his pick up. He wasn't quite sure what to think about Wilson McCann. One thing he was sure of, McCann must have ice water in his veins!

The cattle arrived on Tuesday in two trucks. The younger of the two drivers handed McCann a leather pouch stuffed with papers and asked for a check before the unloading began. The older man knelt and began to pet Ted. He looked up at McCann, a broad smile on his face.

"A fine dog you have here, Mr. McCann. He'll do well with these cattle!" he said in a voice with a heavy brogue to it as he rose and extended his hand. "My name is McIntyre and I know dogs!"

McCann took his hand and smiled. "I don't know about Ted. He was here when I arrived."

"Ah! Ted is it? Well now, we will have to see what you're made of Laddie!"

he said as he stooped to ruffle the fur on Ted's back. The dog wagged his tail expectantly.

McCann tendered the check and the cattle were unloaded into the barn-yard. Several went immediately to the water tank and began to drink. Others ran into the pasture and, with their tails high, began to run wildly about. Ted crouched next to McIntyre, his head on his paws and his tail extended straight out behind him as if expecting a command. McIntyre reached into the cab of the truck and took out a hard wood cane. With the dog following, he walked through the barn yard and out into the field.

McCann and the younger man watched as McIntyre, with a series of low calls, whistles and gestures proceeded to put Ted through his paces. The dog quickly gathered three of the steers and drove them back into the barnyard. Then, at McIntyre's direction, he raced back into the field and cut out one steer from a group of four and brought it in as well. McIntyre patted the dog and made a fuss over him as they walked back to where the two men stood.

"Amazing!" McCann said, extending his hand in congratulations. "I didn't know he had it in him! I'm afraid I do not have your skills, however."

"Easily learned if you're interested in learning," McIntyre responded.

The younger man interrupted. "I have to be going. All of the registration and inoculation papers are in the pouch, together with the bill of sale and the tag numbers. I think you will find everything in order."

"Thank you. I appreciate your help," McCann responded. "Mr. McIntyre, do you have time to give me a lesson?"

"Aye, that I do and happy to do it!" boomed the Scotsman in reply.

The first truck drove out and down the road as the two men and the dog walked back to the field. For nearly an hour, McIntyre instructed McCann on how to direct Ted through various calls, whistles and gestures. By the time he was done, Ted was panting heavily and the cattle were grazing peacefully.

McCann was by no means an expert but his knowledge had been greatly increased.

"I have a small book on the subject that I will send you," McIntyre said, as he enjoyed a cup of coffee in the kitchen. He took down McCann's address as he regaled him with stories of other dogs and other places for ten minutes before looking at his watch and draining his mug.

"I'd best be going. I sometimes get to visiting and forget about the time. Some folks are always in a hurry to get to the next place or the next rung on the ladder. Me, I like to stop and look around a wee bit and visit a while. But, I have a job to do as well so I'd best be getting to it!" he said as he headed for the door. Before climbing back into his truck he handed McCann the cane.

"I have others. It's my gift to you and the dog. I can see you're a man with a quick mind. Your dog is a quick one too. It won't be but a few days and you will be sitting on your back porch while your Teddy does all the work! Good luck to you now!" With that, he drove away leaving McCann and Ted standing in the yard together.

"A very remarkable man," McCann said to Ted as they watched the truck go down the road. Ted wagged his tail in agreement. He considered the two men he had just met. One was very efficient and didn't even offer his hand or his name in friendship. The other had shared not only his hand and his name but his knowledge, his friendship and his love of life. McCann knew that up until a few weeks ago, he had been like the younger man. He hoped that he might put that part of his life behind him and be more like McIntyre. He would have to work at it.

McCann had been so taken with McIntyre and his work with Ted that he hadn't really looked closely at the cattle. He walked back into the field and quietly walked among them, Ted trotting quietly behind him, waiting to see if anything was needed of him. McCann could tell that the twenty steers were prime beef. Ray Priestly had seen to that, no doubt about it.

As he headed back toward the barn, Donna's Forester drove up the road and into the drive. Ted raced ahead and she was standing at the gate with the dog as McCann came up out of the field. She opened the gate and he stepped through it and took her in his arms. He buried his face in her hair and asked quietly, "How are you doing?"

She leaned against him, her voice muffled in his shirt front. "Better. Thanks to good friends like you and Belle and others."

She wrapped her arms around his waist and they stood there in the sunshine. Ted sat beside them. The cattle grazed peacefully in the pasture and

Wilson McCann thought that he had never been this happy and so much at peace in his whole life.

At the Farnsworth Telephone Cooperative, things were anything but peaceful. After what had been a long, loud and contentious Board meeting, Belle and Doug Warner, together with Phil Willard and Fred Penay, knelt in prayer beside their chairs in the conference room. Outside on the street, Arthur Boyington walked away down the street to his car while George Whyte and Joe Rambaugh stood under one of the oaks. Rambaugh's face was still red from his outbursts during the meeting and George Whyte was grim.

"It's going to be a disaster!" Rambaugh said loudly. "They're going to lose the company! We'll lose everything we've put into this! What can we do?"

Whyte looked down the street after the lawyer. He rubbed his hand across his face and turned to face the frustrated auto dealer. "Well, I can tell you what I am going to do. I am going to sell my interest to the highest bidder and I'm going to do it before word of this gets out."

"To who? The Warner's have right of first refusal and they can't pay what it's worth. They'll need every cent just to try to do this crazy acquisition scheme of theirs!" Rambaugh responded, his voice rising.

"I've already offered my shares to the Warners and they have refused to buy them at the price I offered, which was a reasonable price based on current acquisition costs as was quoted by the wonderful Wilson McCann himself," Whyte replied, smiling for the first time. "I suggest you do the same."

He went on to explain to Rambaugh how he had arrived at his offer price of $6 million for his ten per cent interest. Rambaugh scratched his head reflectively. "At that price, I could pay off my floor plan loan and have enough left to get me by until this economic situation we're in starts to get better," he said thoughtfully, his voice quiet for the first time in the last hour. He looked at Whyte and a frown began to gather at the corners of his mouth. "But who's gonna buy the shares? There's no market for them!"

"I've already talked to a broker who handles acquisitions for the larger 'aggregators' as McCann calls them." Whyte responded. "He is interested in talking further. Do you want to go together on this?"

"By all means," Rambaugh replied, "by all means."

The two walked down the sidewalk together, discussing possible maximum and minimum prices for their shares. Back inside the conference room, the four remaining Board members rose as one and sat again in their chairs.

"Mom, with your permission, I'd like to call Wils McCann and get this started," Doug said, looking at his mother.

She smiled and looked at Willard and Penay. "Go ahead. I believe Mr. McCann is a man of great integrity and that he can be of great assistance to us. I would like to suggest that we remember to pray that he will also become a man of the Lord's leading." The others nodded.

Meanwhile, in New York City, a FEDEX delivery arrived at Stu Bailey's offices. It contained the bid package for the sale of LEGENT'S operations in the Mid-West.

Donna stepped back and looked up at McCann. "I've brought you a gift," She said, smiling.

They walked to the Forester. She opened the rear door and took out a gray Stetson hat and a denim jacket with sheepskin lining. McCann smiled as he took them and tried the hat on. "Do I look like Clint Eastwood in 'Unforgiven'?" he asked.

"More like Gene Autry in 'Melody Ranch'. It's going to get cold soon and you'll need that jacket. The hat is just to recognize your transition from desk jockey to cattle herder."

"You should have brought a hat for Ted. He's the real herder! You should have been here earlier. A man named McIntyre came with the cattle and put Ted through his paces. He has talents none of us knew about."

"McIntyre? I've heard of a man named McIntyre who always does well at the Scottish/Irish festivals in the sheep dog trials," she replied, looking at Ted and bending down to scratch his ears.

"Must be the same, he was amazing! So was Ted."

"The touch of the Master's hand ..." she murmured.

"What?"

"There is a story about an old violin that was to be auctioned off as part of an estate. When it came time to bid, there was only a bid of a dollar or so until an old man picked it up and played a beautiful piece on it. It sold for thousands. When someone asked what made the difference, the auctioneer replied that it was "the touch of the master's hand" that brought forth its true worth. Ted's abilities were brought out when a master dog handler put him through his paces. I believe that it is the same as what God's touch can do for each of us. "

"Well, I hope what he was able to teach me in less than an hour will rub off a little," McCann said, wanting to change the subject.

Donna sensed his uneasiness and looked out at the barn with its unfinished paint job. "Where is Nick?" she asked.

"I gave him two days off.....with pay. He's due back tomorrow." McCann replied.

"I think I will take some time off too." Donna turned to face him.

McCann tensed, sensing that there was something more coming. "Well, that might be good for you," he said quietly, waiting.

"I've decided to take a month and go on a Work and Witness Mission for the church," she said, looking into his eyes. The disappointment was clear. He looked away over the pasture before he spoke.

"I'll miss you. When will you go?"

"Not for a month or so. I need to place orders for the Christmas season and get Darcy ready to run the store while I am gone. Oh! I brought something else I know you'll appreciate! I almost forgot!"

She reached in the front seat and brought out a Dunkin Donuts bag and held it up. He smiled and the two of them walked to the back porch, hand in hand. She sat and produced the two donuts and two cups of coffee from the bag. They ate and drank in silence, neither ready to go back to the subject of her leaving. She cupped her hands around the coffee and sipped, looking out past the barn. He looked down at his feet and asked the question that was uppermost in his mind.

"Donna, I need to talk to you about something," he said quietly.

"Go ahead," she said, anticipating what might be coming.

"I've told you that I care deeply for you, more than I've ever cared about anyone. During the last few days I've begun to sense that you care more for me than you have been willing to let on. I guess I need to know where we stand."

He waited, his heart hammering against his ribs as she took another sip from her coffee and glanced over at the Buick, resting on its two flat tires. "Wilson, I have loved you from the first summer we met. I have never stopped loving you in my heart. I love you today more than any other human being. But…"

"But what?" he asked, looking at her.

A tear formed at the corner of one eye and she looked down before brushing it away. "I love Jesus more," she said quietly.

"I know that. It's one of the reasons I care so much for you."

She placed her left hand on his right arm. "You use the word 'care' Wils. Do you love me?"

He knew at that moment that he had to be as honest as he had ever been with another person in his life. He took a deep breath before he spoke.

"I don't know what love is. I don't know whether this feeling I have for you is love or not. I have always had to take care of myself. I never had time to get beyond caring. I…"

"Wils, did you love Dynacom?" she interrupted him.

"What kind of a question is that?" He said it in frustration and stood with his back to her. She remained where she was.

"Wils, you have shared your feelings about Dynacom and what happened. I think you loved that company and the power and the prestige that went with your position. I think that was love."

He turned to face her, his face was angry now. "And that was wrong?"

She looked up and he saw the love in her eyes. "No, it wasn't wrong in itself. The fact that you let it block out your ability to love anything or anyone else was, in my opinion, wrong."

He turned away again. She had touched the nerve that he thought had healed. He fought to control his emotions as his thoughts raced. Why did every conversation have to turn into this psycho-analysis? Why did it seem that Jesus was a part of almost every conversation he had with other people since he came to this town? He felt like screaming "forget Dynacom and forget all this Jesus stuff!" Instead, he scuffed the dirt with his boot. He heard her rise behind him and felt her arms slip around his waist. Her head was against his back and her voice was muffled as she spoke.

"I love you Wils. But, it can never be more than we have today until you find a way to love God and others the way you loved Dynacom."

And, deep in his heart, he knew that his words had been answered with an honesty that was equal to his own. He turned within the circle of her arms and held her against him. He would later say that it was the moment when he took his first step in a journey to find the real meaning of love.

(15)

The next few weeks sped by in a blur. The cattle added a routine to McCann's life that had been missing since he left Dynacom. It was obvious that Nick, working alone, would not be able to get the entire barn painted before winter set in. McCann discussed it with the young man and they agreed that McCann would have to get involved as well. Doug Warner called to advise him that the Board had decided to pursue the acquisition. McCann made arrangements with Stu Bailey to meet with the Warners and Stu's Wall Street and banking partners to review the request for proposals received from LEGENT. His attorney called to advise him that the work McCann had asked him to do was completed and that they were ready to take the next steps in carrying out his instructions to them. He began to realize that all the things he had set in motion could not be completed without some help. He talked again with Nick and they agreed that Nick would take on the job of caring for the cattle and the day-to-day needs of the farm during McCann's absences when he had to go to New York, Dallas and elsewhere to work on the acquisition. The very next day after their agreement, he came home from lunch with Donna at the Diner to find the LeSabre back on four fully inflated tires and sparkling from bumper to bumper. Nick proceeded to tell him that it was his "gift" to McCann for trusting him with added responsibilities.

On a warm Sunday afternoon, he had an unexpected visitor. McIntyre drove into the yard and the two men spent an hour in the field with Ted, practicing the various commands and gestures. Afterward, they sat in the kitchen drinking iced tea.

"You've the knack for it McCann," McIntyre said. "You must have a little of the Scot in you!"

"I think more Irish than Scottish, although my mother's maiden name was Wallace," McCann replied, smiling.

"Ah! Sir William of 'Braveheart' fame, is it?"

"Well, I don't know about that" McCann said.

"Tell me, do you believe in the heavenly being, Mr. McCann?" The old man's eyes were keen as he asked the question.

"I…believe in God….yes," McCann replied, slowly sipping his tea.

"As do I! And a sorry sight I was before I first believed!" McIntyre said, his gaze not wavering.

"Is that so? Tell me about it," McCann said, leaning back in his chair.

"I was a drunk! I lost my wife and my children and my position as a bookkeeper with one of the stores in Bay City. I was sitting in the park down by the river one night having decided to take my life and put an end to it when a street preacher convinced me that there was still hope. God changed me that night and I have never been the same since. And, I've never taken another drink either!"

McCann eyed the other man. His sincerity was impressive and McCann felt himself drawn to him. "And, just like that you were changed?" he asked.

"Ah no! I had to learn a whole new way of thinking and find a new center for my life. There was many a time when I wondered if I would ever be able to get through the day without a drink. Gradually, as the good Lord changed me, I began to see his plan and gave myself over to it. It took many a month for that to happen."

"But you were 'saved' as they say?" McCann asked.

"Call it what you will, I placed my faith in God through Jesus Christ and he took my life in a whole new direction. I don't have the position or the income I once had but I have my wife back and living in God's great outdoors and my children and their children look at me in a different way now."

McCann drained his glass. "How did you cope with the changes in your work? I mean, you went from an office job to working with cattle and …?"

"Did you ever read the story of the 'Prodigal Son', Mr. McCann?" McIntyre interrupted quietly.

"No, I can't say that I have," McCann replied.

"It's in the Bible, the book of Luke as I recall. This young lad squandered his life and ended up in a pigpen. He realized how low he had sunk and went home to his father asking to be made an ordinary field hand. The father forgave him and welcomed him back with full rights as his son. I'm a lot like that young lad, Mr. McCann, and I suspect that you may be too. But, what is important is that our Heavenly Father never gives up on us and welcomes us home to His loving arms when we realize what we need to do."

"A good lesson, Mr. McIntyre. You are not only a good man with directions to a dog but with well aimed advice for mankind as well." McCann said, extending his hand across the table.

The older man took it and gripped it strongly. "I hope you find your way home lad," he said.

That night, McCann read through the 15th chapter of Luke several times.

He and Donna were together often. Dinners at the farm or at her home in town were followed by watching TV together or playing Scrabble or Cribbage. He told her about McIntyre's visit and his story. She persuaded him to bring Fred and Ella's old Bible with him one evening and she outlined a Bible study that he could do by himself or with her. He felt uneasy committing to do this by himself and they agreed to devote twenty minutes of any evening they were together to it. Once, she asked him to think of joining the small group study that she attended on Thursday evenings but he declined. She did not press the issue nor did she press him to go to Sunday school with her. Instead, they met at the church for the Sunday morning service and sat together. After the service, they joined the Warners, Marks, and Willards for lunch. Cheryl and Chris Warner giggled behind their hands as they saw them get out of McCann's pick up on that first Sunday and Lori Warner admonished them sternly to behave. Phil and Martha Willard added "Wils and Donna's relationship" to their prayer list.

As the days went by, the weather began to change and the leaves began to turn. On the colder mornings, he found the cattle bunched in the shelter of the barn instead of out in the pasture. He and Nick started to paint later each day. The days when they could do so were becoming fewer. Finally, three consecutive days of warm fall weather allowed them to finish and all of the buildings stood resplendent in their new red coats. The pleasure that he took in the changes that he had made since coming here were tempered by his knowledge that, within a few more weeks, Donna would leave for a month.

Stu Bailey called to tell him that the first meeting of the group would be held in New York City the following Monday morning. He called Doug Warner and the two of them made plans to fly out of Detroit's Metropolitan Airport on Saturday to allow time to discuss their respective roles before the meeting with Stu and his team. Doug said that Belle and Arthur Boyington would also be attending. McCann felt exhilaration from the thought of the upcoming week. He had not had this feeling in some time and he was surprised at how much he relished it. He spent the following two evenings working on his computer with the files Bailey had provided and the information he had gathered from Doug Warner. His excitement vanished the next morning when the phone rang.

"I've received my visa and I'm to fly out on Wednesday next week for Prague," she said.

"That's good news…for you," he said, trying to sound enthusiastic as his spirits sagged.

"Will I get to see you before I go?" she asked.

"We fly out of Detroit tomorrow afternoon, could we have dinner tonight?"

"Sure, my house or yours?" she replied.

"Why don't we go up to the lake and eat?" he said, wanting to make it special but not really feeling it.

"That would be nice, Wils. Will you pick me up in the LeSabre?"

"Ah! The Ranger isn't good enough for you anymore?" He smiled into the phone as he said it.

"When I'm going out, I like to go in style!" She laughed.

"I'll pick you up at 5:30 p.m., that should give us time to try to find a place that's open this time of year," he said.

After calling three different restaurants in Caseville, he found one that was still open and made a reservation for 6:30 p.m. The excitement he had felt earlier had been replaced by the empty feeling that he wasn't going to see Donna for at least a month. He went out to check on the cattle and leaned against the gate to the barnyard looking out over the pasture. Ted pawed at his leg and waited expectantly.

"Not today, boy, I'm not in the mood for it," he said, scratching Ted's ear.

Ted lay down with his nose on his paws. McCann continued to stare out over the fields. The wheat was a green carpet beyond the pasture. The cattle were grazing on what remained of the summer's grass. The sunshine reflected from the newly painted farm buildings. It was a Norman Rockwell scene that he failed to appreciate. His heart felt like a lump of lead.

(16)

The three men, who walked into the lobby of the Marriott at Perimeter Center East, northeast of Atlanta, represented the best talents in the field of telecommunications network engineering. Myron Martin, 38 years old and built like a Chicago Bears linebacker, knew digital switching like the back of his hand. John Rice, his wire rimmed glasses pushed up on his receding hair line, was a transmission and protection specialist. Elmer Thune, a native of the Kentucky hill country and the oldest of the three, at 42, was a top flight network facilities engineering manager. The three were inseparable. They had risen to the top of Dynacom's engineering group in Chicago and had directed the modernization of Dynacom's network.

When LEGENT acquired Dynacom, the three had flown to Dallas, walked into the office of the VP of Engineering for LEGENT and resigned. Since then, they had been working on a contract job in British Columbia . After a two-week vacation in Vancouver, they were ready to hit the road again. This would be their first overseas job.

A sandy haired man rose from a lobby sofa and greeted them. He was the Atlanta office manager for an international placement firm specializing in providing contract telecommunications professionals for major telecommunications network projects around the globe.

"Good to see you guys. We have a briefing scheduled for 1:00 p.m. I've already checked you in and here are your room keys. I've also prepared a brief summary of the project that you can review prior to the meeting."

"Who's going to be the on-site manager for the project?" Martin asked.

"Congratulations! You are!"

Rice and Thune grinned and looked down at their shoes. "Looks like 24-hour work days again," Rice said, looking at Thune.

"Who's the overall GM?" Martin asked, ignoring the comment.

"We have an interim guy whose visa is up in two months. We're trying to find a permanent GM until the Czechs can take over."

"Too bad McCann isn't available. He'd get it done on time and on budget!" Thune said.

"Who?" the sandy haired man asked.

"He was our CEO. Probably one of the best telecomm managers in the country," Rice replied.

"What's he doing now?"

"Don't know. He left Chicago about the time LEGENT took over and hasn't been heard from since," Martin said.

"Hmmm, it might be worth it to look him up. Do you think he would be interested?"

"Can't hurt. All he can do is say no!" Thune said as they headed for the elevator.

That afternoon, the three men were briefed on their roles in a project to expand and improve the Czech Republic's telecommunications infrastructure. The next morning, they flew out of Hartsfield International Airport, bound for Prague. Myron Martin was reading the specifications for the latest Nortel digital switch. Elmer Thune was reading the latest issue of Sports Illustrated. John Rice was reading his Bible.

McCann's mood was somber as he flew to New York City on Saturday. It had poured all the way to Caseville on Friday night. The view of Saginaw Bay out the window of the restaurant was low hanging gray clouds and a downpour. Donna had talked excitedly about her upcoming trip to the Czech Republic. While he was pleased to see her so animated, he did not share in her enthusiasm. The food had been good – not great, and the drive home on dark, rain slicked roads had been dreary. She had kissed him on the cheek at the door and told him she would write when she got located. She wished him well on his trip to New York City but he could tell that her enthusiasm for his work on the acquisition matched his for her upcoming trip to Prague.

He wakened Saturday morning to a steady drizzle and the flight from

Detroit to New York had been bumpy all the way as the pilot tried different cruising altitudes to find a smoother ride. Doug and Belle Warner sat together and McCann sat with Arthur Boyington, who was busy going through a photocopy of the Request for Proposals that LEGENT had sent out. McCann didn't need to review the material. He was confident that it was quite similar to ones he had sent out many times during his career. He was also sure that any tricky provisions that LEGENT might have inserted would be caught by Boyington or Stu Bailey's team.

The journey into the city was the usual bumpy cab ride with lots of pot holes and horns. Friday's rain storm was now pummeling New York City and the rain sheeted off the windshield as the cab made its way up to the Marriott Marquis at Times Square. McCann was sandwiched into the right rear seat corner with Belle in the middle and Boyington on the left. Doug sat up front with the driver, a Hispanic, who kept the music turned up as high as he dared given the jammed cab and the pouring rain.

They exited the cab and took the elevator up to the lobby. While they were waiting to register, Doug Warner, who had been quiet for most of the trip, turned to McCann.

"Joe and George both have sold their interests," he said, eyeing McCann.

"To whom?"

"A company called HHF. Have you ever heard of them?" Warner asked. At that moment, the clerk motioned him forward to check in. A minute later, McCann was at another position filling out his registration. Accepting his key and declining the offer of a bellman's assistance, he turned to where Warner stood waiting.

"What kind of a company is HHF?" he asked.

Warner fell into step beside him as they headed toward the elevators. Belle and Arthur had checked in ahead of them and were already on their way to their rooms.

"We couldn't find out much about them," he responded. "Arthur did some checking. They are a Delaware corporation with a Chicago office. We checked and the office address is an attorney who had ties to Dynacom. His name is Norman Miller. Arthur called him and Miller told him that

HHF is an investment firm dealing in information technology. Do you know Norman Miller?"

McCann pushed the "up" button and turned to face Warner. "I know him very well. He handled some of Dynacom's minor legal work and also handled some of my personal affairs. Did he say who the principals were in this HHF Company?"

"He wouldn't, or couldn't, divulge any names," Warner said, as the elevator door slid open and the two men stepped inside. A man and woman and two teenagers stepped back as they entered. The two teens were talking excitedly about the day's visit to "ground zero" and the Empire State Building. As they exited the elevator and headed down the hallway toward their rooms, McCann leaned out over the railing and looked down the center core to the lobby far below. He turned to Warner and smiled. "I wouldn't worry about it. Norm Miller is a good man. Do you have any idea how much this HHF outfit paid for the shares?"

Warner paused in front of his room and withdrew the plastic door card from his pocket. "That's what has me concerned. They paid nine million dollars for 20% of my company. As you know, that is way over book value. Something is going on here and I'm not sure what it is. Ordinarily, when someone pays that much for something, you would think they would look over what they are buying, call us up or something. It just doesn't sound right!"

McCann continued to the next door. He inserted his card in the slot and turned to face Warner.

"These are not ordinary times. I'm sure that in due time, you will find out what HHF's intent is. I'll give you a call later and we can all go to dinner."

He stepped through the door and closed it behind him. Doug Warner watched the door close and entered his room. McCann had done nothing to ease his concern. It was almost as if he was hiding something. Doug Warner was not a man who worried unnecessarily. His faith was strong and he trusted that God would reward that faith. Yet, he couldn't help worrying about what was happening to his company. He felt very alone as he looked out the window and listened to the traffic far below. Tomorrow he would be taking a step that could very well cost him his company. He turned toward the bed and dropping to his knees, began to pray.

In his room next door, McCann quickly dropped his bag on the bed, hung his clothes bag in the closet and picked up the telephone. His first call was to Stu Bailey. His next call was to the hotel's guest services department and his third call was to Norman Miller in his room two floors up.

Belle Warner had just finished putting her clothing on hangers in the closet and in the drawers of the chest in her room when her phone rang. "Ms. Warner, this is Gary in the Guest Services department here at the Marriott. Mr. McCann has arranged a private room for dinner tonight. It will be at seven on the 57th floor of the hotel. You'll see the room number posted near the elevators. Is there anything else I might be able to help you with to make your stay here more enjoyable?"

Belle smiled to herself as she replaced the phone. On the floor below, the phone rang in Doug Warner's room. The same message was delivered but Doug wasn't smiling when he put the phone down. He was beginning to wonder if he had misjudged Wilson McCann.

At five minutes before seven, he and his mother stepped out of the elevator on the 57th floor. A smartly dressed young woman wearing a Marriott badge that said "Charlzie" pinned to her jacket smiled as she stepped forward to greet them. "Mr. Warner, Ms. Warner, right this way please. The others are already here."

They walked down the hallway and into a room overlooking Times Square. A table was set for six and the lights were turned down. A single candle glowed in the middle of the table. Wilson McCann and another man stood in a corner of the room talking quietly. Arthur Boyington and another man stood looking out the window at the scene opposite and below them.

"May I get you something to drink before dinner?" the young woman asked.

They declined and she moved away as McCann came toward them. The other man followed.

"Belle, Doug, I'd like you to meet Stu Bailey," McCann said as Bailey stepped forward and extended his hand.

"It's good to meet you both. Wils has told me a lot about you and your company," Bailey said, smiling.

"There is someone else here that you haven't met yet as well," McCann continued, gesturing toward the other two men. Arthur Boyington turned and smiled at them as the other man, a lean, well dressed balding man with a deep tan, stepped forward.

"This is the notorious Norman Miller," McCann said smiling.

"I'm glad to meet you both," Miller said, extending his hand. Belle took it and returned his greeting. Doug Warner looked questioningly at McCann as he stepped forward and took Miller's hand in turn.

McCann read the look and put up his hand. "All in good time, Doug, let's sit down to dinner first."

They sat down to the table where salads were already placed at each setting. Charlzie reappeared with a tray holding six cups of Lobster Bisque soup that she served quickly before withdrawing again. The quiet at the table was deafening. Doug Warner shifted his gaze from McCann to Bailey to Miller and barely touched his soup. Belle ate her salad and soup quietly, her head bowed. Boyington talked about the activity at "ground zero" in the city that he had seen that afternoon. Bailey responded with comments about the work going on to rebuild that part of the city. Miller and McCann talked about the weather in Chicago and the Chicago Bears' chances in the upcoming season.

Charlzie returned to clear away the salad plates and soup cups and then placed their dinner entrees. Belle noticed that each person's meal was somewhat different and that both hers and Boyington's were exactly what their dietary needs required. Bailey's Shrimp Scampi seemed to please him greatly and he nodded imperceptibly to McCann. Doug's Rib-eye steak was just the way he liked it and Miller's chicken breast looked succulent. She smiled at McCann, "You have obviously done your homework in regards to dinner," she said.

"Doug's secretary was most accommodating in filling me in on what you, Doug and Arthur like best and I already knew that Stu likes shrimp and Norm prefers chicken," McCann replied as he took a bite of his broiled Halibut.

They ate their meals in relative quiet and Charlzie returned to clear away and bring coffee in a silver carafe. She poured each person a cup and set the carafe in the middle of the table. She closed the door as she left.

McCann took a sip from his cup and set it down. Turning to Stu Bailey, he said "Stu, why don't you fill us in on what we can expect on Monday."

Bailey leaned forward and looked directly at Belle Warner. "We will be meeting on Monday with representatives of the accountants, law firms and an acquisition management firm that we have retained to assist us with our proposal to LEGENT as well as the follow-on activity. The representatives of the financial firms who will be providing the backing to the consortium will also be present. As you all know, the acquisition business has slowed considerably since the Dot Com meltdown and the problems at Global Crossing and WorldCom. Venture capital is still available for acquisition purposes, but stronger balance sheets and better business plans are being required. Access lines are no longer the price measurement for acquisitions of this type. A multiple of free cash flow is the gauge for making a bid. As these properties are a smaller piece of a larger entity, it will be more difficult to value them. However, I think we can secure the capital we need for the LEGENT properties, but there are a couple of considerations relative to Farnsworth Tele and the LEGENT properties in Michigan."

"Such as?" Doug Warner asked, as he sat his coffee cup down and leaned back in his chair.

"We can probably secure equity funding equal to about forty per cent of your current equity and you will need to discuss your debt financing as a separate matter from that of the consortium," Bailey's tone was matter-of-fact. Doug folded his napkin and placed it on the table as he leaned forward. He looked directly at McCann. "And what is the collateral for the equity funding?" he said.

Bailey looked at McCann before responding. McCann put his elbows on the table and lifted his coffee cup as Bailey spoke.

"You will basically have to sell forty percent of your equity to the consortium in return for the equity participation."

Warner's face flared red and he slapped his hand on the table. His anger was evident. "And that together with the twenty percent that Mr. Miller's mysterious company owns means that we have lost controlling interest in Farnsworth Tele! There is no way ..."

Belle Warner placed her hand on his arm. "Let's hear the rest of what

Mr. Bailey and Wils have to tell us. Mr. Miller, I would be very interested in what you can also tell us about HHF Corporation and their interest in this matter." She seemed relaxed as she spoke and her eyes did not leave McCann who glanced at Miller and said, "Norm, if you will, I think it is time to tell Belle and Doug about HHF."

Miller smiled at them as he leaned forward. "HHF is an investment company owned by Mr. McCann…"

"What?" Doug Warner shouted. His face registered his shock. "What is going on here?"

McCann smiled and raised his hand. "Let Norm finish, please."

Miller nodded at McCann and spoke again. This time he looked down at his coffee cup as he began to speak. "Mr. McCann formed the company about a month ago. He placed a good portion of his personal wealth in it. The farm in Farnsworth is also owned now by HHF which, by the way, stands for Harms Hill Farms. Mr. McCann asked our firm to form the company in secret as it was his intent to secure the minority interest in Farnsworth Telephone previously owned by Mr. Whyte and Mr. Rambaugh. We completed that acquisition last week as I am sure the Warners know. Mr. McCann now controls that twenty percent interest in Farnsworth Telephone through HHF. Shall I go further, Wils?" He turned to McCann as he finished speaking and McCann nodded, keeping his eyes on Belle Warner. Miller reached inside his pocket and produced a document, which he handed to Belle. "This is an ownership proxy giving full authority to you, Mrs. Warner, to vote HHF's shares as you should choose in all matters relative to the acquisition of the LEGENT properties in the state of Michigan."

Belle unfolded the document briefly before handing it to Doug. He looked at McCann before he began to read. Arthur Boyington was smiling slightly as he poured himself a refill from the carafe and offered it to Bailey who shook his head and looked at McCann.

Belle smiled at McCann. "Does this mean what I think it does?" she asked.

"Yes. If you decide to proceed with the acquisition and agree to transfer a forty percent ownership to the consortium, your remaining equity, together with that proxy means that you still have majority control over Farnsworth

Tele in all matters relative to the acquisition," McCann replied. "As to matters relative to the on-going operation of the present Farnsworth Telephone Co-op and the LEGENT properties in Michigan, you will hold the minority interest in the combined operation. Of course all of that depends on securing appropriate debt financing for the remainder of the purchase price."

The Warners looked at each other as the weight of what McCann had said and done settled in upon them. Sixty percent of their family owned company would now be in the hands of others. Doug looked at Stu Bailey and asked quietly, "who exactly is the consortium?"

"Basically it will be controlled by those who have put up the money for the equity portion of the initial funding, including Farnsworth. Your family will have a seat on the Board of Directors of the company that will control the former LEGENT properties in the other states."

"So, you will form an operating company to run the other operations?"

Bailey looked down at his coffee cup before responding. "We will try to do this acquisition in a fashion that creates a holding company that in turn owns the LEGENT property in each of the states." He hesitated and then continued, casting a sidewise glance at McCann. "I must tell you that it is not the consortium's intent to operate these properties for the long term."

Warner sat back in his chair again as he considered the statement. He looked at Bailey and then at McCann before speaking. "So, you intend to acquire them and then sell them again?"

"Within five years, given a turn in the market place as we expect."

Warner leaned forward and his voice showed a deep emotion as he spoke again. "I believe in operating something, not in buying and selling to make a profit. Wils, I thought you believed in that as well."

McCann took a sip from his coffee before responding. Bailey was looking down again and the others were waiting expectantly. "I do. I have to remind you, though, that times are changing. The future of small companies is in some question due to the changes in settlements for long distance revenue, competition and the rise of the Internet and Wireless as alternate technologies."

Belle Warner looked at him as he said it and she smiled as she spoke. "Then, you think our company may possibly fail in the future?"

McCann leaned back in his chair and dabbed at his lips with his napkin before responding. "I have looked at your financials and those of your non-regulated businesses. I'd have to say that you have done an outstanding job of prudently investing your capital and controlling your costs. The impacts of revenue pooling changes are minimal for your company and your operating area has not been impacted yet by competition. If any company can make it, yours can."

"....And if we acquire the LEGENT properties, what then?" she prodded.

"You've seen my projections of the combined operations. If you are successful in securing reasonably priced debt financing and this whole process doesn't result in unreasonable accounting, legal and other acquisition costs, the combined operation should do well. The LEGENT network is, as you know, mostly the network that Dynacom put in place before it was acquired. It is well designed and fairly modern except for the more rural distribution lines. You will need to invest prudently in further modernization just as you did with your existing company."

Doug Warner looked intently at McCann and asked, "and where do you fit in all of this, Wils?"

"I want to help you succeed in this acquisition, if that is what you want to do. If you do not, my interest in your company is for sale at nine million dollars to only your family any time you want it."

"No ties to the consortium?" Doug persisted, watching Bailey's reaction.

"Only as an advisor, nothing more, right Stu?" he asked, looking at Bailey.

Stu Bailey sighed. "Unfortunately, nothing more. You need to know that we offered Wils the opportunity to be CEO of the combined operation and he turned us down. I still can't figure out why."

Belle Warner stood and the others stood in response. "We shall think this over and seek God's guidance over the next few days. I thank all of you gentlemen for your candor and for your support. Wils, I thank you for your friendship and for a lovely meal. Now it is time for an old lady to go to bed!"

She turned toward the door and Doug Warner paused before following her. "How did you get George and Joe to sell to you for nine million?" he asked.

"Let's just say that Joe had a need which I was able to meet and George had some greed that I was able to satisfy." McCann said, putting his arm across Warner's shoulders as they walked toward the door.

Before following his mother down the hall toward the elevators, Doug turned and held out his hand.

"Thanks......partner," he said quietly.

Behind them, Stu Bailey and Norm Miller exchanged puzzled looks.

On Sunday, the Warners went to the Marble Collegiate Church. McCann had a late breakfast with Arthur Boyington and Norm Miller. The three discussed the approach to be followed by Farnsworth Tele in participation with the consortium and the two attorneys agreed to meet again for dinner that evening to work out a set of critical issues for Farnsworth Tele.

In the late afternoon, he walked over to Rockefeller Center and up Fifth Avenue to St. Patrick's. He sat for a while in the great cathedral watching the people come and go. He had visited St. Patrick's whenever he was in New York and always felt refreshed for having spent a few moments in quiet meditation there. Today, however, his thoughts kept turning to the fact that Donna would be leaving on Wednesday and be gone for a month. He admitted to himself that he would miss her more than he had ever missed anyone. While he felt energized by the upcoming activity related to the acquisition, he knew that once the outcome was known, the old emptiness would return. Donna had helped to dispel that feeling. He looked around at the people in the pews. A well dressed woman in a fur coat sat looking straight ahead. A young man with a book bag slouched in a pew, half asleep. A gray haired street woman sat with head bowed next to a black plastic garbage bag stuffed with her possessions. A young man holding the hand of a small girl walked down the aisle to the front where they lit a candle and stood, hand in hand, heads bowed. McCann leaned forward, head in his hands and tried to pray. He found himself distracted by thoughts about Donna and the acquisition. Finally, he sighed and rose to exit the cathedral. He did not feel refreshed as he walked up 5th Avenue to 52nd St. and turned to walk towards Madison Ave. He entered the Kokachin Restaurant and bar at the Berkshire Place Hotel and waited in the bar area for Stu Bailey.

Bailey arrived a few minutes later and the two men were seated at a window table looking out on 52nd St. The waiter brought coffee and the menu and they ordered. When the waiter left, Bailey looked out the window and spoke.

"Well, what do you think?"

"It's going to be hard for them to give up 40% of their company," McCann replied.

"The proxy move was a good one," Bailey said, looking at him.

"They are good people," McCann replied.

"What are you getting out of this, Wils?" Bailey said, raising his coffee cup.

McCann drank from his own cup and sat it down before responding. "I guess I'd hoped to do something good for a change."

Bailey looked at him quizzically. "The last fifteen years weren't good?"

"The last fifteen months weren't. I'm not sure before then." McCann said, looking out the window.

"You ran a major corporation. You made a lot of money. You are respected in your industry. You could be back leading a company tomorrow if you wanted to. I don't see what more you could ask for."

McCann looked at him, "I lost the only company I really cared about. I had no life outside of Dynacom. I don't have a family, other than my mother. I can't even tell someone I care about that I love her."

"The clothing shop lady in Farnsworth?" Bailey said.

"Yes. She leaves Wednesday for a month in the Czech Republic."

"The Czech Republic? Is she touring or what?" Bailey asked.

"She's going on a work and witness mission for her church. She wants to be a missionary."

"I'd say you better find someone else to care for," Bailey said, as the waiter arrived with their food.

The two men ate quietly. Neither spoke and the silence became deafening. Around them, people engaged in animated chatter and two men and a woman at the bar laughed loudly at a story one of them was telling. The waiter returned to check on things and left with a "fine" from Bailey when he asked about their meals.

Finally, Bailey sat back in his chair and eyed McCann. "The Oxbow group is handling the AMS activity," he said, hoping to provoke some conversation.

"Who are the lawyers?" McCann responded without looking up.

"Lassiter Fielding,"

"…and the accounting firm?"

"Rice Waterson. They will do the due diligence on the entire thing unless you want to be involved."

"I'll have to talk to Doug. I had planned to help out on the review of the properties and look over someone's shoulder on the financial side. We need someone good to look at the LEGENT stuff. The old Dynacom areas I know pretty well."

"The fees from Oxbow, Lassiter Fielding and Rice Waterson will be hefty. Will the Warners be able to handle that?" Bailey said.

"I would think that if I help out on the due diligence and do the property review for the Michigan piece and Lassiter Fielding can accept Miller and Boyington participating on the legal side, we should be able to keep the Farnsworth Tele share in line," McCann said, looking at his friend.

"I can't promise that, but we can see how it goes tomorrow. I figured we'd let the Oxbow reps make their pitch and then review the cost estimates, talk about bid prices, and then caucus about lunch time. You and the Warners and your two attorneys can meet separately then if you want to. If you are going to do the property review, you'll need help as we want to wrap that aspect up quickly."

"How involved do you want me to be with Oxbow, Lassiter and Rice?" McCann asked.

"You know the states well and the condition of the facilities. You also know the people counts and what it will take at a central HQ to run it after we acquire it. I want you to make sure they keep it lean and realistic in their projections. I also want you to make sure they don't under estimate the regulatory situation."

"How long do you think it will take until we know who gets it?"

"I'd say six months, depending on who bids and how many re-bids are made."

"Have you firmed up a figure in your mind as to how high we should go?" McCann asked as he took a sip of his coffee. Both men had declined dessert and the waiter had left the bill and a refilled carafe on the table.

"Four times free cash is the going rate these days. It depends on what gets defined as 'free cash'." Bailey finished his coffee and reached for the bill. McCann let him take it. He knew that the one thing they hadn't talked about and wouldn't was Bailey's fee and percentage of ownership. If it had been anyone else, it would have been the first thing on McCann's mind. But he knew Stu Bailey and he trusted him and he didn't need anything more than that.

"I have to get used to not using access lines as the valuator. Have you got a projection on that basis?"

"About $3,500 per customer access line to start. Depending on the Oxbow report and your thinking, we could go as high as $4,000. They aren't bringing what they did back in the 90's." Bailey said as he dropped his credit card on top of the bill and signaled the waiter who hovered near the bar.

The waiter picked up the bill and credit card and returned shortly. Bailey filled in the tip and signed the bill. He put the credit card and a copy of the bill in a leather wallet inside his jacket as they rose to leave. Out on 52nd Street, the two men paused. Bailey turned to McCann and looked him squarely in the eye.

"One thing more, Wils," he said.

"What?" McCann asked, knowing the answer.

"It's up to you to protect the Warners. When this thing gets rolling, they will have to keep up or get out of the boat. Oxbow, Lassiter and Rice won't hesitate to recommend to the financiers that we go for the whole thing and cut Farnsworth Tele out of the deal. I can't protect them. You, Boyington and Miller will have to do that."

McCann smiled thinly. "What else is new?"

"I had to say it. You know that."

"Yes," McCann said as they parted. Bailey walked to the front of the

Berkshire Place and got into a cab. McCann walked up 52nd Street to 5th Avenue and stood for a few moments, watching the traffic flow up and down the Avenue before heading back to the Marriott. He pulled a $20 bill from his pocket and dropped it in the can held out by a blind man standing between 52nd and 51st Streets with a large white dog at his feet.

"Bless you brother," the blind man said as McCann walked away. The dog, his head resting on his paws, did not move.

(17)

The next morning, McCann, the Warners, and Arthur Boyington walked down to the Lassiter Fielding law offices in the 600 block of 3rd Avenue. It was a beautiful fall day and the city was alive with motion and sound. Norm Miller met them in the lobby and they took an elevator to the firm's offices where an attractive receptionist led them to a large conference room. The room was already filled with people. Stu Bailey welcomed them and introduced them to the representatives of the various firms represented. All of the men and women were immaculately dressed and well groomed. The receptionist closed the door and people settled into chairs at and around the large conference table. McCann and the Warners sat against the wall behind Boyington and Miller who sat at the table along with the lead attorneys and partners from Oxbow and Rice Watterson. Stu Bailey sat at the head of the table. Two men from the investment banking firms sat against the wall on the opposite side of the room.

Bailey introduced the Oxbow partner, a young man in his late 30's who quickly outlined the firm's services in the Acquisition Management Services or AMS field. Next, he went through a quick Power Point presentation of Oxbow's current perspective of the rural telecom industry and the financial markets. At the end, several questions were asked, mostly about the valuation mechanisms and various financing methods.

Next, Bailey introduced the lead attorney from Lassiter Fielding and the Rice Watterson accounting firm. The young woman from Lassiter – Fielding reviewed the legal aspects of the process and the procedures that LEGENT had outlined in its request for proposals. The Rice Watterson partner reviewed the steps in the due diligence process. At the end, the two presented a summary of estimated legal and accounting costs.

The Oxbow partner took over at that point and presented the valuation model that would be used to structure the bid. It focused heavily on "free cash flow" and Earnings Before Interest, Taxes, Depreciation and Amortization, or EBITDA. It was evident that everyone was familiar with these terms and the way the model was structured. After a few routine questions about the process to be used , he was asked to present his firm's estimated costs and the three representatives presented a Power Point slide that summarized all expected costs of the acquisition. Doug Warner swallowed hard and looked at his mother whose face held a rare frown. At that point, the young woman turned to Norm Miller.

"Mr. Miller, I understand you and Mr. Boyington will be representing Farnsworth Telephone on certain aspects of this transaction. Who else will be involved?" she asked.

Norm Miller smiled and turned in his chair to look at McCann.

"Wilson McCann, the former CEO of Dynacom is very familiar with the LEGENT properties that were once owned by that company and with the industry in general in the states involved. Mr. McCann will be assisting the Consortium and Farnsworth Telephone in the work. For the record, Mr. McCann has a minority interest in Farnsworth Telephone."

Heads around the table turned to look at McCann. The expression on the faces of financiers was unreadable but those at the table nodded slightly and smiled. It was evident that McCann's reputation had preceded him into the room.

Bailey looked at McCann and asked, "Wils, would you like to comment on the properties involved in what we are considering?"

McCann was somewhat surprised by Bailey's question but quickly realized that he was being given an opportunity to establish his value to the group and to strengthen Farnsworth Telephone's position at the same time. He stood as the others resumed their seats and waited expectantly. He walked to the head of the table and began to speak.

"The LEGENT properties in the four states under consideration are primarily rural, but in several locations, they adjoin larger metropolitan areas. Growth in those areas is especially strong. The rural areas are for the most part agricultural and tourist areas with moderate growth. In a few areas, there is some economic depression and an out-migration. The properties that were formerly owned by Dynacom have, for the most part, state of the art switching and modern feeder and distribution facilities. There is a good bit of fiber optic cable in the feeder portion of the network and some in the distribution networks. DSL and other broadband services are offered in some locations. In the properties that were owned by LEGENT prior to its acquisition of Dynacom, the switching is also digital and the feeder cable portion of the network is modern. The distribution portion of the network has not kept pace with that modernization and there is limited availability of advanced services. Those properties will need some infusion of capital to bring them up to the level of the former Dynacom properties. Because of the network issues, there are some customer service problems and the Cable Television companies in those areas have made significant inroads in the offering of broadband communications services."

He paused for a moment and one of the financiers lifted his hand before asking, "How current is your knowledge of these things, Mr. McCann?"

"Mr. Feldman, my knowledge is about one year old but I doubt that things have changed much in that year," he said.

"Thank you." Feldman replied, smiling.

There were a few other questions relative to capital expenditure needs and personnel issues before Bailey stood and thanked McCann. McCann returned to his seat and saw that Belle Warner was regarding him with a faint smile on her lips.

The remainder of the morning was spent reviewing the LEGENT RFP and in discussing the structure of the initial bid. As the lunch hour approached, the Oxbow partner, Lassiter attorney and Rice Watterson partner presented a milestone chart which plotted the steps to be followed. McCann noted that it called for a completion date of all activity by February 1st of the following year.

"It'll never happen," McCann whispered to Doug Warner who nodded slightly in agreement.

Stu Bailey led the group through a discussion of the Farnsworth Telephone relationship to the consortium and the need for it to raise its own debt financing. He suggested that the Farnsworth Telephone group meet separately with the two investment banking firms during lunch and that the group return to finalize its initial bid proposal at 2:00 p.m. that afternoon.

Cindy Melzy represented Triad Investments. She had already committed one hundred million dollars to the consortium. She knew and liked Wilson McCann. Ed Feldman's investment banking firm had committed one hundred and fifty million to the venture and he also knew and respected McCann. The two had met for breakfast earlier that day and agreed that if McCann's relationship to the venture was suspect, they would pull those commitments. Neither knew the Warners or their attorney, Boyington. Feldman had met Norm Miller and knew that he had been involved in various legal matters for Dynacom. After the morning session, they huddled in one corner of the conference room as it emptied.

"I'm convinced that McCann's participation in due diligence and the financial review is critical," Melzy said.

"I quite agree. I am disappointed that Stu wasn't able to get Wils to agree to be CEO. I'm not sure where Farnsworth Tele fits in our firm's thinking, are you?"

She looked down before answering. "If Wils has a minority interest in it, the people must be either ripe for the picking or good operators. Which do you think it is?"

"I've done some research on it. Farnsworth Tele is well respected within the industry circles. They run a tight ship and they have been a 'fast follower' in adopting technology. The Warners seem like solid people. I doubt, however that they have ever been through something like this. Their family made its money when the Dixie Highway was built in Michigan many years ago."

"They will need forty-five million in financing. How much will you provide?" she asked.

"As of now, nothing. At the most, fifteen million. You?

"About the same, and only because Wils has a minority interest."

Feldman looked at her with a twinkle in his eye. At thirty eight, Cindy was bright, attractive and three years removed from a messy divorce. "He's still available, you know," he reminded her.

She smiled thinly. "Don't get cute, Ed. My interest is purely financial."

"Sure," he responded as they turned toward the door.

The Warners, Boyington, Miller, McCann and the two investment bankers met in a smaller conference room where a soup, salad and sandwich buffet had been laid out. As they filled their plates, Cindy stood behind McCann.

"What have you been up to lately, Wils?" she asked.

He smiled at her as he forked a slice of ham onto a Kaiser roll. "I'm sort of a gentleman farmer. I have some cattle, a couple of tractors, a pick up and a dog."

She reached for a roll and the diamond studded ring on her right hand sparkled. McCann noted that her left hand was bare. He also noted the scent of her perfume. Cindy Melzy was a class act if there ever was one. Her black pant suit with silver buttons on the coat and white blouse with ruffles at the throat accentuated her black hair and fair skin. When she smiled, her whole face lit up. She had the talent of making the person she spoke to feel like they were the most important person in the world. It was a skill that had brought a host of clients to Triad.

"Sounds sort of rustic," she said as she began to build her sandwich.

"It is. How about you? Still in the game, I see."

"Which one, the singles game or the financial game?"

"Both," he said, as he picked up his cup of soup and, balancing a plate in one hand and the soup in the other. He moved toward the table. She followed and sat down next to him.

"Haven't found a good deal that I didn't like or a man that I liked well enough to do "due diligence" on," she said, "Do you have a 'significant other' yet?"

McCann, caught in the act of raising a spoonful of soup to his lips, paused before he replied.

"I'm working on it," he said. She noted the hesitation and wondered what it meant. She decided that, over the course of the next few months, she would find out more about that. She found McCann interesting and challenging at the same time. She had been burned once but McCann was clearly a cut above most men she had met.

The talk around the table was light and helped to acquaint the participants with each other. Boyington was quiet, but Feldman and Melzy detected a competence in his manner. Doug Warner was obviously a little nervous, especially when Feldman began to question him about the area that Farnsworth Tele served and his plans for the LEGENT property, if the acquisition was successful. Belle Warner handled Cindy's questions about her role in the company easily, and Cindy found herself taking an immediate liking to the older woman. Belle's respect for McCann was obvious and yet there was a bit of a questioning look on her face whenever he spoke about the possibilities in the future of the combined operation. Miller was the type of hard-driving attorney that she worked with on a daily basis.

Dessert consisted of chocolate chip cookies and coffee. Doug handed out copies of Farnsworth Tele's latest financial statement and McCann distributed copies of his presentation to the Farnsworth Tele Board. He described his acquisition of the twenty percent minority interest in the company and the proxy he had given Belle. Ed Feldman sat back in his chair and spoke directly to Belle.

"Mrs. Warner, we need to know if your family is prepared to give up control of a portion of your equity in the company in return for participation in the consortium. I understand that that issue is still in question."

Belle turned to Doug and nodded, giving him the role of company spokesman.

"We are prepared to turn over forty percent of the equity to the consortium, provided that we can secure debt financing at reasonable terms."

Feldman smiled. "Excellent. That will provide thirty million of equity capital. You will need approximately forty five million to secure the Michigan properties. I presume you would like to know what we are prepared to invest in that venture?"

"Very much so," Doug replied.

"At the moment, I cannot make a commitment on an amount but I can say that we would not be able to commit to more than fifteen million of what you need if we decided to participate."

Doug Warner sat forward in his chair with his hands in his lap. His eyes moved from Feldman to McCann and finally to Cindy Melzy.

"Cindy?" McCann said.

She looked up from the papers she had been reviewing. She glanced at McCann briefly and smiled before she spoke.

"I'm prepared to commit fifteen million, if Ed will. Where will you get the rest?"

Miller spoke for the first time, "Arthur and I have had some conversations with an investment banking firm in Detroit and we believe we can interest them in participating."

Boyington nodded his agreement at this statement and Belle Warner turned to look at McCann. "When might we know about all of this?" she asked.

McCann looked at the two investment bankers. Cindy sat back in her chair waiting as Feldman flipped through the Farnsworth Tele financial statement that Doug had provided. At last, he put the papers down and looked at McCann.

"I want to make it very clear that we ordinarily would not be interested in something of this size. If it weren't for your participation in this project, Wils, I would have to say that we would pass on it. However, due to your knowledge of the properties to be acquired and what I see here, I think I can give you a positive response by Friday." He placed a slight emphasis on "positive" as he said it.

Cindy also turned to McCann and spoke. "If Ed's in, we're in. You had better turn your charm on that Detroit firm. Ed, would you like me to do the due diligence on Farnsworth Tele for both firms if you come in?"

Feldman eyed her suspiciously. Why would she want to travel to an out of the way town like Farnsworth to spend three days looking at telephone plant and computer-printed financials? Nevertheless, it would save his firm the time and trouble, if they decided to get in on this deal. One thing he knew about Cindy, she would do the job right. "That is agreeable to me," he said, looking at the financials again.

Belle Warner smiled at Cindy. "I'd like to invite you to be my guest while you are in Farnsworth. Our motels are limited and the nearest larger city is about 40 miles away."

Cindy looked from Belle to McCann. "I'd be delighted," she responded, as she noted the faint smile on McCann's lips.

A few minutes later they rejoined the larger group to discuss the outline of a cash bid of three hundred and eighty five million dollars for LEGENT'S one hundred and ten thousand customers in Iowa, Michigan, Minnesota and Wisconsin. The cream of mushroom soup that Doug Warner had eaten for lunch, together with the numbers he had seen in the morning and the concern over the remaining fifteen million to be raised, was upsetting his stomach. He had to leave the room twice before they broke it off at 5:00 p.m. so the attorneys, accountants and financiers could catch their trains home. Miller had a late flight out of JFK to Chicago and Boyington was planning to have dinner with one of his law school classmates. The Warners pleaded fatigue and, in Doug's case, no desire to eat out. McCann ate alone at Menestrellos and went to bed early.

In Detroit the next morning, an investment banker named Smith scrolled down through his e-mail messages until he saw one from Norm Miller. He quickly read it and then opened the attached worksheet and printed both off. He sat back in his chair and considered the situation before picking up his phone and calling the partner in charge of his division. A few minutes later, the two men reviewed the message and the worksheet.

"This is not something we should do," the partner said, as he put the worksheet on his desk and slid it across to Smith. "Telecom is not what we do. Rural Telecom is definitely not what we do."

"They are a good solid firm and they have commitments from major investment banks in New York. Fifteen million is not a big thing," Smith replied. "Let me at least flesh it out. I'll bring in a recommendation at the end of the week."

"Okay, but I think you could use your time more wisely," the partner replied, indicating that their meeting was over.

Smith returned to his office and closed the door. He laid the papers on his desk and picked up a small, framed photograph of the Michigan State University football team from his senior year. He was in the front row, wearing his halfback number 23. Right behind him was Doug Warner wearing his linebacker number 68. He remembered the night when MSU had defeated their hated rival, the University of Michigan, 24 to 20 and the riots that had followed. East Lansing's jubilation had turned to uncontrolled violence.

He had been in the forefront, drunk from victory and vodka. Just as the police car arrived and he threw the empty bottle at it, Doug Warner had grabbed him and virtually carried him into the shadows where he passed out. The next morning, several of his teammates were in jail facing serious charges and possible expulsion. He was sleeping off his intoxication in Doug Warner's dorm room.

"I owe you one, big guy. But how do I pay off?" he said aloud as he put the picture down. He picked up Norm Miller's e-mail and the worksheet and began to think.

The next day was spent in more meetings as the Oxbow group led them through the process once again and the attorneys and accountants went over the bid and made revisions to it. Several calls were made to the LEGENT team coordinating the sale from LEGENT'S headquarters in Dallas. Miller called from Chicago with the news that the Detroit investment banking firm wouldn't have an answer before the end of the week.

McCann worked with the Oxbow representatives and with the Warners during the morning and began to feel energized by the process. His mind continually formulated new approaches and alternative steps that could be taken to restructure both the process and the bid in the event of various reactions from the various participants to the process. He and Bailey walked to the Waldorf Astoria and ate their lunch in the crowded Bull and Bear Steakhouse and Bar. Bailey could sense a renewed spirit in his friend.

"You are enjoying this, aren't you?" Stu commented, as he dipped his spoon in his Lobster Bisque.

McCann smiled at him. Stu Bailey, in addition to his ability to put together deals could, on occasion, be almost perceptive. "I am. I didn't realize how much I missed it," he replied.

"The Warners are great people. I can see how you would want to help them. Cindy has really taken to Belle. Did you know they are having lunch together today?"

McCann looked up. "Really?"

"Yep. They made it clear to Doug and Art that this was a 'girls only' lunch." Bailey said, as he poked at his shrimp salad.

"Cindy had better watch herself. Belle Warner has a way of getting inside your head," McCann said, as he cut into his grilled chicken breast.

"Has she gotten into yours, Wils?"

McCann eyed his friend, "Yes, she has a little."

"I'll have to take the lady to lunch myself. Maybe I can learn why you are wasting your life away up in no-wheres-ville driving a tractor and herding cows."

"Steers, Stu – they are steers. And, I only have twenty of them."

"Okay, steers… and a dog too…and a girlfriend who runs a store?"

McCann's head snapped up and he laid his napkin on the table and pushed back his chair. Stu Bailey watched as Wilson McCann stood and stepped around the table.

"Where are you going?" He asked, as McCann began to walk away.

"What's the matter?"

"I just remembered that Donna is leaving today for Detroit. She flies out for Prague tomorrow. I've got to call her before she leaves," McCann said, as he hurried away.

Bailey continued to eat his soup and salad. A few minutes later, McCann returned, his face downcast. He slid into his chair and looked glumly at Bailey. "She had already left for Detroit. I missed her. I got so caught up in what we were doing that I completely forgot to call her."

"Big deal! Call her on her cell phone!" Bailey responded, finishing off his salad.

"She doesn't have one. I don't know where she is staying. She will be gone a month. She's going on a mission for her church. I don't know how I could have forgotten to call her!"

"I do. You got interested in this acquisition and your juices got flowing and your love life took a back seat to it!" Bailey grinned.

Wilson McCann didn't grin back. The excitement of the last few days had left him. It was as if a gaping hole had been ripped in his heart. He worked through the afternoon. But the excitement was gone and the others noticed it. Belle Warner pulled Stu aside during a break in the meetings and asked what was bothering McCann. When Bailey told her, she smiled know-ingly and walked away. Bailey resolved to get to know Belle Warner better.

In Detroit that evening, Smith attended a fund-raiser for the Governor. As he mingled in the crowd of smartly dressed men and women, he spotted one of his old MSU buddies standing off to one side watching the Governor as he greeted a line of supporters.

"Hello Ross. It looks like the man is on his game tonight!" he said, as he extended his hand and nodded in the direction of the Governor.

"Smitty! How are you? What are you guys doing to stimulate the econ-omy of our fair state? You know we need that money in circulation!?" the Governor's aide said, as he gripped Smith's hand.

"Well, we're trying, that's for sure! But we aren't as free with it as we were a couple of years ago. In fact, I was working on a deal for one of our fellow Spartans just today," Smith replied, turning so that both men were side by side as they watched the Governor.

"Really, who?"

"Remember Doug Warner? His family bought a little telephone compa-ny up in the 'Thumb' and now he's trying to make it bigger," Smith replied, sipping his drink.

"What's he trying to do, become another Global Crossing?"

"No, he and some others are trying to buy LEGENT'S properties in the Midwest. Doug's company is trying to raise forty-five million to buy the property in Michigan. A couple of New York City firms have indicated they might go thirty million and Doug's company has asked us to consider the remaining fifteen. I don't think it will fly, though," Smith replied.

"Doug's company too thin to go that far?"

"No, it isn't that. My boss got burned in the Telecom meltdown and doesn't want to consider it. Doug's firm is solid and they have the former CEO of Dynacom helping them with the deal. I think it would be safe, but I'm not going to be able to sell it."

Ross turned to face Smith and leaned in to speak quietly and still be heard above the chatter of the crowd. "Call me tomorrow morning and give me the details on this, Smitty. We want to be sure that well run small businesses in Michigan are encouraged to expand. I think the Governor might be interested in this."

Smith started to respond, but at that moment the Governor motioned and Ross immediately turned and headed towards him. Smith wandered the room speaking to various acquaintances, but he couldn't get the question out of his mind as to why the Governor would take an interest in a fifteen million dollar telecom acquisition. As he was turning to leave, Ross caught up with him and walked with him to the foyer outside the room. He looked around and determined that there was no one within earshot.

"Smitty, I want you to be sure to get me that information. This is very important to us. I want to know everything there is to know about Doug's company and I want to have your candid assessment of the viability of this deal. Okay?"

"Okay…but why…?" Smith began. He knew that disclosing this type of information was probably illegal and violating all sorts of trust and confidentiality rules.

"Don't ask any questions. Just trust me. This is important," Ross said, as he put his hand on Smith's shoulder before turning away to rejoin the Governor.

Smith punched the button for the elevator and scratched his head as he watched his friend disappear into the crowd. "What is going on here?" he thought to himself, as he stepped inside the elevator and the door closed. He was beginning to get a little nervous.

Later that evening, as the Governor's Chevy Suburban headed for Detroit's Metropolitan airport, Ross briefed the Governor, who listened intently.

"This is very important, Ross. We need to find out as much as we can about this group and in particular this man Warner's company. Where is it located?"

"I took a minute and called our friend at the Commission. It is the Farnsworth Telephone Co-op and it is located in Farnsworth. Our friend says it is one of the better companies in the state."

The Governor looked out the window as the Detroit skyline receded. "Do we know anyone close to the company?" he asked.

"The county Republican Chairman is on the Board of Farnsworth Tele," Ross replied.

The Governor smiled broadly. "Phil Willard! He's a believer! Give him a call tomorrow. Better yet, see me first thing and we will call him from my office!"

The Governor sank back into the Suburban's leather seats. "What did you think of this evening?" he asked.

"I thought we had a good turn out and your talk hit all the right buttons," Ross replied.

"Yes, I think things went well here in Detroit and what you have just told me makes me feel a whole lot better about our little project in the North Country as well," the Governor said, as the Suburban pulled into the private aviation terminal.

The next morning, while Norm Miller, Arthur Boyington, McCann and Doug Warner held a conference call about the expanded data request from Smith and how best to get the information to him that day, the phone rang in the Farnsworth Agway. The store clerk who answered immediately stood up in what was as close as he could get to full attention. "Yes sir! Right away sir! I'll get him!" he said before putting the phone down and sprinting to the garage area where Phil Willard was talking to one of his mechanics beside the big Agway fuel tanker.

"It's him…! It's the Governor…!" the clerk half shouted as several men turned to stare.

"Slow down son," Phil said as he turned toward him. "Now, what is it?"

"It's the Governor, Phil! He's on line one and he wants to talk to you!"

Phil Willard didn't run, but he walked very quickly back into the store and picked up the phone, as the men in the garage area clustered around the clerk to ask what was going on.

McCann was encouraged by the speed with which Boyington, Miller and Doug Warner were able to put the information package together and get it on its way to Smith by FEDEX. An e-mail was also sent out with a summary of the more than fifty pages of detail that had been requested.

McCann was also satisfied that the Detroit investment firm was giving the proposal serious consideration.

Cindy Melzy asked him to join her for lunch at the Hyatt on 42nd Street, and the two walked up 3rd Avenue together. McCann was carrying a new cell phone that Stu had given him that morning. Bailey had told the group how McCann had suddenly needed a phone to call his "friend" back in Farnsworth and had to use a pay phone.

"One of the leaders of the telecom industry and he doesn't carry a cellular telephone or a pager or even a PDA," Bailey mocked. The others had smiled and kidded McCann about it. He hadn't bothered to memorize his new cellular number when he gave it to Doug Warner and Arthur Boyington.

Cindy chatted easily about how well things were coming together and expressed her confidence that Feldman would deliver a commitment at the end of the week. They entered the Sun Garden overlooking 42nd street and were immediately shown to their table by a smiling hostess who greeted Cindy warmly. "We've missed you lately, Ms. Melzy," she said as she pulled Cindy's chair out from the table next to the window.

"Thank you, Marie. How have you been?" Cindy inquired. McCann seated himself as the two women talked animatedly before Marie was replaced by an equally friendly waiter who took their drink order, white wine for Cindy and coffee for McCann, and left.

"Does everyone in New York know you?" McCann asked with a smile.

"Oh, you know, a single woman with money to give away is everyone's friend!" she replied as she picked up her menu.

They bantered back and forth until the waiter returned with the wine and coffee and took their orders. Cindy raised her glass in toast. "To success," she said.

"To success," McCann responded, raising his cup.

"What is success for you these days, Wils? Is it this deal, or do you have something else up your sleeve?" She asked, turning serious.

He held out his arm. "Nothing up the sleeve. See?"

Cindy didn't return his smile. "I'm serious Wils. What is it with you? You live on a farm near a small town. You have a dog and raise beef cattle. Now, you've bought a minority interest in a small family owned telecom company and you're here in the Big Apple helping put together a four hundred million dollar acquisition. Stu Bailey and I are glad to see you back in action, but neither of us can figure out what you are getting out of all of this."

"I'm trying to help some people I've come to like do something that they want to do," McCann replied evasively.

"Belle Warner says you're a man in search of himself. Is that true?"

McCann sighed and looked out the window. The traffic on 42nd Street crawled by amid the usual honking of horns. The people coming out of Grand Central Station were moving up the street faster than the traffic. Suddenly, he missed the farm and Ted and the smell of the hay in the mows. He missed Donna and knew that she was somewhere in the sky overhead, heading happily toward a month of service to others. He wondered if she even thought about him and, if she did, what kinds of thoughts did she think?

"...Wils?" Cindy spoke again and he turned his gaze back to her. She was the face of the world that he had thought he wanted to live in and conquer. He took a sip of his coffee and placed the cup back on the saucer before he spoke. "Yes, it's true. I thought I knew what I wanted in life. Then...when I lost my...when LEGENT bought Dynacom, I found I didn't know what I wanted. I've found something up there on the farm, Cindy. I'm not sure yet if it is what I want but I am working on it. Can you believe it? Just a moment ago, watching the traffic and hearing all the noise, I missed the farm and Ted and...."

"And...Donna?" She peered at him over the edge of her wine glass.

"So, Belle told you about Donna, did she?" He said, looking down.

"Not a lot. She told me about a woman there who loved you very much, and that she was concerned about your feelings for Donna, and that she felt you hadn't found what you were looking for yet. Do you love her?"

"Cindy, I don't really know what love is yet. I'm working on that, too. I have been reading the Bible and going to church, too."

He watched her eyes as he said it. A faint smile played about her lips but her gaze didn't waiver.

"Very interesting, I'm looking forward to coming to Farnsworth and meeting these new friends of yours and finding out more about the Warners and this 'Come to Jesus' business," she said, eyeing him. "Are you becoming a religious fanatic, Wils?"

He laughed lightly, "No, not yet. But, I find a peace of sorts in reading the Bible and talking with those who have a deeper walk of faith than I do."

She put her glass down as the waiter returned with their meals, a Caesar salad and fruit cup for her and a Roast Beef Au Jus for him. McCann welcomed the interruption. He felt uncomfortable talking about his life in Farnsworth. It seemed to pale in comparison with the life he had once lived and with the life he knew Cindy Melzy lived every day.

"Belle talked to me about her faith yesterday at lunch," she said, between bites of salad.

"I'm not surprised. She and Doug are both very open about their faith and they live it. I admire them both."

"I'm impressed with her. I have to tell you that I volunteered to come out to Farnsworth mostly to see what is going on with you. Yesterday at lunch, Belle impressed me so much that I found myself wanting to get to know her better. I'm looking forward to the trip."

"Be sure to bring your blue jeans and your straw hat!" he joked, as he dipped the edge of his sandwich in the Au Jus.

"Oh I will, Wils. I expect this fifteen million to be the most interesting investment I've ever made."

He was about to reply when the cellular telephone rang. He removed it from the holster on his belt and flipped it open. The smile on his face faded as he listened to the excited voice coming over the phone.

"Doug! Calm down! What did he want? When did he call? I don't know. Yes, we'll be back in about 15 minutes. Okay! Yes! I think we should call Smith right away!"

He closed the phone and put it back on his belt. Cindy looked at him, puzzled. "What was that all about?" she asked.

"Your visit to Michigan may be more interesting than you thought. The Governor called one of Doug's Board Members this morning and wants to know all about it!"

Cindy Melzy had been managing investment deals for twelve years. Nothing had ever surprised her. She had met her share of high-ranking politicians, and dined with a New York Senator on two occasions as part of announcing multi-million dollar ventures. Her boss visited with New York's Governor regularly on his farm in the Catskills. But, she had to admit to herself, for its size, this deal was getting more surprising all the time. As she and McCann walked back down 3rd Avenue, she tried to put it all together in her mind. Obviously, there was something here that she wasn't seeing. What was going on in Michigan and what game was Wilson McCann playing?

(18)

Betty Gabor walked across the little garden area between the two condominiums. She was a short, heavy set woman with blonde hair that was turning to gray. Her husband, Art had passed away the previous year and now she lived alone. Ellen was her best friend and Ellen had stepped in when Art died and had helped her get through a very trying time. They had no children and there was no one left of either her or Art's family. Ellen had been like a sister to her. They had started having a meal together twice a week right after Art's funeral. They would eat at Betty's on Saturday, go to church together on Sunday and stop for lunch afterward. On Wednesday, Ellen would fix dinner and they would watch TV until 10:00 p.m. when Betty went back to her own condo. As she walked briskly over the bricked walkway among the flowers, she wondered why Ellen hadn't answered her phone earlier in the day. Betty knew that Ellen stayed in on Wednesday to prepare their meal. She had called twice and the phone had rung with no answer both times. Ellen didn't have an answering machine and neither of the women had a lifeline machine in their condo. They both agreed that they weren't ready for that yet.

She stepped inside the entry to Ellen's building and buzzed her condo. She waited for the automatic door release to buzz. It didn't. She tried again and then buzzed the manager's office. She told the manager she was concerned for her friend and about her earlier unanswered phone calls. The manager quickly appeared and the two women walked down the hall to the door of unit 25. The manager rang the doorbell and knocked loudly before inserting her passkey into the door and opening it. Fortunately the safety chain was not in place and the two stepped into the entry hall.

Ellen was lying in the doorway to the kitchen. The manager knelt to check for a pulse and Betty moved to the phone and dialed 911. As she spoke to the responder, the manager rose and shook her head sadly. "No need for them to rush. She's gone."

Betty sank into a chair and began to sob softly as the manager turned to a wood framed corkboard in the hallway. Ellen's son's phone number was posted on an index card tacked to the board. She knelt next to Betty and put her arm around her as she dialed the number. A message machine answered and she left the message.   Later, Betty watched as the ambulance took Ellen McCann away.

Later that evening at the Marriott Marquis, McCann partially packed his bags in anticipation of his trip with Art Boyington and Doug Warner to Detroit to talk with Smith about the latest developments. Phil Willard's excited message about the call from the Governor, asking about Farnsworth Telephone Coop and the bid for the LEGENT properties in Michigan, had left him in a puzzled state of mind. He reflected back on his phone conversation with Jim Wolfe. What was behind all this interest in what was, in the grand scheme of things, a relatively small deal?   He decided to check his answering machine at the farm and dialed the number and entered the code and listened to the messages. There was a quick, "I'm on my way! I'll see you in a month!" message from Donna that made his heart skip a beat and his mood turn somber. He erased it and waited as the next message started. It was the Manager of his mother's condo project in Ft. Myers asking him to call her and saying that it was rather urgent.

Fifteen minutes later, McCann had changed his tickets from Detroit to Ft. Myers, told Doug and Belle Warner what had happened and checked out of the Marriott. Belle Warner had hugged him as she said goodbye. McCann looked gloomily out the window as his cab headed for the airport. The day was cloudy and rain was threatening. The noise of the city and the bumper to bumper traffic were oppressive. He thought of his mother and their relationship. Ellen McCann had worked long and hard to provide a home for him after his father died. His relationship with her had been distant. He did not come home often from college even though the proximity of Champaign-Urbana to Chicago made weekend trips easy. He had spent his summers on the farm in Michigan and returned to Chicago in time to buy whatever he would need for the next school year and leave for college. Once he began working for Dynacom, he had established his own home in an apartment building on the north side. His mother had continued to work and they had little time or the inclination to do things together. As he rose to the top of Dynacom, he had urged her to retire and had set her up financially to do so. He had purchased the Florida condominium she lived in and had visited her there once a year. His mother had made one return trip to Chicago to see him but his schedule was so packed that she left after three days. After that, his weekly phone calls to see how she was doing and his once a year visit to Florida constituted their relationship.

During the last two years, Ellen had begun to go to church with some friends from the condo project and had participated in weekly activities at both the church and the project. She had, on several occasions went out of her way to tell him how happy she was and how much she appreciated all he had done for her and how proud she was of him. Lately, she had ended their phone calls with, "I love you." He had not been able to respond in kind and now he knew he would never again have the chance. His lips quivered and a sob racked his body as tears flowed down his cheeks. The cab driver, looking in his rear view mirror said, "You okay mister?"

McCann wiped the tears away and raised his hand to the mirror signifying that he was okay. But, he wasn't, and, as the cab crept through the traffic, down deep in his heart he knew it.

In Detroit later that day, Boyington and Doug Warner sat opposite Smith in his office.

"I need to know why the Governor's office is so interested in this deal," Smith said, leaning back.

"You know more than we do," Arthur Boyington replied. "We received a call from one of our Board members who happens to be the County Republican Chairman telling us that the Governor's office had called asking for information on Farnsworth Telephone and its interest in buying the LEGENT properties."

"Do you have ties to the Governor?" Smith asked, eyeing both men.

"Our PAC contributed to his campaign and my wife and I made a personal contribution. Phil Willard supported the Governor as well. That is the limit of our involvement." Doug responded. "I have a question for you as well."

"Yes?" Smith replied, waiting. He knew what was coming.

"Evidently, you spoke with someone on the Governor's staff about this situation and that in turn resulted in the Governor's office calling Phil. What exactly is your involvement with the Governor and what do you know about this that we don't?"

Smith leaned forward and smiled. "I went to MSU with one of the Governor's staff. We discussed the situation at a fund-raiser the other night. That is the first time I became aware of the Governor's potential interest in this whole thing. I must say that it has helped your situation. My boss has now asked for a full presentation on your company and its plans. He had previously been negative on this deal and our participation in it."

"So, evidently someone changed his mind," Boyington said quietly.

"Evidently."

"So, where do we go from here?" Doug asked, leaning forward.

"We have two major tasks. The first is to put together a comprehensive presentation on this acquisition and Farnsworth Tele's position in it. The second is to put together a slightly different presentation on it for the Governor's staff. Frankly gentlemen, I am feeling pretty positive about this, but I caution you, that on the one hand, we need to keep this as quiet as possible while on the other hand, you need to find out what is behind all this and what the possible impacts could be for your company. Usually, this kind of interest can only mean one thing."

"And that is . . . ?" Boyington interjected.

"Something is going on that involves the properties you are seeking to acquire. That could have significant financial ramifications for you in the future. Those ramifications could be positive or negative," Smith replied.

"Or both," Doug Warner said more to himself than to the others. He was beginning to feel a bit overwhelmed by these latest events and he said a quiet prayer as Smith began to review the information in a file folder on his desk.

Ellen had asked that her remains be cremated. The memorial service was held two days later at the little church that she and several of her friends had attended. The minister spoke of the certainty of heaven for God's children and talked of Ellen's work within the church. McCann learned for the first time that she had done the cleaning of the church each week. She had never told him. At the door between the sanctuary and the foyer, the minister spoke to him of the "faithfulness" of his mother and her "stewardship." McCann gathered that her contributions had included sizable donations to the church and its outreach programs. Afterwards, there was a luncheon in the church's fellowship hall. Most of the attendees were from the condominiums. Several came up to him for a second time and told him how much they would miss his mother and what a wonderful person she had been. One lady named Betty was very distressed. She told him of her friendship with his mother and how Ellen had helped her through the death of her husband.

"I just don't know what I will do without Ellen," she said as she dabbed at her eyes with a small pink handkerchief. McCann held her hand and tried to console her. Finally, she wandered off to rejoin some of the others who were seated at tables eating.

McCann returned to the condo later that evening and began to pack up the personal items he wished to keep. He arranged through the condominium manager to have his mother's furniture sold to an estate firm and the proceeds donated, in her name, to the church. He boxed her clothing and arranged for it to be picked up by the local Goodwill Industries. He debated what to do with her four-year-old Jeep Liberty and decided to drive it back to Michigan. The trip would take the better part of two days but he needed time to think. He loaded the boxes of personal items into the Jeep and locked it. He would sleep here overnight before leaving. The Condo Manager would take care of the small amount of food from the cupboards and refrigerator. She would also arrange for the sale of the condo. "There is a waiting list, I'm sure it will sell quickly," she said. McCann gave her Norm Miller's number in Chicago and told her to work it out with him.

It was dark when he finished eating a small meal, and he sat there in the dimly lit living room and thought about the day. In the end, his mother had more friends than he did. He reflected that not one of his many business acquaintances had sent a word of condolence. In fairness, no one knew of his mother's passing. There had been a large bouquet of flowers from Phil and Martha Willard, the Marks and the Warners. Flowers from friends of a few months, not people he had worked with for years. Those years seemed empty now.

His whole life seemed empty. He really had no close friends other than those he had made since coming to Farnsworth. He had failed to have a relationship with his mother and he had no other family. He couldn't seem to find a way to express his feelings toward Donna in response to her openness with him about how she felt. He began to wonder what was wrong with him. There was no question in his mind that he had been successful in the business world. People recognized his ability and valued his judgments. He had the personal wealth that gave testimony to that ability. Yet, since coming to Farnsworth, he had recognized that there was a great emptiness in his life. He thought about what Chuck Hastings, McIntyre and others had said to him about life in Christ. Was that where the answer lay? Did he need to give his life over to some higher power? He had lived his entire life doing what he felt was right and necessary. He had not relied on anyone or anything except himself. Yet, as he sat there staring out the window into the parking lot, he knew that he had relied upon Dynacom to provide that sense of fulfillment that he now missed. That reliance had cost him dearly and it had reconfirmed his determination to go it alone from now on.

Since coming to Farnsworth, he had begun to enjoy the companionship of others. He saw in Belle Warner, Phil and Martha Willard, Jim and Lona Marks, McIntyre and Donna, a strength that he did not have. He enjoyed the quiet evenings with Donna as they talked, played games and studied the Bible. He enjoyed the fellowship with the others on Sunday after church. He felt challenged by their lives and by Hastings' messages on Sunday. Yet he had failed to respond to their quiet invitations to commit his life to Christ. The price of his freedom to act as his own person was too much to pay.

So he sat there as the night deepened and his thoughts raged back and forth. Finally, in frustration he rose and went to bed. His sleep was restless and he wakened the next morning unrefreshed to start on the trip back to Farnsworth.

Donna walked through the lobby of the Hotel Josef in Prague. The glass, steel and stone of the high-tech lobby was impressive. To her left the bar dominated and the glass staircase descended into the conference area. The lounge area on her right was populated by two businessmen talking on cellular telephones. She went into the Garden Terrace restaurant and was seated at a table looking out on the terrace. Three men, obviously Americans from their dress and manner, sat at a table to her left.

The Hotel Josef was her one extravagance on this trip. She had booked a room on the top floor that had floor to ceiling windows and a balcony with a view towards Prague Castle. She intended to go there that afternoon and to also visit St. Vitus' Cathedral. She would visit Golden Lane in the Prague Castle Walls and wander the cobblestone streets. She knew that the accommodations she would experience after her three days here as a tourist before her mission work began would be Spartan at best. She had booked the hotel room as soon as her clearance had come through. She would check in at the team headquarters the next morning.

The waiter arrived promptly and took her order. She settled back in her chair and looked out onto the terrace. She couldn't help but overhear the conversation from the men at the nearby table.

"So, where do we start?" the man with his back to her said in a definite southern drawl.

"Check in with the GM first and get the lay of the land," the man to his left facing the window replied. He was the largest of the three and looked to be in excellent shape.

"Do you think that they will call Wils McCann?" the third man, a shorter, balding man with glasses, said as he spooned some grapefruit. He sat to Donna's left but was looking directly at her as he raised the spoon to his mouth.

Donna's heart skipped a beat. She looked directly at him and her face registered her shock.

"Ma'am, is something wrong?" John Rice said, as he lowered his spoon, the grapefruit section still in it.

Donna's face flamed red. "I...I'm sorry... I couldn't help overhearing you mention a friend of mine," she stammered. The other two turned to look at her. Elmer Thune had swiveled in his chair to get a better look.

The big man smiled, "You know Wilson McCann?"

"Yes...he...he lives in our town. " Donna stammered on, her composure coming apart, "He...I....we...we're....we are ...friends!"

Myron Martin stood and held out his hand to the vacant chair at their table. "Please join us. We have been wondering where our friend Wils had gone to. Isn't it a small world?"

For the next 45 minutes, the four of them discussed the reasons that had brought them together in the Hotel Josef and the coincidence of both their meeting and their common friendship with Wilson McCann. John Rice was very interested in the mission work that Donna would be involved in and she invited him to visit the mission team headquarters at any time to become involved as a volunteer. All three of the men were interested in what McCann was doing and were amazed to learn about the farm, the cattle and the fact that McCann was helping the local telephone company with an acquisition of properties that the three of them were quite familiar with.

The three men told her about the need for a General Manager for their project and how McCann's name came up in discussions with the placement firm's manager. That led to a discussion of McCann and his leadership at Dynacom. It was evident to Donna that these three had a great deal of respect for McCann as a leader. They also showed considerable interest in his current situation as they knew firsthand how difficult the loss of Dynacom had been for them all, but particularly so for McCann.

John Rice listened closely as Donna shared with them about McCann's attendance at church and studying the Bible with her. He took a long drink from his coffee and sat the cup back as he asked, "Has he accepted the Lord?" The other two men's eyes were fixed on Donna. They knew how deeply John Rice's faith was and it was evident that he had found a kindred spirit in this woman from Michigan. While they did not share that faith, they respected the man and his devotion as well as his talent for reaching out to others in a non-intrusive way to share that faith.

"No…he hasn't…not yet," she replied, looking down.

John placed his left hand on hers and smiled. "Don't stop trying…okay?" he implored.

She looked at him, grateful for his understanding. She sensed that he understood how important Wilson McCann was to her.

Martin looked at his watch and pushed his chair back from the table.

"We're due at the GM's office in thirty minutes, guys. Time to get our bags and get going," he said.

"You are leaving? I…I mean the hotel?" Donna asked.

"Yes, they have an apartment for us and we move in today. We start work tomorrow. Here, let me give you the address and phone number. If you need anything while you are here, or if we can be of help, let us know. I'm sure that John will be checking in with you anyway," Martin responded as he handed her a business card with a phone number and address scrawled on the back.

"If you're talking to Wils, give him our best," Elmer Thune said as he extended his hand.

"Thank you. I will," she replied.

The three of them walked with her to the lobby and said goodbye again. Donna returned to her room thinking how God works in mysterious ways to bring people together to fulfill his plan.

(19)

It was cold, and a spit of snow was carried on the wind as he pulled into the drive twenty minutes before midnight. He had called ahead to let Nick know that he would be getting in late that night, and he found a note from Nick on the kitchen table saying that the cattle had been cared for and that Ted was bedded down in the barn. He turned up the thermostat and made a mental note to call Phil Willard to order fuel oil for the furnace. He decided to leave Ellen's things in the Jeep overnight and carry them inside in the morning. He was tired and ached all over. He had left Florida at 4:30 a.m. and had only stopped for gas and a hamburger at a fast food restaurant along the way. He noticed that his message unit was flashing and punched the "play" button hoping that Donna had called. Instead, Doug Warner informed him that Cindy Melzy would arrive on the following Monday to begin the due diligence work on Farnsworth Tele. Doug also briefed him on the work that he and Boyington had done in Detroit and suggested that they both be thinking about how to obtain additional information on what was behind the Governor's interest in the acquisition. McCann made a mental note to call Jim Wolfe the next day. Phil Willard was working within the party apparatus to see what he could learn, but Doug was not hopeful that anything new would turn up there. It was obvious that a tight lid was being kept on whatever was going on.

McCann kicked off his shoes and flopped in the recliner. It felt good to be home. The fact that he considered this old farmhouse to be home was a new feeling and he welcomed it. He had the urge to go to the barn and bring Ted in to keep him company but thought better of it as he listened to the wind howl around the eaves. He leaned back and closed his eyes, and two minutes later, he was fast asleep.

On Monday, the wind and the snow were long gone and a bright fall day welcomed the Fan Jet Falcon as it landed at Caro. McCann and Doug

Warner stood beside the little airport's one building as the plane taxied to a stop. The stairway dropped and a boy about six, dressed in a New York Mets jacket and cap stepped out and looked down at them. He raised his hand against the sun and seemed unsure of what to do next. Doug Warner looked at McCann questioningly. McCann shrugged his shoulders and smiled at the boy who waited, uncertainly at the top of the stair.

Cindy appeared in the doorway and grasped his hand to start him down the stairs ahead of her. She was dressed in Levis and a brown corduroy jacket. She wore black leather dress boots and looked like a model for *Western Wear* magazine as she descended the stairs, dropped the boy's hand and reached out to McCann. The boy shrank back behind her and peered out at the two men.

"Good morning, Cindy! You look like you've come to stay!" McCann said, as he took her hand.

"I thought I should dress the part! Do you think anyone will notice?" She bantered back as she reached to take Warner's hand.

"Only the whole county!" Warner smiled appreciatively.

"Who is this young man?" McCann asked, as the boy continued to peer out from behind Cindy's jean-clad legs.

She reached back and took his hand to draw him out in front of her. He looked up at her with that same uncertain expression that he had worn at the top of the plane's stair.

"This is David…my son – David," she responded, looking McCann directly in the eyes. "David, this is Mr. McCann and Mr. Warner."

McCann caught the look and caught the question that was forming on his lips and reached instead to take the boy's hand. David looked up at him as though he wanted to quickly retreat behind Cindy's legs. McCann squatted to bring his eyes directly level with the boy's.

"Was it fun flying on that plane?" he asked, as he held the boy's hand.

A smile crossed the boy's face and he didn't withdraw his hand. "Are you the farmer?" he asked quietly. "Do you have a dog?"

McCann looked up at Cindy and she caught the look and nervously responded to it. "I told him you had a farm with cows and a dog and tractors and such."

"Can I go there and see the dog?" the boy asked, continuing to look at McCann.

"David! I don't think…" Cindy began.

"Sure! We'll go out there and you can meet Ted! But I don't have cows. I have steers," McCann said as he rose.

The pilot descended the stair and opened the luggage bay and removed their luggage. As he did so, Cindy directed David to go to the waiting car. The boy reluctantly walked off with his head down.

Cindy turned to face the two men. "I'm terribly sorry. My ex-husband had an emergency come up and had to leave for London on short notice. The lady who normally takes care of David for him is ill and he dropped David off at my apartment last night. I didn't know what else to do with him. I'll be happy to pay someone to take care of him while I'm here. I realize this is an imposition but I didn't know what else to do on such short notice. William has custody and I usually only see David one weekend each month."

The way she said it made McCann instantly sorry for the boy. It was obvious that Cindy regarded him as an inconvenience in her fast paced world. He thought of his mother, and the sense of her recent loss made him turn instinctively toward the car where David waited, his hand on the door handle.

"I…didn't know that you and Bill…that is…," he began.

"Didn't know we had a son? Not many people do. David was born the first year we were married. When William and I divorced, we felt it was better for him if he stayed with his father." She looked away across the runway as she said it. Doug picked up the two bags and started for the car. The pilot closed the luggage bay and told Cindy that he would return on Friday to pick her up. With that, he mounted the stair and it quickly closed after him. In a few moments, the Falcon's jets began to whine.

On impulse, McCann slid into the back seat next to the boy who regarded him cautiously. With Doug at the wheel and Cindy in the front seat, the car headed for Farnsworth. Wilson McCann began to tell David about his farm.

By the time they arrived in Farnsworth, David was smiling and talking excitedly about the animals and tractors he had seen in the fields along the highway. Belle Warner had invited Cindy to stay at her home during the week. As they arrived at the Warner mansion, McCann leaned over and whispered in David's ear. Cindy looked back, a smile frozen on her face. "What are you two whispering about?" she asked.

"Oh mama! Mr. McCann has asked me to stay with him at his farm! Can I? Can I, please?"

Cindy's eyes shot to McCann's face, her surprise plainly evident.

"You won't need me to review Farnsworth Tele's operations. Besides, I can use another hand on the farm. We have to get everything ready for winter." He smiled.

"Can I, mama?" David pleaded.

She relaxed and turned to get out of the car as Belle Warner descended the steps to greet them.

"Yes, David. You may."

"Oh! Thank you mama! Thank you!" David shouted as he jumped out the door. McCann thought that it was the happiest look he had seen on the boy's face since they arrived.

He drove home listening to David's excited chatter about the farm and the animals and wondering if he had done the right thing. It was clear that the boy was an unexpected inconvenience to his mother. McCann had not known that Cindy and her husband had a son. She had evidently worked to assure that this aspect of her life remained secret. He wondered why a mother would give up custody of her son and he immediately knew the answer. Cindy had put her career ahead of her family. It pained him to know that he was guilty of the same actions in his own life. Marriage, children and even his mother had been pushed into the background as he pursued his career.

"Here we are," he said as they pulled into the drive. Ted came racing up from the barn. As the car had stopped, the boy unfastened his seat belt and scrambled out the door to wrap his arms around the dog's neck. McCann stood watching as Ted licked David's face and the boy looked up at him, his eyes shining.

"He's beautiful! Just like the dog in my book!" he exclaimed. He released Ted and grabbed a small back pack from the car. Unzipping the pack, he pulled out a child's version of '*Bob, Son of Battle*' with a picture of Ted's twin on the cover and held it up.

"I must admit, they do look alike" McCann smiled, as he reached in for the boy's other bag.

"Can I take him to see the cattle?" David asked, looking out at the steers drinking at the tank in the barn yard.

"Sure, but only go as far as the fence. Don't get too near them," McCann replied, as the boy and the dog ran toward the barn.

He leaned against the car and watched them. The boy stopped at the fence and Ted sat beside him as he extended his hand through the fence toward a steer that eyed him suspiciously before backing away. McCann had never been comfortable around small children, yet he felt himself drawn to David. What would it have been like to have a son? He felt a great emptiness as he watched the boy and the dog run from the barn to the tool shed and peer inside.

"Can I ride on the tractor?" David shouted from the doorway to the shed.

"Let's get you settled in first," McCann replied, walking toward the house with the bags. This was going to be a very interesting week, he thought to himself.

McCann did not have the remotest idea of how interesting the week would become. He settled David into the spare bedroom and waited as the boy changed into a pair of overalls and a flannel shirt from his bag and a pair of well worn sneakers from his pack. The rest of the day was spent with David following McCann as he did routine chores and cared for the cattle. They took the "A" and drove it back into the fields with David riding on his lap and pretending to drive as McCann rested his hands on the steering wheel. By 4:00 p.m., David was fast asleep on the living room sofa and Ted was curled up in the kitchen next to his water dish. McCann smiled as he looked down at the dog.

"Was he too much for you?" he said. Ted opened one eye and wagged his tail twice before going back to sleep.

McCann called the Telephone Co. and spoke to Doug, telling him that he had called Jim Wolfe, but that his call had not been returned. Wolfe was in the field doing service reviews. Warner said that the due diligence was going well and Cindy expected to wrap it up by Wednesday. Belle had asked her to have dinner at the mansion. Cindy took the phone briefly to ask if David was a problem and seemed satisfied with McCann's assurance that he was fine. She returned the phone to Doug who told McCann that he would give him a call in the morning. McCann replaced the phone with a vague feeling of disappointment that his services were apparently not as yet needed during the due diligence review. He was mildly irritated that he was needed more as a baby sitter for David, but quickly reflected on the boy's joyousness during the day and realized that perhaps he could add something to David's life that quite probably was missing a good bit of the time.

The next two days passed quickly and McCann was beginning to regret the fact that Cindy and David would be leaving. Belle Warner hosted a dinner on Wednesday evening and as McCann watched David recount his adventures at the farm, he noticed that Cindy seemed different. He noted that when Belle and Doug bowed their heads before the meal that Cindy took David's hand and bowed her head, telling the boy, "We are going to pray now."

After dinner, Belle announced that she had invited Cindy to stay through the weekend and that she had accepted. David quickly asked if he could stay at the farm rather than move in with his mother.

"Perhaps Mr. McCann would be willing to bring you in on Saturday so that we can be ready to leave on Sunday. I've asked the plane to return on Sunday afternoon," Cindy said, looking expectantly at McCann.

Belle Warner quickly interjected, "I hope that you will be able to go to church with us before you leave!"

Cindy smiled at her and said quietly, "Yes, I would like that."

As they got ready to return to the farm later that evening, McCann noticed that Cindy hugged David tightly and kissed him on the forehead. The boy seemed surprised but quickly wrapped his arms around his mother's neck and returned her kiss. Belle Warner stood watching, a faint smile on her lips.

Cindy walked them to the car and helped David into the front seat. She pulled his seat belt around him and buckled it for him. Cindy kissed David again before closing the passenger side door. She came around to the driver's side and held out her hand to McCann.

"Wils, I want to thank you for…everything. This week…well…it's been very special. The Warner's are wonderful people and Belle has been so gracious and…well… she has shown me some things that I needed to see. And, I appreciate how you have been with David. I'm afraid I haven't been a very good mother to him and his father has a new 'friend' who takes a lot of his time. You have a wonderful way with children."

"A talent I didn't know I had and haven't had a chance to use." He smiled back at her, "David is a very special boy. You are very lucky."

"I'm afraid I didn't know how lucky I was," she said, looking down at the ground.

"And the company? How is the review going?" McCann asked.

"Oh! It's fine. Everything is just as you had said it would be. I am sure there will be no problem with the financing, assuming they can raise the balance. But this trip has been more than a due diligence review. It's been sort of a 'due diligence' review of my life and …and…David's. And for that, I will be eternally grateful to you."

McCann got into the car and closed the door. She stood waving to them from the driveway as he headed the LeSabre out into the night. David leaned against him and was asleep before they left Farnsworth. McCann drove home slowly, thinking about the change in Cindy's demeanor and what she had said. Something was happening here and he wasn't exactly sure what it all meant. He was still pondering it all in his mind as he tucked David into bed and turned out the light.

Thursday and Friday passed with David alternately playing with Ted, following McCann around the farm and having McCann read to him from his book. McCann enjoyed the evenings with the boy sitting close to him on the sofa as he read from the book. Their time together in the evening seemed to place a perfect ending to each day. Cindy borrowed a Farnsworth Tele pool car and came out for dinner on Friday night and David demanded that they have fried potatoes and fried bologna, just like the two of them had been eating the night before. After dinner, she helped wash the dishes and read to David from his book before he went to bed. Ted curled up next to the bed just as he had all week and she smiled at them as she softly closed the door. McCann poured two cups of coffee and they drank them in the living room. He reflected that he hadn't had dinner with someone at the farm since Donna left for Prague. It also occurred to him that he hadn't thought of Donna since Cindy and David had arrived.

Cindy talked with him about the review and the financing and assured him that there would be no problems with either lender. They talked about the mysterious calls from the firm in Detroit and what it all might mean to the acquisition. Cindy was of the opinion that someone saw a chance to muscle in on the deal and that they would drop out when they learned the details of the acquisition. She also mentioned that she had some contacts in Dallas that might be willing to participate, if the Warners were unsuccessful in finding additional capital.

Finally, she rose to go and McCann followed her to the back porch. She stood looking out over the fields in the moonlight and he stood beside her. He could smell her perfume and he sensed that she wanted to say something and was hesitating.

"Cindy, you seem…different," he said quietly.

She turned towards him and placed her hand on his arm. She looked up at him and smiled. "In one week, I have changed more than I have ever thought possible, Wils."

"How so?"

"I have found a new meaning to my life. Belle has shared some things with me that have helped me to see that I have misplaced my priorities. I intend to change that. I have not been a good mother to David and I intend to change that too."

"I'm glad for you."

She leaned against him and brushed her lips against his cheek. "Thank you, Wils. I will always remember this week."

She stepped back and lowered her head. He thought perhaps she was embarrassed by her show of affection but she raised her head and looked into his eyes.

"Wils…..I hope that you will find what I have found," she said and walked to her car. He stood watching as the taillights headed down the road.

McCann took David into Farnsworth the following afternoon. The boy had said a long and solemn goodbye to Ted and had walked around the yard as if to fix everything in his mind before he left. When they arrived at the Warner mansion, he greeted his mother affectionately and she held him close for a moment before turning to McCann.

"Thank you again for all you have done for David this week. Will we see you tomorrow in church?"

"I suppose so. It has become a regular habit since I came here," He smiled.

"Not a bad habit to have, I think." She smiled back. "I may take it up myself."

Doug Warner appeared in the doorway. He beckoned McCann inside and led him to a small study off the main entrance. As the two men entered, Doug closed the door behind them.

"I've heard from Smith. He has all our information and feels he is in position to put a positive presentation before his boss. Cindy's review results will help, I should think."

"Good, is there anything I can do?" McCann asked, turning to face him.

"Is there any way you can find out what is behind all this interest from Lansing? I'm getting a little concerned that we may be buying into something we can't handle."

"I'll call Jim Wolfe again. If that doesn't help, I have a couple of contacts in Lansing that might be able to shed some light on it."

"Good, thanks." Warner looked out the window across the front yard. He seemed nervous and McCann studied him closely as he waited. "Is there something else?" he asked.

Warner turned to face him and rubbed the back of his neck as he began to speak. "Arthur received a call from someone at LEGENT. They wanted to know if you were involved in our interest in the properties and made it quite clear that if you were, they wanted nothing to do with us."

McCann's anger rose immediately and he turned away to compose himself. "I'm not surprised," he said, as he rubbed his clenched fist into the palm of his other hand. "They obviously haven't forgotten what happened when they acquired Dynacom. Did Arthur explain my role?"

"Yes, he told them you own an interest in the company and that you had given management a power of attorney in relation to the acquisition. He was able to persuade them to accept that, provided that you do not participate in the actual negotiations. I'm sorry, Wils."

"No need for you to be. I don't want to become a distraction or a barrier to your success in this. How do you want to play it from here?"

"I need your help and advice. I'm not willing to give that up. Will you be willing to work with us in the background to help us?" Warner's tone was sincere and McCann could sense that he was struggling with this new development on top of the mysterious nature of the Governor's interest.

"Whatever you want, you've got it."

"Thanks, Wils. I wish it were different. I wanted you to be sitting at the table when we make our proposal."

"I'm sure that with Arthur and the other people involved, you will be in good hands. Cindy's review will go a long way toward keeping the New York City interests satisfied."

"She has been great. My mother has really taken to her. I think that she has developed the same kind of relationship with Cindy that she has with Donna. By the way, have you heard from her?"

McCann looked away again. "No, not since she left for Prague. I imagine she is busy and enjoying her work there." He said it almost jealously and Warner sensed it was a sensitive issue.

"Will you join us for church tomorrow? Cindy and David are coming with us."

"Why not? An evil man like me needs all the help he can get," McCann said gruffly, as he opened the door and walked back into the hall. After a quick good bye to David and Cindy, he walked out the door and drove away. Doug Warner watched from the window of the study and bowed his head in prayer.

"Lord, I pray for Wilson McCann and for your guidance and protection in his life and he might come to a saving knowledge of Jesus Christ," he said quietly, before turning to join the others. Cindy turned as he entered the room. "How did it go?" she asked.

"I think it hurt him, and I think he can't take many more hurts," Doug replied.

(20)

Early Sunday morning, Donna climbed into the old International Scout and smiled at John Rice. They were headed for Milovice, twenty-five miles north and east of Prague. From there, they would travel to Uvaly and back to Prague. The Scout was one of three vehicles the mission group maintained and none were in the best of shape. The trip included visits to small churches near the two towns, and she had been told that once they were off the highways, the roads could be treacherous.

She was happy that John was going along. He had shown up at the group's evening group meeting and had volunteered to help out where he could during his days off from the project.

He started the engine and released the emergency brake. "These brakes feel like they are on their last legs," he said with some concern, as he pushed the pedal. "Not much left there. They might want to have them checked."

"They might want to pray for a new vehicle!" She laughed, as she settled back in her seat and the Scout began its journey out of Prague.

Charles Hastings walked to the center of the platform, his Bible open in his right hand. He looked out over the congregation and noted that Doug and Lori Warner were seated on one side of Wilson McCann and that an attractive woman and a little boy sat between them and Belle Warner. He presumed that the woman was Cindy Melzy and the boy was her son David. Belle Warner had called him earlier in the week to request prayer for Cindy and David. He hoped that his sermon for the morning would help to meet the need that Belle had spoken of in her call.

"My text today is Matthew 6:25-34. In my Bible, the heading for that portion of scripture is 'The Cure for Anxiety 'but I want to change it somewhat to 'The Cure for Care'. What do you care about? Is it the right thing? We all have cares. Some of us care about others. Some care about money, power or position. We all have cares. As we read this together, I want us to see what it is that Jesus said we should care about. I want you to look particularly at the 33rd verse. Let me read it to you. *But seek first His Kingdom and His righteousness and all these things shall be added to you'."*

McCann noted that Cindy had a Bible open in her lap. It looked new and he suspected that it was a gift from Belle Warner. David, seated next to him, was studiously coloring a picture of Jesus at the well of Samaria. He had obviously been to Sunday school that morning.

"The verse is really about what you put first in your life. That is what you care most about. Some of you have put family first in your life. That is not bad. It's good! But listen to what Jesus said: '*seek first His Kingdom and His righteousness.*' Some of you have put your job or your farm first. Some of you have put your retirement first. Some of you have put security first. None of these things are evil! They just aren't what we are supposed to put first! By our choices, we have neglected what Jesus said was most important. We care about our family; we care about doing a good job. We care about putting food on the table and clothes on our back. There is nothing wrong about any of those things. Yet Jesus said that the people of his day cared about them also. See what he says in verse 31: *Do not be anxious then, saying 'what shall we eat?' or 'what shall we drink?' or 'with what shall we clothe ourselves?'* Then in verse 32 he says: '*your heavenly Father knows that you need all these things'.* Think about that! God knows what you need! Jesus said that we need to stop caring about what God already knows we need and start looking for ways to participate in his kingdom and doing his work! Some of you have put your trust in power or position or some other substitute and when you find out that doesn't satisfy, you begin to feel the emptiness of life. Only Christ can fill that emptiness."

McCann looked sideways at Cindy. Her eyes were fixed on Hastings. Her hands rested on the open Bible in her lap. It was as if she was there in body but her mind was elsewhere. David looked up at his mother and then resumed his coloring. Belle Warner sat like a statue next to Cindy. Her eyes were closed and McCann didn't doubt that she was praying.

Hastings walked to the far side of the platform and continued to speak, looking out at the people sitting on that side of the church. The congregation's collective eyes followed him back and forth across the platform as he drove the points of his Savior's message home.

He paused in the sermon and turned back to the center, and it seemed as though he was looking directly at McCann. "There is so much more to life in Jesus Christ than there is to a life where all these other things pile up and drain away our energy! Jesus said that God cares about all of life. He cares for the birds of the air and they aren't busy putting silage into the silos and hay into the barns! He cares about the lilies out in the field and dresses them far more finely than even those who go to Sax 5th Avenue in New York City!"

McCann stole another glance at Cindy as the words hung there. A faint smile crossed her face. He knew that Cindy was no stranger to Sax 5th Avenue and many of the other fine clothiers in the "Big Apple."

Hastings closed his Bible and held it at his side in his left hand as he looked intently out at the congregation. His voice dropped to a more quiet tone as he spoke.

"What do you care about today? What's important in your life? If you have turned your life over to Jesus Christ, only you know the answer to these questions. If you haven't, I submit to you that Jesus gives us the answer to the cares of this world. He says that we should stop worrying about all these 'things' and all these 'issues' and all these 'what-ifs' and concentrate on seeking His will for our lives and doing his business. Does that mean that if you put Christ and His kingdom first in your life you can stop caring about your family or your farm or your job or your retirement or whatever else you have first in your life today? No! But it does mean that if you put Christ first in your life and turn your life over to Him, He will help you put these other things in their proper order and He will care for them just as He cares for you! I urge you to make that decision now if you haven't already done so. Take the 'Care Cure' and put your faith in Christ. He'll take care of the rest! Please bow your heads. I'd like to ask you today to answer Jesus' challenge. Have you given Him first place in your life? Are you genuinely seeking to do His will? If you haven't, I ask you to do it today. As we pray, tell Him that you are guilty of putting other things first in your life. Tell Him that you are sorry about that and that you want Him to forgive you and that you want to make His Father's business first in your life. Tell Him that you want to make that change today and that you are asking Him to come into your life and take control of it. If you want to do that today, I invite you to come to the altar here at the front and make that decision known. Let us pray."

McCann had bowed his head and closed his eyes as Hastings began to pray. He felt David move beside him and opened his eyes to see Cindy rise and turn to move past them to the aisle. She walked confidently down to the altar at the front of the church and knelt. David looked up at McCann with a puzzled look on his face. McCann impulsively slipped his arm around the boy and hugged him as Hastings continued to pray.

The Scout had left the main highway and they started the final 15 kilometer drive up into the hills to the church. Initially, the road had been wide and graveled. As they proceeded, however, it became increasingly narrow and the rate of incline became steep. John had joked that the ride gave new meaning to "it rides like a truck" and Donna had laughed as she braced herself against the seat.

She was enjoying the day. The initial work for the mission team had been in Prague. Prague was a beautiful city and she did not dislike it. She had enjoyed her visits to Golden Lane, St. Vitus' Cathedral and Castle Prague. While wandering the cobblestone streets, she had time to think about her relationship with Wilson McCann. She felt that they had grown in their relationship over the past weeks. Their evenings together studying the Bible had strengthened her belief that McCann was genuinely seeking a new way of life. He was the type of man who did not give expression to his inner feelings easily and she was willing to wait for the day that he could speak to her of his feelings in the same manner that she could for him. She wondered when that day came if he would also share the love for the Lord's work in a way that would allow them to work together helping others just as she was doing here in the Czech Republic. She had felt fulfilled here as never before.

Yet she knew that the smaller towns and congregations were where her missionary heart lay. She had looked forward to this trip since coming even though the language barrier would make it difficult to fully communicate with the people of this little church. The educational materials they brought with them would assist the congregation and they would worship together within the common bond of faith in Christ.

She glanced over at John and for about the fourth time that day thanked God for his involvement and willingness to drive today. He had been a blessing to the team in general and to her in particular as he pitched in and helped whenever he could. His schedule during the day made it impossible for him to participate in the team's Bible study and prayer time but he had attended almost every one of the evening group meetings. On one occasion he had brought Myron and Elmer with him. Donna knew that they did not share his faith but she recognized the deep respect they had for him and he for them. Before leaving that evening the four of them had spent a relaxing hour drinking coffee and talking about the three men's days together at Dynacom. They had talked at length about Wils McCann and his leadership of the company. Through their expressed respect for McCann and she began to see more clearly the depth of his hurt in the loss of the company he had led.

She felt guilty for not having called him. Belle Warner had given her an international calling card with a thousand prepaid minutes on it when she left for Prague. She had not used it. She felt that she needed these first days to sort out her feelings for McCann. She had spent many hours on her knees praying about her conflicting feelings. She had been truthful in expressing her love for him and was somewhat disappointed in his inability to say that he felt the same way for her. While she was encouraged by his willingness to study his Bible with her and his attendance in church, she knew that he was not yet ready to yield his life to Jesus Christ. She had prayed about what it would take to bring him to that point and what it would mean when and if he reached it. During her prayer times, she had asked the Lord to speak to his heart and bring him to a point of repentance, confession and acceptance. She had confidently asked for wisdom for herself to deal with where such a decision might lead.

As she thought about this, her spirits lifted in the assurance she felt that the Lord had a plan for both their lives. "Thy will be done," she thought.

The sun was in their eyes as they climbed up the hillside. The valley below was bathed in sunlight and Donna was enjoying the view out the open side window. The sun was so bright that John had to pull his cap brim lower in order to see the road ahead. It had rained the previous day and it had dampened the countryside and eliminated any dust as the Scout chewed its way up the gravel incline.

They rounded a curve and John swung the wheel hard to the left as they turned. The back wheels of the Scout slewed to the right side of the road and fought for traction against the gravel. The same rain that had laid the dust had eroded the edge of the road and washed a three-foot section at the curve down the hillside. The right rear wheel continued to spin as it ran out of gravel and hit the washout. The rear end of the Scout tipped out and down and the vehicle began its backward somersault descent down the hillside. The slope was not steep but the washout had exposed a spine of rock about three feet high. The Scout came down on that spine with its wheels in the air.

The Scout was at least 35 years old and probably more. It had not been built with the same safety engineering of today's SUVs. The weight of the vehicle, its occupants and contents crushed the top down on the front seat before the vehicle turned over one more time and came to rest. As the dust settled, nothing moved except for a few stones that continued down the hillside.

McCann watched the plane climb into the sky and disappear momentarily behind a wisp of cloud. It reappeared again, the sun reflecting from it and then it was gone. He turned and walked to the Ranger, his head down. He suddenly felt very much alone. David had insisted in riding to the airport in the Ranger with Ted beside him. The Warners had brought Cindy.

He reflected on the events of the day. The church had rejoiced over Cindy's profession of faith and she joined in freely, her face radiant as she hugged the Warners, the Marks and even McCann. Her attention to David was marked in its contrast to her attitude upon her arrival in Farnsworth. She held his hand as they left the church and McCann overheard her promise to the boy to be a "new and better mom."

They had gone out for lunch and then returned to the Warner home to pick up their luggage. It was then that David had made his demands to "say goodbye to Ted" one more time. McCann was more than happy to oblige the boy and knew that he would miss him. Sharing the farmhouse with someone besides his dog had been a refreshing time and opened his eyes to things he had missed in his climb up the corporate ladder.

As they prepared to board the jet, Cindy had promised Belle that she would return in the future, and Doug Warner had asked her to "consider carefully what we talked about." McCann wondered what that was all about. Cindy had embraced him and kissed him on the cheek before leaving and thanked him again for bringing her to Farnsworth. David had tears in his eyes as he hugged Ted and again when he hugged McCann.

"Can I come again, too?" he asked, burying his head against McCann's shoulder.

"Any time buddy," McCann had whispered into his ear before letting him go.

He scratched Ted's ears as he got into the truck. The road back to Farnsworth had little traffic. The streets of both Caro and Farnsworth were virtually empty. He turned into the drive and put the Ranger in the tool shed. Ted raced off behind the barn.

He entered the house and glanced at the phone with its answering machine. The digital display showed two messages. He pushed the "play" button for the first message and heard Chuck Hastings' voice.

"Wils, please call me right away. Something terrible has happened."

He picked up the phone without bothering to listen to the second message. Hastings answered on the second ring.

"What's happened?" McCann asked.

"Donna was in an automobile accident north of Prague this morning. I just received a call from the director of the mission team. Wils, she is dead."

McCann stood there, the phone gripped in his hand. Hastings' voice seemed to come into his ear from a million miles away and he felt like he was falling through space into a deep black hole.

The funeral service was to be ten days later and Donna would be buried beside her father and mother in the small cemetery on the eastern outskirts of Farnsworth. John Rice would be buried the same day in a small cemetery overlooking the Missouri River west of St. Louis. McCann had spent the ten days in a fog. He went about the routine chores on the farm during the day and sat in the darkened farmhouse in the evening before going off to bed only to lie awake for most of the nights. He had cried on that first night as he never had before in his life. He had cursed God and hurled Fred and Ella Harms' Bible across the room. It lay where it landed, a crumpled book against the wall.

The phone rang often during the first two days, as Hastings, Doug Warner and Jim Marks attempted to reach out to him. He ignored the phone and let the messages pile up on the recorder. Marks had driven into the yard on the third day and offered sympathy. McCann had thanked him and turned away. Marks left, a bewildered look on his face. Hastings came that evening and McCann listened politely as Hastings talked about God's plan and his feeling that Donna's life had been centered in that plan. Before he left, the minister had offered to pray with him and McCann replied that he had lost confidence in prayer to a God who was so cruel as to take a life as good as Donna's. Hastings prayed anyway, his hand on McCann's shoulder as the two stood just inside the kitchen door. After he left, McCann retrieved the Bible from where it lay and put it away on a shelf in the hallway closet.

Doug Warner came out on the fourth day. He talked briefly about Donna and how her loss had affected Belle. He also talked about the ongoing work on the proposed acquisition and McCann allowed himself to turn his mind to the work involved. Doug asked him to join the Farnsworth Board and McCann accepted. Two days later, the board had met for the first time. As Doug reviewed the financial statements and impacts of the steadily changing telecommunications environment, McCann found himself focusing on what was necessary for a firm, such as Farnsworth Tele, to survive. That night, he sat at his table in the kitchen and re-worked some of the financial numbers for impact of both the changes in Farnsworth Tele's revenue stream and for the possible acquisition of the LEGENT properties. Farnsworth Tele had been somewhat shielded from the loss in revenue to cable television companies due to their own cable operation. The company had also been able to more than offset the loss in second lines by a steady increase in the sale of digital subscriber lines. The changes in long distance access and universal service funding would come in the future. But for now, the company had a sound local base and had made the right moves to protect it. He found the work invigorating and for a few hours that evening he was able to concentrate on something other than Donna's death.

He reflected that it had always been this way. Whenever his personal life had been lacking, he had filled the void with work. With his mind occupied with strategy and financial or operational results, there was no room for any concerns about his lack of close personal relationships or anything else. Dynacom had been his family, his lover and, if he were honest, his God. When he shut down his laptop shortly after midnight, he heard the sound of pellets of snow against the window. He turned off the lights and went to bed. Once there, he was unable to sleep. He could only think of the great losses in his life. Dynacom, his mother, and now Donna. On the day that the attempt to prevent the acquisition of Dynacom had failed, he had felt a great emptiness, but nothing like the gaping black hole that he had fallen into when Donna died. It was three in the morning before he fell into a restless sleep.

Ted thrust his muzzle under the blankets at eight the next morning and McCann let him out into a foot of snow that had fallen during the night. The day had dawned cloudy and cold, a sunless harbinger of the winter to come. The cold that surged in the door when Ted hastily returned from his morning rounds left McCann feeling as cold outside as he did in his heart. After seeing to the cattle, he returned to his laptop. He continued to review the numbers and prepare several strategy oriented documents to discuss with Doug Warner.

Over the next four days, the weather changed and the cold cloudy days gave way to bright sunshine and temperatures above freezing. The two fields of new wheat emerged from the blanket of snow like a green carpet spread below the barn as he tended to his chores. Cindy called on the day before the funeral and expressed her sympathy. She reminded him of the need to trust in God's plan and put David on the line. The boy asked about Ted and whether he had plowed the snow with the tractor. His spirits lifted as David told him about going to the children's museum with his mother and how they had gone to church last Sunday. The boy said that he still had his picture book with Ted on the cover. Cindy came back on the line to say goodbye and to tell him that she was praying for him each day. He thanked her quietly and hung up the phone, reflecting again that his situation was beyond prayer.

The United Methodist Church in Farnsworth was filled to overflowing and people stood outside on the lawn as Charles Hastings brought the eulogy. McCann sat in the middle of the church flanked by Doug Warner's family on one side and Jim Marks' family on the other. He listened as Hastings talked of Donna's love for the Lord and her desire to help others find a life changing relationship with Him.

As Hastings concluded and offered a closing prayer, the congregation stood as one and sang "Amazing Grace" without musical accompaniment. The rich blend of voices filled the sanctuary. At the end there were several quiet "amen's." He watched as the casket was moved out and the line of mourners followed it. Belle and Doug Warner and Nick and Darcy Hardesty, together with two of Donna's distant relatives, led the procession. As the casket disappeared into the hearse, he felt as though a piece of his life was locked inside it and would never again see the light of day. Belle had asked McCann to join the group for lunch at the Warner home but he declined. Instead, he went home to the farm and sat alone in his living room. The afternoon sun faded into dusk as Ted, sensing his master's melancholy, laid his head on McCann's knee and waited expectantly for a pat on the head. When it didn't come, he curled up against McCann's feet and began to lick his paws.

In the little cemetery at the outskirts of Farnsworth, two workmen began to shovel a mound of dirt to close Donna Barnes' grave.

(21)

The Director of the Telecommunications Division left his office and headed for the Governor's offices. His head down, he ignored two staff members that he usually greeted, causing one of them to look over his shoulder before speaking in a subdued voice to his colleague.

"Wonder what's bugging him this morning?"

"I would guess it has something to do with the LEGENT sale. I heard they went to one of the Commissioners," she responded. She knew more than she was willing to share.

LEGENT had indeed gone to one of the Commissioners appointed by the previous Governor. The subject of the call was their concern about the amount of regulatory oversight that they were encountering to their proposed plan to exit the state. The Commissioner listened patiently and pointed out that she and other Commissioners would give careful review of their staff's actions relative to any sale petition and assured the LEGENT representatives of her desire to assure that such a petition would be handled with appropriate regulatory flexibility. The LEGENT representatives left the meeting with the feeling that they had done little to advance their cause.

The Director had been summoned to the Commissioner's office and had reviewed his previous discussions with the LEGENT representatives and reviewed the process that the staff would follow in considering any sale proposal that was submitted to the Commission. The Commissioner requested that she be kept aware of any developments and the Director had assured her he would do so.

Now, the Governor's office had called again. The Director had met with the Governor's aide, Ross, a little more than a month ago and brought him up to date on the LEGENT meeting with the Chairman and their subsequent meeting with him. He had also told Ross what he knew about the level of interest being expressed by various companies in acquiring the LEGENT properties.

The Governor's secretary glanced at him over her half glasses and said crisply, "Good morning, the Governor is expecting you, go right in." She immediately turned back to some documents on her desk and resumed reading. The Governor was standing with his back to the door as the Director rapped lightly on the door frame and entered. Ross was sitting beside the Governor's desk facing the door. The Governor turned, smiling and coming forward to shake hands. Ross remained seated.

"Good morning Fred. How goes the course of regulatory policy?" he asked, indicating a chair in front of the desk.

"That depends on whether you are the regulator or the regulated," the Director responded, trying to keep things light. The Governor responded with a hearty chuckle and Ross smiled.

"The Telecommunications Act of 1996 did you no favors, did it Fred?" he said, leaning back in his chair.

"The Act could use a little tune up."

"I'm afraid it won't get it for a while given some of the priorities the FCC has set,." the Governor responded. "What's new relative to LEGENT?"

The Director was caught a bit off guard by the quick change in subject, but took a moment to cross his legs and drop his hands into his lap, giving himself time to frame his reply.

"Nothing tangible sir. I suspect you know as much about the rumors as I do." It was said frankly and the Governor's smile indicated that the frankness was appreciated.

"I hear that Farnsworth Tele has joined consortium bidding on the entire property with provisions that it would attempt to acquire the properties in our state."

"I've heard the same," the Director responded.

"Give me a minute or two of your estimate of their company." As the Governor said this, Ross adjusted his position slightly and looked directly at the Director.

"They offer excellent service. They haven't had a formal Commission complaint in three years and they have been very prudent in the investment of capital in both the cable television and provision of data and broadband services. The Warner family is well regarded within the industry. They have a couple of young people on the technology side that are among the best in the business. The family would be stretched to acquire the LEGENT properties and would, in my opinion, need to put on some management assistance in the operational management and financial management areas if they were successful."

Ross spoke for the first time. "I understand that Wilson McCann has purchased a minority interest in the company and is advising them in this matter. Did you know that?"

"I had heard that. Nothing official."

"What do you think of McCann?"

The Director considered his answer before responding. Mindful of the Governor's previous admonitions toward candor, his response was direct.

"Frankly, Governor, if Mr. McCann was running LEGENT, the service in both the former Dynacom properties that were acquired by LEGENT and the rest of the LEGENT properties in this state would be far better than it is today and we would be more confident in the future of the networks in those properties."

The Governor leaned back in his chair again and steepled his hands beneath his chin.

"He's that good?"

"He ran a good ship at Dynacom," the director replied.

"Is he a technology whiz?"

"No."

"A financial man?"

"No. He's a good telecommunications man and he's a good business man."

The Governor looked over at Ross before he asked his next question.

"Wasn't he considered to be sort of an opportunist ...somewhat self-serving in his attempt to buy Dynacom?"

"The media, in my unofficial opinion, made more of that than was there. I can tell you that the Dynacom people in Michigan thought highly of him and believed him to be honest and fair ...a man of good ethics."

The Governor leaned forward and looked the Director squarely in the eye. His voice dropped ever so slightly as he began to speak.

"Fred, this is the last meeting you will have with me in this matter. I appreciate your candor and your patience with us in keeping us posted. A member of the Farnsworth Tele Board is the county Republican Chairman in Tuscola County. He is also a friend to this administration. I do not know Mr. McCann personally, but my understanding of him is the same as yours. He is a good businessman. If Farnsworth Tele. makes an offer on the LEGENT properties in this state, I would want you to give their offer the same scrutiny as any others and I would want you to be especially confident of their ability to deploy and maintain a state-of-the-art network and to have every chance to succeed financially. If they need to add to their human capital to accomplish that, I want you to assure yourself that they have a plan to do so."

"You may rest assured Governor that we will do that not only with regard to Farnsworth Tele but any other potential acquirer." In saying this, the Director hoped that he did not sound self righteous.

"I'm particularly interested in this because Farnsworth Tele represents an in-state acquirer with a reputation for investing in Michigan's future," the Governor said, with a smile. "I'm not at all interested in seeing these properties secured, stripped and sold off again."

Ross rose and extended his hand. "Thank you for coming over, Fred. Keep in touch if need be …I'm always glad to talk with you." His message was clear. From now on, any contact would not be with the Governor.

As he headed back to his office, the Director reflected on the message he had been given. While Farnsworth Tele was clearly on the Governor's list of desired acquirers, there was something more to this than a routine Public Service Commission proceeding. He would gather his staff at the appropriate time and make sure that they knew that whoever sought to acquire the LEGENT properties was subjected to the most thorough review possible. Upon returning to his office, he told his secretary to accept an invitation to address an issues forum sponsored by the State Telecommunications Association. It might offer an opportunity to visit informally with Doug Warner and some members of his team.

John King leaned back in his chair and looked out his window at the Dallas Skyline off in the distance. Ten years! He hated Dallas as much today as he had when he arrived a decade ago. One more year, and he would go home to Savannah, Georgia, and play golf three days a week and sit by the ocean with his wife of thirty five-years and watch the container ships go in and out of the river to and from the Port of Savannah . He was sixty-four with a mop of steely gray hair. His two hundred and forty pounds were well distributed over his six foot four inch frame but he still felt small when Sal Piazza was in the room. Sal was lounging his six foot six, two hundred and sixty pound frame against the doorway to King's office. The brass sign on the door said "J. King." His business card said "Vice President - Organizational Re-Deployment". He referred to himself as "The King of Fire Sales." It occurred to King to ask a question he had never asked during his five year association with Piazza, twenty-two years his junior.

"You ever play football for Holy Cross?"

"Nah – clarinet."

King swiveled his chair. "What?"

"Clarinet…I played Clarinet in the band! Why?"

"Geez – What a waste! Are the rooms ready?"

"Yeah, one for each of them. They are all on separate floors. Do you think he'll show?"

"Who?" King asked, knowing the intent of Piazza's question.

"McCann."

"No. Norm made it pretty clear he was *persona non grata*. Norm's an idiot! We would have been better off if Dynacom had acquired us and McCann was Chief Operating Officer!"

"You'd better watch it or you'll be going home to Georgia early and without any severance pay." Piazza smiled and didn't move away from the door.

"So who's where?" King asked, ignoring Piazza's jibe. Norm Lister, the COO of LEGENT, was an idiot as far as King was concerned. LEGENT had bought a lot of property during Lister's tenure on the job and now they were selling off chunks of it and weren't investing anything to speak of in what was left. King had worked his way up from a cable-splicer's helper and had gone to night school at Purdue while raising two kids and learning the operating side of the business over a forty-year career. He had purchased the Savannah retirement home while he was Division President and General Manager of LEGENT'S Southeast Division. He had used his time there to ready himself for a promotion to LEGENT'S Dallas headquarters as Corporate Vice President – Network. Five years later, a heart attack had changed his life and sidetracked his career. Frankly, he didn't mind. His life was much better for it except for his disappointment with what was happening to the company he had committed his life to. He had watched LEGENT grow and prosper and now, in his opinion, he was watching it sicken and die. Didn't these MBAs know that you had to invest in your business to keep it growing?

"…on the third floor, Fairfield on the seventh and the new bunch on ten," Piazza interrupted his train of thought. He knew that the third floor group was headed by a former FCC operative and had a lot of minority group money behind it. Fairfield was a pretty good aggregator in King's opinion. Up to now they had mainly concentrated on picking up small independents in the Northeast, Midwest and West. From what he had seen, they were at least trying to improve their operation. The third group was made up primarily of financial people from New York City.

The wrinkle was this provision that if they were successful in acquiring the LEGENT properties, a small Independent would take the Michigan property. Of more interest to King was the rumor that Wilson McCann had a minority interest in the Independent. What in the good Lord's name was McCann doing fooling around with some mom and pop operation in Michigan? Norm Lester, who didn't know a transposition bracket from a digital line concentrator, was running LEGENT'S operation and Wilson McCann was, if King's informant was correct, living on a farm in Michigan! He was glad he only had to get this divestiture behind him and he could go home to Savannah.

Piazza shifted his weight and pulled on his left ear. "You gonna make the pitch or do you want me to?"

"You do three and seven. I want to get a look at the folks on ten. Let me know when they get here. Hey Sal…Clarinet. ..I mean Geez! What a waste."

Almost as bad as Wilson McCann on a farm, he thought to himself.

Piazza left and King swiveled his chair toward his credenza and picked up his cell phone from its cradle next to the LEGENT phone. He paid the bill for the cell phone. He dialed the country club near his home in the Dallas suburb of Plano and scheduled a 10:00 a.m. tee time for two the next day. He told the assistant pro he didn't want to be paired with any other members.

He swiveled back to his desk and picked up the CD ROM containing his presentation on the sale of LEGENT properties in the Mid-West. If things went as he hoped they would, it would be the last one of these he would be doing. He also made a mental note to check with the head of LEGENT'S wireless division to assure that Sal Piazza was in line for transfer to their engineering division when this sale was finished. Sal was a great guy but ....the Clarinet! Geez! What a waste!

He scribbled a quick note containing Wilson McCann's name and a phone number and the time and location of the country club and left it with his secretary on his way out of the office to go to the tenth floor.

At the same time, McCann and two young CPAs from the Rice Watterson firm were setting up their laptops in a wireless equipped room in the Marriott Suites – Market Center. As he watched the wireless connection boot up, he turned to the others.

"As soon as we check out the connection to the LEGENT room, I want to go over some analysis I worked up last week with you." I'll be out tomorrow until about 6:00 p.m. and I want to be sure that we run whatever comes in from the team at LEGENT through my worksheets."

Both of them nodded their agreement. They had been told quite firmly by their manager to follow Mr. McCann's lead as they monitored the information that would flow from the due diligence team at LEGENT. While LEGENT could keep Mr. McCann from being in their building, they wouldn't keep him from being in their numbers. Cindy, as a member of the team at LEGENT, had the same worksheets in her laptop as she entered the tenth floor conference room and, with a smile on her face, shook hands with John King.

One hour later, she inserted the CD ROM that King had given to each member of the acquisition team into her laptop and began to transfer information from it into McCann's worksheets and data forms. As she completed each sheet, she sent it by wireless to the three laptops at the Marriott. McCann and the two Rice Watterson CPAs began to formulate various scenarios from the data. By the time the team reassembled at 7:30 p.m., a prime rib sandwich or a chicken Caesar salad was on the table in front of each chair in the conference room together with a printed copy of the analysis work McCann and the others had done.

The next morning, the acquisition team split up to go with their LEGENT appointed contacts to various departments within LEGENT for specific presentations. The two Rice Watterson CPAs continued to work on the results of the late evening's discussion, and Wilson McCann met John King on the first tee of the Los Rios Country Club near Plano.

King was an avid golfer. He was deadly serious about his game and it showed. McCann on the other hand, hadn't had a club in his hand for over six months and it showed as well. By the time they made the turn and teed off at number 10, King was giving McCann three strokes per hole and beating him by an average of 3.5. McCann's hooks and slices contrasted with King's straight down the middle shots.

That didn't allow for much discussion other than for King to make it clear that he was happier on the golf course than he was in the office. His disdain for the leadership of LEGENT and his frustration with the dismantling of many of the properties he had helped to build was obvious.

The two men finished up at 2:30 p.m., showered and met in the Club lounge.

"Well, that wasn't pretty!" McCann said, as he sipped on his soda. King was already on his second Perrier. McCann noted the difference in King. He looked much more physically fit than he had when they had last met at an industry meeting some seven years ago.

"Farmers obviously don't play golf! Geez, Wils! You have to get out more!" King grinned. Beating someone of McCann's industry reputation had made his day. He only wished that Norm Lister played golf. He would love to have the satisfaction of beating him. Lister went to symphonies and off-Broadway plays with his new wife who was his former Executive Assistant.

Lister was always talking about getting some clubs and taking up the game. Thus far, it was all talk.

"Tell you what…you come up to Farnsworth and we'll play in one of my wheat fields. They are very green right now!"

"They won't be tomorrow! There's a front going through and the Thumb of Michigan is going to get 3"- 6" of snow," King smiled.

"You watch the weather in the Thumb?" McCann smiled, waiting.

"I watch everything that relates to the dismantling of my company." King said, looking out the window at the practice green. "Wils, level with me. What are you doing and why are you doing it?"

Ten minutes later, McCann had brought him up to date on his life since the failed Dynacom buyout. He carefully omitted any mention of Donna in his discussion of his move to Farnsworth.

"These are good people? They know what they are doing?" King asked, looking at him intently.

"Solid, John. You would like them."

"LEGENT hasn't done you any favors," King said

"Network improvements?" McCann asked, knowing the answer.

"Hardly any since Dynacom. Our outside plant hasn't had anything major in five years."

"Switches? Up to latest generic?"

"Yes. That is the bright spot. The Feeder cable in most of the exchanges is up to snuff. It's the distribution that needs work. Hardly any DSL anywhere."

McCann knew that King was giving information that he didn't need to and probably shouldn't. LEGENT would expect the acquisition team to dig out this type of information as part of its due diligence.

"Can Farnsworth handle the initial investment and capital needed to get it right?" King asked.

"It will be close. With the changes in supports and the flat local service revenues, they will have to watch every penny. But, given a fair price, I think it's doable."

"…and your involvement…just advice?" King asked.

"Just advice," McCann replied quietly.

"Well, I'm out of here when this is done! I'm tired of it. All they do is watch the numbers. No one is taking care of the customers. LEGENT will be gone inside of five years. You should wait. You could get a better price." King said bitterly.

"Will you be happy....just playing golf?" McCann asked.

"I'll try. It sure will be better than the last five years, job-wise."

"You look good, John."

King leaned forward and put his elbows on the table and palmed the Perrier between his hands. "I straightened out my personal life after the heart attack. Stopped the boozing and the smoking and working until all hours of the day and night...started eating right, exercising every day. I even go to church now!"

"Good for you. Born again?"

"Let's just say that the Good Lord and I have made our peace and I've seen the light. I have a different set of priorities in my life now. LEGENT didn't appreciate that. They stopped letting me run things and shuffled me off to a fancy title and told me to start selling off assets that they didn't think contributed enough to the bottom line."

"I'm trying to find a priority for my life." McCann remarked softly.

"Don't wait too long, Wils. I almost did." King said, reaching across the table and laying his hand on McCann's for a moment before withdrawing it. They sat facing each other for a full five seconds before King cleared his throat and spoke again.

"There's something going on in Michigan that you should keep in mind."

McCann waited quietly. King was obviously searching for the right way to tell him something without telling him too much.

"We've had indications that the Commission is going to put this deal through the wringer and that the Governor's office is behind it. We haven't been able to find out why. I'd suggest you see if you can find out what's going on before you finalize your bid. It's obvious that they are very interested in who gets those properties and that they have some expectations that may be beyond what you might expect."

"I've heard about the Governor's interest. One of Farnsworth's Board members is a County Republican Chair. He got a call asking about the company, and it appears that financing loosened up for Farnsworth Tele after a similar call to one of our backers."

"If I know the politicians, they will want their pound of flesh. Make sure you can stomach what they have in mind," King said quietly, taking a long drink from the Perrier. When he sat the bottle down, he checked his watch. It was clear to McCann that he had gone as far as he felt comfortable with.

They talked for a few more minutes about the acquisition and then walked together to the parking lot. As McCann was about to get into his rental car, King extended his hand. "It was good to see you again, Wils. I hope you are successful in whatever you do. If along the way, you have a need for an old plant man who likes to see things run for the customer, give me a call. My consulting fees won't be too high. And…try to work on your golf game, will you? You're not a lot of competition!"

"I'll keep that in mind, John. Thank you." McCann replied.

He drove back into the city thinking over things King had told him. He found himself returning to King's comments about finding a priority for his life that was greater than his LEGENT work. He envied John King. Work, such as it was, was still McCann's only priority.

At the Marriott, he found the team in the midst of a shouting match. The preliminary due diligence work had resulted in a difference of opinion as to the value of the properties. On one side, the Rice Watterson accountants were arguing that the condition of the assets was such that a lower bid price was warranted. On the other side, the Oxbow representatives and the Lassiter Fielding lawyers were arguing for a premium that reflected the market potential as well as the competition they faced from the other two groups expected to bid. The central aspect of the discussion quickly came down to the amount of capital that would need to be invested post-acquisition to maintain or improve the properties. Here again the group divided into two sides. The Oxbow representatives were strident in reminding the others that the ultimate game plan was to re-sell the properties if appropriate. A smaller group, including McCann and the Farnsworth Tele representatives argued for a proposal that would allow them to operate the properties for the long term. The meeting ended with the consensus that a final decision would be made three days later when the review was completed. McCann returned to his room and called Art Boyington.

"Any word on the Governor?" he asked, leaning back against the pillows propped against the headboard of his bed.

"None yet. Phil Willard is to meet with one of the Governor's aides, a man named Ross, tomorrow. My friends in the PSC legal staff tell me that the Director of the Telecommunications Division has instructed his staff to review any petitions thoroughly," Boyington responded.

"Don't they always?"

"It seems that this sale is to receive special attention. The issues of management of the properties post-sale and the willingness of the acquirer to invest in improving and expanding the network were specifically mentioned."

"Do you have any idea why, Art?"

"There seems to be a feeling that LEGENT did not actively manage the properties to the Commission's satisfaction and invested little in them. The feeling is that even your old properties in Michigan have been neglected since LEGENT took over."

"But why is the Governor interested, do you think?" McCann probed.

"We'll know more after Phil has his meeting, but if I were to guess, I would guess it has something to do with the state's encouragement of economic development in the northern Lower Peninsula. As you know, several of the LEGENT properties lie in the area that was studied by the State Department of Economic Development in their recent study. Particular attention was given to the lack of technological investment there."

McCann's appreciation for Boyington's insight continued to grow as he listened to the attorney. There seemed to be a common thread to what King had said, what Boyington surmised, and what Jim Wolfe had discussed. Perhaps it was time to call his contact in Lansing and see what, if anything, he could learn from that source. He also had the numbers Wolfe had provided in a new PDA he had purchased.

"Thanks Art. Things are coming along here. It will all come down to the numbers on Friday."

"What is your current thinking? Should we proceed? I am very concerned for the family's interests," Boyington replied.

"I remain optimistic. I'll talk with you again on Friday," McCann replied.

"Wils....one more thing....I'm very sorry about....Donna. I know how important she was to Belle and I suspect she was important to you as well."

"Thank you Art, she was." And with that, McCann said goodbye and hung up the phone as a new wave of melancholy washed over him.

He was just about to reach for the phone again to order room service when there was a knock on the door. He opened it to find Cindy Melzy dressed in sweat pants and shirt, her hair pulled back in a bun. There was a deep V of sweat from the neck of the shirt down between her breasts.

"Hi. Got a minute?" she asked, smiling at him as he stepped back.

"Sure, come in," he stepped aside as she came in and sat down in a chair opposite the bed. "Can I get you something?" He indicated the mini-bar which as yet he hadn't touched.

"Just a glass of water, thanks."

He ran a glass full at the tap next to the in-room coffee maker and handed it to her. She took a big gulp and sat it down beside the chair.

"What do you think?" she asked, as he sat opposite her.

"About...?"

"What we've reviewed thus far."

"You're the financial guru," he hedged. "Why ask me?"

"You're the famous CEO. Would you buy it?"

"My last attempt at buying something other than a farm, cattle and a used baler didn't come off so good," he teased, matching her smile. Cindy was different. He had noticed it as soon as the team linked up in Dallas. The fine edged impatience he had always seen in her before was gone. She was more relaxed, almost easy going in her mannerisms. He thought it made her seem younger and more appealing.

"If I buy a farm in Farnsworth, will you come and bale my hay for me?" She said it in the same teasing tone but he sensed there was something more there. Before he could think of a retort that would draw out whatever it was, she continued.

"I think the initial price we came up with is too high, but the total capital requirement is going to be higher than we thought because the PSC is going to extract some sort of commitment to improve and expand the network."

"You've talked to Art?"

"At noon. You?"

"Just a few minutes ago. He's a good head."

She stood, clasped her hands behind her head, and swiveled from at the waist, leaning right and then left as she did so. The sweat shirt rode up as she did so. He caught a glimpse of slightly tanned skin and she caught him glimpsing it. He turned away and bent to pick up the glass.

"There's more to it than that. I'm getting the feeling that whatever is behind the Governor's interest in this deal, will cost the acquiring company." He said it coldly.

"Does that mean you will recommend to Doug that Farnsworth Tele pull out?" She asked it in a disappointed tone.

"Not yet, but maybe, if we can't pin something down."

"What are you doing for dinner?" she asked, putting her hand on the door handle.

"Probably room service. I played 18 holes of golf today and I ache all over."

"I know a Tex-Mex place not far from here. Come with me." He sensed seriousness in her invitation.

"Can I wear blue jeans?" he asked.

"I'm going to…and my boots. See you in 30 minutes in the lobby." She stepped through the door and pulled it shut behind her.

She was as good as her word and more, appearing in boots, jeans, a white western shirt with pearl snap buttons and a short denim jacket.

"All you need is a Stetson." He smiled as they walked out the door. He was wearing tan slacks, a blue oxford button down dress shirt and a dark blue golf jacket with "Pebble Beach" stitched on the left breast.

"And you don't look like the man on the farm," she teased back.

"I forgot to bring my jeans!"

The restaurant offered a wide variety of Tex-Mex food and they both settled for a sampler platter. As they ate, they discussed the current state of the acquisition effort. Cindy pointed out the perils of acquiring assets with potentially declining revenue and a largely rural, tourist oriented market. McCann responded with thoughts on how cost reduction and prudent investment in the right package of services, together with a more "bundled" approach to service offerings might produce positive results. As they finished their meal over coffee, they both agreed that, in the end the numbers would tell the tale of whether this would work out or not.

Cindy turned the conversation in a different direction as she put her cup down and asked, "What was Donna like?"

McCann felt the pain rush through him again. He took a sip of his coffee before responding.

"I don't think I realized how special she was until she was gone. She had that wonderful mix of enthusiasm for life, coupled with devotion to a higher calling. She was a good businesswoman and she was a sterling example of her faith…and she was…my friend." He finished and took another sip of coffee, turning his head away to watch a couple exiting the room.

"Did you love her?" He could feel Cindy's eyes boring in on him.

"Too late," he said, looking down.

"It may be too late for you and Donna but it's not too late for you. Look at me. I had my focus on all the wrong things. I lost my husband and almost lost my son trying to be the most successful woman in New York's financial circles. I fell short everywhere."

"But, you have changed. I like the new you better," he responded, trying to lighten the moment.

"Yes, I have and I'm the happiest I've been in a long time."

"You always seemed to be enjoying life."

"I fooled a lot of people. That was part of the whole deal thing. On the outside, I was one thing and inside, I was dying. I met with William when David and I went home from Farnsworth. We talked for a long while. I told him about my faith in Christ and that I was intending to lead a new life from now on."

"Reconciliation?" McCann asked.

"No, it was too late for that. William has a new love in his life. He agreed to grant me joint custody for David. Depending on where our lives lead us, he may be agreeable to full custody at some point. He is leaving for a year abroad next month and I will have David for the next year. "

"I'm sorry that things didn't work out with William but happy for you and for David. He's a neat kid. He loved the farm."

"I know. I enjoyed my time in Farnsworth. I especially love Belle. Do you know that when Donna died, she called me and talked with me for some time? She said that she felt God had given her my friendship to replace Donna?"

"Belle lost her daughter and Donna took her place. I guess you hold that place now." He said it with just a trace of envy in his heart. He wondered who would hold him in a place as dear.

Sensing his mood, she reached across the table and laid her hand on his. "I was sorry to hear that your mother had passed away and I'm even sorrier that you have lost someone as dear to you as Donna was. If you need someone to talk to…anytime…I'd like to be that person."

He thought back to the rainy fall night at the farm when Donna had said she wanted to be his friend. "Thanks, Cindy."

She started to say something and hesitated, then went on, "I'd like to talk with you about some personal decisions I might make in the future when I have them more fully thought out." She said, as she picked up the check. "It's my treat tonight. It'll be yours next time."

As he rose from the table, McCann was both glad there would be a next time and puzzled by Cindy's last comment. He wondered what personal decisions she intended to make and if, and how, it would impact the acquisition.

(22)

Earlier that same day, two representatives of the United States Department of Agriculture stood behind the operator of a feed lot near Hemlock, Michigan. One was dressed in slacks and a USDA blazer. The other was dressed in a grey wool suit, white shirt and dark tie. Both looked on with interest as the operator, dressed in jeans and a denim work shirt, scrolled down through a computer screen displaying a check register.

"Yes, here it is. A shipment from a local dealer... I don't see how..." he began.

The man in the suit bent forward to study the screen. He made notes in a small notebook and flipped the cover shut. These men were here because beef he had sold to a slaughterhouse in Saginaw had tested positive for Bovine Spongiform Encephalopathy, BSE for short or, as it was more commonly known, "Mad Cow Disease."

"I think we'll find that your dealer bought some of his feed from a Canadian firm. That's probably where the BSE came from," he said, in a matter-of-fact manner that made the feed lot operator dread what he knew would be next. "We'll have to put your lot on quarantine and we'll need the names and addresses of any buyers since you took shipment of that feed." The man in the blazer said. His tone was more sympathetic.

The feedlot operator clicked on a screen icon labeled "sales register", and printed off the register. He handed it to the man in the blazer and the two USDA men prepared to leave.

Wilson McCann's name appeared on the tenth line of the fourth page of the register. At 4:00 p.m., the phone at McCann's farm rang and Nick Hardesty took the call. When McCann returned to his room at the Marriott, a message light was blinking on his phone. After McCann finished talking with Nick, he replaced the phone in its cradle and sat on his bed thinking.

"First Dynacom, then my mother, then Donna and now the cattle are quarantined and will likely be destroyed. What else can happen?"

He went to bed with a sense of dread and tossed and turned until 3:00 a.m., when he finally fell into a restless sleep.

The next morning at breakfast, Cindy took note of McCann's weary appearance. He told her of the phone call from Nick, and she sat back from the table with a look of incredulity.

"I don't understand this... I thought Mad Cow Disease was a problem in England, not here."

"There have been cases recorded in Canada," McCann replied, taking a sip from his coffee. "Apparently, the feed lot operator I bought the steers from had purchased some feed from a local dealer, who got it from a Canadian firm. He sold some steers from the same lot as mine to a slaughter house and they tested positive for BSE. Now every steer that fed on that feed is under quarantine, including mine."

"What about recourse?" she asked.

"I instructed Nick to call the feed lot operator and find out what he intends to do about it. Nick was pretty shook up from the USDA call. I guess they were pretty firm with him." McCann smiled ruefully, thinking of Nick Hardesty's panic on the phone the previous evening.

He looked at her and she could see the defeat in his eyes. "It seems as though everything and everyone I touch turns out badly. You had better beware."

She reached across the table and put her hand on his arm. "Don't talk like that, Wils. Think of all the people you have helped in a positive way. I'm convinced that God has a plan for your life just as he does for mine."

"I wish I could see it," he said, drinking the last of his coffee and pushing his chair back from the table. "I'll see you at the meeting," he said as he walked away.

Cindy sat there for a few moments praying silently. "God, I know your hand is in all of this. I only ask that you work out your plan for his life and show him clearly what you would have him do with it."

An hour later, the acquisition team re-convened. The Oxbow representatives seemingly had won over the Rice Watterson people, or at least gained their notable silence. The Lassiter Fielding attorneys sat back and listened without comment as the acquisitions and mergers people reviewed their position. It came down to the fact that if the group wanted to compete successfully, a larger premium than what had been previously considered would need to be added to the bid price. Arthur Boyington asked for permission to speak as the Oxbow speaker finished. He leaned forward as he spoke and his eyes lingered on McCann.

"As you know, Michigan is an hour ahead of us here. Mr. Phil Willard, a member of Farnsworth's Board, met with a representative of the Governor of the State of Michigan at 9:00 a.m. Michigan time. I think you should be made aware of the nature of that conversation."

He pointed to a diamond shaped speaker phone in the center of the table. "I have asked that a speaker phone be brought in this morning and Mr. Willard is standing by to talk with us. With your permission, I would like to call him and have him review the essence of what he learned this morning."

The others looked at each other. McCann noticed that several pairs of eyes rested on him. Cindy, sitting opposite him at the table nodded at Boyington. "I would like to hear what Phil has to say," she said smiling. The others nodded their agreement but McCann noted the puzzlement on the faces of the attorneys and AMS people.

Boyington pushed a button on the speaker phone and, upon hearing the dial tone, entered a number. Phil Willard's voice echoed in the room after the second ring.

"Phil, I have the team assembled here and we are waiting to hear your report." Boyington adjusted the volume slightly.

"I met with a representative of the Governor's office this morning. The Governor's aide told me that the Governor has some interest in the sale of the LEGENT property. He did not explain why and I did not ask. He asked a number of questions about the make-up of the acquisition group and Farnsworth Tele's position within the group. I explained the terms of Farnsworth's involvement and he seemed pleased that a local company might have an opportunity to purchase the property in Michigan. He made it clear that the Governor's interest was in assuring that service in the acquired property would be second to none and that any company acquiring it would be expected to invest at a level appropriate to the needs of the area to assure state-of-the-art service."

The lead Oxbow representative leaned forward to interrupt. "And just what did he mean by that?" he said, in a tone that indicated impatience with this unexpected phone call.

"I took it to mean that the Governor felt that there might, at some future time, be needs within the area being acquired that would require significant investment in telecommunications networking," Willard responded.

"And what does that mean?" the Oxbow man asked as two of the Lassiter Fielding attorneys whispered to each other.

"I have told you all I know about that," Willard responded. "There is one thing more…"

"And what is that?" the Oxbow man said, his exasperation noticeable.

"He asked what role Wils McCann would play in the acquisition."

McCann could feel the eyes of every person in the room and he wished at that moment that he was anywhere but in Dallas, Texas.

Doug Warner left his office as soon as Phil Willard finished his conference call to the team in Dallas. His nerves were acting up and his stomach felt like someone was dragging a straight razor through it. He went to the men's room just down the hall from his office, and then stopped in Belle's empty office to calm himself. He prayed quietly for a few moments. When he returned, Phil had re-seated himself opposite the desk and was waiting. His concern for Doug was evident.

"You okay, Doug?"

"Yes, I guess the pressure of this whole thing is getting to me a little. I'll be fine. What do you think they will do down there?"

"I have no idea, Doug, I'm an Agway dealer, not a Mergers and Acquisitions man," Willard responded, trying to lighten the conversation as Warner settled himself in his chair.

"Who was the guy from the Governor's office again?" Warner asked.

"A man named Ross. He is considered to be the Governor's primary confidante and 'gofer'. Many see him as a sort of manipulator in many of the Governor's initiatives. He has a reputation as a man you wouldn't want to cross."

"Why do you think he asked about Wils?"

"As I told the group, he seemed interested in the role Wils would play in the acquisition. I didn't detect anything favorable or unfavorable in his interest. It's obvious that they know about Wils from his time with Dynacom."

"I am beginning to think that we should re-consider this whole thing," Warner said, looking out the window. It feels like it is getting out of control. We have to give up 40% of the company and now we have to be willing to commit to some unknown amount of investment if we acquire the property. Our chances of success were little better than fifty-fifty before and now I don't know what to think."

"Have you prayed about it?" Willard asked quietly, sensing the turmoil in his friend.

"Constantly. I felt so much assurance at first. Wils coming into the picture and investing in the company was something that seemed so right at the time. Now, I'm not so sure."

"There is one thing more, Doug. I didn't tell the group in Dallas about one other comment that Ross made."

"What?" Warner asked, looking sharply at the older man.

"Ross asked several questions about the management of Farnsworth. He seemed particularly interested in knowing if I felt it was strong enough for the future."

"What did you tell him?"

"I told him that I was confident in the management team and that while it might need to be strengthened if the acquisition was successful, that should not be a problem."

"I hope you're right," Warner sighed.

"With God's help, I know that I am," Willard responded.

Warner turned again toward the window. "I have to fly to Dallas tomorrow to sit in on the final decision making," he said, as the first few flakes of snow began to fall outside.

"Martha and I will pray for your safe travel and for the right decision," Phil Willard said, as he rose and went to the door. Doug Warner was still looking out the window, lost in thought, as Willard closed the door behind him.

Ed Feldman put down his cordless phone and paced to the window of his 3rd Avenue office. The news from Dallas was the final straw in a haystack with no needle! The Governor of Michigan was involved and no one seemed to know what that meant. Feldman knew what it meant. It meant money, money that hadn't been a part of this deal. From the day that Stu Bailey had told him that Wilson McCann wasn't going to be CEO of this acquisition, he had felt that this thing was sliding down hill like an Edsel with no brakes. Well, it was time for him to throw his weight around a little and put some strings on his one hundred and fifty million dollar commitment. He would start with Stu Bailey and then call the Oxbow people and let them know just exactly how he felt. As far as the Farnsworth Telephone Coop was concerned, he didn't care one bit. These conservative Bible thumpers in the Midwest were becoming a pain right where he sat down and he was going to take care of that right away. He snatched up the phone again and punched in the numbers as he continued to pace back and forth between his desk and the window. Thirteen floors below him, the noonday crowds were shoulder to shoulder as the cold November wind began to howl down the canyons of New York City.

Twenty minutes later, Stu Bailey finished scribbling on a lined yellow legal pad and leaned back in his chair as Feldman wound down.

"Ed, I completely understand your feelings. I just don't know if I can deliver everything you're asking for," he said, as he rubbed his forehead. "Let me talk to the folks in Dallas…sure…yes…I'll talk to Wils…I know you're serious. Let's see what we can find out about this business with the Governor. I'm sure Wils can find something out. Maybe the Warners can… yes I know, Ed…I'll get back to you. Yes…today. Thanks, Ed."

He put down the phone and threw the pen across the room. It hit the wall about the same time as Stu Bailey shouted, "JEANINE!"

But Jeanine had gone to lunch and he had to get the number for the Marriott in Dallas himself.

The rest of the morning meeting in Dallas had disintegrated into disarray. By noon, McCann was thoroughly disgusted with the entire business. Between the premium additive and the unknown capital requirement that Phil Willard's discussion with the Governor's aide implied, it seemed that no one was able to bring some sense of direction as to what the next step should be. Finally, at 11:00 a.m., the Due Diligence team members had left. Cindy left with them, pausing to whisper, "hang in there, buddy," in his ear as she passed by his chair.

He decided to skip lunch and went to his room. On impulse, he picked up the phone and dialed Jim Wolfe's number. June answered and after a few pleasantries, she gave him Jim's cellular number. He thanked her, disconnected and then dialed it.

"Wolfe."

"Jim, its Wils."

"Hi Wils. How is it going?" Wolfe sounded wary.

"Frankly, we've had some disturbing news about the Governor's interest in this deal. It sounds like there is something afoot that drives cap-ex."

McCann could sense the hesitation on the other end of the call. Finally, Wolfe spoke. His words were measured.

"Wils, there's something going on up here but I haven't been able to find out what it is. That's about all I can say. But, you could call a man named Dan Ryan in the Dept. of Economic Development in Lansing. I'm sure he knows something. Whether he will tell you anything is another matter."

"Do you have a number?" McCann asked, picking up a pen and using it to pull a pad closer to the phone.

Wolfe gave him the number. "Wils, if Farnsworth acquires these properties, I'd be interested in talking with you and Doug Warner." The words came out in a rush and McCann could feel the relief in Wolfe's voice for having said them.

"I think Doug Warner already has that in mind, Jim." McCann responded quickly, smiling to himself. Wolfe was making a commitment and McCann fully understood what that commitment might result in. "But, I wouldn't burn any bridges just yet. The cap-ex and the premium the AMS people are talking about may sink this thing yet."

"Thanks, Wils"

"Thank you, Jim" McCann replaced the phone. It rang immediately and when he picked it up Stu Bailey swore into his ear.

Ten minutes later he replaced the phone again. Stu had listed Feldman's terms:

No financing for Farnsworth, no financing for the acquisition in general and complete withdrawal from the process unless:

Farnsworth pledged one hundred per cent of its equity as part of the deal and…

Secured commitments for any capital expenditure exposure and…

Wilson McCann agreed to become CEO of the acquired properties, including Farnsworth.

Bailey's voice had become more aggressive as he talked. Now, like an actor delivering the punch line, he lowered his voice, put his mouth against the phone and spoke slowly and distinctly to the man who was his friend.

"It's time you quit screwing around with farming and dogs and cows and started using the talents and abilities that God gave you to help us pull off this deal. Now, you sit there and you think about what I've said and you better well decide what you want to do with the rest of your life real quick, because I've had it with this thing. We need Ed Feldman's money and we need you in the mix. Call me back in an hour and tell me your answer!" Then, he hung up.

In Dallas, Wilson McCann dropped the phone back in its cradle and looked out the window. Stu Bailey had just talked to him in a way he had never done before. He found himself smiling as he thought about it. Good old Stu! He was "cutting to the chase!"

In New York, Stu Bailey mopped his brow and leaned back in his chair. Jeanine, having heard the entire conversation on Bailey's end, stood in the doorway. Respect for her boss was written on her face.

"Gosh boss! That was epic!"

"Yeah, sometimes I surprise myself," Bailey said, looking down at his hands. They were shaking.

Dan Ryan had just finished a meeting and was thinking of grabbing some lunch in the cafeteria when his phone rang.

"Ryan."

"Mr. Ryan, my name is Wilson McCann and I have a question for you."

Dan Ryan sagged back down into his chair. The voice on the other end of the call was firm and businesslike. He didn't like that at all.

Ten minutes later he said good-bye and disconnected. He immediately dialed another extension and waited for the answer.

"Ross."

"It's Dan Ryan. Wilson McCann just called me and I've invited him to come to Lansing and talk with you."

"Because?"

"Your call to Phil Willard in Farnsworth is about to kill the acquisition of the LEGENT properties, not only in Michigan but in the whole Midwest. McCann said he was prepared to leak a story to the *Wall Street Journal* that the Governor is attempting to influence the sale. This thing is getting out of hand and the manure is about to hit the fan!"

"Very good, Dan. I'll be glad to talk with Mr. McCann. When can we expect him?"

Ryan noticed the "we" and knew that he wasn't part of the "we" Ross was talking about.

"Tomorrow morning. He said he's flying in tonight."

"I'll clear a spot on my schedule at 10:00 a.m. Can you advise Mr. McCann?"

"I'll be glad to," Ryan replied thankfully. At least this problem would be someone else's to deal with.

"By the way, Dan, where did he get your name?"

Ryan thought quickly. He wasn't about to disclose who he thought had passed information to McCann. Then a thought hit him.

"I spoke at a Telecom convention four years ago. He was on the panel just ahead of me on the program. I met him then."

"I see. Thanks Dan. I'll be in touch."

Ryan put down his phone. He had met McCann at the convention for only a moment and he was sure that McCann didn't even remember it.

In New York, Ed Feldman's private number rang.

"Feldman," he said, looking at the ID display. The 214 area code indicated a number from the Dallas area.

"Ed, Wils McCann. Have you a pen handy?" The voice was firm and authoritative. Feldman instinctively pulled a gold Mont Blanc pen from a desk set with a golden clock mounted on solid mahogany.

"You have given me your terms through Stu Bailey. While Stu is my friend and I love him dearly, I prefer to deal direct. So, here are my terms." McCann's tone didn't brook any interruption.

"No 1. I attempt to get Farnsworth Tele's shareholders to allow the company to become part of the acquiring company. You agree that those shareholders can buy the company back in the event that the acquired property is put up for sale, at net book value. You further agree that Farnsworth's shareholders can also buy the rest of the acquired LEGENT properties in Michigan at net book value."

"This is..!" Feldman attempted to interrupt. The voice on the other end became colder.

"Don't interrupt, Ed! You've made an offer. Now you are getting a counter offer. If you don't like it, you can walk away."

"No 2. I receive a salary of $2 million per year plus a 25% bonus opportunity for five years cancelable only at my option with all the usual CEO perks."

"No 3. All of the earnings in Michigan for the first five years are put back into the Michigan portion of the company."

"No 4. You use your influence to secure an on-going line of credit of $40 million per year to be used for Cap Ex and you use your influence to accomplish refinancing every two years."

"Are you through?" Feldman asked quietly.

"Not quite. No. 5. The headquarters of the new company is in Farnsworth,

Michigan. I need to be able to keep an eye on my farm when I'm not out hustling a buck for you financial people. Ed, it's been good to visit with you. I'll look forward to hearing further from you."The line went dead.

Back in Dallas, McCann called Stu Bailey. He suggested that Bailey might want to talk to Feldman and that he was catching a plane that evening to Lansing and was talking with the Governor's aide the next day.

"Does this mean you're okay with the terms?" Bailey asked.

"Stu, you do what you have to do. Ed will have to do what he has to do, and I'll do what I have to do. Then we'll talk. Okay?"

"That's no answer, Wils," Bailey sputtered. "I have to tell Feldman something today."

"I've already told him something. If he is a little stressed, tell him to take the rest of the day off. With his money, he can afford to." McCann hung up the phone.

In New York, Bailey threw another pen at the wall.

In Farnsworth, the snow, which had begun as a flurry, had now turned into a full scale November snowstorm. The snow was heavy with moisture and quickly piled up on the streets, parking lots and on the sidewalk of Doug Warner's home. Lori was inside packing Doug's bag for his trip to Dallas. Doug hadn't eaten much for lunch and said he felt a little "queasy". They both had attributed it to the quickly changing events in relation to the acquisition.

"Maybe it isn't God's will for us to do this," Doug had said, as he put on his overcoat to go out and clear the sidewalk before leaving.

"If it isn't, we can live with that...can't we?" Lori had responded as she lifted his chin with her hand and stood on tiptoe to plant a kiss on his cheek.

Now, as he shoveled, the upset in his stomach had returned and suddenly morphed into a searing pain across his chest and down his arms. He felt as though someone had punched him hard in the chest. The shovel dropped to the uncleared sidewalk, its falling muffled by the snow. Doug reached for the wrought iron railing on his front porch and missed. He felt his knees buckle and he slowly collapsed into the snow. Five minutes later, Lori looked out the window and three minutes after that the Farnsworth Volunteer Fire and Rescue Squad arrived with sirens wailing and lights flashing.

The Farnsworth Medical Center was two blocks from the Warner Mansion. Belle's Cadillac made it there just as the ambulance was moving away from the Emergency Entrance. Doug's Yukon was sitting with the door opened just to the right of the entryway. Lori was inside, her face white as a sheet. Doug Warner had suffered a heart attack and the doctors were working feverishly to stabilize him. The two women, wrapped in each other's arms, prayed together as the snow continued to fall outside.

McCann entered the room and conversation ceased. It was evident to him that Feldman's conditions had been relayed to the acquisition team. It was also obvious that his terms in reply were as yet unknown. He walked quickly to the head of the table and looked down at the attorneys, accountants and finance people arranged on either side. Cindy Melzy leaned back in her chair and swiveled it slightly to look him directly in the eye.

"I presume you have heard from Ed. I've talked with Ed and I'm sure we will have further discussions. In the meantime, I think we need to find out just what is involved in the Michigan situation and I've arranged to meet with the Governor's aide tomorrow to try to do that. I suggest you folks put together your best estimate of the total price of these properties as they stand today and add forty million in cap-ex over the next five years. Any questions?"

The Oxbow man pulled his jacket together and raised his right hand slightly before speaking. "What about Mr. Feldman's condition in regard to you being the CEO?"

"I've suggested to Mr. Feldman through Mr. Bailey that he take the rest of the afternoon off. I'm sure he has plenty of things to think about."

"But...," the Oxbow man began.

McCann cut him off. "That's all I have to say for now. I've got a plane to catch."

Cindy Melzy smiled slightly as McCann walked quickly out the door.

"God direct you, Wils," she said quietly to herself, as she flipped open the folder in front of her and began to review the numbers it contained again.

An hour later, McCann was in his rental car headed for the airport. His cellular phone was in his bag and it was turned off. The Marriott operator advised Belle Warner that Mr. McCann had checked out. When Belle dialed the cellular number, she received a recording saying that the called party was unavailable. No one in Farnsworth knew where Wilson McCann was. When Belle called Cindy later that afternoon, the team in Dallas learned of Doug Warner's heart attack and the Warner family in Farnsworth learned that Wilson McCann was on a plane bound for Lansing.

In New York, Ed Feldman smiled to himself as he stuffed some file folders into his brief case. He was leaving the office early to beat the rush. He needed time to consider McCann's terms. In the meantime, he would go home to his house in Scarsdale and sit by the fire and see if any snow fell. He did his best thinking watching the bird feeder in his back yard through his family room window.

McCann's flight into Capitol City Airport in Lansing was about as rough as it could get. By the time the plane hit the runway, he was reaching for the paper sack in the seat pocket and expecting to "lose it" at any moment. The pilot's voice resounded through the plane.

"Sorry about that folks! We are in the middle of our first Michigan snow storm of the year and it was either divert to Chicago or have a bumpy landing. You might want to bundle up a bit before you go outside. Thanks for flying with us and I hope your next flight will be a little smoother!"

McCann breathed a quiet "Amen to that," and leaned back as the plane taxied to the gate area. His stomach began to settle and by the time the flight attendant opened the exit door to the gate area, he was ready to stand, retrieve his bag and head for the exit. What he wasn't prepared for was the gust of cold air that hit him as he entered the ramp.

He had booked a room at the Radisson Hotel on Grand Avenue. The hotel was in the center of downtown Lansing, just two blocks from the Capital and connected to the Lansing Convention Center by a Pedway. The airport shuttle brought him to the hotel. His entrance to the lobby brought a brief rush of nostalgia as he remembered a previous stay when he spoke at the Michigan Telecommunications Association annual convention.

As soon as he checked into his room, he connected his laptop to the hotel's high speed Internet service and checked his e-mails. He was surprised to see one from Cindy asking him to call her immediately. Five minutes later, he learned that Doug Warner was hospitalized in Farnsworth. He put in a call to the Farnsworth Medical Center and asked for Belle. A few moments later, she came on the line.

"How is he?" McCann asked.

"They have him stabilized and they are hoping to run tests tomorrow to see if there is damage and if there is blockage," she responded. Her voice sounded tired but hopeful.

They talked briefly about Doug's condition and McCann asked what, if anything, he could do.

"We can use all the prayer we can get," she replied.

"You might want to consider the quality of the pray-er," McCann replied quietly. "I'm not sure that I'm plugged in to the network very well."

"You are one of God's children, Wils. The Father always responds to his children." She assured him. "Where are you, by the way?"

McCann was glad of the change in the conversation and quickly brought her up to date on the day's activities. He did not share the details of his conversations with Bailey and Feldman.

"It is all a bit much for me at the moment. I have every confidence in you and your ability to advise us on the best course of action," she replied, when he had finished.

He hesitated for a moment, realizing how great the strain must be on her. But, he also had come to know that Belle Warner was not an ordinary woman and her faith was no ordinary faith.

"There's one thing more…," he began.

"Yes?"

"In order to move forward with this acquisition, it may be necessary for you to consider putting all of Farnsworth Tele into the effort."

"You mean…give up the company?" her voice was barely a whisper.

"Belle, I don't want to add to your burden, but there is a lot of pressure being applied by those with the money. They want more of a commitment from Farnsworth and.....from me."

"And is that commitment one that you want to make, Wils?" The voice had regained its strength.

"I'm not sure yet. I'll know more tomorrow," he replied, dodging the question.

"And I am not sure what additional commitment we can make. I will pray about it. Will you call me tomorrow?" He marveled at her strength. She had lost someone who was like a daughter to her and now her son was in the ICU and people wanted her to give up control of her family's company. Of all the executives he had met during his career, McCann thought, none could compare with Belle Warner when it came to integrity and faith.

"I'll be back in Farnsworth by tomorrow evening. May I come to your home when I get back?"

"I'll be expecting you," she replied. "And…I'll be praying for you."

"And I for you," he said quietly, as he hung up the phone.

Sitting on the edge of his bed with his head in his hands, Wilson McCann awkwardly began to pray.

The next morning dawned with dazzling sunshine reflecting on six inches of new, wet snow. The sidewalks had been shoveled by the time McCann walked to the state Capitol. He cleared security and handed his card to the State trooper at the entry level. "I'm supposed to meet with Ross in the Governor's office," he said, and was told where to go.

The receptionist in the Governor's suite greeted him and showed him where to hang his coat. "You're expected. If you will just have a chair, I'll let him know you are here," she said, indicating a set of maroon leather chairs just inside the door.

McCann had been in several Governors' offices during his time with

Dynacom. He couldn't remember one where the atmosphere seemed as calm and quiet as this one. The four doors opening to the reception area, including the one he had entered through, were all closed. A uniformed Michigan State Policeman occupied the only other desk in the area. He was working quietly at a computer terminal and had looked up only briefly as McCann entered.

Five minutes later, a light on the receptionist's phone blinked. She picked it up and listened before smiling at McCann. "He will see you now," she said, putting the phone down and moving to open one of the three doors.

The office beyond the door was paneled in a dark walnut. A couch and two chairs, all in the same maroon leather, fronted the desk. The large high-backed executive chair was turned away from him as he entered. He could see the top of the man's head and heard the clatter of a computer keyboard. A door to another of the offices was closed. The man in the executive chair did not turn to meet him.

"Good morning, Mr. McCann. Have a chair," the voice was businesslike and somehow familiar. McCann settled into one of the chairs as he tried to remember where he had heard it.

The clicking of the computer keyboard continued for a moment and the man spoke again.

"I hear you have been making threats," he said. His voice was matter-of-fact and not accusatory. McCann felt heat rise around his collar. A combination of shame and irritation rose. The man continued to type. McCann could barely see the edge of the monitor around the chair. It looked like an e-mail message but he couldn't be sure.

"I'd prefer to call them promises," he replied evenly. "I need information to help us determine what risks may be involved in a business venture. People are nervous about putting a lot of money on the line. Some of their concerns are prompted by a conversation this office had with Phil Willard yesterday."

"Phil is a fine person. I admire him very much. Do you always keep your promises, Mr. McCann? I hear that you are a man of integrity." The typing stopped as he spoke. The chair tipped forward slightly and he appeared to be reviewing what he had typed.

McCann's irritability increased. Why was this man treating him in this manner? Was he trying to establish some sort of position of control? "Well," McCann thought to himself, "two can play that game."

"I usually keep my word. If I am intruding, I'll be happy to wait outside until you are finished. The young lady said you were ready to talk with me."

"No need for that. I apologize for my pre-occupation. The latest state budgetary report just came in and I need some questions answered before I meet with some of our friends in the media. I'm finished and I am ready to talk with you. When we have finished, I will ask you to agree that we never had this discussion."

With that, the big chair swung around and the man in it rose to extend his hand in greeting. McCann's memory placed the face with the familiar voice. The Governor of Michigan was not someone you could easily forget.

(23)

Feldman and Bailey in New York City, Smith in Detroit, and Cindy and the Oxbow team leader in Dallas convened by video conference to discuss the situation. The Oxbow man was clearly upset with the way things were developing. Bailey tapped his pencil on a yellow legal pad while Feldman reviewed some notes in a manila folder. Smith sat back in his chair with his hands folded in his lap. Cindy watched each as they signed in and appeared on the twenty-three inch screen that she and the Oxbow man faced.

"I think we are wasting time on this situation. I don't recommend that we proceed. With the current situation in telecommunications and the uncertainty of adequate returns on our investments, coupled with the unorthodox approach being considered and Mr. McCann's behavior yesterday, I simply must advise that we terminate further consideration." He finished by slashing his right hand down to the table and allowing it to rest there, while bracing his left hand on the arm of his chair and pushing the chair back slightly from the table.

Cindy noted his use of the term "our investments" even though, from her perspective, Oxbow didn't have any "skin in the game" beyond their time, for which they would be more than adequately rewarded. She waited for a reaction from those on the other side of the screen. Feldman responded and his voice activated the video screen in front of them.

"I am favorably impressed by your thoughts. Mr. McCann clearly has a very high opinion of his ability to influence the direction we take. However, I am still not convinced that we should abandon the effort. Do you have any thoughts, Smitty?"

Smith brought his hands up to the table and leaned forward as he slid a few pages of paper closer to him, looking down at them briefly. His voice was a monotone as it came over the speakers.

"Dependent on the results of Mr. McCann's visit to Lansing, we are willing to continue to consider the project."

"Cindy, what is your perspective?" Feldman asked.

"We continue to think that the acquisition, if it can be done at an acceptable price, and, if there are no additional risks beyond what we currently know and suspect, is plausible," she said, couching her words carefully. She could sense the Oxbow man tensing next to her even before he spoke.

"What do you mean 'suspect'?" he questioned, looking at the screen rather than at Cindy as he spoke.

"My impression is that there is something going on in Michigan that could expose the properties there to additional capital investment. Wils,...I mean Mr. McCann, is in Lansing this morning to see what he can find out about that and I am sure he will be in touch with all of us as soon as he completes his meeting with the Governor's representative."

"What do you think of Mr. McCann's stipulations for accepting the role of CEO?" Feldman asked. Bailey continued to tap his pencil on the pad in front of him. It was evident that Feldman's review of his telephone call with McCann on the previous day had been somewhat of a surprise to him. If this acquisition began to fall apart, it would reflect on Stu more than on any of the others. Word spread quickly in his line of work.

"They are, to say the least, absurd!" interjected the man from Oxbow.

"I was asking Ms. Melzy for her thoughts, Edwin," Feldman responded easily.

"Wilson McCann is one of the best operating men in the business. Having him on board as CEO will add immeasurably to the chances of success for the venture. Some of his requests are a little unusual, but not unheard of in the industry. Look at Bernie Ebbers at WorldCom and Joe Ford at ALLTEL. They and others made sure that the headquarters of their company was in their home town," Cindy responded. She had been caught off guard when Feldman had reviewed McCann's demands earlier in the conference.

"There isn't even a motel or decent restaurant within ten miles of Farnsworth! Having a headquarters there is ridiculous!" Edwin, the Oxbow man, replied harshly, leaning back in his chair and casting a sidewise glance at Cindy.

"I don't think we would want to model ourselves on WorldCom, do you?" Feldman smiled through the screen, ignoring Edwin's outburst. "What about his other demands?"

"I expected the buy-back requirement as part of getting Farnsworth Tele's owners to commit the company to the consortium. The salary and benefit requirements are appropriate for the size of the operation we are considering and the requirement to re-invest earnings and secure adequate capital is what I would have expected from Wils....Mr. McCann." Cindy replied, trying to keep an unbiased tone in her voice. Edwin shook his head negatively as she finished but didn't respond.

"Stuart?" Feldman turned to Bailey as he said it.

Bailey stopped tapping his pencil and laid it down as he gathered his thoughts. He wanted this deal so bad he could taste it. He wanted Wilson McCann in this deal because he felt it would assure success. Deep down, he felt that the deal was slipping away and he felt powerless to stop that slide.

"I think we should defer any decision until we have had a chance to hear what Wils has to say."

He was going to say more but he sensed that, for now, this was enough. He leaned back and looked at Feldman. The others, miles away, waited. Feldman was the lynch pin now. If he decided to fold, it was all over.

"That is sound advice. We will await further word from Mr. McCann. Edwin, I suggest you and your team move forward to complete any issues related to the due diligence review and summarize your review. I suggest we talk next Monday at 10:00 a.m. Smitty, do you have any snow up there?" Feldman asked.

Smith, taken aback by the change in the conversation, looked out his window. "About three inches, but it's melting fast."

"Fine, perhaps it will be gone entirely by Monday. Feldman closed his folder as he said it. Clearly, the video conference was over.

Cindy glanced at Edwin, the Oxbow man. He was still shaking his head as she punched the "disconnect" button on the video conference equipment remote control.

The Governor of Michigan's story was well known. Born and raised in Mackinaw City, he had driven a truck during the summers while attending Central Michigan University. With his business degree secured, he went to work for the trucking firm full time. Three years later he owned it. Expansion followed and soon it was the leading independent trucker in the northern Lower Peninsula and the eastern half of the Upper Peninsula.

He married, had two children and watched his business boom. He became prominent in area politics, chaired the Chamber of Commerce and the Economic Development Corporation and, at age 35, was an alcoholic. His wife filed for divorce and demanded custody of his children and his business began to suffer.

Alone in his home in Mackinaw City, he considered taking his own life and loaded a double-barreled twelve gauge shotgun to do the job. When the doorbell rang, he found himself face to face with a young minister, recently moved to the area and looking to build his congregation and save souls. The young man greeted him by saying, "Hello, I'm Kerry Dollard, the new Pastor of the Wesleyan Church. I am asking people a question. Do you have the time to answer it? With a guilty glance back at the loaded shotgun on the couch, he said that he did. Whereupon the young minister asked, "If you were to die today would you go to heaven?"

By the time they finished talking the future Governor was a convert. Two years later, convinced that the change in her husband and their father was genuine, his family reunited and his business prospered under a slightly revised set of business ethics. His contacts in political circles eventually led to a run for state representative and ultimately to a failed run for Governor. Four years later, he ran again and won as union members defied their unions and women forsook the National Organization of Women - NOW's endorsement of the incumbent to help elect him.

Despite his conservative positions on many issues, he enjoyed a 55% positive rating in the polls. Many people saw in him an example of their own failings and the opportunity to correct those failings and contribute. He did not hesitate to testify to his faith when given the opportunity but rather than turn people off, his "witness" seemed, more often, to engender trust. He had run with a promise to be a one-term Governor and he had, at every occasion, assured the State

Legislature, the media and the voters that he would keep that promise. Despite this, he had been able to secure cooperation within the legislature to pass an aggressive pro-development, pro-environment and pro-education program. One Democratic state Senator from the Detroit area said, "I'd a lot rather work with a Governor I know than wait for one I don't know."

The Governor leaned back in his chair and smiled at McCann.

"What is it that you are about to tell the *Wall Street Journal*, Mr. McCann?"

McCann felt the intensity of the Governor's gaze. There was neither anger nor affection in it. There was expectation. Somehow, he felt he wasn't living up to what that expectation might be.

"I...was expecting a man named Ross..." he began lamely.

The Governor raised his hand. "Ross is my assistant. He is busy at this time on another matter so I decided to deal with this myself." The tone was businesslike but McCann could tell that there was a great deal of emotion lying just below the surface. He felt as though his choice of reply would either restrain or release that emotion. He leaned forward, clasped his hands together and did not look the Governor in the eye as he responded.

"I...overstepped a little. I ...wanted to get someone's attention."

"You certainly did that," the Governor responded, the beginnings of a smile at the corner of his mouth. "Let me guess at your motives. You and your associates are in the middle of due diligence leading to a possible bid for telecommunication properties, including some in Michigan. This office makes inquiry as to your group's leadership and intentions and you decide to try to find out what lies behind that. Am I right?"

"You are quite correct, Governor," McCann replied. He sensed that the Governor's manner had softened just a little.

"Mr. McCann, I was elected to this office based upon my promise to the people of this state to do everything I could to encourage economic development, particularly development of Michigan based small business. As you know, the automotive business has been a bit of a drag on our economy. So when we heard that a Michigan based telecommunications company was participating in a group that was intending to bid for these properties, we wanted to assure several things. Would you like to hear what they are?"

"I would …very much," McCann replied, settling back in his chair.

"First, what is your role in all this, Mr. McCann? I am well aware of your career and your reputation in this industry. I was not aware until recently, however, that you are now a resident of and, I trust, a taxpayer of our fair state."

McCann smiled. "I live in Farnsworth now and, if my farm has any income, which at this time I question, I will be a Michigan taxpayer."

The Governor smiled in return. "Good. Let me welcome you to our state. But, you didn't answer my question. What is your role in the acquisition of the LEGENT properties?"

"I am an advisor to Farnsworth Telephone."

"And…an investor in Farnsworth Telephone?" the Governor prompted.

"Yes, I am a member of its Board of Directors and I own some of the stock. However, I have assigned the voting rights to the Warner family in this matter."

"Interesting. Do you intend to take a management role in the company?" The Governor leaned forward as he asked the question.

McCann hesitated before answering. He decided that the situation called for full disclosure. "The consortium wants me to be the CEO of the new company and we are in the process of negotiating the terms under which I might do that."

The Governor leaned back in his chair and clasped his hands behind his head. He thought for a minute before speaking.

"Mr. McCann, let me be frank. LEGENT has not invested very much in the telecommunications infrastructure of this state both before and after they acquired your Dynacom property. I would not want you to quote me on this to the Wall Street Journal, or any of your other media contacts but…"

"I apologize for that, Governor," McCann interjected.

"I was about to say that I will not be saddened by LEGENT'S departure from our state. I do want to make sure that whoever becomes responsible for their current property in Michigan is willing to do what they did not. And that is to continue to develop the infrastructure of the rural portions of our state to a 'state-of-the-art' standard and to do everything that is reasonable to expect of a member of the business community of our state. I have asked our Public Service Commission to be especially vigilant in assuring this. Would that be your intention if you become CEO of the acquiring company?"

"It would," McCann said, quietly.

The Governor smiled. "You are probably also aware that our office has talked with people involved in the financing of such acquisitions and we have mentioned to them that we are interested in seeing people who have an interest in the economic development of our state succeed in these types of ventures."

"I am aware of that, also," McCann replied.

"Good. I suggest that you tell your associates that we would be very pleased if a company with an interest in improving and expanding its business within the state were to be successful. We would not be supportive of a company whose only aim was to acquire a business and operate it with an eye to selling it off later to another company."

"Governor, you are a businessman. You understand that change is a part of our daily lives in these days. In the telecommunications business, the old monopoly structures are being replaced by a competitive structure and the wire-line infrastructure is under pressure from wireless, the Internet, cable companies and a host of other technology issues. It is difficult to predict what the outcome will be."

The Governor smiled. "I believe God has a plan for each of us, Mr. McCann. I am living proof that someone beyond hope can, if he grasps that plan, succeed within the scope of that plan. I think God has a plan for you. I think the fact that you are here at this time, in this place is an indication that God is at work. I trust that the outcome of your venture will be what He wills. Now, I must go to my budget conference. I have enjoyed meeting you and discussing this with you. I trust I won't read about it in tomorrow's *Wall Street Journal.*"

He stood and McCann automatically rose as well. The Governor extended his hand and McCann took it. Their eyes met.

"Good bye and God Bless," the Governor said, releasing his hand and exiting through the side door into another office.

McCann turned as the door behind him opened. The receptionist handed him his coat with a smile. "Have a nice day," she said, as she guided him out of the office.

He stepped out into the sunshine and was surprised to see Ted Lark standing on the sidewalk beside a white Ford 500 sedan with "Farnsworth Telephone Coop" and the company logo on its door.

"Good morning, Mr. McCann. Mrs. Warner sent me down to pick you up."

"Thank you, Ted. I wasn't sure how I was going to get back to Farnsworth," he smiled, as he walked toward the car. Lark held the door open as he tossed his bag into the back seat. "How is Doug?"

"It's not looking good, Mr. McCann," Lark responded, as he went around the car and got in behind the wheel.

Ted Lark waited with the car while McCann picked up his luggage and paid his bill. The news about Doug Warner's condition was not good. An aortic aneurism and a leaky heart valve had been diagnosed. Once they had him stabilized, the medical staff in Farnsworth had arranged for him to be transferred to Henry Ford Hospital in Detroit where surgery was scheduled for this afternoon. Lark reported that Lori, Belle and the girls were all in Detroit. After trying to make conversation, both men lapsed into silence. Lark sensed McCann's dark mood and wisely left him alone with his thoughts. Lark himself was deeply distressed by Doug Warner's condition and worried about what it would mean to the company, especially in view of the rumored acquisition activity that had everyone in the office stirred up.

McCann stared out the passenger side window as Lark left Lansing and took Interstate 69 toward Flint. The sunlight bounced off the newly fallen snow with brilliance that hurt one's eyes. The beauty of the day following the storm contrasted with McCann's dark mood and the storm that raged within him. He put on his sun glasses and closed his eyes against the light. He thought about his meeting with the Governor. He had learned nothing of any consequence. The Governor had been very skillful in saying much without saying anything. "Like all politicians," McCann thought. Yet, he knew that this man was different from other politicians he had met. He thought about Doug Warner and wondered what impact his situation would have on the acquisition. His thoughts went again, as they had so often, to Donna's and his mother's deaths. It seemed that his life was filled with the passing of the things and people that he cared most for, first Dynacom, then his mother and then Donna. Even his few head of beef cattle were now under quarantine. Everything his life had touched seemed to be contaminated.

His gut feeling was that the acquisition effort would die as well. He fully expected Feldman to withdraw his financial support. Without it, he knew the consortium would fold without making a bid. He realized his demands to Feldman were driven by his own selfish pride. Down deep in his heart, there was emptiness and he didn't know what it would take to fill it. He thought back over the months since he had arrived in Farnsworth and saw the pattern of encounters with those who offered a relationship with God as the answer. But what kind of God would take away everything in a man's life that brought any shred of happiness?

McCann had left the LeSabre at MBS airport and Lark turned north on highway 52 at the Owosso, Perry exit rather than going on to Flint and hitting I-75. As they traveled north through Owosso, Oakley and St. Charles, McCann continued to stare out the window, saying nothing. In Owosso, they crossed the Shiawassee River and he remarked on James Oliver Curwood's Castle situated at a bend in the river, just to the right of the bridge. They engaged in a brief discussion about how Owosso was the former headquarters of one of the Michigan telephone industry's leading companies back in the 50's. Neither of them had been more than a gleam in their father's eyes then but they both knew the history of their industry very well. Today, the buildings that had once housed the headquarters of one of Michigan's largest telephone companies were largely vacant. McCann reflected that they were much like his life . . . vacant.

Lark helped him transfer his luggage to the car at the airport and McCann asked him to call him as soon as the office heard from the Warner family on Doug's condition. They both headed east to Farnsworth. Lark pulled off in Saginaw, presumably to get lunch, but McCann kept going. He was not in the mood for lunch or for any more conversation. He wanted to get back to the farm and check on the cattle.

As he drove, he thought back to the conversation with the Governor. Was there a message there that he had somehow missed? He knew that politicians excelled at talking a lot and telling you nothing but he sensed that there was something more to the man and his message than the typical political rhetoric. He reconstructed the conversation in his mind and ran through it again. Nothing clicked except the Governor's focus on economic development. There was nothing new there. The Governor was widely known for his focus on developing the rural areas of the state. He was especially interested in the northern portion of the lower peninsula of Michigan. There were LEGENT properties in that area that would be part of the acquisition. The key to the Governor's interest had to be there and it had to be tied to economic development. His thoughts turned to Jim Wolfe. Jim had indicated that something was going on. If he could persuade Jim to help him, perhaps he could find out what lay behind the Governor's interest.

He crossed the abandoned railroad tracks at the west end of Farnsworth and drove slowly past the Agway. He hadn't had anything to eat since breakfast and pulled over opposite the Diner. When he entered, Sally McHugh was standing behind the counter, wiping her hands on a towel. Two high school age boys were cleaning up the tables from the noon lunch hour. The diner was empty.

"Coffee, Tea or Me?" Sally smiled, as she approached the table.

"I'd take you except I'm not sure I could keep up…you're high maintenance!" he smiled for the first time that day.

"You men are all alike! All hat and no cattle! I hear yours are in quarantine." She said it with a smile but her dark eyes showed concern.

"News travels fast in a small town," he replied. "How about some coffee and a ham and cheese sandwich?"

"You got it. Nick stopped in yesterday. He was pretty upset. Probably felt you wouldn't have a need for him if they take the cattle," she stood there waiting on his reply.

"Yeah, I'm running out of odd jobs. We'll have to see."

She went behind the counter and poured the coffee. She brought it to him and went back to make his sandwich. He poured in the creamer and a spoonful of sugar and began to stir. One of the high schoolers began to mop the floor. The other started putting out clean silverware wrapped in napkins on the tables. Sally watched him as she worked. He looked tired. "Not much is going right for you, Wils" she thought to herself, as she piled lettuce, sliced ham and cheese on the bread, covered it with another slice and deftly cut the sandwich diagonally. She poured herself a cup of coffee and joined him in the booth.

"You look beat," she said, taking a sip of coffee and watching him begin to eat.

"Dallas to Lansing to Farnsworth in two days. I'm on tour." he said, between bites.

"Did you hear about Doug Warner?" she asked.

"Yes. I understand he's at Ford in Detroit. Any news?"

"Phil was in at lunch time. No one had heard anything. It sounds serious."

"Aortal aneurysm and a leaky valve are serious," he responded, taking a drink from his mug.

Two scruffy looking men in barn coats and jeans entered the diner and sat at the counter. Sally rose to take their order. "You look like you could use a little fun in your life, Wils. There's a dance on Saturday night. You could take me. I'd make you smile."

She said it lightly but there was a hint of expectation in her voice.

McCann smiled back. "I might enjoy that Sally. Can I call you?"

"Anytime," she said, relieved that he hadn't said no.

He dropped $10 on the table and rose to leave. A night with Sally might be fun at that! He hadn't had any fun since Donna left for Prague. And with that thought, his gloom returned.

One of the men at the counter swiveled his stool and gave McCann a hard look.

"Is your name McCann?" he asked.

McCann turned back toward him. "Yes," he said, waiting.

"You brought BSE-infected cattle into this county." The man said it slowly and there was a threat in his tone.

"The tests aren't back yet. We don't know if they have BSE or not," McCann replied.

"You 'Gentlemen Farmers' come in and cause people like us problems. We don't appreciate that," the man replied in the same threatening tone.

The weight of the last few weeks seemed to come crashing down in that moment. McCann felt an animal like urge to pound the man's face to a pulp. He took two steps toward the bar and the man rose from his stool. The other man swiveled to face McCann.

BANG! The noise rang through the diner. Sally McHugh stood behind the diner's bar with a 34-ounce Louisville Slugger baseball bat in her right hand. She had slammed it down about six inches from where the second man's elbow was resting on the counter.

"Not in here and not now! You boys either order up or leave! Wils, I suggest you go check on your cattle." The look in her snapping dark eyes gave little doubt as to the seriousness of her intentions with the bat.

The two men rose and walked past McCann, heads down. He backed away, ready and waiting.

The first man turned as he opened the door to the diner. "You had better watch those cattle, mister. There's more than one way to deal with a diseased steer," he said as they stepped out into the street.

The sunshine that had melted the season's first snow was gone as dark clouds scudded across the sky. Sally McHugh put the bat back in its place below the counter and McCann took a deep breath.

"You have unfriendly customers," he said, looking at her with new appreciation.

"They've been in here before. They run a couple of brush country farms south of the river. I wouldn't worry about them. I could smell liquor on their breath. They spend a lot of time across the street at the tavern."

"Thanks, Sally."

"Call me — okay?" she said as he walked out into an increasingly gray afternoon.

He drove to the farm after picking up some groceries and told Nick to take the rest of the week off, after assuring him that "things will work out" in response to the young man's concerns about what they would do if the cattle had to be destroyed. The quarantine signs on the gateposts to the barnyard and on the big double doors of the barn stood out against the bright red paint.

He called Belle's number and the maid told him that Mrs. Warner had called and said that Doug was in intensive care and that he was resting comfortably. She had told the maid that if Mr. McCann called, to ask him to plan on meeting with her the following Monday, early in the morning, at the office.

Next, he called Bailey and reviewed his discussion with the Governor. He could tell that Stu was surprised that the Governor himself had talked with McCann and Bailey agreed with McCann's assessment that something tied to economic development in the northern Lower Peninsula was behind the Governor's interest. McCann decided to keep his intention to talk further with Jim Wolfe to himself. Bailey advised McCann that discussions would resume on Monday. McCann felt some relief that Feldman hadn't broken off his interest, yet. Bailey told him that the due diligence team was wrapping up its work in Dallas and that Cindy was on her way back to New York.

When he finished talking with Bailey, McCann dialed Cindy's cell number but was routed to a voice messaging system. He left a message asking her to call him. When she called later that evening, she confirmed what Bailey had told him and that the team still felt that, given a fair price for the properties, they should move forward if Feldman could be persuaded to stay in. The report was being circulated to all the parties by e-mail.

"Wils, are you sure about this?" she asked.

"What?"

"About getting back in the game…you gave Ed some pretty tough terms. What will you do if he agrees?"

"I'll see if I can persuade the Warners to go along. With Doug's situation, I'm sure it will be up to Belle. I'm to sit down with her on Monday."

"I spoke to her when I got into the city. She sounded more optimistic about Doug…and about you."

"She knows about my talk with Feldman?" he asked, dreading the answer.

"Yes. I told her. She actually seemed pleased."

"Amazing!"

"What? That she was pleased to see you offer to be CEO?"

He laughed into the phone. "No. I was just thinking what an amazing woman she is!"

"You're pretty amazing yourself…sometimes." She said it straight out. "Don't forget, we need to have a chat sometime about some other things I've been thinking about…but not now."

He hung up the phone, puzzled about what it was that Cindy was thinking about. He sensed that there was a lot about the "new" Cindy Melzy that he didn't understand.

McCann fed the cattle and Ted. He went to bed early after reviewing some of the data from the due diligence team report that he had received by e-mail that afternoon. He busied himself throughout most of Saturday with odd jobs around the farm, while carrying his cell phone. It didn't ring. He readied some of the equipment for winter and put the snow plow on the tractor. Nick had gone to town with the Ranger while he was in Dallas and purchased some bats of insulation. He placed these at various locations in the lower level of the barn in an attempt to make it a little warmer for the cattle. By mid-afternoon, he ran out of things to do and went inside and set the coffee pot to perk on the stove. He had been edgy all day, waiting to hear from someone about the acquisition. He tried Jim Wolfe's number but no one answered and the messaging system had been turned off. Jim and June were obviously concentrating on family activities this weekend. As he turned, the phone rang.

"Well, how about it?" Sally McHugh said into his ear.

"How about what?" he replied, using the delay to make up his mind on what he knew she would ask next.

"The dance…are you taking me or not?"

"Are you bringing your baseball bat?" he asked, smiling at the remembrance of her behind the counter with the bat in her hands.

"I think I can handle you, one-on –one, without it," she laughed.

"Okay, it's a date. Are you driving or am I?"

"Let's see. You have a pick-up and an old Buick. I have a Mustang. Can you drive a Mustang?"

"Last time I checked, my license covered Mustangs," he smiled.

"Okay. I'll pick you up at 7:00 p.m. and you can drive me to the dance in my car."

He enjoyed driving Sally's five-year-old red mustang to the dance in Sebawaing. The dance wasn't as enjoyable despite Sally's enthusiasm. Most of those there seemed intent on getting as drunk as they could before leaving. Never a big drinker, McCann nursed his beer and danced a few times with Sally. Eventually the loudness of both the band and the drink enhanced level of conversation rose to a level that McCann found both irritating and uncomfortable. To her credit, Sally, who was on her fourth beer, sensed this and suggested they leave.

As they drove back toward Farnsworth, Sally laid her head on McCann's shoulder. He wondered what would happen when they reached the farm. He thought he knew what Sally wanted to happen and knew he needed to welcome it or find a way to politely send her on her way. He decided on the former.

They pulled into the yard and he turned off the ignition and killed the lights. They sat there for a while looking up at a full moon. For a few moments, he completely forgot about the acquisition and the impending meetings here in Farnsworth and in Detroit on Monday that could determine the course of his future. This very well might be the last time for a while that he would have the time to look at the moon.

"Want to come in for a cup of coffee? I have hi-test. Just like your diner." He said it lightly.

"Sounds good," she said, looking at him before opening the door and swinging her legs out. Her skirt rode up and he caught a glimpse of a well toned thigh.

He opened the driver's side door and got out. As he closed the door and went around the front of the Mustang, a shot rang out and a yelp of pain filled the otherwise quiet night.

Marv and Steve, the two men who had confronted McCann in Sally's diner the day before, had done their chores and met at the tavern in Farnsworth as they usually did on Saturday night. Both men, for all their meager means, enjoyed Jack Daniels whiskey and beer chasers. They were well into it when their conversation turned to McCann and his cattle. The combination of the liquor and their hatred of "that city slicker and his diseased cattle" slowly built as the evening went on. In the end, they decided that they couldn't trust the government to take care of this problem and that it was up to them. When Marv mentioned that he had a 30-30 deer rifle and a box of cartridges in his pickup, the two men paid for their drinks, bought a bottle for the road and headed out of Farnsworth. They parked below the farm and, carrying the rifle and the bottle, they walked through the orchard to the rear of the barn. The bottle was almost empty and the two men were increasingly feeling the effects of the whiskey when the lights of an automobile lit up the farmyard next to the barn. They were just about to make a run for it when a low growl stopped them in their tracks. Without thinking, Marv swung the rifle and fired.

Ted had made his usual rounds including stopping at the Marks farm where he let the children pet him before trotting home across the fields. He scratched at the door at the rear of the house and whined. No lights were on and he gave up quickly and trotted to the barnyard. He went under the fence and into the feed alley through the partially open door. He lay down on a pile of hay and began to lick his paws when he heard a rustling behind the barn. He rose, listened, sniffed and quietly went back through the door and circled around the end of the barn past the cattle that were lying quietly in the barnyard. As he rounded the corner of the barn, his sensitive nose picked up the mixed smell of unwashed bodies further fouled by alcohol. He crouched low and growled. The explosion was followed by a searing pain in his chest and he yelped in agony before everything went black.

McCann came over the rise by the barn at a run and charged down to where the two men stood over the dog. He hit the first man with his shoulder and knocked him into the second man who held the rifle. Both men went down and the rifle flew out of the second man's hands. McCann quickly picked it up and leveled at the two as they struggled to rise.

"Stay down or I'll shoot you both!" He levered a shell into the breech as he said it. The sound caused both men to drop where they were.

"Sally! Call 911 and get someone out here!" He yelled to her as she stood at the top of the rise. She disappeared back toward the house.

"We didn't mean to…" the first man began in a slurred voice.

"Shut up and stay down!" McCann barked as he knelt beside Ted while waving the rifle in their direction. The dog was still and McCann felt no breath as he cupped Ted's nose. "I ought to shoot the two of you but you aren't worth a bullet!" McCann snarled at them.

"It's… just a… dog …" the second man mumbled, his voice thick.

The roar of the rifle brought Sally back at a run. She looked down to see McCann holding the rifle to the sky while the two men cowered in front of him. He had fired it into the air. As the echo died away, the second man sniffled, "Please…"

Ten minutes later, two Deputy Sheriffs arrived. The two men were quickly cuffed and taken into custody. The first Deputy told McCann that he would send someone out for their pickup. The second Deputy took Ted's lifeless body away. They would need an autopsy to confirm the cause of death in case it was needed at a trial. As the Deputies left, McCann and Sally stood beside the place where Ted had lain. She slipped her hand into his as they stood there looking down at a small spot of Ted's blood that was reflected by the moonlight.

Dean Wilson had been Tuscola County Sheriff for ten years. He had grown up in Farnsworth, played baseball and football for Farnsworth High School and married a local girl. He took some law enforcement training and was appointed Town Constable by the village of Farnsworth. After five years, he became a deputy sheriff and, when his boss retired, he ran for Sheriff. As a local boy who had spent his whole life in the county, he won with 60% of the vote. As the county drifted from solid Republican to a more evenly divided electorate, he made sure that he kept in touch will all the voters and was easily re-elected twice.

The last shooting in Tuscola County had taken place while Dean was a teenager and he always had wondered, with a sense of anticipation mixed with anxiety, when the next one would occur. He rubbed his eyes and looked at the digital clock beside his bed as the phone continued to ring. It was after midnight.

"Yeah?" he said into the mouthpiece, trying to force himself awake.

"Dean, there's been a shooting near Farnsworth," his deputy said, a tone of excitement in his voice.

"What? Who was shot? Do you know who did it?" The questions came rushing into his mind as he swung his legs over the side of the bed and stood, muffling the phone as his wife stirred in the bed.

"Just a dog …a couple of local guys …"

"A dog! You're calling me in the middle of the night because a dog was shot?" Wilson said it too loudly. Now his wife was fully awake, sitting up in the bed and turning on the lamp beside her.

"Yeah, well, there's a little more to it," the Deputy said, impatiently.

"So, let's hear it and it better be good." Wilson sat back on the edge of the bed and shrugged his shoulders at his wife's enquiring look.

"Well, it seems Marv Simmons and Steve Radcomb went out to the Harms farm and shot this guy's dog…"

"Whose dog? Isn't that the new guy that moved here from Chicago?" Wilson struggled to bring to mind the name of the man who lived on the Harms farm.

"His name's McCann and Marv and Steve claim he threatened to kill them!" the Deputy responded.

"Any witnesses?" Wilson said automatically, his training kicking in.

"Yeah, Sally McHugh was with McCann, and Steve and Marv say that she threatened them yesterday at her diner with a baseball bat."

Wilson looked at the ceiling. "What a crazy world this is!" he thought as he scratched his head.

"I'll be right there." He hung up the phone and started to get dressed. His wife sighed and went back to sleep. Her husband was always going down to the county jail to take care of some problem at the oddest hours. She knew that tomorrow morning he would tell her all about it. As far as she was concerned, it could wait until then.

(24)

Janice DeGroot was having her second cup of Sunday morning coffee. Her laptop was on the table in front of her, connected to the Internet through the wireless modem in the den. Janice was in her 10th year as a reporter for the *Bay City Times*. She and her husband lived in Essexville and she covered the Thumb Area of Michigan for the paper. There wasn't' usually much news on a Sunday morning but she checked the latest from the police reports in the various communities around the Thumb. She had worked a deal with the county Sheriff's office in each county to keep her posted on the latest developments. Janice had graduated from Farnsworth High School twenty years before and had taken a Journalism program at the University of Michigan on scholarship after being Salutatorian of her high school class and Editor of the high school paper for two years. Her husband, Dick was still asleep upstairs.

When she saw an entry about two men being jailed for shooting a dog in Farnsworth, she smiled but continued to read. She recognized Sally McHugh's name immediately and her interest quickened. Sally had quite a reputation in Farnsworth. She didn't recognize any of the other names, but one of them stuck in her mind as she rapidly went through the rest of the items from the counties. Finished, she went back to the Tuscola County item and copied down the name. She entered it into her search engine and scanned the results. It was then that it dawned on her who Wilson McCann was.

Janice DeGroot and her husband were LEGENT stockholders. LEGENT stock had rewarded them well for their investment. Wilson McCann had opposed one of LEGENT'S acquisitions. She remembered that the media had made him out to be a very self-centered person. The fact that he was with Sally McHugh and a shooting had occurred automatically made this a news item worth looking into.

≈≈❖≈≈

Sheriff Wilson leaned against the kitchen counter and looked at McCann. He had read through the Deputies' reports and had talked to Simmons and Radcomb. Both men had been evasive when he asked why they were at the farm and what they were doing with a loaded rifle. Simmons said the dog had "attacked" and that he had shot it in self defense. Radcomb said that McCann had threatened to kill them both after knocking them down and grabbing the gun. The deputies had recovered two spent casings from the scene. Simmons swore that he had only fired once at the dog and that McCann had fired the gun as proof of his intent to do them bodily harm. Wilson had called Sally McHugh and was to talk with her after he finished with McCann.

McCann had told him of the encounter at the diner and how he and Sally had returned to the farm late last night to hear a shot and the dog's yelp.

"Was Ms. McHugh planning to spend the night?" Wilson inquired, watching McCann's face.

McCann tensed and his reply was measured. "We had just gotten out of the car. I had been driving. That is when we heard the shot. I had invited Sally in for a cup of coffee. I think that's about it."

"And you say that you fired the gun in the air...to scare them?"

"I was mad. One of them said something about how it was 'just a dog'. I wanted to make sure they stayed put until Sally could call 911."

"Were you mad enough to have shot them?" Wilson's question was matter-of-fact. He had learned to ask such questions in a way that usually produced an honest answer.

"Sheriff, let's get something clear here. Are you more concerned with the facts that two drunken farmers carried a deer rifle onto my property with the obvious intention of killing my cattle and killed my dog, or with my intentions after I knocked them down and grabbed their gun?"

Wilson smiled. "Both."

"I was mad. I would not have shot a man to kill. I can't swear that I wouldn't have blown away a knee-cap if either of them had moved."

Wilson moved away from the counter and stepped toward the door. "Marv and Steve will be in jail until tomorrow. They'll post bail and I'll let them go. Frankly, my Deputy made a mistake with you. You should be in a jail cell for threatening the two of them and discharging a firearm with intent to intimidate. I'll expect you in Caro tomorrow morning to give your statement. You might want to get an attorney to come along with you."

He walked to his car and drove toward Farnsworth. He heaved a sigh of relief as he considered how closely he had come to having his first homicide. He would speak to his Deputies about their failure to jail McCann. It wouldn't happen again.

Sally McHugh verified McCann's version of events except that she had not seen him fire the rifle. She told Wilson that she had run back to find him standing over the two men with the rifle pointed in the air.

"Had the two of you been drinking?" he asked, when she had finished.

"I'd had a few, sure. I don't think Wils had more than one or two."

"You and McCann just friends, Sally?" Wilson asked.

"Just friends, Dean." She looked him squarely in the eye when she said it. He had always liked Sally. As he drove away, he thought probably most men did.

On Monday, McCann called Belle and told her what had happened. He could sense the disappointment in her voice as she agreed to await his call to set up another meeting. He tried to call Bailey but was told that he and Feldman were in conference. He tried to call Smith but was told that Smith was in a meeting. Finally, in frustration, he drove to Caro and gave his statement at the Sheriff's office in the County Court House. Sally McHugh was just coming out of an adjacent room when he got there. It was evident that she had just given her statement as to what had happened. The Deputy who followed her out beckoned to McCann.

"Right this way Mr. McCann. We are all ready for you", he said, smiling and ogling Sally at the same time.

"I'm sorry about this, Wils", she said, as she brushed past him on her way out of the office.

"It's not your problem," he replied, as he stepped past her into the room. A sheriff's Deputy, a Stenographer and a representative of the County Attorney were present.

The deputy who took his statement repeated Wilson's advice on securing an attorney and told him that he might yet be cited for reckless endangerment and menacing. He also asked that McCann inform the Sheriff's office before leaving the state for any reason. He made it clear that Sheriff Wilson was not happy with the way the situation at McCann's farm had been handled. McCann left the County Court House and drove back to the farm in a mood that matched the threatening gray sky. Another snow storm was predicted to hit that night.

When McCann arrived at the farm, the message light on his telephone was blinking. He punched the button and listened as Stu Bailey told him that Feldman had withdrawn his support for the acquisition and that they were returning to New York City. Bailey's voice seemed strangely detached.

Janice DeGroot's story came out in Monday's late edition of the *Times*. On Tuesday, the *Detroit Free Press* summarized the events into one paragraph stating that Wilson McCann, former CEO of Dynacom, was involved in a shooting incident on his farm near the Tuscola County village of Farnsworth. It went on to say that he was in the company of a thrice-married and twice-divorced woman who owned and operated a diner in that village. The two others involved in the shooting, both local area farmers, had been booked on various charges and released after posting bail secured by mortgages on their two farms. The County Sheriff was quoted as having "no comment" when asked why Wilson McCann had not been jailed as well.

The next day, Janice published her second story as a follow-up. She reported that Mr. McCann, who was reported to be a stockholder in the Farnsworth Telephone Cooperative, was also rumored to be involved in a New York-based consortium which was attempting to buy the Michigan operations of LEGENT. By that evening, Smith in Detroit, Ross in Lansing and Feldman and Bailey in New York City had all read excerpts from both stories. Feldman received his by e-mail from Edwin, the Oxbow man. His reply was two words.

"Good Riddance!"

In Detroit, that Tuesday morning, Arthur Boyington listened quietly as Belle Warner recounted what had happened at the McCann farm. When they finished talking, Boyington called an attorney in Bay City and reviewed the situation with him. Later that afternoon, Sheriff Wilson recommended that no charges be made against either Wilson McCann or Sally McHugh, while at the same time saying that McCann should have been put in jail at least overnight. The representative of the County Attorney's office, who had been in his job less than a year, considered the fact that the Sheriff was well connected throughout the county and quickly agreed with his recommendation.

That night over dinner, Wilson told his wife that the resulting publicity would be bad for Mr. McCann, as a newcomer to the county and all. He of course had no idea of the scope of the impact of Saturday night's events.

Leonard Olzewski's station wagon turned in at the long lane that led back to the farm. The farm, five miles south of Farnsworth, sat well back from the road. The house, barn and a one car garage sat on a small rise at right angles to the end of the lane. A small creek crossed the lane about 100 yards in and wandered away south into a wooded area and north to the fields of an adjoining farm. The house had been re-sided and the barn and garage were weathered but in good shape.

Olzewski knew that it wasn't much of a farm. The current owners were retired and had rented out the land. They were now renting one of the townhouses in Farnsworth with an option to buy when the farm sold. Part of the sixty acres was good for pasture land. The ground east of the house and north and west of the barn was good for hay and oats. About five acres at the westernmost end of the property was wooded and Leonard knew there were a lot of blackberry bushes in the woods. The owners had proudly shown him the blackberry jam that they had put up last year when they signed the listing. He wondered if they had put up more this year before they moved to town ahead of the advancing winter. When he had listed the farm this past summer, he had walked back to check the survey stakes and had picked about a quart without any trouble at all.

The biggest problem was the well. It was a shallow well and the water had the "rotten egg" smell of sulphur. The current owners had used bottled water for drinking. The buyer's agent hadn't seemed too concerned but said that one of the conditions of any offer would be a check of the well and a determination of whether or not good water could be assumed if a deeper well was drilled. That suggested to Olzewski that the potential buyer had money. This was the second visit the buyer's agent had made to the farm and the first meeting between the two. She was a local realtor from Farnsworth. She didn't have as big an agency as Olzewski but was a good person to deal with, based upon his few previous encounters.

She was sitting on the front porch looking down at the two walnut trees that fronted the lane where it turned into the drive up to the house. She walked out to meet him as he got out of the wagon.

"Good morning Leo. How are you?" she smiled, extending her hand. She always looked so professional that it made him a little self-conscious.

"I'm good. You?"

"Great. Could we go inside? It's getting a little nippy out here." He took the key to the house from his pocket and led the way inside.

Twenty minutes later, she had finished walking through the house and barn. She had made notations on a yellow legal pad as she did so. He wondered what new issues or concerns the potential buyer might have in addition to the well. She did not offer any information but kept up a steady chat about the weather, prices of property in the area and the general economy. Whenever Olzewski tried to find out anything about the buyer or the buyer's intent, she deftly fended off his inquiries.

They stood in the drive as she flipped up a page on her pad and reviewed a list of jottings that he took to be the things her client had given her to check on.

"Will your client be making an offer?" he asked, hoping that his tone was businesslike and did not sound too eager. He had taken the listing almost three months ago and this was the first real interest.

"I can't say. It depends on several issues my client has to resolve," she smiled back.

"Perhaps if I could meet with you and the buyer, I could help to…" he began.

"Leo, I am under instructions not to reveal the name of my client until an appropriate time. I understand your concern and that this is a little unusual. I can only tell you that my client is from out of state and has given me the authority to act on their behalf both prior to making an offer and to follow up on any conditions after an offer is made. I hope you understand and appreciate my position."

Despite the cool wind that blew across the yard, he instinctively pulled his handkerchief from his coat pocket and mopped his brow.

"Of course. I'll hear from you soon? A fine farm like this won't stay on the market long, you know."

She smiled and extended her hand. "With you on the job, I'm sure it won't. I'll be back in touch as soon as I can."

As he drove back down the lane, Leonard Olzewski thought of at least six questions that he wished he had asked. He wondered who would come from out of state to buy a sixty-acre farm that was mostly good for raising hay and pasturing a few head of cattle. But, the real estate business had taught him to expect the unusual.

Over the course of his career, Wilson McCann had been in many situations where he had to give an account of his management to higher authority. Charlie Corbin and his sycophant Board had been particularly difficult, but he had always looked forward to the confrontations and relished the opportunity to display his ability. On Wednesday morning, as he drove into Farnsworth to meet with Belle Warner, he was not looking forward to the meeting. He remembered Judith Bingham, who had taken a particular interest in him and encouraged him. As a junior, he had let this teacher down through failure to apply himself and spending more time with his friends having fun than studying. On the last day of school, she had called him into her classroom. He remembered the day as if it were yesterday. The sun shone in through the windows and filled the room as she sat there behind her small wooden desk. Her white hair radiated the sunlight like silver. 'I'm disappointed in you Wilson," she had said. He had vowed to try harder. To his credit, he had applied himself well the following year.

He entered the building through the business office and one of the Service Representatives called back to Belle's administrative assistant. A few minutes later, she appeared and motioned him to follow her back to Belle's office. "She is expecting you," the young woman said, as she led the way.

"How…is she?" he asked.

"She looks very tired. She has been through a lot. Go right in."

He stepped through the doorway into Belle's office and had an immediate flashback. The sun shone through the windows and Belle's hair reflected it like silver. Her head was bent over her desk as he entered. She was reading her Bible. As he entered, she looked up and he saw that in the past week she had begun to look her age. She smiled wanly as she indicated a chair.

"Good morning, Wilson" she said quietly. He noted the formality of the greeting.

"How are you Belle? And how is Doug?"

"I'm a little tired as you might guess. Doug is coming along well and we hope to have him home by Saturday. They tell us it will be a month or so before he will be back on the job. I'm thankful that it wasn't worse."

"Amen to that," he said, smiling. The smile was not returned.

She leaned back and closed her eyes for a moment as if summoning additional strength.

"I'm disappointed, Wilson." He felt as if she had slapped him across the face.

"I know. I had hoped that we could pull this deal off. I know how much it meant," he began.

She raised her hand to silence him.

"I'm not disappointed about the acquisition. I'm disappointed about you."

Feeling that he knew where this conversation was going, he nevertheless tried to deflect it. "I probably overstepped with Feldman and I should have…"

She raised her hand again and fixed her gaze on him for a moment before she began again.

"I'm not disappointed with Mr. Feldman's actions or with anything related to the acquisition. The acquisition is not what is important here. You and your life are what are important here."

He started to speak again but she took a deep breath and refused to be deterred. "I have watched you over these past few weeks. I have hoped and prayed that you would find what is really important in life. God has given you so much and you have squandered it! People respond to you, they respect you and they want to follow you. And yet you have failed in the most important thing! You have missed so much and you continue to miss so much!"

The strength of her words and the heat of her emotion slammed into him. He sagged in his chair as she paused to catch her breath and leaned forward toward him. Her eyes bored into his as she closed the Bible in front of her and raised it from the desk. She held it out toward him.

"What is the most important teaching in this book?" She asked it quietly and waited for his response.

"I suppose it is to love others and treat them as you would want them to treat you," he replied, knowing already that he had missed the point.

She smiled and sat back, returning the Bible to the desk in front of her. "Close, but incorrect. The most important teaching in this book is to love God. But you do not love God, do you? And because you do not love God, you cannot bring yourself to love others. You didn't love your mother until it was too late. You couldn't bring yourself to love Donna in the way she needed to be loved until it was too late. You couldn't take the one step that would have brought you so much. Instead you substituted the love of things. Things that, when you and I are both gone from this world, won't matter very much. I've watched you these past few weeks. You thrive on the 'business' of business. You were energized by the challenge that this acquisition offered. You have wasted the talents you have because you sought the recognition of others. You have wasted the love of a godly mother and a young woman who prayed with all of her heart for your soul. You have ignored the counsel of others as to your failure to give your love and your life to Him. I'm not disappointed that we lost this opportunity to expand our business. Doug and I have dedicated our company to God in the hope that he could use it to glorify Himself and draw others to him. We will continue to do that even though this 'deal' did not materialize." She emphasized "deal" in a tone of voice that had the edge of contempt in it.

"I'm sorry that you think so poorly of me," he replied. It was all he could think of to say. But she was not finished. She leaned back in her chair and clasped her hands in her lap before speaking again.

"When we die, every one of us will be required to give an account of his or her life before God. If those two drunken men had shot you instead of that beautiful, wonderful dog who adopted you when you came here, what account would you have given?"

It was then that he saw it. He saw in her eyes the love that stood behind the heated words that had burned into him like a branding iron. Belle Warner's concern was not for an acquisition effort failed or for his personal part in it. She was not concerned with organizations and numbers on a spreadsheet. She was not concerned with the success or failure of an earthly venture. Her concern at this moment was for him and the decision that she, Donna, his mother and others had so earnestly prayed that he would make, the decision that he had not made.

She opened the desk drawer and took an envelope from it and handed it across the desk to him. He opened it silently and took out the proxy that he had given her in New York City.

"You don't need to give this back," he said quietly.

"I think it serves no purpose for me to have it. I hope that you will continue to be a member of our Board and help us with our future direction. Now I must get back to work. I have several things to take care of this morning. I hope that you will forgive me if I have given any offence in what I have said. God loves you Wilson...and I love you."

She rose and extended her hand. He took it and held it while their eyes met. Then, he turned and walked out. He could feel her gaze following him down the hall. In the parking lot, he tore the envelope containing the proxy into pieces and dropped them in a waste can. He sat for a while in the Ranger before putting the key in the ignition. He thought back over his life as he sat there. What account would he have given if the bullet that killed Ted had instead ended his own life?

(25)

John King strode past his secretary and into his office, swinging the door shut behind him. He paced once around his desk and slouched in a chair opposite it. He did this at times when he wished he wasn't occupying this office any longer. This was one of those times. He had just met with Norm Lister. King bowed his head and breathed a brief prayer, "Lord give me strength and keep my attitude focused on you."

King sat there for five minutes and finally rose and circled the desk. He punched in Sal Piazza's extension number. When Piazza answered, King sighed and said, "Can you come over for a few minutes?"

Piazza was there in two minutes. He shut the door quietly behind him and waited for King, who stood looking out the window. King spoke without turning.

"Norm doesn't like the numbers we're giving him."

Piazza took a minute to think about what King had said and lowered his big frame into the chair recently occupied by his boss.

"And he wants us to do what?"

"Tell them to up the ante or forget it," King replied, turning and dropping into his swivel chair.

"We've already lost the New York group," Piazza replied, telling King what he already knew.

"That wasn't because we were being unrealistic," King said, leaning back. "I'm not sure yet what happened there, but I'll bet it had something to do with Wils McCann and that Independent in Michigan."

"So…what is Norm thinking?" Piazza asked, taking a small note pad from his shirt pocket and flipping up the cover with a green LEGENT logo on it.

"Eight times EBITDA," King responded, watching Piazza. He was rewarded by the look of incredibility that washed across the big Italian's face. Piazza flipped the cover back down on his pad and returned it to his shirt pocket. EBITDA, or Earnings Before Income Taxes, Depreciation and Amortization was only one of the traditional methods of measuring financial performance and, therefore, valuation. In the late 1990's, Piazza knew, eight times EBITDA would have been a reasonable valuation for a rural telecommunications property, given its other financial and service results, geography and the condition of its facilities. But Piazza also knew that with the advance of the Internet, wireless and other competing technologies, such valuations were not the norm now.

"We're not going to sell these properties," he responded in a matter-of-fact tone, putting his hands behind his head and rocking back on the chair until all two hundred and sixty pounds were balanced on the back two legs.

"You got that right. I'll call Fairfield and you call the others. We probably better call Regulatory and get them prepared to go see the commissions again to let them know we'll be staying around for a while. I'm sure they will be glad to hear that, especially Michigan."

"Is Norm prepared to spend some money on improving service in those states?" Piazza asked, as he dropped the chair back to all four legs and rose to leave.

"Didn't say so. Based on our track record to date, I doubt it," King replied.

Piazza turned in the doorway. "Are you going down to Georgia for Thanksgiving?"

"Yeah…I may just stay there." King replied, as he swiveled to his computer and brought up his Outlook contact file. He brought up the Fairfield information and thought again of what he had told McCann at the golf course. LEGENT would be gone in five years. Perhaps McCann had taken him seriously and his group was waiting for a better price. He'd have to call him after he had spoken to Fairfield.

McCann drove to the small veterinary clinic on the edge of Farnsworth and picked up Ted's body. The report that had been requested by the Sheriff's office confirmed that the dog had died from a bullet fired from a 30-30 rifle. The bullet, extracted and given to the Sheriff's office would later be matched to the rifle taken at the scene of the shooting.

As he drove home, snow was beginning to fall and the day was darkening. The storm a few days earlier had been the forerunner to this larger storm. It was evident that while it was late November, this would be the beginning of winter.

He parked in the drive and went inside to change his clothes. He came out dressed in jeans, boots and his sheepskin lined denim jacket. He could still smell Donna's perfume on the collar as he buttoned it. He thought back to the sunny day when she had given it to him. If only he could go back to that day!

He took a pick-mattock and a shovel from the tool shed and walked out into the orchard. Near one of the trees, he began to dig as the snow continued to fall. The pick quickly broke through the slightly frozen layer of soil and he was able to dig through the unfrozen subsoil and chop away the roots that he encountered as he dug. An hour later, the four foot deep hole was finished and the pile of newly removed earth beside it was already covered by an inch or more of snow.

He lowered the dog's body into the grave and stood there looking down at the bundle, wrapped in the body bag from the clinic. He closed his eyes and remembered the nights with Ted lying at his feet or resting his head on his knee, waiting for that pat or scratch behind the ear that sent his tail into constant movement. His mind flashed back to his mother's funeral in Florida and Donna's in Farnsworth. He sank to his knees beside the grave and felt the cold, wet snow-covered dirt seep through his jeans. The cold couldn't begin to match the coldness that he felt in his heart. He remembered Hastings' sermon on reaping corruption and, in his mind, he saw himself at the bottom of the hole that he had dug for himself.

Tears began to course down his cheeks and he clamped his teeth together to stop the sob that rose. It didn't work. Once released, the sobs came quickly and the tears dropped into the grave and onto the formless bundle that it held.

"Oh my God!...my God!" he choked out between the sobs. The wind carried the sound away across the orchard. The snow on the sheepskin collar of the jacket began to melt and run down his neck as he bowed his head over the grave. In his mind, he again saw not Ted but the image of himself at the bottom of the hole. What account could he give of his life?

Jim Marks parked his pick-up behind the Ranger and got out. He started for the back door of the house when he saw the figure kneeling in the orchard by a mound of snow-covered dirt. The snow was coming down so hard that the image was blurred behind the fast falling flakes. Marks started to walk toward the orchard but something held him back. His eyes moved from McCann upward to a power pole on the fence line at the edge of the orchard. Only the last six feet of the pole was visible behind the trees. The cross arm fastened to the pole two feet below its tip supported two power lines. The lines were obliterated by the falling snow. Marks' stared at the image of a cross that rose up above the trees and the man who knelt beneath them.

Wilson McCann stayed on his knees for some time. When he got to his feet and began to shovel the snow-covered earth into the grave, he knew inside himself that his life had changed. As he worked amid the steadily falling snow, he felt a peace that he had never known before. He tried to think ahead as to what this meant and how it would affect him in the future. He felt as if he was facing a blank computer screen. He knew it would be up to him as to what would be keyed onto that screen. He was sure of one thing. What would be written there would be written with a different purpose and a different focus than what might be contained in a file of his life thus far.

He finished filling in the grave and went to the fence line where a small pile of stones had been left by some long ago departed farmer. One by one, he carried enough stones to completely cover the grave. He would put a marker there in the future but for now the stones would serve as a visual reminder as to what had just occurred.

He walked back to the shed and stored his tools. He drove the Ranger inside and positioned it so that he could get the tractor with its plow out if needed. As he rolled the big double doors to the shed shut and turned to go into the house, he saw the faint outlines of tire tracks in the snow. Someone had been here and had left. He wondered who it might have been and why they hadn't called out or come to the orchard.

He went into the kitchen and took off his coat and hung it over a chair to dry. He changed the muddy jeans for a new pair and put the coffee pot on to perk. Then he went to the hallway closet and retrieved Fred and Ella Harms' Bible. As he turned toward the kitchen, another thought crossed his mind and he replaced the Bible on the shelf and went into the spare bedroom. The box with his mother's personal things was in the bedroom closet. He pulled it out of the closet and opened it. He remembered a Bible among the things he had boxed up after his mother's funeral. He found it and laid it on the bed. Returning the box to the closet, he picked up the Bible and returned to the kitchen. He poured himself a cup of coffee and took it and the Bible into the living room. He sat in the recliner and leaned back. As he did so, he absently dropped his hand down beside the chair as he had on many occasions in the past. No cold damp nose rose to meet it and no soft ears were there for him to scratch. With a catch in his throat, he opened the Bible and began to thumb through it. He noted that the presentation page showed that the Bible had been presented to his mother a few years ago by "SAM." He wondered who Sam was and what his relationship was to his mother. He made a mental note to call the minister of the little church in Florida to see what light, if any, he might shed on it.

On what had once been blank pages he found various sayings written in his mother's perfect penmanship:

Across the fields of yesterday, there sometimes comes to me a little girl just back from play, the girl I used to be.

And oh, she smiles so wistfully once she has crept within. I wonder if she hopes to find the woman I might have been.

There was a note in parenthesis — "*It is there — potential is there — God is there*" — Phil. 3: 1-14, Eccl. 9:10a

He read on.

If the direction of your life is a peril to your soul — better try another road — Charles L. Allen.

I do not know what makes the tides nor what tomorrow's world may do, but I have certainly enough for I am sure of you!

and...

Often on the rock I tremble, faint of heart and weak of knee. But the steadfast rock of ages never trembles under me.

He turned to the referenced passage in Philippians and began to read. Two verses were underlined in green, the eighth and the sixteenth. He re-read them.

More than that, I count all things to be loss in view of the surpassing value of knowing Christ Jesus my Lord, for whom I have suffered the loss of all things, and count them but rubbish in order that I may gain Christ. I press on toward the goal for the prize of the upward call of God in Christ Jesus.

McCann read the next two verses, removed a pen from his shirt pocket and carefully underlined the sixteenth verse.

However, let us keep living by that same standard to which we have attained.

He thumbed the pages back to Ecclesiastes thinking about Donna and how she had worked with him to better understand how the Bible was organized and where the various books were. The first part of the verse his mother had noted was underlined.

Whatever your hand finds to do, verily, do it with all your might.

He read the rest of the verse and thought of what Belle Warner had said to him earlier that day.

ACQUISITION

..for there is no activity or planning or wisdom in Sheol where you are going.

Thinking about Belle and Donna and his mother, he continued to read until he reached the end of the book. Once again he took the pen from his pocket and carefully underlined the last two verses of the book.

The conclusion, when all has been heard, is, fear God and keep His command-ments, because this applies to every person.
Because God will bring every act to judgment, everything which is hidden, whether it is good or evil.

McCann flipped back to the page at the front of the Bible where his mother's notes were written. There was about an inch of space remaining on the page. McCann began to write in that space. His handwriting looked almost illegible in comparison to his mother's fine hand. When he finished he looked at what he had written.

When day begins, when day ends, all a man has comes from God.
In the time I have left and through the grace of God, I will do my best...
for Him!

He read it again and then placed the date and his initials WJM beneath it.

On the following Sunday morning, Charles Hastings gave the first of three planned sermons leading up to and including Thanksgiving weekend. His text for the morning was Second Corinthians 9:15.

Thanks be to God for his indescribable Gift!

When the invitation was given, Wilson McCann rose from his seat at the rear of the church and made his way to the altar. He knelt there and made public his profession of his new- found faith.

In his seat in the third row, Jim Marks shut his eyes and brought back to mind the image of the man he had seen kneeling in the snow with the image of the cross rising above him. "Thank you God," he said quietly. In the fifth row, a slightly thinner and much paler Doug Warner sat with his family. He wiped away a tear and looked at his mother. Belle Warner's head was tilted up toward the light streaming in through the stained glass windows back of the altar. As the light bathed her face, he saw her smile. Later, he told Lori that he had never seen his mother look as beautiful as she did at that moment.

The Director entered the conference room with two of his staff. The two LEGENT men were the same well dressed duo that had met with him before. The older man's perfectly capped smile was displayed for all to see as they entered.

The two staff people shook hands and sat down with their yellow legal pads at the ready. They were there to take notes, nothing more. When the meeting was over, each would prepare a brief summary of what was said and their impressions. The Director had made it very clear that anything he said was to be recorded verbatim.

"Thank you for taking the time to meet with us. As we mentioned before, we want to keep the staff informed as to the progress of our actions to divest our property here in Michigan or any other changes relative to our decision to do so," the LEGENT man with the capped teeth began. The Director and both staffers took notice of the mention of "any other changes relative to our decision" and waited. The Director already knew that the New York consortium had abandoned its efforts to make a bid. He wasn't sure why and was somewhat disappointed. He knew that the Governor's aide, Ross, would want to know all there was to know about that, and the fact was that the Director didn't know much more.

"As you know, we have a significant investment here in the state and we have added to that investment over the years both through network improvement and expansion and through acquisition. It is of primary importance to our customers and our shareholders that we find a buyer willing to continue to invest in the network here and that we recover a reasonable portion of that investment," the LEGENT man continued. His companion looked straight ahead and appeared uncomfortable.

The Director said nothing. The two staff members were making a few notes.

"The fact is…," the LEGENT man said as he shifted slightly in his seat, "…we have not found a buyer for the properties in the Midwest that meets those two objectives and we are continuing to consider our options."

The Director smiled inwardly. So, LEGENT had not found a buyer that would pay what was no doubt an inflated price for the properties and was now faced with having to continue to operate them.

"Do you expect to receive any offers for the property here in Michigan?" he asked.

The LEGENT man leaned forward and the smile faded a bit. "We continue to believe that the properties should be sold as a package and we have no intention of splitting individual states out. At the current time, we do not have any offers for the properties as a whole."

"Or in part?" the Director responded, noting that both of his staff were writing.

"No…not in part either," the LEGENT man responded.

"Well, thank you for coming in and keeping us informed of the situaton. As I had mentioned during our previous meeting regarding your intention to sell the property here in Michigan, our primary focus is to protect the rate payers of the state. With that in mind, I must make you aware of a proceeding that we will shortly be initiating."

The smile was gone now. Both LEGENT men shifted uncomfortably in their chairs and waited. The Director glanced down at the notes he had made for himself on his own yellow pad.

"We will shortly be opening an inquiry into the levels of service provided by the regulated telecommunications companies operating within the state. We will also be asking for plans from the various companies as to the level of their commitment to assuring that any service deficiencies are rectified within the next two years. I need not tell you gentlemen that the service levels of your company are, in many cases, not meeting our service standards. The Commission is also concerned that the levels of the former Dynacom properties in Michigan have also deteriorated to a point where many of them are also in danger of not meeting our service standards. I suggest that you advise your company of our intention. We will be most interested in LEGENT'S future plans for its operations in the state."

The two staff members were writing furiously now. They continued to do so for the remainder of the meeting. They didn't have to write very much more as the Director had said most of what he had come to say, except for the usual assurances that the staff would be happy to work with the company, etc. etc. The two LEGENT men left quickly. Their smiles were gone.

Later that morning, the Director called Ross and brought him up to date on the LEGENT situation. Ross listened carefully until the Director was finished.

"So they intend to stay for now and you will be investigating the service levels?" He phrased it more as a statement than a question.

"Yes."

"Thanks for the call, Fred", Ross said, as he hung up the phone. Ross admired the Governor and was very careful to insure that his language was restrained whenever he was with him. Alone in his office, Ross leaned back in his chair and swore.

The snow was a foot deep on the fields and wasn't showing any signs of melting in the sub-freezing temperatures that had followed the latest storm. But the cold didn't bother McCann as he went about his chores on Monday morning. He could still feel the warmth of Belle Warner's embrace as he stood at the front of the church when the service had ended. Doug had gripped his hand and clasped his shoulder with a big smile on his pale face. McCann had gone to dinner with Jim and Lona Marks and their children. During lunch, Trent Marks had said, "My dad came to see you last week but he said you were busy burying Ted so he didn't want to bother you. Did you put a marker on Ted's grave?"

McCann had smiled as he remembered the tracks in the snow. So that was who had been there while he was in the orchard! He had looked at Jim but the farmer was studiously checking the menu.

" No, but we will. Perhaps you and Susan and your mom and dad can help me do it right," he said.

Back at the farm, he heard a truck come up the drive. He came out of the barn to find Phil Willard getting out. Phil and Martha had not been in church on Sunday. The Agway dealer's rotund face broke into a big smile as he approached. In his brown barn coat and smallish Stetson hat, his resemblance to Andy Devine was striking.

"Praise the Lord!" he shouted loudly enough that the cattle in the barn yard turned and perked up their ears.

McCann smiled as he was enfolded in a bear hug. "Careful Phil, I'd like to keep my ribs intact!"

Willard rubbed his ruddy face. "Martha and I are just so happy...," he began.

McCann raised his hand and looked him in the eye. "Thank you for your friendship and for not giving up on me."

"Hey, that's what it's all about," Willard responded, as they walked to the house.

Once inside, Willard helped himself to some coffee and seated himself at the table.

"I had a call this morning Wils...from the Governor's office."

"I appreciate the Governor's interest, but one black sheep coming back to the fold shouldn't warrant it," McCann said, hoping that his humor was appreciated.

Willard took a sip from his mug and put it down. "His aide wanted to know what happened to the acquisition."

"Did you tell him?"

"As much as I knew. He seemed pretty upset about it all," Willard responded, taking another sip from his mug.

At that moment, both men turned to the window as a car pulled into the yard. The USDA logo was plain on the passenger side door. A middle aged man wearing a USDA jacket and cap got out and came to the door. McCann rose to meet him and Willard sat watching.

"Mr. McCann?" the man asked, extending his hand.

"Yes," McCann replied, suddenly nervous.

"I'm glad to tell you that your cattle are okay. We are lifting the quarantine and I'll be taking down the signs."

"Praise the Lord!" Phil Willard shouted. While his voice could be heard outside the house, the cattle continued to eat the baled hay that McCann had put in the barnyard earlier that morning.

After the USDA man and Willard had both left, McCann made a few phone calls. The first was to Bailey in New York City. The second was to Feldman. In both, McCann apologized for his behavior and in particular for anything that he might have said or done that had resulted in the collapse of the acquisition effort. Bailey was at first rather cool but became philosophical and, by the time the call ended, had warmed up considerably. Feldman, surprised by the call, was guarded and expressed his view that while McCann's "terms," as he referred to them, were unprofessional, the acquisition could not have gone forward on a sound financial basis. He also told McCann that he had learned that both of the other groups that had been considering bids had withdrawn, evidently because of LEGENT'S position as to the value of the properties.

Next, McCann called Cindy. She seemed pleased to hear from him and shared his disappointment that the acquisition had not gone forward. It seemed to McCann that she was holding something back but he didn't press it.

"There is one thing more," he said, taking a deep breath before continuing, "You know how you said you had found a new purpose for your life and hope that I would find purpose for mine. Well, I think I may have found what you found."

"Oh Wils! I'm so happy for you!" Her enthusiasm washed over him and warmed him.

He told her about the events of the last few days and sensed that her enthusiastic response was dimmed slightly when he told her that Sally McHugh had been with him when Ted was shot. They continued to talk for several minutes about Belle and Doug's condition and Feldman's revelation concerning the sale of the LEGENT properties.

"Tell David that I miss him," he said, as he prepared to hang up.

"He will be heartbroken when he hears about Ted. He has me read *"Bob, Son of Battle"* to him every night and always tells me that Ted is just like Bob."

"Cindy, I'm not sure where our paths will cross again, but I hope it will be soon."

He sensed the hesitation at the other end of the line. "I hope so too, I had thought that ….but my plans have changed."

"Cindy, will you please tell me what is going on? You keep alluding to a decision you were about to consider and if I can help in any way, I'll be glad to do it."

There was a moment of silence before she spoke again. "Doug and I have….had been talking about me becoming CFO of the combined companies in Michigan if the acquisition went forward. I had even taken a look at a little farm near Farnsworth. David and I were going to have a place of our own and…"

He felt like someone had punched him in the stomach. The collapse of the acquisition had collapsed her plans.

"I'm sorry. I didn't know. Doug always said his people could handle the increased responsibilities…I had no idea."

"His Treasurer, Ron Layne, is retiring. He mentioned having to hire a new one and Belle and Doug and I talked and it just seemed so right that perhaps I got ahead of myself a little. Anyway, that's over and done with now. I'll just keep praying that God will direct my path. I'll pray that he directs yours too, Wils."

As he hung up the phone a few minutes later, McCann realized that the collapse of the acquisition effort hadn't really mattered all that much to him until now.

(26)

In Dallas, John King strode by his secretary's desk and into his office, shutting the door behind him. His secretary reflected that every time her boss went to Mr. Lister's office lately, he went into seclusion when he returned. Usually his period of seclusion ended with the arrival of Sal Piazza. She checked her watch and smiled to herself when Piazza arrived at King's office door five minutes later and went inside.

King was seated behind his desk this time. Piazza sighed as he lowered himself into one of the chairs opposite the desk.

"Well, what is it this time?" he asked.

"We've got to get out of Michigan!" King replied with a tinge of sarcasm in his voice.

"You mean...as in 'sell the Michigan properties'? No one is going to pay eight times EBITDA for those properties!"

"The eight times rule doesn't apply to Michigan anymore," King replied. His voice showed that he was getting a little tired of this situation.

"Since when are we so anxious to get out of Michigan but not the rest of the Midwest?"

"Since the Michigan PSC told Regulatory Affairs that they are opening a service proceeding," King replied, reaching into his left hand desk drawer and taking out a bottle of Tetralac. He popped two of the little white antacid tablets into his mouth and chewed for a moment. Piazza smiled as he watched his boss.

"Every action produces a reaction. That's what you've always said." He stood and stretched. He walked to the widow of King's office and looked out. "What are the rules?"

"Norm wants out before we get into the proceeding. You and I both know that the PSC will make service improvement and expansion a condition of their approval for any acquisition. Norm's willing to factor in some sort of adjustment for required investment. I want you to go down to Network Design and get an estimate from them on what it will take to get those properties up to standard and keep them there. We'll take that estimate and reduce what we think is a reasonable price by it. That's the number I'll take back to Norm."

Piazza noted that King had emphasized "what we think is reasonable." He bent to touch his toes and then raised his hands toward the ceiling, stretching his six foot six inch frame. King watched him with a slight smile beginning to form on his face. He would truly miss this guy when he retired.

"Must get tough carrying that clarinet around, huh?" he said.

"Nah, I started playing paddle tennis last night and I'm a little sore."

"Paddle Tennis! Geez! What next? A rousing game of Bocce?"

"Hey! Don't knock Bocce! It's in my genes," Piazza grinned as he went out the door.

King leaned back in his chair and thought for a moment. He knew Fairfield didn't have any property in Michigan. Their closest operation was in Ohio. The other group wouldn't look at anything as small as the Michigan property.

"Well, Mr. McCann, you are going to get another shot at this!" he said, as he picked up his phone.

The phone in the farm house rang and McCann answered on the second ring.

"Wils! It's Dale Dryer in St. Louis. How are you?"

McCann thought for a moment and then recognized both the voice and the name. Dryer was a principal in one of the elite executive search firms in the nation. McCann had often used Dryer's services to find needed talent for Dynacom. At the time of its acquisition by LEGENT, Dynacom had several high level executives that had been recruited from the Regional Bell Operating Companies. McCann had always appreciated Dryer's professionalism and his candor. He knew that Dryer didn't handle just any head-hunting job.

"Dale! How are you? How is the family?"

"Growing like a bunch of weeds. I'm going to have some serious college tuition bills shortly! I've had a dickens of a time finding you. What are you doing in Michigan? Where is Farnsworth, anyway?"

McCann brought him up to date. As he talked, he wondered what had prompted this call. Dryer was not one to waste time on "just keeping in touch" with people. He was always on a mission to find and/or place the best executive talent available.

"So what prompts the call?" McCann asked as he finished telling Dryer about the farm and his cattle. He decided not to mention the acquisition or his activities with Farnsworth Tele.

"Two of your old compadres are working in the Czech Republic on a big network job and the outfit running the job is looking for a GM to head it up. They suggested you might be available," Dryer replied. "Are you?"

McCann's thoughts flashed back over the last few days. Was this "God's plan" that everyone kept talking about? He thought of Donna and her mission trip to the Czech Republic and John Rice and the accident. He knew that the two men Dryer was referring to were Myron Martin and Elmer Thune. His mind was whirling.

"Wils? Are you there?" Dryer's voice came over the connection.

"Yes…I was just thinking…Elmer Thune and Myron Martin are in Prague, aren't they?"

"Yep! John Rice was, too, until he died in an automobile accident north and east of Prague. You knew John, didn't you?"

"Yes…I knew John. And the lady he was with was from Farnsworth. I…I knew her…"

"Really? It's a small world! Well? What do you think?"

McCann rubbed his hand through his hair as he tried to focus his thoughts. "I'd need some time to think it over Dale. Do you have the information on the job?"

Got it right here, description, financial details, contract terms, all of it. Do you want it e-mailed or should I send it FEDEX? They do have FEDEX up there don't they?"

McCann smiled, relieved that he would have time to consider and pray about this. "Yes Dale, we have FEDEX up here. The local company has DSL and Cable TV as well as state-of-the art telecommunications!"

"How about that! You involved in it in any way?"

McCann smiled. Dale Dryer wouldn't know a DSLAM unit from a set top box but he knew how to find the people who did.

"I own 20% of it," McCann replied, enjoying this.

"How about that? I'll send the stuff right out by FEDEX! Let me know as soon as you can. They would like to make a decision and if you aren't interested I'll try to find someone else. You're my first choice though. Good to talk to you, Wils!"

McCann put the phone down. A verse from Psalm 111 that he had been reading the previous evening crossed his mind.

Great are the works of the Lord; they are studied by all who delight in them.

In Dallas, John King, having received a "busy" tone on two attempts to call McCann, decided to try again later.

That afternoon, McCann called the county attorney's office and requested that they drop any charges pending against Marv and Steve. The attorney pressed him, but McCann refused to change his mind. In the end, the attorney said that the County might proceed with the case on its own initiative. If they did, they would call McCann as a witness. He hung up the phone feeling that he had done what he could do and was at peace with himself about the situation.

By mid-afternoon, the snow was coming down heavily. He could hardly see the barn from the kitchen window. He had opened the doors to the run pen on the lee side of the barn and the cattle were bunched inside. He watched the snow fall for a while, thinking about the opportunity in Prague. Was this the direction he should take? What about the farm and the cattle? Ordinarily, he would have felt some tension as he thought of this type of step. Today, he felt none. He would consider the information when it came and somehow he felt he would know at the right time if it was the right thing to do. He turned away from the window just as the phone rang.

"Wils, John King at LEGENT. How are things in Michigan?"

"Great John! Never been better!" he replied, with a smile and told King of the events of the past few days. King listened without interrupting, and when McCann finished he simply said, "Welcome Brother."

McCann could feel the warmth behind the two words spread through him. "I only wish I had found my way earlier in life," he said, quietly.

"Don't we all!" King responded in like tone.

"So, what is going on in the wonderful world of LEGENT? Have you sold the Midwest?" McCann asked, dropping into his recliner and putting up the foot rest.

King proceeded to tell him the situation, holding nothing back including LEGENT'S visit with the Michigan Commission. McCann appreciated the honesty that King demonstrated in a new way.

"So, I'm calling to see if we can resurrect some interest on the part of your group in the Michigan property," King finished up.

"Let me make some calls and I'll get back to you," McCann replied.

"I'm going to Savannah for the Thanksgiving weekend. I'll be back in Dallas next Tuesday. Can you call me then? If you need to reach me in the meantime, here's my number in Savannah."

McCann took down the number and hung up the phone. His mind quickly ran through a series of action steps to respond to this latest development. As they tumbled into his mind, he suddenly realized that his old nature was reasserting itself and the sense of peace that he had enjoyed for the past few days had begun to leave him. He sat back down and bowed his head. "Never the less, not my will, but thine be done," he murmured softly. He sat there until his mind became quiet. Outside the snow continued to fall.

He called Stu Bailey the next morning after tending to the cattle and plowing the drive. A foot of snow had fallen and the clouds still hung heavy. Bailey seemed reserved at first but as they discussed the latest turn in events, his enthusiasm grew. By the time they ended the conversation, Bailey had committed to contact Feldman to determine if there was any interest in considering further action. But, he reminded McCann, this was a much smaller acquisition and Feldman's firm, as well as Triad, might not be interested.

Next, he called Belle Warner at her home. She committed to talking with Doug and said she would contact Arthur Boyington to get his reaction. "What do you think, Wils?" she asked.

"I think you should consider it in light of what you shared with me last week," he replied. "Will this be something that will glorify God?'

"Your priorities have changed," she said. He could feel the smile in her voice.

"A long time in coming, I'm afraid."

"Each of us comes to God at the right time," she responded. "What role do you think you would want to play if we reconsider this?"

"I don't know. I want to help you and your family in whatever way I can. Beyond that, I'm still feeling my way forward."

"I'm confident you will sense God's leading. Please keep Friday evening open for a possible Board meeting."

He put down the phone and considered calling Cindy. He thought better of it and decided he would await the results from Stu Bailey and Belle Warner.

The day before Thanksgiving dawned gray and cold. By mid-morning snow was falling steadily. He checked his cupboards and the refrigerator. He had food enough to get him to the weekend and decided not to go into town. He would spend Thanksgiving alone and somehow the thought made him think again of his mother and Donna and Ted. How much in life he had missed! Jim Marks and his family were going to Detroit to visit relatives during the day. The Warners had invited him to spend the holiday with them but he had declined. He wasn't exactly sure why.

Thanksgiving morning brought sunshine for the first time that week. The wind was still out of the west and cold. But as the sun rose in the sky, snow started to melt and by noon, the snow underfoot was slushy as he went to the barn to check on the cattle.

As he came out of the barn and headed back to the house, Phil and Martha Willard pulled into the drive. Phil bounced out of the car and hustled around to the passenger side to hold the door for his wife. Martha emerged with something wrapped in an insulated covering and headed into the house with a cheery, "Happy Thanksgiving!"

Willard opened the rear door and brought out a large picnic basket and handed it to McCann. He reached into the back seat and brought out a large crock pot wrapped in another insulated covering.

"What's all this?"

"Martha decided to bring Thanksgiving to you this year! I hope you don't mind!" Willard replied as they turned toward the house. His smile clearly said he didn't really care if McCann minded or not.

Inside, Martha Willard had made herself right at home in the kitchen. She turned on the oven and began to unwrap a large roasting pan. She lifted the cover long enough for McCann to see a small Turkey already baked. The rich aroma of Turkey drifted into the kitchen as she placed the roaster in the oven and turned to take the crock pot from her husband and plug it in. Next, she opened the picnic basket and began to lay out the remainder of a Thanksgiving meal; biscuits, jelly, cranberry sauce, a can of green beans and a six-inch pumpkin pie.

"It's not much but it's all we have!" She smiled as she began to take out plates, silverware and cups from the cupboards. "You can make the coffee."

McCann smiled. "It looks like quite a feast to me. Have you checked my larder lately?"

"Yes, that can of spaghetti and meat balls doesn't look very appetizing!" She turned and reached up to pull his head down and kiss him on the cheek. "God loves you and I love you," she whispered in his ear, as she leaned against him. Phil Willard straddled a chair and watched with a smile on his face.

McCann felt a surge of warmth go through him and he instinctively gathered the little woman in his arms and hugged her back. "And I love you too...both of you."

He couldn't remember a better Thanksgiving. Martha had chased both men out of the kitchen and simply taken over. For the first time since he had moved to the farm, the dining room was used for what amounted to a banquet. Martha had peeled, boiled and mashed two big potatoes from the basket and McCann found a can of beef gravy in his cupboard. After Phil prayed, they dined on turkey, mashed potatoes, green beans, biscuits with jelly, cranberry sauce and pumpkin pie washed down with fresh perked coffee. Martha refused to let either of them help in the kitchen when they were finished.

McCann and Willard moved to the living room where they discussed the most recent developments. Willard allowed that it was "something to pray about" and expressed no other opinion. McCann quickly moved on to other subjects and spent a good portion of the afternoon showing the Willards some of his mother's personal things, including her Bible. Martha held the Bible in her lap and ran her hand over the cover with her eyes closed. She spent several minutes reading some of what was written inside the covers. She looked intently at McCann at one point with a small smile playing across her face.

By four o'clock, the sun was fading and a chill was back in the air. Phil and Martha bundled their Thanksgiving equipment up after leaving a good portion of the leftovers for McCann. He bent to hug Martha as she prepared to leave. He did the same for Phil as the Agway dealer opened his car door.

"Thank you," didn't seem like much to say but from the looks on their faces, he knew it was enough.

Bailey came into his office on Friday. The street crews were busy cleaning up the residue from the Thanksgiving Day parade in the city. He had called Jeanine to come in as well but reached a recording. Evidently, Jeanine had either decided to screen her calls or had taken advantage of the four-day weekend to depart for warmer climes. He stared out his window at the scene below and pondered how to proceed. At last, he decided to call Feldman and see if any portion of the bridges that McCann had set on fire with the investment banker could be salvaged.

Feldman was at his home in Scarsdale. His wife answered the call and Bailey could hear the sounds of children in the background. Evidently Feldman's grandchildren were there for the weekend. For a moment, he considered leaving a message for a Monday return of his call. Mrs. Feldman, however, was too quick for him and the next voice he heard was Feldman's.

Bailey outlined what McCann had told him about LEGENT'S desire to sell the Michigan properties as a separate transaction and their interest in re-opening the negotiations.

"Do we know if they intend to re-open discussions with others as well?" Feldman asked.

"We don't, but I presume they will."

"What do you think the reaction will be on the part of the other parties? This is not a large deal."

"Fairfield will consider it. I don't think the others are interested in purchasing just one state."

Feldman was quiet for a few moments. Bailey waited, recognizing that this was a critical moment in whether the acquisition could gather any legs at all.

"LEGENT is trying to unload their properties on someone before the Michigan Commission finds them in violation of its service standards and orders them to make what could be significant investments to remedy that. Do you agree?"

Bailey leaned back in his chair. Feldman's ability to cut to the key elements of any acquisition never ceased to impress him.

"It appears that way. The critical issue is what the impact of those investments would be. Wils McCann has a pretty good feel for what they would be in today's operating environment. We could refine our numbers a little and see what you think." Bailey had introduced McCann into the conversation. In his mind he saw a charred bridge across a wide chasm. Was there any strength in those bridge timbers or not?

"Ah, yes. Mr. McCann. I had an interesting telephone call from him. He evidently has had time to re-think his 'Terms' and apologized to me for any offense. Have you spoken with him?"

"Twice. I received a similar call and then he called again when LEGENT contacted him."

"What do you think of his relationship with LEGENT?"

Bailey considered the question and what lay behind it. He decided to throw caution to the winds and jump in with both feet.

"I think that if we want to do this deal with LEGENT, Wils McCann can deliver it to us. I don't pretend to understand what has happened to him since he left Dynacom but I have to tell you, I like the new McCann better than the old one and I liked the old one very much."

After another long pause, Feldman spoke quietly. "This is not anywhere near the size of what we had been considering. I have a great deal of concern as to whether this smaller acquisition makes financial sense. I am particularly concerned about all the imports of what may be going on in Michigan. Political decisions often do not bode well for business, especially regulated ones. However, I must confess to a degree of admiration for the quality of the people I see at Farnsworth, including Mr. McCann. I think you should contact our friend Smith in Detroit and get his perspective. Next, I suggest you and Mr. McCann put together a revised presentation and, if Smith shows any interest, send it to both of us. We will evaluate and get back to you."

After he hung up the phone, Bailey took a deep breath and stood to look out his window. The cleaning crew had finished their job. The street below was free of debris. He felt in some way that this proposed acquisition was not quite free of debris but certainly in better shape than it had been thirty minutes ago.

Without thinking, he called loudly to the adjoining office, "JEANINE!" Then he realized he would have to get Smith's number from her computer file himself. He also realized that he didn't even know if the Warner family was interested in proceeding with the acquisition.

The Selma Dunt Elementary School in southeast corner of Farnsworth had been built in the early 1950s and replaced 40 years later when Farnsworth's school district approved a new educational complex on the north side of the village. That complex included a new high school, middle school and elementary school. "The Dunt Center," as Selma Dunt Elementary had always been referred to, was named for one of Farnsworth's long time English teachers. It had been used as a sort of unofficial community center since being replaced. The senior community helped to maintain it and the village ran an active schedule of activities for both young and old. The cost of maintaining the building, which included a gymnasium, set of offices, kitchen, library and a dozen class rooms had grown steadily. Two years ago, the village had quietly put it up for sale.

Charles Hastings and his guest for the weekend sat in front of the fireplace in the parsonage and discussed Selma Dunt for over an hour before putting on their overcoats and driving to the school. It was a one story brick building with a large double door at the front and a service entrance at the side. They entered into a long hallway and checked in with an elderly lady at a reception desk to the right of the entrance. They walked through the building, checking the condition of each of the rooms, the library and gymnasium. They spent several minutes in the furnace room which appeared to be clean and well kept. The overall condition of the building was good, considering its age.

They spent about an hour inside and then walked the perimeter as best they could considering the amount of snow on the ground. By the time they returned to the parsonage, the older man was rubbing his hands together and blowing on them. Hastings poured two cups of steaming coffee and the two men sat before the fire and resumed their discussion. Then they knelt in prayer at their chairs, asking God to direct them in their joint venture and to guide them in their decision making.

Rising from their knees, they sat in silence for a while before the older man spoke. He was tall and in his early 70's with a mane of white hair that curled up over his shirt collar. His large hands rested on the arms of his chair. The arthritis in them was evident. He leaned toward the fire and rubbed them together, letting the heat warm them.

"Your cold weather up here doesn't agree with my ailments very well, Charles," he said, leaning back in his chair.

"I'm sorry. Do you think that would deter others from wanting to move here?" Hastings responded.

"Oh, I'm not sure if that would matter. We have a few on staff that came from the Midwest and are used to the weather. Our International Coordinator came from North Dakota. I've never been to North Dakota but I presume my hands wouldn't like it very much!"

"If you were to do this, how many would have the option to relocate?" Hastings asked, taking a sip from his coffee.

"Probably eight to ten. We would need to hire six to eight locally. Most in support functions. As I have said, my concern is for overall management and direction. I must plan for that. Frankly, I would like to retire and write. As you know, I helped to create our initial program material and I enjoyed that. Like many, I do not enjoy the day-to-day management of the ministry as much as the creative part."

Hastings took another sip from his coffee cup. "While we would love to have you come personally, I sense that you would not do that."

The other man sat back and wrapped both of his hands around his cup. "No, I'm afraid not. I sense that the Lord is leading me into the twilight of my career. It's time for new hands and new vision. I have the people to handle the development activities and the training and coordination of our people in the field. I need a General Manager for the day-to-day, especially so if we were to move our staff here."

Hastings rose from his chair and crossed the room. He retrieved a file folder from an end table and brought it to the other man.

"Take a look at this for a moment and then I would like to tell you what isn't there," Hastings said, as he returned to his chair.

The older man opened the folder and began to read a series of newspaper articles that it contained. His face showed his puzzlement, but he read on until he had finished all of them. He closed the folder and held it in one hand as he retrieved his cup and drank from it.

"Interesting. But I don't understand what some sort of business deal in the telecommunications industry has to do with what we've been discussing."

For the next thirty minutes, Charles Hastings discussed what wasn't in the folder. The other man listened carefully and asked several pointed questions. Finally, he leaned back and steepled his hands against his chin.

"I should like to meet this man, McCann. I would like to take the measure of the man. . .and a measure of his new-found faith. Is he aware of Donna's wishes? "

"No, I don't think so," Hastings replied. "Donna was very close to Wils McCann. I think her life and her death had a great deal to do with his new-found faith. But I don't think she shared this."

The older man sighed. He thought back across the years. "She was a wonderful girl. It is so hard at times to know the 'why' of these things."

"We can only trust and move forward in God's direction," Hastings replied. "Suppose I ask Mr. McCann to Sunday dinner here? You can visit a while and see what you think of him."

The older man sat back. His thoughts were still on Donna Barnes. In all the years that his ministry had operated throughout Eastern Europe, Donna was the first person to lose her life in the service of the Lord.

"Yes, I would like you to inquire as to Mr. McCann's interest in having dinner with us. I should like to meet the man who, if God had ordained it, would have captured Donna's heart."

Belle Warner convened the Farnsworth Board at 7:00 p.m. that evening. McCann entered the building through the side door, leaving the cold dark night behind him, and walked down the hall. He stepped into the brightly lit conference room and found that he was the last to arrive. Art Boyington's image was on the video conference circuit. Doug, looking much better than the previous week, sat to Belle's left and Phil Willard at her right at the head of the conference table. Fred Penay sat next to Doug. McCann shed his overcoat and seated himself next to Willard. Belle brought the meeting to order and, at her request, McCann reviewed the telephone call from John King.

"Are we still talking $45 million in your view?" Boyington asked from the TV set at the foot of the long conference table.

"LEGENT is definitely anxious to sell these properties. That works to our advantage. The reason they want to sell works to our disadvantage," McCann replied.

"We would definitely have to improve service to get the acquisition by the Commission," Boyington stated. "What additional investments we would need to make are at this time unknown?"

All eyes turned to McCann. "I think it is safe to say that whatever initiative the Governor is thinking about would have some impact on the properties in the northern Lower Peninsula. Given his background and strong positions on developing the economy of that area, I think that is where the impact would be," he said. He had given this a great deal of thought since returning from Lansing and felt confident that the Governor's interest had something to do with the north country. He made a mental note to try to contact Jim Wolfe again.

"You didn't answer my question, Wils," Boyington prodded. "Is it still $45 million?"

McCann leaned back in his chair. He could feel Belle Warner's eyes on him, waiting. He looked out of the corner of his eye at Phil Willard who was busy doodling on a ruled pad in front of him.

"Valuations of wire line telecom properties are continuing to drop. I think that the initial offer should be in the $35-40 million range to test the waters. If LEGENT doesn't laugh us out of the room, we know we can at least get serious."

The room was quiet for the next few moments. Belle Warner jotted a few notes on her pad and lifted her eyes back to McCann.

"And, where would that money come from?"

McCann felt it was time to talk about his conversations with Stu Bailey. "This would be a much smaller acquisition. I asked Stu to contact Ed Feldman and determine if there is any interest at all there. If there isn't, this will be a very difficult situation to put together. I am assuming that Feldman is the key to this having any chance. If he would stick reasonably close to his original commitments to Farnsworth Tele for the Michigan piece, Triad and Smith in Detroit might provide the balance."

"And the money to finance improvements and any impacts from what-ever is going on in the North Country...?"

McCann folded his hands on the pad in front of him. "I don't know," he replied, looking at Doug.

Belle wrote something on her pad and looked down the table at Boyington. She looked at Doug, Phil, Fred Penay and McCann in turn and then laid her pen carefully on her pad.

"The Chair would entertain any motion not to proceed." The wording caught McCann by surprise and he glanced quickly at Boyington. The at-torney looked straight at Belle from the television set. Doug looked at his mother with a faint smile. Phil Willard looked at the ceiling. Penay looked at some notes he had made.

Belle waited a full thirty seconds before picking up her pen. She looked at McCann. "Please follow up with Mr. Bailey and, if necessary, with Mr. Feldman. Doug, please call Cindy and review the situation with her. Arthur, would you see if you could contact Mr. Smith? You may not be able to reach him before Monday. Phil, do you think it would be wise to contact Ross at the Governor's office to make them aware of this turn of events?"

Willard glanced sideways at McCann before responding. "I think it might be a good idea to do just that. What do you think, Wils?"

"Might as well know what, if any, reaction they would have."

Belle made some additional notes on her pad and put her pen down again. "Let's be prepared to meet again on Monday afternoon. We are adjourned."

McCann rose and took his overcoat from an adjacent chair. As he prepared to turn to the door, Belle laid a hand on his arm. "Could I have a moment?"

"Of course," he said as he followed her from the room and down to her office. As he stepped through the door, the memory of his last meeting in this room flooded back. How much had changed in the past week! As cold and miserable as he had felt that day, he felt warmth and happiness on this dark and wintry evening. A single lamp was lit on the corner of her desk and her office was mostly in shadow. She laid her pad on the desk and turned to face him, leaning back against the front of her desk. He stood just inside the doorway, his coat draped over his left arm.

She picked something up from her desk and smiled. "I have something for you and I have a favor to ask," she said, quietly.

"Whatever it is, if I can do it, I will," he responded.

She stepped toward him and pinned a small silver cross on his coat lapel. "A symbol of the new Wilson McCann," she said. "I hope you like it."

"I'll wear it…always. Thank you."

"She looked down briefly before continuing. "Doug is gaining strength every day but is still weak. The Doctors have said he will have full recovery but needs to avoid unnecessary strain for the next month. If this acquisition were to move forward, you would need to be heavily involved. Can I ask you to do that?"

He thought of the FEDEX package lying on his kitchen table. The material from Dale Dryer had arrived that afternoon. He had opened the package and read the material quickly. He had prayed over it and asked for God's guidance. Was Belle's request part of that guidance?

She sensed his hesitation. "Is there a reason you might not be able to do this?"

He told her about Dryer's call. She listened quietly and didn't respond. He turned towards the window, looking out into the darkness. "I want to make the rest of my life count for something, Belle. It seems I have wasted it and the talents I was given thus far."

She came and stood beside him. "I don't think your life has been wasted...perhaps it was misdirected. You have accomplished much that, by the world's standards, was good."

"But not by God's standards," he replied.

"Perhaps you have been brought to this knowledge and this time for a purpose. The difficulty we face once we ask God to take control of our lives is knowing where he will lead us. That kind of trust comes from the commitment of the heart, not the mind nor the will."

He reached out his right hand and took her left in it. "I know this. If you and your family want to proceed with this acquisition, I want to help in any way I can. Not for myself. I want this to be for you and for your family."

"And for God?"

"...and for God."

Later as he drove back to the farm, he felt again the sense of peace that came and went more often now. He would call Dryer in the morning and tell him that, if a decision was necessary before the end of the year, he was not interested.

(27)

On Saturday, as McCann came in from feeding the cattle, Charles Hastings called to invite him to Sunday dinner at the parsonage after the service. He went on to tell McCann that James Jacobs, the Chairman of Eastern European Christian Ministries was visiting for the weekend and would be attending services on Sunday and joining them for dinner.

McCann recognized the organization as the one which Donna had been serving with in the Czech Republic. The thought brought a rush of emotion with it. Donna's love for the ministry had expressed itself in many ways. She had often spoken of Jacobs and his commitment to bringing the Gospel to the former Communist countries. McCann remembered his jealous feelings at the time. How shallow he had been then! Now, he would have an opportunity to meet the man who had provided an outlet for Donna's enthusiastic zeal.

Church service on Sunday morning included a brief review of EECM's outreach programs by Jacobs. McCann was impressed by the tall white-haired gentleman in his dark pinstriped suit. He remembered Jacobs from the days of his youth. Jacobs had been a "Fire and Brimstone" preacher from the Bible belt. He had visited Chicago once during McCann's teen age years. Turn-outs for his weeklong visit to one of the city's evangelical churches had not been particularly impressive if newspaper accounts could be believed. As the years went by, Jacobs' ministry escaped the scandals that racked other, more famous evangelists. In the early '80's he developed a relationship with one of President Reagan's staff. When the Soviet Union collapsed, he turned to Eastern Europe, and, while he continued to conduct evangelistic programs within the United States, his small group of missionaries and volunteers from churches in the U.S. had become his major focus. EECM was unique in that it carefully selected the missionaries that it sent out. Unlike similar ministries, it trained them and supported them financially. They were not required to raise their own support. EECM raised the funds and disbursed them to the missionaries in the field through a local field organization in each of the countries where EECM had established missions. The difficult thing, in McCann's opinion, as he listened, was continuing to raise the funds necessary to support the people in the field.

After the services, McCann walked with Dorothy Hastings to the parsonage. While old, the parsonage was well kept and radiated a warmth and hominess that were largely due to Dorothy's unceasing efforts and hospitality. With her red hair shining in the mid day sun, she directed McCann in setting the table for the four of them and prepared the meal. The two Hastings children were away for the weekend at a youth retreat and would return later in the afternoon.

They dined on Caesar salad, minestrone soup, warm Italian bread and canned fruit cocktail. Dorothy promised deep dish apple pie for later as she shooed them into the living room despite offers of assistance in clearing away the remains of the meal.

Jacobs had shed his pinstriped suit jacket and his tie and had donned a dark blue cardigan sweater. He sat in one of the two reclining chairs and stretched his long legs toward the fireplace. Hastings motioned McCann to the other recliner and took a seat on a sofa opposite the fire. He took a file folder from the coffee table in front of him and sat back.

"Wils, there is something we would like to share with you. As you know, Donna was actively involved in EECM's ministry and had been for several years."

McCann felt the pain again as he thought back to days when his feelings for Donna had begun to change. He remembered the day that she had come to help him bring in the hay. In his mind he stood again behind her on the tractor, smelling the scent of her hair as they drove into the field. He thought of the rainy night in Caseville as they dined beside Saginaw Bay. With sorrow, he remembered how he had become so preoccupied with the acquisition that he had failed to call her before she left for Prague.

Jacobs, sensing McCann's emotion, leaned forward and spoke quietly. "I too feel a great sense of loss. Donna was all that is good about our work. She was a remarkable person and I am so pleased that she was, if I understand Charles correctly, an important part of your coming to know the Lord."

McCann looked at the old man, liking him more by the moment. "I only wish I could have told her how much I cared at the time. I wish she was here now to share in the happiness I have found."

"I'm sure that in some way, she knows and she shares in your new found life," Jacobs responded. "I'm sorry, Charles, please continue."

Hastings opened the folder and took out several sheets of typewritten paper. He rose and handed them to McCann. As he sat back down, McCann began to read.

It was a will. It specifically covered the proceeds from an insurance policy on the lives of both Donna's father and Donna herself. It directed that the proceeds from the policy be entrusted to Eastern European Christian Ministry for their use in any manner that they might choose. It also requested that consideration be given to making Charles Hastings a member of EECM's Board.

"I wasn't aware of Donna's personal situation beyond what was connected with the Barnes' Loft. I'm not sure why you're sharing this with me," McCann said, as he finished reading.

"I think you should also read this," Hastings said as he rose and handed McCann another sheet of typewritten paper.

As he took it, McCann sensed that the contents of this paper would involve him. It contained two paragraphs. The first paragraph referred to the previous document as to date and purpose. The second paragraph stated that should Wilson James McCann give evidence to experiencing the saving grace of Jesus Christ through a public profession of faith, that he also be named to the Board of EECM.

McCann sat back. His face registered the shock that he was experiencing. "I don't know what to say... what prompted Donna to make these requests....?" he began. Jacobs held up his hand to stop him.

"I think it might help if we mentioned the amount involved in this bequest," he said, glancing at Hastings.

"Over one million dollars," Hastings said quietly.

"One million dollars! But...what...where...how?" McCann sputtered.

"Donna's father took out the policy many years ago when he was a much younger man. He paid the premiums off before he died. The proceeds of the initial policy were set up in a trust for Donna upon his death. The actual amount of the policy, at the time of his death was over $1.5 million. Donna had never mentioned it to you?"

"No...never," McCann said quietly, staring out the window at the sunlight reflecting off the snow.

"I hope that you will honor us and honor Donna's memory by accepting a seat on our board," Jacobs smiled. "Charles has already done so and I am pleased to have him."

"But... I don't know anything about...," McCann began.

".....about evangelical missions ministry?" Jacobs interrupted him. "Perhaps you would like to review this before you make a final decision."

He reached in the pocket of his cardigan and produced a small flash drive. He handed it across to McCann. He noted that it was a two gigabyte drive. "I trust you have a computer with a USB port," Jacobs smiled. "If not, perhaps Charles will let you use the Church's."

McCann rolled the flash drive between his thumb and fingers. "What's on it?"

"All of our current programs, financial situation and our short and long range plans," Jacobs replied. "While I don't know a lot about the telecommunications business, I think you will find that we use a lot of the same principles in our work as you do in the secular side."

"Jim, perhaps now would be a good time to share the 'rest of our story' with Wils," Hastings said, as he leaned back against the sofa's cushions.

McCann wondered what additional surprises were in store as Jacobs rose and stood with his back to the fireplace, his hands clasped behind him.

"I must ask that you keep what we are about to tell you in strictest confidence for the time being. We have not reached a final decision and we're quite aware that what we're thinking of, while not as large as some of the transactions that I am sure you have been and may still be a part of, is still of some significance for us, for Charles and for Farnsworth."

McCann was puzzled by the inclusion of the village in Jacobs' comments. He surmised that Jacobs and Hastings were close and shared a deep commitment to the EECM ministry. He looked down at the flash drive in his hand and knew that whatever Jacobs was about to reveal was not contained there.

"You have my word."

"Excellent! As you'll learn from the information contained on that drive, our ministry is staffed by a small but vibrant group of missionaries. Most of the logistical support comes from a very dedicated group of volunteers in both the U.S. and in Eastern Europe. Our small headquarters staff plays a key role in coordination, fund development and promotion of our work.

"And…your headquarters are where? I've forgotten what Donna told me."

"Weaverville, North Carolina. That is where I began my ministry. Do you know that we had a small independent telephone company there when I started preaching?"

McCann smiled at the question. "I'm sure you did. Back in the '50's there must have been close to 15,000 independent companies."

"Ours was the Western Carolina Telephone Company. I remember it well," Jacobs said with a smile. "We actually have our headquarters in one of their old buildings. We have about twenty full and part time people there. We are considering a move to Farnsworth."

"Farnsworth? I'm sorry but most people are heading south," McCann said, smiling up at the old evangelist.

"Yes, the ways of the Lord are, at times, difficult to understand. We have a solid base of financial support in the upper Midwest and Donna's bequest adds to that. If you choose to join our Board, Farnsworth would have two representatives. There is also another matter to consider as well. Charles, why don't you fill Wils in on what you have in mind?"

McCann turned slightly to face the minister. His mind was already digesting the revelations of the past few minutes. Hastings smiled at his evident puzzlement. "We're giving you a lot to think about in a short time, Wils! What I'm about to tell you is also in confidence. No one outside of our Church Board, Jim here and certain people in the village is aware of it. For some time, we've wanted to start a pre-school and child care center in Farnsworth. There is only one other child care facility in the village and they're limited in what they can accomplish. Obviously we have neither the facilities nor the room to expand our existing facilities to accomplish this. However, we recently became aware that the former elementary school in

Farnsworth is for sale. Our proposal is to create a new corporation under the EECM umbrella, buy it and use it for a pre-school, and child care center as well as some Senior Citizen activities. Jim is considering the move of his headquarters here to occupy a good portion of the facility as well. Whether we can convince him to come personally is still a matter of prayer. Certain representatives of the Village have indicated their support for the project and certain incentives if we go through with it. We anticipate that between the two operations, we would generate about twenty additional jobs within the village."

McCann sat back in his chair. "Why are you telling me this?" he asked, looking first at Hastings and then at Jacobs.

Hastings looked at the evangelist before responding. "Wils, when you came to Farnsworth you said you were looking for something. I trust that you have now found a new focus for your life. Both Jim and I are well aware of your talents and capabilities. Obviously, those talents and capabilities would be very helpful to us if we proceed with these ideas. As a member of EECM's Board and possibly in other areas you could contribute significantly to the Lord's work."

"My cup runneth over," McCann said, smiling.

"I'm sorry?" Jacobs said, leaning forward.

McCann proceeded to tell the two men about the position in the Czech Republic that Dale Dryer had contacted him about. He also told them about the commitment he had made to Belle Warner relative to the possible LEGENT acquisition. "I'm afraid it's my turn to ask you both to treat the latter in confidence," he said, as he finished.

Jacobs looked at Hastings and smiled. "It seems that all of us have much to pray about. Perhaps now would be a good time to start."

And for the next thirty minutes the three men prayed for each other, for God's direction in their lives and for guidance in moving forward. Wilson McCann prayed with an earnestness and confidence that was new to him. Dorothy brought in the deep dish apple pie and coffee. The four of them sat together before the fire eating the pie and drinking their coffee and enjoying each other's company as the sun slowly sank into the western horizon. McCann carried the warmth of the afternoon with him as he went back to the farm. That night, after he finished his chores outside, he inserted the flash drive into his laptop and spent three hours immersing himself in all aspects of EECM.

Ross had a ten o'clock briefing with the Governor on Monday morning. They reviewed the events of the past weekend and various items from the Governor's agenda for the coming week. He also told the Governor of his telephone conversation with Phil Willard earlier that morning. The Governor sat back, looking out the window,

"That is both interesting and encouraging. Do you think it has a chance of coming about?"

"It's a little early to tell. I presume the financing is the issue. This is a smaller deal and the New York money men may not be interested."

"Is there anything we can do to assist?" the Governor asked. Ross waited a moment before responding. These types of questions were always the most difficult. How to use the power of the office in a way that was both proper ethically and legally and yet accomplished goals that the administration had set for itself.

"I could call Smitty in Detroit and see what they think. I could pass along your interest in seeing a Michigan company expand its operation. If you think it is worth the risk, I could contact the Economic Development folks and see if there is any way to have them help."

The Governor stood and paced back and forth behind his desk, tapping a pen against his chin.

"Contact Mr. Smith and let him know of our interest. Let's keep it at that for now. We can always try to help in other ways if this acquisition gets legs. Did you tell Phil Willard to keep us posted?"

"Yes."

"I haven't made a trip to the 'Thumb' in a while. Could we work something in before the year is out?"

Ross smiled. "Not a lot going on in the 'Thumb' these days. There's a hospital addition in Bad Axe that is due for a ribbon cutting in mid-December. They are talking about a few new jobs there."

"Ah! An example of the strength and growth of our rural economy! Can you get me an invitation?" The governor was smiling now across the desk at him.

Ross rose and made a note in his briefing book. "As sure as snow falls in December! I presume you would like Phil and a few of his friends to attend?"

"Absolutely! I wouldn't want to miss an opportunity to see Phil and a few of his friends," the Governor replied.

An hour later, Smith put down the phone and opened the file drawer in his desk. He extracted a folder titled "Farnsworth Acquisition" and laid it on his desk. He clicked on the EXCEL icon on his computer and brought up a workbook containing the financial analysis of the Farnsworth-LEGENT deal and began to review it.

At almost the same moment in New York City, Cindy Melzy began to prepare a summation of her thoughts on the Farnsworth-LEGENT acquisition for Triad's executive group. As she worked on her computer, she glanced at the copy of a real estate listing for the 60-acre farm south of Farnsworth and at a picture of David that sat beside it.

McCann had never minded being alone. His most pleasurable companions throughout his career had been management issues, reports, results, and the challenges of leading a complex organization. But that companionship had not brought him the kind of peace he now relished in his aloneness. He rose early and fed the cattle and was in the kitchen lingering over a second cup of coffee while reading his mother's Bible. Charles Hastings had recommended that he read John's Gospel and the book of Psalms as part of his quiet time each day. This morning, he was reading the fourth chapter of John when he heard a car pull into the driveway. He rose and looked out the window. A familiar red Mustang was parked in the drive and a familiar figure dressed in a fur lined pink parka, jeans and boots was walking to the back door.

"You're out early, Sally," he smiled, as he let her in. "Who's minding the store?"

"I'll open at 9:00 a.m. I'll lose a few of the early birds, but I needed to talk to someone. I picked you. Hope you don't mind." The way she said it made it clear that she wasn't interested in whether he minded or not.

She unzipped the parka and tossed it to a vacant chair. McCann noted that she wasn't wearing her usual make-up, and her hair had been combed but not styled the way she usually wore it. The beige turtleneck sweater that she wore accentuated the curves but did little to enhance her appearance. Sally McHugh was showing her age this morning.

"Sit down. Do you need cream or sugar with that?" he asked as she helped herself to the remaining coffee from the pot on the stove.

"Black will do fine," she said, as she leaned back against the counter top.

McCann sat and picked up his cup. He could feel Sally's gaze on the open Bible on the table. He took a sip from the cup and waited.

"I heard you 'got religion'," she said, eyeing him over the rim of her cup.

McCann smiled up at her. "Farnsworth is a small town. Word travels quickly I guess."

"Tell me about it. If I have a beer at the tavern, everybody knows it."

"I guess it's the price we pay for fame," he said, trying to keep it light. He sensed it would get a little heavier later on. It didn't take long.

"Wils, what would have happened that night if those men hadn't shown up and shot your dog?"

McCann leaned back in his chair and ran his index finger around the rim of his coffee cup before replying. "I think you know."

"I wish it had. I wish that night would have been different. Now it's too late." She half turned as she said it and looked out the window.

"Too late for what?" he asked quietly.

"For us to be...you know...more than...more than friends."

His mind flashed back to the rainy fall night when Donna had asked to be his friend and he felt the pain and knew just how Sally felt.

"We are...friends...good friends," he looked up at her as he said it and he could see the pain in her eyes and her lower lip began to tremble. She turned away and put her cup down, her back to him. She leaned over the countertop, bracing her hands against it. She fought to compose herself, but a great sob came out and she bent forward as another and another came.

He rose quickly and came around the table. He put his hands on her shoulders and turned her to face him. He wrapped his arms around her and she sagged against him. She continued to cry, her body heaving against his. He looked out the window at the cattle standing in the barnyard as he tried to think of what to say.

She pulled away from his embrace and turned again to look out the window as she blew her nose and wiped her eyes. "It's the story of my life. I've really screwed it up!" She said it harshly. He reached back for his cup and walked to the door, looking out over the back yard.

"You have a good business and three great kids. I'd say that is a big positive right there."

"…And three busted marriages and a reputation around here that you wouldn't want your name associated with," she finished for him.

Before he could respond, she dropped into the chair he had been sitting in and pulled the Bible closer to her. "Jesus and the woman at the well…how appropriate to the moment," she said, as she pushed the Bible away.

"You know the story?" he asked.

"I'm not illiterate you know. I read books…even the 'good book' once in a while," she said it accusingly.

"I didn't mean…"

She pulled the Bible back to her and began to run her finger down the page. "Lots of men in her life….bad reputation in town. She had me beat though. She had five husbands and was living with the sixth. I'll have to work on my skill set." He could feel her watching him as she said it.

He sat down at the opposite end of the table and smiled at her. "I sincerely hope that you will try to emulate her in other ways as well."

She looked at him with a question in her eyes. "What's that supposed to mean?"

"Read the whole chapter, not just the first part. She recognized who He was and she told others who He was."

"In other words, I should 'get right with God', like you did."

"It's given me something I was lacking in my life. It sounds like you are lacking something in yours or you wouldn't be here at 7:30 a.m.in the morning drinking the last of my coffee."

"And now that you have it, you wouldn't want to be seen in public with the likes of me."There was both accusation and question in her voice as she said it.

"Try me," he said, looking straight into her eyes.

"I'll make it tough for both of us…church next Sunday morning. I'll drive."

McCann sat back against his chair. A smile grew across his face. "You made it too easy. I've always wanted to go to church in a red Mustang!"

After she left, McCann picked up the cups and washed them. He prayed silently as he worked. He thought about the events of the past few days. His life was certainly interesting!

The phone rang at 8:30 a.m. It was Bailey. McCann smiled to himself as he checked his watch. Stu was "up-and-at-em" early this morning! Bailey brought him up to date on his talks with Feldman. He also said that Cindy Melzy was taking a positive recommendation to her team that morning. The only party as yet not heard from was Smith in Detroit.

"Where are we at with the Warners?" Bailey asked, when he had finished.

"I don't know. I haven't talked to them."

"Come on! You go to church with these people," Bailey's voice rose as he said it.

"That's not what we go to church for," McCann replied, in a matter-of-fact tone. "Or haven't you been lately?"

"Don't get 'saintly' with me!" Bailey said, his voice dropping. McCann could sense the smile across the miles.

"The Board may meet this afternoon. I'll call down later this morning and see what I can find out. I'll get back to you. Okay?"

"Okay. I'll call Smith. Where do we stand with King at LEGENT?"

"He's waiting for a response. We need to make sure we're all on the same page and then I'll call him." McCann said firmly.

"Shouldn't one of the Warners call him if we go forward? Sort of make it official?" Bailey questioned.

"It will be official if I call him. Belle has asked me to help out on this."

"Oh. Okay…well let me know as soon as you can." McCann could sense the question in Bailey's voice but chose to ignore it.

"I will…and Stu…"

"Yeah?"

"Think about going to church, will you?"

"Yeah … right! Call me!"

McCann chuckled to himself as he put down the phone. Stu Bailey in church, wouldn't that be something? Then he thought of Sally and it didn't seem like such a far-fetched idea after all.

(28)

Later that morning, four meetings took place, one in Detroit, two in
New York City and one at the Boyne Mountain Resort in Boyne Falls. The
first took place in the conference room at Triad. Cindy presented her report
and recommendation to Triad's managing partner, Malcolm Shaw. Shaw was
a tall, thin man in his late 60's with a penchant for sweater vests. This morning he had chosen a bright yellow one. Cindy read a "caution" in it and she
was right.

"This isn't worth the time or effort, Cindy. Why are you expending so
much energy in it?" Shaw inquired, as he placed the report in front of him on
the gleaming mahogany table. He leaned his padded leather chair back and
steepled his index fingers at his chin. Malcolm Shaw was Cindy's mentor. He
had watched her rise within Triad over the past ten years. He respected her
drive to be the best at what she did. He also respected her ability to come
through a divorce and loss of custody of her son without missing a beat as
she guided Triad investments into very successful businesses. Lately, however, he had sensed a change. It had all started with this LEGENT acquisition.
He could feel a wavering in her resolve and what he viewed as "softness" in
her approach to this project. He knew that she had recently regained joint
custody of her son and had begun keeping shorter hours than in the past
in order to care for him. Shaw was a family man and respected that. What
bothered him was his inner feeling that Cindy was about to make a decision
that he sensed would not be in the best interests of Triad or, quite possibly,
Cindy herself.

Cindy flipped through the pages of her copy of the report and pointed
to page five of the financial section. "As you can see here, there is a good
possibility that Farnsworth…"

Shaw held up his hand. "You didn't answer my question," he said, looking her straight in the eye. "I've read the report. I've looked at the numbers.

We both know it's a risky bet and you can make the numbers go either way in the projection. Fifteen million is not a big number for a lot of firms. It's certainly not a big number for Feldman. It's mid range for us and you know that. I want to know why you want to do this."

Cindy closed the report in front of her and laced her hands together on top of it. She considered her answer for a moment and decided to be forthright. She took a deep breath and returned his gaze.

"I want to do this because I believe in these people and in their way of doing business and in their dream. I'm afraid I've become quite taken with Farnsworth and the Warner family. You've always told me that we have a responsibility to assure that our investments build something good as well as bring us a good return and I believe this will do both."

"And, if this goes forward and they acquire the LEGENT properties, then what?"

"They will expand to twice their current size and begin to..."

Shaw held up his hand again. He smiled at her and slowly lowered it until his index finger was pointing directly at her. "What will you do?"

Her pulse quickened and she could feel a lump in her throat. How did he know? She felt as though she were in a canoe without a paddle and that she was being taken by the current towards a roaring waterfall. She closed her eyes and took another deep breath. When she opened them, he was still smiling and she knew that she had to tell him.

"I'm thinking of moving to Farnsworth. They will need a Chief Financial Officer and the Warner family has asked me to consider it. I've been looking into a property there." She hurried on before he could interrupt again. "If it happens, I'll stay until someone is ready to take my place. I won't leave you with any open issues. I'll..."

The hand went up again. The smile was gone. Strangely, the look on Shaw's face was fatherly. He leaned forward and dropped his hand to the report.

"We'll do the deal if Feldman comes in and they can raise the rest of the money. End of discussion on that. Beginning of discussion on you...I am concerned that you have not thought this through fully. You are a unique individual with unique talents. We both know that in another five years or

so, you can and should take my place as Managing Partner. Under your guidance, Triad can continue to grow and be successful. But, I want first and
foremost that you be happy. If you can tell me that beyond a shadow of a
doubt, this change, if you make it, would make you happy and that a year
from now, you will feel that you are leading a challenging life in a small town
as the head bookkeeper of a relatively small telecommunications company,
I'll not say another word. But, from where I sit today, I think it would be a
tragic waste of your talent and abilities."

She impulsively laid her hand on top of his. At that moment, her respect
for Malcolm Shaw reached a new high. Strangely, at the same moment, the
first pulse of doubt about what she had been considering crossed her mind.
She smiled at him as she withdrew her hand. "Thank you."

"I do care about you, you know," he said, leaning back.

"Head Bookkeeper? Aren't you being a little tough there?"

The smile returned. "When I compare the responsibilities of the oversight of a few clerks and accountants keeping the books and records of a
company with 30,000 customers to your accomplishments in the private
equity financing business, it pales."

"Malcolm, I've found something that I think I've been looking for all my
life and it has changed the way I view the world."

"Your faith. You've found something besides the almighty dollar to believe in."

She lowered her gaze and smiled. "Does it show that much?" She was
hoping that it did.

"It's hard to miss. You suddenly care about others more than your work.
You care about your son whom you previously were willing to sacrifice for
your career. You aren't here at 9:00 p.m. every night and you didn't come
in the last two Saturdays. Of course the silver cross on your jacket lapel
was also an indicator. It makes you, at least in my eyes, much more likable.
It doesn't make you any less talented and it doesn't change my opinion as
to your capability and your future. I presume you spend a little time each
day in prayer. I hope that includes me and Triad. I hope it includes a request
that our Maker use you and the talents He has given you in the best possible
way."

Five minutes later, Cindy walked back to her office. The doubt she had experienced in Malcolm's office hadn't gone away. Malcolm's loving acceptance of her new-found faith had reassured her and at the same time brought the first bit of confusion as to where she was headed in the future. She dropped the report on her desk and sat looking out the window at a gray autumn day. She picked up David's picture and the real estate listing. She felt that she was at a crossroads and for the first time she was unsure as to which way to turn.

In Detroit, Smith also met with his Managing Partner. The meeting, however, was far less cordial. Smith was subjected to a rant about "the Idiots" in Lansing, "The Idiocy" of investing in telecommunications and "ultimate demise" of the small investment banker if acquisitions such as this one were forced upon the marketplace. Smith endured it all quite stoically and waited for the tide of emotion to break and recede. When it was finally over, he leaned forward and quietly asked, "What would you like me to do and, more importantly, what would you like me to tell the Governor's office?"

"Do? What else can we do? If we don't do this we will be forever branded as lacking in patriotism! Call Ed Feldman and Cindy Melzy and tell them that if they are in, we are in! If this thing goes bottoms up, I want someone else on the deck with us when we go down. Then, call your old school chum in the Governor's office and tell him we wholeheartedly support the Governor's efforts to expand and improve the economic conditions in our fair state. Now, get out of here!"

Smith smiled to himself as he walked back to his office. He thought of Doug Warner up in Farnsworth. "It's first and goal, old buddy, let's see if we can punch it over," he muttered to himself. A passing part time mail clerk who attended the University of Detroit looked at him quizzically before continuing on his rounds. People in high places often behaved strangely. At least that was what his college professor had told him.

In New York City, Feldman met with one of the junior members of his staff. He handed the young woman a copy of the Oxbow report and other material related to the LEGENT properties. He also gave her a sheet from his monogrammed note pad with the telephone numbers and e-mail addresses of Cindy Melzy and Smith written on it.

"Familiarize yourself with this. It's a minor investment, only fifteen million. I'll need someone to coordinate with these two people and a representative of the potential acquirer. We'll demand two seats on the board made up of representatives of the three investing firms. We'll want to form an acquisition shell and subordinate both the acquired companies and the acquiring company under it. I'll want to be kept informed of course, but assuming the numbers are positive, we will proceed. Any questions?

There weren't. Two things were obvious to the young woman. This was not a big deal in terms of its dollar value but it was important to Mr. Feldman for some reason and that made it her most important job at the moment. She hurried back to her office and began to read through the files.

Jim Wolfe was making his monthly trip to the Boyne Falls area and in particular, to one of his largest customers, the Boyne Falls Resort. He met with the Resort's manager in charge of facilities and checked to be sure that everything was fine with their services. As he prepared to leave, the Manager walked him to the door of his small office.

"By the way, do you know anyone at Alcatel-Lucent?" the Manager asked.

Wolfe turned, "A few, mostly sales and technical people. Why?"

"We got a call from some guy who wanted to know how far we were from Brutus and whether it was an easy commute. Said he might be moving here in a year or so as a part of some big operation that they had an interest in. The guy was a big-time skier in the French Alps and wanted to know all about our facilities. Said he might buy a place here and commute."

Wolfe's senses went on high alert. "Did he say what kind of an operation it was?"

"No, just that there were some high tech companies involved and that it was a big project. Said something about the State being involved. Why? Is it something you guys are involved with?"

"Not now, but anything new could have an impact on us down the road," Wolfe replied, thinking of his calls to Lansing and to Wils McCann. "Let me know if you hear anything more, will you?"

"I sure will. I guess the guy will be a little disappointed if he compares us to the French Alps! I suppose it will mean more business for you in the Burt Lake area, won't it?"

Wolfe smiled as he shook the man's hand. "Yes, it could mean that. You never know."

That afternoon, Wolfe made several calls to sales people at Alcatel-Lucent and other suppliers. No one knew anything about a big project in Brutus, Michigan. Jim Wolfe decided to call Wilson McCann.

McCann, meantime, was brushing and currying five of the steers. He herded them into the barn and into the stanchions where he proceeded to brush and curry them down. He found that working with the animals brought a sense of accomplishment. He remembered that he hadn't enjoyed working with Fred Harms' cattle during his summers here. Perhaps, he thought, that was because Harms' cattle were dairy cattle and required daily milking, feeding and care, whereas the beef cattle didn't seem to create the same sort of obligatory responsibility. As he worked, the warmth of the steers' bodies in close proximity to his helped to offset the chill that the late November wind brought into the barn. He thought about the information he had received from James Jacobs and what possible future it might hold for him. He also considered what his involvement in the latest turn of events regarding the LEGENT acquisition should be.

When he finished he walked to the mailbox and retrieved the day's mail. He noted an official looking envelope with a LEGENT logo on it and opened it on his way back to the house. It was a letter from the Employee Relations office advising him that certain stock options granted to him by Dynacom and carried forward to become obligations of LEGENT, had now matured. He laid the mail on the kitchen table and removed his jacket and hat as he mentally computed the value of the options and the resulting gains and tax obligations that would arise if he exercised them. The recent upturn in the markets had carried LEGENT with it. That, together with the pre-acquisition option value of the stocks would net him a tidy sum.

He called Max in Chicago and issued the necessary instructions to start the exercise and sale process. Then he called the Farnsworth Tele office and was informed by Belle's secretary that the Board meeting was scheduled for three o'clock that afternoon. He called John King's office and left a message with King's secretary that the Farnsworth Board was meeting today and that he would contact him after the meeting. As he was putting the phone down, he heard the sound of a vehicle driving into the farmyard.

He looked out the window and saw that it was McIntyre. The old Scot was wearing a pair of brown winter coveralls and a winter cap with the logo of his employer on it. He looked out towards the orchard and then came to the back door. Before he could knock, McCann pulled it open and welcomed him inside. Soon, the two men were seated opposite each other at the kitchen table while the coffee pot began to perk. McIntyre listened thoughtfully as McCann told him of Ted's death and his recent decision. He reached across the table and gripped McCann's shoulder with his weather-scarred right hand.

"Ah, so it is! Out of the sorrow of great loss comes the joy of great gain," he said as he smiled warmly. "You'll no doubt be missing the laddie. Perhaps I have good news in that regard."

"How so?" McCann smiled expectantly.

"Well, I heard about the incident here at the farm. That is really why I've come. I have someone I'd like you to meet."

He rose from the table and was out the door to his pickup before McCann could move. When he came back, he was leading a Border Collie on a short leash. The dog was almost totally white except for its head where the black was broken by a slash of white that began over its eyes and ran down to its nose. There was a splash of black on the left flank and on its right front leg. A black stripe wound almost all the way around its tail. McCann could tell from the way that the white slash on its head became gray at its muzzle that this was an old dog. It moved slowly to sit beside McIntyre's chair and when he sat back down, it lay down, with its head on its paws. McCann fought to resist the urge to reach down and scratch its ears as a surge of conflicting emotions ran through him.

"It's a bit bold of me to do this and if I've offended in any way, I'll take her back out to the truck," McIntyre said quickly, sensing the other man's feelings.

"What's ...what's its name?"

"Her name is Wink and she is eleven years old. She has the beginnings of arthritis in her right hip and she cannot work the cattle as quick as she has in the past. But I can vouch that in her day she was one of the best. She is in need of a place where she can live out her years loving and being loved. My sense is that you might know a bit more about loving and being loved now than when last we met," McIntyre said, as he leaned back, waiting.

"I don't know...Ted and I...it was so hard.... I never thought I could get attached to a dog that way and now...I just don't know," McCann faltered. He wanted to reach down and pet the dog and at the same time he knew that if he did, he might make a commitment that he wasn't quite ready to keep.

"Aye, I know how you feel. I've had three in my lifetime that I thought I couldn't bear to part with and when each was gone I felt I would never want another. But I found that each one added a wee something to my life. Go ahead man, give her a wee pat. You'll nae be obligated unless you want to be."

McCann extended his left hand with the fingers curled back for the dog to sniff. She raised her head and did so and then she licked his knuckles and waited expectantly. He rubbed the top of her head and she stood as he scratched lightly behind the black ears that felt like velvet. Her tail slowly moved back and forth. And as those of her breed had been doing for hundreds of years, she brought him into her life.

An hour later, McIntyre shook his hand as he opened the door to his pickup. The cushion Wink had ridden into the farmyard on was now in the kitchen. McCann and McIntyre had spent twenty minutes working the dog with the cattle. She was slower than Ted had been but every bit as efficient. As the pickup pulled out of the drive, she looked up at McCann and wagged her tail. Together, the two of them walked slowly back to the house. He thought of the handsome amount of money that would soon be deposited in his investment account in Chicago and looked down at Wink. It was very clear in his mind which of his two acquisitions on this cold November day was the more valuable.

Just as he entered the house, the phone rang. Jim Wolfe brought him up to date on what he had learned at the Boyne Falls Resort. McCann thanked him and asked him to keep his ear to the ground for any other hints as to what might be going on in Brutus. He went to the spare bedroom and rummaged through the boxes from his office in Chicago until he found what he was looking for. He went to his laptop and inserted a disk labeled "Dynacom Long Range Plan." A wave of memories washed over him as the disk booted up and displayed an index including a tab for "Network Improvement and Expansion." He clicked on it and moved through a series of windows until he was reviewing the Michigan networks and individual exchange profiles. He re-acquainted himself with the details of the Brutus, Michigan exchange.

He closed out the file and removed the disk. He went to his Microsoft Outlook file and opened his "Contacts" folder and extracted the names and telephone numbers of several executives from firms involved in providing networking equipment to the telecommunications industry. Having loaded them into a flash drive, he shut down the computer, removed the flash drive and prepared to go into Farnsworth for the Board meeting.

At 3:00 p.m., the Farnsworth Board convened. Art Boyington participated by video conference. Belle called the meeting to order and asked him to review what he had heard from the venture capitalists. He reported that firm commitments had been made by Feldman's organization, Triad and Smith's firm in Detroit. The total commitment was $45 million. He also reviewed the conditions associated with the commitments and the general process through which those making financial commitments expected the acquisition, if successful, would proceed.

Doug Warner, still looking rather weak, said that the Warner family was willing to commit an additional $8 million in equity capital. Wilson McCann surprised everyone by stating that he was prepared to keep his ownership at the same ratio to the Warner family's by a purchase of an additional $2 million in equity.

McCann did the math quickly in his head. The Warner family's existing equity was about $32 million plus their new equity contribution of $8 totaling $40 million. His equity share was now $10 million. The three investment capital firms would have an equity stake of $45 million. The Warners and McCann together would control fifty three per cent of the new firm. The longer term issue of how to fund the expansion and improvement of the LEGENT properties could be handled out of the residual equity after the purchase, if there was any, plus debt. He knew that the debt ratio in the current Farnsworth balance sheet was relatively low.

Belle Warner smiled from the head of the table. "It appears we may have the financial strength. Do we have the will?"

Fred Penay looked around the table and raised his hand. "If it is appropriate to do so, I move that the Farnsworth Telephone Cooperative move forward to make an offer for the LEGENT properties in the state of Michigan."

The motion carried. Belle asked Boyington to work with Feldman's people, Cindy Melzy and Smith to put the offer together. McCann volunteered Norm Miller to assist as needed. The Board discussed various aspects of the new corporate structure and Belle informed the group that due to Doug's recovery period, Wilson McCann would be assisting her in the overall management of the company.

The Board agreed to make an initial offer of $35 million and see what LEGENT'S response would be. It was agreed that McCann would contact John King to determine the best course of action for making the proposal. He, Belle and Boyington would work together to formalize the offer.

After the meeting adjourned, McCann walked with Belle to a small office adjacent to the company's computer room that had been set up for his use. A desk, credenza, wooden swivel chair and two mismatched side chairs constituted his "suite."

"Keep in mind, you are only a 'temp' so we cannot afford to spend a lot of money on you," Belle smiled as he dropped his brief case on the desk. He noted that a laptop computer and telephone had been installed on the credenza.

"Didn't I read somewhere about 'How the mighty have fallen'?" he smiled back at her.

"David's lament for Saul and Jonathan – 2nd Samuel 1," she said quickly.

He looked at her and felt once again a surge of appreciation and respect for this dynamic woman of faith. "I hope someday to know the word as you do and to live it as well."

"Where there is a will, there is a way."

"What book is that?" he asked.

"Belle Warner – School of Hard Knocks," she waved her hand at him as she went on down the hall.

He called John King and reviewed the events of the afternoon, skipping specific financial numbers but pointing out that Farnsworth had financial backing sufficient to warrant making an offer.

"What are you thinking, Wils? Give me a range," King said.

"We're looking at something under $2,500 per access line, John."

King was silent and McCann knew he was making the financial calculation. "Under $40 million then."

"Considerably under John, more like under $35 million."

"I serve masters. You know how it is," King said.

"I understand. Why don't you talk with them and call me back. If they are willing to talk, we are willing to talk. Are there others in the game or can't you say?"

"There are others but they're scared of what the PSC may do and why this thing has drawn the attention from the Governor's office. That leads me to a final question. Have you got the horses to pull the load that may come from there?"

"Depending on the size of the load, we've got the horses," McCann said it with as much confidence as he could muster.

"Sounds good. I'll get back to you tomorrow or the next day."

"Fine, John. By the way, I have a new lady living at my farm."

Again there was silence on King's end of the conversation. "Her name is Wink and she has arthritis…she's a Border Collie."

"Geez, Wils. I've got to see this farm of yours when this is all over."

"I'd enjoy that John. See you."

He swiveled the chair and heard it creak. The one small window looked out at a row of parked cars. He watched as the setting sun shot one last feeble ray before it dropped below the horizon. His mind ranged back to his early days at Dynacom. He had occupied an office similar to this one at the end of a hallway next to an elevator. Its one redeeming grace was that it looked out over a busy street at a dry cleaning shop. Each morning he had arrived early and watched the sun come up and transform his darkened cell. His days then had been filled with the diligent pursuit of making a contribution to the growing enterprise. If only he had known then what he knew now, how would his life have been different?

He plugged in the flash drive containing the names and telephone numbers he had recorded earlier and began to make a series of phone calls to old friends in Schaumburg, Illinois, San Jose, California and one to Espoo, Finland. In each instance, he was warmly greeted and after a few minutes of pleasantries he asked his question. In two instances, he was given an "I don't know anything about anything," type of response. The Nortel executive in Schaumburg, whom he had known for over fifteen years replied, "I can't talk about that." McCann thanked each person in turn and after the third call, sat back in his chair and began to put together different scenarios in his mind. None gave him the answer he was seeking. At length, he jotted some notes on a pad and removed the flash drive from the laptop on his desk. Next, he called Stu Bailey in New York and brought him up to date. At the end of the call, he told Bailey about the Boyne Falls Resort information and the results of his calls to the industry's providers.

"What do you think it means?" Bailey asked, when he had finished.

"I think there is something going down in that area that those providers are involved in. If it is tied to the Governor's interest, and I think it is, than it involves some significant investment by the industry providers in conjunction with the state's department of economic development. What they are doing is still not apparent. Can you use your contacts to try and add to what we know?"

"Let me see what I can dig up. I'll call you on Monday," Bailey replied, before hanging up.

McCann spent the remaining part of the afternoon reviewing the Farnsworth operating and construction budgets for the coming year and constructing possible scenarios for the impact of the LEGENT properties on them. Down the hall, in other areas of the office, employees talked quietly about what might be taking place within their little company that had brought this intense stranger into their midst. Several knew of McCann's history in the industry and shared the information about his past. Most were aware of the consideration that the company was giving to expansion although they were somewhat in the dark as to what that meant. Belle Warner had sent out an e-mail late last week advising all employees that Mr. McCann would be assisting her during Doug's recuperation. A few found reasons to walk past the doorway to the little office where he sat, working away at his computer. One or two hesitated long enough to see that the screen was filled with numbers.

Ted had shared the farm and the farm house with McCann on an equal basis. While he was readily willing to accept some affection and spent a good deal of his time lying at McCann's feet while the two were in the house, he wandered often when they were outside. There had been times when he would disappear for hours at a time. Clearly, Ted's life had been his own and not completely subject to or shared with McCann.

Wink, McCann soon found, was far different. She stayed close to him at all times when he was outside. She waited as if expecting some sort of assignment that she might eagerly perform for him. It was clear that the arthritis had curtailed any desire for extra activity and had made her a conservator of her energy for those assignments. When they were inside the house she followed him everywhere. When he went outside and left her in the house, she immediately retreated to a clothes closet in his bedroom and sprawled next to a heat vent to sleep. That was where he found her when he returned late that afternoon. As he took off his jacket and hung it in the closet, she jumped to her feet and stood waiting for a pat on the head and a scratch behind the ears. Then, she padded quietly after him as he returned to the kitchen and lay at his feet under the kitchen table as he ate his evening meal. When he went outside to care for the cattle, she trotted at his side, head partially cocked to watch for any directions he might give. In the moonlight, her white flanks made her look almost like an apparition. Using the commands McIntyre had taught him, he sent her into the pasture to bring in two steers and watched as she slowly and efficiently did so. He noted from time to time the hitch in her gait as she dealt with the pain in her hip. He watched with admiration as she moved the steers quickly to the barnyard and crouched at the gate opening waiting.

"Good girl! Come!"

She rose from her crouch and trotted to him, all the while watching the cattle as if to be sure that none would head for the gate.

He crouched beside her and ruffled her coat. Then, impulsively, he lowered his head to hers and rubbed his cheek along her muzzle. She licked his face and leaned against him.

"I think you and I are going to be a good team," he said, rubbing her hip. For some reason, Donna's face flashed through his mind as he rose and headed into the barn with Wink trotting beside him.

(29)

In Dallas earlier that afternoon, John King and Sal Piazza met in King's office. King and his wife had flown back from Savannah that morning. He briefed Piazza on McCann's call.

"What do you think Norm will say?" Piazza asked, as he settled his big frame into a chair opposite King's desk.

"He'll grouse about how it isn't enough. Then I'll remind him about the Michigan PSC and their service proceeding and he'll tell me to go back and negotiate."

"What about other offers?"

"Haven't heard from anyone, have you?"

"Not a word. I think they are chewing it over."

King leaned back in his chair. He clasped his hands behind his head and looked at the ceiling. He thought of McCann and his "new lady" and he began to smile.

"What?" Piazza said, from across the desk.

"Wils McCann has a new dog. Remember, he almost got himself thrown in jail when a couple of drunks shot his other one?"

"So, what's so funny?"

"It's just that I find it amusing to think of Wilson McCann taking care of cattle, playing with dogs and making multi-million dollar offers on telephone properties all in the same day."

"Maybe he's lost it a little," Piazza said, looking out the window. "You know how you older guys get."

King grinned back at him. "Get smart with me and you'll be a service center supervisor in Fort Wayne next week."

"Might not be too bad. I could drive down to Indy for the 500 and Colts games. Could I get the LEGENT box seats?"

"You wouldn't be able to afford the parking on what you'd be making,"

King retorted. "You know, I'd like to see Farnsworth get these properties. Wils McCann and the Warner family know how to run an operation the right way."

"You sound a little envious," Piazza said, looking at him intently.

"I am. If I were your age, I'd get Norm to sell to Farnsworth and then I'd quit and go ask Doug Warner for a job."

"Is that a message?"

"Naw! I don't think an ex-Michigan State Spartan and a clarinet player from Holy Cross would work out well! You want to go with me down to see Norm?"

"Sure, when you leave, I'll need all the friends I can get," Piazza said, as he stood.

"Believe me, you don't need friends like Norm Lister," John King said, as he dialed Lister's office.

Forty-five minutes later, the two had returned to King's office. Norm Lister had reacted just as King had predicted. After grumbling about the amount of the offer and the fact that Wilson McCann was involved, he had instructed King to find out if any of the other companies were going to make an offer and, if not, to open serious negotiations with Farnsworth Tele. He had then resumed his grumbling about having to deal with "the likes of Wilson McCann." Beyond an initial nod of greeting, he had barely recognized Sal Piazza's presence.

Piazza stood in the doorway as King lowered himself into his chair. "Do you think you will be meeting with McCann?" he asked.

"Probably. Why?"

"I'd like to meet him. It sounds like he is a bee in Norm's bonnet."

"More like a burr under his saddle. Maybe we'll get the jet and fly up to Farnsworth. I'll take you along. You can help McCann feed his beef. It's a skill you might be able to use after I leave!"

Piazza considered this and saw the connection. "Do you want me to call Fairfield and the others or are you going to do it?

King looked out the window. "I'll do it. I want to crowd them a little. I'd like to get this thing agreed to and sent to the Commission before Christmas."

For the remainder of the week, McCann operated on a schedule that started early with morning chores in the barn, followed by breakfast and a devotional period in the kitchen with Wink. Then, he showered, shaved and changed into casual business attire and drove into Farnsworth. He arrived at Farnsworth Tele around nine o'clock each morning and worked until three o'clock in the afternoon. He quickly fell into the same organizational rhythm that had characterized his days at Dynacom. He read reports, asked questions, listened in on meetings and gradually assimilated himself into the affairs of the company. At times he closed his office door and made phone calls to old friends in the industry. Most were glad to hear from him and puzzled by his involvement with the smaller company. A few gave him additional pieces of information that they referred to as "scuttlebutt" from within the industry. He jotted more notes on his pad and continued to run the information he had through his mind.

The people in the office were at first reserved but quickly came to accept this interloper into their daily routine. They found him both intense in his questioning and observations while at the same time a wealth of information on the industry and the reasons for things that they had come to accept without really asking why. They also found him to be full of anecdotes about the past that made them laugh and shake their heads in amazement at the things he had seen and done. Those who knew Donna Barnes and a little of the relationship that had existed between her and their new co-worker, found themselves thinking about the "what ifs" that were eliminated by her death.

Doug came to the office each day and was clearly gaining strength. He appreciated McCann's willingness to be involved and the two men complemented each other in their approaches with no sense of rivalry. Belle came in for one or two hours each day and observed from a distance. She watched McCann with a question lurking in her mind as to what direction his newly found purpose in life would take him.

Cindy Melzy did not call and McCann found this to be somewhat disconcerting. When he mentioned it to Belle, she said that Cindy hadn't called her either. Smith in Detroit was working with Art Boyington on any issues related to his firm's participation in the acquisition and McCann spoke several times with Feldman's representative. Most of her questions related to gaining a better understanding of the due diligence information that she was reviewing.

On Wednesday, McCann, after talking things over with Doug, called Jim Wolfe. He reviewed the situation with Wolfe and made it clear that, if the acquisition was successful, Farnsworth Tele wanted Jim to join its management team as Vice President-Operations. Wolfe indicated he would talk with June about it but his demeanor indicated that he would be more than happy to leave LEGENT and join Farnsworth. McCann told him that until the Governor's interest in the northern Lower Peninsula was resolved, Wolfe would remain in Mackinaw City. Later, he and his family might want to move to Farnsworth. He asked Wolfe if he had learned anything further from his contacts within the industry or in Lansing but the LEGENT man did not add to McCann's meager store of information.

On Friday, John King called to inform McCann that, if "certain issues" could be resolved, LEGENT was prepared to make a counter-offer and engage in negotiations leading to eventual transfer of the properties, subject to Commission review and approval. McCann told King of his call to Jim Wolfe. King's response was that "Jim Wolfe is a good man and I'm glad he will have an opportunity coming out of this." King made a mental note not to tell anyone else about what McCann had revealed to him.

The "issues" King pointed to during the call related to ownership of overfunded pension, work in progress, agreements for transition activity and costs and future impacts of Commission actions in relation to the sale. McCann made notes and discussed these issues with Doug before calling King back to request a face-to-face meeting. King indicated he would bring an associate as well as someone from LEGENT'S legal department. McCann said that he, a representative from the Warner family and Art Boyington would represent Farnsworth. McCann agreed to contact Feldman's office, Cindy Melzy and Smith in Detroit to see who would represent the three firms.

"Where and when?" McCann asked, as he leaned back in his chair.

"I'm going to see if I can get the jet. I need one more company plane ride before I head off to Savannah. Why don't we meet at your office? You promised to show me your farm!" King replied. "I'd like to move quickly before somebody here changes his mind."

McCann didn't need to ask who "somebody" was. He was well aware of Norm Lister's propensity for changes in direction without advance notice.

"Sounds good. How's next Tuesday suit you?"

"Let's work toward that. I'll get back to you," King replied.

McCann put down the phone and thought about what this call meant. Things were underway now. Barring unforeseen events, an acquisition was possible. He was about to reach for the phone to begin calling people about the meeting when it rang. Phil Willard spoke into his ear.

"Ever been to Bad Axe?" he asked.

"Yes, drove up there for a banana split with Donna a long time ago," McCann replied, thinking back to that summer night. He felt the same dull ache that came whenever he thought of her.

"Well, you have an invitation from the Governor to come to a ribbon cutting at the Bad Axe Hospital addition on Sunday afternoon. He's invited Belle and Doug, too."

"And you?" McCann asked.

"Of course. I'm the County Chairman," Willard came back, sounding a little miffed that McCann didn't appreciate his position.

McCann smiled into the phone. "Wrong county Phil, you're not 'the man' in Bad Axe! I wonder what the Governor wants to talk about."

"I think you can guess. It should be interesting. You know, since you came to town, my life has become awfully interesting!"

"Glad to be of help. What time do we have to leave? I'm bringing Sally McHugh to church on Sunday morning."

The silence on the other end of the line told McCann that Willard was either in shock or in prayer. He waited, a smile playing about his lips.

"That's…that's…you're…amazing!" sputtered the Agway dealer.

"So…what time, Phil?"

"We'll have to leave right after church. The wives are invited. Why don't you take Sally along, too?

"Maybe I will. I'll bet she's never been out with a Governor before."

Sally stood sideways to the full-length mirror on the closet door and took stock of herself. As she did so, she was tempted to take a good stiff drink from the bottle of Jack Daniels that was hidden high up in the kitchen cupboard. Contrary to what most of the people in Farnsworth thought, Sally did not drink much hard liquor. Beer was her drink of choice. But, whereas others when feeling stressed might take a Valium, Xanax or Atavan, Sally took two fingers of whiskey to calm down. It didn't happen very often. Sally McHugh was usually pretty confident. That was not the case this Sunday morning.

She did a one-eighty and checked herself again, deciding that Jack Daniels, Rev. Chuck Hastings, and the Governor were not a good mix. She would have to "tough it out" without Jack.

"Not bad if I do say so myself," she said aloud. The dark blue pant suit with the white blouse was a good choice. She had considered the red leather mini skirt and jacket with the blouse but couldn't bring herself to do that to Wils.

She sat down on the bed and stared into the mirror. Donna Barnes was not the only one in Farnsworth who had carried a torch for Wilson McCann all these years. As a senior in high school, her mother had warned her about McCann. "He's only out for one thing and he isn't suitable for you," her mother had said. Her mother was right on the first count and wrong on the second.

Sally thought back over the years. Her mother had always been protective. No one was good enough for her daughter. She was crushed when Sally married after one year of college and had a baby seven months later. The first divorce came at the end of three years. Within a year, Sally had married again, this time to a local football hero from Caro. Two months into that marriage, he beat her for the second time and she got a protection order, moved out with her four-year-old son and filed for divorce. One year later, she was in Saginaw, working in a restaurant as a hostess and going to school at night to learn how to run her own business. She married for a third time. He was a construction worker she met in a bar. They were happy for five years. Two more children followed and then he got the urge to move west just about the time Sally's mother died from cancer. Sally held her father's hand at the funeral and silently cursed herself for being such a failure as a daughter. When her father died two years later, Sally took her small inheritance and purchased the diner in Farnsworth. By that time, husband number three was working in the state of Washington. The child support payments required under her third divorce decree weren't very regular. They stopped about a year later and Sally knew she was on her own. She smiled as she thought about how hard Phil Willard had tried to get her to bring them to Sunday school. But the smile faded quickly. Her kids were good kids. She had been a good mother. But she knew she could have been better.

Some might say that Wilson McCann was what started Sally McHugh down the wrong road. But Sally knew better. She and Wils had enjoyed a "wild oats" summer and she had never forgotten him. The three men she had married were the result of her search for someone like McCann. Just like Donna Barnes, she too had a scrapbook with clippings of McCann's career.

Today she would go to church for the first time in a year. No one in Farnsworth knew it, but Sally went to church every Christmas Eve with her three sons. She went to a small country church north and east of Caro where no one knew her. Communion was served but Sally and her sons sat silently as others went forward to receive the elements. That one service each year was Sally's time of commitment. She promised to be a good mother and she promised to work hard and she promised to try to live a more proper lifestyle. She had kept the first two promises. Her three children were proof of that. The third was too hard and she usually gave up on it by Easter. She took comfort in knowing that she wasn't as bad as most people thought but in moments like this one, she ached to be as good as she knew she could be.

She would go to church this morning on the arm of a man that she was deeply attracted to but would never have. She knew that now. She had seen the look in McCann's eyes last Monday when he had said, "We are... friends...good friends." It was a different look than had been in his eyes the night they came back to the farm and those two drunks had shot his dog. She knew that look well. She had seen it often over the last twenty years or so. Wilson McCann had changed. She knew that no matter what she did or said or how badly she wanted him, he would forever be...a friend. When they walked in, people would stare and whisper to each other and turn away. They would question Wilson McCann's character and that made her feel that this was very wrong. But, just this once, she wanted to walk beside the person she had kept tucked away in the back of her mind all these years. She hadn't told McCann but she planned to beg off on the trip to Bad Axe. She could find an excuse, a headache; something needed doing at the diner, she just wanted one hour of sitting beside him, even if it was in church.

An hour later, it all turned out a bit different. They entered the church together. He held the door for her and she let go of his arm to step through the doorway. She hadn't gotten three feet inside when first Martha Willard and then Lona Marks grasped her hand to welcome her. Their husbands stood beside them and shook hands with Wils as he entered. It was clear that Wilson McCann and Sally McHugh would not walk into the sanctuary alone.

They sat in the third pew from the rear. Sally couldn't keep from smiling as she thought of how they must have given up at least seven rows of seating just to surround her. Martha sat on her right and the little Marks boy sat next to Wils. It was obvious that the two had a special relationship and she thought about the kind of father Wilson McCann would be.

A few people looked at her with some surprise evident on their faces. But, for the most part, her entrance with Wils and six other people had gone unnoticed. She was glad she had left Jack on the shelf in the kitchen.

She found the music to be exciting and not what she had expected. Other elements of the service were those with which she was acquainted from her annual pilgrimage to the little country church. When Charles Hastings walked to the center of the platform, Bible in hand, she braced herself for what he might say. She felt as if he was looking directly at her as he began to speak.

"..Today's reading scripture is from Luke 10, verses 38 to 42. It's a familiar portion of scripture and not one usually associated with the Christmas season. But, hopefully, I can help you see the significance of it for this time of year. Let me read it for you."

Now as they were traveling along, He entered a certain village; and a woman named Martha welcomed Him into her home. And she had a sister called Mary, who moreover was listening to the Lord's word, seated at His feet. But Martha was distracted with all her preparations; and she came up to Him and said, "Lord do you not care that my sister has left me to do all the serving alone? Then tell her to help me."

But the Lord answered and said to her, "Martha, Martha, you are worried and bothered about so many things; but only a few things are necessary, really only one, for Mary has chosen the good part, which shall not be taken away from her."

Hastings closed his Bible, keeping his index finger at the place from which he had read. He bowed his head and prayed a quiet prayer for guidance and then looked out at the congregation. "Are you distracted today? Are you busy with all the preparations for Christmas? Could it be that we get so distracted that we, like Martha, fail to sit at Jesus' feet and listen to what he has to say? How are you doing today in that regard? Are you taking time for Christ or are you busy with the distractions of the season?"

Sally cast a sidewise glance at McCann. He sat back in the pew with his legs crossed and his chin resting in between his thumb and forefinger. To her right, Martha Willard had her Bible open in her lap and Sally could see that there were a number of verses underlined in various colors.

"....or maybe you are like the inn keeper in the story of the Nativity. There's no room in your life for Christ. Maybe you're like the Shepherds, you're out there every day in the hum drum of your job and nothing exciting is happening and the Christmas season is just 'same-old – same-old,' Hastings continued. "I invite you to change the routine that you're in and do what Mary did. Come and sit at the feet of Jesus. Put aside the business of Christmas and get about listening to the business of Christ. We sometimes hear people talk about putting Christ back into Christmas. I want you to consider putting yourselves back into Christ this year. I want you to come and join me at the feet of Jesus and listen to what he has to say."

Sally found herself thinking about what it would have been like to sit at the feet of Jesus there in the heat of Bethany. She felt herself being transported back to that day when Martha was scuttling back and forth with the preparations for the people who would soon enter her home. She looked again at Martha Willard. She tried to envision Martha as the Martha in the story that Hastings was using as the basis for his sermon. She could sense that this Martha was quite a bit different than the Bethany Martha. Sally wondered how she might get to know Martha Willard a little better. Phil was in and out of the diner on almost a daily basis but his wife had never joined him. Sally thought of her mother and the grief that she had no doubt brought to her before she died. She wished that she could go back in time and try again.

The service ended with prayer and a closing hymn. Hastings invited those who wanted to sit at Jesus' feet and learn his will for their lives to come forward. No one did and Sally felt sorry for the minister. The message had been a good one. Why didn't people respond? Then her thoughts turned inward. Why hadn't she responded?

They exited the sanctuary with the rest of the congregation and Martha Willard laid her hand on Sally's arm as they paused in the foyer. "You and Wils can ride up to Bad Axe with us. That way, I will have someone to visit with. I don't know much about the Telecommunications business so we can talk about other things."

Sally McHugh forgot about her intentions to excuse herself from any further involvement in the day's activities.

"Thank you, I'd like that."

"I'll get to know Martha a little better and that will be better than meeting the Governor," Sally thought to herself, as McCann took her elbow and led her toward the door.

The Huron Medical Center was founded in 1903 and had been originally chartered in Michigan in 1906 as the Hubbard Memorial Hospital in honor of Frank W. Hubbard. In 1968 a new hospital was built west of Bad Axe and the Hubbard Memorial and Bad Axe General Hospitals had merged to form Huron Medical. A third floor addition in 1974, a new Physical Therapy Department and a Cardiopulmonary Department and Pharmacy were added in 1976. In 1981 additional Laboratory and X-Ray facilities were added. In 1989, a Computerized Tomography (CT) Scanner was the first in the tri-county area of Michigan. A 15,000 square foot addition including new Operating Room suites and an Ambulatory Surgery to be opened on this snowy Sunday afternoon would accommodate several physicians with a variety of medical specialties and new, more specialized operating room equipment. An additional phase had resulted in renovation of portions of the first and third floors. A new Central Registration area was also added. It was into this new, brightly lit area that Doug and Belle Warner, Phil and Martha Willard, Wilson McCann and a very nervous Sally McHugh walked. The climate controlled area was a welcome relief from the gusting snow and falling temperatures that had greeted the Governor and his entourage about 15 minutes before.

The well-dressed receptionist, a lady in her forties with "Elaine" on her HMC badge motioned them to a semi-private seating area and told them that the Governor's aide, a man named Ross, would be with them shortly. The Governor was touring the new facilities, and the ribbon cutting and a reception in the medical center's dining area would soon follow.

The Farnsworth delegation talked among themselves about how fortunate Bad Axe was to be both a county seat and the home to such a comprehensive modern medical center. While Farnsworth's hospital was adequate to the smaller community's needs, it was not equipped as this facility was.

"Well, at least we beat them in both football and basketball," Doug Warner said, without sounding petulant. Sally thought he looked more and more like his old self as he lounged on a small couch with Belle. He was dressed in a buttoned down white shirt that was open at the collar with a blue sport coat and lighter blue slacks. Both Phil and McCann were dressed in suits with shirts and ties. She thought McCann looked uneasy and uncomfortable as he sat beside her. He had adjusted the knot of the tie he wore twice since sitting down and alternated between leaning forward and leaning back on the couch. She had the urge to slip her hand inside his arm but knew he probably wouldn't appreciate it. Willard, on the other hand was perfectly relaxed. Martha had picked up an HMC brochure at the reception desk and was reading through it.

ACQUISITION

It was Belle Warner that drew Sally's attention. Sally had always been in awe of the older woman. Belle represented "old money" to Sally McHugh. She had heard the stories of how the Warners had made their money. She had gone to school with both Doug and Nancy Warner. She, like others in the community, had been saddened by Nancy's early death. She remembered a night many years ago when she and other young people from the eighth grade had been invited to the Warner mansion for dinner. Her mother had taken her to the Federated store and purchased a new dress for the occasion and had lectured her on proper behavior. She felt again the hot rush of embarrassment as she remembered how she was one of two girls who had worn dresses that night. All the others had been in slacks or jeans. She remembered how Belle had gone out of her way to make them feel comfortable and how Nancy Warner had asked her to sit next to her at dinner. When Sally went home that night she had felt as if she had been at Cinderella's ball and how she had ridden her bike past the mansion many times after that, just to re-create the feelings. Belle had always demonstrated a reserved friendliness toward her. Today, she had welcomed her into the group as though it was the most natural thing in the world. Sally knew it wasn't and that there were probably some questions lurking behind the friendly countenance of the older woman as she sat rather stiffly beside her son.

Within minutes a tall sandy haired man who introduced himself as Ross strode up to them and welcomed each in turn. He motioned for them to be seated and pulled up a side chair to face them all.

"As you know, the Governor will be doing the ribbon cutting and then making a few remarks to the public in the dining area. He'll do the usual 'meet-and-greet' with the audience and then meet with you in the HMC Boardroom. Mrs. Willard and Ms. McHugh, I've arranged for a tour of the medical center for you. Someone from the HMC staff will conduct the tour and they will meet you at the Boardroom after the Governor has had a chance to meet you. I hope you understand."

"Sorry, I should have sold you a share of stock," McCann said, as Ross left them.

"Don't worry my dear, we will have more fun than listening to a lot of political and business discussion," Martha Willard said, as she laid her hand on Sally's arm. "Besides, when you've met one politician, you've met them all."

Phil Willard smiled indulgently at his wife as the group headed back into the reception area where, due to the rapidly deteriorating weather outside, a big blue and gold ribbon had been stretched across one of the hallway entrances. A small podium had been set up and the area was rapidly filling up with people.

The Governor entered with his entourage trailing behind him and rapidly shook hands with many of the assembled crowd. The press, both local and state, was in attendance and there was an explosion of camera flashes as the Governor came in. The crowd gathered behind him. The ribbon-cutting went smoothly and the entire group proceeded to the dining area where the Governor and several community and medical center leaders spoke briefly. As the refreshments were served, the Governor and several of his aides worked the crowd. The press jostled with dignitaries in an effort to stick their microphones close to the Governor to catch his every word and the cameras continued to follow every move he made.

Sally and McCann were standing off to the side sipping their punch when Ross approached.

"If you will follow me, we will move to the Boardroom," he said in passing, as he moved toward Belle and Doug Warner.

They didn't have to wait long before the Governor entered. He moved quickly around the room, meeting each of them and Sally was impressed with how quickly she felt at ease. "I'm glad you could come and be with us today. I understand Ross has arranged a special tour for you and Mrs. Willard. I hope that you enjoy yourselves. If there is anything else I or my staff can do for you while you are here, please let us know," he said, as he held her hand. She tried hard to match the level gaze but found herself looking down at her feet as he moved on to greet Martha Willard. For a brief moment she had experienced the same type of feelings that she had in the Warner mansion as an eighth grader.

As the door closed behind Sally and Martha, the Governor dropped into a chair at the head of the table. Ross sat at the far end of the table next to Doug Warner. The rest of the Governor's aides had left the room.

The Governor looked quickly at the four of them. He knew he was taking somewhat of a risk in having this meeting. He had noted the cross on McCann's lapel. McCann had been the one uncertainty in his mind. The tiny cross had lifted a great deal of that uncertainty. He removed the cap from a bottle of water on the table in front of him and took a drink. Putting the cap back on, he leaned forward and rested his interlaced hands on the leather pad in front of him.

"Let me be very direct with you and I hope that you will be so with me. Let me begin by saying that I trust that nothing that is said here will be repeated outside this room. I wouldn't want the *Detroit Free Press* or even the *Wall Street Journal* to pick up on this."

As he said it, he looked directly at McCann and smiled broadly. McCann's face flushed and he held up his hand, palm toward the Governor.

"No problem here, sir."

"Please forgive me for having a little fun, Wils. I apologize if I have made you uncomfortable. Mrs. Warner, I understand that there is a very good possibility that Farnsworth Tele could be the new owner of the former LEGENT properties in Michigan. Could you bring me up to date on just where that stands?"

Belle Warner swiveled her chair slightly to look at Doug. "Doug, would you bring the Governor up to date on the latest? . . . and Wils, jump in where you feel appropriate."

Over the next five minutes both Doug Warner and McCann briefed the Governor on the status of the negotiations as well as the financial aspects of the proposed acquisition. Ross made several short notes on a small leather covered pad that he took from his suit coat pocket.

When they had finished, the Governor leaned back in his chair. "I want to say two very important things to you and I trust you to keep them within the confines of this group. First, I consider it to be very important to the interests of the state and its economic development that these properties be operated by a Michigan-owned company. With all due respect to Mr. McCann's previous employer and the current owners, they were and are 'absentee landlords.' I am determined that wherever it is fiscally responsible to do so, we encourage an environment in which companies that provide infrastructure within our state be locally owned and operated. I have asked Ross to make our interests in the acquisition known to those whose financial help you need."

"Thank you, Governor. We can use that assistance and we appreciate it. May I ask if there is anything else we might know about that may lie behind your attention to this? It seems that, on the grand scale of things, it would be of minor interest to your office," Belle said, easily. McCann smiled as he considered how deftly she had gotten to the heart of the matter.

The Governor leaned forward and returned her gaze. "That leads me to my second reason for wanting to meet with you and be brought up to date on the status of the possible acquisition. Shortly after the first of the year, we will announce a major economic development project in the northern Lower Peninsula. It will be a project with direct ties to your industry and it will require the most modern telecommunications network to be in place as it moves forward to completion and operation. It will involve some significant investments within the currently franchised area of the LEGENT properties in Michigan that you intend to acquire."

He paused to look at the four of them. He was pleased to see that there was no apparent surprise on any face. He recognized that he hadn't told them much more than they had already probably surmised. He quickly considered how much more he should say. Before he could proceed, however, McCann spoke.

"Are you speaking of significant investments by Farnsworth Tele, others or both?"

"Both," the Governor replied.

"May we know exactly what types of investments and the magnitude?" Belle Warner asked.

"I am not as well versed on your industry as others but I would expect them to include both switching and network investments. I would also expect them to be in both the wire-line and wire-less broadband, data and other information services areas. As to the magnitude, I have not the foggiest idea of what would be involved. I'm sorry I cannot be of more help in that area."

McCann shifted uneasily in his chair and raised his hand. The Governor nodded and McCann asked, "Governor, recently there has been some talk within the industry that would lead one to think that there might be some significant investments by corporations involved in providing equipment and software to our industry. It seems as though these investments would be part of a top secret project that seems to focus on the area around Brutus, Michigan. Brutus is one of the exchanges that would be involved in this acquisition. Could you comment on that?"

Every eye in the room turned toward McCann. He felt a moment of guilt for not having shared what little he knew with the others, but he wanted to judge reaction and he wanted the others to judge it as well.

The room fell quiet for a few moments. The Governor took another drink from his bottle of water and cleared his throat. McCann watched the expression on the face of the Governor's aide, Ross. He thought that Ross looked extremely tense. The Governor seemed to relax in his chair. "I make it a firm policy to try to keep from commenting on 'scuttlebutt' Mr. McCann. However, I do find that it is sometimes helpful to explore all the sources and see what underlies it. As you know your industry as well as anyone, I'll leave that to you."

"Thank you sir," McCann replied. "I may do that."

The Governor let his eyes move around the table before speaking again. "There is one thing more. I know that we all share the same faith. It would personally give me great satisfaction to see people of faith such as yourselves as a part of what we intend to do. I hope that you will pray for me and for those who work with me and I want you to know that I will be praying for you and your enterprise as well. I realize that I have not provided all the answers that you may have hoped for. I must again point out that your acquisition of these properties will be closely monitored by our Public Service Commission. I will in no way seek to influence them in their decisions beyond letting them know that this is very critical to the state's economic development program. You will need to do the best job possible in making presentations that satisfy their requirements for approval. If, however, you need assistance in making those presentations beyond what is normal in these circumstances, please keep Ross fully informed and if he can assist you, he will."

The Governor's eyes moved to Phil Willard. He smiled as he thought of how the Agway dealer had staunchly supported the Republican cause throughout this area of the state. He couldn't help but think about his boyhood when he would hurry home after school to catch the latest "Wild Bill Hickok" episode on TV with Andy Devine playing "Jingles," James Butler Hickok's sidekick. The resemblance was amazing.

"Jingles, would you lead us in a brief prayer?" He asked, smiling. The others smiled in return and absolutely grinned as Willard responded, "Yessireebob."

The Governor and his group exited the room and Belle Warner turned to McCann. "Is there anything else you would like to tell us before we head out into the snow?"

"Belle, I'm sorry to have sprung that on the three of you but I wanted to see what his reaction was and what you made of it."

"You evidently touched a nerve. Ross was about to have a stroke!" Phil Willard said.

"You think whatever it is they plan to do is in the Burt Lake area?" Doug asked.

"The network in Brutus, which includes the lake, is not bad but it isn't state-of-the-art. The switching system is about ten years old. If you dropped all the stuff the Governor mentioned onto that network, it wouldn't support it. The reaction I got from calling companies like Nortel, Nokia and Cisco Systems together with a comment that Jim Wolfe picked up in Boyne Falls that came from an Alcatel-Lucent employee talking about a possible move to the area, makes me think that our supplier friends know more than they are willing to discuss out in the open. I think that is where we have to focus and we need to know more. I've asked Stu Bailey to make some contacts and see what he can find out. He is to call me tomorrow. Doug, if you know anyone in the industry that might add to what little we know, please contact them."

"Will do," Doug Warner replied, the respect for McCann showing in his face.

"We are driving in more than one type of snowstorm, aren't we?" Belle smiled, as she picked up her purse. The others smiled with her.

They were still smiling ten minutes later when they met Sally and

Martha in the reception area. McCann turned to Willard after looking out at the snowstorm which was rapidly growing worse outside.

"Let's go, ' Jingles'! The road may be a bit slippery."

Willard slapped McCann on the shoulder as he shrugged into his overcoat. Sally wondered just what had gone down in the Boardroom!

(30)

The trip back to Farnsworth was slow as M-53 was snow-packed and slippery by the time they were underway. When they reached the junction with M-81, east of Farnsworth, the conditions improved and they arrived just as the gray blustery day turned into darkness.

Charles Hastings was keeping an eye on the red Mustang parked halfway between the church and parsonage. When he saw McCann and Sally get out of Phil Willard's car, he quickly put on his coat and headed out into the falling snow. He was ten yards from the car when he called out to McCann.

"Wils! Do you have a minute? I need to talk with you."

McCann turned toward him as Sally got behind the wheel and started the Mustang. In the weak light of the street lamp, he could tell that the usually ebullient minister was looking grim.

"What is it, Charles?" he said, moving toward the preacher.

"I received a call this afternoon. James Jacobs died this morning from a heart attack!"

McCann cast a quick glance at the car and turned back to Hastings. "Obviously, we do need to talk!"

"I would appreciate it," Hastings replied, looking at the car.

"Does Dorothy have the coffee pot on?" McCann asked, meaning something different.

"Absolutely, can the two of you come in for a cup?" Hastings replied, the relief already showing in his face.

"We'll be right there."

McCann turned back to the car and bent to speak to Sally. A moment later the Mustang's engine stopped and she emerged from the driver's side.

"Church, punch and cookies with the Governor and now a cup of coffee in the parsonage with the preacher's wife. I'm learning a whole new way of life!" she muttered as she pulled her jacket more closely around her. "What's going on?"

"I just need to speak with Charles for a few minutes. You'll like Dorothy. She makes good coffee."

"So do I," Sally grumbled good-naturedly. She was pleased when he put his arm around her waist to support her on what was quickly becoming a slippery sidewalk.

Hastings opened the door for them and the cold of the night was quickly replaced by the warmth of the parsonage and the faint smell of wood smoke from the living room. Dorothy Hastings, in a plaid shirt and jeans grasped Sally's hand in greeting and quickly offered her a cup of coffee in the kitchen, as Hastings and McCann headed into the living room where the logs in the fireplace snapped and crackled. McCann shed his overcoat and sat in one of the two chairs before the fire. Hastings dropped into the other and leaned forward, elbows on his knees and head resting on the steepled fingers of both hands.

McCann waited, wanting to ask the obvious questions about what this meant but respecting the need for the minister to speak first. Finally, Hastings sat back and rested his arms on the arms of the chair.

"He had chest pains this morning at breakfast and by the time they realized what was happening and called 911 he was having a severe heart attack. The EMTs got there too late. It is such a shock!"

"I'm sorry Chuck. I know how much he meant to you. What happens to his ministry and the things we talked about?"

"It's too early to tell but I'm afraid there will be no desire to re-locate the ministry now. I'm afraid that James' passing will make everyone associated with the ministry want to maintain the current situation until new leadership can either validate or re-think its mission. I'm afraid we have lost an opportunity. I was so looking forward to expanding our role in the community. I just don't know…"

"Charles!" McCann said it firmly and strongly, causing the minister to stop and look at him. "You more than anyone I've ever met are the embodiment of the fact that God is at work in our lives and has a plan for our good. Come on!"

The minister rubbed a hand across his face and settled back in his chair. A smile crossed his face and he shook his head. His sense of the loss of something he had put a lot of effort into was something the man who sat opposite him had felt. He immediately recognized that, for the first time in their brief relationship, he could feel the kind of loss that McCann had been carrying when he first came to Farnsworth.

"What?" McCann asked.

"I was just thinking about the times I came out to the farm and talked to you about God's plan and here you are reminding me. We've come a long way, haven't we? More importantly, you have come a long way."

"Yes, thank God."

"I guess I lost my focus there for a while. You know what they say, focus on the giant and you fall, focus on God and the giant falls. I just felt so certain that it was meant to happen. It would have meant so much to Farnsworth to have James' organization here. It would have meant so much to our own ministry to have a facility to offer more to the community."

McCann sat back in his chair. "Let's give God some time to work out what He has in store for us. Will you be going to the funeral services?"

"Yes, I'll leave on Tuesday and be back Thursday evening. I should know more then. I have a meeting scheduled with people from the ministry while I'm there."

"It looks like next week will be a 'big week' for a lot of people," McCann said. I presume Belle and Doug have spoken with you about some things that are happening at the Telephone Company?"

"Yes, I don't fully understand all of it but I know it involves a significant organizational change and expansion of their company."

"Some industry people are flying in on Tuesday for a meeting and it could have a significant impact on their futures," McCann replied.

"I'll remember to pray for them…and for you …for guidance."

"Okay. Let's pray together and then I'd like to have some of Dorothy's coffee before Sally and I leave. I need to get back home and take care of the cattle. This storm is getting worse by the minute."

"I was so pleased to see her in church this morning. I believe that underneath that worldly exterior she likes to project, there is a good person and one that God loves and can use."

McCann looked at the minister and didn't see the unasked question about any relationship. "She is a good person. She is trying to find her way just like I was." From the living room, McCann had heard Sally and Dorothy laughing and talking together in low tones like a couple of school girls. He liked to hear Sally laugh like that. The laughter didn't have the hard edge that it usually did.

"Perhaps we can help her find it," Hastings said quietly, as he bowed his head. The two men prayed briefly together and went into the kitchen where Dorothy and Sally were just finishing their coffee. A plate of chocolate chip cookies was on the table between them.

"That was a good sermon this morning, Reverend," Sally said, looking up at him.

"Call me Chuck. I'm glad you could come. I hope you will come again. Wils and I need all the support we can get, don't we Wils?"

"We all do," McCann smiled as Dorothy poured him a cup of steaming black coffee. He picked up a cookie and began to eat it.

They could see the snow falling heavily outside and while he was hesitant to lose the moment, McCann knew he needed to get home and look after Wink and the cattle. He was also concerned about Sally getting out to and back from the farm. After hastily drinking his coffee and burning his tongue in the process, they said their good nights and left.

The trip to the farm was quiet with each of them lost in their thoughts. Sally was reviewing the events of the day and reflecting on the fact that she hadn't had a day like it in all her life. McCann was thinking about the meeting with the Governor and what it meant for the future of Farnsworth Tele and what the impact of James Jacobs' death would have on Charles Hastings' hopes for an expanded ministry. He thought about the upcoming meeting with the LEGENT people and what the effects of all of these events would have on his own future.

Sally interrupted his thoughts, "What did you think of Dorothy's coffee?"

McCann thought it a strange question and gave her a quizzical look. "I don't know...it was okay I guess. Why?"

"Do you like my coffee at the diner?"

He sensed there was something deeper in her questions. But he couldn't figure out what it was. Then, as she slowed for the turn into the farm, a realization began to dawn on him.

Sally pulled into the drive, circled in front of the tool shed and headed the Mustang back toward the road before stopping.

"Thanks, Wils. For today and for…being a friend." She leaned across the console and gave him a quick peck on the cheek. She wanted it to be more than it was but knew it would have to be enough.

"I'll always be there for you, Sally. No matter what," he said. "By the way, I forgot to tell you how great you look in that outfit, and I'll never forget the day I went to church in a red Mustang!"

Impulsively, he reached across the console and put his arm around her shoulders and pulled her toward him. He kissed her on the cheek and quickly turned back and opened the door and got out.

"I'll be in for coffee next week! Then I'll tell you if it's as good as Dorothy's," he said, as he slammed the door shut. The smile on Sally's face told him that his hunch had been correct. She had wanted something to take from the day into the coming week.

She drove out into the steadily falling snow. The Mustang's rear wheels swerved as she turned into the road and gunned the engine. She easily corrected it and drove slowly until she was a mile or more from the farm. Then, she pulled over to the shoulder of the road and began to cry.

The tears she was shedding were not tears of sorrow. Sally McHugh couldn't remember a day like this in her whole life. The tears that flowed so freely down through her make-up were tears of sheer joy. She thought about the four women she had been with today. Belle Warner had treated her as an equal. Lona Marks had treated her like a sister. Martha Willard had treated her as a daughter and Dorothy Hastings had treated her as a friend. Sally didn't have many girl friends in Farnsworth. Dorothy had asked her to come again and said she would stop in the diner for coffee sometime next week. It would be the first time. Sally resolved to do everything she could to make sure it wouldn't be the last time she and the preacher's wife got together.

For one day, Sally had truly felt like the person she knew she could be. It wasn't Christmas yet, but she vowed that this year she would keep all three of her resolutions. Wiping the tears away, she drove on into the steadily falling snow.

Later that evening as he worked in the barn feeding the cattle, McCann was thinking about four women also. He would never be able to replace the empty spot that Donna's life had left in his life. He thought of her and wished that he could go back in time and change things. He thought of his mother and the sacrifices she had made on his behalf. He thought of Cindy Melzy and wondered what her future would be now that she, like himself, had changed the focus of her life. Lastly, he thought about Sally. He liked Sally. He had meant what he said as he got out of the car. He would always be there for Sally. It wouldn't be what he knew she wanted but it was all he could give, friendship. He prayed that Sally would find that same sense of direction for her life that had guided Donna and his mother and was now guiding Cindy.

He thought about the upcoming week. He still had some reservations in the back of his mind about the wisdom of the LEGENT acquisition. He knew that the future of wire-line telephony was going to be significantly impacted by the change from a regulated service to an unregulated commodity. The changes in the way that revenues were shared within the industry and the impact of technology would all create extraordinary pressures on companies like Farnsworth Tele. While the rural markets that Farnsworth served would be the last to feel all of the impacts, it would come eventually. Farnsworth Tele had done the right things up to now by investing in the modernization of its networks and in expanding into Cable Television, DSL and other unregulated business ventures. His careful review of their financials had shown him that they were profitable in all aspects of their business even though the margins on the unregulated side were small.

He had projected, as best he could, the impacts of the acquisition and felt that there was a good chance that Farnsworth Tele could continue to be successful in the near term. It was the unknown that bothered McCann. The Governor, he was sure, was doing his best to share as much as he could with them about what might be underway in the north country. He did not doubt for a moment the Governor's interest in seeing a Michigan-based company in charge of the service to an area that was critical to his plan for economic growth in that portion of the state. He felt they could trust the Governor to do everything within the scope of propriety to be of help.

He was convinced that the large equipment and systems suppliers were involved in whatever project the Governor had in mind. Perhaps Stu could dig up something additional. Without pride, McCann knew that his contacts within that portion of the industry were probably better than Doug Warner's. McCann had spent large sums of money with those companies while he as at Dynacom and that had led to relationships at the higher echelons of most of them.

But, the fact was that they still did not know enough to accurately forecast what it all might mean. That was a cause for concern, as the clock moved toward the meeting with LEGENT in the person of John King, on Tuesday. He knew that John was a straight shooter who would not try to gain unfair advantage. That same fairness would demand that John do as much as he could to protect the shareholders of the company that employed him. Could they work within that window of fairness to achieve an agreement that would not put Farnsworth Tele in jeopardy?

The cattle crowded into the run pens to escape the snow and falling temperatures. The warmth of twenty animals began to reduce the chill of the unheated barn. He sat down on a stool in the feed alley and watched them. Wink lay down at his feet and rested her head on the toe of his boot. A great feeling of contentment welled up within him. The routine tasks of caring for animals and for the farm itself were now a part of his life that he didn't want to lose. He had to work diligently to keep from allowing himself to be caught up in the excitement of the acquisition. He knew that he could easily lose the focus he had so recently gained. He thought of the four men who had been such an influence in his life during the past few months. Jim Marks with his servant attitude and open, enthusiastic friendship, Phil Willard with his faithful fatherly perseverance, Doug Warner with his knowledge of the business and the strength of character that he brought to the pursuit of providing excellent service to his company's customers, Charles Hastings with his knowledge of God's word and how to apply it to daily living. He needed to be near these types of men. Just as he had formerly modeled his past behavior on those who had mentored him within Dynacom, he needed to take from men such as these the traits that made them worthy mentors for his future.

He sat there in the dimly lit feed alley with Wink at his feet. The minutes stretched into an hour and when he roused himself from his thoughts, he shivered as the increasing cold penetrated the sheepskin denim jumper that Donna Barnes had given him. He wished that he could take her in his arms again and feel her warmth surround him and he felt the pain of loss. He scratched Wink's ears, rose and walked from the barn to the house. Wink, her head down against the snow, trotted along beside him.

While McCann had been sitting in his cold barn thinking, Cindy Melzy was curled up on the couch in front of the gas log fireplace in her apartment. David had gone to bed early after pizza and a chapter from "*Bob, Son of Battle.*" His sadness over learning that Ted was dead had been replaced by an excitement about McCann's new dog. He had been badgering her to call McCann and ask him to send a picture of Wink over the Internet. She had only been able to stave off a phone call by telling him that she didn't think Mr. McCann had a digital camera.

She had changed into her pajamas and robe and made herself a cup of Chamomile tea. She eyed the briefcase on the coffee table and the television in the corner and decided to just sit for a while and watch the fire.

McCann had called her last week to see who would be representing the New York investors. Her assistant had taken the call and checked with Cindy. Cindy, for some reason she couldn't explain, had resisted the urge to call him back and had checked with Feldman's offices. They assured her that they were comfortable with her representing both firms on Tuesday in Farnsworth. She had a flight scheduled out tomorrow into Detroit where she would link up with Boyington and Smith. Together, the three would drive to Farnsworth.

While she was excited about the opportunity to see the potential acquisition move forward, she was also apprehensive on the personal front.

Malcolm Shaw's conversation had unsettled her. She was reluctant to face both McCann and Doug Warner with her future intentions suddenly in question.

She weighed the two paths that were open to her. Obviously, Malcolm had sent a clear message that she could count on being considered for Managing Partner at Triad within the next five years. He had also implied that her new found faith would not be an issue in that opportunity. The financial rewards associated with that path were significant and Cindy felt she could make a difference within the business community that she came in contact with. She had many friends and a lifestyle that was built around the city and she would be able to keep that in place.

She knew that the life in Farnsworth would be far different. The work at Farnsworth Tele would soon lose its challenge. The pace of the small community would be different than in the city. She had made good friends there and she knew that she could concentrate on her personal life and David. The need to work at balancing work life and personal life would be less there than in the city. David would love the farm and the opportunities it would open up for him. She wasn't as sure about herself. She was used to having things done for her. She supposed she could hire people to do things there for her as well.

Money was not an issue either way. Cindy had invested wisely and the divorce had not put any drain on her financially. She could live on far less than she was living on now in the city and still be putting money away for the future. David's future was secured.

Her thoughts turned to McCann. She liked and respected him. She was sure that he respected her as well. Their common backgrounds within the business world and their new found faith had drawn them together and with increased contact might draw them even closer. She had not given any thought to falling in love until she had seen him with David on the farm. The evening they had shared together at the farm house had sparked a flame that had been held in check ever since her divorce.

She knew that McCann felt that he had missed the one great love of his life when Donna Barnes had died. She wondered what kind of a woman Donna had been. From things Belle, McCann himself, and others had said, she must have been exceptional. Was it possible that, in time, she could re-place her in McCann's life? Did she want to try? If she went to Farnsworth with that as one of her objectives, she was sure that she would not be able to recover if she failed.

She had been studying a series on great women of the Bible. She was in-trigued by the stories of Sarah, Deborah, and Rahab. Recently she had been reading the book of Esther. She picked up her Bible from the coffee table and began to re-read the 4th chapter. As she came to the 14th verse, the words seemed to jump from the page....

And who knows whether you have not attained royalty for such a time as this?

She closed the Bible and sat quietly praying. Tomorrow she would go to Michigan and take a step down a path that would ultimately shape her future.

The Governor's plane ride from Huron County Memorial Airport near Bad Axe back to Lansing had been a rough one. The storm made flying at the altitudes suitable for his small plane choppy at best and downright bouncy at the worst. Ross was agitated not so much by the flight as by what he had heard at the Medical Center.

"McCann is getting dangerously close to learning what our little proj-ect is all about. I think we have to have an emergency plan ready in case we need to get out ahead of any leaks," he said, as the plane hit a relatively calm stretch of air.

The Governor took a sip from another bottle of water and looked out the window at the blank wall of dark gray that they were flying through.

"Do you think he would leak?"

Ross considered the question as the plane hit another bump. "No. He is a shareholder in Farnsworth Tele and he has an obligation to tell the Warners to put their interests first. There are people who would like to get hold of that information and use it to try to hurt you and what you are trying to accom-plish. Not everyone will think of it in the same terms of it being good for the state that you do. Our friends in Detroit will be only too happy to say that the effort, and the money, should have been applied downstate. They will accuse you of trying to take care of the 'home folks' before you leave office."

The Governor smiled. "In a way that's just what I'm trying to do. We've poured a lot of money into the southern portion of the state with modest success. I'll take modest success in this venture if I can get it. Do you think I said too much today?"

"I think Mrs. Warner and Mr. McCann will think you didn't say as much as they would have liked to have heard."

"Then I did the job of a good politician. I told them a little and left them wanting more. Tomorrow, I want you to convene a conference call between our friends in the industry, our academic friends and the development group and get a sense of just how close we are to an announcement. Perhaps we should give them a deadline."

Ross nodded. "What sort of a deadline do you have in mind?"

"If Farnsworth Tele and LEGENT reach an agreement on a sale, when do you think a joint petition would be heard by the Public Service Commission?"

"With a little prodding from our office, by the end of the first quarter, if they file in early January. We can't wait that long."

The Governor sighed and automatically grabbed his seat arm as the plane bounced heavily. "We'll announce by mid-January. That's the deadline. It will be up to Mr. McCann and the Warners to get their petition filed before then if they reach an agreement."

"LEGENT may pull the rug on the deal if they learn about what we have planned. It might change their attitude about leaving the state if they thought there was something in it for them."

"We'll have to trust Mr. McCann to protect Farnsworth Tele from that happening. Do you think LEGENT could find out what we plan to do?"

Ross smiled. "If they worked at it like Wilson McCann, they could. I don't think they will be quite as diligent as he will be. Their focus is elsewhere."

"Good, let's hope it stays that way. I won't miss them when they leave."

"I'm surprised at you! They donated heavily to your last campaign," Ross said, enjoying the opportunity to poke at his long time friend and mentor.

"Money well spent. But it wasn't matched by an equal investment in the state or the state's people. Both deserve better. I think the Warners and Wilson McCann will be far more 'diligent' as you put it, in doing that. Let's continue to do all we can, within propriety to assure that they get the chance to do it."

The plane started down, bounced twice more and then settled into a long glide into Lansing's Capitol City Airport.

Charles Hastings sat on the edge of the queen bed on the second floor of the parsonage. He could hear Dorothy brushing her teeth in the adjacent bathroom. He removed his slippers and began to pull off his socks. Then, in response to the burdens he felt, he placed both feet on the floor and bowed his face into his hands, his elbows digging into his thighs. Dorothy opened the door to the bedroom and stood there watching. The moment passed and he raised his head to look at her. She moved to him and took his head in her hands. Looking down at him, she smiled.

"God will provide. He always has. He always will. I remember someone saying that to me many years ago."

He smiled back at her. He had said it to her when the two of them were expecting their first child while pastoring a pair of little churches in the Kentucky hill country. Charles had been attending Asbury Theological Seminary and trying to be a good husband and a good shepherd to his little flocks. The two churches paid almost enough to cover their living expenses. There was nothing in the steel box under the bed in their cramped little country parsonage, where they kept any extra money that came their way. At most, they had never exceeded $150 in that box at one time. She had broken down and cried when he came home late one night from sitting with a family who had lost a loved one. The burden of her pregnancy, and the uncertainty of each week's survival had finally gotten to her usually optimistic personality. He had knelt before her and said the words that had remained their slogan through all of the following years. God had provided. He always had. And somewhere down deep in their souls, they both knew he always would. Yet, there were times, like tonight, when a faith tried and tested, wavered.

"I had hoped it would be the beginning of a chance to….," he began.

"I know," she said. You're going down to Jim's funeral on Thursday and staying for the Board meeting on Friday?"

"Yes. I'll fly back on Saturday. It will be a busy week."

He waited while she sat down beside him and slipped her arm in his. "Is Mr. McCann going with you?"

"I didn't ask him."

"Ask him, Charles…talk to him. I have a feeling about that man."

He smiled at her. When Dorothy had "a feeling" about someone, she was rarely wrong. Her ability to sense certain things in people had been of great benefit to his ministry over the years.

"He's a new Christian."

"But he is long on experience. God will use him."

Hastings bent and began to remove his socks. Then, the emotion hit him. It was a different emotion than the one that had possessed him before Dorothy came into the room. Impulsively, he wrapped his arms around her and squeezed her tightly to him.

"Thank you for being you," he said into her rich red hair, and looking up toward the bedroom ceiling, he said, "…and thank You for giving her to me."

(31)

McCann emerged from the house at 6:00 a.m. to find a world encased in snow. The trees drooped with it. The power line to the barn from the house sagged under a coating. The barn's roof was white and only the hipped aluminum roof of the tool shed was bare. The snow around the shed was at least three foot deep with what had slid down. On the level, the snow was over the tops of his Pac-boots. Wink waited behind him until he stepped off into it. As the two of them moved off to the barn, she made no effort to bound away as she usually did in the early morning before the pain of a new day slowed her down. Instead, she followed, plowing through the snow in his boot prints.

He cared for the cattle and trudged through the snow to the tool shed. Luckily, the big doors slid back into the snow far enough that he could get the tractor out and clear the drive and turn-around, as well as an area in front of the shed. By 7:30 a.m., he was chilled to the bone and ready for his second cup of coffee. Wink had waited inside the shed as he plowed the snow and moved out behind him as they headed back to the house. Using a snow shovel from the shed, he cleared a pathway up to the steps and scraped them clear. Once the two of them were in the kitchen, he took a towel and used it to wipe the snow from Wink. She checked out her food and water bowls, took a long drink of water and headed for the heat vent. She stretched out, and it wasn't long before the kitchen held the smell of wet fur.

He poured the coffee from the pot he had started earlier and sat down to read his morning devotional. Thirty minutes later he looked out the window as the county snowplow came up the road. Soon, his driveway entrance had over a foot of plowed snow in it. He looked out over the fields as the roar of the plow faded into the distance. It was clear that this snowfall wasn't going away soon. He wondered if it would impact those coming to Michigan from Texas and New York. Just as he was about to turn on the television to get the latest news and weather, the phone rang. It was Charles Hastings. The minister seemed more buoyant and asked McCann to go with him to Jacobs' funeral. McCann hesitated, mindful of the activities that this week's visits to Farnsworth Tele could possibly result in, but agreed to fly out with Hastings on Thursday. He would need to get Nick to care for things while he was away. Hastings volunteered to make McCann's airline reservation with a return on Saturday.

He called for Nick, but Darcy answered. He could hear the baby crying in the background. She said that Nick would come out Thursday, Friday and Saturday to take care of the cattle and on Sunday also if McCann was delayed. He put the phone down and said a silent prayer of thanksgiving for the young couple. At times, he wondered if he should just sell the cattle and even consider selling the farm, but they seemed to be an important part of his new life. He knew that to do so would be to give in to the urgency pressures of old drives and old goals that were not as important to him now.

The radio weatherman from Caro said that the main roads were "in good condition," and that the county and secondary roads were "snow packed and slippery." All airports were open but there were numerous flight delays in and out of Detroit. He called the county airport and was told that the runway would be cleared and ready for flights by noon. Barring additional snowfall, King's jet should be able to fly in tomorrow with no trouble. Cindy, Boyington and Smith were to drive up from Detroit this afternoon. Cindy would be staying with Belle at the mansion and Boyington and Smith, who apparently had college ties to Doug, would be staying with him. If the meeting ran long tomorrow, King and his associates would have to be provided for. McCann had no concerns about asking the LEGENT Vice President to stay at the farm, but his associates might be another matter. The lack of a decent motel in Farnsworth was an obstacle. They would just have to work something out.

The house felt warm and snug against the cold and the white landscape outside. He considered whether he should go in to his office at Farnsworth Tele and decided against it. There was nothing further he could do to prepare for tomorrow. He called Stu Bailey in New York and brought him up to date on the status of things. Bailey was working on another deal and, while appreciative of McCann's call, was obviously preoccupied. McCann hung up the phone with a sense of disquiet over the fact that his long time friend wouldn't be in Farnsworth tomorrow when they worked out the details of any possible acquisition. He fully realized, however, that Bailey's interest had been primarily in the acquisition of all the LEGENT properties. With only the Michigan portion involved, it was up to McCann, Cindy, and Smith to handle the financial aspects of the smaller acquisition.

He ate his lunch, surfed the Internet for a while, and caught up on the latest world and business news. He went out and cared for the cattle around 2:00 p.m. and shoveled out the end of his drive. He could have cleared it with the tractor in about two minutes but it took twenty to do it by hand. When he finished he was sweating under his winter coat but felt refreshed from the manual labor and the cold, crisp air.

Back inside, he sat in his recliner and took a nap. Wink padded into the living room and sank down between the chair and another heating vent. She looked up at her sleeping master and waited for him to notice her. When he didn't, she stretched out full length and joined him in slumber.

As the gray daylight began to fade into evening, they both were awakened by the sound of a vehicle pulling into the driveway. McCann got to his feet and made it into the kitchen before he heard a knocking on the back door. He opened it to see Doug's Yukon in the drive and Cindy standing on the steps.

"Surprise! Can I come in?"

"Absolutely! When did you get in?" He stood aside as she entered. She was wearing a long hooded cloth coat over a sweater and blue jeans. Her sneakers had snow on them and she took them off as she entered the kitchen.

"I was late getting into Detroit because of the weather and the delays. The airport was a zoo! Arthur met me and we went to Smitty's office and had a working lunch. Then we hit the road. Arthur is at Belle's for the night and Smitty is at Doug's. Doug insisted that I drive his Yukon instead of Art's car to see you. He said I'd be safer."

Wink had retreated to the doorway into the living room and sat watching as McCann helped Cindy out of her coat and hung it up. Cindy turned and dropped to her knees holding out her hands to the dog. Wink slowly rose and took two tentative steps toward her. Cindy curled the fingers on her right hand and the dog drew near enough to sniff before allowing herself to be petted.

"She's beautiful! I have to take a picture for David before I leave. He has been begging me to call you and ask for one. He still reads about 'Bob' every night!"

She stood and then sat down in one of the kitchen chairs. "Can a girl get a cup of coffee out here in the country?"

He busied himself emptying the pot and refilling it with coffee and water and put it on to perk. Wink came and stood beside him, positioning herself between them. Cindy smiled at her. "I don't think she wants another female in her farmhouse."

"She is much more attached than I thought she would be at her age and much more so than Ted was. He was his own dog. She seems to have adopted me."

"Do you think she would mind if I stayed the night? I have my bags outside."

McCann turned away to reach into the cupboard for coffee mugs. She had caught him off guard and his thoughts raced as to how to respond. She anticipated his reaction and spoke again before he could reply.

"The spare bedroom, Wils…where David stayed when he was here. I need to talk with you about some things and I'm not at all worried about what others might think. Are you?"

He turned to face her and saw the frank open expression on her face and the need in her eyes.

"Not at all."

The room began to fill with the aroma of the percolating coffee and they sat at the table and talked about her meeting with Boyington and Smith and Detroit and tomorrow's meeting with John King and his associates. He told her about the meeting with the Governor and they agreed that while they knew little more than previously, it was evident that something was afoot that would drive the need for capital. He didn't tell her about his meeting with James Jacobs and she didn't tell him about her meeting with Malcolm. She would get into that later in the evening.

Dusk turned to darkness. McCann got some frozen hamburger patties from the refrigerator and unwrapped them. He peeled and quartered a couple of potatoes and opened a can of peas and poured them into a pan.

"Unexpected company gets the deluxe dinner!" he smiled at her. "Now, it's time to feed the cows!"

"Actually, Wils, they are steers. Even I know that!" She joked, as she put on her sneakers and reached for her coat.

"Better leave that here. Take this one instead." He handed her the lined denim jacket that Donna had bought for him. "You won't need mittens!" He smiled as the sleeves hung about three inches below her hands.

"Watch where you walk, lady! I don't need a mixture of snow and steer dung on my kitchen floor!" he said over his shoulder, as he led her toward the barn. Wink went around her and positioned herself between them as they walked down the path he had cleared earlier in the day.

She helped him get bales of hay down from the mow and then sat on the stool where he had sat last evening and watched him as he went about his chores.

"Who is Sally McHugh?" she asked it as he finished up.

"She runs the diner in town," he replied, waiting on the next question.

"And she was with you the night Ted was killed?"

He smiled, "And at church yesterday morning and with me when we saw the Governor."

"And…is she someone 'special'?"

"She is a very good friend. Let's go fry those burgers."

Cindy thought about his response as they walked back to the house. She was tempted to ask if Sally was as good a friend as Donna had been to him, but that would take them somewhere that she didn't want to go this evening. Instead, she stepped past Wink and slipped her arm through his. Wink was forced to tag behind or go into the deeper snow along the path. She chose to walk behind, but her nose was inches from him as they walked. Cindy retrieved her bags from the Yukon and brought them into the house and took them to the spare bedroom.

They prepared their dinner standing side by side at the kitchen counter. He thawed the hamburger patties and she put the potatoes and peas on to boil. He started another pot of coffee and she set the table. Wink chose to lie at the entrance to the living room and keep an eye on them instead of going off to her closet. As they worked, they talked of their mutual friends and their new-found faith. He sensed that the heavier conversation would come later and didn't try to push it by asking questions that would force her to talk now. They ate their meal and took their coffee into the living room. He sat in the recliner and she sat on the couch, her feet tucked up under her. He thought of Donna sitting there in the last days of summer and wished with all his heart that he could go back to that night.

"Wils?"

He looked down at Wink, lying beside the chair and brought himself back to the present. "Sorry, just thinking."

She took a sip from her mug and looked at him over the rim. For a moment, he had been gone away. She wondered where. She thought she knew. Self consciously, she put her feet down on the floor and sat the mug on the end table beside the couch.

"I had a talk with my boss the other day and it started me thinking. I need someone to talk to and you're it."

He thought of Sally and their early morning conversation the previous week. He smiled at her. "Sounds serious. Does this have anything to do with Doug's offer and your intentions to buy a farm here in Farnsworth?"

"Yes it does. I'm having some second thoughts."

She told him about her conversation with Malcolm and how conflicted she felt between what he had held out to her and what she had been planning to do. "What do you think?" she asked, when she had finished.

"What do you want to do?"

"I want to be a witness to what God has done in my life. I want to have a better work/life balance and I want to be a good mother to David. Beyond that, I would like to enjoy my work."

He reclined the chair and put his feet up. Wink raised her head and then went back to sleep. He took a slow drink from his coffee before he spoke.

"You can be a witness wherever you are and whatever you are doing. Can you achieve the work/life balance you want in New York City?"

"I think I can if I keep my mind centered on what God would have me do."

"Can you be a good mother to David in New York City?"

"Same answer."

"Which would you enjoy most, being the CEO of a well respected venture capital firm in New York City or being VP Finance of a small rural telecommunications company in a small town?"

"Before I answer that, counselor, tell me which you would enjoy most, being CEO of a major telecommunications firm in Chicago or living on a hundred acre farm with a dog and twenty steers?"

"Right here, right now, knowing what I know...I'll take the hundred acres and the twenty steers."

She rose and went to the living room window. The moon was rising high in the sky. The front yard and the road, banked on each side with plowed snow, were bathed in its light. She stood for a while looking out. He waited until she turned to look at him. "Now it's your turn."

"I don't really know. It's so hard to know what God's plan for my life is. I thought I knew but now I'm not as sure."

He rose and headed for the kitchen. "Come on. Let's go for a ride."

He began pulling on his coat and held hers out to her. She took it with a puzzled look and sat her coffee mug on the kitchen table. When she had finished putting her coat on, he led the way out into the cold moonlit night.

"Keys please – I'll drive."

She handed over the keys to the Yukon and climbed into the passenger seat as he got in on the driver's side. He started the big SUV up and headed out onto the road.

They drove through Farnsworth and headed out south of the town. Three miles out, he turned onto a well plowed side road and drove for two miles. He turned left onto a narrow road that had been plowed to the width of about one and a half vehicles, one if it were the size of the Yukon. She knew where she was immediately.

"How did you know?" she asked, a smile beginning to creep across her face.

"Don't forget, I'm practically a local now. I have friends in high places, bankers, real estate salesmen, you name it. When you threaten to shoot someone, you become famous," he smiled at her as they came into view of the farm sitting well back from the road. A single lane had been plowed back to the farm house. He turned into the lane, hoping that there was a place to turn around at the end.

He turned the vehicle toward the house at the end of the lane and parked. He turned the lights off and then the engine. They sat there in the moonlight, looking at the old two-story house that seemed to rise up like some ghostly specter against the sky. To her right, the barn squatted below the rise of the ridge upon which the house sat, as if bowing to it. The cold night air began to creep into the Yukon. She pulled her coat more tightly about her. He leaned back in his seat and put his right arm across the back of her shoulders.

"The farm across the road is owned by a couple that work somewhere south of here. They don't have any children. The farm just to the north is abandoned. The owners died years ago and the family only comes up once a year. The farm beyond that is a rental. The family that rents has four or five kids and lives mostly on relief, food stamps and that sort of thing. The farm around the corner is owned by an older couple. They plan to keep it but may have to move to town because of their advancing age. South of here, at the corner, is the old one-room school house. It's pretty much falling in on itself."

She turned in her seat to face him. "You've done quite a bit of homework on the area."

"My friends have lived here a lot longer than I have. I just thought you might like to know a little about the neighborhood you're thinking of moving into. It isn't Broadway and 42nd street."

A little smile formed on her lips as she looked out through the passenger side window at the barn and the cold, barren landscape behind it that stretched back to the dark woods at the back of the property.

She pulled her coat more tightly about her, opened the door and got out. She walked up the slight rise and stood in front of the house, looking at it. He watched from the Yukon as she turned to look back and bowed her head. He bowed his as well and when he looked up again, she was starting back to the SUV.

She opened the door and climbed in. "Thank you," was all she said.

They drove back to Farnsworth, the Yukon's heater bringing warmth back to them. He came into town and turned left at the light. He drove two blocks west and made a U-turn at the corner in front of Phil's Agway. He drove back through the light and two more blocks before making another U-turn and heading back to the light. He turned right and headed back to his farm. In all, they had seen five cars parked on Main Street. Three had been in front of the tavern.

She smiled at him. "It's not 5th Avenue, either."

He smiled back, "Or even 3rd."

"It's not Chicago, either."

"No, it's not. But I don't miss Chicago. Chicago was never 'home' to me."

"Is this home?"

"It's more of a home than I thought it would be. It may become a home I can't leave."

"You could go anywhere you wanted, be anything you wanted to be." She watched his face as she said it. In the dim light of the SUV, it seemed to her that a fleeting sadness flashed across his face.

"My motivation isn't the same anymore. I want to spend the rest of my life giving back for what I have been given and took for granted. I want to count for something besides the ability to 'do deals' and bring more to the bottom line."

Her tone became light as she looked at his face, reflected in the dim light from the dash. "And you take me out into the country on one of the coldest, snowiest evenings of the year to help me see that my future may not be here but in New York City 'doing deals' and making money!"

"Is that what I helped you to see?"

"No. You helped me to reaffirm what I already knew. I have to think about two very important things in my life. I have to consider where I can witness to my faith with the most impact and I have to consider David and what is best for him. I don't think my future lies here in Farnsworth. But I still love that farm."

"Then buy it. Use it as a 'get away'. Some people go to the ocean, some go to the mountains, and some go to a special place where they can rest, relax and recharge. Perhaps this is where you could do that. David would love it and Wink and I could visit."

They pulled into the driveway as he said it. He drove the Yukon around the circle and parked it heading out. She put her hand on his arm. "Would you visit?"

"You couldn't keep me away," he smiled at her.

"And will you farm it for me, Mr. Green Jeans?" she said lightheartedly, as she got out. The moon was riding high in the sky and the red outbuildings reflected the light.

"I've got my hands full right here, but we can find someone who will," he said, as she circled the Yukon and came to stand beside him. They stood together looking out over the snow-clad fields. A semi growled down the highway in the distance.

"You are a very special friend, Wils," she said, looking up at him.

Afterwards, he reflected that it was pretty much what he had said to Sally.

The Hawker 400XP climbed into its flight path out of DFW with three seats occupied and four to spare. King and Piazza sat opposite each other and the attorney sat one row back, engrossed in a file of papers that King had given her upon arrival at the airport. He hadn't wanted an attorney along. In his view, attorneys complicated things. He had considered objecting but thought better of it. He wanted to get this done with no snags. The attorney could, if handled properly, be an asset. She was new to LEGENT and seemed very bright. She was about twenty-eight and not unattractive. What he would give to be twenty-eight again! Piazza had given her the eye. No harm there. King had met Piazza's wife. She was a dark haired Italian who didn't mind letting you know that she didn't buy all the LEGENT party line and that she would fight like a wildcat to protect her family, and her man.

"Where did you meet her?" he asked.

Piazza looked up from his laptop, "Who?"

"Marie."

Piazza looked puzzled. Even after working with King for many years, he still had trouble with these thoughts of his that seemed to come from nowhere. Then, he glanced at the young attorney and immediately surmised where his boss was coming from.

"In grade school at St. Mary's."

King smiled. "You met your wife in grade school? What grade?"

"First, she lived five doors down from me."

"Did you ever date anyone else?"

"Nope. Marie and I started going steady in High School."

King thought this over for a minute. "What instrument did she play?"

"The tuba, how'd you know she played an instrument?"

King smiled as he reclined his seat back. The Hawker leveled out and he could feel the increase in airspeed. He knew the pilot and had flown with him many times. They would soon be clocking five hundred miles an hour. The return flight might be his last for LEGENT, no matter what happened in Farnsworth.

"It figures," he said as he closed his eyes. In a few minutes, he dozed off. Piazza looked out the window and then back at the man in the opposite seat. God, he was going to miss him!

McCann was up early and out in the barn. They had played a game of Cribbage before turning in last night. She had used the bathroom to get ready for bed and then called "all clear" through the closed door of the guest bedroom. He normally slept with the bedroom door open but last night he had closed it.

He came in from the barn to find her frying eggs and bacon on the stove. She was already dressed in a dark skirt and white blouse. She had put on one of Ella Harms' old aprons and she still had a pair of fuzzy blue bed slippers on.

"You need to work on your Martha Stewart image," he said, taking off his barn coat and hanging it on a hook near the door.

"Don't rush me. These things take time and if I smell like bacon in the meeting today, it's all your fault."

"Hey, us farm folks have to work for our bacon. You could smell worse than that!"

"And you do," she said with a smile, as he passed her on his way to the bathroom.

"Ah, but I'm not in my working duds yet!" he called back as he shut the door.

The bathroom was just as it usually was. The only difference was the smell of her perfume and the lingering humidity from her shower. It felt strange to share such intimacy and his thoughts flashed back again to Donna Barnes.

He showered, shaved and was just putting on his slacks and shirt when she called from the kitchen in a Granny Clampett voice.

"You'd better hustle, Clem, the vittles is a-gittin' cold!"

He smiled as he slid into wing tips. "I'm a comin' Granny!"

She had taken off the apron and was half way through with her breakfast when he sat down opposite her and began to eat.

"What's the drill for today?" she asked, looking at him over the top of her coffee cup.

"Doug and I will pick John King and the others up at MBS International and bring them to Farnsworth. We've set the meeting for 1:00 p.m. John is staying the night here and his assistant is staying with Doug's family. I understand they are bringing an attorney with them and she is going back to Detroit with Smith and Boyington. If we reach an agreement, she will work with Art tomorrow to finalize it."

"I'm going back with them as well. What's your feel for the outcome?"

"I think John King wants to get this done. I'm not sure we'll get another chance if we can't reach agreement today. The issue for Farnsworth Tele is what happens after today if we reach agreement."

She insisted on setting up the spare bedroom for John King's arrival before they left. While she attended to it, he cleaned up the kitchen and washed the dishes. Once again the thought of what it would be like to share this place he now called home with someone else crossed his mind. She emerged from the bedroom with her bag and he smiled at the professional that she was.

"Where did 'Granny' go?

"Didn't you hear? They found oil and moved to New York City. She lives in an apartment with her son."

"That's a shame. We'll miss her out here in the country," he said, as he held her coat for her.

She turned into him and looked up into his eyes. "Would you?"

He sensed the meaning behind the question. "Last night and this morning were special, Cindy. I enjoyed having you here."

She turned away to pick up her bag. His answer had been quick and pleasant. But it wasn't the answer she had wanted. She sensed that the memory of Donna Barnes still occupied this place and that it would be a while before that memory would allow new memories to take full possession of it.

They walked to the Yukon and he drove into Farnsworth. He dropped Cindy off at the Warner mansion and went on to Doug's home and picked him up. Together, the two men left to meet the LEGENT plane.

The Hawker XP descended into MBS International Airport just after 10:00 a.m. By noon, they were in Farnsworth. After a round of introductions and the usual patter of talk about snow, remembrances from the industry and other light topics, they sat down to a luncheon of soup, salad and sandwiches topped off with hot coffee and soft drinks. When the luncheon had been cleared away, the discussions began in earnest. King led off with a review of the properties and LEGENT'S interest in disposing of them. Belle Warner responded with a restatement of Farnsworth Tele's sincere interest in making the acquisition and Arthur Boyington reviewed the legal approach that would govern the proposed acquisition. Cindy and Smith presented their financial commitments to the process.

The acquisition of the LEGENT properties, if it was to be accomplished, would be made by a shell company which had been named "Farnet." Once the acquisition had been approved by the appropriate governmental agencies, Farnsworth Telephone would seek approval to combine Farnsworth Telephone Cooperative and Farnet into a single surviving company.

As the afternoon moved along, various acquisition issues were raised and debated. These included valuations for pension funds, billing for transition services to be provided by LEGENT, cut off scheduling for various billing, payroll and investment projects, payment of legal and accounting costs associated with the petition to the PSC and other state and, if necessary, Federal agencies. The Farnsworth team had developed an Integration

Plan and reviewed it with the LEGENT team to confirm its practicability. Several minor changes were made and King made a note to formulate a similar team and plan on the LEGENT side. Each side named coordinators for this integration. As these discussions moved forward, each side kept a running estimation of costs associated with its part of the process.

McCann, from his seat at Belle Warner's right hand, observed quietly that these issues were dividing almost equally between those which resolved to Farnsworth's benefit and those which resolved to LEGENT'S benefit. The attorneys guided the discussion at critical points as to possible legal and regulatory issues and Cindy and Smith stated acceptance or lack of acceptance at appropriate times which helped to move the discussion along. McCann offered his thoughts freely at critical points in the discussion and took some satisfaction from the fact that his opinion seemed to be valued by both sides. Several modifications were made to the transition schedule in direct response to his advice. Belle Warner was especially thankful for his presence.

In the end, it came down, as all things of this nature do, to money. At 4:00 p.m., Belle called for a brief recess to caucus with her group and they moved to her office. The two LEGENT men and their attorney met in the conference room, and Cindy and Smith moved to other offices to make calls back to their offices in New York and Detroit. During the short meeting around her desk, Belle, Doug, Boyington and McCann reviewed the progress made and the impact that it had on their valuation estimates and transition plan. They all agreed that, depending on the final price, the acquisition still held promise.

They all returned to the conference room thirty minutes later. Fresh coffee, tea and chocolate chip cookies had been provided and they all helped themselves.

"These are excellent!" John King said, munching down on one of the cookies. He noted that Piazza had taken three.

"A friend of Wils' makes them," Belle Warner smiled, looking at McCann. She was amused by the puzzled expression on his face. "She operates the diner here in town."

McCann could feel the flush rising on his face as King turned to look at him. "Wils has many friends," the LEGENT man said. Cindy was watching McCann as well, a little smile playing across her face.

King finished off his cookie and took a swallow from his coffee. "It appears we have the framework for a possible transaction. What we lack is a number of a certain size to put in the appropriate places within that framework," he said, looking first at Belle and then at McCann.

Belle Warner leaned back in her chair and glanced first at Doug and then at McCann. "We have put that number at thirty five million dollars, John," she said.

A frown appeared on the face of the LEGENT attorney. Piazza looked down at the one remaining cookie before him and then out of the corner of his eye at King. King took another drink from his coffee and put the mug down. He leaned forward, his hands clasped in front of him.

"As I told Wils, I have masters that I serve. They will not be happy with your figure and I doubt that they will seriously consider it," he said, his eyes locked on Belle's.

"Have you a number in mind, John?" she held his gaze as she said it. Arthur Boyington scribbled something on a note pad in front of him and the sound of his pen was like a roll of thunder in the quiet of the room. McCann leaned back in his chair and thought of days gone by and similar situations when he had been one of the parties involved in stare downs similar to this one.

King did not move a muscle. With his hands still clasped in front of him he said quite firmly, "Forty Million."

Piazza cleared his throat and considered whether to pick up the one remaining cookie. He decided against it. The LEGENT attorney stared at King, a look of puzzlement on her face. Doug Warner looked at his mother. A slow smile spread across her face.

"Suppose we split the difference?" her tone was warm.

King picked up his coffee cup, inclined it toward her and slowly sipped from it. "I'll be happy to take that as a final offer back to my masters."

"…and?" Belle Warner said.

"…and I will recommend they accept it," King replied, smiling.

Piazza decided it was time to eat his final cookie. As he picked it up, the room erupted in conversation. The LEGENT attorney was tapping away on her laptop and Arthur Boyington, tapping on his cup with his pen to gain everyone's attention, rose and lifted his cup. "A toast to a successful petition by both firms before the Michigan Public Service Commission," he said, to a chorus of "Hear, Hear!"

Wilson McCann stood, smiling at his friends, both new and old. A great weight seemed to have lifted from his shoulders. At the same time, a great deal of uncertainty had replaced it.

In Dallas, a LEGENT attorney read the e-mail a second time and then clicked "forward." He entered his boss's and Norm Lister's e-mail address, typed in a terse "this just in from Michigan" message and clicked "send". The e-mail message had come from the young woman assigned to John King from his group. It simply read, "Tentative agreement reached at $2,700 per access line or $37,500,000."

The group discussed the milestone list moving forward from the tentative agreement and adjourned at 5:30 p.m. Cindy, Smith and Arthur Boyington were to leave for Detroit by car. The LEGENT attorney would accompany them. Boyington had been assigned the task of putting together the joint petition to the PSC with assistance from the young woman from Dallas.

Cindy and Smith stood in opposite corners of the room talking on their cell phones to Malcolm in New York and Smith's boss in Detroit. John King, Doug and Belle were busily engaged in conversation and McCann stood in front of a window looking out into the darkness.

Sal Piazza, holding his fifth cookie, came and stood beside him. "I'm very glad to have finally gotten to meet you, Mr. McCann. John speaks very highly of you and I know you've been of great assistance to Mrs. Warner and her family. She is a great lady."

McCann continued to stare out the window. "John tells me he is going to retire soon. You'll have a new boss?"

"I think probably I'll be reassigned. John has been putting in a good word for me with some other departments."

"What's your background?" McCann asked, looking up at him.

"Accounting and finance," Piazza replied.

"Farnet may be looking for a Chief Financial Officer," McCann said, looking at Cindy who was still talking into her cell phone.

Piazza took a bite of his cookie and smiled, "That would be very interesting. I've always been on the corporate side of things. The operating side might be fun."

"Is your family mobile?" McCann asked.

"Yes. I don't know how they would react to a small town like this though."

"Well, you'll have a chance to spend the evening with Doug. You might want to talk about it a little. It never hurts to talk."

McCann turned to move away and Piazza hastily wiped his hand on his trousers and stuck it out. "I'm glad to have met you."

McCann smiled. "Me too. I hope we'll get to see each other again. Good luck."

Later, at the farm, McCann did his chores while John King talked to Dallas from the house and gave his report on the results of the meeting. He checked his e-mail and typed out a brief summary of the agreement and sent it along to Dallas. He knew that his attorney had already filed her report prior to leaving for Detroit. He had asked to speak to Norm Lister, but was told that Lister was unavailable. He changed into some jeans and was just coming into the kitchen when McCann came in the back door.

"Got your cows tended to?" King asked as McCann took off his coat and hung it.

"Steers, John. Steers."

"I keep forgetting. Are we having beef tonight for dinner?"

"I'm thinking pancakes and bacon. How does that sound to you?" McCann smiled, as he washed his hands at the kitchen sink.

King collapsed into one of the kitchen chairs. He swiveled his head and shrugged the tension out of his shoulders. His sigh was audible. "Pancakes and bacon sounds great. I haven't had pancakes and bacon in weeks."
McCann leaned back against the cupboard and dried his hands on a towel. They hadn't discussed the agreement on their way out to the farm. Both

men had been engrossed in their own thoughts. It was as if both realized that a step had been taken into a future that neither could predict and that at least one of them would not be a part of.

"What do you think?" McCann asked.

King looked at him. McCann was dressed in a pair of jeans that were beginning to look the worse for wear, and a flannel shirt. The surroundings here in this old farm house were so out of character with what he had known of the man that King felt as though he were sitting in some sort of time warp.

"A reasonable deal for both sides," he responded. "And you?"

"I agree," McCann said, laying the towel on the counter. "Will it be approved in Dallas?"

"Hard to say. It depends on which way the wind blows at the moment. They probably will bicker about it but I think I can sell it. We'll just have to see. What about the State of Michigan? What's afoot with them?"

McCann paused before replying. "Equally hard to say. I'm guessing it's something that will drive a need for capital improvements in some of the North Country properties. We've tried to provide for it."

"Will the Warners be able to make it?" King asked.

"I hope so. They have a firm foundation and know how to run a tight ship. Doug's health is an issue. I'm hoping they can attract Jim Wolfe to take a role with the new company if everything moves forward. You know as well as I what wireless, broadband data and the Internet are going to do to the future of traditional telecommunications."

"...and you?"

McCann turned to the cupboard and began getting out the things he needed to make their dinner.

"I have a lot of things to think about, that's for sure," McCann replied, as he put a cast iron skillet on the stove.

"Do you miss it...being involved in the management of a company?" King asked, watching him intently.

"At times I do...very much. At other times, I feel like my future lies somewhere else. I feel like I have missed so much and have so much to make up for." As he said it, McCann paused and looked out the window into the darkness. King sensed that he was struggling with some inner emotion.

"Donna...the lady who died...she was special?"

McCann turned toward him. "I didn't realize how special she was until she was gone," he said, and King could see tears welling in his eyes. "That's the way it has been for me lately, I lost my mother, Donna, even my dog, before I realized how special they all were to me. That's what it took to wake me up to what was important in life. I have found a faith that was lacking before. I only wish I could have found it before I lost them."

King smiled. "We share that faith, brother. The important thing is how we build on it in the future. I would say you have found a good replacement for the dog." He looked at Wink, lying near the heat register. The dog was sound asleep. She had checked King out when he arrived and then ignored him from that point on. King had noted how she had followed McCann out to do his chores and returned with him when they were over. The country western song "*Constant Companion*" had ran through his mind at the time.

"Yes, she's a keeper. But she's a little like you....getting old!" McCann replied.

King laughed heartily and then asked his next question. "Cindy stayed here last night. She has found that same faith. Where does she fit in?"

McCann smiled. He looked at King and thought of him as he would have thought of a big brother if he had had one. "Cindy is searching to find her future as well. She is a very good friend, but I'm not sure I'm ready for anything beyond friendship at this point."

King smiled back at him. "And the lady with the diner in town?"

McCann paused in mixing the ingredients for the pancakes. "Sally is another good friend. She was here when my dog was shot. She and I go back a ways."

King was enjoying this. "You seem to have a lot of 'good friends' who happen to be female."

He watched as a bit of color flashed on McCann's face. "You could add Belle Warner to the list, too, along with Martha Willard, and Lona Marks and Lori Warner and Dorothy Hastings."

King pushed his chair back onto the back two legs and clasped his hands behind his head. "Now I know why you like living out here in the country."

McCann filled him in on who Martha, Lona, Lori and Dorothy were as he finished preparing the meal. As the two men ate, he talked openly and frankly about all of the opportunities that had come his way, including the situation with the church and the EECM board. King listened intently and asked several questions.

When the meal was over and they had washed the dishes, they took their coffee into the living room. King asked to see the information on EECM and McCann booted up his laptop and opened the files that Jacobs had given him. King began to review them and McCann watched in silence as the older man spent the next fifteen minutes paging through the information on the laptop. At times, King broke the silence with comments like "interesting" and "hmmm."

When he had finished, he set the laptop aside and picked up his coffee cup. The coffee was already cooled and he walked to the kitchen and poured it out, replacing it with more from the pot on the stove. He stood in the doorway and looked at McCann.

"Wils, I want to ask a favor of you."

"Name it," McCann replied, sensing the seriousness of King's tone.

"I want to be involved in this EECM situation. When do you leave for Weaverville?"

"Thursday. Charles Hastings and I are flying down to the Jacobs memorial service. I understand there is to be a Board meeting afterward."

King dropped his big frame onto the couch opposite McCann's chair. "Wils, go over that operation like you would if you were acquiring it. Do the 'due diligence.' Draw some conclusions and when you do, give me a call. Okay?"

"Okay," McCann replied, wondering what was going through King's mind. "But why?"

King leaned forward. "I'm on the boards of two different mission-oriented organizations. Trust me. I know something about how they operate. Let me show you something."

He retrieved the laptop and his fingers moved over the keys like a pianist playing a concerto. McCann stood behind him as he paged through various documents and reports. Finally, he stopped. Displayed on the screen was a financial report of EECM for four years ago. McCann peered at the numbers.

"How good are you at remembering financial results from year to year?" King asked, looking up at him.

McCann smiled, "Still pretty good I guess. Farm work hasn't addled my mind if that's what you mean."

"Good. Got the picture?"

McCann nodded and King skipped to another report. McCann noted that it was the same report for the following year.

"Got the picture for this one?" King asked.

"Yes."

King skipped to the same report for the following year and the process repeated yet a third time to the most recent year.

In his mind, McCann registered what he had just seen into a comparison sheet that compared the numbers for the four years. The result was a mental image of the revenues and expenses of EECM as filed with the government for the past three years.

"Well?" King asked as he closed down the report screen and sat back in his chair, the laptop on his knees.

McCann moved from behind King's chair and looked out the living room window. The light from the room shone brightly against the darkness and the front lawn's cover of snow.

"I would say that EECM has some significant financial issues," McCann said quietly.

"And we both know that where there are financial issues, there are usually…?" prompted King.

"…operational issues," McCann said, finishing King's observation.

(32)

At that same moment, Cindy Melzy was putting her room service tray in the hall outside her hotel room. The trip to Detroit had been full of discussion among Boyington, the LEGENT attorney, Smith and herself. They had worked out most of the plan of action in the car with Cindy and the LEGENT attorney keeping notes. She had checked into the hotel upon arrival in Detroit and ordered room service.

Now, as she settled back with the TV remote beside her and her laptop opened to her e-mail, she had her first real moment of reflection on her stay at McCann's farm. She had gone there in the hope that spending some time with him would help her think through her own future. Clearly, she had gained a perspective that she needed. She would stay with Triad in New York for now. Last night at the farm, she had realized that what she had been hoping for was the possibility that McCann's future and hers could somehow intersect. It was clear that such thinking was too early for him. She also realized that she would not be challenged by a position with Farnsworth Tele and that living on a remote farmstead in Michigan would not be in the best interests of her or her son. McCann had helped her see all this more clearly.

She opened an e-mail message and clicked in Malcolm's e-mail address. She typed "Thanks," into the subject line and keyed in, "Turning down the Head Bookkeeper job. You'll have to put up with me a little longer. Thanks for the guidance."

She sent it and opened another. She clicked in McCann's address and paused while she thought of what to key in. Finally, she put "Last night," in the subject line and began to type.

Wils:

Thanks for last night. I know I was presumptive in showing up unannounced and asking to stay the night. I hope you didn't mind. I didn't. In fact, I would do it again, but not until you ask me to.

You helped me more than you will ever know. I've decided to stay at Triad for now. But, I do like the country life you lead. Give Wink a pat on the head for me.

Cindy.

She looked at the screen. Somehow she didn't feel it said what she had wanted it to say but she wasn't all that sure what she had wanted it to say. After a moment or two, she sent it. Afterward, she reflected that she hadn't even mentioned the acquisition or the events of the day. Somehow, that hadn't seemed important.

Weaverville, North Carolina's Business Association touts the area's natural beauty, healthful climate and proximity to Asheville as having made the community of 2,300 people "the perfect blend of small town and big city."

Five blocks from Weaver Blvd. a rather plain looking red brick building housed the headquarters of Easter European Christian Ministries. The entrance to the building was stylish but not current. To the left of the receptionist's desk was an office that had been Jim Jacobs'. To the right of the entrance was a doorway that led to the ministry's conference room. The room was well done with dark paneling, a long, boat shaped conference table surrounded by twelve padded leather swivel chairs. A small credenza that matched the conference table was against the far wall and held a silver carafe and some ceramic cups with the EECM logo on them.

Two men, one a tall black man with the look of an athlete and the other white with the look of a tired office worker, were in the room. The tall black man held a white business envelope securely sealed with clear packing tape. The address on the envelope was simply "Wilson James McCann."

The tired office worker said, "Have you any idea what it is, Lark?"

Lark Bishop had been christened Meadow Lark Bishop. His father had been a fan of the Harlem Globe Trotters and had named his only son after the Trotters' Meadowlark Lemon. It hadn't taken long for Bishop to shorten that to Lark. His three years of varsity basketball for Coastal Carolina University had at least brought his father some sense of having done the right thing. More important to Lark Bishop was the degree in business with a major in finance and a Masters of Business Administration he had secured from the Conway school. He looked at John Botek, the Administrative Manager for EECM. The situation outside the conference room was slowly grinding his friend down. Five years ago, Botek would not have been in this room coatless. Four years ago, his white shirt would certainly not have been half out of his suit pants and three years ago his tie would have been securely knotted at his throat. The bags under Botek's eyes only served to compliment his rumpled appearance. Bishop thought for a moment of suggesting that Botek do something about his appearance before the memorial service and Board meeting but thought better of it.

"No idea, John. It was given to Jim by the woman from Michigan before she went to Prague. The envelope that this envelope was in was marked, "To be opened if and when Wilson McCann becomes a member of the Board of Directors of EECM." I opened it this morning when we went through Jim's personal files."

"This guy, McCann, who is he?" Botek asked, leaning on the back of one of the chairs.

"He comes with his own minister and over one million dollars," Bishop replied, smiling at the look of incredulity that spread across the other's face. "Miss Barnes left a will leaving over one million to EECM and asking that her pastor, a man named Hastings, be named to the Board of EECM. She evidently also asked that Mr. McCann also be appointed to the Board if and when he came to know Christ."

"But...that doesn't explain....," Botek sputtered.

"I did a little web surfing using one of the few computers we have that has any capability and found out that Mr. McCann has quite a history in the telecommunications business. He was CEO of a fairly large company and was ousted in a failed attempt to salvage the company, when it was being acquired by a larger company. He evidently has quite a reputation within that industry for dynamic leadership. Next, I called a former classmate named Earl Wood up in Santee, South Carolina. Earl was local manager for the

Santee Office of Dynacom — that's the company McCann headed. Earl confirmed everything I had read on the net."

"The good Lord knows we could use a little of that right now," Botek responded, ignoring Bishop's comment about their computer capability. He was well aware the EECM's information technology was about ten years old with the exception of one or two computers that had recently been acquired through a small grant.

"Thank you," Bishop replied, and watched the red rise in Botek's face.

"Ah…Lark …you know I didn't mean…," Botek stammered.

Bishop moved to his friend's side and put his long arm around Botek's shoulders. "I know. You don't have to apologize. I've done my best just to keep our missions active. We need more help in fixing our administrative problems, fund raising, donor relations, and the whole nine yards."

Botek looked up at the tall black man who towered a full six inches above him.

"Maybe we should pray," he said, quietly.

"An excellent idea. Let's pray that the memorial service will do credit to our founder and all that he did and that God will send us what we need to keep doing his work."

Botek slipped his arm around Bishop's waist. The two men, so different in physical appearance united as one in their prayers. Ten minutes later, Bishop placed the white, sealed envelope inside a "briefing book" binder for board members with McCann's name on it and put the binder in a wall safe in his office. The other binders, including one with Charles Hastings' name on it, remained on his desk. Somehow, he felt McCann's would prove to be the start of something special.

The next morning, Doug Warner and McCann drove King and Piazza to MBS International and watched the Hawker climb into the bright morning sky. Prior to Doug's arrival in the Yukon at the farm with Piazza, John King had briefed McCann on what to look for as a member of EECM's board.

McCann smiled to himself as he and Warner returned to Farnsworth. He hadn't even said "yes" to Jacobs' offer of a Board seat and already he was in up to his eyeballs in EECM's financial results and wondering where all this would lead.

Doug dropped him off at the farm and McCann spent the rest of the day bringing Stu Bailey up to date on the results of yesterday's meeting, reading and responding to Cindy's e-mail and talking with Charles Hastings about the trip to Weaverville the following day. He decided not to mention any of what he had learned from King's Internet surfing and discussion. Hastings had seemed distraught enough about the loss of his friend and the possible disruption of their plans that could be caused by Jacobs' death. Hastings, however, did assure McCann that the Board seat was his for the asking and that they would be meeting with officials from the ministry as a Board following the memorial service.

McCann called Norm Miller in Chicago and had a lengthy discussion with the attorney about Farnsworth Tele and about EECM. The attorney asked several sharply pointed questions and offered equally incisive advice. McCann asked him to take several actions, including calling Arthur Boyington and offering assistance to the team putting together the petition to the state of Michigan. Miller said he would call McCann on Friday evening in Weaverville.

Nick Hardesty was lined up to take care of the farm for the three days McCann expected to be in North Carolina. That afternoon, as the brilliant sun was descending rapidly into the woods a quarter mile away, McCann and Wink walked through the fields, now covered with a foot of snow, to the back of the property.

As daylight turned into dusk, McCann gazed back over the fields to the farm buildings. In the few months that he had lived here, his life had taken some interesting turns. He felt a new excitement about living and where his life was headed. As his mind went back over the events of the past week, he found himself thinking of Donna and wishing he could share that future with her. He supposed it would take time for those feelings to fade into the background. Perhaps they never would.

He slapped his gloved hands together to take away the advancing numbness brought on by the darkening winter night.

"Let's go, Wink."

The dog, who had been sitting beside him, perked up her ears and followed him back to the barn where he did his evening chores. Once they returned to the house, she curled up near the heat vent and, after making sure he was in the kitchen making his evening meal, went to sleep.

While McCann and Hastings were flying to Asheville, where they would pick up a rental car for the trip to Weaverville the following morning, Lark Bishop and John Botek met with Shirley Jacobs in the conference room. The widow of EECM's founder was no more than five feet two inches tall and dressed in a grey pantsuit that matched her steel gray close cropped hair. The strain of the past few days was etched on her face. Shirley Jacobs had worked side by side with her husband throughout his ministry. She had, however, devoted most of her energy to supporting the missionaries in the field in any manner possible, rather than becoming deeply involved in the business side of the ministry. While on the Board of Directors, she had played the role of quiet supporter to her husband's leadership. Two days from now, she would be required to chair the first meeting of the Board since her husband's death. She had seen to her husband's cremation and the planning for the memorial service that would take place tomorrow morning. She had shed her last tears the previous evening and with the grit of her Minnesota- born forbearers, she now was ready to face what lay ahead.

"I must know exactly where we stand," she had said to them. When they attempted to circle the issues that she knew lay beneath the surface, she had pressed them to be frank. They had quietly complied.

Now, she stood and poured herself some water from the silver carafe. They waited, watching, as she drank, swallowed, bowed her head for a moment as if summoning outside help, and turned to them.

"And the money we received from the Barnes estate?"

"About half gone, spent in support of our people on station," Botek replied.

She fixed her gaze on the 28-year-old Bishop. What a fine young man he was. He was forty years her junior and so full of energy and passion for their work. It hurt her to ask the question.

"And the money we set aside to bring them all home if we needed to?"

Botek looked at Bishop before answering. Bishop had told her that he was already sensing that some of their financial support would erode now that James no longer led the ministry. James Jacobs had been the face of the ministry to many individual donors. He was even more than the face to some of the larger organizational supporters.

"Barely enough, but we can bring them home if we need to," Botek replied.

She held her eyes on Bishop. His head bowed slightly and he looked up at her as one who was imploring her not to say what she might say next.

"I've had some contacts from others in ministry. They expressed their sincere condolences and offered to assist us, if it was necessary," she said, evenly.

Bishop couldn't help himself. "Assist us or take over the ministry?"

She smiled slightly. "It might be for the best, you know."

"No!" he said it like a man facing death by drowning, recognizing that if he gave way and took a breath, he would inhale the water and speed his own expiration.

She sat down and patted his hand. "Not today. Not tomorrow. But on Saturday, we need to explore everything. I need you both to be strong… strong as you have ever been. I need you to be honest…pulling no punches. The Board must have a clear understanding of our situation. James would have it no other way." The last words seemed to fade away into thin air.

She leaned back in her chair. "Tell me of the two men coming from Michigan. What do you know of them? I know of James' discussions with Pastor Hastings. I presume any further consideration of that idea is impractical?"

Botek looked at Bishop. "Considering what we have already discussed with you, I would think it is highly impractical to consider re-location of the ministry."

Bishop leaned in toward her. His voice had regained its clear strong tone. "I believe God will provide. Do you believe that?"

She smiled at him. "Powerfully so".

"I don't know Pastor Hastings or much about him. But I've been doing some research on the other man. He has a reputation as a leader even though it is in the secular and not the spiritual. Donna Barnes was quite specific in her bequest that, if he had found Christ, he be extended an opportunity to join the Board. I can't explain it but, somehow I have a feeling that he may represent God's provision."

"Then we shall await their arrival and we shall see what God has provided. Remember, I want everything on the table. I want you to give our new friends a tour of our facilities and I want you to answer any and all questions that anyone, including Rev. Hastings and Mr. McCann, may have."

She leaned in toward Botek and placed her hand on top of his. A slow smile crossed her face. "....and tuck your shirt in John."

At first, the color started to rise in Botek's face. Then, as he saw the love in her eyes, he began to grin. Bishop was more vocal. "Amen to that!" he said, loudly enough that the receptionist in the entrance lobby, startled, paused in her work and looked questioningly at the conference room door.

McCann and Hastings stayed overnight in a small bed and breakfast that had been arranged for them by EECM. Friday morning dawned gray and gloomy as though heaven itself was grieving over the loss of one of its own.

The service was held in one of Weaverville's larger churches. The church had been picked more for its holding capacity than for any affiliation with the ministry or its leader. An hour before the mid-morning service the sanctuary was already half full. When the two men arrived at 9:30 a.m., they were wedged into the third pew from the back. People stood in the gloom outside to listen to the proceedings. Music, scripture reading and prayer were the cornerstones of the service. The appropriate tributes were given by men and women from Jacobs' life experience, from his ministry and from the world wide Christian community. McCann was especially moved by the short talk given by one of EECM's missionaries from Hungary.

They paid their respects to Shirley Jacobs following the service and she introduced them to Lark Bishop and John Botek. Bishop offered to conduct a tour of EECM's headquarters that afternoon and they gladly accepted. McCann noted that both men looked very professional in their dark suits, white shirts and ties. During his career he had been called upon to take the measure of many men and women in leadership positions with companies that Dynacom had acquired. Thinking of King's advice two days previous, he decided that these two were "keepers."

At 2:00 p.m., they entered the reception area and were ushered into the conference room where Bishop greeted them. McCann surveyed the room and noted that while it compared favorably with most corporate board rooms, there was a dramatic absence of current technology. No whiteboards, computer connections or screens in the ceiling, no telephone except a beige princess telephone on a small stand just inside the door. He noted that the receptionist's key system turret was an older version.

After a few preliminary greetings, Bishop led them out into the main office area on the first floor. It was a large room sectioned off with Houserman partitions. The various cubicles and work areas were filled with an assortment of rather drab looking desks and credenzas which McCann knew must go back to the '60's. He noted again the absence of any modern telephone equipment. While most of the work areas and individual offices had computers it did not appear that there was any networking capability.

Bishop described the various functions of the ministry as they circulated through this maze. At the rear, he led them through another door into a large room that was obviously a combination shipping/receiving and printing area. As Bishop described the work being done, McCann again noted a combination of cleanliness and maintenance with older, less current technology. The people they met were a mix of young and old. All were quick to describe in accurate detail what they were doing and as they did so, they exhibited a passion for the work of the ministry. McCann reflected that these were the type of people that had made his years at Dynacom so enjoyable. Their enthusiasm, despite having to work with equipment, processes and an office environment that were far from "state-of-the-art" was, to his mind, exemplary.

As they exited this area, Bishop led them up a flight of stairs into the second floor. They entered another large room. A row of offices with glass partitioning ran up the right side of the room and the occupants looked out into another maze of desks sectioned off by more partitioning. Bishop indicated that this was the administrative side of the ministry and also the coordination area for the missionaries in the field. A large map of Eastern Europe dominated the left wall with appropriately placed pins and notes indicating the names of the various mission teams at work in that area of the world.

"Jim told us that you have a coordinating staff in Eastern Europe. Where are they located?" Hastings asked, as they surveyed the map.

"It is a small logistical team that is located in Budapest. They basically are doing coordination, problem solving, fire-fighting…that sort of thing," Bishop replied.

Again, as they visited each work area, they were greeted with cordiality and a sense of pride in each person's responses. McCann realized that this organization, like many he had known over the years, had a great strength in its people.

At the far end of the floor, they walked down a hallway that opened into another area that McCann assumed was the employee lounge area, kitchen and restrooms. Halfway down the hallway, a door opened into John Botek's office. He rose to meet them and offered them seats around a small conference table.

"Questions?" Bishop asked.

Hastings and McCann exchanged looks. Clearly, the minister was looking to McCann to lead the way. He had been relatively quiet during the tour, asking pertinent questions about materials used to communicate with the ministry's donor base and about the missions in Eastern Europe.

McCann felt uneasy. He recognized that he was not even officially a member of the Board yet and that he was probably viewed with some question because of his secular background. He decided to tread carefully.

"Your people are a tremendous asset to you. I am impressed with the enthusiasm."

"We have a good combination of volunteers, part-time people and dedicated, long-time partners in the ministry," Bishop responded.

"How long have you been with EECM?"

"I came right out of college. I've been here five years."

McCann swiveled to face Botek. "How about you, John?"

Botek, who seemed less relaxed than Bishop, shifted his weight in his chair before responding. "I've been here ten years. I was with a charitable organization before that."

McCann smiled and decided to play a card. "Yes. I understand that was in Michigan. Do you have family there?"

Hastings' eyes widened a little. It was obvious he hadn't been aware of this fact. McCann had been gathering facts from somewhere other than from the flash drive that Jacobs had given him.

"Mother, father and a brother still live in the tri-cities area," Botek replied.

"Not too far from Farnsworth," McCann observed. He smiled, but his eyes bored into Botek's.

But before Botek could respond, Bishop interjected. He leaned back in his chair and let his words come out easily and smoothly. "Both John and I are aware that Jim had spoken with both of you gentlemen about a possible move of EECM's headquarters to Farnsworth."

McCann decided to push a little. Looking at Hastings, he addressed his question to Bishop. "Do the two of you feel that is practical and feasible?"

"We do not know all of the facts that support such a move, but from what we do know we don't think it is practical," Bishop replied easily. Botek nodded his agreement and leaned forward folding his hands on the table in front of him.

Now it was Hastings' turn to look uncomfortable. McCann didn't give him a chance to respond. Instead, he pressed ahead. "Why?"

Botek appeared ready to respond but Bishop raised his left hand as if signaling that he wanted to handle the question. "Mr. McCann, my guess is that you have already identified some of our strengths and weaknesses. Your reputation as a business manager is not a secret to us. As you can probably see, our strengths are our work force and our field missionary operation. Our information systems and our operational practices and procedures are, frankly, behind the time. John can give you the financial picture."

He turned to Botek. Botek leaned forward and McCann was pleased to see the unease leave his face has he began to speak.

"Our financial situation is static. We have been able to maintain a supportive donor base and we have been able to adequately support our people in the field. We have not been able to afford the enhancements in our operational infrastructure that we should have. With Jim's passing, we expect to see some erosion in our donor support base, especially our organizational support. I did talk with Jim prior to his trip to Farnsworth and I did tell him I personally would be enthusiastic to move to Michigan, but that we would lose some of our workforce and have to recruit new people. In addition, the vultures are circling."

Hastings' facial expression had gone from one of shock at Botek's blunt statement to one of puzzlement. McCann immediately grasped the import of the final comment.

"Other ministries wanting to 'help you'?" he smiled as he said it.

"One of them is offering to 'help' us right now downstairs," Bishop smiled back. It was the kind of smile that a brave man puts on when he is tied to a stake and facing a firing squad.

Bishop's comment was accurate but the "helper" had left. Shirley Jacobs was washing her hands in the small bathroom adjoining her dead husband's office. She vigorously scrubbed and decided to wash her face as well. The thought of Jewel Favor's farewell kiss on the cheek as they parted made her stomach turn. She rubbed her face with a moistened paper towel. She dried her hands and face and re-applied her make-up.

Outside, Favor's Lincoln Towne Car pulled away from the curb. Favor was in the back seat with one of his aides. The driver had wisely put up the privacy window between the front and back seats and headed out for Asheville where Favor's chartered plane was waiting.

Jewel Favor leaned back into the padded leather seat and exhaled loudly. "The poor dear lady, she must be just devastated but she is holding up remarkable well," he said, looking out the window. Favor was sixty years old. His graying hair dyed black, his features were tanned by the Georgia sun from his weekly golf outings. While he was getting a little thick around the middle, his well tailored dark suit and white shirt were cut to minimize the bulge.

The aide glanced over at Favor and kept his mouth shut. He knew better than to challenge "God's Favor," as Favor billed himself in his weekly radio and TV messages. But he knew that Shirley Jacobs was not some poor little wall flower wife who would be "devastated." He thought of Favor's own wife, twenty years his junior, who dressed in the latest fashions, smiled at the appropriate time and offered an occasional "amen" or "praise the Lord." Were it not for the prenuptial agreement she had, she would be "devastated" if something happened to her older husband. Shirley Jacobs had grit. The aide knew that if there was a way to keep EECM going, she would work hard to find it.

Favor had immediately seized on the idea of attending the funeral to offer his "Favorable support" to the "poor widow." Favor could have started his own mission ministry in Eastern Europe. The ministry certainly had the money to do it. But why exert the effort when EECM could be taken over under the guise of helping a "sister ministry" and absorbing it into "God's Favor." They would close up the Weaverville site, re-locate any key people to Atlanta and welcome the EECM supporters into the "Favored Family." It would all be done in the name of "doing the Lord's work."

As the Lincoln moved out onto the highway, the aide kept his thoughts to himself and Favor congratulated himself on how well the day had gone. It was just a matter of time. He had plenty of time. He would make a follow up call in a week to see how his "dear sister" was doing. By then, the shock of her situation would have begun to work on her.

He would have been slightly less confident if he could have seen the purposeful steps of Shirley Jacobs as she went up to the second floor conference room to join Bishop, Botek and the others. She had cried and she would cry again in mourning the loss of her soul mate. But this was a time for looking forward, for assessment of the situation and for beginning to develop an action plan.

She rapped lightly on the door and entered just in time to hear McCann ask, "What do you estimate it would take to modernize the systems and equipment in all aspects of the operation?"

"The estimates we have are somewhat dated but we are probably looking at between one million and a million and a half," Botek responded.

All eyes focused on her as she pulled Botek's swivel chair from behind his desk and rolled it up to the table between him and Bishop. "Don't let me interrupt. I'm interested in hearing what you, all of you, have to say."

Two hours later, McCann had a very good grasp of the situation at EECM. James Jacobs had been the principal fund raiser for the ministry. His reputation and contacts around the country and internationally had brought in the most significant part of the ministry's support. Shirley Jacobs had provided the principal direction, guidance and support of the missionaries in the field. It was clear that when there had been any contention between spending money for improvements in the ministry's administrative functions and support for the missionaries in the field, the missionaries had gotten the support they needed.

McCann also had a very good understanding of the situation on the administrative side of the ministry. Passionate volunteers and a core of equally passionate, although poorly paid, staff had, by sheer dint of their passion, overcome antiquated information systems to keep the ministry functioning. McCann had also formed the opinion that Lark Bishop and John Botek were exceptional individuals who were working tirelessly to provide the administrative direction to the ministry, its volunteers and its staff.

Sitting opposite McCann and Hastings, Shirley watched as McCann skillfully probed into areas of the ministry that she had not been exposed to. As the afternoon sunlight began to dim, McCann switched from direct inquisitor to suggesting hypothetically designed scenarios to measure Bishop and Botek's responses. As the conversation moved ahead, she began to see that he was painting a picture of what the ministry's future might look like. The picture was not encouraging.

The conversation turned to Jewel Favor's visit and she candidly told the others that she fully expected further contact with him, clothed in words of sympathy but hiding his real aims. Lark Bishop looked at Botek and smiled. He was happy to see that Shirley saw Favor's attentions for what they really were. McCann noted the look between the two men and quickly glanced at Shirley. He could see in her eyes that "Favor" would not be bestowed on any one who came seeking to take over EECM.

"Thank you, gentlemen, this has been most helpful," Shirley said as she leaned back in her chair. "Mr. McCann, you have asked a lot of questions for someone so new to our ministry. You have also very cleverly suggested some outcomes based on our situation and how we handle it. I wonder if you would favor us with a more direct suggestion as to what we might do. Your reputation in the secular world is impressive and Rev. Hastings and others have given me to believe that your new-found faith in Christ is both dynamic and genuine."

McCann smiled as he considered how best to reply. He decided to be direct. "How would you feel about going on the road for the next couple of weeks?"

She didn't even blink. "To what purpose?"

"I suggest that you visit every major supporter of this ministry within the next two weeks to do three things. One, to make them personally acquainted with the work being done in the field, as only you can do it. Two, to assure them that it is your intention not only to maintain this ministry but to improve and expand it. And three, that you need their continued assistance and, if possible, an increase in their support."

Her eyes glinted as she took in his suggestion. Before she could respond, he turned his attention to Bishop and Botek. "Shirley will need the very best multi-media presentation of the work in the field that you two can put together. She will want to make people feel that they are standing right beside an EECM missionary in the field. Can you do it?"

The two men looked at each other. From his seat beside McCann, Hastings could see some optimism begin to appear on their faces.

"We don't really have any presentation equipment...," Botek began.

McCann was about to respond when a quiet voice to his left said, "Get it!" Shirley Jacobs reached across the corner of the table and laid her hand on top of McCann's. "Lark, put together a list of any individual or organization that has given us in excess of $25,000 in the past year. Then, put together an itinerary that allows for reasonable air travel to every one of them. Anything else, Mr. McCann?"

McCann looked at Botek. "I'll have a couple of my friends call you tomorrow. We may be able to do something to improve those IT systems.

I'd suggest you begin to inventory both the systems and the equipment and prioritize where you feel we should start. Lark, you'll need to sign off on the priorities from a logistical support standpoint to the ministry in the field."

Shirley leaned back in her chair, her hands folded in her lap. "I suggest we have a moment of prayer for guidance and direction. Then, I believe that Lark has something for Mr. McCann, and I would like a few moments with Rev. Hastings in my office. I'm sure that Lark and John will have plenty to do while Mr. McCann continues to use this room for a few minutes."

They bowed their heads as Shirley prayed. When she had finished, Lark Bishop handed the sealed white envelope to McCann and the rest left him alone in the room.

McCann's surprise was quickly replaced by a wholly different set of emotions as he looked at the envelope. He recognized the neat handwriting immediately. It took him a few moments to compose himself before he took a small Swiss Army knife with a DYNACOM logo on it from his pocket and slit the sealing tape and opened the envelope. He took out the single sheet of paper and slowly unfolded it. His heart was racing as he began to read:

My Darling,

Oh, how I have wanted to call you that. How I have wanted to be with you forever and never let you go. I tell you now that I have always loved you and no other save Jesus Christ.

The fact that you are reading this means that I will never be able to tell you how much I love you until we meet in heaven. It also means that my greatest prayer has been answered and that you have found the Savior that I love more than life itself. How I wish that we could have shared a life in Him together.

But, God has a plan and His plan is always best. I pray that you now have found new purpose for your life. I pray that you will apply your God-given talent to that purpose. I pray that perhaps you can be used of God to help EECM. I do not pretend to understand the many difficulties that this ministry faces but

I am sure that you will. Please, for me, help them! I have left a small be quest to help you.

With all my love,

Donna

He held the paper in shaking hands. The first of his tears dropped onto it as he bowed his head. Lark Bishop passed the conference room a few minutes later and paused to consider the man who sat at the table, the letter in front of him. Bishop read two emotions in McCann's face: pain and purpose. Before continuing down the hallway, Bishop said a quiet prayer in support of Wilson McCann. Somehow, he had a feeling that momentous change was about to overtake EECM.

Ten minutes later, McCann folded the letter and replaced it in the envelope. He put it in his inside coat pocket and rose. The emotion had passed but he knew that he would read the letter many times in the future and he would shed more tears when he did. For now, however, he had work to do.

(33)

Earlier that morning, Janice DeGroot looked again at the pictures she had taken at the ribbon cutting in Bad Axe, last Sunday. There were three that she was particularly interested in. She toggled the camera's review button to the first one which showed the Governor leaning forward to cut the ribbon. But it wasn't the Governor that commanded Janice's attention. In the background, at least six familiar faces were evident; Wilson McCann, Sally McHugh, Phil and Martha Willard and Doug and Belle Warner. She toggled again and the second picture appeared, showing the governor exiting the room with one of his aides holding the door was displayed. She toggled a third time and the next picture showed that same aide leaning in to speak to McCann while Sally looked on.

Janice leaned back in her chair and took a sip from her third cup of morning coffee. Something clicked in her mind and she picked up the camera and began toggling the review button again. Finally, the picture she wanted was displayed. It showed McCann, Willard and Mrs. Warner exiting through the same door that the Governor had used moments before.

Janice put the camera down and took another sip of coffee. Her first two stories about Wilson McCann had been short-lived. She had clipped and framed the one paragraph follow-up from the *Detroit Free Press* and when her sources in the Thumb area had not given her any new leads, she had moved on to other stories. One had been the ribbon cutting in Bad Axe.

What had McCann, Phil Willard and the Warners been doing there? Bad Axe and Huron County were outside of Willard's political purview and Janice had never seen him as one of the "hangers on" in the Republican Party. He showed up and was usually involved in party activities in his county but seldom ventured out. The Warners had shown no interest in political activities outside their county either, as far as Janice could tell. Had they been there to meet with the Governor? Was the LEGENT acquisition still alive?

She had made some discreet inquiries around her limited scope of acquaintances that followed such things but they either didn't know or felt that this was "small potatoes." If the Warners and McCann had been meeting with the Governor, what did that have to do with the acquisition? All these thoughts scrambled through her caffeine enhanced senses. Something was going on and she intended to find out what it was!

She booted up her laptop and got some phone numbers from her Outlook files. One was an old high school chum named Joyce Hall. Joyce had married her high school sweetheart and settled down with him in Farnsworth. The sweetheart worked for Farnsworth Tele and Joyce ran a small beauty salon in part of her home. Joyce often passed along little tidbits of gossip about the goings-on in Farnsworth to Janice and had filled in the details when a local farmer had taken a shot from his porch at his wife's lover late one evening when he dropped the farmer's wife off from what the farmer had been told was a ladies aid society meeting. The lover was a prominent Farnsworth pharmacist who sold his drug store a year later and departed Farnsworth never to be seen again.

Twenty minutes later, Janice reviewed the hastily scribbled notes from her phone call to Joyce. Joyce's husband had told Joyce how the office was abuzz about a LEGENT plane dropping off two men who were rumored to be there to discuss a business deal. One had stayed overnight with Wilson McCann and there had been a big meeting with several strangers in attendance that had lasted most of the day and into the early evening.

"You know, Joyce, I had heard that LEGENT was going to sell some properties to Farnsworth Tele a while back but then it sort of died off. Do you think that's going to happen?" Janice had asked her friend.

"Well my hubby says that the boys in the 'bull room' were talking about some big money people and some lawyers being in the meeting. Most of the scuttlebutt around the company is that the deal is on again," Joyce had replied.

"I saw some pictures of a ribbon cutting for that new hospital addition up in Bad Axe on Sunday and the Warners and Sally McHugh were there. What's Sally doing running around with the Warners?" Janice had asked, hoping that Joyce would rise to the lure of small town gossip.

"I haven't the foggiest except that she was at church on Sunday with Mr. McCann. He's the man that has been helping out at the company after Doug had his heart problems."

"Well! What do you know about that – Sally in church!" was all Janice could think to reply.

Now as she sat looking at her notes and the pictures, Janice wondered where to go next. There was a story here. She was sure of it. She just needed to pull the pieces together and make them fit. She poured her fourth cup of coffee and got ready to make another phone call to another one of her contacts. This one worked in Lansing.

After he left the conference room at EECM, McCann met with Shirley Jacobs and Hastings for over an hour. Half way through their discussions Bishop and Botek joined them. McCann laid out his thoughts and the commitments that stood behind them. While he gave no assurances, his firm determination and quiet conviction impressed them all. In the end, Shirley looked at Bishop and he could see the tears beginning to form in her eyes. "Let's do it!" he said. Hastings sat back in amazement. What had just been proposed was beyond his comprehension. He closed his eyes and breathed a silent prayer of both wonderment and thanks for God's timing and provision.

Later that evening, the two men ate a hurried meal and McCann left for his room. He had calls to make. As he climbed the stairs to his bedroom, he realized he hadn't felt this energized in years. As he removed his suit coat, he felt the rustle of Donna's letter in the inside packet. What he planned to do this night would hopefully be the first installment on a journey to realize the purpose Donna set before him.

Mike Divell opened one eye and squinted at the digital clock eighteen inches away from his head. It read 6:00 a.m. He opened his other eye and quietly moved the covers back and swung his legs out. Sitting on the edge of the bed, he glanced back over his shoulder at Moira. She slept as usual on her back. Her red hair framed her face. The freckles weren't as prominent in her 50's as they had been when she and Mike first met ten years previously. What a joy she was! What a rock! He stood and picked up his robe from the love seat near the door to the master suite and put on his slippers. He padded down the hall and down the stairs to the first level of their 4,000 square foot home in Dunwoody, Georgia. Last evening's call from McCann had awakened old memories. Divell had worked for Dynacom in his late 20's and early 30's. His work in the IT department had led to one promotion after another until he was the top IT man. Information Technology was under the umbrella of the corporate finance department and Divell came under the eye of the Chief Financial Officer, Wilson McCann. Five years later, Divell decided to take the Chief Technology Officer position at a company in Washington, D.C. Two years after that, Divell was divorced, drunken and destitute. That was when he met Moira. Moira's Irish strength and AA got him straightened out. Her salary supported them after they were married. That was when he had called McCann to ask back into Dynacom. Surprised, McCann agreed to an interview. He was more surprised when Divell admitted that he was an alcoholic and had lost his driver's license.

As he started the coffee maker, Divell thought about the conversation on that cold windy day in Chicago.

"I'll do anything you ask," he had said to McCann.

McCann had leaned back in his chair and rubbed his chin. "I don't usually take people back who leave for other jobs, Mike. But I'll make an exception with you. One chance, that's all you get. You screw it up and you're gone. And, no one but you and I will ever know about what happened in between times unless you tell them."

Linda McReedy took one last look in the mirror. Everything was in the right place and Linda had all the right things in the right places. Ten years ago, when she turned 18, someone told her she looked like the famous 50's and 60's actress, Kim Novak. She had rented *"Vertigo," "Picnic"* and *"Man with the Golden Arm"* and began to dress and style her hair like the screen siren. While such actions might have appeared "odd" to most, Linda's combination of beauty, brains and drive, all packaged in a statuesque 5'8" body, made customers and co-workers alike drool even when she arrived at a client location in a pill-box hat, matching powder blue skirt and jacket, white blouse and three inch heels.

She picked up her laptop carrying case and headed for the door of the condo she was renting in St. Louis while leading an information technology team on a three-month project for Mike Divell. Just as she turned the knob, her cell phone rang.

Thirty minutes later, she was packing her bags for a trip to Charlotte. She had already called one of her teammates, Al Prince, and pulled him off the job. She had called another teammate and put him in charge of the St. Louis job. Both had been amazed.

"What's going on?" Prince had asked, when she told him to pack his bags and meet her at the airport.

"We're doing a job in some mountain town north of Asheville. Mike says it's top priority. That's all I know," Linda had replied. "Sounds like the outfit needs a complete overhaul from what Mike told me."

"What kind of a business is it?" Prince had asked.

"Some kind of missionary aid society," Linda replied.

"Are you kidding me?"

"I don't kid where Mike's orders are concerned. Now get your bags packed and meet me at the airport."

Prince, two years older than Linda, single and "looking" smiled to himself as he put down his cell phone and began to hurriedly pack his bags. Most men would kill for a chance to spend time with Linda in the mountains of North Carolina but he knew better. Linda had a boyfriend who was into his fourth year in the NFL. He just hoped the little old gray-haired ladies at the mission wouldn't convert Linda. He kind of liked traveling with Kim Novak!

Archie Harold, President of SOTA Solutions, handed two pages of computer print-out to his warehouse manager. "I need this out the door by tonight," he said it loudly and firmly, hoping to silence any reaction. He got one anyway.

"What? Tonight? That's unreasonable! This is a complete mid-size hardware configuration including power and cabling. It can't be done," she said, as she re-read the second sheet which contained the list of components.

Harold leaned in close to make sure she could hear him. He spoke quietly this time, his eyes boring into hers. "I want that gear on a plane by midnight to Charlotte. I want it picked up by FEDEX and in Weaverville at the address listed by 8:00 a.m. tomorrow morning. I don't care what it takes or how much you have to spend to do it. I want it done. Is that clear?"

"Yes sir," she turned away from him and yelled.

"Bill! Frank! Jamie! Get your butts over here! We have a job to do that has to go tonight!"

Harold walked back into the office area that fronted the cavernous warehouse. The call that morning from Divell had been a surprise. More surprising was Divell's comments about Wilson McCann. Harold had been managing one of Dynacom's computer centers when McCann had taken over as Chief Financial Officer. When McCann consolidated Dynacom's computing centers, Harold had opted to leave and start his own company. Rather than react with hostility, McCann had directed that Dynacom's IT equipment vendor list include SOTA, which stood for "State Of The Art." Three contracts later, SOTA was a success. When the IT business began to contract, Dynacom had continued to buy needed equipment from Harold and that had helped SOTA to weather the storm. Divell didn't need to mention that Archie owed Wilson McCann big time, and he hadn't.

Harold printed off another set of layouts and equipment lists and also e-mailed the file containing them to Linda McReedy as directed by Divell. Next, he called Larry Bergman in Tampa. Bergman ran a company that specialized in packaged software applications for various types of businesses including non-profits. Harold told Bergman about his conversation with Divell and the equipment layout. At Bergman's request, Archie e-mailed the file to him as well. Bergman would contact McReedy to get an idea of the project breakdown and timeline.

Based on his review of the layout and equipment lists and his contact with McReedy, he would begin to assemble a software package to fit the customer profile and equipment layout. Bergman had been the systems analyst at Dynacom responsible for implementing the responsibility accounting package that Wilson McCann had ordered up when he took over. The experience he had gained on that job and several others at Dynacom, together with a penchant for running his own show, had led him to establish his own company five years earlier. Contracts with both Dynacom and other telecommunications carriers had resulted in the same survival story that Harold had experienced at SOTA. Bergman suspected that many of the contracts he currently held within the telecommunications industry were due to recommendations from Wilson McCann.

Bergman's natural drive to "give back" to the community in which he lived had resulted in several opportunities to automate the records systems of secular and religious non-profit organizations. His largest non-profit customer was Jewel Favor's ministry in Atlanta. Bergman personally thought that Favor was "gaming the system." But, the TV evangelist always paid on time and Bergman could live with Favor's frequent "Do you know the Lord, Brother Larry?" questions. Bergman was usually playing golf on Sunday when Favor's TV show was on. He wondered how Wilson McCann had become involved with some sort of overseas missionary effort, but he owed McCann so he hadn't asked when Divell called.

Linda McReedy balanced her laptop on her knees as she sat in the gate area for their 9:30 a.m. US Airways flight to Charlotte. She had just received two e-mails, one from Archie Harold and the other from Larry Bergman. She had saved the attachments and was now building a project management schedule that included the information provided by Harold and Bergman. Al Prince, sitting opposite her, had his Toshiba laptop open as well.

"We're going to need file conversion outsource," Linda said, without looking up.

"Who do you want to use? Amrut?" Prince asked.

"He's the best combination of speed and quality work."

"What kind of turnaround are you thinking?" Prince asked.

Linda looked up and then out the window at a big United jetliner that was taxiing down the runway. "One day for outbound, two days for file conversion, one day back, that's four days."

Prince's concern showed in his face. "That's awful tight, Linda."

"Mike wants this baby done and done quickly."

"But, four days?"

"Okay, add in one more day for the unexpected if that makes you feel better," she said, returning to her computer screen. "You call Amrut."

"Gee, thanks for the opportunity," Prince said, as he reached for his cell phone. "Who's doing the hardware install?"

"I called Light and Lively. They are due in tomorrow around noon."

"Only the best," Prince said, as he brought up his cell phone's phone book. "This outfit better have some big bucks to spend."

Linda looked up and sat back in her chair. "That's what gets me about this job. Mike said keep track of the time and make sure no bills are sent by anyone unless they go through him first. We're using the latest hardware and getting specialized software from Bergman and now Light and Lively to do the hardware install. Amrut's bill on this kind of turnaround will be twice what we usually pay. All of it adds up to a big tab and Mike's controlling it. That's unusual, don't you think?"

Prince pushed a button on his cell phone and listened. "I never question those in authority over me," he replied, looking at her.

"Yeah…right!" Linda said, as she went back to her program.

"Hello Amrut, Al Prince here. We've got a rush job for you. Linda says five days."

Prince held the phone away from his ear and Linda smiled at the torrent of East Indian angst that came out of it.

"Well, I've got to get going. I've got two perms and a cut this morning," Joyce Hall said, as she drank the rest of her coffee and began to pull on her hooded coat. Sally swept up the mug and put it in the sink behind the counter. "Well, it was sure good to see you out so early this morning. Be sure to stop in again."

"I will, and you take care. Give my love to the Governor if you see him again," Joyce said playfully, as she headed out the door.

Sally watched Joyce as she walked down the street. Joyce hadn't been in the diner in six months. This morning she had come in at 9:00 a.m., and acted like the two of them were on a weekly school chum friendship basis. Sally had been amused at Joyce's attempts to pry information about Farnsworth Tele, Wilson McCann and the ribbon cutting ceremony in Bad Axe. Joyce told her that she had it on "good authority" that "Wilson McCann and Phil Hubbard must have something cooking with the state if they went to see the Governor." Beyond acknowledging what Joyce apparently already knew and giving out with a few "Is that so?" and "That's interesting!" comments, Sally offered little encouragement to her friend.

She leaned against the counter and considered what, if anything, she should tell Wils. Joyce had mentioned that she had been visiting with Janice DeGroot. If Janice was trying to find information about the telephone company or McCann and the Warners meeting with the Governor, it could only mean one thing and that wasn't good.

She stepped back into the kitchen area of the diner and made a quick phone call to McCann's cell phone. When she reached a "leave a message" recording, she said, "Wils, its Sally, call me. It's important. Someone is snooping around about your trip to Bad Axe last Sunday."

She returned to the dining area just as Dorothy Hastings, Lona Marks and Lori Warner came in. Today was turning into a very unusual day. Dorothy had never been in the diner before as far as Sally could remember!

Donald Straylin was making his second trip to Weaverville in two days. He had driven up the previous day for the memorial services and to pay his respects to Shirley. That was when he learned that the board of EECM would be considering two new members. Straylin didn't mind adding a minister friend of the late James Jacobs to the EECM board even if it was puzzlement to him as to what value Charles Hastings would add. But Straylin was determined to oppose the addition of Wilson McCann to the board with all of his energy. At five foot ten inches and one hundred and sixty pounds, with close cropped dark hair that was tinged with gray around the temples, Straylin resembled a bulldog in his appearance. That appearance and his nature were fully integrated.

Donald Straylin's grandfather had founded a small investment banking company in New York City over a century ago. His father had taken over during the depression and had been able to keep the firm afloat through a judicious mix of conservative investments and tight-fisted cost control. He had even resorted to closing the firm's offices in the mid-thirties and moving its operation into the family home. Donald had taken over in 1968 and had moved the offices again, to Charlotte, North Carolina. He had watched as the dot com boom emerged and the telecommunications industry re-invented itself under the new regulatory framework. His firm had invested in neither and he was happy with that decision. His interest, however, had brought the sale of Dynacom to his attention. He had formed an opinion of Wilson McCann and that opinion was in no way favorable. Simply stated, he felt that McCann was a cold-blooded, selfish opportunist. Those qualities, to the straight-laced Straylin, were not compatible with EECM's Board. Donald Straylin was a "Born Again" Baptist who had joined Jerry Falwell's Moral Majority early on and never wavered. He was not vocal in his views. His personal and business decisions and the actions associated with them reflected his distrust of Washington, Wall Street and most corporate executives.

His dress this morning reflected his conflict with the norm. Yesterday, he had dressed in a dark blue pin-striped suit, dark blue tie and white shirt out of respect for James Jacobs. Today, he had returned to his more customary attire. A brown corduroy jacket topped crisply pressed jeans. A western bolo tie fronted his light green buttoned down oxford shirt. As he got out of his car, his well polished brown cowboy boots reflected the morning sun.

He entered the EECM building and went straight to what had been James Jacobs' office. It was now to be Shirley's office. Her assistant told him to go right in. Shirley sat behind a large desk. As she rose to welcome him, Straylin noted that there was an aura of confidence in her demeanor that he hadn't noticed the previous day.

"How are you doing this morning?" he asked, dropping his portfolio next to a chair opposite the desk.

"I'm doing quite a bit better this morning," she replied, grasping his hand in both of hers and squeezing. He was surprised at the strength of her grip. "In fact, I am doing much better. Please, have a seat," she replied, sitting and gesturing to the chair.

Straylin sat and Shirley leaned back in her chair. The chair seemed to wrap itself around her and make her seem even smaller. Yet the smallness was only one of stature, not in strength of purpose.

"Something exciting has happened and I want to share it with you," she said. "I met yesterday with our new Board members and Mr. McCann has helped me to see what must be done to assure our continued success. He has also put in motion a plan to revitalize and reenergize EECM."

Straylin felt like he had been punched in the stomach. He leaned forward and raised his hand as if to deflect the impact of her words but she smiled and kept going.

"…I realize, Donald, that you probably came here this morning to question the advisability of adding Mr. McCann to our board. I have always admired and respected your ability to judge wisely and well and to sense God's leading in every matter that has come before the Board in the past. I want you to listen to Mr. McCann and apply that same wisdom in judging the authenticity of his faith and his contribution. Will you promise me to do that?"

Straylin was dumbfounded. This was not the same rather introverted woman who had sat in relative silence during previous meetings of the board. As her eyes bored into his, he felt his unvoiced opinions being pushed aside. He struggled to find the right response.

"..of course I will….but…"

"No 'buts,' Donald. Just listen and judge wisely as you always have. Okay?"

He nodded weakly, and she rose to lead him to the adjacent conference room where the board was gathering. The way she said "Okay" made him feel like a lamb being led by a shepherd. It was a feeling he didn't find comfortable at all.

(34)

Traffic at the diner was slow during mid-morning. It began to peak about twenty minutes before noon. By that time, Dorothy, Lona and Lori were long gone. Sally had enjoyed their visit. She had sat with them and bowed her head as Dorothy prayed over their coffee, tea and cinnamon rolls. Dorothy had even complimented her on her coffee. They had chatted with her about her trip to Bad Axe and she filled them in on what it had been like. Lona listened attentively, not taking her eyes off Sally. When they were done, she smiled and asked, "So what do you think of our new neighbor?"

Sally could feel three sets of eyes on her as she looked out the window at one of Phil Willard's Agway trucks passing.

"He's a good man," she quietly said, looking Lona squarely in the eye.

"Amen to that," Dorothy said, taking a sip of her second cup of coffee.

"And good looking too," Lori said, the smile on her face widening.

"Watch it, you already have a man!" Sally shot back, glad for the chance to keep it light.

"I know, and Doug is so grateful to have Wils on board," Lori responded.

With that, Sally filled her in on Joyce Hall's visit and her concerns about Janice DeGroot. Lori listened attentively and said she would pass along the information to Doug.

"See you in church Sunday?" Lona asked as the three were putting on their coats.

Sally took a deep breath. "Why not?" she said, knowing that this time she would be going alone. It hadn't bothered her to go it alone in the past, but church was something else!

As Straylin settled into his seat, he glanced around the table and nodded to his fellow Board members. The EECM Board consisted of the President of one of Weaverville's local banks, a professor of Religious Studies from a small Christian college in Pennsylvania, the Vice President for Administration of a major Protestant denomination, a CPA from Atlanta, representing the firm which audited EECM's books and the CEO of a small modular home manufacturer from upstate New York. Together with the vacant seat previously held by EECM's founder plus himself it totaled seven. Lark Bishop and John Botek sat in chairs behind the CPA and the CEO. A third man, who he assumed to be the minister from Michigan, sat opposite him, and Wilson McCann sat away from the table in a corner of the room. Straylin swiveled to look at McCann who was surveying the room as if evaluating everyone seated at the table. Straylin found his blood pressure beginning to rise already.

Shirley Jacobs took the seat at the head of the table where her husband usually sat. Three folders had been placed in front of her. She folded her hands on top of them and looked around the table.

"Let's open with prayer. Pastor Charles, will you lead us?"

Hastings bowed his head and prayed a short and direct prayer asking for God's guidance and that the Holy Spirit would fill the room and each person in it. He closed by asking that every decision taken would be to move God's kingdom forward.

"Brevity is good," Straylin thought to himself.

"Thank you, Charles. We have three actions to take immediately and I ask that Professor Hayes give us the first," Shirley said, turning to the professor, who sat at the opposite end of the table. The professor picked up a single sheet of paper from the table in front of him and read it aloud.

"Resolved; That this Board, with a deep sense of appreciation for our departed Chairman and Founder, Reverend James Jacobs, does hereby elect Mrs. Shirley Jacobs to the position of President and Chief Executive Officer of Eastern European Christian Ministries."

"Second," said the bank president.

"Discussion?" Shirley inquired quietly, looking at each person in turn. No one spoke.

"Hearing none, all those in favor say 'aye'."

Six voices said "aye" in a somewhat subdued manner.

Straylin was not surprised at this. He had expected it and supported it for now. What took place in the next two hours surprised him a great deal.

Shirley guided the Board through the approval of minutes and review of the financial situation. The CPA from Atlanta asked several questions about the current financials, which represented the first eleven months of the year and were not audited. He also asked what, if any, consideration the Board should be giving to a possible combination of EECM with another ministry, given what he chose to term the "negative financial picture" that the report gave.

That was the first surprise for Straylin. Before anyone could make a comment, Shirley Jacobs stated with a certainty that he found impressive that she would not, at this time, consider any action that would result in EECM losing its independence. She followed that up with a quick summary of her plans for the next two weeks to reassure the ministry's supporters and ask for their continued and expanded support. She called upon Lark Bishop who quickly outlined her itinerary for that effort by means of a well-prepared handout to each Board member. Straylin noted that the CPA from Atlanta appeared somewhat distressed by the rapid nature of Shirley's deflection of his question.

Shirley next asked the Board to approve the addition of Reverend Charles Hastings as a member of the Board. This was done in the same manner as her installation and elevation to the Chair had been. Straylin tensed as he prepared for what he knew would come next.

Shirley leaned forward and looked around the table. Her eyes came to rest on Straylin and it seemed as if she had grown in size. He wondered if Bishop or Botek had raised the level of her chair to make her appear taller.

"Before I introduce a resolution to add Mr. Wilson McCann to our Board, I would like for you all to become better acquainted with him. Mr. McCann, would you please tell us a little about yourself and in particular your relationship with Jesus Christ?"

Straylin couldn't believe what he was hearing. As McCann stood and walked to stand next to Shirley, all eyes swung to him.

He spoke for no more than five minutes. He recounted his youth, his business background, and his recent move to Farnsworth. He talked briefly about his relationship with Donna Barnes. Everyone on the Board knew who Donna was and what had happened in the Czech Republic. At that point, McCann paused as if gathering himself. He looked out the window for a moment and then turned his gaze back to the seated Board members.

"For over forty years, I lived for myself. I have never, to my knowledge, done anything illegal or immoral in my business life. I wish that I could say the same for my personal life but I cannot. I have always been a man of my word and never have cheated anyone in business. But I cheated those who loved me by not returning that love. I cheated God by not loving and living for him. My single purpose in life was to advance my company and myself. Some of you may be aware that my company was sold to another and that I tried unsuccessfully to keep that from happening. While I can assure you that my intentions were honorable in my view at the time, my focus clearly was on preserving something that I loved more than any one person or principle. That has changed. I came to Farnsworth four months ago looking for a purpose for my life. I have found that purpose in a personal relationship with Christ. I have a lot of catching up to do and I believe that He would have me help you and this organization and, with your permission, I intend to do that."

He walked back to his chair and sat down. Straylin thought, "He has just confessed to being everything I thought he was and he has clearly changed. I need to hear more of this." He sat back in his chair and rubbed his hand across his eyes. Shirley Jacobs began to speak about her meeting with McCann the previous day.

"Even as we are sitting here, Mr. McCann has arranged for a complete and total upgrade of our administrative information technology. Within the next ten days, a completely new IT system will be installed together with all of its supporting software. Our fund raising and development systems will be brought to what I believe John calls 'State of the Art', isn't that right, John?"

Botek smiled broadly, "Yes Madam Chairman. That is correct."

Straylin thought he knew the answer already but he asked the question anyway.

"This has to be a multi-million dollar expenditure, where will the money come from?"

He saw several other heads nodding in agreement.

"Mr. McCann, would you care to answer Donald's question?" Shirley said, a faint smile beginning to spread across her face.

"It will all be donated by some friends of mine within the industry," McCann said quietly.

McCann's election to the Board followed with Straylin voting "aye." His eyes were downcast as he considered how far he had come in his thinking this day.

At the conclusion of the meeting, he waited until the other members had left. McCann was talking quietly with Bishop and Botek. Straylin noted that both were making notes as McCann spoke. When the two men left, he approached McCann. He held out his hand which McCann took in a firm grip.

"Donald Straylin of Straylin and Company. Welcome to the Board. I have to say that I am impressed, both with you and your impact on EECM."

McCann smiled, "A small payment on a big debt."

"Never the less, an important step forward. Are you heading back to Michigan?"

"Tomorrow, unfortunately. We have a late flight out of Charlotte," McCann replied, as they moved to the doorway.

"I wonder if I might have the opportunity of filling in some of your time in the morning?" Straylin asked as they moved into the reception area. Charles Hastings was waiting and moved to join them. He had overheard this last from Straylin.

"Wils, that would give me the opportunity to see some old friends in Charlotte while you two get together," he said quickly.

McCann considered for a moment, wondering what this was about. "Let's do it," he said, extending his hand which Donald Straylin took. Straylin had traveled far this day. He expected to travel further tomorrow, both in his understanding of Wilson McCann and the telecommunications industry that McCann came from and which Straylin had watched from afar.

McCann returned Sally's call, but they were playing "telephone tag" so he left a message. He and Hastings ate dinner together that evening at a small restaurant near their Bed and Breakfast. Hastings expressed no small amount of amazement at McCann's activity over the past two days. Shirley Jacobs had asked him to lead a brief devotional at the offices the next morning. He suspected McCann's hand in this as well. The more he was exposed to Wilson McCann in action, the more positive he was that God's hand was working through him.

The next morning, they were up early, had breakfast and checked out of the B&B. Hastings led the devotional period to standing room only. EECM people and volunteers crowded into the main office area and listened as Hastings talked about Gideon and his little band and how God could do a mighty work with what might seem to others as limited assets. He noticed that McCann stood beside two newcomers. The young woman was stunningly attractive in blue jeans and a Jacksonville Jaguars sweatshirt with a big 78 on it. Her face and hairstyle caused Hastings to have a momentary flashback as though he had met her somewhere before. The other newcomer was a sandy haired man with a pleasant open face that almost begged you to be his friend. Later, McCann introduced them.

"Linda McReedy, Al Prince, please say hello to Charles Hastings. Pastor Hastings is my pastor," McCann said. "Pastor, these folks work with a friend of mine in Atlanta. Linda and Al will be leading the conversion of EECM's IT operation."

Linda smiled and extended her hand. Once again Hastings was reminded of someone but he couldn't think who it was. He was surprised at the strength of her grip. Prince smiled and looked at Linda out of the corner of his eye as he extended his hand. "She doesn't have her pill box hat on today, reverend. She's gone casual," he said.

Linda's face flushed slightly as Hastings' eyes registered his recognition. "I...I'm sorry but you look just like..." he stammered.

"Yep! Molly-O herself!" Prince said, stepping back and enjoying himself.

Later, on their way to Charlotte, Hastings smiled again. "I can't get over it. She looks just like Kim Novak! That was pretty funny, Al calling her "Molly – O from *Man with the Golden Arm*."

"If Mike Divell sent her to run this job, she has got to be the best at what she does," McCann replied, staring straight ahead.

At EECM it was organized chaos. Linda and Al directed the receipt and distribution of a steadily growing stream of computers, servers, cabling, and software and laid out a conversion plan involving a growing number of outsiders as well as EECM IT people and volunteers. A few minutes after noon, a young black couple checked in at the front desk. They were both dressed in the latest fashion. Matching dark blue striped business suits over a white blouse for her and a white buttoned-down shirt for him. While she had ruffles at her throat, he sported a dark blue bow tie that was hand tied. She balanced perfectly on four inch black heels, and his black Florshiems reflected the ceiling light. In her heels she was as tall as he. Her face exuded a joyfulness that he matched with a wide smile.

"Good day to you!" he said it rather loudly to the receptionist.

"And what a beautiful day it is!" the young woman added, matching his smile.

The EECM receptionist, who had met Linda McReedy and Al Prince earlier, and had heard about all the material coming in the rear entrance, wondered what these two were all about. She didn't have to wait long. The woman asked for Linda and when she appeared, the three engaged in a group hug.

"The three L's are at it again!" whooped the young man as the receptionist looked on in disbelief. Shirley Jacobs stuck her head out of her office door to see what was causing the commotion. She had been introduced to Linda earlier.

"Shirley, meet Lashonda and Lucien. We call them 'Light and Lively' because those are their last names and more so because when they are around, things are always light and lively! They will be installing all the stuff that's been coming in this morning," Linda said, as Lashonda and Lucien stepped forward to pull Shirley into another group hug. Lucien stepped back from an astonished Shirley and bowed low.

"Sister Shirley, we must pray for this misguided young woman in her ignorance! The items presently coming into your life are state-of-the-art technology and not 'stuff'!" Lucien Lively said in a high pitched voice that could be heard throughout the offices. "And, we are God's appointed guardians of this technological universe!" added Lashonda Light as she duplicated Lucien's bow and followed it with a complete 360-degree turn, her arms outstretched as she whirled in front of a laughing Shirley Jacobs. The receptionist noted that this was the first time she had seen Shirley laugh in a week. Life at EECM was certainly interesting this morning. First Kim Novak had arrived, and now "Light and Lively."

McCann dropped Charles off at the home of one of his former seminary professors. It was clear that Hastings was excited about the opportunity to spend some time with a man who obviously had contributed a great deal to shaping Hastings' theology.

"I'll catch a ride down to Straylin's office around 1:00 p.m. and then we can head on out to the airport," Hastings said, as he shut the car door.

McCann parked in a garage near Straylin's office building and walked in the door at 10:30 a.m. He took the elevator and rode to the seventh floor. An all-glass wall fronted the elevator door and he noted a fish symbol about six inches below the "Straylin and Company" logo that was etched into the glass in silver letters.

Straylin ushered him into his office and McCann noted the various memorabilia scattered throughout the spacious room which overlooked the greater Charlotte downtown area. His eyes were drawn to pictures of Straylin with Billy Graham and Straylin with Charles Stanley on the credenza behind the investment banker's desk.

Straylin offered coffee and the two men settled into their chairs. Straylin leaned back and smiled across the desk.

"Tell me about Donna Barnes," he said.

McCann was somewhat taken back by the directness of the question. He took a quick sip of his coffee as his mind scrambled to collect itself.

"Donna and I were friends of long standing. Very close friends. I miss her greatly," he said, feeling that his response didn't do justice to the question.

"Were you in love with her?" Straylin asked, holding his smile in place.

McCann could feel his irritation mounting and he swiveled in his chair to gain control of it. At the same time, he sensed a purpose behind Straylin's probing.

"I didn't know what love was at the time. I do now."

Straylin looked out the window for a moment. "Please forgive me for my boldness. As you might suspect, I was aware of Miss Barnes' gift to EECM and the contingency that attached to it relative to you. I must tell you that I came to yesterday's meeting prepared to challenge your participation in EECM's affairs."

McCann smiled back, "And why would that be?"

"I have followed the telecommunications industry for some time. We do not have any significant activity in that sector of the economy but I have found it interesting. I was especially interested in Dynacom and its acquisition by LEGENT. You opposed that acquisition and I'm afraid I formed some opinions about your character as a result of that activity. You have a reputation as an outstanding leader of people within the industry but you also had a reputation as being shall we say…," Straylin paused, looking at him over the rim of his coffee mug.

"Cold?" McCann offered.

"Very good!"

"And very accurate," McCann responded. "My motivation for opposing the acquisition was, I now know, motivated by a misguided love for my position and Dynacom at the expense of any other relationships."

"Including your relationship with Donna Barnes?" He could feel Straylin's eyes on him as he looked down at the coffee mug he held.

"Yes," he said softly.

"Was Donna's death the event that brought you to Christ?"

McCann responded, telling this man he had only met a day ago of the events of the last few months including his mother's death, Donna's death and, last of all, the day he had buried Ted in the middle of a snowstorm. Straylin listened quietly, his eyes softening a bit as he heard McCann speak. When McCann had finished, he rose and refilled his mug, offering McCann a refill which the other man declined.

"Tell me about the LEGENT property acquisition," he said, as he resumed his seat.

McCann was surprised that Straylin knew about the proposed acquisition of the LEGENT properties by Farnsworth Tele. It soon became evident that this was not what Straylin had meant.

"I'm talking about a bid you were involved in for a much larger segment of the LEGENT operation. A friend of mine in New York, a man named Feldman, was also involved, I think."

McCann sat back and recounted the details of the failed attempt to acquire the larger properties which had led to Farnsworth Tele's proposed acquisition of the LEGENT Michigan properties only. From time to time Straylin made notes on a yellow legal pad. McCann noted that when he mentioned Stu Bailey's name and Cindy Melzy's name that Straylin's face indicated his knowledge of them. He also noted a wrinkled brow when he mentioned the role of the Oxbow group in what had transpired.

"Bailey is a bit of a wild card," he observed, when McCann had finished.

"But he's a good wild card," McCann replied.

Straylin raised his hand to acknowledge McCann's obvious loyalty to his friend. "If you say so, I'll take your word. He has a bit of a reputation as a gadfly M&A person in our world."

McCann smiled, as he thought about how Stu would react to this characterization. "And Cindy?" he asked, watching Straylin intently.

"An outstanding young woman. She will head her firm when Malcolm Shaw retires."

"She's a Christ follower."

"Really?" Straylin's surprise was evident. "Tell me about this."

McCann did so, mentioning Hastings' role and that of Belle Warner and the Warner family. Straylin asked questions about the various people in Farnsworth. McCann decided to take a chance and mentioned Hastings' relationship with James Jacobs and what had brought Jacobs to Farnsworth.

"An unworkable and impractical idea," Straylin responded to McCann's comment. "EECM will do well to survive where it is without thinking of moving to Michigan."

"I believe it will survive and I also agree with you that any consideration of moving the headquarters to Michigan is impractical."

"And what about your industry? Will it survive?" Straylin asked, switching direction. McCann sensed that they were getting close to one of the major reasons for this meeting.

"I believe it will survive but in a much different form than at present. The direction of our business is increasingly based upon use of the Internet by our customer base. The desire by that base for increased bandwidth and smaller, more capable terminal equipment that will be both wired and wireless and that will possess multi-media capabilities. There will be further consolidation within the industry. That will put pressure on traditional telecommunications equipment suppliers. To survive, companies will need to make significant investments in fiber optic facilities and deploy convergent technologies."

"That makes your willingness to acquire wire line properties somewhat suspect, doesn't it?" Straylin asked, as he jotted notes on his yellow pad.

"Within five years, LEGENT will be gone. It will be acquired by another company. I predict that further fragmentation of existing wire line properties will occur. Companies like LEGENT and those who might acquire it will seek to divest themselves of rural properties, thinking them to be unworthy of the investment required to provide the kind of service that will be demanded. Farnsworth is well advanced into cable TV and the Internet. It has also deployed fiber optics deeply into its networks. It can do the same in the LEGENT properties at an increasingly favorable cost/benefit ratio. The Warner family runs a good operation. What they have learned, bolstered by good people that can be added to help with the increased scope of operation, suggests they will be successful."

McCann had the impression that he sounded a bit like a CEO speaking to a group of Wall Street analysts. He paused and waited. Straylin stopped his writing and leaned back in his chair. He tapped the pad with his pen as he spoke.

"And you would be one of those 'good people' that they would add?"

McCann smiled. "I will do what God opens for me to do in the future. I have spent far too much of my life doing what I wanted without regard to others."

"What if the larger acquisition had gone forward. Would you have become CEO?"

"Your friend, Mr. Feldman and I had a couple of conversations about that. I don't think they ended very favorably."

"Tell me about it," Straylin said.

McCann did so. A smile began to spread across Straylin's face as he listened. "You told him that the headquarters would be in Farnsworth, Michigan?" he interjected as McCann told of his one-way tirade with Feldman.

McCann lowered his gaze, "As you say, I can be 'cold' at times."

"Marvelous! Tell me more about it!"

The two men talked well into the lunch hour, Straylin asking questions and McCann providing answers, opinions and approaches to various scenarios that Straylin proposed relative to the future of the telecommunications industry and its underlying technologies. Straylin's assistant appeared at one point with a tray of sandwiches. By the time Charles Hastings arrived, Straylin's pad was filled with notes, numbers and organizational chart sketches. As McCann and Hastings prepared to leave, Straylin walked with them to the door. Before opening it, he paused and took McCann's hand in a firm grip.

"I've enjoyed our discussion. I'm pleased to say that I feel I have misjudged you in the past and I am delighted that we have had this opportunity to get to know one another better."

He squeezed McCann's hand, released it and took Hastings hand in turn. "You, sir are a good shepherd. Wils has shared with me your impact on not only his life but others as well. I will pray that your hopes for your ministry will be fully realized. Could we pray before you go?"

The three of them bowed their heads as Donald Straylin prayed, "Father, bless both of these men in all of the endeavors they make on the behalf of your kingdom. Help me that I might be of assistance to them in any way you see possible."

"It seems you have made a new friend," Hastings observed on the way to the airport.

"So it would seem," McCann replied, thinking that he had shared a lot more about himself than Straylin had in return.

After the two had left, Donald Straylin sat for a time, looking out the window and occasionally referring to the notes on his yellow pad. He noted the various names scattered through the pages of notes. One name wasn't there. He scribbled for a while on his pad, then turned to his computer terminal and began to key an e-mail to one of his associates. Straylin's well-organized mind laid out a research plan as he typed it into the terminal. He briefly reviewed it and then placed a call to the man whose name wasn't on his yellow pad, John King.

(35)

In Weaverville, later that afternoon, Linda and Al watched as a FEDEX truck was loaded with the data base records, both digital and paper, of EECM. Inside the various office locations, Lashonda and Lucien were deeply involved in the supervision of the network installation.

"Christmas comes but once a year," Prince said.

"That's next week. Tomorrow we train," Linda responded.

"Do we get time off for good behavior?"

"When your work is done, you can play," she responded.

"That's funny; you don't look like my mother at all."

"If I were, you'd have had a better upbringing."

"If you were, could I sit on your lap and have you read me stories about Computer Man and Software Man and Operating System Man?"

Linda smiled and turned away. "In your dreams, pal!"

"Rats!" Prince thought to himself. Then again, he would rather she not be his mother. But he wouldn't mind having her sit on his lap. "Oh well, we all have our dreams," he said under his breath, as he headed into the conference room.

Linda had set up a laptop computer in front of every chair arranged around the conference table. Another laptop was connected wirelessly to a new multimedia projector that Light and Lively had mounted on the ceiling of the room. Linda and Al began to run through the video training program that they would use to bring EECM personnel up to speed on the new system installation beginning tomorrow morning. From time to time, EECM people walked by and paused to look in through the open doorway. The day to day activities of the ministry had been reduced significantly as the installation team had taken down the various systems to replace them. The data base conversion would take place over the weekend and, hopefully, the ministry would be back to "live" operation on Tuesday with completely new automated operating systems based on all new hardware and software. EECM would have part of Tuesday, Wednesday and half of Thursday before shutting down for the Christmas holiday weekend. The systems primarily automated four areas of EECM's operation. Fundraising software would automate everything from producing fundraising program material to recording and acknowledging support to developing statistical analysis of the EECM support profiles. It would link to a revamped accounting system. A new system of logistical support activities for the actual field missions would build from information provided from these systems. A new program outreach system would automate and enlarge EECM's profile to the supporting public as well as provide links to what was needed in the field. For those EECM staff and volunteers who had been around the ministry for any length of time it was truly likened to "the second coming."

In Shirley's office, Bishop and Botek were busily helping her assemble a multimedia presentation that would both assure and challenge EECM's sponsors to not only stick with the ministry but consider enlarging their support.

Around noon, Jewel Favor had called on the pretense of reassuring Shirley of his support. He had heard from his friend, the CPA on EECM's Board, earlier in the day. What he heard upset him. He called Larry Bergman in Tampa and asked what he knew about any large software projects by EECM. Bergman had seemed evasive but didn't deny that his software company was involved with the EECM project.

"While I praise the Lord for the good fortune that our sister Shirley has received at His hand, I cannot but be concerned that the additional financial strain of having to pay for this could be devastating for EECM. Clearly, our dear sister has received some advice that gives evidence to the working of the Adversary," Favor said.

Bergman swiveled in his chair and looked out the window. A slow smile crept across his face and he put both feet up on his desk before he answered.

"Well 'Brother' Favor, as I have heard you say many times, the Lord does work in mysterious ways His wonders to perform."

Two minutes later, Favor hung up the phone and Bergman's smile had broadened considerably. He felt so good he might just call it a day and go play an extra round of golf.

Favor next called Shirley Jacobs in Weaverville. He listened with increasing frustration as she recounted what was, at that very moment, happening at EECM and what she intended to do beginning the Monday after the Christmas weekend. When Favor questioned where this dazzling array of good fortune had come from, she was happy to tell him that it was "as a result of prayer and God's answer through the good offices of our Board."

Favor stormed from his office and headed for the small but ornate chapel that occupied one corner of the executive suite at the ministry. "I am beset at every hand and must find solace for my soul in a period of quiet," he muttered to his aide. The aide went back to his work humming "*A Mighty Fortress is Our God*" to himself. He had always loved the story of David and Goliath. He wished that Pastor Favor would preach on it more often. But today, he felt as though he had seen the story come to life.

McCann and Hastings turned in their rental car and waited in the gate area for their early evening flight out of Charlotte. McCann was already feeling drained. He leaned his head back and closed his eyes. Hastings waited until McCann opened them and began to reach for a newspaper he had purchased at the airport.

"Can I ask you something rather personal?"

McCann nodded, "Not too personal, I hope."

"It's about Sally McHugh. What is your relationship with her? If I'm being too nosy, just say so."

McCann hesitated before he replied. It was just long enough that the minister could see that he was being very careful in what he was about to say.

"My relationship with Sally started a year or two after my relationship with Donna began. I'm afraid it was just as selfish on my part as my relationship with Donna was. Sally and Donna were actually quite a bit alike in those days. Both were rebels. Unfortunately, it appears Sally has continued to be a bit of a rebel although I think that she is, underneath that brassy front she puts on, a good person. She is a good friend."

Hastings considered this and spoke again, "Donna loved you very much. I think that Sally may have some of those same feelings."

"I know. I don't want to hurt anyone like I have in the past. But I'm not ready to take it beyond friendship just now."

Hastings considered the "just now" portion of what McCann had said.

"Another question, if I may?"

McCann smiled, "You are my pastor. Ask away."

"What about Cindy Melzy? What is your relationship with her and her son?"

"I've known Cindy for some time. We crossed paths from time to time and especially so during the LEGENT-Dynacom acquisition and now the Farnsworth Tele acquisition of the LEGENT properties. I would say our relationship was professional until both of us found Christ. Now it has changed."

"More personal?"

"Yes."

"Interesting, two very attractive and intelligent women with totally different backgrounds and perhaps at the present time two different spiritual outlooks, both harbor some feelings for you."

"And…your spiritual advice is?"

Hastings smiled and reached to squeeze McCann's knee. "Love God, love your neighbor and listen to the Lord's leading."

McCann smiled in return, "should we take an offering now?"

"I think you have contributed enough in the past few days that we can dispense with the offering for now. One thing more…"

"Yes?"

"I believe that Sally McHugh is a searcher for God's love. You may be the instrument of that love. Sometimes it gets confusing between loving someone with God's love and with your own heart. I'm going to pray that God will give you the discernment you need."

The flight out of Charlotte to MBS International had a change in Detroit. Hastings spent the first leg working his sermon for the last Sunday before

Christmas. McCann tried to read his paper but found himself thinking of three women, Donna, Sally and Cindy. They arrived at MBS late in the evening and by the time they reached Farnsworth it was close to midnight. The drive from Caro to Farnsworth was into the teeth of a winter storm coming off Lake Huron. McCann dropped Hastings off at the parsonage and when he arrived at the farm, there was five inches of new snow on the ground. He could tell that Nick had plowed the drive and turn around earlier in the evening. He gave silent thanks for the young man and his willingness to step in whenever McCann needed him.

He rolled the double doors back on the tool shed to drive the Liberty inside. He had driven the Jeep on several occasions recently. There was still the faint odor of his mother's perfume in the little SUV and at times he found himself brushing away a tear. He knew that at some time, the smell would be gone, just as she was gone. He wondered what in his future would replace all the good things in his life that he had ignored.

Nick had left Wink in the barn. McCann dropped his bags in the kitchen and put on his boots for the trudge to the barn to release her. She came to him, tail wagging, and resisted the urge to jump. She sat, tail sweeping an arc in the chaff of the feed alley floor as he stroked her head. Once outside, she ran through the snow in widening circles until she had spent her happiness and trotted along with him toward the house. He paused, looking out through the curtain of falling snow at the fields below the barn. Two feelings flooded through him. One was a combination of relief and gladness to be home. It was closely followed by the realization that this was, indeed, home. Tired, but content, he walked through the snow to the house and its relief from the cold and snow outside.

Inside, he found a phone message from Sally earlier in the evening saying that she was at the high school basketball game and would call him in the morning. There was also a message from Stu Bailey, saying, "Call me. Something has come up that you should know about."

McCann was too tired to care. He didn't bother to hang up his suit as he headed for bed. Wink followed him into the bedroom. She rarely stayed in the bedroom with him but tonight she curled up on the floor at the head of the bed. From time to time during the night, she rose, lifted her head, and looked at him, making sure he was still there. Then, she quietly curled up again. Outside, the snow continued to fall.

He woke to the sound of pounding on the back door and Wink whining. He tumbled out of bed and quickly pulled on a pair of jeans. He glanced at the alarm clock by his bed and noted that he had slept for nine hours. The cattle would be fed late this morning!

He stumbled toward the door as the pounding continued. He pulled it open and was face to face with a smiling McIntyre.

"The top of the morning to you laddie!" boomed the smiling Scotsman.

McCann rubbed his eyes and looked out beyond McIntyre. The snow had stopped but there was at least eight inches of new sunlit snow on the ground. McIntyre's truck had left two deep furrows in the turn around.

"You've gone to seed man! It's nine in the morning! What ails you? Are you sick?"

McCann couldn't repress a grin as he stepped back into the kitchen to let his ruddy visitor in.

"I got in late last night. I must have overslept."

"Ah …! Affairs of state or affairs of the heart?"

"Affairs of state," McCann said, and told him a little of the events of the last few days as he readied the percolator for the morning coffee.

"It's the Lord's hand that's at work here! That's for sure!" McIntyre said loudly, when McCann had finished.

"I need to feed the cattle. Come to the barn with me and by then this coffee will be ready," McCann said, as he pulled on his work shirt and jacket.

"Better yet, I'll move my truck and plow your drive and turn around for you while you work."

McCann walked with him to the tool shed and together they rolled the doors back. McIntyre quickly went over to the tractor and made sure he was familiar with its operation. McCann and Wink headed to the barn as the roar of the machine filled the sunny morning.

Thirty minutes later, the two men sat down at the table. McCann had scrambled some eggs and diced a slice of ham into them. He had toasted four slices of bread and placed a jar of strawberry jam on the table. McIntyre at first protested that he had already eaten but after asking a blessing on the food, he took an ample helping of the eggs and ham and two slices of the toast. He drank his coffee black and McCann filled one of Ella Harms' mugs to the brim.

"How about some orange juice?" McCann asked as he watched McIntyre ladle a heaping forkful of eggs and ham into his mouth.

"Mmff," the Scotsman nodded. Wink looked up at him and then went and lay down beside the heat register. McCann had noted that while she showed initial affection to McIntyre, she had remained closely by McCann's side all morning

Later, they lingered over a third cup of coffee. McCann could feel the effects of it washing away his fatigue. Outside, the sun rose higher in the sky and the cold air warmed. Soon, he could hear the "plop – plop" of melting snow outside the entry way.

McIntyre was on his way to Harbor Beach to pick up five yearlings for his employers. He had decided to stop and wish McCann a Merry Christmas and see what was going on in his friend's life.

McCann felt at ease in sharing more of the details of the events of the past week except for the meeting with the Governor. McIntyre listened thoughtfully and took a sip of his coffee when McCann had finished.

"And you've had the company of a pretty lass, too?"

McCann hadn't mentioned either Sally or Cindy and wondered where McIntyre had picked that up. His quizzical look brought a broad smile to the Scotsman's face.

"Ah! Twas in the paper that I saw it! I do read, you know!"

McCann remembered Sally's call. "What paper?"

"The *Times*! You were front page on the business section, hobnobbing with the Governor! And with as pretty a lass as ever I've seen sitting beside you!"

So McCann told him about Sally and going to church and the trip to the ribbon cutting. He didn't include the meeting with the Governor but he could tell by the sly smile on McIntyre's face that he knew there was more to the story.

"This purchase you talked about…will you be back 'in the business' so to speak?"

"I don't know. I want to help wherever I can."

"And this ministry in North Carolina… you've done God's own work there. Will you involve yourself more there?"

"As a Board member at least. Beyond that, I don't know."

"And the lassie…can you win her to the Lord?"

McCann hesitated, he hadn't thought of Sally in that way. "I don't know. I'm not a very good witness."

McIntyre emptied his mug and stood. "None of us are laddie! But we must try. That is what is important." He moved to stand over Wink, who lifted her head expectantly. "The Lord has work for each of us to do. Just as this lady here gets stronger the more she works, we get stronger the closer we draw to God and try to do his will. Well, I must be going, a very Merry Christmas to you!"

He put on his coat and hat and moved to the door. He reached into his coat pocket for gloves and stepped back toward McCann.

"Ach … I almost forgot…I've brought you a wee gift!"

He brought out a small velvet box which he gave to McCann who opened it. A small delicately carved Pewter figure of a Scottish Piper rested inside.

McCann stared at it and smiled. He looked up into his friend's eyes as McIntyre placed a rough hand on his shoulder.

"God bless you, laddie!"

Instinctively, McCann pulled him into an embrace. He had never been one to hug but it seemed the right thing to do. When they stood apart, he brushed a tear from his eye and noted that the Scotsman's eyes were also moist.

"Thank you….for everything."

"Now don't be lying in tomorrow. It's the Lord's Day and we must be about his business!" McIntyre said, as he got into his truck and drove away.

McCann and Wink stood there in the sunlit yard, watching until the truck turned onto the highway at the end of the road. McCann made a note to himself that he needed to pick up his Christmas gift orders at the Barnes Loft. When he had said as much to McIntyre, the Scotsman had smiled and said, "I trust there's one for your lass. That will be your gift to me. It's paying it forward … that's what it is."

As he was thinking about what he intended to give Sally, the phone rang. Stu Bailey was calling from New York City.

John King had left Dallas early for the holidays. He and his wife had flown into Savannah on Friday morning. He was looking forward to a solid two weeks before having to go back. He was also looking forward to the day when he wouldn't have to go back. That day would come as soon as the divestiture of the Midwest properties was completed. He felt good about the Michigan sale to Farnsworth. Norm Lister hadn't been as enthusiastic because of McCann's involvement with Farnsworth Tele. But he had agreed to take the agreement offering to the CEO for his approval. Hopefully, when King got back to Dallas on the first Monday of the new year, that part of this would be on its way to completion.

They had lunch along the riverfront and then went to their home. King practiced his putting on an artificial green in his basement and sat down for a nap which was interrupted by Straylin's call. An hour later, as he put the receiver down, he realized that his two week holiday was already over!

Two hours after King put down his telephone, Arthur Boyington took a call in Detroit. He listened carefully, making notes on a legal pad as the caller outlined what he had in mind. At the end of the call, Boyington said, "I don't believe there is any interest there, but I recognize that as legal counsel to the company, it is my responsibility to discuss it with them. I will do that. I cannot promise to get back to you until Monday but I will do my best."

He put down the receiver, reviewed his two pages of notes and leaned back in his chair. After thinking the whole matter through again, he picked up his telephone and placed a call to Farnsworth.

At about the same time, in New York City, Cindy Melzy's telephone rang.

"Hello, Cindy. Ed Feldman here. I have an interesting proposition to put to you."

When she put down her telephone an hour later, Cindy realized that she would be working on Saturday. Before leaving the office, she called Stu Bailey. Bailey immediately called McCann. McCann didn't answer his phone and Bailey left his "Call me, something has come up" message. He next tried McCann's cell phone. McCann had turned it off while he was in Straylin's office and hadn't thought to turn it back on. Bailey left a voice message. Bailey sent an e-mail but McCann didn't answer. Bailey paced back and forth in his office fuming. Jeanine put on her coat and headed for the door. As she opened it, she heard him talking to himself.

"Communications! We have all this communications technology and I can't communicate with the one man I need to communicate with and he's a communications guy!"

"What is going on?" Bailey barked, as soon as he heard McCann's voice.

McCann sensed that something was wrong. For all his faults, Bailey was cool under fire and now he was obviously agitated.

"Suppose you tell me."

"I'm talking about the deal for the LEGENT properties," Bailey responded.

"I haven't heard from King. I presume he put Farnsworth's offer forward to Lister and they are thinking about it."

"I'm not talking about your little deal out there in Michigan! I'm talking about the deal for all of it…all of the properties!" Bailey's voice rose as he said it.

"What?"

There was a moment of silence at the New York City end of the line. "You don't know?" Bailey's voice had returned to normal levels.

"Stu, you obviously know something I don't know. What is it?"

"An offer has been made for all the LEGENT properties. I'm told another offer is being made to purchase Farnsworth Tele and combine it with the LEGENT properties."

McCann turned to look out the window over the snow-covered fields. The cattle were slowly moving around in the barnyard. He could hear the sound of a semi out on the highway. Wink had lain down next to the heat vent and was cleaning the frozen snow from between the pads of her front paws. His mind raced to digest what Bailey was saying.

"Wils? Are you there?" Bailey's voice came into his ear.

Then it hit him. "Straylin!"

"What? Who? Are you saying Donald Straylin has something to do with this?"

"Stu, tell me what you know and I'll try to tell you what I think is going on."

Bailey told him about the call from Cindy. Basically, she had said that the original deal was being resurrected. Feldman, Triad, and Bailey had been asked to review a proposed offering that was to be e-mailed to them this morning by eleven o'clock. Oxbow was no longer involved. No indication had been given as to who the sponsor of the offer was or if she knew, Cindy wasn't telling anyone. No mention of McCann had been made but Cindy had indicated that an offer would also be made to Farnsworth Tele to sell to the sponsoring partners. Basically, Cindy felt that the proposal would be much the same as the original plan had been.

McCann filled Bailey in on his meeting with Donald Straylin and Straylin's obvious interest in both the industry and the LEGENT property acquisition in particular. McCann recalled that Straylin had been very interested in the details of the original failed proposal offer. Bailey agreed that Straylin's firm was an obvious source of the resurrection of the acquisition offer. Straylin knew Feldman and Cindy and Bailey. McCann remembered Straylin's comments about Bailey. That might explain why Cindy had called Stu and not Straylin himself.

McCann agreed to try to contact Doug or Belle Warner, and Bailey agreed to call back as soon as he had seen the prospective offer.

McCann clicked off from talking to Bailey and placed a call to Doug. No one answered. He left a message asking Doug to call him. He called Belle at home.

"Good morning Wils. How was your trip?" She sounded relaxed and in a good mood.

"Great! We accomplished a great deal. Speaking of which, Stu Bailey just called me and told me that the original acquisition proposal is being resurrected and that an offer for Farnsworth may be part of it. Are you free to talk about that?"

"As a minority shareholder, you are most definitely entitled to know what's going on. We have been told that an offer will arrive later this morning. Why don't you come in to the office and we can review it?"

Somehow, he got the sense that Belle Warner was enjoying this conversation and that bothered him.

"I'll be right down."

"Good. Oh, and you might want to turn your cell phone on?"

"Why?"

"Because I gave your number to someone and you might get a call, silly! Bye!"

Irritated, McCann dug his cell phone out of the pocket of the suit coat that he had hung on the back of a chair the previous evening. No sooner had he turned it on than it rang and a "message received" screen lit up. He punched the "voice mail" button and listened to Donald Straylin's voice.

"Good morning, Wils. You did such a marvelous job of wheeling and dealing to take care of EECM's problems that I decided to do a little wheeling and dealing of my own just to see if I still had the touch. I hope you will like the results as much as I admire the results you produced at EECM. By the way, I spoke to Shirley earlier this morning and she tells me the team worked all night and all the hardware and software is up and running. They are running training sessions this morning and this afternoon. As soon as the data base comes back from India or wherever you had it sent, they will load it." You might want to check your e-mail. I've just sent you what I hope you will find to be an interesting document. I've talked to John King about it already and he is definitely intrigued! Call me after you've read through it. Here's my number."

McCann jotted down the number and moved to his computer. He felt like a teenager on a scavenger hunt. Where would the next clue lead?

"Come on! Come on!" he growled at the computer as it booted up. Wink raised her head and looked at him before going back to her paw cleaning.

The e-mail from Straylin was among a dozen others that downloaded into Outlook Express. The Adobe Acrobat and EXCEL attachments were titled "Acquisition – General" and "Acquisition – Financial Structure." He opened the "General" file first.

The five-page document outlined the key points of a proposal by a consortium of parties including Straylin and Company, Feldman's firm, Triad and Stu Bailey's firm to acquire the LEGENT properties at a price that was slightly in excess of four hundred million. It further called for the acquisition of Farnsworth Tele and for the eventual merger of the LEGENT properties and Farnsworth Tele into an unnamed operating company with corporate headquarters in Charlotte, North Carolina and operational headquarters in Farnsworth, Michigan. A Board of Directors consisting of Donald Straylin, Cindy Melzy, Douglas Warner, Feldman and Wilson McCann was named. Straylin would be Chairman and Chief Executive Officer. McCann would be President and Chief Operating Officer. It also pointed out that, upon his retirement from LEGENT, John King would join the Board. The rest of the information provided the various terms of the offer and a target date for acceptance or rejection by LEGENT of twelve noon on Christmas Eve.

McCann quickly opened the "financial" document and reviewed the numbers. He printed both documents and looked again at the one sentence contained in the e-mail. It read, "If you're going to be an Operational Headquarters for a big company like this, you had better find a good hotelier and a good restaurant operator!"

McCann didn't think about the fact that he was still in his barn clothes as he sped down the road. He called Bailey and filled him in. Bailey sounded a little hurt that he wasn't proposed to be on the Board. "Always the money man, never one of the top bananas!" he grumbled. Never the less, it was clear that he liked the deal.

McCann clicked off and called Sally at the diner. She filled him in on her conversations and he quickly surmised that Janice DeGroot was going to be a problem for the Governor and for the acquisition. Right now, he had other things to think about. Sally was busy getting ready for the noon crowd. Before he hung up, he asked her one more question. "Did you ever think about running an executive restaurant?"

Her puzzled, "Sure, I used to have that dream," left him smiling as he pulled into the Farnsworth Tele parking lot.

As he got out of the Jeep, he paused to think about the fact that it hadn't bothered him a bit that Straylin had presumed to name him as Chief Operating Officer and not CEO. Operations and Farnsworth was where the fun was anyhow!

The atmosphere in the conference room was electric. Fred Penay, Phil Willard, Doug and Belle were already seated when he walked in. Arthur Boyington was on the video conference screen. Willard looked at McCann's clothes and smiled. "Please sit at the other end of the table," he said as he pushed the chair next to him in tightly to block McCann. McCann felt the color rise and noted Belle's amused smile. He peeled off his denim jacket and hung it on the back of the end chair opposite Willard. He noted that Boyington was covering a small smile on the screen as well.

Doug Warner handed him a printout of the offer being made to Farnsworth Tele. Its terms dovetailed with those of the document that McCann had received from Straylin.

"You've made quite an impression on this Mr. Straylin," Belle commented from the head of the table. "Tell us about him."

McCann did so, leaving nothing out. The others asked a few questions and the conversation turned to the offer documents.

"We're on a rather tight timeframe," Boyington said, from the TV screen.

"Fred, I would like your comments and Phil's as well," Belle said, turning to the two businessmen.

"Before I answer, I would like an estimate from Wils on the number of jobs that would be created by basing the operations here," Penay said, swiveling to look at McCann.

McCann leaned back in his chair. He hadn't had time to think about something like this. "Using typical ratios of manpower to customers and allowing for the existing staff here at Farnsworth, I would say that we are talking between 35 and 50."

Penay scribbled something on his pad. "And what kind of jobs would these be?"

"Primarily administrative, including financial, human resources, marketing as well as engineering."

"Where would these people come from?" Penay continued to probe.

"Many of them will come from within the area. The more specialized positions would have to be filled from within the industry and the people re-located here. We would have to look at the capabilities of the people we get with the acquisition and see if any of them would fit the bill and be willing to move here."

"That's a problem, isn't it? Would people move to a small town like this?" Willard interjected.

"A lot of people are looking for a challenge. They are also looking for a smaller town to raise their kids. From what I've seen since coming back to Farnsworth, we have a good school system, good medical facilities and good available housing. Our retail, restaurant and motel facilities will be drawbacks," McCann replied. As he did so, he thought of Donna Barnes and Sally McHugh.

"The Chamber could work on those issues, don't you think, Fred?" Willard said, turning to the banker.

"Maybe your friends in Lansing could help," the banker smiled back.

"Point taken," the Agway dealer smiled.

The conversation went on for another hour. In the end, Belle led them in prayer for guidance and then Penay offered a resolution that the Board approve the sale of Farnsworth Tele contingent on the consortium's purchase of the LEGENT properties, the signing of firm agreements placing the operational headquarters of the new company in Farnsworth, Michigan and Wilson McCann's acceptance of the position of President of the combined operation. McCann voted "aye." For better or worse, he had made a very big decision.

"Next time we get together, could you clean your boots and try to dress a little more appropriately?" Willard said, as he reached across the table to shake McCann's hand.

Boyington was appointed to convey the necessary paperwork to the other members of the consortium. Later that afternoon, John King and his wife flew out of Savannah on a LEGENT jet bound for Dallas. His wife wasn't bothered by the fact that they probably wouldn't be spending the Christmas holidays in Savannah. She knew that once this business was over, they would have all the time they wanted there. She was also happy that, if this acquisition went through, John would still have a connection with the industry that he had given his life to. She was looking forward to visiting Charlotte again and even this little town in the "Thumb" of Michigan which was about to become much more important.

(36)

Sally McHugh's three sons sat around the kitchen table in her house on Grant Street. Robert, the eldest at 22, had returned from college for the Christmas holidays. His dark hair and slightly brooding features contrasted with the fair hair and round, open facial features of his two half-brothers, David, age 15 and Kenneth or "Kenny," age 13. On the table in front of them was an issue of the *Bay City Times*. Prominently displayed was the picture from last Sunday's ribbon cutting in Bad Axe. They were looking at their mother sitting beside a well dressed, handsome dark haired man as the Governor addressed the audience.

"So, what's going on?" Robert asked. "This is the same guy she was with when the dog was shot."

"Well, you'd have to agree, he's a cut above the ones she usually picks," David responded. Kenny said nothing. Quite frankly, he thought it was kind of neat having his mother's picture in the paper.

The three of them were used to Sally's boyfriends. Robert had been five when David was born and by then he knew that his mother's choice in men was somewhat flawed. By the time Kenny came along, he had accepted it as a part of his life. Robert had taken on the role of father figure to the two younger boys when their father left. Sally's Saturday night partying had meant that the three were often left to shift for themselves. The fact that they had not gotten into any trouble was, in no small part, due to Robert's influence.

"She went to church with him, too," Kenny offered.

"Church?" Robert's brows came together, accentuating his stare at the picture.

"She wants us to go with her tomorrow," David put in. "Can you get us out of it?"

Robert sat back and rubbed his chin. "We'll go. I need to meet this guy."

"I suppose we'll go again on Christmas Eve too…like we always do?" David said it in a complaining tone of voice.

"Twice in one week won't kill us," Robert said, clapping him on the shoulder. "Let's go shoot some hoops."

David was a member of the Farnsworth High School basketball team as a sophomore. Kenny was a member of the Junior High team. Robert, not as athletic as the others, had been a team manager in high school. As a member of the current team, David had access to the school gym on Saturday afternoons during the season. As the three headed out the door, Robert thought back over the last ten years. He had first seen a picture of Wilson McCann when, as a twelve-year-old, he had been rummaging through one of his mother's closets. He had found an old picture album. Among the pictures was one of a teenaged Sally with a dark-haired boy at a party. Both looked to be about 18 years old. Six years later, he had been looking for his birth certificate when he came upon the picture again. This time it was in a file folder in his mother's desk. The folder contained several newspaper clippings about Wilson McCann. He had asked his mother who McCann was and, a bit flustered, she had replied, "Someone I once knew who is doing well."

Just before he had left for Central Michigan University in late August, he had seen his mother looking through the file folder and he had heard that Wilson McCann had moved to the Harms farm outside Farnsworth. When McCann's dog had been shot, the news about his mother's involvement had reached Mt. Pleasant.

With earnings from summer jobs and some help from Sally, Robert had purchased a four year old Ford Explorer. Now, as David and Kenny piled into the SUV, Robert considered the latest developments involving his mother and Wilson McCann. "Anyone who can get mom to go to church and meet the Governor on the same day must be quite a man," he thought to himself as he got into the Explorer.

At the same time that Sally's three sons were talking about him, Wilson McCann was on the phone with Donald Straylin. The two men discussed the acquisition and Straylin was pleased that McCann had readily accepted the COO role. Straylin had no real interest in being CEO on a permanent basis. He had deliberately set himself up in that role to help ease what he sensed would be a contentious issue with LEGENT as to McCann's involvement in the acquisition and to see how McCann would react to a non-CEO role. As the two men talked, McCann's thoughts were constructive and supportive. There was no sign of ego as McCann made suggestions as to how the properties should be operated if their offer was accepted. He also offered solid thoughts on organizational structure, staffing and publicity for the acquisition. He added what he could to Straylin's understanding of the situation involving Michigan's Governor. Finally, an hour later, they were finished. They agreed to keep in touch over the remainder of the weekend. Just before the call ended, however, McCann sprang his surprise.

"We need another half million," he said, smiling into his cellular phone.

There was a long silence on the Charlotte end of the call. "I'm sorry?" Straylin finally said. "Did you say another half million? What would that be for?"

McCann told him. Ten minutes later, he walked into the diner just as Sally was getting ready to lock up for the day.

"Let's take a ride," he said, as he held her coat for her. "I have something I would like you to give me some advice on."

An hour later, he dropped her off beside her Mustang behind the diner. Sally's head was swimming. If what McCann had showed her and talked to her about happened, her world would change significantly! The tough part was that, for now, she couldn't tell anyone about it!

That evening, after doing his chores, taking a quick shower and changing out of his work clothes, McCann had dinner with Phil and Martha Willard at their home in Farnsworth. The Willards listened thoughtfully as McCann outlined his idea and they exchanged smiles as he mentioned getting Sally's advice. McCann left around 9:00 p.m. Although it was getting late in the evening, Willard placed a call to Ross in Lansing. He told the Governor's assistant about the potential acquisition of all the LEGENT properties and the impact on Farnsworth. After answering a few questions, he told Ross about McCann's idea.

"We'll need some help," Willard said.

"You'll get it," Ross said. To use a basketball term, it seemed to the Governor's right hand man that this was a "slam dunk!"

It was after eleven when Ross left the Capitol for home. He had summarized his conversation with Willard into a three-page memo to the Governor and e-mailed it. He had also prepared a one-page directive for the Governor's signature. He had no doubt that it would be signed and delivered early Monday morning. As he strode to his car, he looked up at a cloudless sky. The moon and the stars were shining brightly and, it seemed to him, were coming into alignment!

The cloudless, moonlit sky of the previous evening exploded into a brilliant sunshine on Sunday morning. McCann, up ahead of the sun, watched it rise over the eastern horizon as he fed the cattle. The temperatures were well below freezing and his breath floated before him as he spread the bales of hay for the steers. Wink lay in the doorway of the barn, letting the rising sun warm her.

He made the mistake of checking his e-mail when they went inside. A barrage of messages filled his Outlook Express folders. Most were the back and forth of terminology and specific points to be or not to be included in the acquisition plan. Cindy, Stu and Feldman in New York and Boyington and Smith in Detroit as well as a man named Nixon, working with Straylin in Charlotte, were all involved. Few invited comment from McCann but where he felt it important to, he did so. He changed into a suit, dress shirt and shoes, foregoing the tie, and started for the door as the phone rang.

It was Bailey, checking various minor points that McCann chafed at while watching the clock slowly tick down toward the time for the start of Sunday services. Just as he was about to try to terminate the conversation, it dawned on him what Bailey was doing. He was checking McCann's mental attitude about accepting a lesser role in the proposed organization.

"Stu, I'm fine with everything," he said, "Stop playing mother hen! It doesn't suit you!"

"I just want to be sure you are solidly in this thing and that you're okay with the COO role," Bailey responded.

"Stu, for the first time in my life, I have my priorities straight and being CEO is not at the top of the list. I want to do what God leads me to do. I want to stay here in Farnsworth and I want to pay back for years of putting myself and my personal goals above everything else. So, stop worrying! I've got to go now. Church starts in five minutes."

"Fine, I just wanted to...," Bailey started.

"Stu, you are a good friend and I appreciate you. I've got to go." With that, he hung up and headed out the door.

In New York, Stu Bailey put down his phone and looked out the window. He had spent the night in his office working on the details of his firm's participation in the acquisition. For some reason, this deal was more personal to him than most. It felt different than most of the M&A activity he participated in. McCann had changed. Bailey had been concerned that McCann's ego would get in the way of taking a lesser role but that appeared to be unfounded.

"Amazing," he said, as sagged back into his chair. He looked at his watch. He decided to go home. His wife would be surprised. She was used to his eccentric work schedule when a deal was about to come off. Maybe he could take her to lunch. Afterward, they could take a walk in Central Park. That would surprise her even more!

Even as Bailey was heading home, McCann was striding down the sidewalk to the church. It was the last Sunday before Christmas and there wasn't a parking space within three blocks! He entered just as the *Gloria Patri* was being sung. Thankfully, there was a seat in the last row. He much preferred sitting in the back as it gave him a full view of the entire congregation. He could watch others, while they would be hard pressed to watch him watching them. There were, however, three sets of eyes that had seen him enter. Fred Penay, from his seat on the far left, Phil Willard from his seat on the far right and Sally McHugh from the pew she shared with her three sons and the Marks family, three rows in front of him. All three were trying to re-focus on the services and refrain from thinking about the impact of the acquisition on Farnsworth.

The children presented a short program of recitations and two Christmas carols before Charles Hastings led the applause and waited while the children scurried down from the platform to re-join their families. Trent Marks, spotting McCann in the last row, walked right past his family and slid into the pew next to McCann. Lona Marks looked over her shoulder to see where her son had gone and smiled broadly as she spotted him leaning against McCann, whose arm now encircled the boy's shoulders.

Another carol was sung. The announcements including the Christmas Eve Communion service for the following Friday night were read. One of the young women of the church sang "Oh Holy As her voice resounded through the church, the congregation became still. When Hastings walked to the center of the platform, Bible in hand, the hush continued.

"My text for this morning is Luke 2:8-20. Let's read it together," he said, opening his Bible.

The congregation stood as one and began to read the account of the shepherds and the angels. When they were finished, they sat and Hastings put his Bible on the lectern and, without notes, began to speak.

"The shepherds are my favorite characters in the story of Christ's birth. If I could be any character in the story, I would want to be a shepherd. Now, you have to consider that shepherds get much more favorable treatment in our re-enactments of the Christmas story than is probably due them. We portray them with nice clean shepherd costumes and we wouldn't think of allowing someone to play the part of a shepherd if he or she hadn't taken a bath for a couple of weeks. Usually, if there are any live animals in our manger scenes, they are kept away from our shepherds, neatly penned to make sure they don't run away. Today, if someone plays the part of a shepherd; he or she is usually at least a high school graduate and maybe even holds an advanced degree."

"But let's be clear about something. Shepherds, on the day that Christ came into this world were at or near the bottom of the social order. They were illiterate, dirty, and smelly! They had to get 'up close and personal' with their sheep, and the smell of sheep was all over them. If you were one of the band of shepherds, you probably had smelled it and seen it so long that it didn't faze you. If you weren't one of the band, you would probably be holding a hankie over your nose and trying to get as far away from them as you could."

"But, God sent his angels to announce the birth of his son to this bunch! That brings me to the first reason I respect the shepherds and would be proud to be one. They were on the job! It says in verse 8 that *'and in the same region there were some shepherds staying out in the fields, and keeping watch over their flock by night.'* They were doing what they were paid to do and they were there to receive God's message of 'Joy to the World.'

"So, the first angel delivers the message of God to this group and they are scared out of their wits! But, God isn't finished with them yet! The angel tells them not to be afraid and delivers the 'good news of great joy'. That brings me to my second reason for respect. They stayed to hear the whole message. They could have run away! The Bible says they were terrified! Why didn't they run? If they had run away, they would have missed the message and they would have missed the directions on how to find this 'Savior'."

Then, God gives them the grand finale. The Bible says, *"And suddenly there appeared with the angel a multitude of the heavenly host praising God, and saying, 'Glory to God in the highest, and on earth peace among men with whom He is pleased'".* "That had to be something that would lift you right out of the sheepfold! Can you begin to imagine what a 'great company of the heavenly host,' sounds like? WOW!"

"I want to take a minute to play something for you. Tim, if you will, please play it now."

Hasting pointed to the sound booth at the rear of the church. A man in head phones reached forward and pushed a button on a control panel and the church was filled with the sounds of the Mormon Tabernacle Choir singing *Gloria In Excelsis Deo*. The volume grew until it was almost too much. Trent Marks looked up at McCann and covered his ears with his hands. The volume, having reached its upward limits, began to recede until, as the final words were sung, it faded away to nothing.

Hastings smiled as he took a step forward toward his audience. "Multiply what you just heard by ten and maybe it comes close to what this band of dirty, scruffy, smelly shepherds has just heard."

"This brings me to my final four reasons for wanting to be a shepherd. I'll give them to you quickly. They **went,** they **saw,** they **spread the word** and they **went back to work, glorifying God.**"

"They found something that was more important at that moment than doing their job. They had to stop keeping watch over their responsibilities and hope that the sheep would be safe while they responded to a higher calling. When they saw who was in the manger, they couldn't keep quiet about it. They told others. Then, they went back to work but they went back changed. They glorified God in their daily living."

"This Christmas, will you join me in being a shepherd? Will you come and see Jesus? Will you tell others about Him? Will you let Him change you to the point where you can't keep quiet about him? He doesn't care about how dirty you are with the world's filth. He doesn't care about how you smell from the day-to-day battles of living in an unclean world. He doesn't care if your clothes aren't from the most fashionable store in the mall. He doesn't care if you don't have a PH.D., M.B.A., J.D. or even a GED. He just wants you to come and see, to come and see and tell, to come and see and tell and live for him. Will you do it? Let's pray."

The congregation stood to sing the final carol. After the benediction, people engaged in quiet conversation but the mood was reflective without the usual chatter that followed a morning service. Trent Marks looked up at McCann.

"I'd like to have been a shepherd, wouldn't you?" he said quietly.

McCann place his hand on the boy's head. "That would have been pretty neat!" he said.

Monday's dawn came cold and damp with a wind out of the northwest. McCann pulled his sheepskin lined denim collar up as he fed his cattle. Wink stayed well inside the barn and waited to return to the house.

After breakfast, he changed into a pair of clean jeans, white shirt and a sleeveless sweater vest before driving into Farnsworth for an early morning conference call between the parties. Cindy, Stu and Feldman in New York, Smith and Boyington in Detroit and Straylin and his assistant in Charlotte discussed follow-up options based on both acceptance and rejection of their offer.

Theirs was not the only conference call going on at that time. Ross chaired a video conference between Lansing, three other points in the U.S. and three international locations. His message to the participants was crisp and clear.

"Lady and gentlemen, I need your commitment by January 3rd at 10:00 a.m. Eastern Standard Time. We need to make an announcement within that week."

The participants had little to say beyond a few questions about form and follow-up once each party had received copies of the others' commitments. Ross provided a summary of the time line milestones for the week following the receipt of the commitment letters.

Following the call, he handed Dan Ryan the Governor's directive. Ryan looked it over and dropped it back on the conference room table. His questioning look was not surprising to Ross.

"I presume there is more to this than you want to tell me right now?" he asked.

"It's conditional but we need to be able to announce it on Friday," Ross replied.

"When will we see the commitments on behalf of the investor and the village?" Ryan asked.

"They should be here by tonight, tomorrow morning at the latest."

"Job counts, economic impact, lease agreements, management agreements? That's a lot to pull off in one day." Ryan's tone conveyed his skepticism.

Ross leaned back in his chair. "I have confidence in the parties' ability to do it."

"This thing is like a spider web," Ryan said, gathering the paper up and stuffing it into his portfolio.

Ross frowned. His irritation showed as he said quietly, "Tell me again what you do?"

Ryan sighed, "Work with the state and county economic development entities to facilitate economic development."

Ross let his temper recede. Ryan was a career public servant and, Ross suspected, not a great supporter of the Governor or his programs. But he would do his job and he would do it well.

"We are developing the economy. The people involved have to do their part. If they don't, or if they don't do it the way it needs to be done, you have my permission to file that directive away in your 'failed projects' file," Ross said, as he left the room.

Leonard Olzewski's phone rang at home before Lottie was out of bed. He grabbed it before it could ring a second time. Fifteen minutes later he stuck his head in the bedroom doorway to tell her he was leaving for the office. Before she could ask why he was leaving so early, he was out the door. Ten minutes after that, he was reading the first of twenty pages on his office computer. He printed the agreement, signed and scanned the signature page into his computer and e-mailed it back to the sender. Then, he picked up the phone and placed a call to the Village Manager in Farnsworth. Next, he brought up a commercial real estate offer document on his computer and used the document he had just signed to fill in the blanks. He e-mailed it to the sender of the agreement he had just signed. Ten minutes later, the signature page of the offer document came back attached to an e-mail. He printed it off attached it to the offer and made three copies of the offer. He put all of it into his briefcase and walked out of his office, locking the door behind him. Twenty minutes later, he walked into the Farnsworth Village offices. At that same time, Phil Willard placed a call to the Executive Director of the Tuscola County Economic Development Corporation at his home. By the time the Director had hung up and called the Michigan Economic Development Corporation in Lansing, they were expecting his call because Dan Ryan had already talked to them. While Leonard Olzewski waited outside the Village Manager's office, the Village Manager received two phone calls. One was from Lansing and one was from Caro. He looked out the doorway of his office at Leonard Olzewski. He had known Leo for over twenty years. He had never been very impressed with the realtor, until today.

"Leo! Come in! Come in! I have to tell you that I am impressed at how quickly you are moving on this!" He boomed in his most citizen friendly voice.

As Olzewski crossed the threshold he felt like Julius Caesar crossing the Rubicon. He took the proffered chair and waited until the Manager was seated behind his desk. Olzewski reached into his briefcase and produced a copy of the offer which he handed to the Village Manager.

"My client would like a decision within twenty four hours," he said.

The Manager quickly scanned the offer. "It's a conditional offer, Leo. What's the hurry?"

"My client has several projects underway that together represent a significant amount of money. While this is an important part of the overall program, it is not the keystone project. My client has to know that this offer is accepted based upon the conditions put forward in the offer so that he can concentrate on the larger parts of the overall projects," Olzewski replied. The response sounded rehearsed because Leo had spent the entire twenty minute drive from Caro to Farnsworth committing it to memory. The speech had been written out for him and attached as an addendum to the original document that he had signed.

"Leo, I have to know more in order to ask the Village Council to go into emergency session to deal with this." He said it in a forceful tone.

Olzewski squirmed a bit in his chair but held firm. He had his marching orders and he wasn't about to deviate from them. There was a large commission tied to this offer and he wasn't about to do or say something that would put it in danger. He hadn't rehearsed his reply and it came out sounding plaintive.

"I'm not at liberty to say anything more. The offer my client has made is very fair and deserves consideration. It has a time limit and my client would appreciate an answer within twenty four hours…please."

The Farnsworth Village Manager could see that Olzewski was not going to give him anything more. It was obvious that Leo was a man on a very short leash and the offer that lay on the desk was, indeed, a very fair one.

"I'll get back to you before the end of the day with a status," he said, rising and extending his hand.

Olzewski took it gratefully and left to deliver the other two copies of the offer to Fred Penay and Wilson McCann.

King had waited as long as he dared. He was already five minutes late for his meeting with Lister. He made another call to the CEO's office.

"Is he in yet?" King asked.

"He just got in. I'll give him your message. You'll be in Mr. Lister's office?" the Secretary asked.

"Yes, but remember to tell him that it needs to be..."

"Yes, I know, 'casual'. I'll see to it," she said. He sensed the tone of a fellow conspirator and gave thanks for experienced secretaries.

He took the elevator up to Lister's office and was ushered in. Lister was a tall, thin man with graying hair. He was an avid runner and his physical condition reflected it. He consistently wore a look that said "challenge me if you dare." As King entered, he looked up over his half glasses and then down at his wrist watch.

"What kept you?" he asked in his "challenge me if you dare" tone.

King was used to this. He slid easily into the subservient role that Lister wanted.

"Sorry Norm, I was putting the final touches on the summary. Here it is."

He handed the document across the desk and settled down in one of the side chairs. "The top two pages are the summary," he said.

"That's what it says – summary," Lister responded, sitting back in his chair and beginning to read.

King took a surreptitious glance at his wrist watch. Lister caught it. "In a hurry John?" he asked, returning to the document.

King shifted a little in his chair and smiled, "Just thinking that I had planned to be playing golf this morning."

"Stuff happens," Lister responded, not looking up. He flipped to the second page.

"Where does McCann fit in?" he asked, not looking up.

King had known that this would be the first question. Lister had an absolute phobia where Wilson McCann was concerned. When LEGENT mounted its acquisition of Dynacom, the word at LEGENT was that, had the venture gone smoothly, McCann would have been sitting in Lister's seat. Lister knew that too.

"He's not on the Board," King replied, stating the obvious. The summary listed the principals of the acquiring consortium. He had purposefully left McCann's name out of the summary. If Lister chose to read the detailed proposal he would find McCann's name on page 3 listed as President and Chief Operating Officer of the acquiring company.

"Straylin is CEO? That had to be tough for McCann to swallow," Lister observed. He put down the report and looked at King. His voice rising, he said, "John, cut out the crap! I know that you went through McCann to bring this deal. Now, what's his role?"

King let his gaze sweep the room including the doorway to the office. It was empty.

"He will be Chief Operating Officer."

Lister flicked the middle finger of his right hand and snapped it against the report, sending it half way across the desk in King's direction. "No deal! We aren't doing it."

"Norm, be reasonable. This is the best price we are going to get for these properties and we can divest all of them in one transaction. The backers are vetted. They will do what they say. Don Straylin has been watching this industry for years and this is his first major investment in it. He will do everything that agreement says they will do," King replied, trying to keep his voice reasonable. He eyed Lister as he said it. This was going to be difficult.

"No. No deal. We aren't doing it…"

"Doing what?"

The voice from the doorway surprised both men. King felt his hopes return. He turned his head to see James "Stormy" Weathers, the CEO of LEGENT standing in the doorway.

Weathers' thinning hair was combed straight back which emphasized his bullet-shaped head. He was wearing a green sport coat with light green slacks and a white oxford shirt, open at the throat. He stood six feet even and looked like a professional prize fighter. His shoulders and arms were muscular and there was no bulge at his beltline despite his sixty five years.

King turned back to Lister, waiting. Lister's discomfiture was apparent. Stormy Weathers was a formidable figure.

"John's brought in an offer for the Midwest properties. I don't recommend it."

"Who's it from? I thought we had about run out of suitors!" Weathers said, walking a few steps further into the room. "I was just going to wish you a 'happy holidays' but now that I'm here, let me take a look at it."

King glanced at Lister. Lister's face betrayed his skepticism. He knew that he had been "set up." King didn't care. He had thought his flight to Michigan would be the last one on a LEGENT jet. Now, he had logged one more from Savannah to Dallas and, with some luck, he might make a couple more. Hopefully, he wouldn't have to deal with Norm Lister beyond today. He leaned back in his chair and waited for Lister to hand Weathers the report. It was obvious that Lister had been hoping that King would do so. He reluctantly leaned across the desk, retrieved the report, aligned the pages, and handed it to the CEO. Weathers dropped into a vacant chair and began to read. King noted that he didn't merely read the two page summary but read on into the report. The silence was deafening. By the time Weathers reached the middle of the report itself, Lister cleared his throat and spoke.

"I just don't think this deal represents full value for the properties, after the first of the year, we can re-solicit and I'm sure that we will get a better offer."

"From who?" Weathers replied without looking up.

"There are rumors that other groups are forming; perhaps we can re-attract one of the original companies. Maybe an RBOC could be attracted…"

"Come on Norm! We want to get on with our optic programs in our major metro areas and we want to fully develop our cellular presence. This is money in the hand that cuts both ways. We shed some properties that frankly we aren't doing so well operating and we get some cash flow to fund the two programs we really care about."

"I just don't think..." Lister began.

"That's right. You're not thinking. Not on this one. This is a reasonable offer and I think we should take it to the Board," Weathers said, rolling the report into a scroll and leaning forward. "We have to move quickly, right John?"

"The offer expires Friday evening," King replied, not looking at Lister.

"Good, I'll call an emergency teleconference of the Board tomorrow and recommend we move forward on this. Good job John! This will send you off on a high note!"

King smiled at his CEO. He and Weathers had started out together years ago. It was obvious from the start that Weathers' star would rise far and wide. On this day, King was glad for that and the enduring friendship they had been able to share.

"Speaking of high notes," Weathers said, rising, "I see where Wils McCann will be Chief Operating Officer of the new company. I envy that son-of-a-B. Operations is where all the fun is. Right, Norm?"

King bit down hard on his lower lip to keep from laughing out loud at the look on Lister's face. "Thanks, Norm," he said, as he rose and followed the CEO out the door.

(37)

Robert had been awakened by a dim light coming from the kitchen. He looked at the clock on the bedside table. It read slightly before 5:00 a.m. He knew that his mother usually was at the diner at 6:00 a.m. each morning, but this was early even for her. He glanced over at David in the other twin bed. David was breathing heavily.

Robert slid into his slippers and quietly stepped out into the hallway. He walked down to the kitchen to find Sally, fully dressed, hunched over a large sketch pad on which she was making notes. A ruler and various colored pencils were spread across the pad.

"Mom, what are you doing?" he asked, moving closer.

Sally turned her chair to place herself in his path. It was obvious that whatever she had been doing on the pad, she didn't want him to see.

"I'm sorry honey; I didn't mean to wake you. Do you want some breakfast?" she asked as she stood and flipped the pad over. The ruler and pencils scattered with some landing on the floor. She began picking them up.

"Mom, what's going on? What are you doing?" His tone was urgent.

Sally finished replacing the pencils on the overturned pad and spoke without looking at him.

"I'm working on a project."

"What kind of project? Why are you being so mysterious?"

She let out a sigh and turned to face him. "Can you keep a secret?"

He felt like he did years ago when Sally would hide things in their little apartment for him to find. They hadn't had much but they had each other. No matter what she did or what others said about her, he always remembered those days. Now, he could see the same light dancing in her eyes that he had as a four-year old looking for the hidden "secrets" that she gave him.

He smiled at her, "Sure, mom."

She turned the pad over and began to tell him. As her fingers traced the drawing on the pad and she told him about the ideas she had, he was taken aback by the awesome opportunity that lay on the papers before them. When she finished, he smiled at her and said, "This is Mr. McCann's doing, isn't it?"

He saw the color rise in her cheeks. "Yes."

Robert knew that for most of his life his mother had been looking for something in the wrong places. He still loved her despite the mistakes that he felt she had made. Now, he saw a glimmer of what could be and he silently hoped that this time she would find it.

Darcy Hardesty looked out the window of the Barnes Loft onto Farnsworth's main street. She saw Leo Olzewski scurrying down the street toward the bank, a leather portfolio clutched beneath his arm. She could see Sally McHugh serving coffee to two men at the diner across the street. She turned back to the counter and eyed the two large cartons that UPS had just delivered. Wilson McCann had placed the orders two weeks ago. There was over $1,000 worth of clothing, jewelry and toys in those cartons. A smaller box containing more gifts was behind the counter. She had already guessed that one of the jackets in the box on the counter was for her and knew that there was a snow suit in it for her baby. The small box behind the counter held a small electronic automotive testing tool that Nick had been coveting. The cartons would have to be opened where they were and the contents moved to the storage area for wrapping. The Christmas wrap, bows and name tags had arrived last Friday. McCann wanted everything wrapped and the bows attached by tomorrow night. She would put the name of the item on post-it notes and stick them on the packages so he would know what was in each. The addressing of the cards was his job.

These merchandise orders would ensure that the Barnes Loft would finish the year in the black. She still struggled with the enormity of it all. When Donna died, McCann had come to the store and asked her if she thought she could run it. He had assured her that between Fred Penay at the bank, Phil Willard and himself she would have the support she needed. Since then, she had studied, worked and trusted that God would take care of her little family, and He had. Nick was working part time for Phil Willard at the Agway and for McCann at the farm. From time to time, he took on auto repair jobs using a small garage on the outskirts of Farnsworth. An elderly mechanic owned and operated it and Phil Willard had arranged for Nick to use it in the evenings for a reasonable fee.

Since Donna's death, Belle and Lori Warner, Lona Marks and Dorothy Hastings had all become more frequent customers of the Barnes Loft. When they couldn't find what they wanted in the store, they thumbed through catalogs that Darcy kept under the counter and ordered from them. A month or so ago, Darcy had received an e-mail order from Cindy Melzy in New York City that more than paid the lease payment for November. Three weeks ago, Sally McHugh had come in and ordered gifts for her three sons and a winter barn coat in McCann's size. Regular customers whose business had dropped off in the period after Donna's death had begun to return with the onset of the holiday season.

After New Years, Darcy was scheduled to go to Chicago to a fashion show and buyers' seminar. McCann had given her the name of an attorney who had handled the flight arrangements and hotel reservations. A clerk from his law firm would meet her at the airport.

She slit open the top of the first carton and as she did so, a tear coursed down her face and dropped on the cardboard. She wiped her eyes as she began to take out the items inside. She thought again of the Sunday morning when she and Nick had walked down to the altar at the end of the service. She breathed a silent prayer of thanksgiving as she carried Wilson McCann's Christmas gifts back to the storage area for wrapping.

George Whyte and Joe Rambaugh were the two men having coffee at the Diner. Rambaugh's cell phone had gone off just as Sally brought their check, so she retreated behind the counter and tried to ignore the conversation. People seemed to talk louder when they used their cell phones and Rambaugh's voice was loud anyway. She couldn't help but hear his end of the conversation and smiled to herself knowingly. Rambaugh turned off his phone and leaned in toward Whyte.

"That was our good City Manager. There's an emergency meeting of the Village Council at noon." He had tried to lower his voice but Sally could still hear it quite plainly.

Whyte had been reaching into his pocket for his money clip. He paused and looked at his fellow City Council member. "For what?"

"Someone's made an offer for the Dunt school building and they want an answer by tomorrow morning."

Whyte stopped reaching for his money and leaned back in his chair. "Who?"

"He didn't say. He just said to be at his office at noon."

"What's the hurry?"

Rambaugh looked out the window and saw Leo Olzewski walking rapidly down the street toward the Agway. He thought it seemed strange that the realtor, whose office was in Caro, would be in Farnsworth this early in the morning.

"The offer expires at 9:00 a.m. tomorrow," Rambaugh said.

"There's something funny going on here. I hear rumors that the telephone company is involved in some big deal and the Warner's are seen with the Governor up in Bad Axe. Now somebody wants to buy a 40-year old school building and gives the town 24 hours to take their offer," Whyte grumbled as the two men rose, dropped some money on the table and left.

Sally moved to pick up the two coffee mugs, the three $1 bills and the $2.95 bill. She watched Whyte and Rambaugh as they headed up the street. Rambaugh was gesturing animatedly at the other man.

"If only you knew, guys! If only you knew!" she thought to herself as she wiped the table.

"You missed a spot!" McCann said, as he came through the door.

She turned, smiling as he took off his sheep lined denim jacket. It was beginning to look a little worn and she thought about the new barn coat that she had ordered from Darcy Hardesty. It had seemed like an odd Christmas present at first, but she had decided it would be something of hers that would be close to him.

"A lot of work for a five cent tip!" she shot back.

McCann looked out the window and up and down the street. "Aha! Must have been my friends George and Joe!"

"They just got the call from the City Manager," she said, as she retreated behind the counter and dropped the two mugs and spoons into a tub of hot soapy water.

McCann dropped into a chair at one of the tables and smiled up at her. "Had any more thoughts on the matter?" he asked.

Sally reached under the counter and pulled out several rolled-up papers. "I'm losing my beauty sleep over this!" she said, as she dropped them on the table in front of him. There was no one else in the diner, so she sat down opposite him and unrolled the papers. When Phil Willard and Fred Penay walked in ten minutes later, McCann and Sally's heads were close together as they concentrated on Sally's drawings and notes. The two men poured themselves cups of coffee from the urn behind the counter and joined them.

Promptly at noon, the Village Council convened in emergency session. The town Clerk took minutes and noted that all five council members plus the Village Manager were present. The Village Manager passed out photocopies of the offer sheet that Leo Olzewski had given him earlier that morning. After an hour of discussion including a lot of questioning by Council members Rambaugh and Whyte, the Chairman, Earl Hardesty, called the question.

"I move we accept the offer as presented," Phil Willard said.

"Second the motion," Fred Penay said.

"I will now poll the council as to the matter of the sale of the Selma Dunt Elementary School. Mr. Whyte?" Hardesty inquired.

"Nay," Whyte replied. "I want to know more before I agree to this."

"Mr. Penay?"

"Aye," the banker replied.

"Mr. Rambaugh?"

"Nay, I agree with George, we need to know more about this. There's something fishy here," the auto dealer blustered.

"Mr. Willard?"

"Aye," Phil replied, looking at Fred Penay.

Hardesty looked down at the pad in front of him. He looked at the Town Clerk who looked right back at him.

"The Chair votes Aye. The motion is carried. The Village Manager is instructed to accept the offer subject to the conditions listed in the offer sheet."

Fifteen minutes later, after a barrage of objections, complaints and ominous threats by Whyte and Rambaugh, the meeting was adjourned. Whyte and Rambaugh noisily gathered themselves and their papers and stalked out of the room. Willard and Penay followed. The Town Clerk left for her office and Hardesty and the Village Manager sat alone in the room.

"The offer was a very reasonable one," the Manager offered.

"Yes," Hardesty replied.

"Do you think we did the right thing?"

Hardesty leaned back in his chair and looked at the ceiling. A lot had changed in his life in the past few months. His son and his family would be coming for Christmas dinner at the end of the week. It would be the first Christmas in eighteen years with gifts for a baby under his tree. His son had "cleaned up his act" and was working at three different jobs. Earl had taken to walking down the street to the Barnes Loft on most days to look in on his grandson. The girl not yet out of her teens that he had thought of as a "tramp" six months ago had blossomed before him into a young woman who was running a business while being a wife to a reformed son and a mother to the start of the next generation of Hardestys.

"I have come to believe that great things are possible in this world if we truly believe them to be," he said as he stood, shook the Manager's hand and left.

At the Agway, Phil called McCann and reported the results of the meeting. At the same time, Fred Penay called Leo Olzewski and informed him that the Village had accepted the offer and that their acceptance would be coming shortly.

McCann hung up from talking to Willard and immediately placed a call to Norm Miller in Chicago.

"It's a go," he said.

"Conditions accepted?" Miller asked.

"Yes."

"Well, everything depends on LEGENT now," Miller said.

"Their Board meets tomorrow afternoon by teleconference. King tells me that Stormy will push it through."

"Christmas Eve should be pretty exciting up there in the country," Miller said.

"Very much so," McCann replied.

When he had hung up the phone, he sat back and closed his eyes for a moment. Wink, sensing the opportunity, came and rested her head on his knee. He stroked her head. "If only Donna were here," he said, quietly.

That evening, Shirley Jacobs called McCann and brought him up to date on the planning for her fundraising trip. He could tell from the moment that she said "Hello Wils" that it was going well. She had already secured five telephone commitments from existing support organizations. All of the commitments were above their previous levels and three were five-year commitments that replaced three-year ones. He sat back and listened, patting Wink on the head as Shirley talked. She stopped abruptly. "Wils, tell me what's been happening in your life since we last were together."

He smiled at the abrupt change in direction. "Well a few things are going on, that's for sure."

"Tell me about them," she said, and he did.

"I'm as excited for you as I am about what is happening at EECM! When will you know about all of this?"

"Friday is the day, one way or another," he replied.

"I'll be praying for you! God bless." They said goodbye and McCann put the phone down only to have it ring again.

It was Lark Bishop reporting on the IT installation. All systems were up, training was complete and they were awaiting the arrival of the re-constituted data base. McCann shared what Shirley had told him and there was a long silence on the other end of the connection. Bishop finally spoke.

"Wils, I don't know how you did this but you have totally changed the outlook for this ministry. God has his hand on you, that's for sure."

McCann felt the color rise. "Thanks Lark. Donna had a real interest in EECM's ministry. I feel that she would be pleased with what you are going to be doing as you move forward."

"If I don't talk to you again before Christmas, I'm praying that you will have a very blessed one," Bishop responded.

The two men spoke for a few more minutes and then the call was over. McCann looked at his watch. It was a little early to take care of the cattle. He sat back in his chair and closed his eyes. Wink circled the chair, looking up at him and then lay down and put her head on her paws. Just as she closed her eyes, a car pulled into the drive. Both man and dog came alert as one. McCann strode to the kitchen window and looked out. A three-year-old Toyota Camry had circled the drive and was parked opposite the back door-way. A woman in a blue Beret and a rather worn looking cloth coat got out. As she turned to walk up to the back door, McCann smiled, "Well, Wink, I think Janice DeGroot has arrived!"

While Janice was walking up to the back door of Wilson McCann's farmhouse, Sally McHugh was walking the halls of the Selma Dunt School with Al Strahl of Sheppmann Engineering. Strahl had arrived at the diner a few minutes earlier and she had hung a "be back soon" sign on the door, locked it and driven with him to the school.

Strahl was making notes on a section of the school's floor plan as they walked. On the drive over, she had reviewed her notes with him. She was surprised at how readily he had picked up on her thoughts and added to them. It was obvious that someone had prepped him to what he would hear on this trip.

"Help me understand how it is that you are here so quickly and seem to be so well-informed on this? . . . .I mean, we don't even have a formal answer yet and . . .," she began.

Strahl paused from looking into a small wash-room and turned to face her.

"Mr. McCann's attorney, a man named Norm Miller, filled our Chicago partner in on the broad outline of what you folks have in mind and he called my boss in Detroit. I was told to get up here, meet with you, listen to your ideas and put together a high-level outline that could be priced out and used as an information piece. I'm to have that done by Thursday noon."

Sally was amazed. "How can you do all that in such a short time?"

"Easy. We feed the data from these building plans into a CAD-CAM system and then we make the changes that you and I agree on and produce a cost estimate and a time-table. We give that to our own PR person and she writes up what she thinks are the most important aspects that the public will want to hear about and gives it back to me. I look it all over and send it to you. By the way, I'll need your e-mail address so I can send it to you. From there, it will be up to you and Mr. McCann to handle the announcement."

Sally's stomach tightened. She could feel her nerves kicking in and she wished she had a drink to steady them. Then she realized that a drink and what she had given herself over to wouldn't go well together.

"But...I've never done anything like this... I don't know...," she stammered.

Strahl smiled at her. "Ms. McHugh, our firm has been doing business with Wilson McCann and his organization for the last ten years...right up until Dynacom was bought out by LEGENT. I'm proud to say that every project we did for Dynacom was brought in on time and on budget. I've seen the type of people he picks and they are all first-class. If he says you are going to head up this project. Then you will be a success. And we are going to make sure that happens!"

He put his hand on her shoulder and looked her squarely in the eye. "Now, we've got a lot of work to do and it starts with making sure we know all about this building. I understand you went to school here?"

"Yes, it seems like an eternity ago."

"What better person to work with than someone who spent several years here?" Strahl said, as he walked on down the hall. Sally followed after him. She felt a new surge of confidence. She could do this thing and, when she got home tonight, she was going to pitch that bottle of Jack Daniels into the trash can!

Two hours later, Strahl dropped her off at the diner with a promise to be in touch the next day. She glanced at her watch and noted that she had just enough time to get ready for the dinner customers.

Janice reached for her Beret and stood as she put it on. McCann held her coat for her and opened the door. She paused as she picked up her tape recorder.

"And you're sure there is nothing I could take with me for a lead-in story prior to Friday?" she asked, knowing the answer.

McCann smiled broadly. "Janice, we have an agreement. I expect to keep my part of it and I expect you to keep yours. I imagine you wouldn't tell your kids what they are getting for Christmas today, would you?"

"Well, no but...,"

"Exactly. Your little gift for your readers will come, if it comes, on Friday. If it doesn't come, I will give you a second interview on Friday afternoon that will be on the record. If it comes, you have it all nicely wrapped up in your little recorder. But make no mistake. If you breathe a word of what I've shared with you before we announce on Friday, you and your paper will have a lawsuit of epic proportions under your Christmas tree on Saturday morning. Now, I have to take care of twenty hungry steers. It's been nice meeting you and I hope we will be seeing you on Friday. I'm sure Sally will be pleased if you can come."

With that, he placed his hand on her back and, without seeming to push, escorted her out through the door and toward her car.

As she drove away, she saw McCann and his dog head for the barn. She drove to the end of the road and stopped to gather herself. She had just been handed what was potentially the biggest news story of her career. She had also sworn to speak to no one about it until McCann called her on Friday. At that time, she would know if she was coming back to Farnsworth to listen to a blockbuster announcement or to interview McCann again on what had gone wrong.

She thought of Sally McHugh. She and Sally had been best friends and co-editors of the Farnsworth High School newspaper as seniors. Janice had gone on to college and continued to study Journalism and earned her Masters degree. Sally had gone on, too. But Sally's life had had a few bad bounces along the way. It had all started that summer between their junior and senior years. Donna Barnes had gone on a mission trip and Sally McHugh had picked up where Donna left off and sowed her wild oats with Wilson McCann. Now McCann was back in Farnsworth and it appeared that Sally McHugh might have something really exciting to celebrate on Christmas day. Janice thought about McCann. Those eyes of his seemed to look right inside your soul. She found herself hoping that everything he had talked about would happen. She even found herself envying Sally McHugh for the first time since high school. She turned west and headed back to Bay City. Christmas was going to be interesting this year!

Tuesday dawned cold and cloudy. After tending to his chores and eating his breakfast, McCann went through his e-mails, showered and shaved and went into Farnsworth. He stopped at the Barnes Loft and picked up several shopping bags full of gifts that Darcy had wrapped for him. He noted the yellow post-it notes that she had placed on each one to tell him what was inside. He went to the diner and had coffee with Phil Willard and Sally. Sally reviewed the walk-through with Al Strahl. McCann was pleased to see that she seemed more confident than she had been about her role in the plan that was unfolding.

He went to the Telephone Company offices and participated in a last-minute run-through of the details of the offers to Farnsworth Tele and to LEGENT. At 11:00 a.m., the final sign-off was given by Arthur Boyington to the LEGENT attorney in Dallas. Now they would wait. In the meantime, McCann printed off several agreements that had been e-mailed to him by Norm Miller in Chicago. He gave one to Belle Warner and dropped the other two into his portfolio. He phoned Charles Hastings and arranged to meet him at the diner.

"We can try out the new cook's offerings," Hastings had said. When McCann asked what he meant, the minister had replied, "See you there."

Light, powdery snow was being blown by a cold wind across the street as he walked the three blocks to the diner. He had forgotten his gloves and shoved his hands into his coat pockets to keep them warm, his left arm clutching his portfolio close to his side.

The diner was busy with almost every seat taken. Sally was working behind the counter and he was surprised to see Dorothy Hastings shuttling between the tables and the kitchen. Christmas carol music played quietly in the background. Charles occupied a small table in the corner and watched the look of puzzlement spread over McCann's face as he hung up his coat.

"What's going on?" McCann said, as he dropped into the vacant chair opposite Hastings.

"Dorothy came in at 6:00 a.m. this morning and started helping Sally out. She's learning the ropes so that she can help whenever Sally needs her. All this new opportunity that you have brought to Farnsworth is having an impact at the parsonage too! This is something Dorothy has dreamed of trying all her life and, with the children in their teens, she decided to give it a whirl."

McCann sat back and watched Dorothy as she moved back and forth, serving customers, slapping bills on counter top and table alike and running the cash register on occasion as customers departed.

"I suggest you have the lemon meringue pie, it's Dorothy's," Hastings commented as he looked at the menu.

"Amazing!" McCann said, turning his attention to the menu as well.

After the two men had ordered, Hastings said a quick prayer and McCann extracted one of the contracts from his portfolio. He slid it across the table.

"Can you take a look at this and get the church board to approve it by Thursday?" he said.

"That's not a problem. I anticipated you would be moving quickly and our board will meet after prayer tomorrow night."

The two men quickly ran through the contract while they waited for their lunch. After five minutes, Hastings folded the contract and put it in the inside pocket of his sport coat. "I'm sure that this will be fine with our people," he said quietly.

"Great. We'd like to have everything ready if things break the way we hope they will," McCann said quickly. He saw the emotion begin to build in Hastings' face and knew what was coming. The minister reached across the table and laid his hand on McCann's.

"God bless you, Wils. This means more to me than you will ever know."

Just then, Dorothy Hastings arrived with their orders, which included two big slices of lemon meringue pie.

"Can I get you anything else, gentlemen?" she asked, with a smile on her face.

"Can you bring another slice home tonight for dinner, honey?" Hastings replied as he winked at McCann.

While McCann and Hastings were finishing their lemon pie, Stormy Weathers was finishing up an 11:00 a.m. Board teleconference call. Despite former Dynacom Chairman Charles Corbin's dissenting vote, the LEGENT board approved the sale of its Midwest telephone properties to the consortium led by Donald Straylin. Two other former Dynacom board members joined Corbin in voting against the sale but it passed on a 14-3 vote. Norm Lister returned to his office, told his administrative assistant not to put through any calls and slammed the door to his office behind him. John King called Donald Straylin in Charlotte to inform him of the LEGENT board's action and then called McCann. He left a message for McCann to call him and settled back in his chair to wait.

Wednesday morning brought snow flurries and a flurry of activity between Charlotte, New York City, Detroit, Chicago and Farnsworth. Rumors of the impending sale began to circulate through the offices in Dallas and Farnsworth and by noon, someone in the news media called both LEGENT and Farnsworth Tele. Both responded with "no comment at this time" as per their agreement. That response served to whet the media's interest and by the early afternoon similar calls were received at Straylin's office in Charlotte and Feldman's office in New York. Both calls were handled by designated underlings who could truthfully deny any knowledge of an impending deal. By mid-afternoon, both the *Tuscola County Advertiser* and the *Farnsworth Chronicle* had called Belle Warner. She graciously took their calls and told them that she would be happy to grant an interview on Friday morning. Both papers were weeklies and Belle's response did not satisfy their Wednesday evening content cut off. There was nothing the publishers could do but grind their teeth at the fact that by the time they got the full story, their daily counterparts in the larger cities would have a "scoop." Phil Willard was assigned to call the *Advertiser* and Fred Penay called the *Chronicle* to try to allay their concern and suggest, "Off the record" that extraordinary access would be given for any follow-up stories that their paper would want to do.

Janice DeGroot's editor called her at 11:00 a.m. to ask what she knew about the rumors being circulated. She replied that she was "chasing them down" and offered nothing else. She called McCann to make him aware of what was happening. McCann was in the middle of reading through a stack of agreement details that had been delivered by FEDEX that morning.

"Hang in there Janice!" he said to the urgency in DeGroot's voice. "Isn't this fun?"

Janice allowed as to how she had never been a part of something so frustrating and at the same time so exciting. McCann reminded her again of their agreement and the penalty for any breech and returned to his reading.

Meanwhile, John King, Donald Straylin and a public relations firm hired by Cindy, Bailey and Feldman worked through the logistics of a joint announcement for Friday morning. A video transmission link would connect Straylin's office in Charlotte with LEGENT'S Dallas office and the Selma Dunt Community Center in Farnsworth. When the three in New York questioned the Farnsworth location, Straylin was quick to state rather strongly that it was "part of the deal."

LEGENT'S human resource department was brought into the loop at approximately 4:00 p.m. They were assigned the task of working with McCann and Farnsworth Tele's Personnel representative to put together a message from McCann to all of the employees in the LEGENT properties that were to be acquired, as well as to the Farnsworth Tele employees. Using the terms contained in the acquisition agreements and his previous acquisition experience, McCann dictated a letter to all employees of the new corporation. In Dallas, a former Dynacom Human Resource Manager who had moved from Chicago to Dallas when LEGENT acquired Dynacom listened to McCann and upon going back to her office, immediately brushed up her resume and e-mailed it to McCann in Farnsworth.

In Prague, Myron Martin received a cellular phone call from a former co-worker in Dallas telling him about the rapidly spreading rumors of the sale. Martin and Thune immediately conferred and sent a one sentence e-mail to McCann: "If you need us, we can be there in 60 days." That was the notice requirement of their contract. In Farnsworth, McCann read the two e-mails and smiled at the thought of putting some of his old team back together.

At the same time that the Human Resource people in Dallas were talking with Wilson McCann, Phil Willard received a call from Dan Ryan in Lansing advising him that a Job Development Grant of $400,000 by the state's Economic Development Corporation had been approved. Phil immediately called the Tuscola County Economic Development office and was advised that, based upon the state's commitment, an additional grant of $100,000 would be made by the county. Willard hung up and called McCann. McCann was in the barn putting down hay for the cattle when his cellular phone rang. Wink, startled by the noise, rose from where she had been lying down in the feed alley and went outside into the gusting snow. She burrowed down into the snow in the lee of where the two sections of the barn came together and watched as the cattle stood in the barnyard waiting to be fed.

McCann hung up from talking to Willard and called Straylin in Charlotte. Fifteen minutes later, $500,000 was wired from Straylin's firm to a bank account in HHF Corporation's name at the Farnsworth State Bank.

All in all, Wednesday had been a very busy and productive day. As he and Wink walked back to the house at 6:00 p.m., McCann knew that the next two days would be just as busy. He stood for a moment in the dim glow of the yard light and looked out over the fields. Through the lightly driven snow he could make out the headlights of the traffic on the highway a half mile south of the farm. So much had happened since he had come back here. He bowed his head and thanked God for His love and guidance and asked that it would continue for the days ahead.

(38)

On Thursday morning, one of the news services broke the story of the rumored sale by LEGENT of its Midwestern telephone properties to a consortium headed by Donald Straylin. In response, Straylin and LEGENT issued a statement that a joint announcement would be made at ten o'clock on the following morning. The announcement would be made from a conference room at Straylin and Company's offices in Charlotte, LEGENT'S corporate offices in Dallas and the Selma Dunt Community Center in Farnsworth, Michigan. The news services responded to this by breaking a secondary story that the same consortium would acquire the Farnsworth Telephone Cooperative from the Warner Family. They included references to a rumor that the village of Farnsworth would become the headquarters for the newly formed corporation. For the rest of the day, Sally McHugh listened in as an unusually large lunch and dinner crowd discussed what was happening in Farnsworth. Several of her regular customers asked her questions about what she knew, to which she gave the same answer, "You'll have to wait 'til tomorrow to find out!"

By noon, she had received calls from the *Detroit Free Press* as well as the papers in Lansing and Flint. Each of them began the conversation by stating their understanding that she was a close friend of Wilson McCann who was rumored to be involved in an impending acquisition. Sally gave the same response to each of them. "Mr. McCann and I are friends but you will have to discuss anything related to his business interests with him."

They called McCann at the farm but he had unplugged the telephone. They called Farnsworth Tele but were told that "Mr. McCann is on our Board but is not in the offices today." Frustrated, they called the Editor of the *Chronicle* who told them that he didn't know any more than they did and probably not as much.

Ross briefed the Governor at 9:00 a.m. that morning. The Governor immediately scheduled a brief news conference for 1:00 p.m. the following day.

"This is outstanding, Ross! We couldn't have asked for more! We can follow this up with our own announcement right after New Years," he said, leaning back in his chair. He looked over the briefing sheet that Ross had prepared. It contained the statistics related to both acquisitions and projections of the economic impacts on Farnsworth, Tuscola County and Michigan's "Thumb." He pulled a file folder from his drawer and skimmed through a similar briefing paper on the Wolverine Property Management project. He quickly added the impact of the two projects together and smiled.

"Yes sir! This is great!" He swiveled in his chair and tapped his computer keyboard. His e-mail came up and he typed in an address and a quick message. He hit the "send" button and turned again to Ross who looked at him quizzically.

"I just sent our friend McCann a Christmas message."

Ross waited, thinking that the Governor was like a kid with a new toy.

"I told him that perhaps he would make the *Wall Street Journal* now and for the right reasons!" the Governor said. "Merry Christmas, Ross!"

Ross returned to his office and began to draft a statement for the Governor's Christmas Eve press conference.

At 1:00 p.m., McCann and the Warners visited the Dunt building and looked over the preparations going on in the old school auditorium. Three wide screen TVs had been set in place on the stage. Several rows of chairs had been placed on the floor of the auditorium below the stage. A podium was being put in place as they entered. Technicians were running the necessary communications cables that would connect to the head-end equipment at the company and allow the various news media to connect their satellite trucks back to their studios. T-1 lines had been installed the previous day for expanded voice and data communication. In deference to the local media, the *Advertiser, Chronicle* and Janice DeGroot had been given front row center seating. The Mayor, City Manager, the State Senator, and State Representative for Farnsworth had also been given front row seating along with representatives of the county and state Economic Development agencies.

Adjourning to a smaller room which had previously served as a school library, they were joined by Sally McHugh and Al Strahl. Strahl set up a small lap-top connected to a large screen monitor and ran through Sheppmann's situational analysis and cost projections. When he had finished, McCann turned to Sally who was obviously ill at ease.

"Well coach, what do you think?" he asked.

"I can't believe how quickly they did this. It's great," she replied looking at the screen.

McCann sharpened his tone, "I didn't mean how great it looks, and I want to know if you think it will work?"

She turned to face him, her face reddening. She could sense Belle and Doug watching her reaction.

"I'm no expert but …," she began.

"Yes you are! A lot of this represents your ideas. I want to know if you think we can announce tomorrow with good confidence that this will work," McCann said. His tone was sharp and his eyes bored into hers. Strahl watched them both, a faint smile on his lips. He had been the target of McCann's pointed questioning in the past.

A defiant gleam came into Sally's eyes. She turned slightly to face McCann squarely.

"You're damn right they will work! I'll see to it!"

The silence was deafening. Belle Warner looked at McCann with a small smile playing about her face. Doug Warner looked out the window and Al Strahl grinned openly. "Good for you!" he thought as he looked at McCann.

McCann tried to keep a straight face as he looked at Sally. Her eyes were still flashing and the color on her face was turning from red to white as she realized what she had just said.

"Good. You're beginning to sound like a project manager," he said evenly.

"Oh God!" she said.

"Indeed! Let's ask Him to guide this venture to His glory," Belle Warner said. Bowing her head, she led them in prayer.

At six o'clock the next morning, J. W. Storey availed himself of the "Free

Deluxe Continental Breakfast" at the Sleep Inn on West Wackerly Street in Midland, Michigan. As he ate, he scanned through the free *USA Today* newspaper. He paid particular interest this morning to the "Money" section of the paper but could find no mention of LEGENT or Farnsworth Tele. He glanced out the door as he settled his bill. The snowfall that had begun as snow showers two days ago was intensifying. The drive to Farnsworth might be a little more challenging than he had anticipated when he had made his decision yesterday afternoon.

J.W. was a well built 24-year old. He stood an even six feet tall and weighed in at 180 pounds. He had black hair and green eyes. Two and a half years of service in the United States Army had taught him the importance of focus, discipline and staying in shape. He hadn't really needed some of that army training. Frank and Francis had prepared him well for life. Frank and Frances Storey were both loving and protective while at the same time stern disciplinarians and firm in raising their son. Frank was a "lifer" at Midland's Dow Chemical plant. Frances was a stay-at-home mom who volunteered at their church, the school's PTA and the Red Cross. J.W. had graduated just past his 18th birthday and immediately enlisted in the Army. Frank had driven him to the recruiting office and saw him off at the train station with a firm handshake. When he was discharged, his parents met him at the airport with another firm handshake from Frank and a hug from Frances. He had immediately enrolled in college. He was ready to prepare himself for the rest of his life. The focus and discipline he had learned at home and in the military resulted in completion of his college studies in three and one half years. On Monday, the four sheets of paper in an envelope that was in the inner pocket of his jacket had shaken that focus to its very core.

He stowed his duffle bag in his snow-covered car and started it up to warm it while he brushed off the night's snow accumulation. As he did so, he could feel the envelope rustle against the fabric of the jacket. The family attorney had read its contents to him on Monday morning and it had taken him until now, four days later, to get over the shock and decide what he wanted to do.

J.W.'s duffle contained another document that he had thought would mark the beginning of the next stage of his life. He had finished his undergraduate studies at Central Michigan University just last week. In accordance with his parents' last will and testament, he had come home to meet with their attorney to read the codicil to their will.

Two years ago, just as he had been finishing his second year of college, Frank had died in a nursing facility here in Midland. Frances had died four years ago from a sudden heart attack. "Frances and Frank — F&F — just like the cough drops," his mother always introduced themselves to strangers. "And this is our son J.W — for 'just wright'," his father would add with a smile. The way he thought of them before Monday had been altered forever by the contents of the envelope.

J.W. had sat in the attorney's office after Frank's death, wondering if he would be able to finish college. The elderly white-haired lawyer had read the will to him and put his concerns at ease. While his parents hadn't left much of the world's goods behind, they had left enough money in a bank certificate of deposit to pay the last two years of his college education.

"There's one thing more," the attorney had said as he handed over the will for J.W. to take with him. "Your parents added a codicil to the will about ten years ago. It is to be opened and read upon your graduation from college."

"Any idea what it is about?" J.W. had asked.

"I'm not at liberty to say," the attorney had responded.

J.W. assumed then that "F&F" had provided some extra money for him at graduation to buy a car or furniture or something. That was how they usually thought about things. He had found out on Monday that the codicil would impact his life more than money ever could have.

J.W. had never been to Farnsworth. What little he knew came from surfing the Internet and some research he had done yesterday at the public library. It was while he was at the library that he had seen a brief news clip on CNBC's afternoon financial program that talked about a rumored acquisition involving the Farnsworth Telephone Cooperative and the LEGENT properties in the Midwest.

The reporter had mentioned some names connected to the acquisition including Wilson McCann. That was when J.W. had made up his mind to go to Farnsworth. The news program had mentioned that an announcement would be made at a former elementary school at 10:00 this morning. As he drove east, he wondered if he could get there in time. Without thinking, he increased his speed and reached up with his free hand to touch his jacket where the envelope was.

As he drove, he ran the same question through his mind again and again just as he had since the Monday morning meeting at the attorney's office. "Why? Why did they do this?" The attorney did not have an answer except to remind him that his parents had loved him very much.

He drove through Caro and the snow increased. The highway was a set of snow- packed tracks. He caught up with a slow-moving truck and waited for three miles to get around it. He kept checking his watch. He drove into Farnsworth at 10:15 and stopped at the Agway to ask for directions to the cemetery and the Selma Dunt Community Center.

"You from TV or one of the papers?" the young sales clerk asked him. When he replied in the negative, the young man said, "There's a ton of 'em in town. They're all over at the Dunt School listening to Mr. McCann."

J.W. had been looking up the street. He could see the sign for the Barnes Loft about a block away. He would have to stop there. At the mention of McCann's name, he turned back to the clerk.

"Do you know McCann?" he asked.

"Sure. He comes in here a lot. He and Phil, that's the owner, are real close."

J.W. glanced at his watch. Time was slipping away. "What's he like?"

"Phil says he's the best thing to happen to Farnsworth in a long time," the young man replied.

"Thanks," J.W. replied, turning and stepping out through the door into the snow.

Earlier that same morning, McCann had faced a tough decision. He had taken care of the cattle early and fed Wink. Now he stood in his bedroom, a mug of coffee in his hand, looking at his wardrobe. Should he go for the casual "farmer" look or the "Chicago Executive" look? He wanted to wear the sport jacket, light blue dress shirt and slacks that lay on the right side of the bed. He thought about the "message" a casual approach would send. He looked at the pin striped suit, white shirt and dark tie that he had laid out on the left side of the bed. He thought back over his career. Whenever he had stood in front of microphone or in front of a TV camera, he had worn a similar set of clothes. Would wearing them this morning seem to be too "big city executive" for Farnsworth?

In the end, he compromised. He put on the light blue shirt and the pin striped suit and left the tie. "It's casual city," he said to Wink, as he put on his overcoat. From her place next to the heat vent, she looked at him briefly and went back to sleep. She had no desire to go back out into the rapidly falling snow.

McCann drove into Farnsworth and met Belle, Doug, Phil, Fred Penay and Arthur Boyington at the telephone company. From the conference room, they held a thirty minute videoconference with Cindy, Stu and Feldman in New York City and Straylin and his public relations team in Charlotte. When they came out of the conference room an obviously nervous Sally McHugh was waiting for them. At 9:00 a.m., they drove to the Dunt Community Center. The large parking lot in front of the school was almost full. Two TV satellite trucks were parked in the "staff only" parking lot and a Sheriff's Deputy waived them into that lot. All others would have to fend for themselves.

The auditorium was rapidly filling up. The media were making last minute adjustments to their equipment. The three large television sets were live, showing Straylin's conference room, a conference room at Triad and a conference room at LEGENT'S headquarters in Dallas.

At precisely ten o'clock, the TV sets were populated with Cindy, Feldman and Stu Bailey in New York City, Straylin and his PR person in Charlotte and John King and one of LEGENT'S PR people in Dallas.

A moment later, Belle Warner, dressed in a black skirt and jacket paired with a white blouse walked to the podium and welcomed everyone. She then asked each person on the TV screens to introduce themselves. Next she introduced the Farnsworth Tele Board and Arthur Boyington. Finally, she recognized the local and state elected officials in attendance. Each stood as they were introduced and were greeted with light applause.

She then advised the media that copies of statements and announcements would be made available to them at the conclusion of the meeting.

She then re-introduced Donald Straylin. Straylin looked directly into the camera and began to speak. McCann would learn later that Straylin's remarks were on a teleprompter.

"Good morning ladies and gentlemen. I am pleased to announce this morning that an investment consortium led by my firm, Straylin and Company, in partnership with the firms represented by Ms. Melzy, Mr. Feldman and Mr. Bailey have reached an agreement in principle to acquire the telephone operating properties of LEGENT in the states of Iowa, Michigan, Minnesota and Wisconsin. Mr. King?"

John King, looking just a trifle nervous, looked down at the paper in front of him and spoke into the camera.

"The agreed upon purchase price is slightly over $400 million. We expect to file the necessary papers seeking approval of this sale with the appropriate Federal and State authorities within thirty days. We are committed to continue to operate the properties in the interests of our customers until the approvals are received and the transfer is complete. We will work with the acquiring parties to facilitate a seamless transition to the new organization."

As King stopped, Straylin resumed. "We do not as yet have a name for the new company but will announce that within the next couple of weeks. I can tell you that the operating headquarters for our new corporation will be located in Farnsworth, Michigan. In that regard, I believe Mrs. Warner has an announcement as well, Belle?"

There was a noticeable stir and buzz among the audience.

Belle Warner stood and walked to the podium. She did not have any notes but was every bit as relaxed as Straylin had appeared.

"As you know, the Warner family acquired the controlling interest in the former Farnsworth Telephone Cooperative many years ago. Since then, we have consolidated our holdings and have continually expanded and improved the service to our customers. I think it is only fair to say that the service we offer to our customers is every bit as technologically advanced as any in the country."

" We believe in the future of Farnsworth, the Thumb, and the state of Michigan. It is with that in mind that we have only considered opportunities for expansion that will benefit not only ourselves and our people but the community and the state's economy. We have agreed in principle to sell the Farnsworth Telephone Cooperative to the company headed by Mr. Straylin..."

At this, there was another noticeable stir among the audience. Belle waited, a smile playing about the edges of her lips until it subsided.

"...It is never easy to see a smaller, family-owned enterprise disappear into a larger one. History shows that in many cases such sales have worked to the disadvantage of the local economies and to the communities served. We are pleased that this sale will run counter to that trend and that Farnsworth will become the operational headquarters for the new enterprise. Farnsworth will be represented on the Board of Directors of the new company. The President and Chief Operating Officer of the new corporation will be Mr. Wilson McCann of Farnsworth who is currently a member of our Board. At the close of this meeting, several of our people will be distributing copies of informational bulletins and media releases giving additional details. Mr. Straylin, I believe we have one more announcement."

Straylin looked into the camera as Belle returned to her seat on the stage. All eyes in the auditorium swung to the TV again. As they did so, one of the Farnsworth Tele employees who had been standing at the doorway handed Fred Penay a handwritten note. The banker read it and immediately rose and left the room. McCann could see a look of shock on Penay's usually stoic features.

Straylin spoke again. "We are very pleased to have our operational headquarters in Farnsworth under the direction of a man with Wils McCann's experience and reputation within the telecommunications industry. I want to make it very clear that we intend to operate and succeed in this increasingly competitive industry and that we will apply the principles that Farnsworth Tele has utilized in the past to improve and expand services to all our customers within the three states. Shortly after the first of the year, representatives of LEGENT, Mr. McCann and I will be visiting the individual states to meet with our people and begin to plan for our future programs."

"Our assessment indicates that Farnsworth is a community that offers a great quality of life not only for our existing staff but the professionals and technicians we expect to add within the next year. Our current estimates are that we will be adding between 35 and 50 people to the existing staff in Farnsworth. We will need space for that expansion. Farnsworth currently has a shortage of office space as well as overnight accommodations. Straylin and Company has made a significant investment in HHF Corporation, an investment firm specializing in technology innovation. Mr. McCann is the founder and CEO of HHF. I believe Mr. McCann has an announcement to make."

As McCann rose to walk to the podium, Fred Penay returned to his seat. The 57-year- old banker had aged ten years in five minutes. McCann was caught up short by Penay's demeanor and had to struggle to focus on his remarks. He looked away and then out over the audience as he began to speak.

"Through the additional investment that Mr. Straylin and his firm have provided, we are pleased to announce that HHF Corporation and the Village of Farnsworth have agreed to the sale of this building and grounds by the Village to HHF Corporation. It is our intention to renovate this facility to do several things. First, it will house office space for the additional staff that Mr. Straylin just mentioned. Secondly the entire east wing of the building will be reshaped into a set of overnight rooming accommodations sufficient to handle the needs of many of the people coming into Farnsworth for meetings, conferences and so forth. This will be done to today's standards to serve as a facility that can provide breakfast to those using the facility on an overnight basis and those who will be using the facility for these meetings, seminars, etc. We intend to renovate the south wing of the building to provide for state-of-the art conference and research facilities. Lastly, the extension of the west wing beyond the south wing, which includes all the rooms and conference rooms, will be remodeled into a pre-school and day-care center which will be operated by the Farnsworth United Methodist Church under a renewable ten-year agreement between the church and HHF.

The stirring among the audience was back. McCann waited for it to subside, looking over at two of the dignitaries sitting in the front row. "You are probably wondering where the capital will come from for this. I believe we have two gentlemen here who can speak to that. The first is Mr. Dan Ryan of our State Economic Development Department and the second is Milton Showmeister of the Tuscola County Development office. Gentlemen?"

The two men stood and walked up the three steps onto the stage. Ryan spoke first. "I am pleased to announce that the State Economic Development Department has approved a grant of $400,000 for the development efforts Mr. McCann just described. The project qualifies under both our community development and job creation programs. Our Governor will be making a statement later today about this entire project. Mr. Showmeister?"

Showmeister, a tall thin man with silver hair appeared very nervous as he took the microphone and cleared his throat before speaking. "We are very excited about all this. Our Board met yesterday and we advised Mr. Ryan here that we could put an additional $100,000 into the pot."

The audience laughed at this and then began to clap. It was obvious that, of all the speakers, the locals identified most with Milton Showmeister. The applause died away as Showmeister impulsively grasped McCann's hand before the two men went back to their seats.

McCann smiled as the applause quieted down. He looked down at Sally, seated in the front row next to Phil Willard. She was in a black skirt and blouse with a short red leather jacket. He smiled more broadly as she nervously ran her hand through her hair. She knew what was coming next.

Before I turn it back to Don Straylin, I would like to introduce the persons who were largely responsible for many of the suggested renovations that will occur in this facility and who will serve as the engineering firm and HHF's Project Manager. First, let me introduce Al Strahl, from Sheppmann Engineering. Al will be in charge of seeing to it that things are done as planned and on schedule. The overall project will be under the management of Ms. Sally McHugh. Sally has offered many suggestions which have been incorporated into our plans for this building. Al and Sally, please take a bow!"

Strahl and Sally both stood as another buzz went through the crowd. Several elderly women in the back were seen to cover their mouths as they whispered to each other. Sally's face flamed crimson, but her three boys, standing at the rear of the room, whistled and clapped loudly. Kenny yelled "Way to go, mom!" As she dropped back into her chair, Sally vowed to strangle all three of them!

McCann, who had joined in the boy's applause, smiled down at her.

(39)

After a twenty minute question and answer session with the media and the audience, everyone adjourned to the center's cafeteria for coffee and donuts. Belle had recruited Lori and her two girls and Lona Marks to act as hostesses. Sally tried to help out but was quickly shooed away and forced to visit with some of the local media who wanted to know more about the plans for the Dunt Center. McCann was tied up with interviews back in the auditorium. As he completed the last one and walked down the hall toward the cafeteria, he noticed Fred Penay talking quietly with a dark haired young man. As he approached, the banker turned toward him. Penay's face displayed a grave uneasiness as he looked from McCann back to the young man. For his part, the young man gazed intently at McCann as Penay introduced him. McCann had the vague impression that he had seen him before but he couldn't place him.

"Wils, I would like you to meet J. W. Storey. J. W., this is Wilson McCann," the banker said, stepping back as the two men shook hands.

"Glad to meet you J. W. Have we met before somewhere?" McCann said, as he shook hands. The younger man's grip was firm.

"I am sure that we have not." The response was quiet but firm. There was a hint of something unsaid and McCann wondered what it might be. Whatever it was, it was apparent that this young man had unsettled Fred Penay.

"J. W. has brought something with him that I think you should see, Wils. But, if you don't mind, I would like to talk with you first."

McCann eyed the young man suspiciously before turning to Penay. "What's this all about Fred? What's going on?"

Penay removed his glasses and nervously wiped them on the sleeve of his jacket. "I think we should find somewhere that we can talk privately."

"Okay. There are a couple of small conference rooms off the old library.

Let's go there," McCann said, leading the way down the hallway. The former school library had been converted to a sort of lounge with various pieces of furniture in various stages of disrepair occupying it. Two doors in one wall led to a pair of small conference rooms. Signs over the doors identified them as A-1 and B-1. McCann turned the handle on the door to A-1 but it was locked. B-1 opened at his touch.

"I'll wait out here," Storey said, turning away to the side of the lounge and heading for an overstuffed chair.

McCann walked into the room and Penay followed. The banker dropped into a side chair. McCann walked to the opposite side of the table and turned.

"Fred, what is this about?"

The banker leaned forward and clasped his hands on the table in front of him. "I think you should sit down, Wils. What I have to tell you will come as a shock."

"Who is this guy and what has he said or done that has you acting this way?" McCann said, as he sat down opposite Penay.

Penay looked at him and began to speak. As he did so, the effort was obvious. His hands, still clasped in front of him, turned white at the knuckles.

"The last summer you were here living with Fred and Ella Wils, do you remember it?"

"Yes, but what..?"

Penay unclasped his hands and put them down on the table. The words came out in a rush.

"You will remember that Donna Barnes had gone away on a mission trip that summer. She wasn't here. Well, that wasn't entirely true. Donna Barnes went on a mission trip alright but it didn't start until about the middle of July. In May, before you came back to the farm for the summer, she went to Midland, Michigan and delivered a baby. Ed Barnes and I arranged for that baby to be placed with a couple who had no children of their own. Besides Ed and Donna and that couple, I'm the only one who knew about what had happened. Donna was able to keep her condition a secret from everyone else. Not even her school friends knew about it. I had hoped that the secret would remain but today, it has been revealed. J. W. Storey is Donna's son.

The couple who adopted him never told him that he was adopted. They waited too long and both died. Before the husband died, he added a codicil to their will that instructed their attorney to make J.W. aware of his birth mother and the man she named as the father of her son on the birth certificate and the adoption release that she signed. You are that man. J. W. Storey is your son."

McCann felt as though he had been hit with a club. The room seemed to whirl about him and he gripped the edge of the table with both hands. The urge to hit Penay was strong and yet he knew in that instant that the old banker was telling the truth.

"How could you ....?" His voice croaked.

Penay seemed to relax. The color returned to his face. "I never dreamed that you would return to Farnsworth. Donna was happy. She had patched up her relations with Ed and she was accepted in the community. You were successful. She never mentioned it to me and I felt I should just try to forget it. When you came back, I felt that if she wanted to tell you, she would. The fact that she didn't indicates that she had put it all firmly behind her and saw no reason to involve you in what was past."

McCann sat back, trying to regain his composure and curb his raging emotions. He squeezed his eyes tightly shut and sat rigidly until he felt he could speak without saying something that would hurt.

"What proof is there? What is it that this young man wants me to see?"

"The family attorney gave him his birth certificate and the medical record from the hospital where he was born. He also has the certificate of adoption."

"I want to see them."

"Fine. There are just two more things."

"What?" McCann leaned back in his chair and put a hand up to support his head.

"J.W. just found out about all this on Monday. He doesn't show it now, but his shock is just as great as yours is.'

"No way that's possible, Fred," McCann said quietly. "What else?"

"J.W. stands for James Wilson. Donna specifically stated that was to be his name when she put him up for adoption."

Wilson James McCann absorbed this new piece of information like a man carrying a load of bricks to which another had just been added.

In New York City, Stu Bailey shook hands with Cindy and Feldman, wishing them a Merry Christmas and walked briskly back to his office.

"How did it go, boss?" Jeanine asked, looking up as Bailey came in.

"Without a hitch," Bailey replied. "I think I may take the rest of the day off. Why don't you do the same?"

Jeanine looked at her watch. "It's almost noon. I get the rest of the day off as a holiday. We usually close at noon on Christmas Eve or did you forget?"

Bailey chuckled. "Well, take Monday off then."

"I get that as my Christmas holiday, boss."

"Well, have a Merry Christmas and don't spend this all in one place," Bailey replied, reaching inside his jacket and removing an envelope which he dropped onto her desk. Turning, he walked out, shutting the door behind him. She could hear him whistling "Here comes Santa Claus" as he walked down the hall. As the sound faded, she opened the envelope and removed a check for $5,000. The apron of the check said "Good Job!" in bold black type.

Cindy went straight back to her apartment and picked up David. Together, they headed off to Macy's. They were going to see Santa Claus, something they had never done before.

Feldman returned to his office and called Straylin.

"I thought it went well. How did you feel?" he asked.

"I was pleased. Somehow, I feel we have a real interesting and rewarding year ahead."

"I was impressed with Mrs. Warner. She's a class act. The gal in the red jacket is the same one that was with McCann when the dog was shot?" Feldman asked.

"Yes, she's the one. She operates a diner in Farnsworth. I checked her background. She has some interesting life experiences. McCann trusts her. That's all I'm concerned about."

Feldman wasn't about to ask what Sally's "life experiences" were. He thought he probably knew. No need to micromanage. Straylin wished him a Merry Christmas and he responded with a Happy Hanukkah and left early for his home in Scarsdale.

In Lansing, shortly after 1:00 p.m., the Governor held a short press conference. He briefly reviewed his administration's work to promote economic development to date. Next, he commented on the news out of Farnsworth that a new corporation would have its operational headquarters there and would employ between 35 and 50 additional administrative and professional personnel. He also pointed out the involvement of the state's Economic Development Office in providing funding for the renovation of the Selma Dunt Community Center to keep pace with the expansion of this new corporation. He pointed out that one of the aspects of that program was the provision of additional pre-school and child care services to the community.

The question and answer session following his remarks had to be cut off after twenty minutes. The Governor was asked if the state's Department of Public Service should approve the acquisition of the former LEGENT properties in Michigan and the former Farnsworth Telephone Cooperative. He replied that the PSC would review both acquisitions and work to assure that they resulted in continued improvement and expansion of telecommunications services to the state's residents and to keep telecommunications rates at reasonable levels. He added that, assuming that both of these criteria were met, he was hopeful that the acquisitions would be approved. The reporter asked a follow-up question as to whether the Governor felt it would be good to have LEGENT, an "absentee landlord," out and the new, Farnsworth-based corporation in. The Governor glanced briefly at Ross and then gently reminded the press that the corporate headquarters for the new organization was in Charlotte, North Carolina. He then reiterated his pleasure that operational control would be exercised from Michigan under the direction of people who resided within the state. Before another question could be asked, he wished all a very Merry Christmas and ducked out the side door of the briefing room. All in all, Ross thought the press conference had gone very well. Wolverine Property Management hadn't been mentioned.

In Dallas, John King met his wife for a late lunch. They decided to catch a Christmas morning flight out to Savannah. Norm Lister hadn't bothered to come in to the office that morning. He decided to buy himself an early Christmas present, a $2,000 set of golf clubs. He took them to his club and played nine holes before noon. His first attempt at golf hadn't erased his frustration. He spent the early afternoon in the club's bar and because he was in no shape to drive, he called his LEGENT driver to transport him home. The driver, who had previously been given the day off, was understandably unhappy about this. Listening to Lister's drunken ramblings, he concluded that some guy named McCann was responsible for all this misery.

Sally brushed the snow off her Mustang and started out of the parking lot. As she hit the street, she gunned the motor and the car's rear wheels spat out a stream of snow as it fish-tailed down the street. At the first intersection, she stopped and let her temper cool a bit before continuing on across the main street in the direction of the UMC Church and Parsonage.

She had walked into the cafeteria after the presentations were over and had tried to help with the refreshments but quickly noted that several of the locals were eyeing her with questioning looks. Several were whispering to each other and she could guess what they were whispering about. When she saw Joyce Hall and Janice DeGroot sipping coffee and whispering together off to the side, she decided to try to lose herself in the crowd. Then, she saw the Editor of the *Chronicle* headed her way and had ducked out into the hallway.

She saw Wilson McCann, Fred Penay and a dark haired younger man heading into the former library. She started that way but saw that McCann and Penay had gone into one of the conference rooms and shut the door. The young man had sat down in one of the chairs in the lounge area and was idly thumbing through a magazine. That was when Sally decided to leave.

She pulled up in front of the church and went inside. She headed down the hallway towards the Pastor's office. She had seen Charles Hastings leave just ahead of her. Hastings had made the rounds of the crowd in the cafeteria, grabbed a quick cup of coffee and left. It seemed no one in particular wanted to talk with him about the new pre-school and child care center. "A lot of them were too busy wondering what the town tramp did to get herself named to a big job with Wils McCann!" Sally had fumed to herself as she drove down the street.

The outer office was vacant and she could see Hastings hunched over his computer terminal. She rapped lightly on the door frame. Hastings looked up and smiled. He swiveled in his chair to face her and waved her in.

"Sally! Congratulations on the new job! I haven't had a chance to thank you for all you are doing for the village and, in particular, our church. Your sketches of how the pre-school and day care could be set up in the southwest wing were great!"

"I'm afraid that some people are wondering who I've been 'doing' and not what I've been doing," Sally said as she sat down opposite the minister's desk.

Hastings leaned back in his chair and drummed his fingers on his desk for a moment. "It's been my experience that reasonable people will think reasonably and unreasonable people should sometimes be prayed for and then ignored."

"Kind of tough for a man of God, aren't you?"

"Sally, each of us is a sinner. You and I and everyone in this town fall short of God's standards. It's what we choose to do about that that is important. Some people continue to reject and resist God's call on their lives and continue to live for their own interests and desires and not God's. Others, seeing where they have gone astray, make a decision to answer His call and begin to live for Him. Where are you?"

Sally ran her hand through her hair and then gripped the arms of the chair. "I'm in the first category, Reverend. But I'd like to move over into the other category if God would have me."

"God will have us all, if we will only ask. Why don't you ask him and I'll listen in and then add my input as well."

Sally McHugh bowed her head and did just that.

J. W. sat down opposite McCann as Fred Penay left the room, closing the door behind him. He sat down in the same chair that J.W. had just vacated to make sure that the two men behind the door were not interrupted.

McCann looked him over. Now he saw the resemblance to Donna. The green eyes, the little turned-up nose. He also saw the dark hair and the broad forehead. J.W. Storey had inherited something from each of his parents. McCann inhaled deeply and leaned forward. The younger man met his gaze, waiting.

"As I'm sure you can appreciate, I'm in a bit of a state of shock right now. If you don't mind, I understand that you have some documents. I would like to see them."

J.W. reached inside his jacket and retrieved the envelope. He passed it across the table to McCann who noted the name and address of the attorney in Midland. McCann opened the flap and extracted the three documents. The first was a birth certificate giving the mother and father's name. His heart began to beat a little more rapidly as he saw his name recorded there. He laid it aside and looked at the second document. It was a medical record from Mid Michigan Medical center on Orchard Street in Midland, Michigan, recording the birth of a 9 pound 2 ounce baby boy on May 7th, 24 years ago this past May. Handwritten notes at the bottom indicated that both mother and baby were "doing well." McCann swallowed hard and took the third document.

It was an adoption release prepared by the same Law Office named on the envelope. It recorded that on May 8th Donna Barnes, a minor, had placed her baby boy for adoption by Frank and Frances Storey of Midland, Michigan. The release was co-signed by Edward M. Barnes and Frederick J. Penay.

McCann carefully folded each document and returned them to the envelope. He slid it back across the table and J.W. put the envelope back in his inside jacket pocket.

"I didn't know…I don't know…,"McCann said softly.

"where to begin? Neither do I," J.W. replied.

"Perhaps if you told me a bit about yourself and I did the same, we could….you know…get to know a little about each other," McCann said, sitting back in his chair and rubbing his hand across his eyes.

J. W. spent the next five minutes describing his boyhood, teenage years and military and college years. As he talked, McCann was impressed that this was a good young man who had been raised by good people. He felt a sense of pride and wondered how Donna would have felt if she had been sitting with them. That caused him to think back to their brief time together since he had returned to Farnsworth. Why hadn't she told him? He knew the answer. He hadn't deserved to be told.

"So that is about it. I've read some about you. You have been in the news a little more than I have," J. W. summarized.

"Thank you. I'll start with my boyhood as well," McCann said. He proceeded to describe his boyhood, teenage years, college and career. He skipped over the details of his summers in Farnsworth but he sensed that this would be where J. W. would be focused. He was right.

"So you and my…Donna…you…," J. W. began.

McCann leaned back as if to avoid the question but knew he had to answer it both for this young man's and his own sake.

"Donna and I were typical teenagers. We had a lot of good times together. Donna's father was quite strict and she rebelled. I fully aided and abetted that rebellion. Whatever you do, please don't blame her. I realized too late how much I loved her and how much I had hurt her. If you want to hate anyone, hate me."

J. W. turned to look out through the window at Penay who still sat in the lounge.

"I don't want to hate anyone. I just want to try to understand. I am struggling with what to do with all of this. I can't call you 'dad' and ….Donna 'mother'.

"And you don't need to. You obviously were raised by two wonderful people who deserve those titles. Only time will tell you what you should think and do. I would like to know you and be known by you, but I need time to struggle through all of this too. In some ways, I feel betrayed. I'm sure you must feel the same to some extent."

"So…I am the product of a summer's fling…is that it?"

McCann could feel the heat of the question. The green eyes were boring into him. The rage was there. He could see J. W.'s jaw working as he tried to control it.

"We were two teenagers who thought we knew what we were doing and who, twenty- four years later found out that we really loved each other. I found that out too late. Donna Barnes never stopped loving me. I didn't know it. I'm sure that, in the same way, she never stopped loving you as well."

"I don't know where to go from here," J.W. said, looking down at the table.

"Are you staying in the area?"

"I hadn't planned to. I really hadn't planned anything except to find out as much as I could. I stopped at the bank and asked for Mr. Penay and they said he was here. I knew you would be here. So, I came here."

McCann leaned forward, lacing his hands together on the table in front of him. "Let me take you out to the cemetery where your…where Donna and her father and mother are buried. Let me take you to the store that she ran here in town. It's Christmas Eve and it's snowing pretty hard. Come out to my farm and stay the night. I've got a spare bedroom. We can talk some more, maybe get to know each other a little better."

J.W. hesitated. He hadn't planned on this. Yet, somehow, it seemed the right thing to do.

"I'll think about staying overnight. I would like to visit the cemetery and the store. I saw it from the car as I drove in."

"Good. Let's go," McCann said, getting to his feet.

"Don't you have some things to do relative to the big deal today?" J.W. said, rising as well.

"Right now, you are more important than anything I have to do," McCann said, as he led him out the door.

McCann was as good as his word. He shook hands with Penay and said a brief "Thank you" to the obviously nervous banker. He and J.W. moved out into the hallway and headed towards the front door. A group of reporters with recorders and microphones in their hands moved to head them off. McCann raised his hand and with a brief "excuse us, thank you," they were outside into the falling snow. McCann moved toward the Jeep and J.W. hesitated.

"Where's your car?" McCann asked.

"Over there in the general parking lot, in the back row."

"Leave it here. We'll come back and get it later," McCann said, resuming his fast walk toward the Jeep. J.W. hurried to keep up.

They drove first to the cemetery where they stood for a few moments in the snow looking down at the graves of Donna and her parents. After a few moments, McCann stepped back and waited while the younger man remained rooted to the spot, gazing at the grave markers.

McCann pulled his coat collar up around his neck and thrust his gloved hands into the pockets. His mind was a whirl of thoughts and he assumed J.W.'s was as well.

At length, the younger man turned and faced him. "Thank you. It's all so much to absorb. My feelings are all over the place."

"I know. I feel the same. Would you like to visit the store? A young woman named Darcy Hardesty runs it now. She worked with Donna." McCann said, as the two men headed back to the Jeep, which was already covered with a new layer of snow.

"This storm shows no signs of letting up. Where are you going when you leave here?" McCann asked, wondering what the answer might reveal.

"San Jose."

"California? Do you have a flight?"

"I intend to drive. I have a job offer there with a technology company," J.W. replied, as they reached the Jeep.

"It's a long drive. You might run into rough weather along the way." McCann said, as he started the Jeep. His thoughts were conflicted. He admired the young man's confidence while at the same time a new sensation of concern for his welfare rose within him. He was beginning to recognize what it might feel like to be a father.

"I have to be there by a week from Monday to begin work. I'll see some of the country along the way. I've never been west of the Mississippi."

"Where were you stationed in the army?" McCann asked, as they headed back down the main street of Farnsworth.

"Fort Drum in Upstate New York, the 10th Mountain Division, part of the 18th Airborne," J.W. responded. McCann could sense the pride in the younger man's voice.

"Light infantry, right?"

"Yes sir, I was a heavy equipment operator. We kept the base free of snow and up there you get a lot of snow."

McCann did a U-turn two blocks past the Barnes Loft and came back to park in front of the store. Despite the snowfall, which was intensifying, the main street of the village held a lot of parked cars and trucks. The activities of the day and J.W.'s appearance had caused him to forget that it was Christmas Eve. Evidently there were quite a few people who were doing some last- minute shopping in the village stores.

They entered the store and McCann's thoughts were confirmed. Darcy was waiting on two ladies while two other people waited and two more examined racks of clothing.

McCann and J.W. spent several minutes walking around the store under the guise of looking at various items. When the last of the shoppers had left and there was a lull in activity, McCann introduced J.W. as a "friend of Donna's" and Darcy and the young man shared a few moments of discussion about Donna before another customer entered. The two men quickly wished her a Merry Christmas and began to leave.

Darcy watched as they left. There was something vaguely familiar about the young man. She couldn't place it but she wondered about it as she moved to meet her next customer. Something in his face reminded her of someone and it was someone she was certain she should remember.

McCann looked at his watch and westward into the snow which was falling harder and being swept along by an even stronger wind. In another hour, it would be dark. They drove back to the Dunt Center and into the nearly empty parking lot. J.W.'s car was now covered by at least five inches of new snow. As he turned off the engine, McCann turned to face him.

"Look…it's snowing pretty hard and the roads are going to be getting worse. There won't be a lot of maintenance crews out. Do you have a place for the night?"

"I'd thought to get a room in Saginaw," J.W. replied, taking his hand away from the door handle.

McCann took a deep breath. His emotions were running high and he struggled to keep his voice calm and businesslike. "Come home with me. You can spend the night at the farm. I have a spare bedroom and you can head out in the morning. They say that tomorrow will be clear." Despite his attempt at control, the words came out in a rush.

"I...I don't know..."

"Please?" McCann laid his hand on J.W.'s arm. He let it rest there a moment before he withdrew it. The younger man looked at him for a moment and then out the window into the falling snow. Finally, he turned back to face McCann.

"Perhaps we could...you know...talk some more...if I stayed?"

"I'd like that," McCann said.

And so it was settled. The two men brushed off the car. McCann noted that it looked a little travel weary. He wondered how it would handle the trip across two thirds of the country through widely divergent terrain. Once again, he felt the fatherly concern rise.

J.W. followed him out to the farm. By the time they arrived the drive and the turn-around were under another eight inches of snow. McCann rolled back the tool shed doors and drove the Jeep inside, motioning for J.W. to pull his car in tight so that they could get the big tractor with its snow plow out.

J.W. pulled a rather worn looking duffle from his car and the two men walked to the house. J.W. stopped twice to give the farm buildings and surrounding countryside as good a look as possible considering the fast falling snow.

Inside, they were greeted by Wink as she rose from her place beside the heat vent. Before McCann could send her outside, J.W. dropped his duffle and bent down to extend his hand, fingers bent back, for her to sniff. She did so and wagged her tail in acceptance. He stroked her head and scratched behind her ears. She moved forward to him and he rubbed her back.

"Well, you have been accepted..," McCann had almost added, "as a member of our family," but bit the words off.

"She's beautiful. I have always wanted a dog," J.W. said, standing as Wink headed for the back door.

"You never had one...as a boy...I mean?"

"No, mom and dad Storey didn't have any pets. I had a couple of goldfish once but they died pretty quick and I didn't get any other pets. Mostly, I played with other kids in the neighborhood and a couple of them had dogs… one neighbor girl had a cat."

McCann showed him the spare bedroom and went to check his voice mail. Among the messages was one from Sally which sounded rather breathless, reminding him that he had promised to go with her and the boys to the Christmas Eve Communion service at the church. In the rush of events during the last few hours, he had completely forgotten. He stood looking at the phone, wondering what to do when he sensed J.W. watching him from the hallway.

He turned and saw the question in the younger man's eyes. "Sally is a friend of mine. She has three sons. There's a communion service tonight at the church and I had promised to go with her. She doesn't usually go. I'll call her and tell her I can't make it."

Once again, the words came out in a rush as he sought to answer the questioning look. "Do you go to church in Farnsworth?" J.W. asked, not moving.

"Yes, it's rather of a long story. I'd like to tell you about it. My aunt and uncle, the ones who owned this farm, went there. My neighbors across the fields go there as well," he said, pointing out through the front windows into the darkening afternoon.

He hesitated, wondering how J.W. would react to the question that was forming in his mind. He plunged ahead. "Do you go to church?"

J.W. shifted his weight to the other foot before moving into the living room and looking out the window. "Not a lot. We went when I was a kid and I went to a few services when I was in the military. I've never been much of a church go 'er. But Mom and Dad Storey always made it a point to go on Christmas Eve."

McCann paused while he processed what J.W. had said. Then, acting again in impulse, he asked, "Would you like to go tonight…with me, I mean?"

J.W. turned toward him and he felt the green eyes travel over him. "Sure. Let's do that."

McCann couldn't keep the satisfaction he felt from his voice. "Great! I need to feed the cattle and we can get some supper around and we'll take the Jeep and go. I'll just call Sally and let her know we're coming."

"Interesting!"

"What?" McCann asked.

"You said 'supper,' Mom Storey always called it supper. She never said 'Dinner.' That was 'lunch'."

"I guess it's the farm rubbing off on me, "McCann replied. "Fred and Ella always said 'Supper' too."

"While you're doing your chores, can I clear the drive and turn-around? I've got a bit of experience with snow removal and I'd enjoy driving that rig of yours!" J.W. responded, a note of excitement coming out in his voice as well.

He retreated to the bedroom and closed the door while McCann called Sally. She shared the afternoon's event with him and a surge of joy went through him. He felt the impulse to tell her about J.W. but thought better of it and only told her that he would be bringing "a friend" who was spending the night with him prior to heading for the west coast.

When he returned to the kitchen after changing into his work clothes, J.W. was standing there in a pair of old, well worn army coveralls.

"I've kept these for times when I needed to work on the car and other stuff," he said, noticing the appraisal McCann had given him. "I'll need a pair of boots."

"I've got an extra pair behind the door there…size 11?"

"They'll do." J.W. replied. "I'm a 10 ½."

By the time McCann had finished taking care of the steers, J.W. had cleared the drive and turn-around and put the tractor back in the tool shed. McCann observed the clean lines around the edges of the freshly plowed snow. As he was working in the barn the sound of the tractor had been a continuous roar. There was none of the starts and stops that usually accompanied McCann's handling of the big machine when he was clearing the drive.

The two men ate a hastily prepared meal of cubed steak, canned green beans and hash brown potatoes. By 6:45, they were out of their work clothes and dressed for church. They drove out into the snow which was diminishing in intensity.

"I believe our storm is running out of steam," McCann observed.

"I hope so. I'd like good roads tomorrow," J. W. replied.

McCann wondered what it would be like to watch him drive away in the morning. Would he ever see him again? Would he want a relationship with someone he had only met today? What did the future hold? As he drove through the snow, he thought of a young woman centuries ago in strange surroundings with a new baby in her arms. Did she wonder what would happen to her son? For the first time in his life, the story of Christmas took on a new meaning for him.

(40)

The Farnsworth Methodist Church foyer and the sanctuary beyond it were bathed in candle light as McCann and J.W. entered. *"While Shepherds Watched Their Flocks by Night"* was playing softly over the speaker system. Several families were scattered throughout the pews. Sally and her three boys were waiting in the foyer.

"I'm not sure what we are supposed to do," she whispered, as McCann approached. The oldest boy, Robert, looked at J.W. and McCann could see that he recognized him.

"Pastor explained it to me. We go in, have a seat and meditate, pray or sit quietly for a while. When we are ready, we go up to the altar rail and he will serve the elements," McCann replied.

"Did you go to CMU?" Robert asked J.W.

"Yes, I just finished up. You?"

"Yes. You played baseball too, right?"

J.W. glanced at McCann, a small smile on his face. "Yes, I played a little."

"Small world, I guess," Robert said, looking first at his mother and then McCann.

"This is J.W. Storey, he's a friend of Mr. McCann's," Sally whispered to the boys. The two younger boys, gave nods and half waves in recognition.

More people were coming in and a few were leaving. They glanced at McCann and Sally and the others as they did so. He could see the looks of puzzlement on their faces as they looked at the six of them.

"We'd better go in," McCann said, leading the way. J.W. stepped back, allowing Sally to go ahead of him. He followed her with Robert and the other two boys trailing along behind. When they reached the pew, he stepped aside to allow the three boys to sit beside their mother.

A couple knelt at the altar rail and Charles Hastings knelt in front of them, talking quietly as he served the elements. When they were finished, he resumed his seat behind the altar as they continued for a moment at the altar before rising and turning to exit the sanctuary. As they left, another family came. McCann bowed his head and closed his eyes as he quietly prayed. He thanked God for Sally's declaration of faith and prayed that her sons would soon follow her. He prayed for a continuing relationship with J.W. and for J.W.'s safety as he traveled to California. He thanked God for the events of the past few months and for all that had taken place. He asked that he put God's will first and that he be given the wisdom to know what God would have him to do in the future.

He was lost in his prayers, not paying any attention to those who came or went. Finally, he could hear the silent rustling of the younger men stirring in the pew. He raised his head and looked around. Those seated in the sanctuary had all come in since they had sat down. He sensed that they were waiting for the six of them to go forward. He leaned forward and looked down the pew at J.W. who was sitting on the end. The younger man caught his eye and immediately stood to allow the three boys and Sally to exit the pew. As McCann neared the aisle, J.W. stepped toward the altar and they walked forward to kneel.

Hastings waited a few moments before picking up the trays with the bread and juice. He moved in front of them and knelt.

"We celebrate Christmas as the wonderful gift of God coming to earth as a baby in a manger. The story of God's love for us reaches its climax at Easter when we celebrate the victory of Jesus over sin and the grave. Without the manger, there can be no cross. Without the cross there is no hope. Before he left this earth, Jesus gave us an example of his love for us in the last supper. Tonight as you take the bread and the cup, you have but a brief glimpse of what we have to look forward to when we celebrate it with him in heaven. Take, eat and drink and be thankful," he said as he passed the elements to each of them. As each one took the elements, Hastings spoke their name and added, "God Loves You." In the dim candlelight, he noted the young man kneeling next to McCann. He had seen him earlier in the day at the Dunt Center. There was something strangely familiar about him. As they rose to leave, a question began to rise in his mind. The scripture from

Isaiah 9:6 flashed through his mind and he marveled at the thoughts that accompanied it.

Outside, McCann gave Sally a hug and whispered "I'm so happy for you!" The men shook hands with the boys. With calls of "Merry Christmas" they parted and headed for their cars. McCann noted that the snow had stopped and the sky was clear with stars shining brightly.

At the farm, the two men pulled the doors of the tool shed closed and looked up into the starlit sky. On impulse, McCann walked to the edge of the small rise facing west from the barn. The view of the fields and the woods a half mile away was bathed in moonlight and starlight.

"Pretty isn't it?" J. W. said, coming up behind him.

"It has become one of my favorite places since I came here," McCann replied.

"Did…my…did Donna come here?"

McCann continued to stare off into the distance. "She came here several times after I returned. She loved this place too."

Standing there, he told him about the haying and the other nights when Donna and he had shared time together. For the first time in a long time, it felt good to talk about her. He didn't feel the pain that usually accompanied memories of her. So, he told J. W. that as well.

They continued to talk as they walked back to the house. Once inside, they drank coffee and ate some cookies that Martha Willard had given him for Christmas. J. W. told him more about his life in the military and in college. He told him more about the Storeys as well and McCann breathed a silent prayer of thanksgiving for the goodness that the couple had shared with J. W. He could see that their qualities and value systems had become J. W.'s.

McCann told J. W. about his own career and didn't hide the fact that his priorities had been misplaced for a long time. He talked about his mother and how she had struggled to provide a good home for the two of them. As he did so, an idea that had come to him earlier returned. He rose and went to the hall closet. He rummaged around in the closet for a while and returned with a Bible and a large brown envelope.

"This was my mother's Bible. Would you let me give it to you? I think she would have been very happy to know that her…that you have it."

He handed it to J.W. who took it and leafed through it. As he did so, he noticed the notes and underlining and highlighting. "Are you sure? Wouldn't you want to keep it?"

"It means a lot to me but it would mean a lot more knowing that you have it," McCann said.

J.W. continued to thumb through the Bible. After a long moment, he looked up at McCann . "Thank you. I'll take good care of it."

"I hope you might read it from time to time as well," McCann said, hesitantly. "I never paid much attention to the Bible until recently. It has helped me a great deal. Donna helped me to see that I needed it."

J.W. closed the book and rested his hand on it. "Maybe I'll give it a whirl," he said quietly. McCann sensed a promise in his words.

"There is one thing more," he said, opening the envelope and extracting a piece of paper. "This is the title to the Jeep. It was my mother's also. I'm going to draw up a bill of sale and sign it and sign this over to you. I want you to take the Jeep to California."

He could see the resistance forming in J.W.'s face and he hurried on. "Look, that car of yours is a little the worse for wear. I'll have a young friend of mine tune it up for you and we'll keep it in the tool shed. You can come and get it any time you want. I'll just feel a whole lot better if I know you are driving the Jeep through the Rockies. Please, as a favor to me? I've just met you for the first time and I find myself not wanting anything bad to happen to you. You'll have to forgive me but I've never had these kinds of feelings before in this kind of circumstance and I don't quite know how to act."

He felt lame and silly as the words rushed out. To his relief, a smile of understanding replaced the resistance on J.W.'s face.

"I wouldn't want to end the first day of getting to know you by causing you to worry. Look, I can't call you 'dad' or think of Donna as 'mom'. I hope you understand that. I've had a really good life up to now and mom and dad Storey were responsible for most of that. But, I don't want to lose touch with you either. I'll pay for having my car worked on and I'll drive the Jeep to California. Once I get there, I'll decide whether to re-register it in my name or bring it back some day. Okay?

McCann felt a surge of hope at the idea that J.W. might come back in the future. It was something to hope for and look forward to and to pray about.

Shortly after midnight as Christmas day came upon them, the two men went to bed. As he paused in the doorway to his bedroom, McCann turned to J.W. "I'm glad you agreed to stay the night and that we had a chance to get to know each other better."

J.W. smiled back at him as he moved to shut the door to his room. "So am I. Good night and Merry Christmas!"

McCann heard the sounds of water running in the bathroom before dawn. He rose and dressed. By the time he walked into the kitchen, J.W. was already fixing breakfast. The two men ate and then went to the tool shed where they transferred J.W.'s few belongings from the car to the Jeep. The sun was just beginning to creep over the eastern horizon when they shook hands and J.W. got into the Jeep and drove out of the driveway and down the road. McCann watched the taillights until they turned onto the highway and headed southwest.

He turned and walked to the top of the rise beside the barn. As the sun came up in the east, the fields behind the barn and the woods in the distance began the transition from darkness to light. He watched for a long time as the line of sunlight slowly advanced. Wink trotted up beside him and sat down, looking off in the distance as though seeing it through the eyes of her ancestors who might have helped to herd the sheep on a Judean hillside some two thousand years ago. The cattle in the barnyard began to move stiffly toward the water tank, leaving tracks in the deep snow. The sun bounced off the blanket of white into a clear sky. Far off in the distance, he could hear the sound of a church bell.

He looked down at the dog and bent to ruffle her head. He thought of Ted and Donna and his mother and Dynacom. All of them lost to him. And then, as the sun continued to rise, he thought of Jim Marks and his family with whom he would eat Christmas dinner. He thought of Macintyre and his gift of Wink. He thought of the Warners and their example in his life. He thought of Phil and Martha Willard and the Thanksgiving meal they had shared. He thought of Charles Hastings and how his ministry had impacted his own life and those of others. He thought of the opportunity that had been provided him to share in EECM's ministry and the strength of Shirley Jacobs. He thought of Sally and her boys and Cindy and David and the decisions that both had made to change their lives just as he had. He thought of Straylin, John King and the LEGENT acquisition. So much had changed in his life in the past few months. He had gained so much since coming to this farm. He looked out over the fields and thought about the wheat and the hay now covered by the snow waiting for the coming summer's harvest. He looked at the buildings with their fresh coat of paint standing out against the background of white. A surge of gratitude ran through him for God's blessings. Unless God directed otherwise, this was home.

As he turned to go down into the barn and feed the cattle, he thought about the two greatest things he had acquired in the past few months. One was the new found friendship with J.W. "My son," he said out loud. Wink cocked her head at the sound as she trotted along beside him. Lastly, he thought of his new found faith in Jesus Christ, the greatest acquisition of his life.

EPILOG

During the first week of the New Year, Michigan's Governor announced the creation of a new center for Telecommunications Technology Research, Development and Training. The center would be financed by continuing investments and staffing from a combination of leading telecommunications equipment manufacturers and telecommunications service providers together with support from the state's economic development corporation. The center would occupy land purchased by Wolverine Property Management near the small community of Brutus in Michigan's northern Lower Peninsula. The center, when fully operational, would occupy a one-hundred-acre tract that would include not only research and development facilities but training and dormitory facilities and "application test" facilities designed to provide on-site application testing and demonstration. The Center would initially focus on technologies that would frame the telecommunications network and services of the 21st century. When employment reached its projected 250 people, the Governor said it would have a $200 million dollar impact on the economy of the northern half of the Lower Peninsula.

The newly named Tachyons Telecommunications, based in Farnsworth, Michigan was commissioned to provide initial facilities and to maintain and operate expanded facilities under a contract with Wolverine. Tachyons would also serve as a "Test Bed" for new technologies under consideration for introduction in the marketplace. Tachyons would form a separate, unregulated subsidiary to carry out that purpose. Tachyons' newly appointed State Manager for Michigan, Jim Wolfe, was named to an Advisory Board for the center. Tachyons took its name from a putative class of particles which are able to travel faster than the speed of light.

Eastern European Christian Ministries increased its donor base by over five million dollars in the first three months of the New Year. While attending the

Spring EECM Board meeting in Weaverville, McCann received a phone call from Boyington saying that the Michigan Department of Public Service had approved the acquisitions subject to continued expansion and improvement of service and limited rate impact on Michigan consumers. Michigan was the final state to approve the acquisition. Myron Martin and Elmer Thune were already working with a newly hired group of engineers to design the service improvements and expansions that would constitute a three year capital expenditure program.

In New York, Stu Bailey was already at work scouring the country for potential acquisitions that would augment the new company. In a display of unusual consideration, he had granted Jeanine an additional week of vacation with pay and increased her salary. Jeanine was somewhat surprised when her boss started taking Sundays off on a regular basis so that he and his family could go to church.

In April, McCann sold his twenty steers for a small profit. He also contracted for a fall shipment of thirty yearlings to feed through the winter. Sally McHugh and Dorothy Hastings agreed to share the day to day management of the diner as Sally became more involved in the renovation of the Dunt Center. Sally's former classmate, Janice DeGroot, was named a recipient of a Michigan AP Journalism award for her exclusive story on the LEGENT acquisition and her first person interview with Tachyons' President and Chief Operating Officer, Wilson McCann. In May, the *Wall Street Journal* reported Cindy Melzy's promotion to CEO of Triad. John King retired and saw an immediate improvement in his golf handicap. He was named to Tachyons' Board of Directors. Sal Piazza resigned effective the date of King's retirement and moved his family to Caro when he became the new Controller for Tachyons.

Belle Warner was honored by the Michigan Telephone Association for her contributions to the industry and to the state. Doug was named to the Association's Board of Directors. Belle stopped coming into the office after the acquisition was approved. She flew to Charlotte and drove up to Weaverville where she had lunch with Shirley Jacobs. The Warner family soon made a substantial contribution to EECM. Belle became a frequent visitor at both the diner and the renovation project at the Dunt Center. Phil

Willard decided not to run for County Republican Chairman and took on the job of organizing the new pre-school and child care facility that would occupy the west wing of the Dunt Center. Martha remarked that she had not seen him this excited since he had started the Agway.

In early June, Wilson McCann and J. W. Storey traveled to Eastern Europe together. In his role as a member of EECM's Board, McCann reviewed the progress being made in EECM's programs and the two men traveled to a lonely stretch of road in the Czech Republic where, on a rocky hillside, they planted a cross and a wreath in honor of a woman whose dedication to her faith had resulted in a similar dedication by both of them. J. W. read a passage from 2nd Samuel as they stood together overlooking the valley below. He read it from his paternal grandmother's Bible, a book he had become very familiar with:

The Lord is my rock, my fortress and my deliverer;
My God, my rock, in whom I take refuge,
My shield and the horn of my salvation.
my stronghold, and my refuge;
My savior, Thou dost save me from violence.
I call upon the Lord, who is worthy to be praised;
And I am saved from my enemies.
The waves of death encompassed me; the torrents of de struction overwhelmed me.
The cords of Sheol surrounded me, the snares of death confronted me.
In my distress I called upon the Lord;
Yes, I cried to my God.
And from His temple He heard my voice; my cry for help came into His ears.

2nd Samuel 22:2-7

Breinigsville, PA USA
01 April 2011
258900BV00001B/2/P